Only the deepest desire could bring them together. Only the darkest betrayal could tear them apart.

OLIVIA AND JAI

She was fascinated and baffled by this strange conundrum of a man, yes; but she was not yet sure that she even liked him! He was hard, opinionated, arrogant, twisted with hate and cynicism. He believed in adventurism, thought nothing of flaunting his moral turpitude before come who may and had no scruples about achieving his ends with whatever dubious means happened to be available at the moment. Arvind Singh had professed profound admiration for Jai as a man of rare courage. In Olivia's view, however, there was nothing especially admirable about a man merely because he was foolhardy enough to challenge the gods themselves.

All this Olivia recognized with extreme clarity. What she could not identify was the capricious, obscure, utterly illogical reason why she could not shake Jai Raventhorne out of her thoughts no matter how hard she tried. Inexorably, the world in which she lived was becoming unreal, like a fantasy. Something sly and unwanted was creeping into her life, taking her away from her roots. And somehow, at the crux of her disorientation, stood Jai Raventhorne....

CRITICAL PRAISE FOR *OLIVIA AND JAI*!

"A splendid book that should give millions of readers great pleasure."

—*Greenwich Times*

"Ryman, a spellbinding storyteller, captivates the reader from the first page."

—*Publishers Weekly*

"Has it all: history, villainy, heroism, romance."

—*Boston Sunday Herald*

"A first novel so sweeping in scope, so melodramatic in incident, that one realizes immediately it is headed straight for the bestseller lists."

—*El Paso Times*

"Good, old-fashioned, epic entertainment, told with admirable vigor and style."

—*Kirkus Reviews*

"You won't be able to put it down...an enthralling story of love, mystery and betrayal."

—*Shreveport Times*

REBECCA RYMAN

OLIVIA AND JAI

Taj Mahal photo courtesy of Stockmarket.
Inset art by Addie Passen.

Library of Congress Catalog Card Number: 89-77952

ISBN: 0-312-92568-9

Printed in the United States of America

St. Martin's Press hardcover edition published 1990
St. Martin's Paperbacks edition/August 1991

10 9 8 7 6 5 4 3 2 1

For my parents
In ever-loving remembrance

AUTHOR'S NOTE

I would like to express my deep gratitude to my husband for his many accurate observations and rectifications, and for his tolerance of domestic disarray over long periods while this book was being written. My warm thanks also to caring friends and relations who donated freely of their time and thought, not to dismiss with facile praise but to compliment with painstaking and productive criticism. To others who advised with wisdom and steered the manuscript into publication, I owe a debt that will ever be outstanding.

Special thanks are due to Mr. Thomas J. McCormack, whose often relentless but always inspired editorial guidance has resulted in a better book than I had envisaged. And for those whose formidable task it has been to question, to suggest, to correct, and to finally bring order to a chaotic typescript, I record not only my gratitude but my unqualified admiration.

Calcutta

1848

1

The city sweltered.

Monsoon clouds, pregnant with rain, growled and grunted across a swollen pewter sky. The dome of afternoon pressed down on the earth like a soggy blanket, trapping the oppressive humidity and laying low even the most fortitudinous, their bodies robbed of energy and their minds of will. Slashing across the city, the river Hooghly crawled as if on leaden feet, waiting for the gales that would whip it along and relieve it of its torpor. Not a leaf moved, not a dust devil stirred; but in the very stillness there was promise. When the storm did break it would bring with it blessed coolness and once again the earth would breathe.

But in the meantime, Calcutta sweltered.

Standing in her kitchen house doling out rations for the evening meal, Lady Bridget Templewood appeared untouched by the heat. As always, her stance was ramrod straight. The hand holding the long wooden spoon swooped in and out of the groundnut oil jar, moving with the mechanical precision of an instrument devised solely for that purpose. As she counted, her lips framed silent incantations, giving her the appearance of a vestal high priestess immersed in some esoteric ritual upon which depended the fate of the Empire. Had anyone told her this, Lady Bridget would have been flattered. She believed devoutly that even in this distant outpost of Her Majesty's burgeoning realm, as an English noblewoman she had obligations to Queen and country from which not even the kitchen house was exempted.

The rice, lentils and green beans, all carefully weighed, had been dispensed. The potatoes—two for each of them and none for Estelle—were in the process of being peeled by the scullion. Two chickens, plucked and cleaned, squatted by the coal range awaiting dismemberment into manageable pieces. On the white marble tabletop waiting to join the sizzling onions for the *vindaloo* curry were turmeric paste, chillies, coriander and cumin all ground in vinegar. Hardened by the pungent flavours of the East, Sir Joshua's palate demanded sharp spices although Lady Bridget herself would have gladly done without.

Watching his lady memsahib go through her conscientious daily rituals, Babulal stood by in silence and impassivity, but within himself he simmered. For two whole days now he had been patiently waiting for an opportunity to replenish his own family's depleted larder and he considered it scandalous that it should be so. For one, his wife nagged him incessantly. For another, if cooks in prosperous *firanghi* households with bulging stores had to stoop to making their own purchases, was it not a matter of shame for his entire community? Not for the first time Babulal wondered if his own meagre pickings from the daily bazaar were worth it considering how well his counterparts did for themselves in other less stringent households.

"Memsahib, *mem*sahib . . . !"

The ayah's sudden scream from the compound shattered Lady Bridget's concentration. Her hand jerked and sent oil splashing all over the immaculate flagstone floor. "What on *earth . . . ?*"

"Memsahib, come kweek, *kweek!*" Still shrieking, the ayah flew through the kitchen door, the whites of her eyes rolling fearfully amidst the chocolate brown of her face. "Umrican missy mem fall from gee-gee into nullah . . . !" Breaking into hysterical Hindustani, she burst into tears.

Lady Bridget congealed. The cornflower blue of her eyes stilled with shock; incantations forgotten, her mouth rounded in horror. Dear God, if the reckless girl had really damaged herself, how would she ever face Sean again? Not that Lady Bridget particularly wished to, but that at the moment was beside the point. Mindless of greasy fingers, she dropped the ladle to clutch at her starched muslin skirt and ran out into the compound followed by the rest of the staff. Keeping time with her feet, her mind ran wild with conjecture; what if Olivia had broken her neck, injured her spine, disfigured her *face . . . ?* Shaking with fear, Lady Bridget flew around the double-storied bungalow towards the front garden, uncaring of her hemline trailing mud through the residual puddles, mentally expecting the worst. She rounded the final corner—and stopped dead in her tracks.

Far from having broken her back, Olivia was, in fact, in the process of heaving herself out of the ditch next to the casuarina hedge that separated the front lawn from the drive. Filled with stagnant rain-water, the ditch was now churned into a viscous brown soup, much of which clung to Olivia's person. On the other side of the hedge stood Jasmine, the white mare, neighing apologetically with her saddle askew and her reins draped around her neck like streamers. Olivia's new riding cap (fresh from London and bought only last week from Whiteaway Laidlaw for a rupee and a half) was floating down the muddy stream visibly unworthy of retrieval. Worse, the groom's cheeky son—too big for his britches by half anyway—was gripping Olivia's hands in his own in an effort to help. There appeared to be equal hilarity on both sides.

Lady Bridget's short-lived relief turned into annoyance and her lips thinned. Even so, she waited. It was unthinkable to castigate kith and kin in front of the servants no matter how hideous the crime and how grave the provocation. Clapping aside the insolent lad, she stalked grimly towards the site of the mishap. "Are you hurt, Olivia?"

With a final heave Olivia swung out of the ditch and onto the swampy lawn. "Only my pride, Aunt Bridget." Her grin beneath the drying mud on her face was rueful. "*Damn!* I was so doggone sure she'd be able to do it again!"

Lady Bridget blanched but decided to ignore the sotto voce expletive. In all fairness, the child's barbaric speech had improved considerably. And one could hardly expect miracles in eight weeks as one might with a decently brought up English girl. "Can you walk?"

"I think so. I reckon only my knees are bruised and I've had worse, believe me." Rising unsteadily to her feet, Olivia lifted her dripping skirt to examine the extent of her injuries. "Bucktooth always says that knowing *how* to fall is the name of the game. Being a rodeo man himself, I guess he should know." She laughed, gave her aunt a dazzling smile and started to wring out her skirt.

Lady Bridget was neither amused nor dazzled. In fact, she shuddered. Pointedly, she refrained from asking who Bucktooth was apart from a rodeo man, whatever that might be. Engaging her attention entirely was the horrifying sight of Olivia's bare legs at which she tried desperately not to look, knowing that that was an exercise in restraint not shared by her servants. Never having before seen a white mem's legs—not even sure that they possessed them—they stared openly. Astonished at the sudden revelation, the groom's son almost fell backwards into the ditch himself.

Lady Bridget leapt into action. "Go up immediately, Olivia, and get Estelle's ayah to pour you a hot bath. I'll be with you as soon as . . . ," she looked around and realized to her dismay that Babulal was no longer part of the audience, ". . . as I've finished with the stores." Grimly, she positioned herself between the knot of ogling onlookers and Olivia's bare knees.

"Mama, what's happened . . . ?" A highly alarmed Estelle came running down the portico steps followed by her yapping King Charles spaniel puppy. Catching sight of Olivia she broke off, stared, then doubled up with loud laughter. "Ooh, I *told* you so, didn't I? I *told* you it was a fluke—Jasmine would never be able to take that hedge again! Well, that should learn you, Miss Devil-May-Care, and oh *my,* you do look a proper sight!" Holding her sides she hooted.

"That's enough, Estelle!" her mother snapped. "I fail to see anything funny in this deplorable exhibition! Now help your cousin up the stairs and see to her bath, will you? Take out the iodine tincture, the bandages and cotton wool and send to the pantry for some boiling water. I'll be up in a few minutes." Clapping her hands together she briskly rattled off orders. "Come on now all of you, back to your posts *juldee, juldee,* chop, chop. Rehman, get the water boy to carry up four buckets from the hammam. You there, stop staring like an ape and see Jasmine back to the stables. If she's hurt that foreleg again it's your hide sahib will want, I promise you. Ayah, take missy mem's clothes to the dhobi this instant for a boil wash."

Wasting no more time, Lady Bridget hurried back to the kitchen. No doubt that wretched Babulal had already stuffed his turban with whatever he could lay his hands on for that disgustingly large brood of his. And if the level of port was further reduced, Josh would be livid. It was his second to last bottle and the replenishments ordered a year ago for Estelle's ball were not due for another two weeks. Thankfully, Olivia's injuries were minor. They could wait a few more minutes.

As Sir Joshua often had occasion to remark, there was nothing ambiguous about his wife's priorities in life.

"I thought it was understood, Olivia, that riding out in the heat of the day was inadvisable, and even more so without an escort?"

Scrubbed back into pristine respectability, Olivia reclined on a chaise-longue in the upstairs parlour. Her skin shone pink with the effort, her tall, coltish figure encased again in a feminine calico, this time of apricot and olive green. The offending knees were not only covered but also swabbed, medicated and bandaged. On a cushioned towel behind her head, her heavy chestnut hair fanned out like a mane, giving her even more the look of an unbridled filly. The soiled riding habit had been dispatched to the dhobi house in the servants' quarters, the mutilated cap had been joyously claimed by one of the gardeners and the groom had confirmed that Jasmine's foreleg was in no way damaged. But that was by no means the end of the matter. Lady Bridget was far from having had her say.

Olivia sighed. "The heat doesn't bother me, I promise you, Aunt Bridget. And I do know the station well enough by now not to need an escort."

"The heat you are used to is not tropical heat, Olivia. Here, it can ruin delicate white complexions and produce dreadful skin ailments." Even as she said it, Lady Bridget faltered. Olivia's robust, glowing complexion might not be of a hue suitable for Europeans but it looked anything but delicate. "More to the point," she added quickly, "you could have met with an accident elsewhere and been at the mercy of the natives."

From the window seat where she was occupied with a watercolour still life of a fruit bowl she regularly depleted, Estelle snorted. "Olivia has the best seat Papa says he's ever seen on a woman. She only fell off because she was being pigheaded."

Her mother withered her with a glance. "I know Olivia rides well, but that is irrelevant. *No* respectable European woman here invites trouble by venturing forth on her own!"

"Well, where she comes from they teach women to look after themselves," Estelle retorted hotly. "They don't tie them down with their mama's apron strings."

Before the familiar argument could blossom further, Olivia hastily intervened. "I only rode down to the embankment, Aunt Bridget, and I had no intentions of staying away long."

"I have never doubted your intentions, dear child," her aunt sighed, "only your methods. In India it is unsafe to be on one's own if one is a woman. A white woman here is an object of curiosity to the natives. They stare, make impertinent remarks and start entertaining ideas far beyond their station." She spoke with studied patience, wondering how often she would have to repeat her warnings to the headstrong girl.

Struggling to sit up, Olivia balanced herself on an elbow. "The natives stared far less than *I* would have if one of them had suddenly turned up in the middle of Sacramento! In fact, the villagers were most kind. I was watching this snake charmer with his cobras and they gave me a stool to sit on. They also gave me some very sweet tea in a clay pot." She met her aunt's eyes without flinching. "It was delicious."

It was Lady Bridget who in fact flinched. Drinking tea in clay pots with filthy peasants? Ye gods, what *would* the child think of doing next! She simmered with slow anger; what a mess, what an appalling mess Sean had made of Sarah's lovely child! Given the right upbringing in England, the girl could have had the world at her feet. Lady Bridget's anger melted and instead she was filled with pity. She rose to sit on the chaise-longue beside her niece and took both her hands in hers.

"Our life here must appear strange to you, my dear. I do understand that—especially in view of your own . . . unconventional upbringing. But in the colonies we must remain aloof, a little distant from the masses. Superior civilisations can survive only in exclusivity—you do see my point, don't you, dear?"

It was a variation on a theme Olivia had heard incessantly since she had arrived. As always, it left her unconvinced. "From what little I've read, it would seem that superiority is a relative term, it—"

"What is true in theory is not always the reality, Olivia!"

"Perhaps, but Papa says that an old civilisation such as this—"

"Your father is an idealist." Lady Bridget's mouth crimped as if having said a word not to be repeated in front of children. "And he has never been to India. No matter how old, this is a pagan country. Its culture reeks of superstition, of savage belief abhorrent to all true . . ." She stopped. Once again she was being drawn into an argument she considered futile and irrelevant. Olivia had an annoying habit of using logic as a weapon; it was not a habit Lady Bridget approved of in women. There was right and there was wrong, and word juggling could not make them otherwise. She stood up to indicate the termination of the debate. "Anyway, to return to the point, I would be obliged if you would not ride out again on your own. That stable-boy is an impudent, disreputable lout but at least he can keep pace with a horse and return with a message in case you have trouble with the natives."

Estelle giggled. "If Olivia has trouble with the natives, I'd give my sympathies to the natives! She'd just take out her derringer and shoot them dead straight through the heart, wouldn't you, Coz?"

"Indeed!" her mother exclaimed with cutting displeasure, and inwardly Olivia groaned; the giddy girl was really the limit! "If your cousin does carry a weapon, Estelle, perhaps it is because she is not aware that India isn't *quite* the Wild West yet, nor by England's grace is it likely ever to be. In the meanwhile, I would prefer you not to meddle in matters that in no way concern you." Sweeping out of the room she slammed the door behind her.

Olivia glared at her cousin. "I wish you would stop championing my causes with such unnecessary fervor, Estelle! Your efforts always seem to end up making even more trouble for me—and for yourself. Now she knows I have a derringer and she's livid."

"Oh, fiddlesticks! Mama bullies you the same as she does me, and I just don't think we should stand for it." Her blue eyes, so much like her mother's, showed no sign of repentance.

"She doesn't bully either of us," Olivia said sharply. "She has her principles like everyone else, that's all." That she considered some of her aunt's principles absurd she had no intention of telling Estelle.

"Principles, *huh!*" Estelle pouted and gazed thoughtfully at an orange. "It's all very well for you. *You'll* have to suffer them only for a year; *I* have to put up with them for *life!*"

"Only if you choose to remain a spinster and, somehow, I can't really see *that* happening!" She grinned.

Estelle tossed her flaxen curls with an air of disdain and jabbed her paintbrush into a pool of crimson lake. "I'll make sure it doesn't! When I'm eighteen, I shall do exactly as I please, so there!"

"You do pretty much as you please right now."

"Not as much as Polly does. *Her* mother lets her use lip salve and kohl and go to *burra khanas* with her beaux—and Polly's a whole six months younger than I am." The enormity of the injustice depressed her. She pushed away her water-colour, picked up the orange and started to peel it, scowling. "Uncle Sean never bullied you, did he? Can you imagine Papa letting *me* carry a derringer and taking me on a wagon train?"

"There aren't any wagon trains in India," Olivia pointed out.

Estelle dismissed the technicality with a wave. "If Uncle

Sean always treated you as an adult, why can't they me? I'm not even allowed to *eat* what I want to when I want to without Mama making a fuss." She glowered at the orange segments, demolished them in a single mouthful and spat the pips out of the window with deliberate defiance.

"But you still manage to," Olivia remarked drily. "What you can't have at table you bribe Babulal to give you later in the kitchen—and I've seen those biscuit tins under your bed, remember?"

"Well, I'm not going to let Mama starve my body to death like she tried to crush my spirit, am I? I'll lay a wager Uncle Sean *never*—"

"Our circumstances were quite different, Estelle," Olivia said hastily, uneasy in her cousin's persistent and misplaced admiration. Estelle was as lovable as she was exasperating, but Olivia had no intention of being blamed for inciting rebellion. "Now tell me," she changed the topic swiftly, "is Uncle Josh absolutely certain the ship will reach here in time? There's no chance of your dress being held up, is there?"

Forgetting everything else, Estelle brightened. "Papa has *promised* he won't allow anyone to let me down. Oh, Olivia . . . ," in her sudden change of mood she squealed, swept her puppy Clementine up in her arms and hugged it, ". . . I'd die, just *die,* if anything went wrong now. I'd never be able to look that silly Charlotte Smithers in the face again, not after everything she's been saying to Jane about my ensemble. Do you know what Jane actually had the gall to tell Mrs. Cleghorne, who told Marie who told Polly? She said . . ."

Olivia closed her eyes and stopped listening, satisfied that with the floodgates once again open her cousin's energies would all be expended on the most momentous future day of her life—her eighteenth birthday next month and the coming-of-age ball being planned for it. As the familiar torrents of gossip flowed out of an excited Estelle, Olivia allowed them to wash over her unnoticed, her monosyllabic responses all that Estelle desired.

A year.

Twelve months.

Three hundred and sixty-five days—minus only sixty!

Against the soothing murmur of Estelle's unheard chatter, Olivia's own familiar torrents of thought flooded her mind. How would she ever survive these three hundred and five remaining days of an exile that stretched ahead like a sterile desert, dull and joyless? She should never have come, never have given in to her father's well-meaning persuasions, insisted that he take her with him, as he had often done in the past. Glumly and for the thousandth time, Olivia decided that her coming to India had perhaps been a mistake . . .

Which was an introspection very similar to the one Lady Bridget was indulging in as she absently supervised the pruning of the bougainvillea above the front portico. Had Olivia not taken so impartially and so equally from both parents, she mourned silently, there would have been no problem. That wilful stubbornness and hard set of the chin, those disarming hazel eyes so filled with innocent fire, that smile of blinding radiance that seemed to illuminate her face from within, the vulnerability behind the defiance—all these had come from Sarah. If one could overlook her disastrous taste in husbands, Sarah had many virtues even though high intellect and the ability to articulate it had not been among them. These, definitely, Olivia had acquired from her outrageous father. Whatever Lady Bridget's opinion of him—and it was unambivalent—she could not deny that Sean O'Rourke did have brains. That he chose to fritter them away in chasing rainbows Lady Bridget might have considered *his* business, had he not driven poor Sarah to her grave and defiled his daughter so thoroughly with his radicalism. Why, she had never even had an English nanny! And which high-born English gent would want to wed a lass who debated like a politician and gave a lecture where only a kiss was called for?

Irascibly Lady Bridget rebuked the gardener for having let the vine grow wild and promised a deduction of four annas from his wages. But she remained abstracted. Certainly, Olivia's growing influence over Estelle was not Olivia's fault. Despite her fearsome spirit, Olivia was practical, resourceful, unspoilt and (when she chose to be) eminently sensible. That she had been allowed to run wild in a country already a wilderness was not her fault, any more than the fact that it was her less sterling qualities that Estelle chose to emulate. And it was her daughter's growing insurgency that alarmed Lady Bridget. English society forgave the Americans much because they didn't know any better; in an English girl born and bred amidst the most hallowed traditions of the aristocracy, radical behavior was neither easily forgiven nor quickly forgotten.

As far as Olivia was concerned, Lady Bridget not only knew her duties but was determined to fulfil them to the best of her considerable ability. It was Estelle's future that was now beginning to cause her concern. *Had* it been a mistake, she wondered also for the thousandth time, to bring Olivia out here before Estelle was suitably wed? . . .

"*Vindaloo?* Oh, splendid." Estelle attacked the curry with gusto. "Is Papa going to be late again?"

"Your father said not to wait dinner for him. He and Arthur will eat later in the study." Lady Bridget signalled Rehman, the chief bearer, to remove the serving dish from her daughter's purview.

"It's that *Sea Siren* business again, isn't it?" Estelle adroitly outmanoeuvred the bearer to add one last spoonful of rice to her plate. "They say she was pirated because of all that opium on board."

"Was she? Ask your father. I have no idea. Incidentally," she frowned, "Jane Watkins sent a note to say she's bringing both dresses in the morning. If you wish to still fit into them, Estelle, I suggest a little more restraint at table. I will not allow another gown for the Pennworthys' *burra khana.*"

"Oh, I'd forgotten all about the *burra khana!* But can I at least be measured for the green georgette, Mama? That is, if Olivia doesn't mind the beige."

"No, I don't mind the beige." Olivia's heart sank—*another* dinner-party? Did folks in these parts have no other means of entertainment? Since she had arrived she had been to one, sometimes two, each week and more over weekends. "In any case, I don't need another dress. I have more than I can use. Thank you."

"Estelle has two other greens. I think you should have the georgette, Olivia," Lady Bridget said firmly, determined to make no differences between the girls. "Green suits you well, you know."

"Oh, but it suits Estelle better," Olivia said, her eyes twinkling. "As the dashing Captain Sturges has no doubt already noted."

Estelle blushed and tossed a napkin playfully at her cousin. "Well, who cares? It's *you* who has poor Freddie Birkhurst mooning like a lovesick duck, hasn't she, Mama?"

"If Olivia has aroused the interest of Mr. Birkhurst," her mother said with a smug smile, "I see nothing wrong in that. Your cousin is a very personable, very eligible young lady with impeccable antecedents on . . . ," she almost said "on her mother's side" but thought better of it. "I should have told you earlier, Olivia, but it slipped my mind—Freddie Birkhurst has written to ask if he may escort you to the Pennworthys next week. Naturally I have been pleased to accept. I take it the arrangement finds favour with you?"

With great restraint Olivia forbore from informing her aunt that it certainly did not! Freddie's obvious infatuation with her embarrassed and irritated her, as did the unilateral acceptance of his wretched invitation. "Do I have to go to the party at all?" Olivia asked bluntly, side-stepping the issue.

"I thought young girls *liked* going to parties!" Inwardly Lady Bridget seethed again—what was wrong with this child? Had that wild Irish father of hers given her no social graces at all? "And it wouldn't do to disappoint poor Mr. Birkhurst now, would it?"

"Olivia doesn't want to go *because* of Freddie," Estelle took it upon herself to explain. "She says he keeps staring at her and his eyes remind her of boiled gooseberries." She giggled and sucked noisily on a chicken drumstick. "They do rather, you have to admit, Mama."

Under her breath Olivia muttered a strictly forbidden oath and her aunt bristled. "If Olivia finds Mr. Birkhurst's kind and entirely courteous attentions irksome, she is at perfect liberty to tell me so herself." She paused, but no response was forthcoming from her intimidated niece. "You see? Olivia has no such reservations. And I do think it's wicked of you to make idle mockery of the brave young men who sustain the outposts of our Empire with such dedication, Estelle!"

It was a reproof for them both but, catching her cousin's eye, Olivia nearly giggled too. Everyone knew that if there was anything Freddie Birkhurst was dedicated to, it was devout self-indulgence. As for the Empire, in Freddie's own opinion, it could sustain itself very well without his help. Or, as many felt, better for that reason precisely.

"Oh, Mama, stop *worrying!* You don't have to make matches for Olivia," Estelle offered without being asked. "She'll trap her own husband without even trying. Freddie isn't the only prospect in station ready, willing and able; they all are."

A shocked silence ensued. Furious, Olivia broke it before her aunt could recover. Under the table her palms itched to smack her cousin's bottom. "I shall be very pleased to accept Mr. Birkhurst's offer," she said behind clenched teeth, somehow raising a smile.

"It is kind of him to have made it." Crushing her cousin with a look, she excused herself from table and escaped into the back verandah.

At last the storm had broken.

In a clamour of thunder and lightning the still of the afternoon vanished to give way to whipping gales that raced across tree tops, making them dance like dervishes to rhythms dictated by arcane music. Jagged bolts of white light cracked open the skies, turning night into day bathed in eerie phosphorescence. Through the frenzied acacias at the foot of the garden, the Hooghly peaked and pranced as it joyously joined in the impromptu monsoon ballet, its waves rising in walls of animated abandon. If there was anything Olivia had come to love in Calcutta, it was these nightly seasonal rituals. Curled up in a cane chair in the verandah with Clementine in her lap, she sat and watched the play of earth and sky and water, comforted by an odd kind of security. Even half-way around the globe, a million years and miles away from her roots, this at least was familiar. The rolls of thunder, the gush of water down the drainpipes, the rain insects fluttering around the sconces, the rich smell of wet earth, the slush, the splashing sprays, the brilliant intensity of the nourished greens—these were the same here as at home.

Home!

Suddenly, she felt washed away again with nostalgia. Her eyelids started to sting and her throat hurt but, chewing hard on her lip, Olivia swallowed her homesickness. *I will not cry,* she vowed softly into Clementine's warm, musty fur. *Come what may, I will not cry.*

It was past nine when carriage wheels rumbled up the drive and Sir Joshua's hearty bellow of *"Koi hai?"* sent the household again scurrying into activity as he rattled off orders in his fluent Hindustani.

The storm had long subsided, leaving an aftermath of cool. Against a clear sky galleons of clouds skimmed tree tops, urged on by gentle wind. The inevitable chorus of cicadas and deep-throated frogs was in full concert around the verandah where Olivia still sat brooding. With the arrival of the master, fresh human sounds started up. Servants, barefooted and hushed, scampered up and down stairs like mice; overhead, punkahs squeaked as they circulated air, and in the pantry, under Lady Bridget's crisp supervision, glasses tinkled, crockery rattled and the pungent aroma of warming food arose. Sir Joshua's deep chuckles and Estelle's prattle floated in Olivia's direction from the front portico and a moment later heavy footsteps strode purposefully down to where she sat.

"Jasmine threw you today?"

"Well . . ." With a reproachful look at her cousin, Olivia lifted a cheek to receive Sir Joshua's peck. "I guess so."

"Not hurt badly, I hope?"

"Not hurt at all! Just a few grazes. Jasmine took that hedge so perfectly yesterday. I could have bet a silver dollar she'd do it again." Olivia made a wry face. "Fortunately, the ditch was full of water."

"Fortunately?" Sir Joshua cocked an eyebrow. "Well, I could bet a silver dollar your aunt didn't see it quite like that! You had no business to try and turn poor old Jasmine into a steeplechaser. Don't risk it again, eh?" His eyes twinkled and he winked. "Let's keep that pioneering spirit on a shorter leash, shall we? I won't say more because I have no doubt Bridget has said it all. Had dinner?"

"Yes," answered Estelle, "and there's chicken *vindaloo* curry with loads still left for you and Uncle Arthur." She nuzzled her father's arm fondly.

"There is? What did you do then, starve yourself?" He laughed, patted his daughter's well-rounded behind and turned again to Olivia. "We had fun and games in the Chamber this morning. Those new tea levies seem to have opened a pretty can of worms, as you Americans might say. Come and join us later if you like. I'll tell you how we worthy boxwallahs become squabbling fishwives when it boils down to rupees, annas and pies." With Estelle still hanging on to his arm, he strode away.

Olivia's spirits lifted, as they always did in the presence of her uncle, whom she liked enormously. As senior partner of Calcutta's largest tea exporting house, Templewood and Ransome, he was a merchant prince in stature, recently elected chief official of Calcutta's Chamber of Commerce. If Olivia found anything intellectually stimulating amidst the narrow confines of colonial society, it was the rough and tumble of the city's corporate life. Here, as in New York and Chicago, according to what her father had told her, murderous rivalries prevailed, especially in the China Coast trade where dog ate dog with neither compunction nor compassion and only the most primeval laws of the jungle applied.

This complex, cold-blooded mercantile world fascinated Olivia. From her uncle she had learned much of the honourable East India Company, the world's largest trading establishment and bastion of English enterprise in India. From books borrowed from Sir Joshua's ample library, she had gathered that the rise of the establishment—known locally as John Company or Company Bahadur—had been spectacular. It virtually ruled India under charter from the Crown, or that part of India not ruled by the princes, and wielded immense power with its own army and the right to wage war if necessary. Founded in 1600 by eighty canny, hard-headed English businessmen, John Company capitalised with great profit on the open-ended wealth of the Orient: spices, silks, China teas, indigo, jute, cotton for Lancashire's mills, opium, camphor, shellac, perfumes and countless other commercially lucrative commodities. The cut and thrust of commercial life here reminded Olivia of her own country, where vast industries such as railroads, steel, and coal and other mining were burgeoning and competition on ever-expanding frontiers was as violent and fierce as in these imperial market-places.

But if Olivia's interest in Calcutta's commerce amused Sir Joshua, it aggravated her aunt even more. After the men had eaten in the study, she cornered her husband in the bedroom when he came up for a wash. "I do wish you wouldn't encourage the girl, Josh, in these silly pursuits. Don't you consider her ideas forward enough as they are?"

Standing before the mirror brushing out his mutton chop whiskers, Sir Joshua grunted. "The lass has a good brain between her ears. Let her use it if she wants to."

"If she has a good brain between her ears let her use it to find a decent English husband!" his wife retorted. "She's here only for a year and she's not getting any younger. Would you approve of a spinster daughter almost twenty-*three?*"

Having no particular opinion in the matter, he merely shrugged. He gave his whiskers a final pat and strolled out of the room, having no doubt dismissed the subject entirely from his mind. In the art of solemnly hearing his wife without listening to a word she said, Sir Joshua was something of a master.

It was around ten that Olivia walked into Sir Joshua's study followed by Rehman bearing the coffee salver. Sir Joshua and his junior partner in the firm, Arthur Ransome, both held snifters of brandy and the air was thick with Havana cigar smoke. "Ah, there you are, m'dear." Lifting his chin Sir Joshua inhaled appreciatively. "I'm beginning to agree with Olivia, Arthur. There is a great deal to be said for Brazilian coffee."

Arthur Ransome rose to his feet with some awkwardness and bowed. "Indeed there is. Could be we've been chasing the wrong beverage all these years."

The banter continued through the appreciative sipping of coffee as Sir Joshua regaled them with a literally blow-by-blow account of the morning's rumbustious proceedings in the Chamber. Then Ransome made a comment, which Olivia missed. Sir Joshua sobered. "I was not being frivolous, Arthur. I think it's a perfectly viable project and draconian situations call for draconian action, at least that much you will agree?"

It was evidently the thread of an earlier conversation that was being picked up. Ransome shook his head. "Draconian yes, but not suicidal! To act rashly now would be to lose sight of the reality, Josh."

Without comprehending the background to the dispute, Olivia listened intently. Although Ransome was her uncle's closest and dearest friend apart from business partner, the two men could not have been more different. Whereas Sir Joshua was large, loose limbed and dominated with ease whatever environment he happened to be in, Ransome was visibly sedate, squat, fastidious and content to remain in the background. If there was occasional flamboyance and a certain simmering ruthlessness about Sir Joshua, Ransome's middle name was caution, perhaps because as an accountant said to be a genius with figures, he liked precision and propriety. Olivia had met him before, of course, and had been impressed by his unfailing courtesy.

"We can't sit back and let them beat us at our own game, dammit! It's a challenge that must be answered." Sir Joshua stood up to tower above his seated partner, his face even more florid than usual.

"It will be answered by others."

"Maybe. But I don't give a damn what others do. There are rich pickings here, Arthur, richer than available in London. I think we must bid for our share of them *now.* Isn't that right, Olivia?" He suddenly spun around and impaled her with a stare.

"Isn't what right?" Quickly, she reassembled her thoughts.

"Would you not say that our chances of making hard dents in your American markets are again good considering that three quarters of a century has elapsed since those infernal Tea Parties?"

Olivia pondered. Her uncle's habit of frequently asking her opinion on matters she knew little about pleased her, since at home her father had always treated her as an equal even when she was much younger. This time she knew to what her uncle was referring—the Tea Act, which had imposed a threepenny per pound levy on teas imported from England into America. The opposition to the levy had been bitter and the first consignments received in 1773 in Boston, Greenwich, Charleston, Philadelphia, New York, Annapolis and Edenton had been unceremoniously dumped into the harbours, the incident earning the jocular nickname of the "Tea Parties." In fact, it was this indignation that had struck the first blow for the American War of Independence and, understandably, soured American taste for tea.

Olivia recalled these facts now in answer to Sir Joshua's query. "Well, I do know that some folks back home still will not buy anything imported from England. Besides, almost everyone we know drinks caw— coffee." Remembering her aunt's advice, she hastily amended her long vowel. "And, surely, whatever little demand there is for tea is satisfied by American importers who also sail to the China Coast?"

"You see, Arthur?" Sir Joshua smacked his thigh and looked pleased. "Olivia has hit the nail on the head. It's because there *is* a demand that Astor, Griswold, Howland and that bunch are making fortunes. By Jove, I'd dearly like to have another poke at Boston!"

Ransome continued puffing quietly at his pipe, unimpressed. "Not now, Josh. Maybe later. We do pretty well in Mincing Lane and in the domestic market. Why reach for the moon when we don't need it?"

"Because when we do need it, it will have waned!" Exasperated, he controlled himself with an effort. "Listen, Arthur, the Americans have an edge on us at the moment, and do you know why? Not because they're better, not by a long-shot, but because they're *faster.*"

"Agreed. But we simply cannot afford one of these Baltimore clippers at the present time. We have to operate with what we have, our ugly little tea wagons, and do the best we can, which is pretty good."

"Precisely, old boy! But if we modernised the tea wagons they could still be a match for the clippers."

The expression on Ransome's round, plump-cheeked face turned wary. "How?"

"By refitting them with coal engines."

Ransome laughed. "Coal engines! My dear fellow, that's a pipe dream, a pie in the sky. It will be years before coal-powered navigation becomes commonly available, within the reach of private merchants."

"You're wrong there, Arthur." Hands clasped behind his back, Sir Joshua walked to the glass-fronted cupboard in which reposed all the memorabilia of his sailing days—carved ivory ornaments, jade figurines, etched metal vases, urns and incense stands, brass Buddhas and Ming jars—and stared into it hard. "John Company already uses steam packets for coastal and river traffic. England and America have coal engines pulling trains. Why should we not make a start here?"

"Well, for one," Ransome asked drily, "where's the coal? The Royal Navy maintains its own coaling stations, which we cannot touch. Every lump mined at Raniganj—and ninety thousand tons a year is still precious little—is being stockpiled for the Bombay-Thana railway already under construction. Let's not daydream, Josh." His tone sharpened. "Whatever coal exists at the moment is not available for private business."

Sir Joshua turned and strolled back toward Arthur, his face suddenly blank. "Raniganj will expand. Other mines will open up. We know, for instance, that there is coal in . . ." He paused and pulled in a deep breath and his half smile was suddenly very sly, "in Kirtinagar."

"Ah!" His partner's intake of breath was audible. "I've suspected for some time that *this* is what you've been building up to, Josh. And now I know you *are* reaching for the moon!" He laughed but with irritation.

"Why? I know the calibre of these native princes, Arthur. Show them a few pretty baubles from Europe, tickle their fancies, prime their egos and pleasure them well—and they'll sell their mothers to you if the price is right." His face was now set and his voice harsh.

Ransome sat up slowly and subjected his partner to a surprised stare. "But we both know the reputation Arvind Singh has, Josh. He's not one of those maharajas you have in mind."

"Pshaw!" Sir Joshua threw up his hands in a gesture of

contempt. "Underneath, they're all the same—and there's more than one way of catching a monkey. Arvind Singh wants big money for that irrigation project of his. If the Europeans formed a consortium with merchants like Jardine, Gillanders, Schoene, a jute man or two, we could afford to make Arvind Singh an offer he would not be able to refuse. There isn't a single merchant in Calcutta who wouldn't sell his soul for steam navigation. What we need is some hard bargaining power."

All at once, it seemed to Olivia, the timbre of the debate had changed subtly from healthy disagreement to something else. There was tension in the air, an unspoken feeling of disquiet. For a long while Ransome did not speak as he exercised his right leg sorely afflicted by gout, and when he did speak it was so quietly that Olivia could barely hear him.

"I'm not certain, Josh, if you are forgetting the crux or missing it deliberately. We both know that it is hardly the Maharaja's fancy that needs to be tickled, and I can't bring myself to believe that you, especially you, are up to the alternative." Presenting the expanse of an angry back to his partner, Sir Joshua clenched his fists by his side but remained silent. Doggedly, Ransome ploughed on. "It sours me too, Josh, that the man has had his clipper refitted in Clydeside with a coal engine, which makes him twice as fast as any of us, but he is an exception. Yes, I too am envious as hell of his successes, *but* we must accept that we cannot match him in the American market. Not anymore. Kala Kanta has too much of a head start. And now that he's devised this clever novelty of selling tea in smaller, individual packets—"

"I thought of that two years ago, dammit!"

"True," Ransome agreed calmly, "but it is Kala Kanta who has *done* it."

"Are you chickening out of a challenge, Arthur?" There was anger in Sir Joshua's hard, intractable tone. "He hasn't cornered *all* the market yet; that moon still has slices for others, for *us!*"

"It may well, yes. But to match him in the West, we would have to cut investments in the East, and I'm not prepared for that. Our foundations are in the China Coast. We are neither ready nor equipped for reckless adventurism in another hemisphere. As for the challenge," he shrugged, "ten years ago when we were younger, healthier, more foolhardy, yes, I would have taken the gamble, but not now. Let us abandon thoughts of the Kirtinagar coal, Josh. We both know that it can never be ours."

Sir Joshua's volatile temper, always quick to ignite, strained to explode. "It can be ours, Arthur, it *must!* If we play our cards right we *can* bypass him!" He strode to his desk and thumped a fist on it.

"Bypass Kala Kanta?" Ransome echoed. "In Kirtinagar? My dear fellow, have you taken leave of your senses? Even trying such a tactic would be an insanity!" He held up a hand to tick off his fingers one by one. "A warehouse lost in a mysterious fire. The *Sea Siren* stripped at sea of valuable cargo by unidentifiable privateers—by no means a first act of piracy with our opium consignments. Mincing Lane in London continues to receive from our Canton establishment inexplicably adulterated teas. What Marshall dispatches are the best souchong and pekoe. What mysteriously arrives is ash and sloe leaves tanned with japonica and molasses. Leave aside our sinking reputation; we could earn hefty fines under these new anti-adulteration laws, even prison sentences. Suddenly no one remembers our magnificent first and second flushes of the best teas in the world, teas for which we've been renowned. Now even our insurers are starting to ask damned embarrassing questions." For a man as taciturn as Ransome, it was a heated speech. He slumped back in his chair and mopped his forehead. "But then I don't need to remind you of all these disasters, Josh. They're emblazoned boldly enough in our ledgers."

Gazing out of the window Sir Joshua nodded, but absently, as if he had heard nothing. "We must remain the best, Arthur," he said softly, "the *best.* It is what we have striven all our lives to be. If we are to be second, it cannot ever be to him, *never to him.* As for the rest, Kala Kanta is not invincible. He *can* and *will* be beaten!"

"No Josh, he is not invincible," Ransome sighed a trifle wearily, "he is merely *mad.* And he is violent, which makes him doubly dangerous. Heaven knows we too have fought dirty in our time, our hands too are not all that clean, but I don't have the strength or the stomach for retaliation now. Our only defence against this mad dog is to stay well out of his way."

"And what have we gained so far by staying out of his way?" Sir Joshua asked, his eyes rife with contempt. "Shall I repeat to you those calamities you have yourself just recounted?"

"I still have no stomach for provoking more trouble." Ransome's jaw set in a stubborn line. "Let the bastard do his worst, and we have to concede it could have been worse than it has. Maybe, given enough rope, he'll do us the favour of hanging himself some day. But for the moment, Josh, leave it be. Leave it be, my friend."

Sir Joshua fell silent, refraining from the heated rejoinder that obviously trembled on his lips. Instead, he stood glowering at a moth fluttering across a maroon shantung silk drape as if about to swat it, but he didn't. Unaware of its brush with death, the moth found a chink in the curtain and flew out into the garden. Sitting in her wing chair partially concealed from both men, Olivia remained very still. The silence seemed so total and yet so turbulent that she finally couldn't contain herself. Inching forward to the edge of the chair, she asked with a touch of nervousness, "Who is this . . . this Kala Kanta you've been talking about?"

Both men started. It was obvious they had entirely forgotten her presence. For a moment neither volunteered an answer. Then, with a visible effort, Sir Joshua recovered. "Just a man, a business competitor," he said shortly. "No one of any consequence."

It was Arthur Ransome, courtly as ever, who hastened to repair his partner's brusqueness. "Kala Kanta is a scoundrel, to put it bluntly, Miss O'Rourke. There are many such fly-by-night operators in Calcutta who are a disgrace to ethical business, if you will accept a seeming contradiction in terms." A brief smile flickered across his lips. "But this man has gone beyond all limits. Be that as it may, I apologise on our joint behalves for subjecting you to a deplorably dull discussion and for excluding you from it so rudely. I hope you weren't too dreadfully bored?"

"Oh no," Olivia replied quite truthfully. "I was fascinated. These calamities you spoke of—are they serious?"

The endless, often naive, questions she had got into the habit of asking Sir Joshua usually received indulgent, good-humoured answers, but now his expression showed a flash of annoyance. "No, of course not. Ups and downs are facts of corporate life, ours included. Overnight, men can become millionaires on the China Coast, or go bankrupt. Fortunately, those with the kind of resilience we have bounce back like rubber. Isn't that right, Arthur?" Buoyant again, he clasped his hands together and smiled.

"Oh, absolutely." Ransome heaved his short, stocky frame out of the chair and stretched each leg in turn. He did not, Olivia noticed, lift his eyes to meet his partner's.

It was almost midnight. Since Ransome was a bachelor and lived alone, he often spent nights at the Templewood house. A bed had already been prepared for him in the downstairs guest-room. Olivia summoned Rehman, dozing behind the study door loyally waiting for his master to retire, to remove the coffee tray and soiled brandy glasses. She bid good night to both men, received a peck on her cheek from her uncle, now seemingly recovered and again his usual urbane self, and allowed him to usher her out of the room. As she turned to smile her thanks before the door closed again, Olivia's smile froze on her lips and her eyes widened.

The expression on Sir Joshua's face was one of such virulence, such naked spite and tangible hate that she stood rooted. It was only a flash and in a flash it was again gone, but there was something so ugly about it that Olivia shivered.

"I say," Freddie Birkhurst asked, "do you like croquet?"

Two months ago when she was fresh from home, Olivia would have had no hesitation in demanding bluntly, "What is croquet?" However, eight weeks of Lady Bridget's assiduous tutelage in the art of polite English conversation had taught Olivia caution. The problem was, for the life of her she could not remember whether croquet was a game or some kind of mutton cutlet. Morosely scanning the earnest countenance of the Hon'ble Frederick James Alistair Birkhurst, her escort for the evening, she decided to play safe. "Croquet? Well, I'm not sure that I've ever enjoyed . . . any."

Freddie stared, his protuberant eyes poised precariously at the edge of their sockets, then he chortled. "Oh, Miss O'Rourke, you do have such a divine sense of humour! Tell me, are all Americans so delightfully witty?" In the width of his smile his limited chin disappeared altogether.

"There are seventeen million Americans in America, Mr. Birkhurst," she said coldly. "Not having met them all, I can hardly hope to answer your question with any degree of accuracy."

Two and a half hours of Freddie's uninterrupted company had begun to wear Olivia down. Except to refresh his whisky, he had not left her side for a moment since he had fetched her to the Pennworthys in his splendid brougham with the crested doors. As Lady Bridget's American niece, Olivia effortlessly invited attention at *burra khanas,* even though it was the last thing she wanted at these dreary social occasions. Tonight, however, she craved attention from others if only to make Freddie's worshipful presence less intolerable. Her jaws ached with the mandatory smiles and her temples throbbed for want of fresh air in the crowded rooms, but there was no avenue of immediate escape. Even Estelle had vanished from sight on the arm of her dashing Captain Sturges, and Olivia had no desire whatsoever to exchange notes on fleas, bedbugs or thieving cooks in the company of Lady Bridget and her friends.

In a room teeming with vaguely familiar faces to which she could put few names, Olivia circulated with some desperation. As at all *burra khanas,* there was the same sprinkling of uniforms and the customary contingents of merchants, bankers and John Company officials. Those gents not in uniform wore frock-coats and shirts with stiffly starched frontages. One or two of the younger blades ventured sporty jodhpurs and fancy silken cravats. Among the ladies crinolines and chintzes were the favourites, allover hoops and fussy petticoats, with bodices adorned with frilly collars, bows, buttons, ribbons and yards of lace made limp by constant dhobi washings. Had Olivia given in to her aunt and worn tusser silk, she knew she would have expired with the heat. Her chosen lavender organdie with short cap sleeves and boat neckline was singularly unelaborate but at least it allowed for ventilation.

Circulation among the guests held other hazards for Olivia and small talk was a penance. She was constantly being asked to repeat herself and, worse, was having to constantly do the same to others. If her speech sounded odd to the English, their accents—ranging from Cornish to cockney—baffled her equally. As for frequently used colloquialisms such as "tiffin," "the mofussil," "gymkhana" and "chota peg," she couldn't make head or tail of any of them without explanation. Especially annoying, she found, was the appalling ignorance that existed about her own country. But if it was any consolation, information quotients were equally low about India—the country of their residence—and indeed about England, yearningly talked of as "home" but which many had never seen.

"How do you tolerate it here, Miss O'Rourke, considering the diabolical boredom of life? Enough to send one potty, wouldn't you say?"

Olivia turned to face Peter Barstow, a friend of Freddie's, also a man of leisure and private means whom she had met before and thought frivolous. "I tolerate it very well, Mr. Barstow," she countered, more out of loyalty to the Templewoods than truth. "If you cannot, then why do you stay?"

Barstow grimaced. "Same reason as Freddie. Pater's orders."

"Pater?"

"His father," Freddie translated. "We were both sent down together from Oxford. Our old boys were livid, justifiably I daresay. Awful disgrace, blot on the family escutcheon and so forth. Everyone thought we were less likely to soil the family linen further in the good old colonies, eh Peter?" He hiccupped, pardoned himself and staggered off towards the bar.

Olivia stared after him helplessly. "Sent down?"

"Expelled. You know, kicked out." Barstow grinned. "Stroke of luck, really. Couldn't stand the musty old mausoleum anyway." He sipped and over the rim of his glass surveyed Olivia reflectively. "Tell me, Miss O'Rourke, since you do tolerate this blasted country so well, how *do* you fill the long, dismal hours of the day? Believe me, it is truly for knowledge that I thirst."

The mockery was thinly veiled but Olivia let it pass. "Well, I ride every morning and explore the town, I read a great deal and I enjoy making mundane, everyday discoveries. There's so much to learn, I find, about this strange subcontinent."

"Learn?" He looked astonished. "Come, come, my dear Miss O'Rourke, we're not here to *learn,* we're here to *teach!*"

This time Olivia bristled under his patronization. "Oh really? Then you tell me, Mr. Barstow, having been *sent down* from Oxford and banished to the colonies, what precisely are *you* qualified to teach the Indians?"

He flushed but covered up with a murmured "Touché!" Nevertheless his faded blue eyes showed pique. "I hear from Calcutta's other gentry that you, Miss O'Rourke, are a young lady of considerable spirit. As such, might I inquire how you agreed to become a willing member of the fishing fleet? I'm sure you will not resent the question since American women are so admirably blunt and forthright."

"The fishing fleet?" Olivia looked blank.

"You are not familiar with the term?" He ran the tip of his finger along a well-waxed moustache. "Permit me then to enlighten you. Each year hordes of young ladies come to India with the specific purpose of finding a husband. In local parlance we refer to them as the fishing fleet. If they are unsuccessful in their hunt, as some sadly are, and are forced to leave without having made a catch, we call them returned empties." He chuckled, then added quickly, "Not that anyone as lovely as you, Miss O'Rourke, could possibly be a part of the return contingent, and certainly not if Lady Bridget's endeavours succeed."

The arrogant smartass! Olivia went cold with fury, but silently. Death rather than let him have the satisfaction of knowing that she was in any way riled! "Because we American women are blunt and forthright, Mr. Barstow," she said with a pleasant smile, "some might consider your generous words to be a proposal of marriage. Are they?" She had the great pleasure of seeing his face turn purple and his jaw loosen. "No? Well, I can't deny that I am relieved. There are some fates in life possibly worse than being a returned empty after all. *Do* excuse me." With a tinkling laugh she swept away from him and plunged into the crowd, inwardly fuming.

From the far end of the room Lady Bridget beamed. How *well* Olivia was conducting herself with the young men if that smile was to be believed! Of course, Barstow's family even with a titled second cousin was not in the same class as Freddie's, but they were not to be scorned. Satisfied for the moment, Lady Bridget happily returned to the subject of prickly heat with her hostess.

Blissfully, Olivia saw that Freddie had disappeared from her immediate vicinity. Taking quick advantage of his absence before it was too late, she pressed through the room towards the verandah, which led into the back garden. En route a Mrs. Babcock, wife of a Methodist clergyman, complained bitterly about the miserable, utterly miserable, subsidies her husband received from the church compared to those dispensed by the American Missionary Society in Bombay and seemed to hold Olivia solely responsible for the inequity. Estelle floated by briefly for reassurance that her emerald georgette was indeed superior to Charlotte Smithers's overdone London confection. And a Lieutenant Pringle, resplendent in naval uniform, and some others asked for their names to be added to her dance card.

The back garden was deserted. Only two bearers, turbaned and white coated, stood silently on call. Trained never to stare sahibs and memsahibs in the face, they lowered their eyes and salaamed as Olivia ran past onto the lawn. The wall that demarcated the Pennworthys' property from the embankment was high, but the wrought iron gate set in it, though locked, was manageable. With a quick glance over her shoulder Olivia hitched up her skirts and easily swung over the gate to the other side.

The hour was late and there was no one about on the embankment. Grateful for the privacy, Olivia swallowed huge lungfuls of cool air and sighed with relief. It was a remarkably clear night. Clusters of stars hung low against the smooth black satin of the sky. A melon moon, yet to rise fully, hovered over the horizon entangled in silhouetted palm fronds. Save for nature's orchestrations, the silence was untrammelled. Leaves rustled; occasionally the distant splash of oars echoed across the Hooghly. Nightjars bickered, river frogs croaked and the inevitable symphony of cicadas struck varying chords in the dark. In the flickering light of a rising moon Olivia saw a flight of stone steps leading to the river. She ran down it, removed her sandals and sat down on the last step to trail her finger-tips in the welcome coolness.

In the immense dark the distances seemed endless and unfettered. As always, the solitude of the night brought with it a soaring sense of freedom, a vast liberation of the spirit. Memories stirred, surged and flew across space and time to evoke visions and voices that would not be stilled. Olivia's mind raced back to other nights similar to this when she was with her father and rain smell steamed up through the earth to fill the world with freshness. It was on one such night that she had stood beside him by the mighty Mississippi gazing across its steady flow crinkled in the silvery moonlight. In the infinite silences where only the wind made footfalls in the mind he had said, "The virgin land you see before you, my darling, is a wilderness today, but tomorrow, within our very lifetime, this barrenness will explode and the blessed earth, this earth of America, will throw forth giants. One day we will be proud of what this fallowness will produce, for its fruit will startle the world. It is a grand scheme, Olivia, and you and I too are part of it."

She had been barely twelve then but she had never forgotten his words. He had spoken with awe, with such passion and simple faith, that now the remembrance again tightened her throat. It had seemed like a miracle that she too could have a share of this promise, of the future of this sweet-sour, soft-savage land out of which people like her father were hacking a nation. Transported across oceans and continents and chasms of dividing loneliness, Olivia thought of Sally and One-Eyed Jack and Bucktooth and Red Feather and Sally's boys, and of Greg. Especially of Greg. She saw that careful smile, those quiet, clear eyes and that sadness in them when she had left. She thought of Spike, her untidy mongrel rescued as a pup from coyotes, and of her Appaloosa, Domino, with his white hide and black spots with a touch of roan, which her father had given her when she turned thirteen. In her inner vision she saw the orchards and the corrals and the paddock rife with the scent of newly mown hay, and in her nostrils she smelt the generous promise of Sally's frying doughnuts to be smothered in sugar and cinnamon, the hickory smoke from the barbecue pit and the foul odour of those cheroots her father refused to abandon. She wondered if it was day or night in California, and was it warm? Wet? Who was frying her father's morning eggs in grease sunny side up on that Nantucket whaler? Reminding him of letters to be written, shoe-laces to be tied, ink stains to be removed from shirt cuffs that never seemed without them . . . ?

The lump in Olivia's throat hardened; self-pity bubbled up and spilled out, overwhelming her like a shroud. What oh what was she doing here, an eternity removed from her beginnings, from everything and everyone she loved? Consumed by melancholy and despair, she cushioned her cheek on her knees and did precisely what she had vowed she would not. She cried.

How long Olivia wept softly to herself she could not assess. But, as she was drying her tears and feeling better for having shed them, she stiffened. She felt, suddenly, that she was not alone. Peering over her shoulder she could see no one, but the sensation of being watched was so strong that one by one the hairs at the nape of her neck started to tingle. Nervously, she turned again. And stilled. Something had stirred against a shrub. Then, in the shadowed dark, the faint movement resolved slowly into the outline of a human form.

As her aunt's repeated warnings rushed back to her, Olivia felt a prickle of fear. In a reflex action born of habit she groped for her purse, which carried her derringer. Reassured, she breathed more easily again. Who was this person sitting behind her? Why? What could his intentions be if not criminal? She was about to get up and hurry away from what might well be trouble, when he spoke.

"Do not be alarmed. I sit here doing exactly what you are—savouring the solitude." The voice was cultured and the language he used was English. Olivia was on the point of relaxing her guard when he asked, "Why were you crying?"

She went rigid again. He had sat in silence while she *cried?* As an invasion of privacy it was unforgivable! "I was under the impression, obviously mistaken," she said stiffly, "that I was alone."

"Oh, but you are alone." He rose, walked unhurriedly down the steps and stood against a tree trunk with his arms crossed. "We are all alone. That is how we come into the world and that is how we will go. Alone and, in both instances, unconsulted."

A wit to boot! She was not impressed. "Courtesy required

that you make your presence known to me." She was both annoyed and embarrassed. Who on earth was he—another refugee from the Pennworthys? "I dislike being spied upon."

"If I took you by surprise, I apologise willingly. I had no intention of spying, I assure you. I usually walk my dogs here at night. They enjoy the exercise and I the solitude."

In the distance Olivia picked up the sounds of barking, and the slight emphasis on the word *solitude* could hardly be missed. "If it is I who have unwittingly poached on your preserve," she said with a private heightening of colour, "then it is from me that an apology is due."

"You misunderstand me. My solitude is enforced so I make a virtue out of a necessity. Your presence is in no way intrusive, on the contrary." Unlocking the shadow of his person from the foliage behind, he sat down at the far end of the step.

He had spoken politely enough and Olivia's resentment changed into curiosity. She could discern nothing of his face, but she could see that he was tall and wore a light-coloured shirt above dark trousers. Surely he could not have been at the party in that apparel? Betty Pennworthy would have had a fit!

"Well, what is the caper like?" He broke the silence to dispel her unspoken conjectures. A flash of white indicated that he had smiled. "But you don't really need to answer that question. The fact that you yourself choose to sit out here on your own is testimony enough."

Sour grapes? Someone chagrined at being left off the guest list? "It was hot. I felt the need for some fresh air, which is the only reason I'm here." She asked pointedly, "Do you know the Pennworthys?"

He uncrossed his arms and shrugged. "Calcutta is a strange animal. In size, it is a town; in commercial and political importance, a city and a capital. But in terms of social maturity it is a village. And, as in all villages, whether deserving of acquaintanceship or not, everyone knows everyone else."

It was an observation, however acerbic, that could hardly be denied, so she nodded. "Yes, I guess it's the same in all closed communities." At that he laughed under his breath but said nothing even though she had the feeling that he almost had.

Etiquette demanded that he withhold his identity no longer, but he made no effort to introduce himself. Nor did he seem to wish to learn her identity! The lapse, obviously deliberate, made Olivia uneasy again. Apart from his reticence, his manner was altogether unusual. Had she been at home, she would have thought nothing of his unorthodoxy. In America's diverse melting pot, oddballs proliferated; but here, where society was mannered and rules clear-cut and rigid, the man seemed strangely out of place for a European. Intending to leave forthwith, she rose to her feet. However, before she could either move or speak, two enormous black dogs came bounding out of the night to circle her with angry barks and root her to the spot.

"Don't be frightened," the man assured her calmly. "They won't harm you unless they have instructions to do so. If you stand still for a moment they can satisfy themselves that you bear *them* no ill will." He sounded almost amused, as if explaining an elementary fact to a child.

With no other option, Olivia did as suggested while the dogs conducted their investigations with sniffs and squeals and suspicious growls. Both animals were sleek and obviously well trained, for at the sound of their master's low whistle, they immediately abandoned her to flop on either side of him with tongues hanging out and ears still erect and on guard.

He patted each head in turn with obvious fondness. "This is Saloni and this handsome brute glaring at you rudely is Akbar. They are the best friends I have. They protect me with their lives."

Olivia's trapped breath exhaled in a gush of relief but she remained standing. "I'm not surprised you need protection," she said severely, "if you sneak up in the dark and frighten the unwary half to death!"

He laughed. "Had I frightened you half to death you would have returned the compliment by pulling your derringer on me."

Astonished, she sat down again. "How do you know that I carry a derringer?"

"Doesn't every sensible American woman in a precarious situation? And what could be more precarious than one of these infernal *burra khanas?*" He laughed again.

Olivia drew in her breath sharply. "How, may I ask, do you know that I am American?"

"And sensible?" He stretched out his legs to make himself more comfortable. "Because Calcutta *is* a village and the grapevine is extremely effective. And a sensible white woman stands out here like a bird of paradise among cackling hens."

She found the compliment dubious and offhanded, and the direction of the conversation uncomfortably personal. Furthermore, his deliberate refusal to announce his identity was disconcerting. Once more Olivia decided it was an opportune moment to leave, but as she got up, both dogs also rose in unison and growled. Irritably, she sat down again. "Do you think you could possibly instruct your life's protectors to allow me to go?" she asked acidly. "Any moment I expect a search party to come looking for me and it would be humiliating."

He made no move to call off his dogs. Instead, he settled back even more comfortably and laced his fingers behind his head. "I assure you that you will not be missed, except by one or two. And since it is to avoid the one or two that you are here in the first place, a precipitous return would defeat the object of the exercise. Besides," he smiled caustically, "the dancing will have already started and dinner will not be served before eleven. And there will be plenty of simpering girls only too willing to grab those dances you have promised and missed."

His assessments were so accurate that despite their bluntness Olivia had to smile. Her aunt *would* perhaps be looking for her, but then, so also might Freddie! Apart from other considerations, however, it was soothing to stay out here by the river, and she could not deny that there was something about this anonymous stranger that intrigued her, much as his perceptions made her uncomfortable. Against her better judgement, Olivia hesitated.

He misinterpreted her hesitation. "I have already pleaded guilty to having surprised you, Miss O'Rourke, but I assure you I am not in the habit of actually attacking the unwary—especially those who are armed."

She sat down heavily. "You know my name?"

"Obviously."

"How do you know who I am?"

"I don't, except in social parlance. Strictly speaking, it can never be said that anyone truly *knows* anyone else."

"That is either very lofty metaphysics," she scoffed, "or very low prevarication. Which are you—a philosopher or a double-dealer?"

He threw back his head and laughed with such genuine amusement that Olivia could not restrain her own laugh. "You know, sometimes I wonder myself! But is it possible to be one without the other? Let's just say that I have a touch of both, depending on the circumstances."

She frowned. "I find that deplorably cynical!"

"Perhaps. It's difficult to live in this world and not be a cynic."

"And that," she said firmly, "I find cheap. My father says cynicism is a convenient disguise for moral cowards."

"Your father is a man of words, not action. Maybe that's why."

Olivia had not considered that this outspoken stranger could have surprised her further, but this time he startled her. "You . . . *know* of my father?" she gasped. "How?"

He hesitated briefly. "I have read some of his writings."

"Where?" she cried, excited. "Here in India?"

"No. In San Francisco. He wrote an exposé of the conditions under which miners worked along the Coal River. His sincerity and depth of feeling impressed me."

"Then you have first-hand knowledge of my country?" For no reason other than she was so desperately homesick, Olivia involuntarily warmed to him, instantly forgiving him his many excesses. "You have lived in America?"

Again he hesitated. "Yes." Abruptly he rose to his feet, picked up a stone and sent it skimming across the surface of the river. In some subtle way the gesture indicated an end to the subject of himself. "Is that why you are unhappy? Because you are separated from your father?"

"I miss my father but I am not at all unhappy!"

The sharpness of her tone didn't seem to trouble him. If the correction was meant as a reprimand, which it was, he appeared not to notice it. Instead he asked, "Is he still active in his journalistic endeavours?"

Since it was a question less impertinent than his others and since she rarely had the opportunity in Calcutta to talk about her father—never with anyone who knew his literary work first hand—Olivia answered willingly, indeed, enthusiastically. "Very much so. He has recently sailed for Hawaii to investigate the reported massacre of whales in the Pacific, about which he feels strongly. He is urging strict legislation to halt the rampant killings."

"So!" Even in the half light the inquiring lift of an eyebrow was visible as he turned to face her. "He still believes in tilting at windmills even when he knows the fight is hopeless?"

"He believes in principles," Olivia amended, stung. "And that it is better to have fought and lost than never to have fought at all. Isn't that what every decent man believes?"

"Possibly. Not claiming decency, I don't. I believe in winning, or not fighting at all. The world is intolerant of losers."

"And do you always win?" she demanded heatedly, wondering at the same time if she was mad, trading arguments in the middle of the night on the river with a man whose name she did not know and whose face she could not see! The situation was bizarre.

"Yes, always."

She was appalled by his conceit. "In that case you must be singularly lucky or given to self-delusion. Or both."

"I don't believe in luck and only fools delude themselves. I may be many unblessed things but I promise you I am not a fool." His lofty self-assessment was touched with sarcasm as he added, "For a white mem you do have an admirable wit, Miss O'Rourke. I see that my information about you has not been inaccurate."

Information about her? Nervously, she searched her memory again; *could* it be that she had met him before somewhere? She dismissed the probability. It was impossible that she could have met so outspoken a person and forgotten him! "What . . . information do you have about me?"

She heard him fumble in the gloom, retrieve something from his clothing and then strike a light. It was a pipe and he took his time igniting it. The flame cupped between his palms gave her a brief glimpse of a pale face and a mass of very dark hair, nothing else. He puffed a few times before he answered her question with eloquent readiness.

"I know that your mother, Lady Bridget's only sister, died when you were seven, in giving birth to a still-born boy. Her elopement with your father from her family home in Norfolk was violently opposed by her parents and sister, Lady Bridget. Since they refused to accept the marriage, your father took her to America, where you were born a year later in New Orleans. In those days Sean O'Rourke had no gainful employment and the times faced by all of you were hard. After his wife's death, which shattered him, he took you to California on a wagon train. He arrived in Sacramento penniless but was eventually staked by a man called MacKendrick with whose help he built a ranch, which is presently your home and where he writes while you help breed cattle and horses."

While Olivia stared in dumbfounded silence, he turned his face upwards to squint thoughtfully at the sky. "What else? Oh yes, the freedom that your father gave you has made you alarmingly independent with ideas that find little favour with your dyed-in-the-wool English aunt in these socially conservative colonies. The reason your aunt has summoned you here is to find you a rich English husband. The front runner at the moment, I learn, is the Honourable Freddie Birkhurst, Calcutta's most eligible bachelor but also the station's prize buffoon. Now let me see, is there anything I have omitted?" He cogitated, then shook his head and smiled. "No, I think not. At least, that is the extent of my present information. Undoubtedly there is more but then not every village grapevine can be exhaustive."

Through the lengthy recital Olivia had gone very still indeed. For a moment or two silence reigned between them; then, as her paralysis receded, she filled with outrage and sprang to her feet. Instantly the two hounds leapt to theirs and snarled with their fangs bared. Had the man not issued a swift command to them, they would have certainly attacked her.

"Considering you've been brought up in a country where men understand beasts," he reprimanded with ill-concealed exasperation as both his hands firmly clasped the animals' collars, "you should know better than to make sudden moves. Petulance is a stupid reason for bravado."

Shaking partly with fright and partly with rage, Olivia managed to issue a request through clenched teeth. "Would you kindly command those damned animals to let me leave?"

"Why? Because I spoke the truth?"

"No. Because I find you offensive, presumptuous and unbearably self-opinionated and wish to terminate this futile encounter." She was so angry that she could barely enunciate the words.

"Oh? I'm sorry to hear that. I was quite beginning to enjoy our contretemps—an oasis in the arid mediocrity of Calcutta's conversational opportunities." He gave no further instructions to his dogs, both of which remained very much on their guard and ready to charge.

Incensed beyond measure, Olivia began to feel a fool in her enforced immobility. "Why do you continually insult your own community? Do you think that by doing so you add to your own prestige?"

He did not answer for a moment. "What makes you so certain it *is* my own community that I insult?" he then asked softly.

His counter-question confused her. "Why, are you too not English?" she blurted out, furious for having done so. How did it concern her what or who he might be?

"Why should you think that I am?"

"I don't give a *damn* what you are but you don't look a nat—" Flustered and embarrassed, she choked back the rest of her comment to chew angrily on her lip and fumble warily with her feet for her sandals.

"How should a native look then?" he demanded tightly, and

suddenly Olivia saw that he too was angry. "Servile? Obsequious? A humble groveller at the feet of the white memsahib?"

"No, of *course* not!" She was appalled that he should have deliberately chosen to misinterpret her. Forgetting the presence of the vigilant dogs she stamped her foot and immediately earned another snarl. "You know *damn* well I didn't mean that!"

From within the shadows she felt his eyes boring into hers, but when he spoke again it was with control. "What you meant was that if I were black as the ace of spades, you would accept me as a native. Well, in this country, my under-educated Miss O'Rourke, we belong to all colours of the spectrum from the lily white to the blue black and all the rest in between. Somewhere within that spectrum is my own colour, *and it is not English white.*" He snapped a comment under his breath and released the dogs. Without even a glance in her direction, they turned and bounded up the steps to disappear into the night. For a moment longer he stood where he was, unmoving, with averted eyes staring steadily into the middle distance across the river. He seemed to arrive at some decision, for he suddenly turned to move closer to her. "Perhaps you would be kind enough to convey my regards to Sir Joshua and Lady Bridget? My name is Jai Raventhorne." It was said coldly and with clipped formality. Then, with an almost imperceptible bow, he spun on his heel and vaulted up the steps after his dogs.

He did not turn to look back at her.

Transfixed, Olivia stared after him until he melted into the dark. In his fleeting proximity he had offered her a glimpse of his face, and what she had seen had startled her. In his pale face, in vivid contrast to his dense black hair, were set eyes that appeared almost opaque in the light of the moon. Olivia had never seen eyes like that on anyone; they were unearthly in their opalescence and also frighteningly lifeless. She shuddered. Then, in an effort to cast off her sense of unease, she pulled herself up and threw back her shoulders. Giving a hearty dusting to the skirt of her dress, she ran back up the stone steps and hurried towards the Pennworthys' garden.

"Where in heaven's name have you *been?*" The moment Olivia slipped through the wire mesh door, Estelle grabbed her. "*Everyone's* been asking after you, and Mama is *beside* herself with worry."

"Don't exaggerate, Estelle! I only went to . . . powder my nose." A glance at the clock surprised Olivia by announcing that she had been away more than an hour!

"Where, in the garden? I saw you sneak off earlier." Estelle giggled. "Where have you left poor Freddie—underneath some secluded hibiscus with his manly stamina exhausted?" She sniggered again.

"Don't be absurd! If you must know, I went for a walk to get some air. I thought I would faint with the heat."

"Well, wherever you were," Estelle said clearly unconvinced, "if I were you, I'd hurry and make my peace with Mama before she's driven to announce happy nuptials." With a pointed smirk she turned and waltzed away in the arms of a patiently waiting John Sturges.

The peace making with Lady Bridget went off better than Olivia had expected. In fact, as she accepted her niece's explanation and apology, Lady Bridget's reprimand was remarkably mild. The flush on Olivia's face, the nervous twitch of her clasped fingers, the evasively lowered eyes—all these were portents that Lady Bridget chose to interpret to her own satisfaction. "And where," she asked with a touch of archness, "have you left the charming Mr. Birkhurst?"

"I haven't left him anywhere," Olivia replied crossly. "I haven't seen him myself in quite a while." Her aunt's knowing smile told her she was not to be believed, which made her more cross. She turned quickly to the young man hovering diligently behind her. "Oh, Mr. Pringle, *do* forgive me for having kept you waiting and *do* tell me what you had started to about your encounter with the thuggees . . ." Honour bound to make reparation for her lapse of courtesy, Olivia surrendered herself to the rhythm of a polka being strummed more energetically than tunefully by the small string ensemble hired for the occasion by the Pennworthys.

Jai Raventhorne.

It was impossible to cast aside the extraordinary encounter by the river or the man who had dominated it. Over the buffet supper, served deplorably late as predicted, Olivia listened only absently to the sotto voce flirtatious banter between Estelle and John on either side of her. Jai Raventhorne certainly was an unusual name, neither Anglo-Saxon nor Indian. Who—and what—was he? For a European (which he had strongly denied being), his manner was much too uncivilised, his liberties far too many. On the other hand, what Indian would have the courage to bandy words quite so brazenly with a white woman in Calcutta's segregated society? Whichever way she considered Jai Raventhorne, he was a misfit with no familiar slot in which to be placed. As for his prying into her life, it showed a despicable lack of form, an excessive rudeness that she had already been subjected to once this evening. But whereas Peter Barstow was an easily forgettable dandy with a wholly unjustified conceit, this man could not be dismissed quite so lightly. Olivia had to concede, however grudgingly, that whoever or whatever Jai Raventhorne might be, she was finding it difficult to shake him out of her thoughts.

"Another spoonful, perhaps, Miss O'Rourke?" John Sturges was looking at her with a hand poised over a dish of prawn curry that a bearer presented.

Olivia shook her head and smiled. "I don't think I could, Captain Sturges, delicious as it is."

He doused his own fluffy rice and Estelle's cheerfully. "I should imagine our curries *are* too spicy for you. They're not everybody's cup of tea, if you will forgive a shockingly mixed metaphor."

Olivia laughed. "I enjoy spiced food. Because of the Mexicans, we are well used to it at home. Estelle tells me you leave for home shortly on furlough. Will you be away long?"

"The usual. A year or more. When I return I hope to persuade my parents to accompany me. My father used to be in the Civil Service in Peshawar." He threw a meaningful glance at Estelle, who promptly blushed. It was definitely a hopeful omen.

Olivia liked John Sturges immensely. He was a sober Yorkshireman, matter of fact and endowed with an abundance of both common sense and a lively taste for humour. Because he was so eminently sane, he seemed a perfect balance for Estelle's giddiness. Olivia hoped fervently that he would make known his intentions towards her cousin soon. Not only were they well suited in every way but one wedding in the family might well divert her aunt's attention from trying to force another.

Having spent much of the evening in the billiards room with his host, Clarence Pennworthy—manager of the merchant bank with which Templewood and Ransome did business—Sir Joshua suddenly materialized in their midst. "And where might your worthy escort of the evening be, my dear?" he asked Olivia with a heartiness she found rather overdone.

"I have no idea," she answered frostily. Why the *hell* did everyone think she was Freddie Birkhurst's keeper!

"Not taking his escorting duties seriously enough, eh?" he teased, chuckling at her unconcealed chagrin. "Well, don't tell your aunt you've been careless enough to lose him, will you?"

"Lose who, or is it *whom?*" Betty Pennworthy, a vague, twittering woman with perpetually untidy hair that looked like a nest and gave her the air of a sparrow, appeared, casting quick glances at everyone's plates.

"Young Freddie. Haven't seen him all evening."

"Nor likely to, Josh," his hostess said sternly with a firm grip on his arm, "if all you men do is closet yourselves in corners talking politics and money. If I hear another *word* about that wretched Afghan problem, I swear I shall have hysterics. Clarence?" she issued a command to her husband, who was engaged in hot argument with a portly gent with a walrus moustache. "I wish you would persuade your guests to start eating, dear, before the dinner turns stone cold and absolutely *in*edible!"

"In a moment, pet," her husband responded impatiently. "Another beer, Josh?" Wiping speckles of froth from his whiskers, Sir Joshua patted Betty Pennworthy on the hand absently and both men walked off, waving their empty tankards in the direction of a bearer.

It was while the pudding, a rather flattened caramel custard, was being passed around and Olivia had resignedly joined her aunt's circle for a dutiful discussion on heat boils and the iniquities of native servants that a diversion occurred to put an untimely end to the evening jollifications. Freddie Birkhurst was discovered in the garden under a croton bush, drunk and out cold. In the commotion that ensued, with Dr. Humphries bellowing for smelling-salts, American ice and hot tea, the party inevitably disintegrated, with the caramel custard forgotten by everyone except Estelle, who, under cover of confusion, gave herself several generous servings. Escorted by Lady Bridget, Mrs. Humphries, and one or two others, Betty Pennworthy repaired to her bedroom to have her vapours in comfort and, one by one or in couples and families, the guests started to discreetly go home.

The ride back in the Templewood carriage was conducted mostly in grim silence. "If he can't hold his liquor, the silly ass has no right to drink!" Sir Joshua made no bones about his disgust.

Behind a lace hanky, Lady Bridget sniffed. "I can't see what the fuss is all about," she murmured, bravely making the best of her own mortification. "Gentlemen do occasionally go one over the eight—*you* should know that as well as anyone, Josh." Pointedly, she sniffed again.

"One over the eight? *Twenty*-eight more likely!"

Only Estelle dared to giggle. "He has much more, Susan Bradshaw says her brother tells her, at the Golden Behind where—" Too late, she broke off and clamped a hand to her mouth.

There was a moment's ominous silence. Then, in a voice hushed with anger, Sir Joshua asked, "And what may you know of the Golden Behind, my lass?"

Estelle gulped. "I'm only s-saying what everybody s-says, Papa—"

"No daughter of mine is *every*body!" her father roared. "My daughter is—or is expected to be—a *lady*, not a crude-tongued gutter-snipe, is that clear, Estelle?"

"Y-yes, Papa."

"And if this is the language you share with your friends, I must say I approve of your mother's reservations, is that clear too?" Lips trembling at her father's rare display of temper against her, Estelle nodded. "Very well, we will say no more, but such language will not be used in our presence again or, indeed, anywhere. Understood?" For the third time Estelle nodded, then sank back in her corner to sulk in silence.

Olivia said nothing but, privately, considered the reprimand overblown. The Golden Hind, to give its seldom-used proper name, was a "club" of dubious reputation in Lal Bazaar patronised by a strictly male clientele. The name by which it was universally known gave ample indication of the pleasures it offered its members. Olivia could see no reason why a whorehouse should need a euphemism, but she doubted if anyone in Calcutta would have agreed with her.

The journey back was completed with no more talk.

It was not until later that night when they were on the landing preparatory to withdrawing into their respective bedrooms that Olivia suddenly recalled the cryptic message she had been asked to deliver to her aunt and uncle. Was it, she wondered, worth delivering at all? She still smarted under the onslaught of the objectionable Mr. Raventhorne but then she shrugged to herself. Why not? The few words were of no great consequence one way or the other.

"I almost forgot to tell you, Uncle Josh," she began casually, "that I happened to go out on the embankment briefly this evening and I met someone who knows you."

"Oh?"

"He asked me to convey to you and Aunt Bridget his regards. He said his name was Jai Raventhorne."

As Olivia pronounced the final two words, something strange started to happen. Everyone froze into a sort of grotesque tableau. Lady Bridget's hand, half way up to the sconce to extinguish the wall lamp, remained suspended; Sir Joshua's right leg, partially through the doorway to the master bedroom, halted in mid-air, his eyes wide and still. About to say something, Estelle had her mouth open and it stayed so, her saucer eyes glazed with horror. Uncomprehending of what was occurring around her, Olivia stared at each in bewilderment, the residue of whatever else she was about to add forgotten in her throat.

The silence was long and noticeably tense. Lady Bridget was the first to move. She sighed and her arm dropped to her side. Without saying anything she sank slowly to the floor in a swoon.

2

"But what did I *say,* Estelle? What in heaven's name was it that I said *wrong?*"

Olivia and her cousin were, at last, by themselves in the privacy of Estelle's bedroom. Lady Bridget had been carried to her bed, revived with whiffs of ammonia and finally put to sleep with a dose of her usual draught. Apart from what was strictly necessary, there had been no exchanges among them. Not even Sir Joshua, silent and stern faced, had offered any explanations or, indeed, recriminations. The very lack of them and the continuous leaden silences were to Olivia intolerable. She was deeply distressed.

Estelle locked the door behind them. "You should not have mentioned that name," she whispered severely, her own face pale. "It is not permitted in this house, not that you could have known that."

"But why?" Olivia's bewilderment remained. "What has he done, this . . . this Raventhorne?" Unconsciously, she followed Estelle's example and lowered her own voice.

"*I* don't know, nobody tells me anything." With an aggrieved sigh, Estelle reached under her bed to pull out a biscuit tin. "All I know is that everyone hates him."

"There has to be a reason," Olivia persisted. "What has he done to deserve such universal hate? Is it something to do with business?"

"I suppose so." She started to munch on a ginger biscuit. "They say he's unprincipled and unscrupulous and a blackguard without morals. Besides, he hates us too."

"Us?"

"The English. They also say he's plotting to turn us out of India." She laughed scornfully. "You see? He's mad as well."

Olivia digested the information thoughtfully. "Then he is not . . . English?"

"Good Lord, no!" Estelle looked horrified. "He's *Eurasian.* If he *were* English he'd have a good bit more sense." She picked up a second biscuit and, with a sly glance at the door, lowered her voice further. "What did you talk about with him? Anything interesting?"

However fond Olivia had become of her cousin, she certainly wasn't fool enough to answer that truthfully! With her penchant for avid gossip, Estelle kept nothing to herself for more than five seconds. "Oh, this and that. Nothing very much. Tell me, what is his background? I mean, what is it that he does in business?"

Estelle shrugged. "No one knows much about his background, not even Mrs. Drummond—and there's precious little that misses her!" She looked briefly envious. "He has this tea business, like Papa. And he has his own ships, which are better than everyone else's tea wagons. That's *one* reason for hating him."

Well, that made sense considering the fierce rivalries in the city. What didn't make sense was why, not being a European, he chose to live in the White Town, especially in view of his avowed contempt for the English. "And the other reasons?"

Pleased at suddenly being considered the repository of useful information, Estelle preened herself. "Well, Mrs. Drummond says he grows his own teas in Assam and, you see, we *can't.* We have to get ours all the way from China to send to England. He sends his to America, which is what sticks in everyone's craw."

For a moment Olivia wondered if Estelle was making all this up. Surely, no one had yet grown tea in India successfully enough to send it anywhere. Then something stirred in her memory. "Is he the man they refer to as Kala . . . something?" she inquired slowly.

"Yes, Kala Kanta." Estelle looked surprised. "Did *he* tell you that?"

"No, of course not! Uncle Josh and Mr. Ransome were talking about him the other night." Which made the matter more perplexing: If the men could discuss him freely, then why should her aunt's reaction have been so extreme? "Does Kala Kanta mean anything in Hindustani?"

"Yes, *kala* is black and *kanta* is a thorn—clever, isn't it? Black like a raven and because he's a thorn in—"

"Yes, I do get the import, Estelle," Olivia said, impatient to learn more. "I accept that the man is a villain and universally hated, but that still doesn't explain why Aunt Bridget had to swoon at the mere mention of his name! Can you think why?"

Estelle clucked. "No one can understand the way Mama's mind works; certainly *I* can't. Look at the pet she gets into about Polly Drummond and her mother. I mean, what's wrong with having gentlemen friends if one is a widow? And why shouldn't Polly use cosmetics and wear lace underwear if her mother lets her? Clive Smithers says—or so Charlotte told me—he's even *kissed* her once when—"

"The English hate him but they still maintain business relations with him?" Olivia cut in firmly, not interested at the moment in listening to Estelle's familiar list of grievances. "Isn't that odd?"

With an effort, her cousin pulled away her thoughts from problems she considered far more pertinent. "They have to," she sighed, consoling herself with the last biscuit in the tin. "Those clippers of his are so fast that the holds are always full of cargo. And he has warehouses that people hire to store their teas and indigo and all that. They can't *afford* to ignore him."

"But then if he is a business colleague, whether liked or not, why is he never seen at *burra khanas?* Surely he's invited to them."

"Oh, he's *invited* all right," Estelle said with a short laugh and a knowing gleam in her eyes, which were alive with sudden interest. "It's *he* who maintains that he wouldn't be seen dead in an Englishman's drawing-room. Everyone knows there isn't a pukka mem about who wouldn't give her best wig and whalebones for J— this man's favours. Polly says he has a native mistress who actually lives in his house *with* him, and Dave Crichton told Mrs. Drummond he has positive proof that when Barnabus Slocum's sister from Brighton went missing last year and wasn't seen for a week, she was with him—not Dave but this man we're talking about—for seven days and seven *nights.* The Slocums told everyone she had gone to the hills." She gasped for a fresh supply of air and smiled triumphantly.

Overwhelmed by this barrage of unsolicited gossip, Olivia subjected her cousin to a stern look. "Considering you're not allowed to even mention his name in this house," she remarked drily, "you seem pretty well informed about the man!"

Estelle tossed her head and pouted. "Well, you're the one who is dying of curiosity. I'm only repeating what I know, what everybody knows. *He* doesn't give a hoot who says what about him so why should you?"

"Oh, I don't! And just to get this straight, I am *not* 'dying of curiosity' about the much-talked-about Mr. Raventhorne. I'm only trying to figure out why I should have upset Lady Bridget so much." She frowned and sucked on a lip. "But I haven't really, have I?"

"No, nor will you, I promise." Estelle swallowed a yawn and stared into her empty biscuit tin with regret. "If I were you, I'd forget all about it. Mama is unpredictable at the best of times; it's useless trying to get to the bottom of her mind. And in any case," she opened her mouth and yawned fully, "you're not likely to meet him again, are you?" She slipped under her sheet and pulled down the mosquito-netting.

"No," Olivia agreed slowly with a hand on the door knob. "I'm not likely to meet him again."

Unaccountably, she felt a small twinge of regret.

Future prospects notwithstanding, some form of apology was certainly due to her aunt, Olivia decided. Next morning—Sir Joshua having left for work earlier than usual—she found Lady Bridget alone in her bedroom sipping tea.

"I'm extremely sorry about what happened last night, Lady Bridget," she began without preamble as soon as a cold cheek had been presented for the morning kiss. "If I hurt or offended you in any way, it was entirely without intention."

Lady Bridget's cup rattled once as her hand shook. She did not look up to meet her niece's eyes. "You are in no way to blame, child. I do know that. It's not . . . ," she swallowed, "not anything to worry about, but some . . . explanation is due to you. Josh will speak to you later. I . . . we will consider the matter closed . . ." Her voice faded and she turned away, again visibly agitated.

For the moment there was nothing more to be said. The subject was not referred to again through the day.

Even though it was too soon to expect mail from her father, Olivia had got into the habit of writing to him almost every day. She also wrote regularly to Sally and her boys, to other friends she had left behind and to her father's spinster sister in Dublin, his only surviving relative still close to him. While she waited impatiently for mail packets to start arriving from home and from Honolulu, she found the enforced discipline therapeutic, for it assuaged her homesickness. Normally she enjoyed writing letters, but this morning, somehow, her concentration wavered. Instead of her thoughts dwelling on what they should, they kept wandering back to Jai Raventhorne.

What lingered most in retrospect was not the physical man but the atmosphere he had created around himself of something amorphous and indefinable. There seemed to have emanated from his person a strange nervous, darting energy, almost a turbulence, that on those river steps had packed the space between them with tension. Beneath his occasional insolence there had been an underlying hostility that baffled Olivia. No, she had not been comfortable in his presence. As for his scandalous reputation, she paid it little heed; among her father's friends she could name at least two whom various sheriffs would be happy to accommodate as their guests, and there were many drawing-rooms in Washington where her father himself was strictly non grata because of his free and frank political opinions. The reason Jai Raventhorne intrigued her was because not even in America had she met a man so out of tune with the majority.

When Sir Joshua's summons finally came, following a noticeably awkward atmosphere at dinner, Olivia was expecting it. Even so her breath quickened; she felt riven with anticipation as to what exactly was to be revealed. As usual, her uncle sat at his enormous mahogany desk, its surface littered with ledgers and papers, sipping his favourite port and puffing on a cigar. He had changed into his blue silk dressing-gown and his feet were encased in carpet slippers. Even at ease and dressed informally, he radiated power, both mental and physical, the dominant set of his chin giving little indication of his modest beginnings as the humbly brought-up son of a penniless baronet and a low-paid writer with John Company.

"A tot of port, m'dear?" Olivia accepted the offer with a nod and positioned herself opposite him at the desk. It was, after all, for him to decide the direction of the conversation. "Young Marshall returned yesterday from Hankow with some weird tales about the hongs. One or two might amuse you," he began, handing her a glass. "The Russians buy their teas in Hankow, you know. Any idea how long it takes them to make the round trip? Sixteen months! Hah! And we complain because it takes us less than six!"

The anecdotes that followed, Olivia sensed, were to put them both in an easier frame of mind, for he too was far from comfortable. The stories were related with humour and wit and she listened with attention, joining in with his intermittent laughter willingly. It was only after several tales had been recounted and much scorn poured on the Russians that he sat back, lit another cigar, threw up a perfect smoke ring and said, "About last night, Olivia . . ."

Again her breath went tight. "I have been hoping for an opportunity to apologise, Uncle Josh. I am so terribly sorry for—"

"It was not your fault." He waved away her expressions of remorse. "You only delivered an innocent message. How were you to know with what malicious intent it was dispatched?"

Malicious intent? What dark plot could possibly be contained in a few words of harmless greeting? But waiting for more, Olivia refrained from comment.

"This man," Sir Joshua did not repeat the name as he picked up a pencil and idly toyed with it, "is a scoundrel, a debauch and a charlatan of the first order. That he should have had the audacity to accost you—"

"He did not accost me," some inner devil prompted Olivia to point out, "it was genuinely a chance encounter. I went out for some air at the same time that he happened to be walking his dogs."

The amendment did not please her uncle. He frowned. "Regardless of the circumstances, he should have known better than to overstep his bounds to speak to you. He is known as a manipulator, a master of evil designs habituated to turning even the most simple of situations to his best advantage. Was his manner towards you courteous?"

Olivia took both the seeming over reaction and the abrupt question in her stride. "Perfectly. There was no reason for it to be otherwise." It was, she considered without compunction, a justifiable lie. To reveal the reality of their abrasive encounter would be to invite even more trouble.

"What was it that you talked about?" There was a strange watchfulness, even anxiety, in Sir Joshua's eyes as he questioned her.

Olivia hid a sense of irritation—did it matter? "We merely made idle talk," she replied evenly. "It appears that he had read some of my father's writings in American journals. Mostly we discussed those."

Whether it was in her imagination or not, Sir Joshua seemed to loosen. His wariness dropped; he steepled his fingers against his chest and smiled. "In that case I am relieved. It is not often that he chooses to play the gentleman, which is of course why your aunt went into such an unholy flap last night. You are well aware of the high moral standards she maintains and how assiduously she values social propriety in all matters. It shocked Bridget that a scalawag of such despicably low calibre should have had the gall to actually hobnob with you, her own flesh and blood." He gave a quick laugh. "Of course it was absurd of Bridget to faint, utterly ridiculous! But then, we must make some allowances for her little whims and excesses, must we not?"

For all his apparent earnestness, his good-humoured indulgence for his wife's "whims and excesses," Olivia knew that her uncle prevaricated. He had not told her the real reason for her aunt's distress. Torn for a moment between tactical withdrawal (which would be wise) and a bold attack (which would not), Olivia eventually settled for the latter. "This Mr. Raventhorne," her chin firmed as she fearlessly mouthed the forbidden name, "who exactly is he and what exactly does he do?"

"He is in the tea business." The curtness of his reply gave ample indication of his reluctance to pursue the subject.

"On the China Coast?"

"No. He grows his own."

So, Estelle's snippets of gossip were not wholly incorrect! Ignoring her uncle's obvious displeasure and assuming innocence, Olivia pressed on. "He does? But did you not tell me that European planters in Assam are having serious labour problems and that it would be years before China tea could be grown domestically with commercial success?"

"He does not fall in the category of European planters." It was with difficulty that Sir Joshua appeared to be restraining his exasperation. "He cultivates indigenous Indian tea trees, not Chinese."

This time she had no need to simulate surprise. "Indigenous Indian tea trees? I had no idea that tea plants are also native to India!"

"Assam has had native tea trees for centuries," he said impatiently as he swung forward to place his hands palm down on the desk, "but that is neither here nor there in the present context. The reason why I have brought up the subject of Raventhorne," his mouth twisted with distaste, "is because I felt that some explanation was due to you of your Aunt Bridget's silly melodramatics yesterday. I could see that you were frightened out of your wits," he raised a small smile, "and as such an apology from me was certainly in order. Will you accept it, my dear, and forgive us for having alarmed you unduly?" Olivia had no choice but to nod her acquiescence, albeit reluctantly. "In that case, shall we now consider the entire unfortunate matter closed?"

Matter closed. Her aunt's words exactly! What was it about this man that made him such a pariah? Now, of course, there was no possibility of probing further. "By all means," she murmured, hiding her disappointment.

"Tell me, m'dear," suddenly, he was all smiles again, "are you truly happy with us?"

The sharp change in topic took Olivia aback. "Why, of course I am!" she cried, flushing. "Why do you even need to ask, Uncle Josh?"

"Because sometimes I do get the impression that you are not, that life here is not entirely as you would wish it to be."

She was dismayed by his perceptions and hastened to refute them. "Apart from the fact that I miss Papa, I assure you I am marvellously content. How could I not be in your kindness and generosity to me?"

He nodded absently. "Yes, all said and done I must say you have adjusted remarkably well considering how different your environment must have been at home. Well, Bridget and I enjoy having you with us and Estelle, of course, admires you no end." He flicked a tube of cigar ash off his lapel and sighed. "We've rather spoilt her, you know. The truth is, she came to us so late in life that neither of us quite knows how to handle her. We tend to be over protective sometimes, but we mean well."

"Estelle is not yet eighteen," Olivia answered quickly. "She will grow up in time, but . . ." Taking advantage of his sudden mellowness, she dared broach a subject brewing in her mind for a while. "Could not you and Lady Bridget see your way to giving Estelle a little more, well, independence to manage her own affairs?"

"Independence?" He looked surprised. "Bridget says the little minx has far too much already!" He chuckled. "She certainly gives her mother a hard time now and then, I understand, but then that is a daughter's privilege, I'm told. In any case, all that is Bridget's domain. Talk to her about it when you can." He waved away a domestic triviality he considered of no great consequence as his eyes twinkled and his lips trembled with restrained merriment. "Now tell me, what do you think of this fellow Birkhurst? Does he please you in any way?"

"No." Olivia met his look squarely.

"Oh dear, Bridget will be disappointed to hear that! She's rather set her heart on making a match of you two. I daresay you are aware of her ambitions?"

"I would be a congenital idiot not to be," Olivia retorted drily. "And so would everyone else in station." Including, she added in her mind, the noxious Mr. Raventhorne!

Sir Joshua laughed. "Well, I don't mind confessing that I carry no brief for any man who can't hold his liquor. There's no better measure of a gentleman than that."

"Goodness, I sure am pleased to hear that—I was beginning to think that everyone was part of the conspiracy!"

"*On* the other hand," he waggled a warning finger, "let us not forget that old Caleb Birkhurst's Agency House practically mints its own currency. Caleb prefers to live the life of a nabob in England, but the wealth he continues to amass here is still considerable. That indigo plantation in northern Bengal alone is worth a fortune, to say nothing of the Esplanade manse. Does all this not impress you?"

"No." Better frankness now than unpleasantness later. "I have nothing against Mr. Birkhurst, but his wealth and titled family make him no better and no worse in my reckoning." She gave an impish smile. "I hear despite everything that he is still considered the station's prize buffoon."

Sir Joshua threw back his head and roared. "By Jove, you Americans don't mince words, do you? Know what I'd like to do if I didn't fear that Bridget would throw another faint? I'd dearly love to let you loose in the Chamber one day to sort out all those lily-livered nincompoops!" He broke into fresh guffaws and dabbed his eyes dry with a handkerchief. "But yes, I have to agree with you. Birkhurst is a blithering ass, entirely unlike his father or, for that matter, his mother. What the devil Bridget sees in him is beyond me." He patted back a yawn and rose from his chair.

Olivia heaved a sigh of relief; even a minor ally was better than none! "Thank you for the moral support, Uncle Josh; it's greatly appreciated. I'm sorry if I have kept you up with my chatter. You look tired."

"No, no, not at all, lass. I enjoy our little chats." Nevertheless he suppressed another yawn as he stretched with obvious fatigue. "You're a good girl, Olivia, much too good for sots like Birkhurst; but don't for heaven's sake, tell Bridget I said so or she'll have my guts for garters." Fondly, he pinched her on a cheek. "All said and done, Sean has managed a neat job of rearing you, my dear. It could not have been easy. About the other business," he stared down at the carpet with a hard frown, "no more need be said. Your path will not cross Raventhorne's again."

For a long time after the rest of the household had retired that night, Olivia stood by her window listening idly to the hoot of the owls and to the regular *"Khabardar, khabardar!"* of the night-watchman on his rounds as he warned intruders away. Finally she settled down at her desk to complete the letter to her father and to make an entry in her diary. In both, boldly, she wrote, *Last night I met a man.* She cogitated for a while before adding firmly, *I think I would like to meet him again.*

Estelle Templewood, born fifteen years after her parents' marriage when all hope of offspring had been abandoned, had been named after her grandmother, the late Dowager Lady Stella Templewood, and had inherited more than just the name. A woman of iron will and lofty ambition, Sir Joshua's mother had determinedly headed for Calcutta with her young son shortly after becoming a widow in order to manipulate for him a job with John Company that allowed him to earn while he learned. Cannily, she had spurned titled but impoverished prospects to forge for him an alliance with the daughter of a wealthy Norfolk flour mill owner so that the substantial dowry she brought could set up young Josh in his own enterprise. His subsequent success had been his own, but it was this initial impetus that had given a head start to Templewood and Ransome. Until her death shortly before Estelle's birth, the dowager had ruled her son's household with dictatorial firmness. There could not be, she had decreed, two Lady Templewoods under the same roof, and since she herself disliked being called a dowager, it was her daughter-in-law who became simply Lady Bridget, and the name had stuck. Lady Bridget had learned much from her mother-in-law, whom she had feared and respected, but the dowager's eventual death had come as a relief. Which was perhaps why the old lady's portrait had since been relegated to the darkest corner of the Templewood dining room, from where the gimlet gleam that issued forth from the pale, unwavering eyes continued to survey the household with grim disapproval.

It was this same gleam that had now taken up permanent residence in Estelle's eyes as the household plunged into a flurry of preparations for her coming-of-age ball. "Mama insists on saddle of Canterbury lamb," she protested to Olivia, stamping her foot angrily and close to tears again. "*Every*one has saddle of Canterbury lamb and it's so . . . so *common!*"

"But that's not all you're having," Olivia sighed, worn out by the constant demands on her talents as moderator as the arguments raged hourly. "What about the sides of Aberdeen beef, chicken breasts, boned quail, Norwegian anchovies, plovers' eggs, *bhetki* fish and the dozens of other courses? Why not let your mother have her way with the lamb?"

"She's having her way with everything, even the flowers. Why can't I have chrysanthemums instead of those silly roses? And why does Jane Watkins have to arrange the bowls?"

"Because," Olivia explained with miraculous patience, "chrysanthemums are not yet in season, for a start. And all Aunt Bridget wants is for the bowls to be arranged well, which Jane will do since she's been trained in the art."

"Well, that's only because Jane schooled in England and I *didn't.* If they'd let me go like everyone else I'd have been trained too, wouldn't I have? Charlotte says in Tonbridge—"

"All right, all right," Olivia cut in wearily. Her cousin's grouses against the world in general and her mother in particular again dovetailed into each other with bewildering lack of logic and, for that matter, truth. "I'll see what I can do, but nobody can produce chrysanthemums in September, honey, and that's that."

All in all, it was an exhausting time for Olivia. She helped willingly, of course, to lessen the burdens of an occasion such as she had never known; but, plunged into a confusion of tailors, jewellers, shoemakers, embroiderers, carpenters, upholsterers, painters and pedlars, by the time night came her head spun and her feet throbbed with the effort. Catering for the hundreds of guests had been arranged with Spence's hotel, reputed to provide the best fare in town. The long-awaited ship had docked on schedule with its massive cargo of wines, liquors, liqueurs, beer, cigars, chocolates, cheeses and tobaccos, as well as with Estelle's exquisite robin's-egg blue organza gown with frothing Brussels lace, seed pearls and diamanté, which was quite the finest dress Olivia had ever seen in her life. On the back lawn of the Templewood bungalow a wooden dance floor was being laid under a giant canopy. A raised dais had been constructed for the Army band, which was to be in attendance throughout the evening.

In her unwanted and thankless role of arbitrator, Olivia tried to be as fair as she could, but it was not always easy. Secretly she often found her sympathies with her aunt, but in one matter she was firmly on her pampered cousin's side. "To Estelle her eighteenth birthday is the most important day in her life, Lady Bridget," she pleaded following yet another storm of tears from Estelle. "Could you not make some allowances and let her invite whomsoever she wishes?"

Lady Bridget chilled. "Polly Drummond is a common little flibbertigibbet, and her mother is no better than a . . ." She left the word unsaid. "And I have made allowances. That Dave Crichton is a cockney shippie with atrocious grammar and worse manners. Everyone knows his father runs dogfights in Whitechapel. He's not even trade, and goodness knows that's bad enough! Well, he's coming, isn't he?"

"Yes, but Polly *is* Estelle's best friend, and however, well, overblown, Mrs. Drummond isn't entirely unattractive."

Olivia's choice of adjectives elicited cutting comments on the worthlessness of cosmetic appeal when there was moral odium within, but eventually Lady Bridget capitulated, perhaps through sheer exhaustion.

The one person in the household who successfully avoided being dragged into the onerous preparations and disputes was Sir Joshua. Lady Bridget complained stridently about his convenient absences from home, but since he was never to be found anyway, the complaints remained unheard by him. One very early morning, however, she did manage to corner him in his study to present her long list of questions and to demand the required answers.

"I've ordered American ice, Josh, for the sherbets and the white wines. The Bassetts served their wines warm and they were a laughing-stock, remember? Well, how much will we need, four maunds?" The grunt that issued from behind the newspaper could have indicated anything, but his wife chose to take it as an affirmation of her estimate and neatly ticked off an item on her list. "And I've asked for a hundred bearers for the serving. Do you think that will be enough?"

"Quite enough, dear." Had she said two or two thousand, his response would have probably been the same.

"Will you wear your maroon or your navy blue? I've had them both cleaned and pressed just in case."

"Good."

"And you must tell me, what do these native princes drink? Isn't alcohol against their religion or something?"

This time she had her husband's total attention. "As far as

I know," he said, setting aside the newspaper and concentrating fully, "Arvind Singh appreciates a good Scotch as well as the next man. Keep the Glenmorangie aside for him, will you? It's not an old whisky, but Willie Donaldson recommends it thoroughly. I've been informed that His Highness will bring an entourage of twenty-five. They won't touch the beef, of course, or the pork. Neither will Das and his bunch. Make a separate table for them with plenty of fish, fowl and vegetables."

Lady Bridget's lips thinned in disapproval. "What a silly fuss, Josh! The more you pander to them, the larger the swell of their heads."

Sir Joshua returned to his newspaper. "Arvind Singh is an investment, Bridget. Let's leave it at that."

"And that man Das? Vain, dressed-up toad that he is?"

His expression thoughtful again, Sir Joshua fingered his whiskers as he stared out of the window. "When one wishes to catch a monkey, my dear, one has to employ all one's resources," he said softly. "Das is a resource, no less, no more. Besides, he is a money-lender, a rich one at that. He has his uses." He smiled. "They all do, my dear, they all do."

With her head spinning with exhaustion, her feet throbbing and her nerves torn to shreds, Olivia prayed only for the great day to come and go. Save for its lavish dimensions, there was no reason why this *burra khana* should be any less boring for her than the others she had been subjected to. The sole silver lining she saw was that the benign hand of fate had withdrawn Freddie from station and borne him away to his north Bengal indigo plantation. Even so, she decided glumly, the evening for her would be a penance.

But in her pessimism Olivia was to be proved wrong. During the course of Estelle's coming-of-age festivities she was to have an encounter destined to change the direction of her life.

Each year Estelle's birthday missed the last of the monsoons by a hairbreadth. Consequently, it was amidst a glorious post-rains sunset of scarlet and orange and purple that the carriages started to arrive in an endless procession. Smart gentry in their best bibs and tuckers spilled out onto the manicured lawns massed with banks of flowers. Pale faced and shivering with excitement, Estelle took her place in the receiving line together with her parents and Olivia. Her spectacular blue gown suited her well, and in the middle of her elaborate coiffeur (subject of another fierce battle) nestled the priceless diamond tiara given to her by her parents as a birthday gift. The cosmetics on her face were heavy (the fight to have them even more so), but she looked enchanting as she dispensed curtsies, kisses and handshakes, and gave and received compliments with the perfect poise of the adult she considered herself to have now become.

For Olivia, this evening her aunt's will had prevailed. She had not been able to avoid wearing the shimmering aquamarine sateen specially ordered for her by Lady Bridget at enormous cost. The beautiful gown had a waspish waist that necessitated the ultimate horror, whalebone stays. Her aunt had also insisted on lace gloves, high-heeled gold sandals and long stockings. To her pained protest that nobody would see the stockings anyway, Lady Bridget had snapped, "Well, I should hope not!", closing the discussion. But however self-conscious she felt, Olivia would not have been human not to feel some thrill at what the mirror offered. Brought up in wholesome cottons, sensible shoes and no-nonsense underwear, she blushed at the vision of unaccustomed elegance that confronted her, especially at the exquisite emerald necklace and pear-drop earrings her aunt had loaned her to wear through the evening. Secretly twirling and twisting before the full-length mirror, Olivia could almost hear Sally MacKendrick's admiring gasp. "Why Livvie honey, you look fit to be eaten by the Queen, pips and all, I do swear!"

Estelle's fervent plea to her had been to keep an eye on Mrs. Drummond. "If Mama were to be rude to her in front of my friends, I'd die, just *die,* Olivia." But, as it happened, Lady Bridget's mood was expansive. The Governor-General, His Excellency Lord Dalhousie and Lady Dalhousie had sent their regrets since they would be out on tour, but they had also sent a handsome silver creamer engraved with their crest as a gift for Estelle. In her pride at the honour, Lady Bridget radiated impartially in all directions, one of which happened to be where Mrs. Drummond sat. The unexpected smile of approval she received quite confused the lady; in her nervousness she promptly downed two more glasses of claret in rapid succession.

As per her aunt's stringent instructions, Olivia grimly and dutifully circulated. The lawns, both front and back, now thronged with guests and the crush was considerable. The happy clink of glasses sounded across the easy laughter and the hum of well-bred conversation. An inordinate number of bearers, in starched turbans, white liveries and red cummerbunds, scurried to and fro with their splendid array of refreshments. Although Olivia could not remember the names of all those to whom she had been introduced, she exchanged pleasantries and made small talk with finesse, staying well away from the two topics her aunt had proscribed—politics and commerce.

"You ride exceptionally well, Miss O'Rourke, that too astride, which is unusual for ladies here. I see you often in the mornings."

The speaker was a rotund young man with a goatee and humorous brown eyes. His name was Courtenay or Poultenay; Olivia couldn't remember which. "Thank you. Yes, I do enjoy exploring the town—not the native quarters, of course," she clarified quickly in case it was somehow passed on to her aunt. "I restrict myself to the White Town and the embankment."

He raised a questioning eyebrow. "Oh, but you shouldn't! The true heart of India beats where the natives live. The bazaars, the gullies and alleyways are far more interesting than this dreary part of station."

Taken aback, Olivia surveyed him with interest. "You know them well?"

"Oh, indeed. I share a chummery with friends in Neeloo Dalal Street." Noting her look of astonishment, he laughed. "You see, Miss O'Rourke, I belong to that happy, exclusive band of Europeans who are said to have 'gone native.' We don't serve by standing and waiting, but not even Milton could fault the salutary service we perform for the European community. Were it not for us renegades, what on earth would you ladies talk about?" He laughed again, obviously content in his alleged notoriety.

"When you say 'gone native,' " Olivia asked, lowering her voice with a hasty look over her shoulder as she warmed to him, "what exactly do you mean?"

He pinked and his lips twitched. "I regret that such information you will have to extract from one of the ladies, Miss O'Rourke. I'm in enough trouble as it is."

By which Olivia presumed it was something to do with Indian mistresses and suchlike and was much intrigued. She would have dearly liked to pursue the matter, but, catching Lady Bridget's hawk-eye across a jasmine bush, she regretfully excused herself to move on to her next duty. Privately, however, she decided to include Mr. Courtenay or Poultenay in her diary the next day as her accolade to a rather intrepid young Englishman.

In her shimmering beige taffeta cuffed with café au lait lace, Lady Bridget looked intimidatingly regal. Her fair hair, streaked only lightly with grey, was coiffed with such perfection that not even the breeze dared to disturb a single strand. Hers was that effortless elegance that only those who are rich and have never been otherwise can carry off with grace. She patted the chair next to her and Olivia seated herself. The conversation between her aunt and her surrounding friends was about hill stations, the frantic need each summer to flee the blazing heat of Calcutta, and the woeful dearth of any suitable hills to retreat to in this part of the country. "From Rawalpindi," mourned a Mrs. Dalrymple who obviously came from there, "Murree is a hop, skip and a jump. One can abandon the burning plains to be within viewing distance of snowy peaks in the Himalayas in no more than a *day!*" She fanned herself vigorously. "But where does one go from here, I ask you, *where?*"

"Well, there's always the sea," Lady Bridget replied a trifle coldly. It was all very well to curse Calcutta oneself; no such liberty could be allowed a newly come northerner bent only on finding fault. "Many consider the beaches of Puri, for instance, far more invigorating than the hills. I must say, I do myself."

Which successfully put paid to any further comments Mrs. Dalrymple might have been intending on the subject. Sitting next to Mollie Bassett on her right, Olivia picked up her whisper to Betty Pennworthy seated on Mrs. Bassett's other side. "It's the heat that does it, you know. Makes them, well, more *ardent* than we English." They were staring at a knot of Indian gents dressed in awkward broadcloth frock-coats and stiff shirts, looking dreadfully gauche and self-conscious.

"You're not speaking from *personal* experience, now are you, lovie?" Mrs. Pennworthy giggled and jabbed her neighbour with an elbow. "If so, *do* tell. I hear a toss in the hay native style can be very, well, *spicy!*"

Mollie Bassett squealed. "Ooh, *Betty!* Not in front of Arabella and our innocent Olivia, to say nothing of," she dipped her voice, "Bridget!" Holding her sides, she fell about with laughter.

"You don't have to worry about me, ducks," sniffed Arabella Winter drily. A spinster, she was known universally behind her bony, angular back as "the Spin." "I used to teach biology in Middlesbrough—there's not much *I* don't know about our bodily functions. It's young Olivia here you're shocking out of her wits."

"Not at all, Miss Winter," Olivia hastened to assure her,

equally drily. "Believe it or not, we Americans too have our bodily functions."

There were more helpless hoots all around and a shocked "Tut, tut!" from one or two despite the exclusively female company. Just then Estelle hurried up to claim Olivia and drag her behind a tree. "There's something I have to know this *instant.*" She looked flushed and flustered. "It's about John. He *kissed* me, right behind the stables, and put his tongue in my mouth. Is that . . . *normal?*"

"No. If it were normal, he would have kissed you on the *mouth,* not behind the stables," Olivia said, grinning.

Just at that moment Sir Joshua appeared to grab Olivia's arm. "Can you spare a few moments, my dear? There is someone I especially want you to meet and be charming with."

There was a curious urgency in his voice. A fine film of sweat shone on his forehead. Delighted at the reprieve from boring conversational duties and a possible chance of some stimulating talk, Olivia agreed with alacrity. As Sir Joshua guided her with rapid strides across the lawn, there was a spring in his step that spoke of high excitement. They walked to a far corner of the garden where a secluded seating arrangement had been improvised overlooking the river. As they approached, a small cluster of men leapt aside to reveal a seated figure. The figure rose and stepped forward.

"Your Highness, may I present my niece by marriage, Miss Olivia O'Rourke. She has arrived only recently from a country I know Your Highness admires greatly, the United States of America. Olivia, my dear, His Highness the Maharaja of Kirtinagar. He is one of those royal gentlemen who are held in high respect by my own countrymen."

For a moment Olivia was rendered speechless. The Maharaja's name had not been on her guest list, nor had her aunt made mention of him. Never having met royalty, much less Oriental royalty, she was thrown off balance. In some confusion she dropped a hasty curtsy and hoped that it would do. In response, the Maharaja folded his hands in the traditional Indian greeting, bowed courteously and smiled. "I am indeed delighted to make your acquaintance, Miss O'Rourke. Yes, I am an admirer of your country. It appears to me a nation in which the first requisite is courage, the second hard work—am I correct?" His English was curiously accented but fluent.

Olivia pulled a deep breath. "If we seem to have courage, Your Highness, then it is by God's grace. But yes, we do all need to work hard. Life in my country is still demanding and often precarious."

He nodded in approval. "Nevertheless, God's grace is often a euphemism for sheer elbow-grease, is it not?"

"Yes, I guess you could say that!" They shared a small laugh and Olivia's shyness started to wane. Despite his awesome regalia and formal bearing, he seemed extremely congenial. "In our own little ways, we all have to contribute to the process of nation building."

"Ah, nation building." He flicked what was undoubtedly an imaginary speck of something off the front of his splendid scarlet and gold brocade coat that reached down to his knees. "The processes are complex, Miss O'Rourke, but they are also greatly invigorating. From what I have learned of your country, I have no doubt you will attain all your lofty goals in time." He paused to adjust the gold cummerbund at his waist from which hung a jewelled scabbard. "As, perhaps, some day we will too."

Olivia wondered if those last few words constituted a political double entendre meant for the benefit of his colonial host, who was listening intently to the exchange. She quickly filled the gap with an inquiry. "Does Your Highness have first-hand knowledge of America?"

"Sadly no. I have not yet had the good fortune to visit your country. But I do meet many American visitors here, such as yourself, and I take pleasure in reading your newspapers even though several months old."

"And then, of course," Sir Joshua entered the conversation for the first time, "Your Highness does employ American engineers at the mine."

There was a noticeable pause. "Indeed. But they will not be here much longer. Our own men have been trained with sufficient competence to take charge shortly." He took another appreciative sip of his whisky. "An excellent malt, Sir Joshua. I compliment you on your choice. But I see that you are making me drink alone."

At a snap of Sir Joshua's fingers, a bearer sprang forward to serve him a whisky and Olivia a frosted sorbet. Sir Joshua raised his glass. "To your health, Your Highness, and to the continued prosperity of your mine." The Maharaja acknowledged the toast with a gracious inclination of his head. The slight gesture caused the light of a Chinese lantern to catch in the jewelled ruby brooch affixed to his yellow ochre turban and its sudden spark of fire so dazzled Olivia that she had to squint her eyes. "I have learned that the Kirtinagar mine is already considered to have better potential than Raniganj?" Sir Joshua's comment was casual but his forehead was beaded with perspiration.

"Yes. Excavations and predictions are encouraging."

If Sir Joshua was even aware of his royal guest's reluctance to talk of the subject, he chose to ignore it. Instead he continued to ply him with questions, all of which the Maharaja answered readily but with replies that were noncommittal. It seemed to Olivia, as she listened in interested silence, that his quietly dark Eastern eyes against a complexion of ripening wheat were alert and that his medium height and slender build gave him a mildness that was deceptive. Beneath the immaculate courtesy there was still arrogance, the manner of one born to power, of generations of controlled breeding that had perpetuated forever strict codes of ethics, honour and chivalry. The very casualness with which the Maharaja's fingers rested lightly on the bejewelled handle of his sword was that of a man who took for granted his destiny to rule over others.

"The very first Indian-owned and operated coal mine is of prime interest to the merchant community, Your Highness," Sir Joshua was saying. "I have no doubt Your Highness, with his reputed business acumen, is already aware of that. The project shows considerable foresight on your part, Your Highness, especially since it can be of mutual benefit."

Olivia's interest quickened. So this was the native prince who would "sell his mother" if pleasured well and if the price was right! Observing Arvind Singh now, Olivia wondered. His concentration was flatteringly close as he listened; but even though it was Sir Joshua who was doing most of the talking, in some strange, subtle way it was the Maharajà who seemed to control the conversation. The man, Olivia decided, was shrewd.

"How soon does Your Highness propose to make the coal commercially available in Calcutta's markets?" Sir Joshua asked with just a hint of impatience, since Arvind Singh's reaction to his compliments remained bland.

"That is difficult to say, Sir Joshua. You see, I am not yet certain that it will be made commercially available. I am anxious to introduce industries within Kirtinagar, and my domestic requirements might not allow for any surplus." The smile that accompanied the blunt declaration was one of continued graciousness.

Sir Joshua's jaw tightened perceptibly. "A British consortium would be willing to offer extremely favourable terms that might help considerably in, for instance . . . ," he took a sip of whisky and allowed a minim to pass, ". . . Your Highness's irrigation project. Naturally, part payment would be made in advance."

For the first time, interest flickered in the Maharaja's hooded brown eyes as he fingered his clean-shaven chin and reflected. "You already have such a consortium, Sir Joshua?"

"Yes. A draft agreement is in the process of being approved."

"How would Company Bahadur react to the idea?"

"Favourably. They are as hungry for coal as we are."

For another moment the Maharaja stared at his exquisitely tooled gold leather shoes heavy with embroidery and turned up at the toes. "Very well." The sudden decisiveness sounded characteristic. "I would like to see the draft at your convenience, Sir Joshua. And now," he dismissed the subject and turned to Olivia, "I must ask forgiveness for having neglected you, Miss O'Rourke. We men have an incorrigible habit of sacrificing etiquette to mundane business, which is inexcusable." He drained his glass and a uniformed aide-de-camp materialised to claim the empty goblet. The Maharaja declined politely as Sir Joshua ordered a renewal. "It is kind of you to have indulged my weakness for Glenmorangie, Sir Joshua, but in whisky drinking—if not in other matters—one must bow to the wisdom of one's wife. The Maharani disapproves of excesses."

It was said shyly and with such boyish guilelessness that they all laughed and the atmosphere became once again convivial. The gentle dismissal contained in the Maharaja's apology to Olivia, Sir Joshua took in his stride, too buoyant to care. "Well, if I may now leave Your Highness in Olivia's splendidly capable hands, there are duties to which I must attend as a host or Lady Bridget will be extremely cross." He bowed and backed away.

Thoughtfully, the Maharaja watched the distinguished, imposing form till it merged with the crowd. "An admirable gentleman, Miss O'Rourke. And a determined one. I am flattered by the honour Sir Joshua and his colleagues do me as pillars of Her Majesty's enterprise in the colonies." Whether or not there was sarcasm in the remark Olivia could not say, because his expression was quite serious. Then, swiftly, he cast Sir Joshua and his colleagues aside. "Now tell me, Miss O'Rourke, how do you consider the chances of Mr. Zachary Taylor in the elections? Is he likely to get the better of Mr. Cass and Mr. Van Buren in this significant contest when for the first time all your States will vote simultaneously?"

Olivia was amazed. "Your Highness keeps in touch with our American presidential politics?"

"Why not?" By tacit consent they had started to stroll along the paved path that adjoined the embankment wall. Although no one approached, the curious eyes watching were many. Whatever English opinion about native princes in private, in public they aroused keen interest. Not only did the rulers wield enormous power over their subjects, but in some cases their kingdoms were larger than England and certainly richer. "Politics are politics no matter what their nationality, Miss O'Rourke," Arvind Singh continued, "mainly because everywhere people are people. Yes, through friends I do maintain an interest in presidential power play. But you have not answered my question."

"Well, my father believes that Mr. Taylor has the better chances. He might not be a seasoned politician, but he is known as a good soldier and his victory at Buena Vista has already made him a national hero. The Whigs chose him because he appeals to the common people." She smiled. "They call him Old Rough and Ready. I guess that is as good a selling slogan as any."

The Maharaja, listening closely, nodded. "But is he not also a slave owner? How will he rationalise that when admitting new States into the Union on a free-or-slave basis?"

Olivia made a face. "He will change his stance, Papa thinks. In politics, Papa says, only fools keep principles lifelong. The wise stick only to expediency." Quickly she added, "He doesn't mean that as a compliment. Papa has not much respect for politicians."

Arvind Singh laughed. "Your father is, of course, right. In fact, I must remember that observation when I wish to appear wise before my counsellors. I am told that your father is a highly regarded writer."

"Yes. Did my uncle mention that?"

He stopped and rubbed the tip of his nose with a forefinger. "No. It was told to me by a friend who informs me that Calcutta is a village in which everything becomes known to everyone sooner or later."

Olivia's breath knotted. It was not difficult to guess to whom he referred. Her steps too halted in their tracks. "I . . . see." Lightly, she asked, "May I ask who that friend might be?"

"I believe you have already met him. His name is Jai Raventhorne."

The turn of the conversation was so unexpected that Olivia was again thrown off balance. Raventhorne had actually spoken of her to the Maharaja? Why? In what context? "Oh yes, so I have." She kept her gaze fixed steadily on the river. Even though details of her uncle's argument with Arthur Ransome that night now became clear in her memory, she asked, "Mr. Raventhorne is known to Your Highness?"

He did not answer at once. In fact, he took an inordinate amount of time over a question that Olivia had asked with deliberate offhandedness. "Jai Raventhorne is not known to anybody, Miss O'Rourke, maybe not even to himself. But as far as it is possible to know him, yes, he is known to me."

That made her smile. "But Mr. Raventhorne believes that nobody ever truly knows anyone else!"

"In the final analyses, I suppose he is right."

Unexpected or not, the drift of the conversation was too tempting a prospect not to explore further a man who had strangely dominated Olivia's thoughts over the past weeks. Surprising herself with her forwardness, she asked, "Since Your Highness does know him as a friend, does Mr. Raventhorne deserve the hideous reputation he has with the European community?"

"Certainly. He not only deserves it, he enjoys it. In fact, Jai is flattered by the list of charges the Europeans prefer against him. Indeed, he works hard to extend it. That his efforts are recognized is a matter of great satisfaction to him."

Whether or not the Maharaja spoke in jest, Olivia was nonplussed. "But why?" Nervously, she cast a glance over her shoulder to ensure that they were not within listening distance of anyone. Even so, her pulse raced. "Why should any man enjoy being known as a reprobate and a rogue?"

The Maharaja shrugged, amused by her bewilderment. "*Why* is not a question that can be asked of Jai Raventhorne, Miss O'Rourke. His motives are as obscure as the man himself."

Olivia frowned and shook her head. "I'm afraid I don't understand—"

"I wonder if it is even worth trying to," he interrupted quietly. Some subtle signal must have been made, because an aide emerged suddenly out of nowhere to present the Maharaja with a prettily enamelled silver snuff-box held deferentially in one palm balanced upon the other. Taking from it a delicate pinch, the Maharaja dabbed each nostril with a red silk handkerchief into which he then received a subdued sneeze. "You must forgive my little indulgence," he apologised with a half smile. "It is an unfortunate addiction but I choose to believe a harmless one."

They continued their stroll in silence for a while before the Maharaja picked up the thread of their conversation. "Jai is my dearest friend. There is no man I admire quite as much, for he has the courage to wage war on the gods themselves. But," his footsteps halted as he shook his head sadly, "sometimes I am convinced that Jai Raventhorne is utterly . . . insane."

Arthur Ransome, Olivia recalled, had gone a step further—he had called him a mad dog! "Insane?"

"In some ways, yes. But then, on the other hand, one must concede that every man is entitled to his obsessions. Jai Raventhorne too has his." They had arrived back at the point from which they had started. The Maharaja held out a chair for Olivia and then slipped into one opposite her. "Tell me, Miss O'Rourke, why does this man interest you so much?"

Olivia felt the heat climb up her face. The casual façade she had assumed had not deceived the Maharaja. Suddenly, she found the inside of her mouth oddly dry, but she met the probing gaze with contained calmness. "Only because even during that brief encounter, your friend struck me as . . . unusual. I have not met many men like Mr. Raventhorne."

"Many?" he smiled. "If you had met any, I would have been surprised."

Not so much by what he said but by the tone in which he said it, Olivia surmised that the matter of Jai Raventhorne was once again closed. The hundred new questions surging through her mind with even more impatience now would have to remain unasked and unanswered. The conversation slipped back into neutral channels as they chatted informally of Kirtinagar, of America and India, of cabbages and kings. The Maharaja, Olivia saw, was an enlightened, well-informed man whose interests were catholic and with whom it was easy to converse. Apart from Jai Raventhorne, the other subject she did not bring up again was that of the coal mine, as outside her ethical limits as was the Maharaja's enigmatic friend.

"Has Olivia been looking after you well, Your Highness?" Sir Joshua rejoined them eventually, still full of high spirits. "She has a sharp intellect, as I'm sure Your Highness has already deduced, and like many of her countrymen never fails to call a spade anything but that!"

"Yes, indeed. I am charmed by such refreshing candour," the Maharaja agreed with alacrity. "I have greatly enjoyed our little chat."

Olivia blushed. "Well, I hope the candour has not been *too* refreshing! I have never before been in the company of royalty, and so my knowledge of appropriate protocol is deplorably lacking."

The Maharaja grimaced and arched an eyebrow. "You have no idea, Miss O'Rourke, how tired one tends to get of protocol. Your 'deplorably lacking' knowledge, believe me, comes as a breath of fresh air." He bowed. "I thank you for a most entertaining interlude. I have learned much. Perhaps some day you will give the Maharani and myself the privilege of offering you our humble hospitality in Kirtinagar." He turned to Sir Joshua. "And, of course, yourself, Lady Bridget and the delightful Miss Templewood."

Olivia watched as her uncle bore off his prize guest to present to him the waiting line of people ranged underneath the canopy. Many already knew the Maharaja, but there was still a formality about the presentation that impressed with its air of ceremony. However elated Sir Joshua appeared to be in his effusive bonhomie, even from a distance Olivia could see that it was not shared by Arthur Ransome as he solemnly shook hands with his partner's royal guest. Ransome, in fact, looked visibly worried. Obviously, there were undercurrents in the occasion but, as far as Olivia was concerned, none as insidious as those now running within herself. Why had the Maharaja brought up the subject of Jai Raventhorne at all with her? What was it that he might have seen in her face that had urged him on to question the source of her interest? In retrospect, she felt a sense of disquiet, of unreality, about their conversation, for it had been about a man she had met only once and whose face she still had not seen clearly! What an absurd situation!

"Come and join us, Olivia. What on earth have you been doing with all those antiquated fuddy-duddies?" Estelle's voice was loud enough to be embarrassing. Quickly, Olivia joined her cousin and her friends.

"Yes *do,* Olivia," seconded Lily Horniman, a tall girl with ginger-colored hair and an acute case of enlarged adenoids. "Estedde's been regarding us with such tades of your derring-do and they're a *hoot,* readdy they are!"

"Estelle maintains," John Sturges said with a wink and his tongue resting in his cheek, "that you were champion shotgun rider with the wagon train and once fought off five redskins with your bare hands."

Olivia cursed silently; Estelle was incorrigible! But it was difficult not to laugh at her cousin's fertile imagination. "Actually," she said lightly, settling herself down in their midst, "there were ten. And I didn't just fight them off with my bare hands, I *strangled* half of them. If I didn't ride shotgun, considering I was only eight, I still sure was champion of *some*thing."

"Wot?" Polly Drummond asked wide eyed, not certain if all this was serious or a joke.

"I was champion of the buffalo chip collecting team, *that's* what!"

They stared at her blankly, then Estelle asked with marked suspicion, "What's a buffalo chip?"

Olivia told them and John bellowed with laughter while everyone else looked taken aback. "Well, you must admit Estelle's imagination does her credit and she does spin a yarn well!"

"*Ugh!*" Marie Cleghorn shuddered delicately. "How *could* you, Olivia?"

"It was quite easy," Olivia assured her callously. "They were old and perfectly dry, our only assured source of fuel."

"Well, I don't believe it," Marie said flatly.

"Oh, *I* believe it," Charlotte Smithers sniggered. "I'd believe *any*thing about Americans. My aunt comes from Memphis and she once hit my uncle on the nose with an umbrella and he couldn't smell anything for a *week!* Isn't that gruesome?"

"But since 'e could'n' breathe neither, presum'bly, I s'pose she was quite 'appy, eh luv?" Dave Crichton added with a broad wink.

Charlotte Smithers tossed her head haughtily but everyone else laughed, except for Estelle. "Well, that's what Olivia told me herself," she muttered, snatching her hand out of John's. "At least that's what I *think* she told me."

Dinner was announced with a silver gong, then served and eaten with considerable aplomb as tribute to the splendid display of wines, viands and three kinds of dessert. After dinner the long trestle tables were removed and the arena cleared for dancing.

"Disgusting!" Lady Bridget pronounced fiercely under her breath, "dis*gus*ting!" Sitting down briefly next to her aunt to cool her aching heels, Olivia followed Lady Bridget's shocked gaze fixed on a corner of the tent. Next to the liquor table, Mrs. Drummond clung tenaciously to the arm of a retired naval admiral. It was obvious that both were in an advanced state of intoxication. "How Bertie can encourage the woman I don't know. I've never seen such a shameless display of immodesty." Angrily she tapped on her knee with her fingertips. "I shall have words with Estelle tomorrow, believe me!"

Olivia believed her. Mrs. Drummond was making rather a spectacle of herself, but it was obviously with the approval and participation of "Bertie," who made no secret of enjoying the coquettish attentions. But there was evidence of lack of inhibitions elsewhere, too, which was not surprising since an inordinate amount of liquor was being consumed. Nevertheless, Olivia remained silent in the knowledge that it was her intervention that had included Mrs. Drummond in the revelry, and that Lady Bridget's promised "words" would have to be shared equally between her cousin and herself.

"And how Josh can *demean* himself so by pandering to the man's vanity is beyond me! I'm astonished he can't see how it debases him in the eyes of his equals."

Her aunt referred, of course, to the Maharaja. Immediately after supper Sir Joshua and some of the other prominent merchants had withdrawn with him to the formal sitting-room in the house. A flurry of bearers was now busy flitting to and fro with choice brandies, cigars and liqueurs. "The coal is of importance to Uncle Josh," Olivia started to explain. "He is preparing the ground for further negotiations, that's all."

A strange, indecipherable expression came over Lady Bridget's features as she slowly swivelled to face her niece. "Josh will never get that coal, Olivia, *never!* If he thinks he will with his clownish endeavours and his grovelling, he is an even greater fool than that native prince must consider him to be."

It had never ceased to surprise Olivia that her aunt's interest in and understanding of her husband's business should be so minimal, indeed, so grudging. She spoke of Sir Joshua's professional affairs so seldom that Olivia was beginning to wonder if she even knew what he did! But now, the categorical remark she had made seemed so knowing, so profound, that Olivia stared. Lady Bridget's eyes glittered like icy blue shards of glass, but her voice shook with rare passion and her hands were clenched by her sides.

"By gad, Bridget, splendid bash, splendid! Never saw anything like this in Dacca, 'pon my word!" A pompous jute manufacturer with a bright red nose and the strutting gait of an old Army hand strolled up, waving a glass erratically and splashing his drink in all directions. "Can't say I've enjoyed myself so much in years!"

"I'm *so* glad, Tim." Carefully, Lady Bridget wiped the front of her dress with a serviette without dropping her gracious smile. The fierce expression of only a moment ago was gone as if by magic. "You must come round for a quiet tête-à-tête and tell us all about your furlough home."

As the mood became more boisterous, so did the dancing, which continued till the early hours of the morning. By then the gathering had thinned considerably. Only the younger group remained, along with some sporting elders blessed with more energy than their peers. Having danced every dance, Olivia's soles were afire in the unaccustomed gold sandals, but there could be no question of abandoning the party while the younger crowd persisted; Estelle would never forgive her if she did not stay until the bitter end. Eventually, a hearty breakfast of bacon and eggs was served to the determined handful that remained until dawn, Sir Joshua and Lady Bridget having long since retired. Crippled with relief and fatigue, Olivia dragged herself up to bed just before the first streaks of daylight started to stain the eastern horizon. She was asleep even before her head touched the pillow.

Her slumber, however, was fitful and her dreams mysteriously ominous. Two black mastiffs with blank, silverfish eyes had their fangs securely embedded in her flesh. They were by the river and she was being dragged along the embankment. Even so, she could not recognise the environment in which she was any more than she could divine the direction in which she was being pulled. All she knew was that the force with which she was being carried away was magnetic, and that she no longer had the power to deflect it.

3

It was Sunday.

In the early morning the Maidan, a vast parkland across the White Town known as the "lungs" of the city, had its usual complement of brisk walkers, casual strollers and horsemen out for an hour or two of exercise when the city was at its most pleasant. Water carriers jogged rhythmically, balanced by their evenly distributed loads; palanquin carriers transported their customers with geometrically measured steps; and a monkey man with his animal perched cheekily on his shoulders looked around for an audience with the help of a small drum. Along the Chowringhee Road, the town's main thoroughfare, sluggish bullock carts creaked with the weight of fresh fruit and vegetables for the markets, and a few carriages clip-clopped along with European passengers. Farther along, at the Chowringhee-Dharamtala crossing, sweepers cleaned the steps of a church in preparation for the morning service, although the congregation on this Sabbath was yet to arrive, no doubt still asleep in bed after the Templewood ball at which many had been guests.

Despite her exhaustion, or perhaps because of it, Olivia had not been able to sleep for long. She had risen early long before the household had even stirred, to set forth on her customary ride. One of the incidental benefits of Estelle's elaborate party had been that in the confusion that had prevailed throughout the lengthy preparations, nobody had noticed that Olivia went out riding on her own. On this morning, too, with all of Lady Bridget's servants still dead to the world after their arduous labours of last night, Olivia had been unobserved as she left the house on Jasmine. She had long wanted to explore the colourful bazaar near the Chitpur Road, and Mr. Courtenay's (or Poultenay's) recommendation last night had compounded the desire.

That circumstances had turned out to be favourable for such a forbidden excursion was, of course, fortunate; that she was disobeying her aunt's express dictates, Olivia did not think of at all in her state of pleasant excitement. It was unlikely that her casual and, in her opinion, entirely harmless sortie would be discovered.

In the roseate early morning light filled with the pungent aroma of wood stoves, the gracious buildings she passed along the Esplanade and Tank Square looked very imperial indeed. The juxtaposition of elements from Eastern and Western cultures never failed to fascinate Olivia. Outside Writers' Building, seat of the East India Company, Brahmin priests stood waist deep in the Tank chanting with strings of holy beads and their sacred threads looped over one ear. Groups of Indian children, their oily hair slicked over their heads—some with topknots—stared at a group of men in Armenian clothes arguing hotly by the wayside. And a camel with brass rings through its nose trailed behind its keeper and did not even cast a glance at a passing European carriage.

For all her nostalgia for home, Olivia could not deny that she found India as a country intriguing. Here one saw strange mixtures of the mundane and the esoteric, of the old and the new, of gross superstition and astonishing ancient wisdom, of gentleness and savagery, cruelty and compassion. Paradoxes abounded and life was often tragically hard for unwary Europeans at the mercy of strange diseases, furnace-hot summers and death that struck with frightening suddenness when least expected. Infant mortality was high, leaving parents bereft overnight; loved ones could vanish in a trice in sweeping epidemics. All this Olivia had learned, but she also sensed that for those Europeans who opened their minds—and there were undoubtedly many—India could also be a garden of joy, as generous as a spring blossoming.

Despite the earliness of the hour, the Chitpur markets bustled with business. Under slanted awnings serried stalls offered a bewildering array of wares: bamboo basketry, wooden sandals with thongs, brass idols, books, pottery and kitchen goods, cotton bolts, jute ropes and mats, wooden toys, glass bangles, groceries, spices and grain, green produce, spectacular displays of freshly cut flowers, and every conceivable household essential. In some stalls stoves blazed to dispense freshly cooked sweets and savouries served on disposable plates of banana leaves. Captivated, Olivia dismounted opposite a tall Hindu temple with cupolas to stand and observe one confectioner sitting cross-legged before a gigantic pan, frying yellow circles of batter and then dipping them into sugar syrup. She had never tasted Indian sweets, since they were not served at European tables. These reminded her of Sally's doughnuts and for a moment or two she struggled with temptation. *Should* she . . . ?

"I would if I were you. Fresh, they are perfectly safe to eat."

Olivia whirled round in surprise at the unsolicited recommendation, and that too in English. If the features were unfamiliar, there could be no mistaking the rich, deep-timbred voice of Jai Raventhorne! Even less, the pair of piercing eyes that still startled with their opacity. Shocked, she could think of nothing to say.

"I can endorse the sweets, Miss O'Rourke; what I cannot endorse is for to you stand and eat them in the bazaar." Ignoring her speechlessness, he turned to exchange some words with the confectioner and a moment later was handed a neat little packet made of banana leaves. He touched her lightly on her elbow and relieved her of Jasmine's reins. "Come. I will show you a place where you can eat in private comfort."

Still tongue-tied, Olivia could only nod and meekly follow him across the street. It was only as they were about to enter a wide black painted gate that she suddenly returned to her senses. "Where . . . where are you taking me?" she stammered.

In the act of unlatching the gate, he paused. "To my home."

Instantly her eyes filled with suspicion. "But I thought you lived near the Pennworthys!"

He raised a sardonic eyebrow. "I should imagine that not even in the most conservative of English circles is it considered a crime for a man to own two homes?"

"Oh." Feeling foolish, Olivia allowed herself to be ushered in through the gate without further comment or question.

The court-yard into which they stepped was a rectangle of elegant dimensions, marble tiled and shaded on three sides by an arched verandah that rose into a double-storied house. A fountain spraying faintly green water made a cool centrepiece. As they entered, two men glided out silently from a doorway beyond one of the verandah arches, like genies conjured out of some invisible lamp. They bowed, and one, obviously from the north-eastern hill region, as apparent from his Mongolian features, took charge of Jasmine while the other relieved Raventhorne of the packet of sweets that he carried. Some instructions were dispensed in either Hindustani or Bengali—Olivia couldn't tell which—and then Raventhorne turned to her again. "Shall we go inside?"

Hearing their master's voice from one of the upstairs balconies, the dogs had started to bark vociferously. All at once Olivia was overcome with apprehension. "I . . . shouldn't really be here at all," she murmured. "Perhaps I had better . . . leave." It was unavoidable to look directly into his eyes as she addressed him and once more she was struck by their strangeness. Pearl grey, like the inner shell of an oyster, they shone with a translucence that seemed bottomless and, at the same time, cold.

The hint of a smile appeared on his lips as if excavated from within with considerable effort. "I was merely trying to make it possible for you to sit and enjoy your tidbits in privacy. I wasn't intending to make you one of *mine!* Surely your derringer ensures your protection from big bad wolves such as me?"

Again he was making her look foolish and her chin lifted. "It does," she retorted with marked coldness. "Although I have no information as to which animal family you pride yourself on resembling most, I'm willing to accept your own assessment."

The smile widened into a low chuckle. "Well aimed, Miss O'Rourke! But then, why all the fuss? Could it be that in the interim since we met so fortuitously, you have learned something frightening that gnaws away at your American courage, in spite of being so admirably equipped for self-defence?"

"Your reputation, Mr. Raventhorne, whatever it might be, is no concern of mine," she said stiffly, aware that she had coloured and annoyed that she had. "But yes, I do happen to have a bone to pick with you."

"Bones are better picked on a full stomach. Come." Without another word he turned and with loose gait, long strides and not even a glance over his shoulder, walked away inside. With no choice left, Olivia followed. His manner had in no way improved with the passage of the many days since she had first encountered him, but she could not deny that there was something exciting about this second meeting, for she had truly never expected to see him again.

The salon into which Raventhorne now led her was large, also tiled with black and white marble squares, with a high ceiling supported by stone pillars that were heavily carved. It was, Olivia guessed without having knowledge of the subject, a traditional room. A row of windows, screened with delicate filigree in symmetric patterns, ran the length of one wall overlooking another verandah and court-yard on the other side. On a patterned Bukhara carpet at one end of the salon, a seating arrangement had been made with mattresses covered with pristine white sheets and banks of fat bolsters. A *sitar,* a pair of *tablas* and one or two other musical instruments stood in a corner. There were no pictures on the whitewashed walls, no drapes at the windows or doors, no cluttered bric-a-brac so beloved of other drawing rooms Olivia had seen. Only one wall had any adornment—an arrangement of swords, scimitars, daggers and shields—and even those looked more functional than ornamental. It was a room almost defiantly bare with no personal possessions at all, no indications as to the personality and character of the man who occupied and used it.

"Please do be seated." He indicated the mattress. "Or would you prefer a chair? Sitting on floors is a primitive custom not usually favoured by memsahibs, I know."

"I am well used to sitting on floors, thank you." His tone irked her as she sank onto the mattress and started to remove her heavy riding boots. "Not all memsahibs consider chairs necessary."

Patting a bolster into shape, Raventhorne lowered himself onto the other end of the mattress, leaned back and extended his legs over the edge so as to keep his own boots off it. Olivia placed herself comfortably, crossed her legs Indian fashion and fixed him with a stern look. "About that bone I have to pick with you . . ."

"After breakfast."

"No, now!"

He shrugged and crossed his arms against his chest. "Very well. Since you insist."

It was not easy to stare into those opalescent eyes without wavering, but Olivia held her gaze. "The message you sent to my aunt and uncle—were you aware of the upset it would cause them?"

"Certainly. It was the only reason for sending it."

His easy admission galled her. "Did you not think it a dirty trick to play on *me,* an innocent courier of the wretched message?"

"Dirty tricks are a part of life, even in America. One more or less makes little difference."

"It made a difference to me!" His cynicism was, if possible, worse. "Whatever your rivalries with my uncle, you had no business to make me the ham in the sandwich. Surely you must have some scruples about the means by which you achieve your dubious ends, especially when making use of *petticoats!*" High spots of colour glowed on her cheeks.

He looked amused. "I don't consider you a petticoat any more than I consider myself a scrupulous man, Miss O'Rourke.

Fortunately," he smiled, "I suffer none of the constraints of being a gentleman."

Olivia had a rash urge to ask him what he *did* consider her but of course did no such thing. It was bad enough not to have rejected his invitation out of hand and sent him packing when she should have. "You *do* actually enjoy the diabolical reputation you have, don't you? Well, I think that childish and perverse!"

"Perversity carries its own pleasures, Miss O'Rourke," he said lightly, unaffected by her show of temper. "But since you, I suspect, do not believe that diabolical reputation, perhaps you at least will forgive me my trespasses."

The lines of his angular face with so little evidence of softness seemed all at once not so hard. There was also a flash of hitherto unsuspected charm. Olivia wasn't sure she liked any of it, because he was making her unsure again. "Knowing you as little as I do, Mr. Raventhorne, the question of believing or otherwise simply doesn't arise," she said with haughty dignity.

"But considering the extent of your questions to Arvind Singh last night, perhaps you know me better this time than you did the last?"

It was with considerable restraint that Olivia didn't jump right out of her skin! She had met the Maharaja no more than a few hours ago—and he had heard already? Suddenly, the respect she felt for the ubiquitous village grapevine turned close to reverence, but she also felt a small sense of betrayal. "Did the Maharaja tell you that?" she asked, embarrassed.

"No. For his sins, Arvind Singh *is* a gentleman. I have other sources of information."

A timely diversion occurred to plug a line of conversation Olivia had no wish to pursue. One of the men who had received them in the court-yard entered to engage Raventhorne in brief conversation. With his attention elsewhere, Olivia could study him more closely. Yes, his skin was pale beneath the leathery sunburn, justifying the impression of a European. The disturbing eyes, even now as they focused on the face of the attendant, appeared restless, burning with a fierce inner light that was demonic. His shock of hair, black and untamed, tumbled down his neck in a confusion of upturned ends. Thin lips—a clean gash in a shaven chin—showed ruthlessness, but his profile of aquiline nose and high, wide forehead was almost patrician. If clothes maketh the man it was obvious that man was not Jai Raventhorne; his garments were carelessly worn, a white shirt tucked casually into plain black trousers secured with a black leather belt and silver buckle. Yet, the power of the man was such that it was neither increased nor diminished by what he wore. That he was volatile and mercurial Olivia already knew, but there was again that air about him that seemed designed to make others uncomfortable and ill at ease. Had she told him that, she had no doubt it would have afforded him considerable pleasure, for his perversity was abundant.

The attendant left and Raventhorne glanced at a watch attached to his belt with a clip and chain. "There appears to be a problem with one of my ships due to sail on the afternoon tide. I shall have to leave soon."

If perversity was Raventhorne's pleasure, it seemed by no means only his prerogative. In his imminent departure Olivia felt an annoying stab of disappointment. "In that case, let me not delay you—"

"I said soon," he cut in gently, "but not that soon. There is still time for breakfast." He laced his fingers behind his head and half lowered his eyelids. "Why are you frightened of me?"

"Frightened? Surely you flatter yourself!"

"All right then, nervous. Let me assure you there is no cause even for that. Neither of us is likely to inform your distinguished relatives of this encounter! I have no more messages to send." He made no effort to disguise either his mockery or his amusement.

"I am relieved to hear it." Olivia matched mockery with sarcasm, but the discomfiting facility he seemed to have of dipping into her thoughts produced further annoyance. "Are you a musician as well?" she asked, pointing to the instruments in an attempt to change the subject.

"As well as what?"

"As well as . . . whatever else you might be." She was careful not to say "tea exporter," since that would certainly inform him that she had been inquiring about him from others.

"The current, popular descriptions are unmitigated scoundrel, moral degenerate, debauch and unscrupulous villain, but they vary with the season."

It was difficult to suppress a smile; these were near enough the descriptions her uncle had used the other night. "You take pride in being called those? They give you pleasure?"

He shrugged. "Neither pride nor pleasure nor anything else. They don't touch me."

"What does touch you then?" The question escaped on impulse and Olivia regretted it instantly, for it again opened wide the avenues of impertinent counter-attack. But Raventhorne showed no reaction one way or the other. He merely looked away, faintly puzzled, and his eyes became distant.

"Nothing." His face was like a blank even as the smile returned. "Nothing *they* say touches me." She too belonged to the world he dismissed with such contempt, and for an instant Olivia had an insane urge to say something, anything, that *would* touch him. But she could think of nothing. He spoke again in an entirely different tone. "I can see that Lady Birkhurst will approve of her son's choice this time. She at least is a woman of considerable vigour and vitality even if that is more than can be said of the Honourable Freddie."

Olivia struggled between outrage and curiosity—and curiosity won. "Lady Birkhurst?"

"The Honourable Freddie's mother. She is due shortly, no doubt to short-list the finalists for fair Freddie's hand, money and title. I can't see you finding much competition in the home stretch."

To fly again into a temper would be to play into his hands; it was what he was waiting for. "I am obliged for your words of comfort and your vote of confidence," she said with every sign of pleasantness. "But it surprises me that you should be so well informed about my affairs even though I have little knowledge of yours." She added quickly, "Knowledge of or interest in."

"Oh, you have interest all right, Miss O'Rourke," he remarked with an easy laugh. "And if the knowledge is lacking it is certainly not for want of trying. If there is anything you want to know about me, why don't you just ask?"

Were it not for that utterly unlikely charm in one so undeserving of it, Olivia would have been disgusted at his monumental conceit. "And if I do ask will you tell me?"

"No, but you can ask anyway."

She had to laugh.

Another diversion occurred, this time startling. A young girl entered bearing a silver platter, followed by a succession of servants bearing more. With subtle gestures she issued commands, and a low table was placed in front of Olivia on which were then arranged an array of bowls, silver plates and European cutlery. It was a smooth, economical operation, but Olivia's attention was riveted to the girl. Even by exotic standards she was breathtakingly lovely. Dark satin eyes were set in a sandalwood-smooth skin; she was tall and moved with the unconscious grace of a dancer motivated by unheard rhythms. Under a loose tunic of yellow gauze fringed with tinsel, her breasts thrust outwards in perfect cones. Her legs were slender and long with small ankles and voluptuously curved calves, all encased in fitted pyjamas crinkled at the ankles. As she swept past Olivia in pursuit of her duties she did not look at her, but she exuded a strong fragrance reminiscent of roses. Her sculpted fingers—deft and light in their labours—were patterned with filigreed henna, which looked like deep orange lace gloves.

A slight chill travelled up Olivia's body. She knew instinctively that this was Jai Raventhorne's mistress.

He offered no introductions. Instead, quite unperturbed, he said, "Sujata is an excellent cook, as you will shortly see for yourself. It is she who is the musician."

Hearing her name spoken, the girl smiled, but only at him. The sidelong glance might have been coy and coquettish had it not been so full of love and longing. As she bent down to place the last of the bowls on the table, her flimsy veil slipped from her head, slid down and settled over a breast. Without embarrassment or hesitation Raventhorne reached forward to readjust the veil in its former position. Between them passed a look; his retreating hand lingered just a shade longer than it needed to on her shoulder. The fleeting gesture, the shared look, lasted barely a second or two, but to Olivia somehow they conveyed an impression of such intimacy, such explicit sensuality, that she felt her cheeks warm and the back of her neck tingle. A smile still playing on her glistening coral lips. Sujata walked out of the salon. All the while she had been there she had not looked at Olivia even once.

Placing small portions into each bowl, Raventhorne started to serve the food. He offered no explanations for Sujata but merely concentrated on the job at hand with brief descriptions of each course and its preparation. Olivia listened abstractedly, shaken by what she had seen. This was the woman who shared Raventhorne's home and bed; the ravishing image seemed etched into her brain and it was not an image that brought her any pleasure. Unaccountably, she disliked it.

"Eat while it's hot. *Jalebis* cannot be enjoyed when cold." A touch on her hand jolted Olivia back to reality and she coloured. He was pointing to the sweets she had fancied in the shop.

With an effort she smiled. "You should not have gone to all this trouble. I only wanted to satisfy my curiosity about these." The array of courses included far more than the modest *jalebis*.

"The trouble was not mine. I only gave the order. Sujata likes to please visitors."

For devilish reasons of his own he seemed set on thrusting

his mistress down her throat, perhaps because Olivia's discomfiture was obvious and it gave him some impious pleasure. She was again annoyed, not only by his lack of delicacy but by her own irritation; what business was it of hers whom he chose to have in his bed? She found herself again regretting her rash decision to stay, but it was too late to do anything about it now. In any case the food was delicious.

"To where does your ship sail this afternoon?" she inquired to fill the gaping silences. "Canton?"

"No. I no longer involve myself in the China trade."

She had heard that already, of course. "But isn't the China trade the commercial arena that holds most promise of riches?"

"I already have riches. I have no need for more."

"In business, surely, there is always need for more!"

"Well then, let us accept that in my needs I choose to be different. To me money is only a means, not an end in itself."

"And the end?" She threw him an oblique glance and saw that he too was suddenly not at ease. The compacted tension she had sensed that night by the river was making him restless. He rose and walked to the window, the expanse of his shoulders forming a dark silhouette against the light.

"To ensure survival in an environment that is essentially hostile."

Olivia sat up slowly, food forgotten for the moment. She wondered again about those "obsessions" the Maharaja had refused to amplify or even disclose, perhaps rightly so. "But is not the environment hostile because you yourself encourage it to be so through your own wilfulness?"

He walked back to sit down again, still restive. "Wilfulness is a privilege I have earned for myself, Miss O'Rourke. It is a very small reward for very hard labour. Surely you will not deny me such meagre pickings?" Then with a mercurial shift of mood his eyes narrowed. "Tell me, what bribes is your uncle offering Arvind Singh for his coal?"

The sudden question startled her, but she answered calmly enough, "None that I know of. Even if I did know, it is hardly likely that I would tell you. Besides, why should he have to bribe to get the coal?"

"He will not get the coal with or without bribes." A cutting edge sharpened his tone. "Everyone is aware of that except your uncle."

Olivia's mind went back to her aunt's remark of not so many hours ago. How odd that she should share even this thought with a man whose very name had made her faint! "You mean you will use your friendship with the Maharaja to block the sale? Because you want to monopolise the coal for your own steamship?"

"Ah, you *are* better informed about me this time!" The realisation seemed to afford him unconcealed satisfaction. "Sir Joshua's words?"

"Hardly!" Olivia retorted. "One doesn't need a complicated espionage system or secret briefing to learn what the entire business community is up in arms about." But she had no desire to expand this particular dispute. What intrigued her about Raventhorne was not his professional ethics or otherwise, it was the essential contradiction inherent in the man. She had never met anyone so paradoxical, so cussed, so uncaring of opinion. She wanted to ask a hundred, a thousand questions, but then a servant entered to place before her a finger-bowl of warm water with a slice of lime and to clear away the table. In the lost opportunity all she could think of saying was, "You did not join me for breakfast."

"I have already eaten. I rise early so that, like you, I can ride and exercise in peace. It appears we share this habit," a fractional pause, "among others."

The pause, minimal but heavy with thoughts unsaid, made Olivia's mouth again run dry. "What . . . others?"

He did not reply immediately. His brows met in a frown that indicated perplexity as he gazed beyond her out of the window. "Let's say excessive mutual curiosity and the . . . curse of being different from the herd." He sprang to his feet and stretched a hand in her direction. "Come, we must be away or my ship will miss the tide and I will have given my rivals something to be happy about. She is on charter to a jute manufacturer who wants her in Dundee on time or he will cancel my contract."

Olivia rose too but quickly detached her hand from his. Even the trivial physical contact had accelerated her pulse in a manner that was unsettling. She bent down and quickly laced up her riding boots. "Thank you for breakfast. I enjoyed it very much."

"Perhaps you might have enjoyed it more had your thoughts not been elsewhere!"

Even after so brief an acquaintanceship—if it could even be called that!—he had learned to pin-point her passing contemplations with an accuracy that dismayed Olivia. "They were as much here as I was," she corrected sharply. "I tasted and enjoyed every morsel. You must extend my thanks and appreciation to . . . Sujata."

"She does not expect to be thanked. It is her pleasure." He turned and strode impatiently out of the room.

Olivia followed but more slowly. Through a perfect arch, one of many that lined the verandah, she observed the tall, erect figure call for their horses. How old was he? Thirty-five? Forty-five? A hundred and five! It was impossible to tell. His body, lithe, healthy with an abundance of energy, gave indication of a youthful prime, of a male at the peak of his manhood. But it was what Olivia had glimpsed lurking in his eyes, or behind them, that puzzled her. Dark, looming shadows barely concealed a world weariness that gave an odd impression of agelessness, as if he had lived long beyond his years. It was yet another of the maddening contradictions in which Jai Raventhorne abounded.

In the court-yard together with Olivia's own mare, Jasmine, awaited a midnight at least sixteen hands tall with fiery red eyes and a fiercely swishing tail. As Olivia approached with caution, he snorted and his nostrils flared. Knowing horses well, she stood rapt with admiration, for he was an extraordinarily perfect specimen of horseflesh. Glaring at her, he kicked his back legs and sent the attendants skittering. Olivia laughed. "I see that he too is trained to guard you with his life!"

"Since my head is greatly in demand, yes!" Raventhorne fondled the midnight's forehead with surprising gentleness and, pulling down his head, whispered something in his ear. The animal seemed to listen intently, eyes barely moving. Then he neighed softly, pawed the ground and rubbed his nose in the palm of his master's hand. There were men Olivia had known in her own country, where a horse was more often than not a meal ticket, who could establish almost human rapport with their steeds. Raventhorne obviously was one of those. The horse trusted him implicitly.

"What did you say to him?" Olivia asked curiously.

He shook his head. "Secrets between a man and his horse are sacred. It is an impertinence even to ask." He broke off two lumps of jaggery from a large piece that one of his attendants presented and fed one each to the two horses. "His name is Shaitan, which means *devil.* Sometimes he can be a vicious brute, perhaps to justify the reputation that name gives him."

"Very much in the manner of his master, no doubt!"

Raventhorne looked nonplussed at Olivia's tart observation but then flung back his head and roared. "No doubt at all, I assure you!" He continued to laugh as a Nepali arrived leading a third horse, a dun with white stockings. "My man Bahadur will follow you home from a discreet distance."

Olivia's protest was almost a reflex. "Oh, that will not be necessary—"

"It will be necessary!" He interrupted her with a decisiveness that called for instant obedience. "I know that you are American and given to postures of defiance and independence, but please humour my whim, if only so that I can prove I am not entirely without social refinements."

Without another word Olivia got onto the box and mounted Jasmine. Raventhorne ensured that she was well settled in her saddle before vaulting into his own. At the moment of parting the question trembling on Olivia's lips could not be restrained. "In return for your many impertinences, will you allow me one more?"

A wariness settled over his face. "Ask."

"At least partially, you yourself are European," she said meeting his suspicious eyes steadily. "Is it not hypocrisy to profess to hate those to whom you too belong in part?"

She wondered if he would answer at all, for instantly his jaw cemented. But then he did. "It is because I do belong to them partially that I have the right to hate them. And the reason?" The pewter eyes were icy. "In America livestock carries its brand on its haunches; in India the Englishman's bastard is branded forever by his face."

He dug his spurs into Shaitan's sides and at the same instant the huge black gates swung open soundlessly. Like a gigantic wind machine the midnight charged forward to blow a storm around him. For a second, man and beast stood poised at the gate. Then, crouching low in the saddle Raventhorne nudged his horse again and in a burst of speed vanished into the thoroughfare. He did not look back at her. But then Olivia knew from past experience that he wouldn't.

Shaken by the extreme bitterness of his answer, she sat for a moment, unmoving. Then, remembering the open gates and the waiting Bahadur, she urged Jasmine forward. Before the black gates finally closed behind her, Olivia turned for a last look at the house and caught a flash of yellow in an upstairs balcony. It was Sujata watching her leave.

Whether or not it is possible for human beings to define in their minds moments of destiny, Olivia did not know. But what she did know was that her second unsolicited encounter with Jai Raventhorne was like a signpost confirming a direction that confounded her. She was fascinated and baffled by this strange conundrum of a man, yes; but she was not yet sure that she even liked him! He was hard, opinionated, arrogant, twisted with hate and cynicism. He believed in adventurism, thought nothing of flaunting his moral turpitude before come who may and had no scruples about achieving his ends with whatever dubious means happened to be available at the moment. Arvind Singh had professed profound admiration for Jai Raventhorne as a man of rare courage. In Olivia's view, however, there was nothing especially admirable about a man merely because he was foolhardy enough to challenge the gods themselves.

All this Olivia recognised with extreme clarity. What she could not identify was the capricious, obscure, utterly illogical reason why she could not shake Jai Raventhorne out of her thoughts no matter how hard she tried. Involuntarily, as part of the same thought chain, she saw Greg in her mind. Dreamy, gentle, patient Greg with whom she had grown up. She loved and respected and trusted Greg, but suddenly he seemed to exist only on the fringes of her memory. She could barely see his features now and it disturbed her badly. Inexorably, the world in which Greg lived—in which she too had once lived—was becoming unreal, like a fantasy. Something sly and unwanted was creeping into her life, taking her away from her roots. And somehow, at the crux of her disorientation, stood Jai Raventhorne.

There was a time, only a few days ago, when she had longed to meet him again. But now in her revived sense of aloneness, of this strange alienation from her past, Olivia determined that accidentally or otherwise, she would not see Jai Raventhorne again.

"Fancy! I'm actually *eighteen*—I can hardly believe it!" For days after the birthday ball this was the theme on which Estelle harped constantly.

"Well, what does that make you, except longer in the tooth, miss?" Olivia demanded irritably as they sat dispatching the piles of thank-you notes that Lady Bridget insisted Estelle send in acknowledgement of the mountain of gifts she had received, Olivia's being a beautiful doeskin skirt.

"It makes me an adult, that's what! Now I can marry anyone I like whether Mama approves or not, except of course Freddie. He's reserved for you, Coz, isn't he?"

Before Olivia could give a suitably cutting return, Lady Bridget bustled into the room. "Aren't you girls going for your evening drive at all? There should be considerable excitement on the Strand today with this new ship in from Portsmouth. I hear Lady Birkhurst is one of the passengers on board. Freddie must be delighted."

Olivia was not at all surprised at Lady Bridget's announcement. As usual, Jai Raventhorne's espionage network had been dead accurate in its information.

That depressing news aside, the evening drive or stroll along the Strand Road was one that Olivia looked forward to. The outings were a daily sacred ritual with most Europeans in the city. As a rule, white women did not venture out during the day when the sun was relentless and liable to brown delicate complexions maintained scrupulously for their peaches-and-cream pinkness. The evening sorties with their cool and fresh river air were therefore not only entertaining but considered medically advisable. They were also pleasant opportunities to chat with old friends, make new ones, examine at close quarters those newly arrived from home if a ship happened to be in and see the latest modes in frocks, hats and shoes. Even more important, the sorties made it possible to learn what everybody in town was doing (and with whom!) and then to dissect and disseminate the information depending on its value.

Olivia and Estelle were sometimes accompanied by Sir Joshua and Lady Bridget, but this evening Millie Humphries was calling with her recipe for Christmas mince pies and Sir Joshua had promised Tom Henderson a game of billiards at the club.

"Good!" Her parents' absence pleased Estelle. "Now we can go and have a proper look at *his* ship. One of the clippers docked last night." Olivia said nothing; it seemed that her resolution to avoid Jai Raventhorne did not preclude his presence in their midst one way or another. Even so, she felt an involuntary frisson of excitement. "The clipper did the New York to Hong Kong run in a hundred and four days and then returned to New York from Canton in only eighty-one—can you believe it?"

It was certainly an incredible feat, but Olivia did believe it; grudgingly, she was beginning to develop a very healthy respect for her cousin's talent for gathering information that turned out to be true. "Oh?"

"Yes. Susan told me. Her father knows the captain. And Susan's mother's *durzee,*" she leaned sideways in the carriage and lowered her voice even though there was no one listening, "also makes clothes for . . . for this man's mistress, that native woman, Susan says. They say she's a dancing girl from Fenwicks Bazaar Street and very beautiful—in a native sort of way, of course. Susan says the tailor told her mother that she—"

"Estelle, I wish you wouldn't listen to so much gossip! It's . . . *cheap.*" Olivia's reprimand was sharper than she had intended.

"Cheap? My goodness, if I don't listen to gossip how will I ever *learn* anything about what's happening in the world?"

"Well, you could read books and newspapers if it's world happenings you want. If that succession of long-suffering nannies taught you anything at all, surely it was to read and write at least."

Her cousin's sarcasm flew right over Estelle's untroubled head. "Oh, I don't mean those kind of happenings, I mean *real* news. Anyway, Susan Bradshaw's mother's tailor says he's *bought* her, like one of those—"

"Why don't we stop the carriage and walk, Estelle? It's such a lovely evening and it's a pity to waste it." Before her cousin could react, Olivia was down on the pavement, and furious with herself. Estelle's silly chatter had once more evoked that distasteful vision of Sujata's voluptuous body bared for Raventhorne's pleasure, and of his own no doubt ardent responses. It was a vision that Olivia was beginning to hate.

But the evening was indeed lovely. Puffball clouds winged their way across a slowly reddening sky, looking like pink flamingoes. The promenade and its gardens were full of families. Some people walked alone, briskly; others ambled arm in arm in leisured groups chatting in low voices. In between the strollers children wove hoops and shouted with an excess of boisterousness that earned frowns from mothers and guardians. Many were the hats doffed and smiles thrown in their direction as the cousins walked side by side, for only the very new additions to town remained unacquainted with the Templewood daughter and niece.

"Look, there!" Estelle suddenly hissed, clutching Olivia's arm. "*That* one anchored mid stream near the *dhoolie* boats. You can't miss it."

Olivia looked in the direction Estelle pointed, trying to locate the clipper. Vessels of all classes, sizes and flags dotted the river surface—Indiamen, the Company's tea wagons, sloops, square-riggers, Royal Navy men-of-war, country row-boats and fisher craft. This was one of the busiest ports in the East and, as with all ports, Calcutta's was touched with adventure, with magic and mystery. Despite her attempt at nonchalance, Olivia felt her stomach lurch as she focused the opera-glasses Estelle handed her. Yes, among the untidy assortment of vessels the clipper was unmistakable. It was three masted, long and elegant, and stood higher than any other ship. Its sails were furled; one could see small figures scampering about on the deck, lighting buttery yellow lanterns. On the prow was mounted an exotic shape, obviously metal since it glinted in the sun.

"Is that his emblem," Olivia asked, "that odd motif with the three prongs?" It looked familiar but she could not place it.

"Yes. That's a *trishul,* a trident. Something to do with the heathen god Shiva, Dave Crichton says."

"Does it mean anything?" Olivia recalled she had seen the same trident above some Hindu temples she had passed by.

"Who knows? The heathens worship everything, don't they? Dave says he has that on his pennant, saffron and black, but the flag he flies under is yours, American." As Olivia again marvelled at her cousin's cache of information, Estelle snatched the glasses to squint through them, breathing hard. "I wonder if he's actually on board now, this very minute . . ."

Estelle's sense of thrill was infectious; fantasy flared also in Olivia's secret mind. On the clipper's quarter-deck she saw Jai Raventhorne watching her. On the same wind that ruffled his untamed hair she heard his voice, deep and rich and commanding, boom out orders to be obeyed this instant. In her imagination he even taunted her—unlikely to miss the chance!—for her fluttering heartbeat, her soaring excitement, the flush on her cheeks, knowing all about them as he seemed to know everything else.

"And I found out something else about him." Estelle's voice disturbed Olivia's daydream and cut it short.

Embarrassed by her own childishness, Olivia thought, I shouldn't be encouraging her in all this dreadful gossip. But aloud she asked, "What?"

Estelle looked over her shoulder, then pulled Olivia to one side. "They say he's a . . . a *bastard!*" She gasped at her own daring and clamped a hand over her mouth. Then, for Olivia's benefit, she added, "That means his father and mother were never married—isn't that *awful?*"

The information did not surprise Olivia. Most Eurasians in India and the Orient bore the stamp of illegitimacy—the *brand!* Raventhorne's bitterness was neither unfair nor excessive. "Especially for him," she murmured, astonished that she could feel pity for someone who deserved it so little.

"Mama says bastards are born out of sin," Estelle said piously, disappointed at her cousin's lack of shock.

"Bastards are born out of women, just like everybody else! It's we who make illegitimacy, not God. Who were his parents, do you know?"

Estelle brightened again, pleased at being asked. "They say his father was some drunken English sailor, or at least white man, who jumped ship in port, and his mother was a servant girl. He seduced her and then ran away. That means—"

"Yes, I do know what 'seduced' means. He never came back?"

"No. At least, Mrs. Drummond believes that Jai Raventhorne knows something more than he . . . oh! I said his name, how *dreadful!*" She gulped and again her hand flew to her mouth.

"Why?" Olivia surprised herself with her sudden spark of anger. "If your parents do not wish his name mentioned in their house, I respect that. But that doesn't mean we must never talk of him anywhere else at any time. Oh, don't be so silly, Estelle!"

The reprimand halted Estelle in her steps. "Well, *I* don't want to talk about him at all," she said, aggrieved. "I've only been gathering all this because *you* keep asking." Raising her nose, she walked away.

Which was, of course, quite true. Reluctantly, Olivia bit back all the other questions tumbling around in her mind and hurried behind Estelle to smooth her ruffled feathers. "It's just idle inquisitiveness on my part, my dearest *Coz,* and hardly worth arguing about." With a laugh she gave her cousin a hug. "Come on, let's go and see what all the pother is about at the jetty." Perforce, the subject of Jai Raventhorne was dropped.

At the wharf there was chaos. Europeans, newly arrived, and those who received them jostled each other among piles of cabin trunks, carpet-bags, wooden crates, tin boxes, gunny sacks, bedding rolls, furniture and mountains of cargo from the recently docked ship. The noise was cacophonous. Everyone talked at once as Customs and Port Trust officials fought to hold tempers trying to answer a dozen questions at the same time. Clad in loin-cloths, mahogany-skinned coolies bargained hotly as *budgerow* boats delivered more passengers to the jetty.

"I say, what a splendid coincidence! Are you here to receive the unfortunates arriving from the good old mother country?"

Olivia and Estelle turned to see the vapidly grinning face of Freddie Birkhurst. "No," Estelle answered, "but you are, we know."

Freddie's mouth dropped. "Indeed. The mater is about to land and take charge of her wayward son. You must both come for tiffin anon to meet her."

They made polite noises. Then Olivia inquired, "This isn't Lady Birkhurst's first visit to India, is it?"

"Good God, no. Mother is an old India hand. Lived here for years when the pater was doing his bit for the Empire—and taking his bit in return." His glumness deepened. "She's a tough old rhinoceros, you know. Laps up this damned country like whipped cream."

"Well, never mind, Mr. Birkhurst," Estelle comforted cheerfully. "Olivia will help revive your flagging spirits. She's *dying* to meet your mother."

"*Are* you, Miss O'Rourke?" If anything, he looked astonished. "Well, in that case, would you both do us the honour of lunching with us at the Tolly Club next Sunday? There's a frightfully exciting polo game on. Of course I shall get Mother to write to Lady Bridget immediately on arrival." He brightened considerably.

Olivia was furious but Estelle was not yet done. "A polo game? Oh, how adventurous! Just yesterday Olivia was complaining of how little she understood this native game that is suddenly all the rage with you English gents. I'm sure she'd *adore* some explanations."

He went purple with happiness. "I would be delighted, er, *honoured* to explain the game to you in detail, Miss O'Rourke! Shall we then take luncheon next Sunday as said?"

"Oh, would you please excuse me for a moment?" Avoiding her cousin's outraged glare, Estelle started to move away. "I've just seen Charlotte, I think, and there's something I absolutely *must* . . ." She waved and vanished.

It was impossible for Olivia to follow suit without seeming unforgivably rude. Trapped within the adoring gooseberry gaze of Freddie Birkhurst, she relapsed into sullen silence. He coughed and cleared his throat. "I have, er, been waiting for an opportunity to, er . . . ," he ran a finger inside his collar, "apologise to you most profoundly for my unfortunate, ah, lapse, yes *lapse,* at the Pennworthys the other night, Miss O'Rourke, er, Olivia. I should have written but my, ah, nerve failed me. Are you totally disgusted with my behaviour and with me?"

He looked so woebegone that it was difficult not to feel sorry for him. "No, of course not. I had already forgotten all about it." She smiled with as much warmth as she could muster.

It was as if heaven had opened up for Freddie. "You had? Oh, ah, splendid, *splendid!* Not for anything in the world, Miss O'Rourke . . . Olivia, would I wish you to think badly of me. I—"

"I don't think badly of you at all, Mr. Birkhurst, I promise you . . ." Frantically, she looked around for escape but none seemed possible. She cursed her cousin roundly and soundly, but then fate intervened.

"Damn, I think I spy the mater . . ." He clasped Olivia's hand warmly. "I'd better be off. Until Sunday then. I can hardly *wait* . . ." He hurried away.

It wasn't until they were both back in the carriage again that Olivia could vent her exasperation. Estelle, however, was unrepentant. "My dearly beloved Coz, you are now all of twenty-two years old, and Freddie Birkhurst is not only the biggest catch in station, he's passionately in love with you—"

"I don't care how big a catch he is and I'd rather he kept his passionate love to himself. I'm *not* going to marry Freddie!" Olivia was very cross indeed. "And if he is such a big catch, why hasn't Aunt Bridget tried to make a match between you two?"

"Oh, she tried all right. But Papa put his foot down; so did I." She shuddered. "Fancy waking up to Freddie Birkhurst's boiled gooseberry eyes every morning. *Ugh!*"

"Well, thank you very much! Having decided that, you now want to palm him off on *me!*"

"No, Olivia, that isn't the idea at all," Estelle explained patiently. "It's the practical aspect of the matter that you must consider. Papa's money guarantees a title for me anyway, but Uncle Sean doesn't have any money. If you married Freddie you wouldn't *need* a portion because he's already got plenty and he'd sell his soul to have you at any cost. Besides, you'd have one of the best titles in England and estates in Suffolk and India—now, wouldn't that be perfect for everyone?"

What a calculating little minx! Even so, it was impossible to remain angry with such barefaced effrontery for long and Olivia laughed. "Everyone except me! Why don't you just worry about your John and leave me to my fate as an old maid?"

"Oh, John I can have any time. He absolutely worships me." Estelle looked smug as she waved the familiar contender aside.

"But *he* doesn't have a title."

"He will one day, maybe soon. You see, John's father's older brother is the Marquis of Quentinberry and he's a bachelor. So John's father is his heir, unless of course his uncle marries and has children, which he won't because John says he's impotent—not John, the Marquis." She paused to give a maidenly blush, then opened her mouth again.

"Oh, you don't need to explain," Olivia said, greatly amused. "I also know what impotent means."

"Yes, well, John's father is already ailing," Estelle continued unfazed, "which is why John is going home on furlough. The chances are John will outlive both his uncle and his father, so there! The Marchioness of Quentinberry . . ." She rolled the name around on her tongue a few times and looked satisfied. "Yes, that will do nicely, I think. Unless a, well, dukedom *with* money happens to turn up. Especially since John is going to be away for a year and there are other fish in the sea." Eyes narrowed in cold-blooded speculation, she absent-mindedly tapped a tattoo on the window with her fingers.

Olivia was so taken aback by this new aspect of her cousin that for a moment she could only stare. "Other fish?" she then asked suspiciously. "Who? Not Clive Smithers, by any chance? I hear he cuts quite a dash in his naval uniform, and since his arrival Charlotte has suddenly developed a whole new rash of friends including you who couldn't bear her not so long ago."

Estelle first looked flustered, then haughty. "Huh! I *don't* have a case on Clive, so there! I don't want to marry *anyone* yet, I just want to go to London and have fun and be *free.*" Her lips suddenly quivered and her eyes welled. "I've never been anywhere, done anything, met anyone truly wonderful. Do you know, I've never ever even seen *snow . . . ?*"

Lady Birkhurst's formal letter of invitation to luncheon at the Tollygunge Club the following Sunday duly arrived. The invitation kindly included Sir Joshua in case he were not otherwise occupied, which, he lost no time in informing his wife, he would make certain he would be. Lady Bridget, however, was openly thrilled. To have so fortuitously outdistanced all the other ladies in Calcutta also with marriageable girls on their hands!

"You must wear your blue linen with the white organdie

ruffles and, of course, that white leather belt since it suits you so well." Lady Bridget got down immediately to essentials. "Or do you think the lemon with the polka-dots? No, perhaps not. It heightens far too much the sunburn on your face and arms. Mind you, I wouldn't entirely reject the pink. It does bring out the . . ."

Steeped in depression, Olivia listened morosely. Inwardly, however, she burned with resentment. No matter how diligent or well meaning her aunt's matchmaking efforts, they had to be stopped. Should she do it now or later? Well, perhaps later; after all, it was presumptuous to accept as granted Lady Birkhurst's approval of her no matter how positive Jai Raventhorne's uninvited vote of confidence! And it might never happen. With all her heart Olivia prayed that Lady Birkhurst would absolutely hate her!

That night in their bedroom Lady Bridget tackled her husband firmly. "I wish you wouldn't make these unkind remarks about the Birkhursts, Josh. I don't want Olivia to become unnecessarily prejudiced against Freddie."

Lying on his bed face down, eyes closed and a bath towel wrapped around his torso as Rehman gave him his nightly massage, Sir Joshua made little grunts of contentment. "Birkhurst is a walking testimony to his own God-given idiocy. My intervention is scarcely required to prejudice an essentially intelligent girl." He signalled Rehman to punch and pummel even more vigorously.

"All right, I concede that Freddie isn't, well, cerebral," she ignored his derisive hoot, "but what he *has* more than compensates for what he is not. Olivia will live like a queen."

With an effort Sir Joshua drove himself to open one eye. "Olivia might not wish to live like a queen with a king who is a brainless ninny. Besides, if I didn't want him for my daughter I certainly don't want him for my niece. Whether half Templewoods or half O'Rourkes, future broods of imbecilic Birkhursts make me shudder with alarm."

His wife was very cross indeed. "Olivia needs to make a good marriage, Josh. I'm not sending her back to swill horse slop again, or to marry some foul-smelling cowhand with neither grace nor grammar. Olivia needs a decent life with decent people in England, not all this modern rubbish Sean has filled her head with." She prodded her husband's forearm with a finger. "*You* haven't been giving her ideas, have you?"

"No." He turned over and Rehman attacked his stomach

with gusto. "Leave the girl alone, Bridget. Don't try and make her into something she isn't. Olivia has spunk and she has brains; let her enjoy herself as she pleases while she is with us. Unless she herself wishes otherwise, let her go back when her year is up." He turned on a side and faced her. "The girl loves and admires her father, Bridget, and rightly so. Whether you approve or not, she is a product of the New World. Accept it and let her return when the time comes."

"Let her return? You can't be serious, Josh!"

"I am. If that is what Olivia wants."

"At her age they don't know what they want! Did Sarah know what she wanted when she ran away with Sean? She learned her lesson the bitter way, through suffering and torment and terrible sicknesses—"

"Sarah was happy with Sean," Sir Joshua said sharply. "Don't distort facts to suit your arguments, Bridget. It was a good marriage, unfortunate but good. Sean loved his wife. He did the best he could for her."

Suddenly Lady Bridget's face crumpled. "And I want to do the best I can for this child, Josh. I have to, I must. I wronged Sarah. If it hadn't been for me she might still be alive . . ." In her distress she crushed her handkerchief against her mouth and started to sob quietly.

Sir Joshua quickly sat up, dismissed Rehman and put an arm around his wife's shoulders, startled by the uncharacteristic show of emotion. "Now, now, Bridget—I will not allow you to go through all that again. Sarah is dead and gone and history cannot be reversed. Stop punishing yourself for whatever happened. By marrying Olivia off to some well-heeled loon you still can't make Sarah come back."

"No, but I can at least make reparation, Josh," his wife sobbed. "If I hadn't persuaded Father to cut her out of his will, to disown her, she might have lived on in London in civilised comfort instead of dying in such penury, and Olivia would have been brought up a lady . . ."

Gently, he took her in his arms, his expression soft. "All that is hypothetical, Bridget. Sean made the decision to emigrate long before he met Sarah; he told me so when I met him in London. Sarah didn't want material comforts any more than Olivia does, my love. She was happy to follow Sean wherever he went and in whatever circumstances." Not knowing what else to do, he patted her back awkwardly. "And he's not a bad sort, you know.

He might be an idealistic crusader without two cents to rub together, but he's given Olivia an education to be admired—"

"I loved Sarah," his distraught wife interrupted, not listening. "I would give anything to receive her forgiveness, but I can't! The only way I can make my peace with her soul is through Olivia. I at least have to give her a wedding she will never forget. And all that Sarah spurned."

"You can't force a headstrong lass into a marriage she doesn't want, Bridget!" He sighed and started to stroke her hair.

His wife's head jolted up from his shoulder. "Force her?" She looked surprised. "Oh, I won't have to *force* her, Josh! Olivia will marry Freddie of her own free will, of course."

Sir Joshua said nothing; he merely shook his head pityingly and reached for his clothes. He rose from the bed, secured his towel more firmly around his girth and started to shrug into his shirt.

Lady Bridget blew her nose, patted her eyes dry and vacated expression from her face. "Could he have . . . planned that meeting with her, Josh?" She did not look at him.

His hand paused briefly in mid air. "Don't be absurd, woman!" His rebuke was unduly incisive. "Olivia went on the embankment on an impulse that night."

"He is the devil incarnate, Josh . . ." Her voice trembled.

"No. Nothing as exalted. He is only a sewer rat, a guttersnipe, who has recklessly stepped out of his place. Don't elevate him with false values, Bridget!" He was visibly angered.

Lying in her lap, her fingers plucked nervously at each other. Nothing in her face moved except her bloodless lips. "He will do what he has said he will. His kind never forgives, never forgets. You should have listened to Mother, Josh. You should have killed him when you had the chance."

"Perhaps," he said tightly. "There will be other chances."

"And one day he will talk . . . !" Her voice withered into a frightened whisper. "And one day *you* will again weaken to—"

"That will be *enough,* Bridget!" He strode up to her angrily and pincered her chin between his fingers. "*Talk* is one thing he will never do! That is all you need to remember." Releasing her roughly, he snatched his remaining clothes off a chair back and stalked into his dressing-room.

Lady Bridget stared at his vanishing back, then at the door that slammed behind it. Her eyes were still wide with fear, but in them there was also hate.

On Friday morning a courier arrived from Kirtinagar. He brought an unexpected invitation from Their Highnesses. A tiger shoot had been arranged for the weekend now upon them. Sir Joshua, Lady Bridget and their family were cordially invited to join the royal party. The extreme shortness of notice was profoundly regretted; the tiger, a troublesome man-eater, had been resighted only the day before and the expedition hurriedly organised. It was begged that Sir Joshua would overlook and forgive the inadequate notice and give Their Highnesses the pleasure of offering the Templewoods their humble hospitality. It was emphasised that Sir Joshua's renowned and expert marksmanship would prove an invaluable asset to the hunt.

In the family everyone reacted as expected. Sir Joshua was immensely flattered, Estelle was indifferent, Olivia was frankly thrilled and Lady Bridget was furious. "I wish you would occasionally listen to me, Josh," she flared. "I've been telling you for days about Lady Birkhurst's kind invitation to luncheon on Sunday. I wouldn't dream of sending regrets at the eleventh hour for this thoughtless last-minute summons!"

"Damn!" Sir Joshua sucked in his cheeks as he pondered. "Saturday evening is our meeting with the insurance underwriters. There's no question of my not being present." He tapped the letter. "The old boy has something up his sleeve; I smell it. By Christ, I'd like to find out what it is!"

Lady Bridget's anger soared higher with the profanities. "If you want to go running because he snaps his royal fingers, then cancel *your* appointment and take Estelle with you. Olivia and I will certainly not cancel *ours.*"

"You never listen to anything *I* say either, Mama!" Estelle warmed to the fray. "I'm spending Sunday with Charlotte to practise some new carols her brother has brought out from England. Even if I weren't, I'd rather stay here on my own than go on another silly shoot. Last time I was bitten half to death by midges."

Nobody paid her any attention.

"There is a motive behind this," Sir Joshua mused, still lost in his own introspections. "They're wily fellows, these princes, and touchy as all hell. I can't refuse out of hand; he'll take umbrage and instantly sense slights where none are intended."

"Well, he should have given us more notice then!" Lady Bridget cried.

Her husband appeared not to hear her as he suddenly snapped his fingers, having arrived at a solution. He turned to Olivia as she sat in discreet but breathless silence. "Arvind Singh has our written proposal. I'd give a great deal to know how it has been received. The man seemed to take quite a shine to you, my dear. Would you be interested in going for the shoot? One member of the family is better than none, unless Estelle reconsiders."

Estelle merely rolled her eyes and left the room, but Olivia's heart leapt. "Oh, indeed I would . . ." Catching her aunt's enraged expression she hastened to add, "that is if Aunt Bridget doesn't object."

"Aunt Bridget *does* object, and most strenuously! Josh, I think it's wicked, utterly *wicked* of—"

"I cannot risk Arvind Singh's displeasure; it's as simple as that." He waved all the rest aside and stood up. "The native mind is known to take offence all too easily, all too easily." He started towards the door.

"And what if Lady Birkhurst also takes offence all too easily?" Lady Bridget demanded, hand on hip.

"Tell her the girl has fever or something; you women are good at alibis. Now, I can't keep the man waiting any longer . . ." Muttering to himself he disappeared in the direction of his study.

"Well!" Indignation robbed his wife of further speech. *"Well . . . !"* Flouncing out of the room she went in search of Estelle with a view to expending her wrath on her. How dare Estelle accept an invitation from anyone without the prior sanction of her mother!

Unnoticed, Olivia remained where she was, trying hard not to reveal her own jubiliation at the utterly unexpected reprieve contained in the Maharaja's eleventh-hour letter. But underneath her jubilation there was perplexity. Like Sir Joshua, she smelled a motive in the invitation; unlike him, she had an uncomfortable instinct that it had nothing to do with the coal . . .

4

If her journey through Bengal was hot and tiring and the road appallingly rutted, Olivia barely noticed; it was her first venture outside Calcutta and she was enthralled. The Empire's majestic capital was a British creation and as such many of its trappings were European—the architecture, its political and commercial life styles, its social ambience, the thinking patterns of its mercantile complexes and the dominating influences of the all-pervasive East India Company. Cocooned perforce within these narrow boundaries, Olivia had seen little enough of the true colours and character of the land. Even her brief glimpse of the Bengal countryside out of a moving carriage window she therefore found captivating.

The passing panorama was mostly of paddy fields, lime green and washed clean by the rains. In between were palm leaf–thatched mud huts tucked amid bamboo groves, clusters of banana trees and tracts of water covered with proliferating lilies. Farmers, wearing wicker hats, stood in ankle-deep water transplanting the paddy plants in neat, geometrical rows. In the ponds, fishermen trapped sweet-water shrimp in baskets. Women and children worked alongside the men, and in one pond a group of boys had devised an impromptu ball game with a coconut shell. The Templewood carriages with their armed outriders were an impressive sight, but the interest they created among the villagers was brief; with no more than perfunctory wide-eyed stares they continued undisturbed with their labours.

Very different from the rustic simplicity of the rural area was the walled palace of Kirtinagar, Olivia's destination. At the gates of the royal complex she was received by an imposing posse of mounted guards who then ceremoniously escorted the carriages inside. The landscaped gardens that formed the setting of the palaces—for there appeared to be more than one—were beautifully maintained with their cascading flowers, mango groves and shady forest areas of banyan, peepul and *gulmohar,* this last aflame with orange blossoms. The carriages swept up elegant driveways to a portico, on the white marble steps of which, surrounded by a positive army of aides and attendants, the Maharaja waited.

"Welcome to Kirtinagar, Miss O'Rourke!" With a folded-hand greeting he came forward personally to help Olivia alight. "I am delighted that the unavoidably short notice did not prevent you, at least, from accepting our humble invitation."

Somewhat nervous at the awesome formality of her reception, Olivia made her responses with due regard to the strict coaching she had received from her uncle. The Maharaja, however, presented a picture of complete informality both in manner and in dress, for he wore the traditional garments of a white cotton dhoti, loose silken shirt and a draped shawl. In his own environment, clad in everyday clothes, he seemed very different from how Olivia recalled him in his formal regalia. His head was uncovered and he wore no jewelry save for a diamond ring. He looked younger without his turban, perhaps not yet forty, for his thick, dark hair was as yet untouched by grey. The initial formalities exchanged included the expression of deep regrets from Sir Joshua and Lady Bridget at their inability to avail themselves of the Maharaja's kind invitation—and the presentation of a mahogany chest containing gifts for Their Highnesses.

"Come, Miss O'Rourke," the Maharaja said finally after the preliminaries were over and done with. "I must now escort you to the Maharani. She awaits impatiently to make your acquaintance. My wife looks forward to meeting English-speaking ladies so that she can practise her own English conversation—although, I hasten to add, that is not the only reason for her impatience."

"But surely there is no dearth of English-speaking ladies in Bengal?" Olivia inquired as, with a retinue following at a discreet distance, they walked side by side across a trim lawn bordered by flowerbeds. "The British civil service has many officers in the districts."

"True, but then," he smiled, "my wife does not choose to mix with English women. And, of course, she never appears before the men."

The system of purdah, Olivia was aware, existed widely in India and she was a little embarrassed not to have remembered that. At all the *burra khanas* where an occasional Indian gentleman had been present there had never been any Indian women. She wondered again what the Maharani would be like, steeped as she inevitably must be in conservative living with little experience of the outside world. Lady Bridget had warned her of the risks of boredom. "Native women, especially the high born, can be dreadfully tiresome. All they do is sit and simper in corners and jabber away in their own lingo." Still vastly annoyed at the disruption of her engagement with Lady Birkhurst, she had been witheringly pessimistic about the entire Kirtinagar weekend.

The Maharani's palace—and the zenana, as the ladies' quarters were called—stood away from the main building and were screened off from it by a forest belt of tall, leafy trees. Alongside was a small lake dotted with pink and white lotus blossoms as large as dinner plates. It was a very pretty scene indeed. The Maharani's personal apartment was on the first floor. It was spacious, bright and sunny, and at one end was a covered balcony where the Maharani waited. Formal introductions were made, greetings were exchanged and a tray of cold refreshments was passed around. Then, a little shyly, the Maharani said, "You must be tired after your journey, Miss O'Rourke. Four hours on an imperfect road must make you want to rest perhaps."

"No, not rest," Olivia quickly assured her, unable to stop staring. "I am much too excited for that. A bath and change would do me nicely for the moment." The woman who confronted her looked no more than about thirty. She was slim of build and not very tall, and had alert, intelligent eyes in a face of dusky smoothness. The English she spoke was not as fluent as her husband's but it was correct and clear and gave indication of much easy familiarity with the language. When Olivia remarked on this, unable to conceal her surprise completely, the Maharani blushed.

"I was tutored by an English governess until I was fifteen," she said, obviously pleased with the compliment, "but now I rarely have an opportunity to speak your language."

After a few more moments of small talk the Maharaja excused himself, pleading unfinished work in his office. He regretted that he would not be able to join them for luncheon but promised they would meet again at length in the evening. In a way Olivia was relieved; it would be so much easier for her to get to know the Maharani better if they were on their own, as it appeared they would be. There was something very appealing about the young woman whose manner—apart from the mandatory touch of formality—seemed suddenly almost girlish to Olivia, which was surprising since, according to Sir Joshua, she was the mother of two children. The fact that, despite her aunt's dire predictions, communication between them would not be a problem was especially gratifying. Olivia started to relax; her apprehensions about the weekend promised to have been groundless.

"I confess that I am pleased you do not wish to rest, Miss O'Rourke," the Maharani said when her husband had left. "Time is short and there is much that we have to talk about." She made a signal and a maidservant materialised. "Your apartment is immediately below mine. Your bath awaits you. I hope you will find everything to your satisfaction." She paused and looked away, minimally awkward. "I have arranged for your ayah and other staff to be housed comfortably. I assure you, you will not require your personal attendants. Two of my maidservants will be entirely at your disposal, day and night."

It was only later that Olivia was to realise the significance of this arrangement. For the moment she accepted it at face value. Her aunt, determined to fulfil all proprieties despite her displeasure, had insisted on sending Estelle's ayah with her. In addition, Sir Joshua had arranged for two khidmutgars, a young errand lad and two armed outriders since bandits, particularly the dreaded thuggees, were not unknown in the area. And then of course there were the coachmen and their assistants in the cavalcade of three carriages. Apparently, it was customary in India for guests to take with them their own attendants. Olivia had considered all the fuss quite unnecessary but she had bowed to the rule without argument.

The apartment assigned to Olivia was on ground level, opening onto an enclosed patio filled with fragrant plants, and quite charming. Like the rest of the palace complex this too had white marble walls, carved ceilings and arched windows inset with filigreed marble screens. The red velvet drapes had gold tassels; burnished brass vases held sprays of blossoms—some recognisable, others strange. There were touches of thoughtfulness everywhere: a mosquito-net on the canopied four-poster made less ugly with silken embroidery, a pair of damask slippers by the bed, a selection of feminine house robes in a closet, thick Turkish towels and a range of English toiletries in the bath-room. In a crystal glass bowl by the bed was a heap of French bonbons.

Olivia could not help being enchanted. Her clothes had already been unpacked and arranged neatly in a glass-fronted almirah. In a sunken bath enclosure of veined marble awaited warm water scented with sandalwood and rose petals. Sir Joshua had explained to her that the hospitality that Indian princes extended to their guests was generous. Her own welcome had been more than cordial and she was undoubtedly awed by it. But at the same time she could not help being puzzled: Was all this cordiality laid on for her personally, or because she was Sir Joshua's representative?

Half an hour later, bathed and refreshed and changed from a linen travelling suit into a cool chartreuse muslin with white lace cuffs and collar, Olivia was escorted back to the Maharani's sitting-room. Appointed in Western style with French furniture, Belgian glass chandeliers and a rich plum-coloured Aubusson carpet, there was again a touch of formality in the air. Further refreshment came with lemonade in tall, frosted glasses that tinkled with the ice within.

"Since this is your first journey outside Calcutta, I must apologise for the deplorable state of the roads, Miss O'Rourke," the Maharani said. "The rains have again created havoc, as they do each year."

"Oh, we have far worse roads where I come from," Olivia assured her brightly. "Indeed, I felt quite at home on yours."

She went on to inquire about some sights she had seen en route, and as the Maharani answered her questions, Olivia studied her with interest. The features on the smooth, café au lait face were clear-cut, almost Mogul in their classic sharpness of line. What gave the Maharani's face its striking quality, however, was not mere superficial appeal, Olivia felt; it was the animation in her eyes. From time to time they seemed to flicker with something deeper than intelligence—watchfulness? With a shade of unease Olivia recognized that if her observations of the Maharani were keen, the Maharani's assessment of her was no less. She appeared to be studying her with a concentration that was almost intense. Why?

Then luncheon was announced.

"Not knowing your tastes in food, Miss O'Rourke, I have ordered a wholly Indian meal." They had risen and walked into an adjoining room. "Will that suit you or would you prefer something more familiar to your palate? I assure you I will not be offended if you do."

"An Indian meal would suit me fine!" Olivia exclaimed. "I have so far eaten only curries prepared in English homes." She thought involuntarily of that unexpected breakfast with Jai Raventhorne and half smiled.

"In that case," the Maharani nodded, "I am pleased. Shall we commence to eat?" At the nod a dozen maidservants hurried off and presently reappeared carrying large circular trays bearing food in an astonishing variety.

They ate in traditional style sitting cross-legged on plump cushions placed before low stools on a sparkling granite floor. On the silver plates in which the food was served was a series of individual bowls to segregate one course from the other so as not to mingle flavours, as Olivia had seen in Raventhorne's house. This time, however, with no hovering tensions, she could pay attention to the Maharani's careful descriptions of each dish and marvel with awareness at the ingenuity of Indian cuisine. Inevitably, there were comparisons as the Maharani questioned her about the kind of fare Americans put on their tables at home.

"I presume Americans have to hunt frequently for their meats," the Maharani remarked when luncheon was over and they sat again in the balcony sipping rich, sweet Turkish coffee, "so you are well used to handling fire-arms?"

"Well, we have to be in my country," Olivia replied, surprised once more at her hostess's observations about a region not many knew much about. "We use weapons not only for hunting. Few Americans would risk venturing forth unarmed on long journeys, and in new settlements such as mining towns, there is still a great deal of lawlessness. Many homesteads are isolated—ours happens to be, too—and cattle-rustlers are a perpetual menace."

"Rustlers?"

"Cattle thieves. If you don't keep watch you're likely to lose your herd overnight. My father insisted I learn how to use a gun when I was knee high to a tadpole. Very young," she added quickly at the Maharani's look of incomprehension.

"Yes, I see. My father too gave me lessons in marksmanship when I was very young. We also have our share of lawlessness."

"He did?" Olivia scanned the delicate, small-boned hands in amazement, unable to imagine them grappling with anything as unwieldy as a rifle, or indeed ever being required to. "But aren't hunting and shooting considered strictly male preserves in India?"

"Not in families that rule." There was more than a hint of unconscious pride in the Maharani's regal response. "History records many cases of maharanis and princesses abandoning their veils to ride into battle against invaders who have killed their menfolk." She spoke casually, almost offhandedly, indicating an inner strength Olivia would not have expected in one so utterly feminine. "But now tell me about your home, Miss O'Rourke. I understand that you farm quite successfully."

"Well, most everyone does own some land to work. On ours we raise horses. We also have about a hundred head of cattle under our own brand, Durhams mostly, although we have recently acquired longhorns too so as to breed a sturdier mixed stock."

"But with so much work to do," the Maharani exclaimed, "surely you employ staff?"

Olivia smiled. "Oh yes. We have a pretty good foreman and several cowhands. But because my father has to travel a lot the responsibility of seeing to things is mine."

"My husband told me that your father is a writer. What does he usually write about?"

"Whatever touches him deeply," Olivia shrugged. "Inequities in our society such as slavery, violation of citizens' rights, unhealthy conditions in sweat-shops—anything he considers worth exposing. At the moment, for instance, he is in the Pacific because of the wholesale slaughter of whales." In a gesture of pride, she straightened her back. "My father believes in justice for all. He's an absolute squareshooter."

"Squareshooter? You mean with a gun?"

"No, I mean he believes in fair play." Olivia frowned and then laughed. "Yes, I can see why my speech sometimes confuses people."

"No, no, it is my understanding that is limited," the Maharani said modestly. "But tell me, do you yourself not feel inspired to write in the manner of your father? With so much inspiration, surely books interest you more than the labour of farming."

Olivia made a rueful face. "Well they do, and I do read a great deal, but I'm honest enough to see that I lack my father's natural flair. When I return home I want to start a small school in Sacramento. We have a couple but we could certainly do with another. But until then, I indulge my passion for books by helping Sally—Mrs. MacKendrick—our closest friend and neighbour, with her lending-library in town."

At that, more questions followed, all of which Olivia tried to answer as carefully as she could. The Maharani's curiosity about her life, it seemed to Olivia, was endless. Of course she was gratified since to talk of home to someone so deeply interested was a pleasure, but at the same time she could not rid herself of a strange feeling; it was almost as if, for some inexplicable reason, the Maharani was, well, *interviewing* her—which was, of course, absurd. With the passing of the hours, that initial watchfulness in the Maharani's dark eyes had subsided, but even though the formality and the shyness had lessened, there was still about her inquiries a calculatedness that was puzzling. Somehow, with one topic merging into another, they found themselves discussing politics, in which the Maharani appeared as interested as her husband.

"Is it only in America that you are curious about the running of government," she asked, "or does our Indian situation also intrigue you?"

For a moment Olivia pondered. "Well, it certainly does intrigue me, but I have to confess I know little apart from what I overhear others discussing. Your system here is so different from ours at home. Not better or worse," she added quickly, "just different. "But one thing certainly perplexes me: Why are the English here in India so . . . so vastly removed from those I have met in America? They come from the same stock, yet their thinking and attitudes vary so greatly from those at home."

The Maharani considered her question with great seriousness. "Well, I presume that in your country the English are like everyone else," she finally replied, "social equals forced to struggle for survival. Here, they are virtual rulers. Once their political power wanes in India, as it has done in your country, I suppose they too will merge with the rest."

"Do you really believe their power will ever wane in India?" Olivia asked dubiously. "On the contrary, they seem to be becoming more strongly entrenched with each passing year."

"That is a phase. It will pass."

There was such conviction in the Maharani's expression that Olivia was surprised. "Are there many Indians who subscribe to that theory?"

"Perhaps not at the moment but some day there will be. Or so," she suddenly smiled, "we are constantly assured by a good friend to whom the theory is almost sacrosanct."

The Maharani had refrained from naming the "good friend," but then there had been no need to. The fleeting, oblique glance she cast in Olivia's direction was indication enough as to his identity. A small shiver climbed up Olivia's spine and it was all she could do not to react visibly. Ever since she had arrived in Kirtinagar, she had been wondering just how much of her conversation with the Maharaja at Estelle's birthday ball he had shared with his wife. Now she saw that there was not much about it that the Maharani did not know, including, no doubt, her own excessive interest in Jai Raventhorne. In the sudden realisation that the Maharani was aware of far more than their hitherto casual conversation had revealed, Olivia knew that she had blushed. Desperate for a change of subject, she let fall the first remark that occurred to her, a compliment to the Maharani on the gracefulness and colour of her apparel. Perhaps for the same reason, the Maharani allowed the conversational diversion with alacrity. An offer was made—and instantly accepted—to show Olivia her wardrobe of traditional clothes.

What the Maharani and the ladies of her household all wore were very full ankle-length skirts edged with gold, long-sleeved blouses and billowing gauze veils that covered their heads. The ensembles subsequently displayed to Olivia in the royal dressing-room were even more breathtaking. Everything was embellished with gold and silver thread embroidery, sequins and semi-precious stones in colours that left Olivia gasping: peacock blue, scarlet, flaming ochre, saffron, brilliant pinks, parrot green, imperial purple, oranges and reds. During the display Olivia learned more about the royal couple's children, a boy and a girl, both away at present with their maternal grandparents in the north. It was also revealed that, like her husband, the Maharani held court but only for the women.

This surprised Olivia anew. She could not imagine this fragile woman brought up in such luxury sitting and dispensing justice any more than she could see her holding an invading army at bay. "And what is it that the women come to complain to you about?"

The charcoal eyes twinkled. "What women everywhere complain about—their husbands mostly. One doesn't give his wife adequate household money, another drinks and beats her and the children, a third is indolent and neglects his crops. Criminal complaints, of course, go to my husband. I only try to encourage the women to strengthen their inner resources and stand firm by their legitimate rights."

Olivia could not deny that the Maharani amazed her. To be so self-contained and so decisive in such a heavily male dominated society could be no mean triumph. Obviously, she received much support from her husband, himself a man of enlightenment. Wryly, Olivia thought of her uncle's airy dismissal of Arvind Singh as a man who could be beguiled through pleasure; the Maharaja had barely glanced at those costly "baubles from Europe" that she had brought with her as gifts from Sir Joshua ("bribes," according to Jai Raventhorne!). If Sir Joshua truly believed that he could grease the Maharaja's palm in order to get at that coal, then it was a tactic that so far showed little indication of succeeding.

It was much later that afternoon, after the frivolous matter of the Maharani's wardrobe and the serious discussion on the low social status of women in India had been set aside, that Olivia first started to sense a subtle change in the Maharani's attitude. It was difficult for her to pin-point the change, but it was as if some invisible barrier between them had gradually been lowered. Afternoon tea, very English and picnic style, was being served by the lake under a tree resplendent in small yellow blossoms. They sat on a cotton drugget with arms resting on fat bolsters, nibbling at buttered scones, cup cakes and wafer-thin chicken sandwiches. With no warning as she poured out cups of pale gold tea from an egg-shell–fine teapot, the Maharani suddenly remarked, "We belong to very different cultures, but even so we appear to agree on so much. I feel we are destined to be friends. May I therefore call you Olivia?"

Olivia was surprised but pleased. She had the odd feeling that somehow she had passed a test, but what that test could possibly be she could not fathom. "Oh, I wish you would," she cried with great sincerity. "I am not at all used to being called anything else and seldom am at home, where we tend to be informal."

"In that case, you must call me by my name, which is Kinjal." She went on to explain that *Kinjal* was another word for lotus. As such it could not have been more fitting. "After tea you must allow me to show off to you my medicinal plants garden, of which I am immodestly proud, so that I can exhibit my prowess as a gardener."

While they strolled down smooth hedge-lined paths and the Maharani talked about the arcane, ancient system of indigenous herbal medicine called Ayurveda, around them peacocks strutted with sublime arrogance but with such beauty that one could forgive them anything. There was, Olivia felt, a wonderful serenity about the place, a harmony, that she could only describe as spontaneous. Everything around them—the people, the plants, the very air and the manifestations of nature—sprang from the same culture. Everything fitted, and everything seemed relevant. How different was Kirtinagar from Calcutta, with its alien superimpositions!

Under a spreading banyan tree dripping sinuous tendrils,

two women crouched on their haunches beside a modest little whitewashed temple. With dexterous fingers they wove garlands of orange marigolds, which they then coiled like snakes inside the rim of a large brass tray. "They are preparing offerings for my evening rituals," Kinjal explained, noticing her interest. "I am a devotee of Ma Durga, whose festival we will shortly be celebrating. Ma Durga is the consort of Lord Shiva."

Shiva!

Slowly Olivia's glance crept upward to the pinnacle of the temple. Glinting gold and fiery in the sunset was a trident. Its two outside prongs were curved slightly inward. The third, straight as an arrow, was aimed at the centre of the sky. Mesmerised, Olivia could not drag her eyes away from it. "That . . . trident. Does it mean anything?"

"It is the *trishul,* the weapon of Shiva. It is found wherever Shiva and his consort are worshipped."

They sat down again and Kinjal poured out fresh cups of tea. "Does that weapon hold any special significance?" Olivia asked, eyes still transfixed.

"Everything in our rituals holds special significance. In our belief, three forces compose the cycle of life. The godly triumvirate consists of Lord Brahma the Creator, Lord Vishnu the Preserver and . . ." She paused.

"And Lord Shiva?"

"Yes. The Lord Shiva is the Destroyer. The trident is known as his weapon of destruction." Her hands stilled and her gaze locked with Olivia's. "Yes," she said quietly. "That is why Jai Raventhorne has chosen it for his emblem."

The sense of shock that exploded in Olivia's mind was so violent that she almost dropped the cup she held. Suddenly, in a flash, she knew that it was toward this, Jai Raventhorne, that their conversation had been building up all day. And now that the name had been said, it hung suspended between them like a fine mist, unseen but chilly. This time she actually shivered. Raising her cup to her lips, she drank deeply. "Whom or what does Jai Raventhorne wish to destroy?" Her tone remained steady.

"Everyone. Everything." Kinjal sounded sad. "Perhaps, in the end, even himself."

"Why?" A thin trail of ants skirted a corner of the drugget. Olivia kept her eyes fixed on it.

"Jai has within him an anger that will not be contained. It

forces him to be forever apart from the world. He cannot, perhaps never will, be otherwise."

The curse of being different from the herd! Like her in India . . . ? It was cool by the lake but Olivia felt perspiration on her brow. "And the cause of that anger—foreign presence in India?"

"Not only that, although that too. There is a canker in Jai's soul. I wish it were not so because it saps his reason and fills his blood with venom." Noticing a ladybug on her skirt, Kinjal lifted it onto the tip of her forefinger and gently blew it away. "Jai . . . interests you, Olivia?"

The same question the Maharaja had framed! "I barely know Mr. Raventhorne," she replied, unable to prevent a tempering of her voice. "I have met him only very briefly."

"Had you met him a hundred times," Kinjal exclaimed with a shrug almost of exasperation, "you would know him no better. My husband says that Jai is like an onion. Just when you think you have reached the core, another layer appears unexpectedly." Her laugh defused the moment of its tension and, relieved, Olivia laughed with her.

"In that case I guess Mr. Raventhorne is right in his contention that nobody really *knows* anybody else!"

"Well, Jai certainly is an example of his own theory: His inner self is a blank even to us." Her expression changed to turn serious again. "By tying the sacred red thread around Jai's wrist each year, I have accepted him as my brother. But," she shook her head as if in sorrow, "sometimes he is like a man possessed. He frightens me."

Olivia was spellbound, and at the same time resentful. Why was the Maharani telling all this to *her,* who knew Jai Raventhorne scarcely at all? Was her interest in him that obvious, that demanding? And yet, Olivia could not help feeling that there was a purpose in Kinjal's revelations. A thought suddenly occurred to her that was so ridiculous, so wild, that she very nearly laughed at the impossibility of it. Were Kinjal's words meant as some kind of *warning* to her? If so, for heaven's sake, why?

As it happened, Olivia's agitated questions to herself were destined to remain unasked and unanswered for the moment. A maidservant appeared to announce the Maharaja's imminent arrival in the zenana. It was almost dusk, and evidently court matters for the day were being adjourned. With an exclamation and a hurried apology, Kinjal excused herself to go to the temple for the forgotten evening ritual. From a distance and in contemplative silence, Olivia sat and watched the pretty ceremonies. The trident on top of the temple was now cloaked in gloom. Despite the dark, however, its presence seemed to her as eloquent and as pervasive as the brassy tinkle of temple bells that were part of the ritual.

For Olivia's entertainment that evening, the Maharaja had arranged an elaborate ballet in the crimson and gold audience hall of the main palace, quite the largest room Olivia had ever seen. She felt deeply honoured and touched at the thoughtfulness. Attended by a host of ladies and chattering maidservants, she and Kinjal sat in a curtained enclosure, for the hall was packed with people. The Maharaja was in another enclosure with leading dignitaries of his court. The ballet unfolded a story from the Hindu epic *Ramayana;* the dancing was full of fluid grace, captivating rhythms and intricate footwork. Court musicians swayed with the beat and made music on strange instruments—wind, string and percussion—and the dancers all wore bands of brass bells on their ankles. For Olivia it was an alien experience but nonetheless pleasant, for the innovations and improvisations of the musicians, as explained to her by Kinjal, showed complexities that were disciplined if not easily understandable.

At the dinner that followed, served Western style in the Maharani's palace, there were just the three of them. From the Maharaja's talk, wide ranging and informal, Olivia learned much about the mystique of kingship as practised in India with subtle balances between pragmatism and tradition, at least in Kirtinagar. The Maharaja's plans for his State were ambitious and imaginative, and his concern for his people was evidently foremost in his mind.

Two subjects were not touched upon, among the many that were—the coal and Jai Raventhorne. Olivia was certain that the omission in both cases was calculated.

"Our base for the shoot will be my hunting lodge in the jungle." Dinner was over and the Maharaja was almost done with the gurgling hookah at which he pulled with unalloyed pleasure. "We have to make a dawn start so as to reach it before the sun rises high."

An early night was called for, but, still charged with excitement from everything she had seen, experienced and heard, Olivia felt not the least sleepy. "I am in the habit of reading awhile before I go to bed. My uncle tells me you have an extensive library here with a fine collection of rare books. May I be permitted to browse there for a half hour?"

Olivia's request pleased the Maharaja, and an aide was immediately dispatched to unlock the library, housed in a separate building, and prepare it for her perusal. She bid Kinjal good night, for they would not now meet before the morning, and followed the Maharaja across the compound. During the slow, leisured walk they discussed books. "Bernier's travel diaries about India might interest you, Miss O'Rourke, and perhaps Kalidasa's epic poem, *Shakuntala.* I have translations of both in English." They chatted for a few more minutes on the steps of the library, a handsome white single-storied building with scarlet bougainvillea spilling over the portico, and then the Maharaja excused himself, pleading matters still to be attended to for the shoot. "We are truly delighted that you are with us, Miss O'Rourke," he said; then, with visible hesitation, he added in a murmur something that was extraordinary, "but I sincerely hope you never have occasion to regret your visit."

For a moment Olivia stood rock still. There was a gusty breeze blowing and the Maharaja's voice had been low; after brief introspection Olivia decided that the two had combined to deceive her ears, for there could be no logical explanation for what she thought he had said. With a shrug, she abandoned her bafflement and went inside.

Like the evocative aroma of damp earth, there is also something universal in a room filled with old books. Glass-fronted cupboards lined with velvet stood open for her benefit; calf-bound volumes, neatly labelled and stamped in gold with the crest of Kirtinagar, were arranged in order of language and subject. Ledgers, also bound and crested, gave cross references and relevant information in that immaculate, decorative calligraphy that was a natural product of Indian aesthetics. On the reading desk a paraffin lamp threw a bright pool of light in which were placed three or four books meant for her attention. With a discreet cough the aide walked into an adjoining chamber and left Olivia to her own devices.

As she slipped into the seat and cautiously fingered the bound volumes, Olivia washed over with nostalgia for her father's precious collection of books, which had been her responsibility to look after, and for Sally MacKendrick's one-room lending service, which went by the rather grand name of the "library." Sally too loved books and they had together spent many hours of contentment labelling, cataloguing and arranging the collection her father had helped Sally acquire as a small business after Scot MacKendrick had fallen prey to a band of claim jumpers at the mines where he worked. The lingering mustiness in the air of the Maharaja's library was like a whiff of home, but the rest of the environment she was in now contained an element of unreality, a dreamlike ethereality that seemed to remove her into quite another dimension, one she could not quite assimilate. It was as if, ever since she had arrived in Kirtinagar, she had been waiting for something to happen; she appeared to be poised on the verge of a dark chasm filled with uncertainties. Books forgotten for the moment, Olivia sat clasping and unclasping her hands, toying with a gathering malaise made more irritating because it defied identification.

A clock in the next room struck eleven and she jumped back into full alertness. With a sigh she closed the book before her without having read beyond the title. Picking up the rest of the books, feeling somewhat foolish at having had the library unlocked without having benefitted from it, Olivia rose, fitted the chair neatly back under the desk and turned to seek out the aide waiting in the adjoining chamber. She stilled again with a sharp intake of breath.

The apparition of Jai Raventhorne greeted her eyes from a far corner.

He was sitting with his legs outstretched over a stool, his arms crossed against his chest, his face shadowed. For a wild moment Olivia believed it was truly an apparition, but then he spoke.

"Why are you startled to see me?" He uncoiled himself from his seat and stood up. "Didn't you know that I would come?"

It was a moment before Olivia could speak, but when she did, what she said surprised her. "Yes. I knew you would."

Suddenly, everything fell into place: the short notice that made it impossible for Sir Joshua to accept the Maharaja's invitation; the prescience that Lady Bridget would not wish to accept for herself without her husband and that Estelle would not wish to accept at all. Even easier to guess would have been Sir Joshua's reluctance to let pass such a golden opportunity to ingratiate himself with Arvind Singh, as would have been the only alternative left—to dispatch Olivia as a surrogate.

Instinctively, she also realised that Jai Raventhorne had master-minded this weekend for only one purpose—to meet her again.

Walking over to where she still stood in confusion, he reached out for the book on top of the pile she held in her arms. "Hmmm. Did you find Bernier informative?"

"Yes. Very much so." As she struggled for composure, Olivia

could feel the warmth in her cheeks. "His Indian journeys seem to have been as tireless as they were perceptive."

Raventhorne raised an eyebrow. "You learned all that merely by staring at the title-page? You must be more clever than I thought, Miss O'Rourke."

Her colour deepened. How long had he been watching her? "You seem to have an incorrigible habit of scrutinising people when they are unaware of your presence, Mr. Raventhorne," she said coldly but uncomfortably conscious of her erratic pulse rate. "Obviously you apply your lack of scruples with prolific indiscrimination."

"Indeed! There is not much point in the lack if it is not made use of for all kinds of profit." He sounded unworriedly cheerful as he relieved her of the books. "Come, let us go outside. Confined spaces suffocate me."

The aide having materialised again, Raventhorne handed over the pile and indicated that the library could now be relocked. Olivia stood aside with nervousness and an odd sense of anticipation that made her tongue feel clumsy against her palate. "I . . . I presume you will be one of the guns at the shoot tomorrow?" Even as she asked it she knew it was an inane inquiry.

He touched her arm lightly, anxious to be gone. "Naturally. Arvind expects some return for the trouble I have made him take on my behalf to fetch you here!"

Olivia's breath ran shallow again; the Maharani's conversation and the Maharaja's parting remark suddenly appeared pertinent in some way she could still not fully grasp. "May I ask why the trouble was necessary?" Her breathlessness increased as she tried to keep pace with his impatient strides. Even to her own ears, her voice sounded unfamiliar.

He did not answer immediately. When they were half way across the garden he stopped so abruptly that she almost cannoned into him. He turned to face her with his brows pulled together in an edgy frown.

"You and I come from two widely mismatched hemispheres, Olivia." He spoke carefully, almost quietly, but with an undertone of bewilderment, "But between us there is an . . . affinity. I want to find out why, for I don't like it. It . . . disturbs me."

Her face burned; she almost stopped breathing. The unexpected sound of her first name on his lips had produced sensations within her stomach that made it feel hollow. "I . . . don't understand what you mean . . ." Her whisper sounded so patently false that he smiled.

"Don't you?" He did not challenge her lie further. "The gross pity of it is," he took a long, sighing breath, "that we are so irreconcilably on opposite sides."

Olivia's short laugh was as inadvertent as it was incredulous. "You think of me as an . . . *enemy?*" She could not have been more astonished.

He pondered as he stroked his chin between a thumb and forefinger. "Perhaps. But more than that I think of you as a surprise. And I have never cared much for surprises." He turned away and resumed his strides towards the Maharani's palace.

Less energetically, Olivia followed. The drift of the conversation alarmed her. Unerringly, he had touched a chord she recognised. He had vocalised with a single word something she would have chosen not to have acknowledged yet. An affinity! Even as they walked across the deserted lawn with its no-doubt unseen eyes, untouching and unspeaking, they seemed bound by a common thread, intangible and at the same time forceful. Between them was a mute communication, unenunciated but eloquent, that resonated behind the carefully erected façades they maintained. Yes, she was drawn towards Jai Raventhorne. Whatever that mysterious power that propelled her in his direction, it was potent enough to be sensed also by him. Despite her alarm, Olivia felt a surge of elation.

"We went to see your ship." Olivia spoke not so much as to convey something important as to break a silence far from easy. "It stood out from the others and looked very graceful."

"We?" They had arrived in the private garden adjoining the apartment she was occupying.

"My cousin Estelle and I."

"Ah yes. Estelle Templewood." He pulled his pipe from his belt and sucked on it without lighting it. The name of her cousin had been said as if some comment was to follow, but it didn't. Instead, he paced idly, seeming to be entirely involved in the action of his feet.

"Your emblem . . ." Olivia hesitated.

"Yes?"

"What made you choose Shiva's trident?"

"Why? Do you disapprove of it?"

She ignored the causticity. "No, but I do believe it is another of your flamboyances devised to produce, well, a feeling of intimidation in those you dislike . . ." It was an absurd observation considering that it in no way concerned her!

"Good. If it does, then that gives it sufficient justification."

"You mean you like the idea of frightening people?"

"Before the gods destroy, it is said, they make people mad. And fear is as efficient a means of provoking madness as any."

"It is also said," she pointed out quickly, "that *you* are mad! Since I doubt if it is fear that makes you so, what is your excuse?"

She knew he would answer with an evasion, and he did. "Does a madman need excuses for his lunacy?"

"All right then, *causes*—and I'm sure you have some because, as Voltaire wrote, madness is to have erroneous perceptions and to reason correctly from them."

He laughed. "At least you do concede that my reasoning might be correct even though to ask a lunatic to rationalise his lunacy is surely a contradiction in terms!"

Olivia sighed; the exercise in dialectics was as futile as always, but she refused to be diverted. "To return to your emblem, Shiva's trident is a symbol of destruction. Whom do you wish to destroy?"

Raventhorne thrust his pipe back in his belt and shrugged. "Let us just say . . . the destroyers."

"You equate your progenitors with your destroyers, is that it?"

It was not a remark designed to please him, nor did it. "My progenitors, as you call them," he snapped, "are what I equate with greed. It is neither to be indulged nor tolerated."

"Not all are greedy," Olivia observed with matching asperity. "Many Europeans come out here for reasons that are selfless."

"Like you?" His low laugh was derisive. "Greed comes in many shapes and colours, my dear Olivia. Yours, for instance, is for a rich Anglo-Saxon husband. Harmless enough and shared by many spinster mems but hardly *selfless!*"

She was intolerably incensed. To rise to his poisonous bait, however, would be to pamper his perversity. She forced herself to remain unruffled. "You mean the fishing fleet? You consider me to be one of that?"

"Well, aren't you?" He threw her an insolent smile. "Even though it is unlikely that our prize buffoon will allow you to be one of the returned empties, *hah!*"

"Why, *thank* you," she cooed, utterly livid but not dropping her flinty gaze an iota. "I already have had that assurance from others whose business my affairs are as little as they are yours."

His sudden nod of approval was, if anything, even more infuriating. "You know," he said, satisfied, "anger really does become you. Now come here, I want to show you something interesting." With yet another mercurial change of mood he strode off towards a cluster of trees, leaving her standing and stiff with outrage. "See that?"

Olivia swallowed her chagrin and allowed curiosity to take over. Slowly she followed him into the trees, where he sat balanced on his haunches, peering into the undergrowth where something glowed eerily. "Well, what is it?"

"Wild fungus. It shines in the night with its own inherent phosphorescence. Isn't it amazing? I found it by accident last week and have been fascinated ever since."

In great detail he launched into an explanation of wild fungi in India, waxing lyrical about their beauty. Obviously, he had made a study of the subject, for his information was prolific and authoritative. Something about the way he spoke, in short excited sentences and with immense enthusiasm, reminded Olivia suddenly of her father, who also often went into raptures over some new and trivial discovery. Overcome again by consuming curiosity about this most contrary of men, she was once more driven by an irresistible urge to reach the core of that "onion," which had eluded even his closest friends.

"Where was it," she asked in wonder, "that you received all your education. Here, in India?"

He rose and dusted his trousers. "In those best possible of institutions," he replied drily, "the school of hard knocks and the university of experience."

"But in India?" she persisted.

"Everywhere. The institutions are universal."

Olivia was sorely tempted to stamp her foot. "You ask me such grossly personal questions," she said petulantly, "yet you refuse to answer a single one of mine! Is that just?"

Even in the gloam she could see his eyes harden. "I would hate you to run away with the idea that I am a just man. I am not. And my life, such as it has been, is of little consequence to you, whatever its inadequacies."

"But it is in those inadequacies that you revel, isn't it?" she cried, unbearably frustrated by the stone wall with which he blocked questions.

"No, but I accept them. They give me pride of possession because they are among the few things that are mine and mine alone." Aborting all further conversation, he stalked away from her.

At the entrance of the zenana two maidservants awaited them, but as Raventhorne approached they melted into the shrubbery with their veils over their faces. A signal flashed through Olivia's brain, tying up yet another loose thread; Raventhorne's presence here over the weekend was the reason why she had seen no sign either of her ayah or of Sir Joshua's other servants who had accompanied her. Servants in India were the means often used to ferret out information of people's secret doings (which was why Calcutta was such a village!). As such, Raventhorne had ensured that there would be no risk of their meeting in Kirtinagar being reported to the Templewoods. His deviousness was indeed far reaching, but Olivia could not help a sense of relief at the vital precaution.

"Are you good with a shotgun?" he asked suddenly.

"I can shoot straight, if that's what you mean."

"You're not likely to faint and fall off the elephant when the tiger appears?"

She regarded him coolly, put out by his patronization. "I doubt it. I have hunted before, if not tigers then animals equally savage."

He chuckled under his breath. "I forget sometimes that you are American with hackles that rise like those of a prairie wolf when he senses an attack." The hard lines of his face seemed to thaw and, without warning, he reached out to touch her cheek. "From which parent did you inherit those deceptively ingenuous, disconcertingly lovely eyes?"

Olivia recoiled; his fingers were icy. "My mother. She . . ." Her voice died in her throat.

His hand did not retract. Instead it lingered to lightly trace the line of her jaw. Carefully he brushed a strand of hair off her forehead and looped it behind an ear. "You delude yourself, Olivia. You have no idea in how vulnerable a position you stand." He spoke in a flat monotone, his mood more indecipherable than ever. "I see you as I would the wing of a butterfly, fragile and trembling on the point of dissolution at a touch. You play with toys that are not toys." He sighed and let his hand drop. "It is this that disturbs me most about you. Good night."

And with that she was left alone.

For a long while Olivia stood motionless, staring into the dark. Her body was numb; even her mind seemed static. The only sensation she felt was on her cheek where the imprint of his finger-tips burned as raw as if branded into her skin. An instinct then stirred in some far-away recess of her brain, ominous and gathering strength. She knew that with that touch, subtly but irrevocably, Jai Raventhorne had succeeded in altering the course of her life. Something insidious had ruffled the placid surface of her existence; given a chance, it had the power to blow a storm and divert her into spaces unknown and uncharted. Like a deadly undertow in the ocean, it threatened to drag her down into depths she would not know how to negotiate. That Raventhorne with his feral instincts knew it was only too obvious.

Olivia was frightened. Force, power, *affinity* . . . call it what they might, something also told her that however loud the alarm bells ringing around her, however dire the warnings she received, she would not heed them.

She knew it was already too late for that.

Heavily timbered and built on stilts, the royal hunting lodge was set deep in the jungle. Over its red tiled roof sal branches interlocked, filtering shafts of early sunlight that dappled the clearing. The air was heavy with sound and smell; rustling leaves, chirping birds, tunelessly croaking frogs, muted human voices and swirls of wood smoke announcing imminent breakfast combined to make it a lively scene. From a distance came muffled drum beats, rhythmic and steady, like the pulsing of some primeval heart. It was in the bowels of this dank, dense underworld that the tiger prowled, unaware that with those drum beats were also ticking away the last hours of its life.

An armed cavalry unit had escorted Olivia and the Maharani and their attendants in carriages, whereas the men had ridden out earlier on horseback. In the verandah of the lodge the Maharaja and Raventhorne were already at work checking guns and ammunition, working out strategy and assigning jobs. In the clearing were the four caparisoned elephants, now being fed rice balls and molasses, who would bear them into the jungle. The mahouts stood by waiting to mount the foreheads of their massive charges. Early breakfast was being served to the retinue of hunters and attendants who squatted on the grass and ate out of banana leaves while hundreds of villagers watched in barely suppressed excitement, secure in the ability of their ruler to make their lives again safe from danger.

On the verandah a light meal was on offer—glasses of hot milk and savoury triangles of pastry stuffed with vegetables. Sitting next to Kinjal, Olivia spent all her time trying to avoid meeting Raventhorne's eyes, not that they sought hers anyway;

for all intents and purposes, he seemed barely aware of her presence. The Maharaja, on the other hand, greeted her effusively.

"I trust your ride was comfortable and has given you a fair appetite, Miss O'Rourke. We will eat more fully on our return."

"Most comfortable, thank you, although I would have preferred to make the journey on horseback," Olivia answered with frankness.

He spread his hands ruefully. "Forgive me, Miss O'Rourke, for not allowing you that. My people are conservative and the sight of a lady, even European, riding a horse is one with which they are not yet familiar."

"Of course I understand," Olivia said quickly, ignoring the pointed, tacit comment contained in Raventhorne's smile. "I was merely expressing a regret, not a complaint."

But it was impossible to ignore the flesh and blood presence of a man who had spent the night haunting her fitful dreams. What had transpired between them last night had shaken her far more than she would have thought possible. The prospect now of spending more time in his company, even with the safeguards provided by the presence of the Maharaja and the Maharani, was nerve racking, for she needed time to assimilate what was happening within her. Whatever it was, she didn't like it. It had taken her by surprise, and Raventhorne wasn't the only one who didn't care much for surprises.

As they ate and drank, Kinjal pointed out various things to her over the wooden balustrades about the flurry of preparations below. It was as the breakfast dishes were being cleared that she took Olivia into a room away from the others and said, "You must excuse me, Olivia, if I do not accompany you into the jungle. You know that I do not appear before men not of our household, and to enclose the howdah would be such a wasted exercise."

Olivia was not only greatly disappointed but also perturbed. "Then I will stay back with you. It is so serene and pleasant right here."

"My husband would not hear of that and neither would I," Kinjal said firmly. "We would not like you to miss an experience as colourful as a tiger shoot."

It was churlish to argue further so Olivia did not pursue the subject, but her alarm persisted. "How many guns will there be?"

"Eight. One on each elephant and four on foot."

Would Jai Raventhorne ride with the Maharaja? Olivia

prayed that he would. The howdahs were comfortable and well appointed but by no means spacious enough to ensure privacy for two people. But when the starting signal was given and the elephants lumbered up to the ground below the verandah to trumpet and then kneel in obeisance before their king, it was obvious to Olivia that her prayers would not be answered. The Maharaja's elephant stood apart with its royal pennant hoisted and the two other elephants already had their marksmen in place, which left only one more animal. Damn! She turned to see Kinjal watching her closely.

"It is Jai who asked to ride with you, Olivia," she said, her eyes strangely unhappy. "Would you prefer it otherwise?"

The facility with which Kinjal had read her thoughts brought a fierce blush to Olivia's cheeks. *Yes!* she wanted to shout, I would prefer it otherwise! But she shook her head quickly and ran down the stairs where everyone waited.

The sensible hunting clothes she wore had been provided by her aunt, who had been in the jungle many times and knew exactly what was needed. Her skirt, divided for easy movement, was of hardy brown twill. The cotton blouse, high at the neck and long sleeved, was a protection against insects and the sturdy, knee-high leather boots were to guard against snakes and scorpions that might be lurking in the undergrowth. Beneath the skirt, as her aunt had insisted, she wore long johns. "If you fall off somewhere at least you won't make a spectacle of yourself in front of that uncivilised crowd."

As Raventhorne helped her up the ladder onto the howdah, his expression showed approval of her gear. His own, of course, was as careless as ever, the only addition being a gun belt. To Olivia's enormous relief as she settled herself inside the howdah, he stepped across its low surround and perched on the elephant's head next to the mahout, his rifle across his knees and his arms folded. Warily, Olivia stretched out her legs in the opposite direction from him, wondering if by any chance he suspected the unkind thoughts that had crossed her mind.

He did. "I told you I am not totally without social graces," he murmured, enjoying her discomfiture, "although I find it difficult to believe you have never been close to a man before. After all, you are twenty-two and not entirely ugly."

"I have," she retorted with only a slight rise of colour, "but never to one as bumptious as you."

He laughed and let the matter drop.

The procession, ceremonial in its grandeur, moved lugubriously into the dense trees, followed by many on foot. Daylight was now bright although filtered through the dense canopy of branches above. Around them birds squabbled for choice worms, butterflies swooped and glided around spectacular wild flowers and squirrels darted up and down tree trunks, chittering excitedly. From a wedge of lime green moss between banyan roots a family of fat toads watched with impassive expressions. The majesty of the jungle was impressive; it was a world of remarkable efficiency in which everything and everyone knew its place and kept it. In the far distance the drums still beckoned, hounding the tiger relentlessly into the final trap.

Raventhorne sat in silence, occasionally lifting his rifle to squint through the sight, his hands brown and strong but his fingers surprisingly shapely, long and tapering. A picture flashed through Olivia's mind as she watched him out of the corner of an eye and she hated herself for it: It was of Sujata in his arms being whipped into passion by those very fingers that had branded her own cheek last night. Flushing, she looked away to concentrate on a band of black-faced monkeys showing off their skill at acrobatics in a display that she felt was meant solely for her benefit.

"Why are you not married?"

Olivia had by now ceased to be startled by his habit of asking questions no one else in the world would dream of. "You sound like my aunt," she said drily. "It is a question that troubles her greatly, too."

"No doubt, but that does not answer it."

"It is not necessary for you to have an answer!"

"Oh, but it is." His expression as he turned to look at her was quite serious. "You owe me an answer."

"*Owe* you an answer?" she echoed. "Why?"

"Because I have rescued you from luncheon with Lady Birkhurst. Whatever your intentions towards her unfortunate son, I doubt if that prospect could have pleased you much."

Olivia had to laugh. Odious insinuations apart, there was truth in what he said. "I was under the impression you believed *both* the Birkhursts were valuable to my scheme, in which case you have done me a very definite disfavour!"

He rubbed his nose with a thoughtful frown. "I see that I am hoist with my own petard! Be that as it may, my question still remains unanswered."

"I am not married because I have chosen not to be. Does that answer it?"

"No." He shifted positions again and leaned back. "Young men in America are healthy, full blooded and unlikely to let pass an eligible woman who is *not* altogether ugly! Perhaps you are already reserved?" His narrowed eyes were full of cunning and scarcely likely to miss the flush that slowly crawled up Olivia's face.

"You must decide which of my intentions satisfies you more—to trap Freddie Birkhurst or to return an 'empty' and spring my trap back home!" The conversation was again becoming impossibly personal! "Either way your concern is uncalled for." He merely laughed. Cross and anxious not to let the subject be revived, Olivia asked quickly, "Have you lived in America long?"

"Yes."

"What was it you did there?" She expected more stonewalling, but to her surprise he answered readily enough.

"Many things. I worked, I learned, I earned."

"What did you learn?"

He smiled. "The white man's magic."

"Such as?" His ready answers, she realised, were singularly lacking in information. "What actually did you *do?*"

They had been talking in whispers, a prime rule on a jungle shoot. He shook his head and raised a finger to his lips. "It would be easier if you asked me what I did *not* do."

"All right," she lowered her voice further, "what did you *not* do?"

"I did not become president of the United States."

Olivia stared uncertainly. "And why not?"

"Because I never tried to. If I had, I would have." He grinned. "I told you, I believe in always winning, remember?"

The arrogant angle of his head, the proudly perpendicular back, were characteristic, but the smile was uncommonly easy. Olivia tussled mentally with a question again in the forefront of her mind, then, throwing caution to the winds, asked it. "Even when it means pirating ships and burning warehouses?"

"Why not," the admission came with surprising lack of hesitation, "if the ships carry opium and the warehouses stock it?" His manner was still relaxed; only a slight tightening of the jawline and the barely perceptible stiffening of his back indicated a reaction. "I do not believe in selling death," he said shortly.

Olivia was as shocked by his offhanded confession as by the suggestion of moral scruples. But about the adulterated tea chests referred to by Arthur Ransome she had no opportunity to ask, as, in pursuit of her advantage, she had every intention of doing. For, suddenly, Raventhorne's air of casual amiability dropped and he became alert. Even his eyes stilled as he listened motionlessly. Between him and the mahout a look passed, and, minimally, Raventhorne nodded.

Olivia became aware of the eerie hush that seemed to have settled over the jungle. Above their heads a band of noisy monkeys huddled together and buried their faces in each other's pelts; a herd of spotted deer, fleeing silently past through the trees, vanished into the opposite distance. Even a cloud of orange and lilac butterflies hovering over a wild hibiscus seemed to change its mind and collectively shoot away in agitated formation. The drums, so frantic and urgent just a while ago, had fallen silent. Not a leaf moved, not an insect stirred; the very air seemed to have come to a standstill. Then, beginning like a low, subterranean rumble from the very bowels of the jungle, came a sound that grew into a full-throated roar. It was unmistakably the tiger, obviously now trapped in the clearing that was to be its final resting place, although without its knowledge. The kill was imminent.

Olivia's heartbeats galloped. It was impossible not to be infected by the piercing suspense of the moment. Raventhorne half rose from his perch to slide smoothly into the howdah, checked his rifle again and cast a swift glance at the gun rack on which other weapons were arranged as alternatives. In the holster at his hip was the remarkable new revolver designed only last year by Samuel Colt and, Olivia knew, was much talked about at home. She felt a quick stab of sympathy for the doomed animal; certainly he stood little chance of survival against such overwhelming odds. Slowly, purposefully, their ponderous procession crept into the clearing by the river on the banks of which had been tethered the six goats that were the tiger's bait. The beaters had all slunk away into the safety of the undergrowth away from the river. Now only the four elephants and a ring of poised spearsmen remained. Somewhere amidst the tall grasses, Raventhorne pointed out to Olivia silently, was their fearsome quarry.

The elephants fanned out to form a semicircle. As they did so, Raventhorne touched Olivia's arm with a fingertip and nodded in the direction of a rock formation shielded by a stubbled bamboo grove. Framed by the greenery was a hazy blur of yellow ochre, crouching in wait. Olivia's breath caught; it was indeed the royal Bengal tiger, the most majestic, most feared predator of the

Indian jungles. So cleverly had he concealed himself that only the practised eyes of a hunter could have detected his presence in that profusion of natural colour. He had already killed one of the goats, Olivia saw; now he waited to return for his easily earned meal. Raventhorne pointed a questioning glance at her and then looked meaningfully at his rifle. Alarmed, Olivia quickly shook her head. It was one thing to bring down a buck or a bison, but it was quite another to match wits with an animal she had never seen before, much less hunted. He shrugged and, smiling, turned away with an extravagant gesture of disappointment.

For a while nobody moved in the tableau. With the target still partially obscured by the rocks, it would have been foolish to fire. After what seemed an eternity but could not have been more than ten minutes, the tiger finally risked movement. Cautiously, crouching on its stomach, it slithered forward in the direction of its kill. It couldn't avoid a break in the rocks and, all at once, there it was in full view, in all its formidable majesty. In the same instant a gun roared; it was the Maharaja's, the first shot his privilege. He missed; the tiger leapt into the air, its enraged screams reverberating through the forest in crashing waves of sound.

"Damn!" The Maharaja's shouted curse came just as Raventhorne's gun spat fire and a second shot hit the beast's flailing hulk. "Good shot, sir!"

"He's not dead yet!" Raventhorne shouted back, reloading rapidly to once more take careful aim, but the animal had again disappeared behind the rock. "I missed the neck, damn, damn, *damn!"*

Badly wounded, the tiger continued to roar furiously and then, suddenly, maddened with pain, it flew out of its niche and charged. Muzzle-loaders fired and a dozen spears spun through the air, but, dodging in and out of the scrub, the tiger evaded them neatly. For a second it was lost to sight but then, like a mighty trajectile, it took a flying leap to land on the hind quarters of their elephant. Olivia gave a half scream but stuffed her handkerchief in her mouth to abort it. She was terrified. Only Raventhorne remained quite calm. Swiftly moving his rifle balance from one surround of the howdah to another, he pointed its muzzle towards the elephant's tail.

"Hold on tightly," he warned Olivia over his shoulder. "The elephant is going to bolt any minute."

Bucking and trumpeting, their massive mount went round and round in circles, kicking up its huge hind legs to try to shake off the tiger clinging for dear life, its claws dug deep into the tough hide and its roars still deafening in their fury. Customarily, during a hunt like this, a gun bearer was positioned on the back of an elephant, Olivia had been told, but Raventhorne had preferred to have a gun rack in the howdah instead. Just as well, Olivia thought in her terror; by now the poor man would have been crushed or clawed to death. Even with the tiger's enormous head just a few feet away from the muzzle of the gun, it was impossible to take aim with the elephant so completely out of control. The clamour around them was ear-splitting, but Olivia heard none of it. Hypnotised, she stared fixedly at the gaping, gnashing jaws, the unbelievably mammoth head and the baleful yellow eyes that stared back at her with such hate. Raventhorne got up with one hand clasped to a wooden pillar for support, and put a foot over the surround on the elephant's back. Within the howdah he firmed his other leg and, still holding on for support, transferred his rifle from one hand to the other. Just then, the elephant bolted. Screaming with fright, it careened off along the river bank at a tremendous speed, still not having shaken off the tiger. Chalk faced, Olivia cowered in her corner, not seeing anything except those snapping, snarling jaws not two feet away from Raventhorne's boot.

"All right. Come over here." Still perfectly calm, he looked back at her and beckoned with his head. "Let me see just how straight you can shoot." Olivia stared at him in horror; had he gone *mad?* "Come *on,*" he repeated impatiently. "He's not going to wait for you all day!"

Propelled undoubtedly by divine power, since she had none of her own, Olivia moved. Raventhorne clenched the barrel of his rifle briefly between his teeth and extended his free arm to curl around her waist. With her back tight against his chest, he made a lightning move and, suddenly, his Colt was in her hand. "Aim for the forehead," he instructed, dropping his own weapon to support her firmly. "He doesn't have much strength left so try to be quick."

Olivia hesitated but only for a frozen second more. Held securely by the waist, she lifted the Colt, aimed and fired. For a horrible fraction of an instant, she thought she had missed, for the tiger's head remained exactly where it had been. Then a rush of blood spewed forth from a neat hole between its eyes. With a final dying roar and one last virulent glare, the magnificent head dropped entirely from view. Unaware that the drama was over, the elephant continued on its flight down the river bank.

Taking her with him, Raventhorne fell back into the howdah, and the Colt in Olivia's numb fingers went flying over the side onto the ground racing past below. For a moment they lay unmoving, side by side, their arms and legs entangled. The silence outside was suddenly deathly. Tiring, the elephant finally began to slow down.

"You dropped my gun." Propped up on an elbow, he stared down at her with an annoyed frown.

"But at least," she managed to murmur weakly, staring back into his eyes so close, so terribly close, "I didn't faint."

And with that, she fainted.

When she came to, Olivia lay on a carpet underneath a tree. In the clearing, pandemonium reigned. Hundreds of people sang and danced and jubilated all around, and the drums had started up again. One of the Maharani's veiled maidservants was sitting and fanning her; another offered her a drink of water. Olivia blinked to clear her head, sat up slowly and drained the cup in a single draught. Her vision started to return; gulping in huge lungfuls of air, she looked up into the worried eyes of Jai Raventhorne.

"Are you all right?"

Olivia nodded and asked for more water. "What . . . happened?"

"You fainted."

"Oh." She averted her head. "Is the tiger . . . dead?"

"Very." He pointed to the crowd dancing in a circle. "They're measuring him out and singing your praises." His eyes were disturbingly soft, almost as soft as his smile.

"Magnificent shot, Miss O'Rourke, *magnificent!*" The Maharaja joined them, rubbing his hands together in obvious delight. "Although Jai had no right to place you in a position of such danger." He threw an accusing glance at his friend, trying to look stern but not succeeding.

"I could have hardly missed at point-blank range," Olivia protested. "In any case, he is Mr. Raventhorne's prize. The mortal wound had already been inflicted."

The tiger, a full ten feet two inches long between the pegs, lay stretched on the grass, as resplendent in death as in life. Two blood-encrusted holes showed on its beautiful yellow and black fur, one in the shoulder and one in the dead centre of its forehead. Olivia stared at it in fascination and then with involuntary compassion. What a sad end to such a superb creature!

"Don't waste your tears on him," Raventhorne said carelessly at her elbow. "He's eaten more people than even the villagers can count."

"Is the elephant badly hurt?" she asked, anxious. "Those claws seemed to go in very deep."

"No. They have tough hides. The mahouts are expert medicine-men; they know which healing leaves and plants to use."

Olivia turned to face him severely. "You really had no business doing that, you know. Supposing I had missed?"

"At point-blank range?" He tilted his head sideways. "If you had, I promise I would have used my second bullet on *you* as a disgrace to your nation."

Back at the lodge, luncheon was served to hundreds of people from nearby villages sitting in long lines on the ground before the ubiquitous banana leaves that did for plates. On the return journey the hunters had bagged several deer and black buck and the meat was roasted on giant spits out in the open. As a treat the Maharaja had ordered tots of local liquor for all and the resultant revelries were already well under way. On the return, Raventhorne had ridden with the Maharaja and Olivia had shared her howdah with the maidservant. Whether or not she preferred this arrangement she never decided because, drained by the morning's excitement, she slept all the way back.

In the compound of the lodge there were a few embarrassing moments when some overjoyed villagers garlanded both her and Jai Raventhorne and danced around them singing paeans of praise for their marksmanship. Her red-faced protests that the kill had been *his,* not hers, were drowned out by the clamour. Raventhorne enjoyed her embarrassment, making no attempt to convey her protests to the crowd. "Since you concede there is an affinity between us," he murmured with a faint curl of his mouth, "is it not appropriate that we should share the honours? I have never done so before with a woman; it makes an intriguing change."

"I conceded no such thing, Mr. Raventhorne!" she retorted, vexed by his presumption. "You are allowing your imagination to run away with you."

He made no reply except for that maddening smile. Perhaps he knew there was no need to.

Luncheon for the Maharaja, the Maharani and their two

guests was served in the cool privacy of the lodge dining-room, and the variety of spiced meats cushioned on snowy white rice was delicious. Olivia was well used to game meats, having subsisted on them frequently, and the pungent spices gave them added flavour. Through the meal, eaten with their fingers, the conversation was almost entirely about the hunt, mostly for Kinjal's benefit. The Maharaja, in excellent form now that the menace threatening the lives of his people had been conquered, regaled them with accounts of previous hunts, and the mood was generally casual.

It was after they had eaten and were enjoying some sweets presented to the Maharaja by the villagers that he suddenly said, "What is so urgent that you have to hurry back, Jai? Surely you could delay your departure until the morning?" He sounded piqued. "I was looking forward to our customary game of chess tonight."

Raventhorne shook his head. "Not tonight, Arvind. There are important matters that await me in Calcutta."

"What important matters?" the Maharaja queried with a frown.

"Well, that fur consignment for one. Khan is a wily Kashmiri and I know he has been negotiating with Smithers."

"So let Smithers win one round, what does it matter? You have beaten him to it often enough."

Raventhorne smiled. "One round is one too many."

The Maharaja threw up his hands in irritation. "Must you be like a dog with a bone all the time, Jai? Can you not let go once, just *once?*"

Raventhorne stood up. "When I let go, Arvind, I fear my teeth will go with the bone," he said lightly. "Now, would you like to show me your American reloader? I shall have to leave within the hour."

As Kinjal retired into her room following the luncheon, Olivia stood at the verandah balustrades and watched the activity below, but distractedly. Her increasing contrariness was beginning to bewilder her; on the one hand she felt desperately uncomfortable in the presence of Raventhorne, but on the other she was sorely disappointed to see him go! What was it that she wanted? For the first time in her life Olivia found herself facing a dilemma that had no simple answers, a mass of complexities she did not know how to untangle. Her fascination for this volatile man whose directions changed with the wind, like a weathervane, was incomprehensible. He was everything she disapproved of, nothing her reason urged her to admire. Yet the prospect of not seeing him again was intolerable. And impossible! As surely as she knew that the sun would rise in the morning, Olivia knew that she would see Jai Raventhorne again.

Below in the court-yard, his midnight Shaitan was being led out of the clearing by Bahadur, the attendant who had escorted her home the morning she had met Raventhorne in the bazaar. Absurdly dismayed at the prospect of missing Raventhorne's departure, Olivia hurried down the wooden stairway without giving herself time to think. The ache to see him once more, to exchange some meaningless words and delay him a few minutes, was so acute that it was almost like a catch in her side. Then, feeling foolish, she stood behind the trunk of the *gulmohar*, regretting her rashness but unable to retreat. Raventhorne descended the stairs and walked to his horse, then, with one foot in the stirrup, halted as he sighted her. He released the reins and sauntered up to where she stood.

"I hear the Templewoods are planning a visit to Barrackpore."

There was no point in even pretending surprise at his information. "There has been some talk about it, yes. My aunt feels strongly that my uncle needs a rest from—"

"All his misfortunes? Yes, I daresay he does." His manner changed. "But you do not wish to accompany them?"

He had again verbalized something that was still only a vague seed in her own mind. Now that he had, however, Olivia recognised that he was right; no, she did not wish to accompany them! "Of course I wish to accompany them," she contradicted with undue force. "Why ever should I not? I hear Barrackpore is a most agreeable place."

"Agreeable, yes, but it takes you away for a while from your ever-ready Romeo, Freddie!" He scowled.

This time she did stamp her foot. "I wish you would refrain from throwing that damned name in my face quite as often as you do!" she cried, clenching her fists in frustration. "It infuriates me, which is, of course, the sole reason you do it!"

He laughed. "Well, can you think of a better one?" The wave of some invisible magic wand then whipped the humour off his lips. The pale, pale eyes went metallic, as did the voice. "If you do not wish to go to Barrackpore, you will not. Take my word for it."

Olivia remained staring at his vanishing back, mouth open with astonishment.

It was not until late in the evening that the excitement of the shoot subsided enough for the royal party to return to the town of Kirtinagar and the palace. It had been a long, physically wearisome day. For Olivia it had also proved emotionally harrowing. But, despite her mental and physical fatigue, her mind raced. Whatever the paradoxes and the confusions, there was one truth that could not now be dismissed: Her interest in Jai Raventhorne was by no means academic as she had once insisted. This, at least, had been resolved during the day. Nor was she curious about him merely because he was a person cast in a mould of extraordinary dimensions. Between them, inexplicably, there *was* an affinity, an invisible filament, a *bond.* However unwanted and unsolicited, it was at the same time wildly stimulating. Olivia could no longer deny that it was as a man—attractive and exciting and sensual, yes, *sensual*—that Jai Raventhorne affected her most.

"Tell me about him, Kinjal."

Once again they were by themselves, strolling among the bushes of the aromatic herbal garden fanned by the bracing nightly breezes from the south. Above them rotated the arc of the night sky with its burden of stars spelling out by their movement the irredeemable and irreversible passage of time. In Olivia's request sounded a note of urgency to which the Maharani reacted without surprise. It was, after all, too late for pretences. Nor did the Maharani need to ask to whom Olivia referred. The thought between them was shared, tacitly understood.

"Yes," she answered simply, "you of all people have the right to know more."

Olivia halted. "Why do you say that?"

"Because . . . ," Kinjal paused, as if to select the right words, "because you have provoked Jai's attention. It is not an attention that is aroused with ease but it is an occurrence that sometimes," she paused again to breathe a small sigh, "extorts heavy compensations." In the large sloe eyes there was something that momentarily startled Olivia. It was pity.

"Tell me about him anyway." Impatience and that all-pervading sense of urgency cancelled out every other consideration. The look of pity she decided to ignore. "I would like to know everything."

"And so you shall, my friend, so you shall." Smiling a little at Olivia's impatience, Kinjal summoned a maidservant from a knot of women who sat not far away singing softly among themselves, and ordered carpets and cushions. "We might as well make ourselves comfortable. The story is long and the telling will take time."

5

Surprisingly enough, Kinjal said, our chief source of information about Jai Raventhorne's background has been my husband's father, the late Maharaja. A man greatly interested in his fellow human beings, rich or poor, he was in the habit of travelling incognito to Calcutta and elsewhere. On one such journey he happened to stop at a wayside tavern for refreshments for himself, his single attendant and their horses. As he sat in the courtyard chatting with other travellers, his eyes fell upon a young lad of about fourteen busy washing heavy kitchen utensils at the well. The boy was clad in tatters and was far from clean. And his body looked horribly emaciated.

What encouraged the Maharaja's attention, however, were two rather unusual characteristics; even though he was under no supervision by his employer, the boy performed his menial task with single-minded effort—and his curious silver eyes were empty of all discernible expression. The boy was obviously of mixed blood, for beneath the film of dirt his skin was unusually pale. In India there is no dearth of destitute half-breeds forgotten by transient fathers; this one looked unprepossessing, but there was something about him that struck the Maharaja as unusual.

He called the boy over and asked his name. The boy answered but with visible reluctance, almost as if the simple question had somehow insulted him. He refused to respond to all other questions, his manner becoming more and more resentful. Finally, for no reason other than the boy's curious air of dignity and a feeling of pity for his abysmal condition, the Maharaja offered him a handful of coins. The boy's reaction amazed him. Throwing back his shoulders he straightened into a stance of lofty arrogance and his grey eyes became ashen with contempt.

"I do not accept money when I have not worked for it," he said scornfully. "Keep your charity for others who do."

Far from being offended, the Maharaja was deeply impressed. It was rare indeed to find such fierce pride in one who could so little afford it. From that day on the Maharaja made it a point to stop at the tavern each time he passed. He never made the mistake of offering charity again but instead worked hard to win the confidence of the lad. Gradually over the months the boy's attitude towards him loosened and an unlikely friendship of sorts developed between the king and the dish-washer. But the boy seldom smiled and never talked about himself. What he did do a great deal was ask questions, mostly about ships and the sea and the world outside his own meagre one. The Maharaja made handsome offers of employment in Kirtinagar or of education in some forward-looking institution. He liked the boy, was convinced that he had worthy potential and wanted to give him a chance to exploit it. Each time the boy refused.

"Then what do you want to do with your life, Jai?" The Maharaja repeatedly asked, exasperated by this inexplicable stubbornness. "Do you want to spend the rest of your days washing other people's dirty dishes?"

Finally one day, instead of prevaricating as he usually did, the boy volunteered an answer. "No. I want to be the richest man in the world. And I will be some day." He spoke with no passion at all, merely as if he were stating a foregone conclusion.

"Well, that certainly is an understandable ambition," the Maharaja said with matching solemnity although suppressing a small smile. "But for that you have to at least make a start."

The boy looked surprised. "I already have."

"True, but to improve in life substantially you need . . . equipment."

The boy held out his hands. "I have equipment. These, and," he touched his forehead, "this."

"Your equipment is undoubtedly excellent," the Maharaja said gently, "but to spend a lifetime washing dishes will not make you rich."

"No," the boy conceded, "but that is not how I will spend it."

"Then how?"

The boy took a long time to give an answer, the Maharaja later recalled. A strange, far-away look came into his eyes as if he were transported into quite another time. Then, slowly, he smiled. "I will spend it," he said in a purr that was almost catlike, "in fulfilling my destiny."

For an instant the leaden, secretive eyes took on a look of naked spite. There was such malice in them that the Maharaja was disturbed. Not even the most persistent interrogation, however, could get the boy to say more. Once again he had relapsed into silence and the disturbing expression was again impassive. The Maharaja abandoned his inquisition for the next time, but two months later when he came to the tavern again he learned that the boy had left. Nobody knew where he had gone and the tavern owner neither knew or cared. Urchins like this one, anonymous and rootless, were a penny a dozen in India and a replacement had already been found. The rumour around the tavern was, however, that the boy had stowed away to sea.

At this point in her story, the Maharani paused. For a moment or two a silence reigned between her and a rapt Olivia. Lying back on her cushion staring up at the recognisable constellations moving westward in a clear, cloudless sky, Olivia remained very still. In her mind was a vision of the man as he now was, and the metamorphosis defied belief. She rolled over on a side to prop herself up on an elbow. "Then?"

"Then," Kinjal resumed, "for many years nobody heard of or from Jai—not that there was anyone with whom he would communicate. Perhaps my father-in-law was his only friend, and in those many years he had died. In any case, Jai neither knew his name nor was curious enough to inquire."

Arvind Singh became Maharaja of Kirtinagar. He had heard of his father's dish-washer friend but as time passed the story slipped his memory. Twelve years ago, having ferreted out the Maharaja's name from an old groom at the tavern, the impecunious boy reappeared in the form of Jai Raventhorne and asked to see the Maharaja. When Arvind Singh's memory revived, he was staggered at the picture of impeccable, expensive and masterful gentlemanliness the man presented. He found it impossible to believe that this urbane, self-confident stranger who spoke in such cultured tones was indeed the disreputable ragamuffin his father had spoken about so often. Raventhorne was genuinely distressed that the benevolent old man who had showed him such kindness was no longer alive. Despite Arvind Singh's sense of shock, his admiration for the success Raventhorne had achieved and the monumental effort that must have gone into achieving it was instant. There seemed to be some strange empathy between the two men. "And," Kinjal said, concluding her narrative, "they have remained close friends ever since."

Even though it was Kinjal who had been speaking at such length, it was Olivia's throat that felt arid and tight. It was an incredible story, unlike anything she had anticipated; she felt immensely moved. "Jai's father," she finally asked after lubricating her mouth with sherbet, "who was he?"

There was sadness in the look Kinjal gave her. "We do not know. If Jai does, he will not talk about it. Rumour says he was an English sailor, perhaps neither seen nor remembered by his son."

"And his mother?"

"They say she was a tribal from the hills."

"Was? Then is she dead?"

"In all probability. Jai does not talk of her either. Had she been alive I feel that Jai would have wanted us to meet her. My husband did ask him once but Jai became so agitated at the question that the subject has never been raised again."

Olivia's emotions, already melting with compassion, emulsified further although she could think of no man less deserving of that compassion than Jai Raventhorne. Nevertheless, to have won when the deck was so heavily stacked in his disfavour could not have been easy; the uneven battles could scarcely have left him unscarred. Grudgingly, she began to understand if not all, at least a few then of his perversities, for some wounds heal fast while others suppurate for a lifetime. "Was it to America he sailed on that ship?"

"Eventually. He says it took him twice around the world first and it was during this time that he learned about navigation."

"He talks about these experiences freely?"

Kinjal made a wry face. "When he is in the mood. It was America, he says, that finally made him into a man. A Boston merchant hired him as a shop hand. Jai was an eager apprentice and worked diligently, and he ended up as the man's partner." Uncovering her head, Kinjal opened out her long, flowing hair to re-plait it carefully. "That merchant's name was Raventhorne, Jai told us."

Olivia sat up. "Raventhorne?"

"Yes. Jai's own father's name is unknown to him. Until he adopted that of his benefactor, he lived with only one name."

To be so deprived, so discriminated against by fate! Olivia

filled with an involuntary ache. "That one name, what does it mean?"

Kinjal smiled. "*Jai* means *victory*—what else? You must know he can bear to be nothing but a winner. It is one obsession of which he makes no secret."

"That destiny he spoke of, has he fulfilled it yet?"

"Ah!" Kinjal lay back to scan the stars. "That remains the darkest area of all. Jai dismisses it as a joke, a childish flight of fancy."

"Do you believe that?"

Kinjal pondered, then shook her head. "No. Jai is not given to flights of fancy. My father-in-law's indelible impression was that he was repeating some sort of vow. And it has not yet been fulfilled. Had it already been, Jai would not still be a man possessed, a man of such burning inner anger. Which is why, Olivia," she sat up again and her frown was worried, "I do fear for you."

"*Fear* for me?" The word Kinjal had chosen was so unaccountably strong that Olivia stared. "But why?"

"You must forgive me, Olivia, if I presume on a new friendship and exceed my limits." The Maharani took her hand and pressed it. "I feel it is my duty to warn you that Jai Raventhorne is a dangerous man."

The familiar phrase brought an involuntary smile to Olivia's lips. "So everyone tells me!"

Kinjal did not share in her smile. "The English consider him dangerous for other reasons. I consider him dangerous for . . . *you.*" Her unmistakable sincerity washed away Olivia's smile. "You cannot conceive of the lengths Jai went to so that you could be here this weekend."

Olivia flushed. "And that is a matter for . . . fear?"

"You must understand, Olivia, that Jai is very dear to me." Suddenly there was even more concern in her tone. "Nothing I say to you is a disloyalty to him for he knows my views. In Jai's life there have been endless women. He has treated them with scant respect and has used them only for physical gratification." She peered anxiously into Olivia's eyes. "Am I embarrassing you?" Olivia shook her head even though her cheeks felt warm. "In a way I do not blame Jai. He is rich, good-looking and visibly virile so the women flock to him like bees to a honey pot."

"Like Sujata?" She had not meant to ask, for there was something humiliating about her nagging interest in the woman.

"You have met Sujata?" Kinjal exclaimed in astonishment.

"Once." Unable to withdraw the question, Olivia fumbled through a hasty explanation of the circumstances, then inexplicably committed another unwanted indiscretion. "Is he not in love with Sujata?"

Listening not so much to the words but to the impulse that had prompted the inquiry, Kinjal turned melancholy. "Love is an emotion with which Jai is unfamiliar," she said sadly. "He neither understands it nor accepts it in his vocabulary. No, he is not in love with Sujata or with any other woman." She paused as if to underline the significance of her forthcoming words. "Nor, perhaps, can he ever be."

This then, these final six words, were the crux!

They dropped one by one onto Olivia's ears but penetrated her consciousness only superficially. He did not love Sujata! For the moment nothing else that Kinjal had said made any resounding impact. The haunting image of that swift moment of intimacy that had been gnawing away at Olivia's inner mind receded. Now she thought only of another vision, equally haunting, when she had lain in the howdah pressed to his chest, when warmth from his breath had fanned her cheek, when she had glimpsed something in his eyes as nebulous as a passing cloud. Making a circle of her arms, she hugged her knees but kept her face averted so that Kinjal could not observe her contented expression.

"I accept everything you say, Kinjal," she murmured, following with her smiling eyes the path of an owl as it swooped past into the trees, "but I am curious to know why you should consider it necessary to *warn* me. True, I find Mr. Raventhorne intriguing and his background is remarkably unusual, but"—to give her subterfuge credence, she raised a laugh—"on the strength of such slender interest, I am unlikely to become one of those endless women!"

"I have said all this to you, Olivia, because although I am overjoyed that you did come, you must be made aware of the false pretences that have engineered your visit." She spoke with a great gentleness. "Had I not found you so compatible, so unlike other white women I have met, I would have held my tongue. But I think of you already as a friend. I owe it to you to be honest. Please tell me that you are not offended."

"No, I am not offended in the least!" Olivia exclaimed, touched by the sentiments and the concern. "I am only . . . amused. Mr. Raventhorne might be admirable in many ways, but I assure you I find him eminently resistible."

Had she lied? In the conflicting dictates of her emotions, Olivia was again unsure. The reality of Jai Raventhorne was still too outrageous to have taken root in her mind; *was* it only her active imagination that gave him an aura of such disturbing magnetism?

Olivia was relieved that the opportunity to talk about Jai Raventhorne did not arise again for the remainder of her visit.

"You paid *one anna* each for the alligator pears?"

"One anna each."

"And you say you bought *two* chickens? I counted only two drumsticks in the mulligatawny last night!"

Lesser mortals might have quailed before Lady Bridget's gimlet gaze but Babulal was made of sterner stuff. "*Two* fowl, *four* drumstick," he intoned without flinching, his eyes turning accusingly in Estelle's direction as she sat apparently engrossed in one of the melodramatic novelettes that circulated tirelessly among her friends.

Lady Bridget's eyes were the first to drop. She abandoned one battle front to open another. Tapping her household accounts ledger, she attacked from an unguarded flank. "I myself bought two dozen kitchen dusters not more than three weeks ago. Do you mean to tell me that *twenty-four* brand-new and sturdy pieces of cloth . . . ?"

Sitting quietly in a corner reading the very first mail packet she had received from her father, Olivia resolutely shut her ears to the daily harangues. She was beginning to believe that hot wrangles over bazaar accounts were the favourite entertainment of Calcutta's mems, the consequent victories and defeats premier topics of conversation at *burra khanas.* Most European women were contemptuous of their retinues of domestic staff even though they could hardly do without them, but Lady Bridget's aversion to those who inhabited her vast servants' compound appeared to be excessive. True, the population below the stairs, figuratively speaking, was massive; there were bearers, *abdars,* khidmutgars, gardeners, coachmen, *chowkidars,* punkahwallahs, water carriers, sweepers, kitchen boys, stable boys and the two ayahs, and in addition, their prolific families. They all had the length of Lady Bridget's tongue from time to time and, Olivia had heard it said, also a taste of Sir Joshua's hunting crop, for his temper could be volatile. It was a situation Olivia abhorred, but attitudes and prejudices were so deeply entrenched, she could do nothing about it and seldom interfered.

Estelle, of course, had no such inhibitions. "If you detest servants so much, Mama," she lost no time in pointing out as soon as Babulal had been dismissed, "why do we have so many? It's only because you can't do without them, isn't it?"

"And you can, I suppose? Don't *you* talk, miss, until you can learn to keep your own room from looking like a shipwreck! You'll find out soon enough when you have your own household what thieving, indolent—"

"Papa sends everyone his warm regards." Noting that Estelle was still spoiling for a fight, Olivia quickly intervened. "He says the weather in the islands is glorious even though the stench of blubber isn't. He's still on that whaler."

Blubber! Lady Bridget controlled herself with an effort. "How very kind of Sean," she murmured, trying to look interested. "Do reciprocate on our behalves when you reply. Anyway," she closed her ledger with a snap and rose from her desk, "I'm pleased that you enjoyed your weekend and that the Maharani wasn't too dreadful, but how odd that there should have been no other European guests. Generally these shooting parties are like tamashas, circuses really." She frowned, still smarting under her husband's wilful destruction of her carefully laid plans. "I hope he at least had the decency to keep you away from his harem."

"Well, if Arvind Singh has one, we saw no evidence of it," Olivia answered, amused by the comment. "He doesn't appear to be that kind of a gentleman."

"They're all that kind! Do you think the sanctity of marriage means anything to people who burn widows on funeral pyres?"

"Well, *I* haven't noticed much sanctity in the Haworths, for instance, Mama," Estelle piped up. "Everyone knows what *she* does with Bill Corliss when he comes to tune her piano each week, and it's common knowledge that *he's* gone all native with that woman from Cossipore. To say nothing of the taradiddles they tell about that half-caste brat passed off as . . ."

Silently, Olivia crept out of the room, despairing of Estelle ever learning how to keep her mouth shut and when.

Upstairs in the quiet of her room, Olivia sat down to read her father's letter again, her throat tight with happiness. He had not yet received any of hers, of course, but when he did the flow would be steady. Much of what her father wrote had to do with his investigation, which was proceeding satisfactorily. The information he was collecting, he said, was very significant and useful. There was a paragraph or two about the forthcoming elections at home, where the heat was on. The rest of the letter was about Hawaii, where, he thought, Honolulu was emerging fast as the most important port and town in the Pacific. "However, the verdant scene one sees from the ship is deceptive. Except for the mountains and some valleys, the land is hard, dry and barren, and water is not easy to come by. But I might be fortunate in getting some land with natural irrigation near by although it is rare."

Olivia frowned. Was he planning a long stay on the islands? She would have to wait to find out, for he gave no further explanations. A separate letter was all about Sacramento and the ranch. Greg was managing well in her absence (ten more longhorns from old Matty gotten dirt-cheap since he's moving to Texas), and Sally's Dane and Dirk were beginning to sprout 'taches. Sally had had a good offer for her lending-library from an ex-Yale man and was thinking of selling because there was grave concern among the locals about the recent discovery of gold in California, of which the papers were full. "It will start a stampede," her father warned. "Every scoundrel, murderer and rotten apple in the United States will be heading West, Livvie. I fear for our State, darling, for there is no end to man's greed and lust for gold." He concluded the letter with "Enjoy yourself, sweetheart, and do your best to utilise the opportunity your aunt has made available to you. I know it cannot be easy for you, for the rules that prevail there are different from what you have known. But England too, my dear child, is part of your heritage. However strange, you must never reject it, for it comes to you from your beloved mother. Use her gift to the full but remember when you go to bed each night and commune with your heart in silence that you have an old Dad somewhere who holds you more precious than his life."

Olivia refolded the letter, the ache in her heart fierce and her eyes brimming. What would she not give now for an hour, just one hour, of her father's infallible advice when her unwanted "heritage" was drawing her into a maze of such terrible indecision!

A knock sounded on the door and her aunt entered. "I forgot to mention, dear, that Lady Birkhurst has kindly invited us for tea tomorrow. We will leave at four. I have had your blue linen pressed, and you won't forget the white belt, will you, dear?"

"No, I will not," Olivia assured her gloomily, then stood up and decided to take the bull by the horns. "I am deeply grateful for your concern and for everything that you are doing for me, Aunt Bridget, but I feel I must now make something clear to you. I have no intentions whatsoever of marrying Mr. Birkhurst. It would be wrong to raise any false hopes he might be entertaining."

"Marry?" Lady Bridget's expression was of innocence incarnate. "My dear child, nobody has said anything about *marriage!* Surely you do not object to sharing a few casual moments with someone who has been kind enough to seek our company, especially in view of our previous cancellation, which she accepted most graciously."

The aggrieved tone did not fool Olivia, but she had made her point. "No, of course not," she agreed grudgingly, "I would be pleased to accompany you and Estelle to Lady Birkhurst's."

"Incidentally, dear," Lady Bridget hesitated, "I called on her personally last Saturday to inform her that you were ill. It would therefore be imprudent to mention anything about your weekend in Kirtinagar. Will you remember that?"

Olivia sighed. "Yes, Aunt Bridget. I will remember that."

But after five o'clock that afternoon, nobody was to remember anything save that Sir Joshua had returned home surprisingly early and that his face looked like thunder. Without exchanging a word with anyone, he had stormed into his study and slammed the door behind him. "What's happened, Mama?" Estelle looked nervous. "Why is Papa in such a terrible rage?"

As she descended the stairs, Lady Bridget's face was equally pale. She did not answer Estelle's question, or rather, chose not to. Instead, she merely stood staring at the study door as if mesmerized into immobility. Then, attempting a recovery, she continued her passage down the flight. "No doubt some fracas at the office," she said calmly. "You know how strongly your father tends to react to trivialities. He will be over it by supper-time." But in her blue eyes the fear remained.

Sir Joshua was not "over it" by supper-time. Indeed, his mood was such that he refused food entirely, preferring his own company behind barred doors. Through their own meal in the dining-room, Lady Bridget remained abstracted and there was little conversation. Even Estelle did not dare to chatter as she usually did. When the meal was finished, Lady Bridget prepared a tray of food in the pantry for her husband and entrusted it to Olivia.

"Josh likes to talk to you about his affairs, dear. Perhaps you can find out the reason for his foul mood." She smiled bravely. "You see, he won't believe me but he does need a holiday. He works too long and too hard for his health to bear the strain."

Inside the study there was darkness. Olivia could discern her uncle's outline against the window, since the curtains had not been drawn. In the gloom the tip of his cigar glowed a dull red, brightening each time he pulled on it. Olivia stood watching for a moment, then cleared her throat.

"Bridget?"

She groped for his desk and put the tray on it. "No, Uncle Josh, it is I, Olivia." He did not speak. "Aunt Bridget has sent in some cold meat and a fresh bottle of port."

It was only after she had lit the paraffin lamps and tidied the desk to make room for his plate and glass that he finally turned. "Sit down, Olivia."

She did, watching him in worried silence as he walked to his chair and sank down heavily. "What is wrong, Uncle Josh? You look so . . . strange. Are you not feeling well?" There was no longer rage in his face, but what lurked in the rutted lines that radiated from his set mouth was still ominous.

"We have had bad news from Gupta." His tone was clipped. Without paying attention to what he was doing he speared a slice of meat with his fork, shoved it roughly into his mouth and champed on it. Olivia waited while he chewed grimly through the piled meat and washed it down with a glass of port. "Our consignment of opium from north Bengal has been looted en route."

"Looted? By thuggees?"

"So Gupta concludes." He dabbed his mouth with the corner of a napkin, tossed it carelessly on the tray and leaned back.

"But you obviously believe otherwise?"

He smiled very grimly. "Yes. I believe otherwise. Gupta writes that he was badly wounded but nobody was killed. Either the thuggees are getting soft or Gupta is a bloody liar!"

A cold prickle touched Olivia's heart. The thuggees, she had heard, were a fanatic religious band who believed they could murder by divine sanction. Until a decade ago, when John Sleeman became Commissioner for the Suppression of Thuggee and Dacoity, they perpetrated widespread slaughter across northern India using lassos to rope in victims as expertly as any cowboy on the range. The one virtue thuggees were not known for even now, when thousands had been apprehended and condemned to death, was mercy; nor had they ever believed in half measures.

"Why should Gupta lie?" Olivia asked. "You have always considered him a loyal retainer."

"Why?" he barked, his anger surfacing again. "For the oldest reason in the world—thirty pieces of silver! Loyalty, my dear girl, is a highly negotiable commodity among natives, more so when they close ranks against what they believe to be a common enemy, the British. Gupta is a *bania,* a caste loyal only to mammon. When the price was right, he reverted to type."

"Was the opium worth much?" She did not ask who the donor of the thirty pieces of silver might be; she already had a fair idea.

"A hundred thousand pounds in profits from Canton, if a tenth of that here. But the opium is insured." He waved it aside angrily. "What we stand to lose with those hongs is face, and credibility. In this race, time is money, and we've also lost time." He snatched up some papers to make rapid calculations.

Olivia had learned from him already a great deal about Bengal's thriving opium trade, the only remaining and inviolate Company monopoly. With tea also thrown open to private enterprise since 1833, it was now opium—and the Company's massive land revenue collections in India—that provided its shareholders in London with their rich annual dividends. The Company supervised strictly the cultivation and sale of opium in India, although illicit trading also thrived. In theory, British merchants operated in Canton under licence from the Company, but in practice foreign traders in opium also flourished, cocking a snook at the Company's rules. Indeed, many British traders also evaded the rules neatly by taking out foreign naturalisation papers and sailing under alien flags. In the China Coast trade, opium and tea were inseparable. Even though opium was contraband in China, it was the only commodity against which tea could be purchased from the hongs, powerful Chinese merchants. Many believed, including Sir Joshua, that without these charmed twins of trade, the very Empire would be hard pressed to exist. Annual trade figures told their own story: In the last year the Company's revenue from opium was nearly three and a half million pounds sterling; in England alone more than fifty-six and a half million pounds in weight of tea had been sold. Each shipload of opium that Templewood and Ransome dispatched to Canton therefore translated into tea and, consequently, into enormous sterling profits at home and in domestic Indian markets. So Olivia could understand the extent of her uncle's fury.

"Can the police do nothing to identify the . . . culprits?" she asked. If Raventhorne *had* engineered the theft, it seemed monstrous that he should be allowed to get away with it.

Sir Joshua's laugh crackled with contempt. "Old Slocum will go through the motions, but he will discover nothing; he never does. Not one native will squeal. They never do."

"But weren't there European escorts with the consignment?"

"Two." His lips curled with greater contempt. "What makes you think thirty pieces of silver are unwelcome to John Company's officers on starvation wages in their army? Both claim to have been away from the scene answering calls of nature when the ambush occurred. Our own twenty mercenary soldiers naturally tell twenty different stories." He sank into an incensed silence.

Not wishing to throw salt on substantial wounds, Olivia considered it best to steer the conversation into more agreeable channels. "How did you find Arvind Singh's note, Uncle Josh? Was it encouraging, do you think?"

He roused himself and his expression appeared to clear. "Yes, I would say so." He adjusted his gold-rimmed half-moon glasses, opened a folder and withdrew a sheet embossed with the Kirtinagar crest. He nodded in some satisfaction as he read it through again. "Yes, definitely encouraging, I'd say. It was good of you to carry it back with you."

"Then he accepts your proposal?"

"Not yet, but it will come. It's too early for a full-mouthed bite, but he's certainly sniffing at the bait. He said nothing more to you, did he, by any chance?"

Olivia had already given her uncle a fair (albeit abridged) account of her weekend. She shook her head and examined her nails. "No. But Arvind Singh didn't strike me as a man greedy for money, Uncle Josh."

"Greed is a matter of degree. The language of money, my dear, is sweet—and Arvind Singh is as hungry to hear it as anyone. He desperately needs funds for that irrigation project. He would give his right hand to start right away, and his coal will not yield profits for years. We offer him immediate gains. Oh, he's greedy all right, only the price he wants is higher. But there's a long way to go still, a long way for us." He closed his eyes and massaged his lids with his finger-tips, suddenly weary.

The lines of fatigue on his face were very obvious and Olivia filled with concern for him. "Aunt Bridget is right," she said gently, leaning forward to touch his hand, "you do need a holiday, Uncle Josh. A few days in Barrackpore will work wonders. I hear the fishing there is excellent."

"Barrackpore?" His eyes shot open and he frowned. "Don't be absurd, Olivia, I can't possibly leave station now with this police investigation pending! Bridget will have to go on her own with you girls."

Again alert, he sat up to gather a sheaf of papers and start reading. Olivia knew that she was being dismissed.

If you do not wish to go to Barrackpore, you will not. Take my word for it. It was while Olivia was supervising the nightly ritual of having the mosquito-net tucked around the mattress on her bed that she suddenly remembered Jai Raventhorne's parting sentences to her. Quickly sending away the ayah, she sank down in a chair to think, the sick feeling inside her stronger than ever. Who better than Raventhorne could have given her that assurance? And what more substantial proof could one need of his complicity in this spiteful and petty act of vandalism?

There were many in India, Olivia conceded to herself, who had grave reservations about the opium trade. But she doubted personally if Jai Raventhorne's aversion was based on any lofty principles of morality. His motivations were purely vengeful. Whatever compassion she might have recently felt for that miserably deprived urchin of Kinjal's tale died. However wronged he might have once been by the divinities, now he deserved only censure.

"The trouble with cucumber is," Lady Birkhurst remarked as she nibbled a scone and avoided the sandwiches, "that it makes one repeat. Would you agree, Lady Bridget?"

"Er, yes. Yes, of course."

"Tomatoes, on the other hand, do not." As endorsement she chose a sandwich from a second plate. "At least, not that I've ever noticed. Have you?"

"Er, no. Not at all."

"The seeds are a nuisance certainly. They stick between the teeth, which is embarrassing at parties where they *will* give you those coarse bamboo splints that make discreet toothpicking such an impossibility, don't you think?"

Trying bravely to make the best of a one-sided conversation,

Lady Bridget again hastened to agree. Lady Birkhurst's marked preference for the sound of her own voice to the exclusion of others was, Olivia considered, a distinct advantage. Her single choice of topic, however—food, the passion of both her life and her conversation—was becoming dreary. They had now been at the splendid mansion on the Esplanade for almost an hour and the matter of gustatory delights or otherwise still prevailed with unflagging energy. Sitting to Lady Birkhurst's right, Olivia listened in glum silence, having long since abandoned her monosyllabic contributions as unnecessary. Her aunt, hawk-eyed and eager, sat opposite her across the low onyx-topped table with burnished brass legs. Freddie, hair slicked back and collar as stiff and starched as his face, perched on a window seat conversing in low tones with Estelle. He did not look comfortable; his face brightened only when he cast longing glances at Olivia, who carefully did not return them.

"I am not at all certain," Lady Birkhurst was saying, suddenly deserting her favoured subject, "that I approve entirely of Freddie's domestic arrangements. He has too many servants and his control over them is deplorably inadequate." She had a habit of talking about her son in the third person even when he was present. Freddie didn't appear to mind; in fact he beamed.

Lady Bridget looked visibly relieved to be once again on familiar, well-trammelled territory. "Oh, I quite agree that to have too many is to invite trouble." She avoided her daughter's eye. "Especially in a bachelor household." Her emphasis on "bachelor" brought colour to Olivia's cheeks, but her aunt was not to be thwarted now from the course she had charted for herself. Turning to Freddie she pronounced, "Tight control is the answer, Mr. Birkhurst. I trust you do see to that at least sometimes?"

Freddie continued to beam. "Certainly. I give them my instructions and then, well, let them get on with them."

"And, of course, you do keep a strict account of your daily disbursements?" Lady Bridget's eye glinted.

"Most definitely, Lady Bridget. At least Salim, my bearer, does. On the first of the month I hand him one thousand rupees and between him and my cook, Rashid Ali, the house runs like clockwork."

Lady Bridget paled. "One thousand rup—?" Words failed her. Picking up her fan she waved it vigorously across her face. "Dear me, dear *me,* Mr. Birkhurst. I run my household on *half* that!"

Catching Estelle's eye, Olivia quickly averted her head to suppress her impending giggles. Estelle coughed, thrust a biscuit into her mouth—making the most of her mother's diverted attention—and got up to examine with apparently consuming interest the exquisitely appointed drawing-room with its gilded mirrors, Louis Quinze chairs, ebony and walnut cabinets, brocade drapes and finely woven French tapestries. Forced to remain where she was, Olivia merely continued to look demure in her pressed blue linen (with white belt), her lashes lowered modestly, but within her hating every moment of the pointless charade.

Lady Birkhurst listened closely to Lady Bridget's earnest dissertation on the need for vigilance with a native staff, then snorted. "My son has very little sense of money, Lady Bridget," she commented drily, signalling for the cake stand to be passed around. "He believes it grows on trees and can be depended upon to provide two healthy cash crops a year." She raised her lorgnette and withered him with a look. "What Freddie needs is more occupation."

Nominally, Freddie was head of his father's thriving businesses but it was known that he seldom attended his office. The Farrowsham Agency House was run very competently by a dour, canny Scotsman called Willie Donaldson, who made no secret of the fact that his theoretical superior was paid his handsome sinecure to leave well enough alone rather than participate in the firm. A much-favoured joke of Calcutta was that Freddie and Willie scarcely saw each other because the former went to bed when the latter woke up to go to work, and vice versa. But in spite of his short-comings, Freddie was astonishingly popular in station, and not only with mothers of marriageable daughters, for two reasons: He was generous to a fault and he was so good-natured that it was almost impossible to give him offence. He grinned sheepishly at his mother.

"What Mr. Birkhurst needs," Lady Bridget said, firmly getting down to brass tacks, "is a wife."

Olivia's eyes shut in a storm of embarrassment; Estelle's back was towards them as she gazed intently into a glass-fronted display cupboard with an arrangement of enamelled French snuff-boxes, but her shoulders shook silently. Lady Birkhurst shifted positions to swivel her lorgnette in Olivia's direction and examined her closely. "Ah yes," she murmured. "That too." Olivia simmered in silence but there was little she could do to escape the meticulous scrutiny. "I understand you are from our colonies across the Atlantic, Miss O'Rourke?"

It was the first direct question Olivia had been asked. "Yes, Lady Birkhurst, but America is no longer a colony. We declared our independence way back in 1776."

There was a short silence. Lowering her lorgnette, Lady Birkhurst set about polishing it briskly; Lady Bridget merely gazed out of the window as if fascinated by a crow. "Once a colony, always a colony," the baroness declared, challenging a denial. "It is a matter of principle. I take it you do miss your home?"

"Well, I—"

"Olivia adores to travel, Lady Birkhurst." Her aunt's interruption aborted possible further indiscretions. "Alas, like other gentlemen of achievement, her dear father can spare little time for it himself. Olivia is delighted with the opportunity to be with us for a year."

"Hmmm." The lorgnette polished to her satisfaction, Lady Birkhurst replaced the energy thus expended by helping herself to a slice of cherry cake. Back in her window seat, so did Estelle. If there was one person in that room who was warming towards Lady Birkhurst as a kindred soul, it was Olivia's cousin.

"The O'Rourkes live in California, but of course Sean has residences elsewhere as well, isn't that right, dear?" Olivia opened her mouth more in amazement than to issue an indignant denial, but her aunt forged ahead anyway. "Had my beloved sister been alive, she would have ensured that Olivia came out properly in a manner befitting their station. With so many other corporate responsibilities, poor Sean has little time for social conventions." She sat back and dabbed each eye with a puff of lace.

"Quite." Lady Birkhurst nodded in sympathy, a large glass bowl of fruit now claiming her entire attention. "I was greatly disappointed at having missed the mango season this year. Caleb's health is far from satisfactory and he insists that no one can tend his carbuncles as well as I can. I'm never sure whether to be flattered or not. However," she leaned forward as if about to deliver a message of unique importance to the gathering, "what has truly caught my fancy now is a funny little thing called an alligator pear. I don't remember ever having seen any in Hogg's market. Are you at all acquainted with this quite delicious novelty, Lady Bridget?"

"Alligator pears?" Lady Bridget was instantly alert. "Yes, I do know them. I understand they are being cultivated in the south by some adventurous army wives who secured the seeds from a passing Brazilian. Could you possibly tell me how much you paid for them, Lady Birkhurst?" The glint in her eye boded no good for Babulal.

Lady Birkhurst looked at her son and Freddie looked blank. "Haven't the foggiest idea, I'm afraid, but I could easily find out for you."

Lady Bridget was unlikely not to strike while the iron was hot. Nor, for that matter, to kill two birds with a single stone. "Perhaps, with your permission, I can find out for myself." She rose with alacrity. "In any case, Estelle and I have been looking forward to inspecting your kitchen house, Mr. Birkhurst. Would you be so kind as to lead us to it?"

"What an excellent idea!" Lady Birkhurst looked pointedly at her son. "Rashid Ali is greatly concerned about termites. They get into everything, he says. With your own vast experience, Lady Bridget, perhaps you could give him some advice. And of course Freddie will escort you and Estelle there."

"Oh, splendid!" Not quite sure what was happening, and looking a little bewildered, Freddie nevertheless rose to the occasion. "I'm not absolutely certain which the kitchen house is but I daresay we can sniff our way to it eventually."

They trooped out in single file with Estelle casting her eyes heavenward and surreptitiously extracting another biscuit for sustenance en route while Olivia's spirits plummeted downward into her dainty blue sandals purchased that morning to match her dress. She was furious with her aunt for letting her into a situation she found so utterly untenable, and waited with visible anger for the dreaded inquisition to commence.

"Would you care for an apple, Miss O'Rourke?" Olivia shook her head. "You need to put on some fat, my dear. Your hips are far too narrow. Good breeding stock is never lean and hungry like Shakespeare's Cassius, and the secret lies in the haunches. Here." Lady Birkhurst patted her own ample derriere, and Olivia looked away. "Tell me, did the tiger shoot come up to your expectations?"

Olivia gasped. She *knew* the truth about her weekend?

Lady Birkhurst reached for a grape and placed it delicately between her teeth. "I remember my first shoot in the jungle way back in twenty-two. We never even saw a whisker of the wretched tiger, but one young cavalry officer in our party got carried away and shot a shikari in the knee. There was an almighty uproar over that. The poor man had to face a court martial, give the hunter all kinds of compensation and then be posted in some remote swamp infested with crocodiles. Ruined his engagement, too—the girl wouldn't hear of settling down in a bog. So much for true love." She bit into a second grape.

Olivia swallowed, red faced and still speechless.

Lady Birkhurst's watery blue eyes twinkled faintly. "Don't worry, Miss O'Rourke, we all tell social white lies on occasion. It's quite the accepted thing, I assure you. If I had been in your shoes I too would have chosen a shoot rather than a dismal luncheon at the Tolly with a lot of stuffed-shirt gas-bags and all that horse dung."

Finally, Olivia's breath released itself with a whoosh. "I enjoyed the shoot very much, Lady Birkhurst," she said steadily. "We managed to bag the tiger. It was a man-eater."

Lady Birkhurst nodded her approval, then laid a plump, spongy hand over Olivia's. "I would rather you did not tell your aunt that I saw through her little fabrication. It would embarrass her and I would not like to do that. Now, to come to my next question, what do you think of Calcutta?"

Olivia hesitated but only briefly; if her aunt refused to take her attitude seriously, she would see that no such misapprehension remained in Lady Birkhurst's mind. "To be frank, Lady Birkhurst, I am not much taken with it although India as a country I realise is fascinating."

"Indeed! May I ask what your objections are to Calcutta?"

"Well, in the main, I find society here narrow, frivolous and quite uninspiring, especially the ladies. I am not used to an environment in which there are so many restrictions, not that my aunt and uncle have not been kindness itself to me," she added hastily. "My life here is marvellously comfortable in every way. It is just the artificiality of our existence so divorced from the surrounding realities that I find difficult to adjust to." She was surprised that she should be talking so openly to an Englishwoman she had met not two hours ago, but if she didn't say all this now she knew she might never have another chance before matters got out of hand.

"Upon my word!" Lady Birkhurst peered narrowly into Olivia's face, flushed and defiant. "I see that you *do* have a mind of your own!"

"I am sorry if I have been blunt, Lady Birkhurst, but in America that is our way. I do not mean to give offence, I merely wish to be perfectly straight in my answers to you."

Quite unexpectedly, Lady Birkhurst laughed. It was a strange sound, almost a cackle, and her pendulous jowls shivered like blobs of blancmange. "Well, good for you, my dear! I like women who show spirit and call a spade exactly what it is. For one, it saves time. We will get on well, Miss O'Rourke, I can see that." Raising an imperious finger, she summoned a uniformed bearer.

As she dipped each finger delicately into the bowl of warm water the bearer laid before her, Olivia examined her hostess with interest for the first time. With her obvious eccentricities she fitted into no mould Olivia had seen so far in Calcutta, and her attitudes, to say the least, were most unusual. She was a very large woman with a strong, decisive voice, and her hair, white and shiny, was arranged in a series of tight curls in a style far too young for her. Waves of loose flesh hung everywhere, from under her chin right down to her flabby wrists, and the hanging jowls gave her the look of a rather mournful spaniel. Her appearance, to all intents and purposes, was formidable, but her small, button-like eyes that dug deep into heavy lids showed signs of a humour Olivia would not have earlier considered possible.

"Are you serious about returning home when your year is up?" Lady Birkhurst dried each finger-tip with a napkin and sat back again.

"Quite serious."

"And the prospect of extending that period does not appeal to you under any circumstances?"

An unexpected and flash image rose in Olivia's mind's eye of Jai Raventhorne, but, angry with herself, she discarded it immediately. "No. Much as I enjoy being with my uncle and aunt and, of course, Estelle, I have to think of my father, who is alone in . . ." She stopped; in view of her aunt's dreadful fictions, was it wise to mention her father?

"I see." Lady Birkhurst seemed uninterested in her father. "Now tell me, Olivia—I may call you that, may I not? All these formalities are so tedious and goodness knows I get enough of them at home with Caleb's pompous friends in the House of Lords." With some difficulty she heaved herself onto a side so that she could face Olivia. "What do you think of my son?"

The bald question, without either preliminaries or warning, winded Olivia. With all Lady Birkhurst's forthrightness she had not expected so frontal an attack. "I . . . he . . . that is . . ." She faded into scarlet-faced silence, threading fidgety fingers through each other.

"Freddie is, of course, besotted with you," Lady Birkhurst proceeded calmly, "which is hardly surprising. You are most presentable and I myself have seldom seen such long legs on an English girl. So far, my son's taste in women has been, frankly, deplorable. However," she paused to offer Olivia a sweet mint from a silver bowl, took one herself and continued, "I have the impression that Freddie does not appeal to you as much as you do to him—am I right?"

"I . . . hardly know how to answer that . . . ," Olivia muttered unhappily.

"Answer it with perfect frankness. I would appreciate it." A sudden shudder rippled through her huge frame and she sank back into the cushions. "My son, Olivia, is the most sought-after bachelor on two continents. He can have the pick of London and colonial society, and why not?" She snorted. "His family is wealthy, titled, with a seventeenth-century seat in Suffolk and one of the most elegant estates in England. Freddie will one day be the eighth Lord Birkhurst of Farrowsham since our two other children are girls. In the marriage market that alone makes him a plum prize." She paused to let it all sink in. "At the same time I am also aware that my son is an idiot, unblessed by anything even closely resembling intelligence."

"Oh, that is perhaps—"

Lady Birkhurst stayed Olivia's gallant attempt at protest with an impatient gesture. "I have long since come to terms with the truth, Olivia. Freddie is not only a fool, he is an inebriate, a weakling and a dedicated debauch." She emitted a short laugh that had no humour. "It no longer wounds me as it once did, Olivia. I am a confirmed realist, which is why I know that if Freddie marries one of his own—rich, spoilt, mindless and self-indulgent—he will be destroyed." The diluted, darting blue eyes went as flat as her tone. "Freddie is headed for perdition. He drinks like a fish, whores like a randy beggar and abuses his body without remorse. I am not a prude, Olivia, far from it. I accept that young men need to expend certain energies in order to expand others. When Caleb was younger, his doxies were black, white, blue and brindle—and in plenty. But Freddie's constitution is weak; it cannot tolerate his excesses much longer. If he is not leashed soon, within a year he will be dead."

Olivia was shocked. Yet, beneath the seeming lack of emotion with which Lady Birkhurst had made her terrible pronouncement, she sensed the profound sorrow of an embittered mother. Determined as she was to reject the ludicrous proposition, sheer compassion silenced Olivia for the moment.

"For his salvation Freddie needs a woman of strength," Lady

Birkhurst continued in the same unvarying tones. "A woman of character, of good horse sense, sober, and unused to frivolous luxury. Whether or not she loves him is irrelevant. As long as she takes care of him, stiffens his spine, accepts and forgives his faults, which are many, and of course provides him with an heir, I will be content."

Olivia stared at her, almost laughing out her incredulity. Could any girl of "strength" and "character" possibly agree to such a nefarious bargain? And with what cavalier disregard the need for love had been dismissed! As if reading her thoughts, Lady Birkhurst said sharply, "Love passes; material compensations persist, Olivia." She leaned towards her, the watery blue eyes hard and her voice even more matter of fact. "Consider, Olivia, that there would be no threshold in the world over which Freddie's wife would not be welcome. An English title, even without money, is held in high regard also in America; *with* money it is the key to every door. Besides, there is one compensation I have not yet mentioned . . ." She paused and stared at her corpulent knuckles. "Whatever his inadequacies, Freddie is generous of heart. He asks little of others, which is perhaps, why he is such a fool. His wife would enjoy many freedoms not available to others. Do I make myself clear?"

If Olivia was shocked earlier, she was now scandalised. "Yes, *quite* clear, Lady Birkhurst. Obviously, you do not find it iniquitous that a man should be expected to tolerate an openly unfaithful wife!" Her mouth swilled with distaste at the callous "compensation."

"Freddie would not complain," his mother said drily, "if indeed he noticed at all!"

Taking a deep breath, Olivia rose to her feet to stand by a window. She could not believe that she could be participating in a conversation so bizarre and so offensive. She felt humiliated and revolted, and outraged that her aunt should have plunged her into a situation of such monumental indignity. Her inclination was to walk out of the room in disgust, but certainly not until she had expressed that disgust in terms as blunt as those Lady Birkhurst had used. She pulled herself up to her full height and turned to face her. "I am flattered by your extraordinarily high evaluation of me, Lady Birkhurst," she said as briskly as she could without sounding offensive. "I assure you that I am undeserving of such praise. And, therefore, I feel I must tell you before you proceed any further that what you suggest is impossible! I hold nothing personal against your son, but a cold-blooded bargain such as this revolts me. Since you asked me to be forthright, Lady Birkhurst, I have to say that I find your proposition utterly unacceptable—although I have no doubt that some others might not." Having said her piece she sat down again, her cheeks hot with the effort.

Lady Birkhurst appeared untroubled by her outburst as she leaned forward to pluck a grape from the fruit bowl. "The others!" she rasped in contempt. "They see nothing beyond the glory, the title and wealth—"

"And are you so certain that eventually *I* too will not turn mercenary?" Olivia cut in spiritedly. "We Americans are also snobbish about titles, as you yourself pointed out. Also, you must be told that my father isn't—"

"My dear child, I wasn't born yesterday! I have married off two daughters and I know that in the marriage market there are certain permissible liberties one takes with the truth. Frankly, I do not much care who or what your father is. As the daughter of Lady Bridget's sister, you satisfy any requirements of pedigree I might have. I am interested only in what and who *you* are."

"But you know nothing about me!" Olivia cried in mounting desperation. "And if you did, you would also know that I could never barter away my life for—"

"I know what is necessary for me to know." She waved away Olivia's protest almost with anger. "You are young, healthy, lovely to look at, of sound character and mind, straightforward, intelligent, with a will of your own and—as long as you put on some weight—excellent breeding stock. Also, let us not forget that Freddie worships the ground you walk on." She clucked as if in exasperation. "Not one day passes without some silly woman dragging her pampered little brat here for my inspection, like a milch cow up for auction. Every one of them has reduced me to nausea. They are already die-hard mems, infantile and indolent, with no thought in their empty heads save the next *burra khana* or cricket game or pig sticking tamasha where they can ogle and be ogled by young men. They come here with probing, avaricious eyes evaluating my jewels, already arranging and rearranging my furniture, practising silently their new signatures on documents that will make them rich overnight."

Pinned to her chair by the needle-pointed stare, Olivia started to feel trapped even as her temper rose. Whatever Lady Birkhurst's problems with her wretched son, why should *she* be involved in devising solutions? But, out of consideration for the woman's obvious unhappiness, Olivia kept her tone controlled.

"First appearances are deceptive, Lady Birkhurst. Among those you discard there must be at least one who will be as you wish."

Lady Birkhurst sighed. "I am more than sixty years old, Olivia. If I have learned anything as the wife of a gentleman farmer, it is to separate the wheat from the chaff. When you walked in today you looked neither left nor right. You had no desire to impress, although your aunt did. You, in fact, showed signs of deep resentment, of anger. You still do." She chuckled softly. "No other girl would have agreed to miss luncheon with us last Sunday. Indeed, they would have all come leaping and bounding like spring lambs anxious to put in their bids before others did. Even now, though you do me the favour of listening to me, all that is on your mind is flight." She laughed again and patted Olivia's hand. "No, Olivia. In this case, first appearances are not deceptive, which is why I have taken the liberty of making you a proposition that would be, to a woman such as you, iniquitous. And," she breathed in sadly, "also a seeming paradox. I choose you because you are not impressed by money and title, and yet these are the very inducements I use to tempt you!"

Despite her inner rage, Olivia could not suppress an involuntary stab of admiration for Lady Birkhurst's courage. It could not have been easy to swallow pride and resort to such brutal honesty. "I am sorry that my answer has not come up to your expectations," she began gently.

"You have made your opinion known to me frankly, Olivia, and for that I am grateful," Lady Birkhurst interrupted, clasping her hand. Her tone was pleading. "But I beg of you, don't say anything more yet. All I ask of you is the favour of giving at least some more thought to what I have been bold enough to suggest. I have opened my heart to you, Olivia, because you are too astute to be given less. If after further thought you still refuse, as I fear you will, I will of course be bitterly disappointed and poor Freddie will be distraught, but I will accept your decision without either argument or rancour. Freddie intends to speak to you soon, but he will, as usual, make a hash of it. This is why I wished to say my piece earlier." Like a deflating balloon she shrivelled into her chair and her shoulders sagged. "You must forgive me, my dear, for having shocked and perhaps repelled you, but I am so tired of pretences, so tired. I am just an unhappy, aging woman, perhaps foolish and garrulous as well, who would like to see her only son produce an heir before he dies." Tears glistened in the corners of her eyes. "No matter what Freddie is, Olivia, I do love him to distraction. To balance his faults he has many fine qualities and in his own way he deserves the best from me. In my panic to ensure his salvation I have perhaps not been tactful, but it breaks my heart to watch him destroy himself while I stand by unable to do anything . . ."

Olivia would not have thought it possible to feel sympathy for anyone who could have originated so immoral and insulting a scheme, but that was what she found herself feeling. It astonished her to realise that, in spite of everything, she actually liked this extraordinarily forthright woman. "I wish that I could have comforted you in some way, Lady Birkhurst, but it would be so wrong of me to fill you with vain hope . . ."

"All I ask is that you *reconsider* your answer, Olivia," Lady Birkhurst reminded her tearfully. "And I feel we must keep our little . . . discussion between ourselves for the time being. Your aunt is a splendid woman, Olivia, but I would be distressed if she were to pressure you into a decision not of your liking. Come and see me when we return from the plantation. We plan to leave within the week."

As the rest approached from the verandah, making further discussion impossible, Olivia was flooded with relief. "How long will you be away?"

"As long as I can keep Freddie tethered away from the Golden Behind," Lady Birkhurst assured her with a grim smile.

Lady Bridget and her reluctant entourage entered noisily. "*Lids,* Mr. Birkhurst, that's the secret of hygienic kitchen management." Flushed with triumph, Lady Bridget settled herself comfortably in her chair. A visibly baffled Freddie and a rudely bored Estelle did likewise on the window seat. "All containers need lids, and Rashid Ali can easily make them out of old kerosene tins. As for white ants, I will send you some of my own home-made solution. All you must do is spray the burrow heads and, if possible, inside the holes in the walls."

There followed an energetic discussion between Lady Bridget and Lady Birkhurst about the menace of weevils in the flour and semolina and about how much extra money the cook and the chief bearer were making on the side, considering Salim had recently bought two new pairs of shoes and Rashid Ali was thinking of acquiring a third wife. Lady Bridget continued to shower Freddie with salutary suggestions on kitchen-house economics (since his mother made it quite clear she had no intentions of interfering in his messes), and then it was time to leave.

As they were about to climb into the open landau with its matched greys, Lady Bridget appeared to have a brain-storm.

"Olivia is extremely fond of riding and exploring the town, Mr. Birkhurst, and since it is unthinkable for her to wander about on her own, would you perhaps oblige by providing escort?"

Just as Olivia's face collapsed, Freddie's lit up like a beacon. Freddie as an escort? Olivia wailed inwardly, oh mercy, *no!* But it was too late. "By Jove, Lady Bridget, I would be delighted, *privileged!* We leave for the blasted plantation—begging your pardon, ladies—within the week," briefly he looked stricken, "but until we do, I am *entirely* and most *decidedly* at your service."

Mortified by her aunt's transparent ploy, Olivia glared. "I ride *very* early in the morning, Mr. Birkhurst, I warn you."

"Er, how early?" Freddie asked with a hint of alarm.

"Just about the time you eventually get to bed," Estelle muttered from behind a hand and grinned.

"No later than five o'clock," Olivia answered, deliberately moving the time back by an hour.

Freddie's Adam's apple bobbed up and down as he gulped. "Oh, ah . . . splendid, *splendid.* Then shall we say five tomorrow morning?"

"If you absolutely insist," Olivia mumbled ungraciously. With her aunt listening and watching closely, it was hardly possible to say more, but silently she fumed. As if her conversation with Lady Bridget hadn't been harrowing enough, she was now faced with the diabolical prospect of the insufferable Freddie in tow on her precious and enjoyably solitary early rides each morning! It would be an invasion of her privacy that was unforgivable, and Olivia determined not to put up with his presence for more than one occasion. But for the moment there was little she could do but concur.

"What did Lady Bridget talk to you about, dear?" The moment the carriage left the Birkhurst compound, Lady Bridget turned eagerly to her niece. "Was she . . . cordial?"

"Yes. Very. We talked about London and the life there."

"Nothing else?" Lady Bridget sounded disappointed.

"Oh, and about America and all kinds of things," Olivia said vaguely.

"Did she ask about your . . . father?"

"No."

Her aunt's sigh of relief was audible if not tactful. "Well, I'm glad she was cordial. You must go and see her again, of course, when they return from the north."

Olivia stared out of the window, her mind still clogged with the unbelievable conversation she had had. Staves of pity stabbed repeatedly at her heart. How was she ever going to face poor Lady Birkhurst again?

"I told you I was right, didn't I?" Lady Bridget suddenly exclaimed with considerable exultation.

"What about?" Estelle asked.

"I *knew* Babulal had overcharged for those alligator pears!"

6

"I say, wasn't old Lady B an absolute scream this afternoon? As for your face, darling Coz, well I thought I'd die, just *die,* trying to stifle my giggles." Sitting cross-legged on her bed, Estelle layered her cheeks with another generous coat of lanolin.

"Well, I'm glad you didn't," Olivia retorted as she brushed out her hair in front of the mirror. "If you had, who would have finished all those biscuits?"

"She'd have! Have you ever seen anyone so besotted with food?"

"Yes," Olivia teased, "you."

Estelle ignored the barb. From beneath the oily slick of face cream, her eyes glinted like those of a fox on the scent of a choice prey. "I hear that his clipper docks tomorrow night, the one that's been outfitted with a coal engine. Won't Papa be livid!"

Poker faced, Olivia gave no hint of the quick leap of her pulse. "Really? How do you know?"

"From Charlotte's cousin who works in the Customs office. He told her and she told me this morning in Whiteaways while you were buying your sandals. Imagine! The *Ganga* could do the Calcutta-London run in *thirty days!* No wonder everyone's in such high dudgeon. He threatens to wipe out all the opposition." But since her interest in the trials of the business community was minimal, Estelle soon returned to more personal worries. Throwing herself back on her pillow, she glared petulantly at the ceiling. "I'd give anything, *anything,* to be in London in thirty days! Marie says she changed her hair colour twice in three months and nobody in London batted an eyelash. God, I'm so *sick* of this same old face in the mirror every day! And compared to what Susan brought back with her, I have to dress in rags, I swear!"

Olivia laughed. "Well, it's the only face you have, sugar, and when it's not sulking it's really quite pretty, even without hybrid hair. As for your clothes, if you call them rags then the rest of us lesser mortals have to make do with sackcloth!"

Estelle refused to be comforted. "It's all very well for you," she grumbled. *"You'll* have London round the corner when you marry Freddie—"

"I'm not *going* to marry Freddie!" Olivia assured her waspishly. "And I simply won't have you spreading such a wicked canard!"

"Why ever not?" Estelle demanded. "Because of that Greg?"

"Because of *no* one. I just am not, so there." Grabbing her hairbrush and tucking it under an arm, she flounced out of the room extremely annoyed with her cousin. But even more annoying than Estelle's loose tongue was the grisly prospect of having to tolerate Freddie's tedious company on her ride the very next morning.

"I say, I'm looking forward so frightfully to these jolly old trips with you every day, Olivia." Even at five o'clock in the morning, Freddie could barely control his enthusiasm. "Where to, dear lady—the Tolly for breakfast?"

In the unflattering grey pre-dawn light, Freddie looked dreadful. His face was haggard and putty colored, the eyes shot with red. He was trying desperately not to yawn. Olivia almost melted, but didn't. On the one hand it was hardly the poor man's fault that he ruined so totally her day's greatest pleasure; on the other hand didn't he have enough sensitivity to see that he was not wanted?

"I usually cover about five miles every morning," she said heartlessly as they trotted side by side down Chowringhee Road. She sat defiantly astride, rather than side-saddle, as she always did, much to the displeasure of her aunt. "The idea is exercise and exploration rather than a social outing. Today I had planned to visit the fish market near Kidderpore."

Freddie paled further. "The fish market? Oh, I say Miss O'Rourke, er, Olivia . . . isn't that rather . . . extreme?"

"No, I don't think so," she replied very firmly. "I'd like to see the morning haul. Some of the fish brought in are quite exotic, I'm told, such as sharks and barracuda and giant turtles."

"But these native bazaars are diseased places, Olivia, filthy and smelly and with overflowing drains. And those hordes of naked brats with runny noses . . . ," he shuddered, starting to look quite sick.

His alarm was so acute that, resentfully, Olivia relented. "Oh, very well then, shall we take the horse ferry and explore the Botanical Gardens instead? I hear that the banyan tree forest is quite astonishing."

He almost collapsed in relief. Taking note of his mottled complexion, tired eyes pouched heavily with signs of high living, and the stooped shoulders that put years on him, Olivia could not but feel some sympathy for someone so bent on reaching an early grave. Inwardly, however, she reinforced her resolve; no matter how genuinely she felt for his poor mother, there was no compensation large enough to make her ludicrous proposition even remotely acceptable, even *remotely*.

They cantered past St. John's Church, said to be a replica of London's St. Martin-in-the-Fields, along the Great Tank in front of Writers' Building, and past John Company's headquarters and focal point of Calcutta's cosmopolitan mercantile world. The nucleus of the three obscure villages of Sutanuti, Kalikata and Govindpur, which Job Charnock, a Company agent, had selected in 1690 as a place for "quiet trade," had indeed mushroomed into an imposing, architecturally elegant centre of commerce and politics. They rode through Clive Street, where Sir Joshua and, ironically, also Jai Raventhorne had their offices. The Trident building, gaunt and grey and defiantly unadorned, stood silent in the early morning, its windows shut and only the cold metal emblem above its front door identifying it for what it was. With the triumphant return of the *Ganga,* the first private steamship in the country, there would no doubt be plenty of activity later. All at once Olivia felt strangely exhilarated. By the time they arrived at Old Fort Ghat past the New Wharf, her resentment against Freddie had subsided to the extent that she could actually smile at his trivial conversation.

The crossing on the ferry to Sibpur on the West Bank of the Hooghly opposite Garden Reach was very pleasant and did not take long. With their arrival at the Botanical Gardens, Olivia's mood became almost cheerful. The gardens themselves were quite splendid, with many stretches of apple green water covered with gigantic water-lilies, a special South American species now named after Queen Victoria. Founded in 1786, the gardens had as their prize display a massive banyan forest more than twelve hundred feet in circumference and soaring to eighty-eight feet at its highest, every tree in it sprouting from tendrils dropped from one central trunk. Wandering through the unique forest, listening to Freddie's chatter, Olivia realised with some surprise that he was far more entertaining a companion than she had anticipated. For one, he was a lively raconteur with an endless fund of stories about his escapades in London and at Oxford, and about his father, with whom, she gathered, he enjoyed a rather less than cordial relationship. He was, however, devoted to his mother despite his nervousness about her. "She's a bit of a dragoness, I know, but the Mater can be remarkably understanding," he confided. "It's the old boy who's the stickler, rather a dried-up prune, really. He genuinely believes that God created the world so that England could have its House of bloody Lords."

Olivia laughed. Indeed, the flavour of their conversation was so light-hearted that she loosened her defences. The stories Freddie told were mostly against himself. He said not a single cruel word about anyone; in fact, there seemed to be no malice in his heart. But Olivia's relief was to be short lived. It was as they were recovering their breath after a vigorous gallop and had dismounted in a clearing to rest that Freddie suddenly said, "There is something, Olivia, that I must say to you . . ."

Instantly she congealed. "Oh, please don't, Mr. Birkhurst," she exclaimed in alarm, knowing what was coming, "I . . . I'd rather you didn't!"

Whatever little chin he had firmed. "I have to, Olivia, I *have* to get it off my damned chest or I'll just *explode!*" He looked so desperately unhappy that she didn't have the heart to protest further. At least he was unaware of her conversation with his mother, which was some small mercy. "I know that I'm not much of a . . . man. I suppose I really am what everyone says, a fool . . ." He gulped like a fish and looked at his feet. "I know I'm not worthy of . . . of a single, ah, *hair* of your head, Olivia, because you're beautiful and clever and so . . . so *p-perfect* that I, well, I feel even m-more of a . . . a . . ." He choked with the effort of untangling the knot of words in his throat and coughed at some length. "D-dash it, what I'm trying to say and m-mucking it up as usual is," he cleared his throat noisily to remove the croak from it, his heart in his eyes, ". . . is—will you, *would* you possibly by some bloody miracle, c-consider becoming my . . . my w-wife . . . ?" Exhausted, he collapsed weakly onto a fallen tree trunk, almost convulsing with the effort of regaining his breath.

Olivia was riven with pity, with embarrassment. Hot faced,

she sat silent for a moment not knowing with what words to wound least this hapless young man whom she found she did not entirely dislike. He seemed so defenceless somehow, so vulnerable, so utterly without physical strength, that she shrank at dashing his pathetic hopes with a single blow, as honour demanded. But, as it happened, while she stared at the ground hunting for suitable words and phrases, it was Freddie himself who came to her rescue.

"Don't say anything now, Olivia. I . . . I'd rather you didn't." His chest heaved with emotion. "If you refuse me out of hand I'll just be sh-shattered. Let me live in hope at least until we return from that blasted plantation. It will give me time to harden myself against what I fear is inevitable disappointment."

She sagged with relief at the reprieve, ashamed at her cowardice but grasping the device with both hands. Her eyes, however, softened. Poor, poor Freddie! "All right, but on one condition."

"Anything, anything!"

"That you will not breathe a word of your proposal to anyone, especially not to your mother and my aunt."

His hand shot out with alacrity. "Done. My lips are sealed. It will remain between you and me until . . . until you give me your answer. But in the meantime," he looked down at his feet, shuffled them and blushed, "I too have a condition."

"What?" Olivia asked in renewed alarm.

"Would you, *could* you, perhaps, force yourself into calling me F-Freddie?"

Olivia laughed and quickly took the hand he held out. "Agreed. As we say back home, it's a deal."

Freddie took out his handkerchief and dabbed his forehead. "My God, it's a relief to have got that over with! I was sure I would . . ." He stopped and listened, his hand still.

Their peaceful privacy was being broken by the staccato sound of approaching hooves. The forest, not far from a British military encampment, was a favourite riding ground for cavalrymen, but this galloping horse seemed headed straight in their direction. Tendrils of mist hung from the trees in wraith-like formations undisturbed by the still-dormant river breezes and in the cool early morning the grass verges were jewelled with dew. A few moments later a rider burst into the clearing, reined his horse abruptly and slid to the ground before them. He was Indian, barefoot but dressed smartly in native garb with a yellow turban swathed around his head. As they stared at him in vague surprise, he bowed and, approaching Olivia, handed her a white envelope. She took it wonderingly and noticed, with a twinge of unease, that stamped on the back flap of the sealed envelope was the name Templewood and Ransome. Worried, she tore it open and quickly read the note contained within. *Sir Joshua requests Miss O'Rourke's presence immediately aboard the Daffodil. The bearer will act as escort.* That was all.

Olivia's hand flew to her throat in alarm. "Is my uncle ill?" she asked, handing the letter to Freddie. The rider merely shook his head; it was obvious he did not speak English. Freddie read the note, replaced it within the envelope and spoke a few words in halting Hindustani, but he was unable to elicit more information from the youth, who merely kept shaking his head.

"I think I had better go, Freddie. It must be a matter of some urgency for my uncle to have summoned me like this, especially on board his ship."

"Of course." His face fell. "Perhaps I should come as well?" he asked hopefully. "I could be of some assistance in a crisis."

Olivia hesitated. Her uncle's latest disaster might be common knowledge, but considering his opinion of poor Freddie it would be unwise to make him privy to whatever else had happened, as something obviously had. She shook her head. "I think not, Freddie, although it is kind of you to offer. It might be a . . . private matter."

He accepted that with his characteristic good humour. "Right ho, until tomorrow then? Same time, same place?"

Olivia sighed. "Yes, I guess so."

At the river bank to which the youth guided her, a *dhoolie* boat waited. Another youth stepped out from the trees to take charge of her horse and a third helped her onto the boat. The *Daffodil,* having arrived only recently from England, was anchored close to the opposite shore, being unloaded and refurbished for the return voyage scheduled two weeks from now. Through the silent journey across the Hooghly, Olivia's thoughts raced; what new calamity had necessitated this early-morning summons? As the creaking, bobbing row-boat threaded its way between the hulks of scattered vessels, there was another thought in Olivia's mind; it was of poor Freddie's final muttered words to her as he mournfully helped her mount Jasmine: "In my own inept fashion I do love you, Olivia . . ." She sighed heavily; there was something essentially decent about Freddie, for he had so few pretensions.

They seemed to weave their way interminably among schooners, cutters, men-of-war, Royal Navy frigates and sloops before the *dhoolie* showed some signs of arriving at a destination. Out of the diaphanous vapours shrouding the river a hull loomed ahead and the little row-boat slid alongside. A wooden stairway threaded on rope snaked its way down and dangled in front of them. Two Lascars, gripping either side of the ladder, helped Olivia climb her way on board. It was her first visit to a ship since she had arrived in India and, in spite of her worry, her spirits soared. There was something elating, intoxicating almost, about the smell of water and grease and jute and holystone and lingering salt that went with seagoing ships, something that spelt adventure and derring-do.

It was only when she was half way up the ladder that a tear in the mist and a sudden shaft of buttery sunshine through it dazzled her with a sharp, metallic explosion of light. Olivia shut her eyes in a swift reflex and by the time she opened them again, an instant later, what she had seen mounted on the prow had registered in her consciousness.

It was a golden trident.

"You frightened me out of my *wits*—I thought something terrible had happened to my uncle!" Olivia's immediate reaction was one of chagrin.

"Sadly, no." Still holding her hand in the clasp that had pulled her aboard, Jai Raventhorne smiled acidly. "As far as I know, your uncle is in bed with health quite unimpaired."

She snatched her hand out of his. "You had no business playing such a despicable trick on me!"

"I have as much business as you have to traipse the countryside with that idiot loon in tow. Do you have to make such a spectacle of your hunt for a husband?"

Breathing heavily, furious now, Olivia leaned back against the rail and crossed her arms. "Why should any spectacles, as you call them, I make be your unwanted concerns? Evidently, your genius for espionage exceeds those alleged social graces you seem so proud of!"

"Espionage, *hah!*" He threw his arms in the air, spun on his heel and walked off in a huff. "It hardly needs genius to follow *your* blatant cavortings," he flung back over his shoulder.

"And why need my blatant cavortings worry you, pray?"

Striding after him, still angry, Olivia struggled with parallel elation at so unexpectedly meeting him again.

He stopped and turned to glower at her. "They need not but they do!" he snapped. "For whatever my sins might have been."

"*Might* have been?"

He breathed in deeply and combed his hair with impatient fingers. "Are you going to stand there wasting time in petty argument or do you want to see my ship?"

Olivia suddenly remembered where she was—aboard the *Ganga!* Anger fizzling, she felt a rush of renewed exhilaration; she was actually on the *Ganga* with Jai Raventhorne! "I want to see your ship, of course," she murmured meekly enough.

"I thought you would. As first visitor aboard you should be honoured. She only docked at midnight."

"Oh, I am honoured," Olivia assured him lightly as they walked side by side down the deck and she looked around with avid interest, "even though I have no idea why I should be so singularly privileged."

"Haven't you?" His churlishness returned as his pace increased. "For a girl as intelligent as you I find that remark unforgivably stupid."

Heavens, he *was* in an odious humour this morning! But she was in no mood to retaliate. His unexpected proximity, the daring of his ruse and the personal risk she faced in being here at all, scuttled all taste for debate. Besides, there was much that was exciting to see. "So, this is the refitted clipper causing so many waves in town!"

He scowled. "I don't see why. I much preferred her the way she was. Well, will you have breakfast first or be conducted around?"

He was so certain of her coming he had even arranged breakfast? "I would like to be conducted around," she said with suitable docility. "I wouldn't want you to think I'm not duly appreciative of the honour."

He merely grunted.

Despite his pique, however, his pride of possession was fierce. Understandably. The *Ganga* was an extraordinarily elegant vessel with grace, beauty, speed and power written into every line of her sleek body. The ugly "cod's head and mackerel tail" of the tea wagons was nowhere in evidence. Her curved stem lengthened the bow above the water-line, and her raking masts carried tier upon tier of sail (thirty-three in all, she was told), now furled with neat cross-bands. She was three hundred and fifteen feet long, an astonishing dimension; the shining white hull was adorned with gold scroll-work, the wood all burnished Spanish mahogany with gleaming brass fittings. Being scoured and scrubbed even now as they watched from the quarter-deck were the long, pine-boarded decks holystoned further into pristine paleness by teams of Lascars on their knees armed with mops and buckets of sloshing water. Each of the *Ganga*'s twenty-eight guns, of sparkling brass, was capable of firing at thirty-second intervals, a feat of ballistic superiority not to be scorned, Olivia was informed with forgivable arrogance.

Raventhorne fondly patted the snout of one of the guns. "To sail without broadsides is plain suicide. There are as many pirates on water as there are brigands on land. The *Ganga,* as you can see, is a formidable adversary. There's no contingency she isn't prepared for." In recounting the virtues of his ship, his manner had improved appreciably. He actually smiled.

Feeling wonderfully light-headed, Olivia abandoned her nervousness to follow him down a narrow companion-way. The prospect of being with him even an hour was insanely intoxicating, the element of risk spicing rather than subtracting from her enjoyment. Emboldened by his turn of temper, she pulled out a snippet from Estelle's fat dossier of gossip. "I believe you once had a price on your head?"

"Once? You do me a disfavour! The Chinese put prices on the heads of most foreigners, prices that vary with the weather and are quite harmless. The English offer bounty for heads they believe will look good on their walls mounted alongside their game trophies. Whatever its worth, they considered mine would have been a handsome addition."

"Then how did you escape being mounted?"

"The bounty I offered them *not* to was more tempting."

"You mean, you bought yourself a pardon?"

"Why not?" He waggled a finger in her face. "Together with opium, the Company also makes generous profits out of selling respectability, when it suits them to do so."

At the mention of opium, Olivia struggled inwardly. Should she now demand an explanation for the consignment he had looted from her uncle? Then she decided against it. However cutthroat prevailing business rivalries, they really were no concern of hers. Washed over with emotions that defied identification, logic or control, in her state of mental limpness she let the matter rest. Instead she remarked drily, "I doubt if anyone thinks of you as particularly respectable, pardon notwithstanding!"

At that he laughed. "I'm as respectable as I'm ever likely to be, I suppose. I don't aspire to be more, not being a . . ." He hesitated.

"A gentleman?"

He laughed again. "Yes, that too. Come," he touched her hand as they stood watching two seamen coil a giant rope with such expertise that they seemed like precision machines, "let us go farther below."

En route he explained at great length the working of the *Ganga*'s Kew barometer, that most invaluable aid of all sailors, this modern English model the most accurate one on the seas. Olivia did not understand everything about the bewildering nautical data he dispensed with such fluency—"dead rise amidships," "breadth of beam," "belaying-pins," "hawards and halyards"—but it didn't matter a jot. She understood that the vessel was a masterpiece of naval architecture and performance (if she could forget the fleeting sight of an unpleasant little eyesore on deck in the shape of a smoke funnel), and for the rest it was enough just to be where she was, in the company of a man breathtakingly dynamic, and the pox on his scruples! Merely listening to his voice, rich and resonant, she felt vibrantly alive. His exuberance stimulated her beyond belief, almost beyond tolerance; she was no longer embarrassed by what was indeed magnetic between them—that affinity! Unashamed, Olivia savoured it fully. Yes, she was captivated by Jai Raventhorne, spellbound by his personality. She could not help herself, nor did she want to now.

"When she was launched a year ago from the Smith and Dimon shipyard in New York, not many believed she would ever sail successfully. *Hah!*"

"Why ever not?" She ran a palm down a spar, smooth as silk, varnished so that she could see her face in its surface.

"Because of her revolutionary bow line. The English scoffed louder than anyone else, until she docked in Southampton with an eighty-one-day run from Hong Kong under her belt. *Then* they sang a different tune! They confessed they had never seen anything like her, nor had hoped to. They wrote paeans to her in their newspapers, calling her a wonder of construction. The final accolade was a leader in the London *Times.*" His smile turned even more complacent. "And she certainly had many extremely worried, I can tell you *that!*"

"But surely the English too will build clippers of their own soon?"

"Oh yes, they've already started, having to stay in the race." He knocked solidly on a panel of wood with his knuckles. "But they will never match John Willis Griffiths, who designed this. He's the best they have in your country." With his palm he caressed the satin-smooth wooden panelling in which their reflections shone. "The *Ganga* is not only a ship," he said softly, "she is poetry in motion." His brief show of emotion quickly turned into ill temper again. "All right. Enough about her beauty. Now let me show you some of the ugliness on board; then you will understand why I am like a bear with a sore head this morning."

"Ugliness?" She almost ran behind him to keep up with his rapid pace as he swung down another companion-way. "I cannot imagine any ugliness amidst such perfection!"

"No? Well, you will see."

The bowels of the ship were dark and below sea level. They wound their way through a maze of corridors and climbed into a huge, shell-like capsule of a chamber in which, presently dormant, was a tangle of black boilers, pressure gauges, cranks and rods, all horribly encrusted with oil and soot. Facing them was the cavernous mouth of a coal furnace, now fireless but still belching noxious gases. Gone was the fresh saltiness of the sea, the reviving tang of clean air, the smell of varnish and newly washed decks; their nostrils stung with the odium of burnt oil, blistering paint and stale coal. Olivia started to cough.

"*This* is the price one pays for alleged progress!" Raventhorne said bitterly. "This is what is turning my angel of sublime dignity into a god-rotting slut."

Certainly it was an appalling sight. "But still the swiftest slut on the seas," Olivia reminded soothingly, clamping a handkerchief to her nose.

He refused to be consoled. "My captain's account of the journey has destroyed whatever triumphs there are in the logbook. When the boilers work full blast the funnel spews smoke that coats the sails with black that is impossible to wash out. The pistons thunder, the furnace roars and the entire ship shudders with the vibrations of the paddles beneath the stern. The noise apparently is deafening, the heat like a blast from hell—and *this* is what coal does to my men."

A sailor, obviously the stoker, came up to join them and silently tipped his cap with a forefinger. Amidst a mask of black, only his eyes showed white. Rivulets of sweat had made jagged lines down his face and bare chest and the odour he exuded was foul. He made a move to pick up his shovel but, with sharp words, Raventhorne stopped him. The man paused and a row of white teeth slashed his face in a smile. Saluting smartly, he turned and scurried back the way he had come.

Raventhorne cursed under his breath and kicked one of the boilers with such viciousness that something loose clattered to the iron floor. "These men are simple sailors," he muttered savagely. "They place their faith in the stars, the wind and God. Now we tell them to forget their traditional beliefs and pay homage to *engineers!*" His anger cooled and the lines of his face lengthened. "It is the end of a chapter, Olivia. For me, perhaps for others too, the romance of the sea is no longer what it was. The wilful seductress still beckons, but her charm for me diminishes with each modern innovation."

The depth of his emotion startled her. "Then why do you subscribe to a change that causes you such unhappiness?"

He sighed. "Because like the rest of the rats, I too am part of the tedious race to which there is no end. I am on a treadmill."

"You can get off it—"

"No!" His reaction was sharp. "No. It is too late for that."

Olivia had no occasion to press her point further, for he walked away.

Their return path passed through what appeared to be the crew's quarters. Having seen the accommodation on the Indiaman on which she had arrived, Olivia was surprised at the comparison. The dormitory was neat and well scrubbed, and the tiered bunks had cotton mattresses, thick sheets and woollen blankets. There were portholes along a side bringing in fresh air, a rare luxury since most crews' accommodation was below the water level with no light and less air. Deviating from the path, Olivia investigated the rows of adjoining bath stalls and lavatories. They were clean and smelled strongly of carbolic acid.

"Well, do I pass inspection?" Leaning in a doorway, Raventhorne looked on with a sort of resigned indulgence.

"Not until I've examined the galleys. Most ship owners feed their men on cattle slop and vermin. I want to make sure *you* don't," she said, knowing that the kitchens too would be spotless.

Watched by two astonished sailors in white aprons, Olivia went through the ranged vats of rice, lentils, wheat flour, semolina, oil and molasses, poking with a finger for signs of weevils or fungus. There were none. Everything was labelled, dishes and saucepans were sparkling clean, giving evidence of much elbow-grease, and there were racks for all the utensils and taps of running water over the huge sinks. Even the garbage pails were tidy with no messy remnants around which rodents and cockroaches prowled, as she had seen on the other ship. In the canteen next door there were trestle tables and benches and stacked metal bowls and mugs.

"I see you do treat your men well," she said, impressed.

"Why does that surprise you? Don't you think men deserve to live and work with dignity instead of with degradation like worms in a cesspool?"

"Oh, *I* think they do but not many ship owners will agree."

"That is because not many ship owners have lived like worms in a cesspool. I have. Come," he straightened and glanced at his pocket watch, "it is time for breakfast. Today we will be very English and feast off bacon, eggs and muffins."

In the main cabin, just below deck, they were served breakfast by the discreet and attentive Bahadur, his Gurkha face as unrevealing as ever. The cabin was commodious and airy, arranged more like an office than a private chamber, well appointed for functional nautical living. There was a royal blue pile carpet, curtains over the portholes, scuffed leather furniture and, almost incidentally, a four-poster bed with cushions. The desk, a mahogany roll-top, was set against a shiny wood-panelled wall mounted with navigational maps and charts, and there were bookcases against another wall. There were no signs of opulence, as one might have been led to expect from the *Ganga*'s smart exterior. In spite of the cabin's look of practical comfort, the keynote was still that defiant austerity that Raventhorne seemed to prefer in all his living arrangements.

Olivia found it difficult to eat although the array of breakfast dishes could not be faulted. Opposite her, Raventhorne sat without joining in the meal, one arm draped across the back of a chair and the other resting on the table with an unsmoked pipe clasped lightly in his hand. Olivia found his gaze on her unnerving; it was indecipherable and once more, not intended to put her at ease. Raventhorne was a man who carried his tensions with him, and the space between them again crackled almost tangibly, making idle conversation an effort. There was nothing about him that was casual; he appeared perpetually on the point of saying something that she expected would unbalance her. Yet, her curiosity about him was unsatisfied. There was so much more to this man who had woven such an unbreakable spell over her that she felt she had to know. Kinjal's story was merely a framework, a skeleton, which she had an insatiable urge to now flesh out. Her opening came when Raventhorne answered one of her neutral questions with, "No, the American presence in the China trade is still limited in spite of the repeal of the Navigation Acts. The clippers will make a difference although not much in my opinion, but then I don't interest myself in the China trade any more, so my prognosis might not be accurate."

"When you did interest yourself in the China trade," Olivia asked, spearing a last piece of bacon and avoiding his eyes, "what kind of ships did you sail?"

"Sieves!" He grimaced. "The first was a brig we chartered from a ship graveyard. It had one rusty gun mounted on the fo'c's'le, a cask full of inoperative small arms and a basket of stones with which to bombard pirates when the triggers jammed." The recollection seemed to amuse him and the flash of humour brought to his face a boyishness it could not have known for years. "I was a damn fool, of course, but like a cat I have nine lives. I survived."

Olivia's hopes fluttered; he seemed not to mind the probing. "You said 'we'; who were the others?"

"In the main, my American partner."

Raventhorne? But that Olivia dared not ask. "What was your partnership for?"

"For a journey into Eldorado," he said with a dry smile. "We bartered furs for silks, teas and jade. The capital outlay was his."

"And what was your contribution?"

"Navigational expertise, muscle power," he finally lit his pipe and inhaled, eyes crinkled against the spiral of smoke he blew out, "and guaranteed rewards from the China Coast."

"Guaranteed? What if there had been losses instead?"

"Losses?" He looked vaguely surprised. "The thought never crossed my mind. There were no losses. That damn brig sank in the West River after our second trip, but by then we could afford something better and with each voyage our fortunes improved." A distant look came over his features. "Those were good days back in the thirties."

Olivia sat back, enjoying from behind lowered lashes the sudden relaxation of his expression, the far-away eyes usually as restless as quicksilver. "Then why did you return?"

It was the wrong question. His eyes snapped back into wariness, the softness again hardening into impassable granite. "Because India is my home," he said shortly, rising to his feet and waving a hand impatiently for Bahadur to clear the table.

You had no home then, tell me the truth! Olivia wanted to cry out.

What is this destiny you returned to fulfil, this corrosive canker that pulled you back?

But she did not dare speak her thoughts. The gossamer filament between them was tenuous enough as it was; if it snapped altogether, she felt she would forever be shut out of his life with no more opportunity to share the shadows that lay beyond. She could not risk that, not any more. To be barred now from entering his secret, inner world would be to leave her own life incomplete.

"Why do you want to know so much about me, Olivia?"

The thrill of hearing her name on his lips was still unfamiliar enough to bring a flush to her cheeks. His quiet question from the other side of the room, where he stood staring out of a porthole, set her heart galloping again. "Because I know so little at the moment," she answered with perfect truth, her tone wistful.

"Why is it necessary to know more?"

"Because there is so much I don't . . . understand."

He turned. "Such as?" He walked back to sit down again.

"Such as . . . ," she swallowed hard and took the plunge, "why you persist in hounding my uncle." Her chin rose and so did her voice. "You arranged for that opium consignment to be looted, didn't you?"

For a moment he did not answer, but it was obvious that her bold question angered him. "I told you, I don't believe in selling death." He did not deny the accusation she had hurled at him in a second of rashness. "Have you ever been inside an opium den?" Desperately sorry that she had brought up the subject, she shook her head. "Have you ever personally known an addict, been close to one, stood by and watched helplessly as death came, inch by inch, second by second?"

The passion with which he flung the questions at her was consuming; there were tremors in his hands, and his expression was almost maniacal. Shaken, Olivia leaned over to lay a hand on his arm but, leaping out of his seat, he shook it off. "No, I haven't," she began in an effort to redeem herself in his eyes, "but I—"

"Then go and first *learn* from experience. Why come to me with all your pious, mealy-mouthed accusations?" He was shouting at her and his tone was insufferably rude.

Olivia felt her own temper stir in the unfairness of his attack. "*I* did not come to you," she cried, rising to her feet. "*You* tricked me into coming!"

"Tricked but not *forced.*" He controlled himself enough to lower his voice and edge it with ice. "You were free to leave my ship any time you pleased." He spun on his heel to stride up to the porthole. "Don't involve me in your petty inquisitions, Olivia. I dislike being questioned, especially by those who understand nothing of the East."

"I am not an imbecile child," she grated, humiliated by his cavalier dictates. "If made to understand, there is no reason why I shouldn't."

With a muttered oath he threw up his hands in frustration, then roughly combed back his hair with his fingers. When he spoke finally his voice was again level. "We are all afflicted by the same disease, Olivia. No one can boast immunity." He turned slowly to face her with a sickle smile that was as thin as it was dispassionate. "I do what I do because I must."

Olivia's defiance collapsed. Through unalloyed impulse she had deliberately destroyed the few moments of rapport between them. Once again she had fallen prey to the curiosity he hated so much, and once again he had retracted out of her reach. His expression was closed, his eyes openly hostile. Close to tears, she sat down again and ran a hand across her eyes. "I am so totally confused," she whispered miserably. "I don't know what to do . . ."

He wiped himself clean even of anger. "Shall I tell you what I think you should do?" He ambled towards his roll-top desk and leaned his elbow on it. "I think you should marry Freddie Birkhurst."

If he had suddenly pulled the rug from under her feet, she could not have been more stunned. She stared at him, aghast, then very slowly, filled with pain.

"I mean it, Olivia." For all the emotion he showed, they could have still been discussing topgallants. "Your aunt has made a wise choice for you. Birkhurst may be a prime idiot, but he is at heart a good man. He will be kind to you."

She was wounded beyond measure. "How can you, *you* of all people, make a suggestion that is so grotesque, so monstrous . . . ?" Her voice was low but impassioned. In her moment of panic her tongue loosened; she was hardly aware of what she said.

"I can because I am a grotesque, monstrous man."

Olivia flung herself out of her chair to confront him where he stood. "Don't throw that damned notoriety of yours into my face again like an . . . an *award* for meritorious service! I am sick of hearing you crow about your evil self, *sick* of your self-denigrations. Your reputation, such as it is, is meaningless to me."

"If it were," he replied, untouched by her indignation, "you would not want to keep our meetings secret from your family, or anyone else."

Uncaring of anything but his growing distance from her, Olivia no longer heeded how much of herself she was giving away to him. "And what about that . . . that wonderful *affinity?*" she mocked. "I should marry Freddie in spite of that?"

"Not in spite of it." He moved farther away. "Because of it. You will be safe with Freddie."

"Safe from *what?*"

"From me," he said mildly enough. "I will harm you, Olivia."

By her side her hands clenched. "*Why* am I constantly being told that? *Why* do you talk to me in riddles?" Tears glittered in her eyes, unbidden.

"There are riddles because you happen to stand where you do." He remained cold and unyielding, immune to her torment.

"And where exactly might that be, pray?" A far corner of her brain warned her that she was losing dignity, stripping herself bare, debasing herself horribly, but she could not stop. Driven by some hideous compulsion, she continued to expose herself.

"In my way."

The gentleness with which he said the three words was more cruel than a hundred lashes; Olivia was shocked into silence. *In my way!*

He straightened himself to pace with his hands clasped behind his back. "Yes, I tricked you into coming here this morning. I should not have. It was a mistake." His pace increased and his knuckles shone white with the grip of his hands. "But where you are concerned, Olivia, I seem to lack sane judgement. I become rash and fallible. I neither understand it nor like it. It still . . . disturbs me." He spoke in jerks as if unsure of himself, and his eyes were baffled.

She had a violent urge to rip off his mask, to wrench off his insidious, cowardly armour, to force him to denude his soul just as he had forced her to bare hers. But, lacking courage, she kept her hands clasped too and her eyes lowered. "There are dark areas in your mind that I need to reach, Jai . . ." Her voice trembled as, for the first time, she spoke his name.

"You cannot be part of those areas, Olivia."

"Don't lock me out now, Jai, not *now!*" She was leaving nothing with which to cover her nakedness, but it didn't matter any more. He knew everything anyway. "Is it because of . . . Sujata?" She sickened at the depths to which she was sinking, but ravaged by his categorical rejection, she could no longer control herself.

"Sujata?" Brief astonishment widened his eyes. "No, it is not because of Sujata. It is not because of anything that I can make you understand." Suddenly he banged his fist on the desk top with such force that an ink-well jumped and dark blue drops splattered a sheaf of papers. *"Don't* ask me any more questions, damn you! I cannot, *will* not give you the answers. Do you not see that simple fact?" His grey eyes turned ashen with rage. "Your inquisitiveness about me is like an . . . affliction. I find it obscene, do you hear me, *obscene!"*

Between them silence fell. At the far end of the cabin the sound of his rapid, raspy breathing kept time with a handsome marine clock on the wall. The battlements of suspicion, of hostility, that separated them showed no signs of a breach. Olivia's face was pale, her eyes beset with the same deadness she felt within. With a small sigh she roused herself out of her stupor. "I have to go now."

He swore again under his breath and walked back to her. *"Christ!"* he muttered softly. "Don't cry."

She wasn't aware that she had cried. Quietly, she wiped her cheeks. "It is getting late. I must leave." She could not look at him.

Suddenly, he touched her face. "I can't bear to see you cry." He made a gesture of defeat and let his fingers stray over her eyes to brush them with the tips. "I wish we had never met, Olivia . . ."

"Yes," she whispered mindlessly, hollow of feeling but eyes welling again.

Very gently, he took her wrists and pulled her to him. "My God, how vulnerable you really are!" His voice shook; for the first time there was anguish in his face.

His breath carried the words and buried them in the abundance of her hair. She felt the warmth of his mouth against her scalp and shuddered. Eyes closed, body trembling against his, she pressed her lips into the column of his neck, his thick metal chain cutting into them with coldness, but the taste of his salty skin was incandescent. Against her temple he murmured something and it was like the hum of bees on a summer's day, a lullaby in some dream space between illusion and reality. She did not listen to the words.

"I have no answers for you, my innocent victim . . ."

Victim.

Unnoticed, the word slipped through her fading consciousness like dew through the sun's vapour. His closeness, the heat from his body, the quivering fingers brushing her skin with feather strokes entranced her. Sour memory blew away like a troublesome cobweb; she was a bird who, having braved the storm, was now again safe in a nest she should never have left. An instant or an eternity passed, Olivia didn't know which; time petrified like a fossil. Then, still with gentleness, he unlocked her fingers from behind his neck and guided her arms down to her sides. All too fleetingly he cupped her face within his palms and skimmed his lips over hers.

"Now you must go."

Startled out of their trance, Olivia's eyes flew open. He withdrew from her, in body and in spirit. Before her gaze fixed on his face, he again became a cipher. In silence, he led her out of the cabin, up the companion-way and onto the deck. There was no expression in those maddening, mistlike eyes. Once more the seamed mouth was rigid and once more they stood on opposite sides of a chasm without a bridge between them. The instant or the eternity might never have been.

"Bahadur will guide you back to your horse and see you safely home." Raventhorne's tone was flat. The sun behind his head shadowed his features so that she could not see them; she knew that even if she could they would not give her any more. "I will not see you again, Olivia."

Before she could step onto the rope gangway, he had been swallowed up by the door. He had not touched her again, not even with his eyes.

"Well, which do you think—caramel custard or trifle?" Brow furrowed in thought, Lady Bridget flicked another page of her recipe book.

"Both," Estelle decided firmly. "Knowing Lady B's appetite you'll need to. She . . . *ouch!*" This to Olivia, who stood behind her with a pair of curling tongs. "That nearly singed my scalp!" Olivia mouthed an inaudible apology.

"Yes, that's not a bad idea." Pleased, Lady Bridget shut her recipe book and stood up. "We'll have saddle of lamb—not that it's lamb, of course, it's that dreadful goat meat that smells high—if I can procure a leg of good Canterbury. And the Bengal Club keeps a reasonable Stilton, *if* one can get there fast enough after a ship docks . . ." Muttering to herself, she went out of the room.

"Bother Lady B!" Estelle grumbled. "Why do we have to have them *tonight?*" She had to repeat the question before Olivia answered.

"Because they leave tomorrow. Anyway, what's so bothersome about having them tonight?"

"I had other plans," Estelle said loftily.

"Oh? What kind of plans?"

"Just plans." She waited for Olivia to shower her with questions, and when she didn't, added, "Charlotte wants to take me for a ride in their new carriage, if you must know."

"Does the ride have anything to do with Clive Smithers, too?"

Estelle tried to toss her head but, restrained by the tongs and the paper curlers, couldn't. "Perhaps."

"Is that why the hoity-toity, much-hated Miss Smithers is suddenly your bosom companion?" Estelle maintained a haughty silence. "Well, you could ask your mother if you can be excused tonight."

"Huh! You think she'll agree? Mama doesn't like Clive. Just because he plays the horses she thinks he's fast. *She* thinks I should sit and pine for John. God, how *boring!*"

"And so you should, miss, if you are serious about him."

"If he were serious about *me* he'd have taken me to London! He can't expect me to live for a whole year like a *nun!*"

Olivia smiled. "Nuns don't go to parties and have their hair done up with tongs."

This time Estelle did toss her head, sending two paper streamers flying to the floor. "Well, I'm *going* for that ride and Mama will never know. I'll slip out through the back door."

"That's wrong, Estelle. It wouldn't be right to deceive your . . ." Olivia broke off and flushed; who was she to be giving pious advice?

Through the silence that followed, Estelle fidgeted, then caught hold of Olivia's hand and stilled it. "Is anything the matter, Coz dear?"

"The matter?"

"Yes, matter! You've been going round all week like a duck lost in a thunderstorm. What is it? Those rides with Freddie?"

Olivia bent down to replace the tongs on the stove. "No."

"That letter then? From your friend Mrs. MacKendrick? It's made you homesick all over again, hasn't it?"

"Yes."

Estelle's attention span, fortunately, was brief; it seldom stayed away from her own problems for long. "When *I* leave home, I'm never going to be homesick. At least I won't have to go through all this bother for a silly little carriage ride!"

As soon as Estelle's coiffeur was done, Munshi Babu arrived. At Olivia's request, Sir Joshua had arranged for one of the clerks in his office to give her tuition in Hindustani. He had now been coming for a week and for her he offered one more means of filling her empty days with diversion. For the rest, she threw herself into a frenzy of letter writing and books, reading whatever she could lay her hands on, from Charles Dickens's moving novels to the lives of Lord Clive and Warren Hastings, histories of Calcutta's commercial evolution and Tom Paine's incisive writings, with which she was already familiar.

There were also those dreary morning rides with Freddie, which she had now accepted with resignation. Since she could not be on her own, Freddie's company was the next best thing. He was the least demanding man she had ever met, asking nothing of her but her presence. He even submitted to explorations of the bazaar in Kumartuli, where sculptors preparing for the Durga festival sat moulding hundreds of images for worship and for the ritual immersions in the Hooghly that marked the end of the ten-day celebration.

Olivia's attempts at self-beguilement were only partially successful; the pinpoints of pain, of self-debasement and twisting humiliation, could be suppressed only fleetingly, not erased. Ugly furry little creatures scuttled about in the corners of her sleep, making the nights as intolerable as the days. If she hated Raventhorne for his callousness, she hated herself more for allowing him to visit it upon her with such impunity. But in the dark entrails of despair there still flickered sparks of hope in the remembrance of what had been left unsaid between them, of distant echoes of emotion, of silent flashes in those tormenting eyes. And there was that gossamer filament between them, Olivia knew, that could not be denied.

Never to see Jai Raventhorne again was a living death to which he might have condemned her, but she could not—would not!—accept that as the finality.

Among the dozen or so guests at the Templewoods' dinner-party for the Birkhursts, Olivia was faintly surprised to see Mr. Kashinath Das. He had been present at Estelle's birthday ball with other eminent Indians, but Olivia had never seen him in any informal European gathering such as this. Short, wiry, with side-burns and bouncy movements, he looked odd in his stiff dinner-jacket and white boiled shirt. He assumed an affected speech and pretensions with an English briar pipe that were more amusing than offensive, but Olivia could not deny that there was something not quite wholesome about Mr. Kashinath Das. She wondered why he had been invited at all.

"Everything tickety-boo with Sir Josh?"

Freddie's sotto voce inquiry puzzled Olivia until, flushing, she recalled her abrupt departure on that first morning of their rides. Discreetly, Freddie had not mentioned the subject since. "Oh yes. It was only a minor matter on which he needed my opinion." Another lie! How many had she already told because of Jai Raventhorne? How many more?

"Splendid. I haven't said anything to anyone. I felt you would not have wanted me to."

On a sudden impulse, Olivia touched his hand. Yes, there was something very kind about Freddie Birkhurst. For all his inanities, he deserved far better than she could ever give.

The touch of hands, the exchanged look of understanding, the warm smile—Lady Birkhurst's limpet gaze missed none of them. Wherever Olivia went, the needle-pointed perceptions of the baroness followed.

For all Olivia's evasive tactics, they met in the downstairs guest bedroom, where Lady Birkhurst had gone to freshen up before dinner and where Olivia was forced to be on hand at her aunt's command. Taking advantage of the momentary privacy, Lady Birkhurst came to the point immediately. "In my preoccupation with my own thoughts the other afternoon, Olivia, there is one possibility I appear to have overlooked." Warily, Olivia waited while the baroness settled herself in a chair, her fingers grouped primly in her lap in a fat, meaty ball of flesh. "Could it be that your vehement refusal of my proposition is due to your, ah, romantic involvement elsewhere?"

It was not a question Olivia had been expecting and she was flustered. Since an immediate answer was impossible, she merely stood in awkward silence, biting nervously on a lip. In those few seconds of undeniable embarrassment, Lady Birkhurst drew her own conclusions.

"I . . . see." The fleshy folds of her face drooped visibly. "In that case, my dear, you must forgive the presumptions of a silly, voluble woman. And you must, of course, cast our discussion out of your mind, unless," a sad little hope struggled vainly in her eyes, "that is not so and you still might reconsider."

However awkward, it was an avenue of escape. Without thinking twice, Olivia took it. "It is I who must ask for your forgiveness, Lady Birkhurst. I should have myself clarified my . . . situation." In yet another lie (what exactly *was* her "situation," and with whom?) Olivia might have felt shame were it not for her overriding sense of deliverance.

Lady Birkhurst heaved herself out of the chair to lay a plump hand on Olivia's shoulder. "I do not need any clarifications, but if you do have any, I suggest that you make them to your aunt. She is unaware that her strenuous efforts in your direction promise to remain fruitless."

Oddly enough, it was Freddie who sustained Olivia through the evening. He needed neither attention nor answers. It was so easy to pretend that he wasn't there at all. In return, Olivia sheltered him from her aunt's barrage of questions about lids and kerosene tins and termites. "Between you and me, Olivia," he confided glumly, "I couldn't care less if that damned kitchen house sank into the Bay of Bengal. Incidentally, where is Miss Templewood? I have not seen her all evening." His inquiry was one of relief rather than concern. Estelle's constant teasing made Freddie nervous.

"She has a bad cold," Olivia explained, her eyes grim. "I believe she's sleeping it off." In fact, Estelle was not in her room, as Olivia had already ascertained. The stubborn girl *had* slunk out through the back door and was no doubt cavorting uncaringly somewhere with that Clive Smithers. She only hoped Estelle would have the good sense to return before her mother found her out and another almighty row descended.

"Tomorrow being our last morning here for a while, may I beg to be allowed to ride out with you again, Olivia?"

Freddie looked so doleful that Olivia almost acquiesced. Then, because it *was* his last morning here she hardened her heart. He might wax unbearably sentimental again, perhaps expect an affectionate parting, even a kiss or two. She shuddered. "I think not, Freddie. I'm not sure I'll ride at all since I fear I might be catching Estelle's dreadful cold." She sniffled convincingly and pulled out a handkerchief.

"Oh." He looked crestfallen but then rallied with a manful grin. "Well, so be it. Let it not be said we Ditchers don't bear our crosses with forbearance."

"Ditchers?"

"Yes, don't you know? We from Calcutta are called Ditchers. Because of that Maratha Ditch, you see."

She didn't see but looked dutifully amused.

"Madraswallahs are, of course, the Mulls," Freddie went on, encouraged by the smile, "and Bombaywallahs the Ducks."

"Ducks? Why Ducks?"

"Because of the Bombay duck, naturally! Except that it isn't a duck at all; it's a fish." He slapped his thigh and roared.

Olivia laughed too. Poor Freddie was not to know, of course, that her amusement was not at his joke, which she didn't understand, but out of relief that she would not be seeing him again for several weeks.

7

It was nothing more than idle curiosity that took Olivia riding out to the Maratha Ditch, which ran north and south to the east of the city. All in all it was a disappointment. Excavated a hundred years ago as a defence against a Maratha attack, it was never completed because the Marathas failed to launch their aggressions on Calcutta. Now it was a sorry, smelly sight, an insignificant trench filled with stagnant water. Crinkling her nose, Olivia turned towards the forest, a delight of freshness, where billowing bridal veils of mist still draped the trees and the shaggy carpets of grass were sequined with dew.

With Freddie finally away, Olivia once again felt free and unfettered, at liberty to wander where her fancy dictated. The scullion, designated by her aunt to alternate with the stable-boy as her morning escort in Freddie's absence, posed no great problems. Given the price of a hearty breakfast in the bazaar, he was only too happy to save himself an arduous run and wait for her in a tea shop till she chose to return home.

The splintered path that zigzagged through the yellow jacaranda, the sinuous banyan, the mango and the peepuls was suddenly invaded by green parrots making spiralling loops through the trees, their squawky cries indignant at the human intrusion. A family of fat, green buds separated to reveal the questioning face of a beady-eyed mongoose; keeping warily to the top branches, a band of black-faced monkeys followed her passage with apparent distrustful curiosity.

Olivia reined sharply, all at once confronted by a most unlikely barrier: a massive spider's web spread across the lower branches like a magical curtain so fine that she almost didn't see it. Enchanted by its delicacy, she dismounted to watch the incredible labours that went into the fashioning of so intricate a maze.

The home-maker, a plump little black berry of fur and bristles, stilled at her approach to glare with beady, suspicious eyes that seemed not at all pleased at the visit. For a while they stared at each other, then Olivia laughed softly. "Don't worry, little fella, I shall not damage your premises." The spider seemed to understand the reassurance, for, turning its back to her, it continued with its spinning.

It was just then that Olivia noticed the barking of the dog.

Persistent and getting louder, the bursts of sound seemed to be heading in her direction. It could, of course, be someone's friendly pet, but it could also be a stray, since the city abounded in them, many of them diseased and mad. Her aunt had warned her to be careful. Leaving the spider to its travails, Olivia turned to quickly remount Jasmine and be on her way. But it was too late; before she could haul herself up, the animal came bursting out of the bushes. Olivia nervously remained standing where she was.

The dog, large and shiny black, pranced around her feet for a moment in a state of some excitement. His intentions, however, seemed not to be belligerent. Then he sniffed her feet and her clothes with a quite professional thoroughness. His jaws opened and something fell out—a piece of fabric. The dog settled back on his haunches in front of her and whined.

Olivia's stomach hollowed. In the same instant she recognized both the dog and the piece of fabric. He was Akbar, Raventhorne's pet, and the lace-edged white cloth was the handkerchief she had left inadvertently on the *Ganga* that calamitous morning.

With an agonised sob trapped inside her throat, Olivia galvanised into action. In a trice she had mounted Jasmine, dug her heels into the mare's side and was flying towards the heart of the forest guided by Akbar, who, overjoyed at the success of his mission, raced ahead. The wind roared in her ears and stung her cheeks into fiery life; in her temples her blood pounded, reducing her breath to gasps. And in her heart an overwhelming happiness exploded; she was going to see Jai Raventhorne again!

He sat on a boulder by a stretch of water, shoulders hunched, tossing sticks into the trees, which Akbar's mate dashed to retrieve. Nearby, his midnight Shaitan grazed languidly on a verge. Beyond that Olivia saw nothing.

He looked up as she arrived in the clearing and for a moment their eyes locked. He rose, walked towards her and took charge of Jasmine's reins. Then he held out a hand and helped her dis-mount. Slowly, against him, Olivia slid to the ground. Anxiously, her gaze scoured his face but it told her nothing—and yet so much! His arms opened for her and, without a sound, she slipped into the shelter they offered.

Against her, he trembled. "Forgive me . . ."

She laid an ear against his chest and, for the first time, listened to his heartbeat. It galloped, like hers, telling her more than words ever could, his breath, hot and uneven, fanning her own cheeks into warmth. She kissed the pocket of his rumpled mull shirt beneath which lay his heart. There was nothing she could think of saying, nor was there any need for words.

"I wounded you," he murmured, heaving with remorse. "I made you cry. Can you forgive me?"

"Yes," she murmured back mindlessly, hearing neither what he had asked nor what she had answered, "yes . . ."

"Did I make you very unhappy?"

Olivia shook her head, inhaling the freshness of his skin pressed into her face, the misery of the past few days obliterated in blinding happiness. He laid small, frantic kisses on the side of her neck, her ear lobes, her temples—and she shivered. "No."

He released her abruptly to return to the boulder to sit down again, his brows drawn together in self-anger. "People say I have a streak of madness in me. They are right. I have."

Olivia perched herself on a tree stump opposite him, pulled up her knees and hugged them tightly. Just to hold him in her vision, to caress him with her eyes, was enough to content her. "Yes, I know."

"You know and you are not alarmed?"

"No."

"But you should be!" He picked up a stone and flung it into the trees to send Saloni bounding after it with excited yelps. "I carry within me a poison that infects everyone around me." He looked deeply perturbed.

"Poisons have antidotes, or they can be cast out if one wishes." Dreamily, Olivia shut her eyes as if wanting to preserve in them forever this rare moment of something precious shared and harmonious.

"No." He shook his head fiercely. "I do not wish it cast out. Without it I would be half a man. You see?" His bark of a laugh was harsh. "I *am* mad!"

Jolted out of her soporific trance, Olivia paid attention. His expression was one of anguish. Concerned, she rose and walked over to him, squeezing herself into the space beside him on the boulder. "I cannot understand that, Jai," she said gently, smoothing his hair back with a hand that still trembled with welling love. "You know I cannot unless you explain it to me."

"There is no explanation possible that you will accept."

"At least let me be the judge of that!"

"You cannot judge something you cannot understand."

Then make me understand! Olivia wanted to cry out in mounting frustration but held her tongue. They were again teetering perilously close to the limit of his endurance; she could never again risk losing him, forcing him into corners from which he needed to battle his way out gasping for air. Even now, it wounded her unbearably to see his silvered eyes swim in pain that she would not have thought them capable of feeling. He had fallen once more into those vast, private, secret silences from which she was so mercilessly excluded. She watched helplessly, searching for a crack, a chink, through which to peep into his cloistered mind, but there was none. Only his pain persisted.

"You are young and untouched and a stranger to sorrow, Olivia," he said, breaking his silence, his voice heavy with those unsaid burdens he would not allow her to share. "And you have come into my life, uninvited and unexpected, like some unseasonable storm delighting in its capacity to surprise, unsettling everything. I feel uprooted. My foundations are shaken and I have been made defenceless. I am horribly disturbed at having to do battle with a force that is totally strange to me."

Olivia listened without breathing and now she exhaled cautiously, fearful of again upsetting the fragile balance of his curious mind. But what he implied filled her with aching, enchanting joy. "Is it necessary to . . . do battle?" she asked, treading on egg-shells. "Is it not possible just to accept that force?" She reached up to smooth his forehead, to press out the creases of worry, and he rewarded her with a smile.

"No," he said. "Oh no."

The tinge of uncertainty emboldened her. "I too feel uprooted, Jai," she ventured, holding his hand and pleating her fingers through his, frantic not to ruffle the communion between them yet hungry for his confidence. "My foundations too are shaken. I did not seek to feel for you what I do. For me too it is an . . . unseasonable storm neither invited nor expected. As such," she took a deep breath, "at least something is owed to me."

"Yes. Something is owed to you." He unlaced his fingers from hers and moved away to stand at the edge of the water and peer down into it. "Since you risk so much by including me in your thoughts, it is my duty to repeat my warning."

"Duty!" His sudden, stiff formality was hurtful.

"Perhaps unthinkingly I used the wrong word but I am unable to think of another."

"So, it was a sense of duty that made you send your dog to sniff me out this morning?" she asked, again disconsolate.

"No!" He spun around and there was passion in the way he threw out the denial. "I sent Akbar after you for purely selfish reasons. The memory of those incredible eyes bruised with unhappiness haunts me, Olivia. It ruins my sleep and fills me with shame and guilt, both of which are alien to me. They are feelings I resent even more than I resent you for causing them." His shoulders dropped and the passion faded. "I sent Akbar to fetch you because I have a degrading need to see you."

The sun exploded through the clouds and drenched her world with radiance again. She ached for him, yearning for his embrace and the taste of his lips, but she forced herself to be content with only his closeness as he sat down again beside her. "It is a need that is mutual, you must know that." Her whisper trembled.

With an absent-minded smile he trailed the back of his hand down her cheek, making the nape of her neck sting. "There is no decision in my life that I have not made for myself, Olivia. Many of them have been cruel. I have made them in spite of that. But now, I must ask you to make one for me."

Again she stopped breathing. "Yes?"

He turned to take her face gently between his palms. They felt cold and moist. "Since I seem unable to, you must make the decision not to see me again."

A sinuous chill crawled up Olivia's limbs. To make a wilful, self-destructive, masochistic decision as vile as this? Never to sit like this with him again? To abandon willingly the taste of his lips, the touch of his hands in her hair, the sight of those ashen eyes now looking into hers with such soft confusion? To be denied forever the chance of entry into the lost, melancholy worlds that lay beyond his stubborn barricades and turn her life into a desert? She might as well be dead!

Olivia covered his hands with hers and pressed them into her face, fingers of panic clawing at her insides. "You know that that is a decision I can never make, Jai." Her voice shook. "I am not afraid of taking risks, I am not afraid of *anything* as long as I can see you."

"You can invite disaster so blithely?" He seemed puzzled, and he stared into her distraught eyes as if to search for an answer there. "What is this stubbornness that drives you?"

She laughed shakily. "It is a stubbornness called . . . love."

He echoed the word with some slight mockery, then repeated it several times, feeling it with his tongue as if sampling a morsel with an unfamiliar taste, unaware of just how irreversible a commitment, how much of herself she had laid at his feet. "It is not possible to love someone like me," he said curtly but with wonder, looking at her as if she might be a wayward child bent on some whimsical mischief. "Even to myself I am sometimes reprehensible, an eccentric not to be tolerated."

"I can tolerate anything you choose to be."

"Anything?" He continued to humour her.

"Yes, anything!" she said fiercely, clenching her fists, knowing that her eyes were beginning to fill. It twisted her with pain that this once loveless, lonely boy cast out by the world should still be so deprived as to not know a word of such universal understanding. "Why do you not take me seriously?"

"If I did not take you seriously I would not be here! But what you profess for me is perhaps a chimera, a mirage, an illusion of your mind." He tilted his head and observed her through slitted eyes, wary and suspicious. "I know that you have learned much from Kinjal," he said softly. "Considering your obsessional curiosity it could not have been otherwise. Is it therefore *love* you feel, or pity?"

The ease with which he seemed to delve into her thoughts and pull out the most immediate one made her heart miss a beat, but she was not intimidated by the tautness of his jaw line, the angry twitch of a muscle just below his temple. "If I feel pity for anything," she said, irked, "it is for your *mulishness* that makes you so unworthy a recipient of either!"

He broke into a laugh that loosened the lines of his face and brought genuine amusement into it. "For you to complain of my mulishness is the height of impudence, my obstinate American!" His arm brushing her shoulder slipped down to her waist and he drew her close to him. With infinite tenderness he kissed her behind an ear. "You are very stubborn, Olivia," he breathed with a heavy sigh, "and I am weaker than I had thought."

"You, *weak?*" She laughed, shutting her eyes, not daring to move.

"Weak *and* insane, a vicious combination." His voice turned husky as he stroked her hair lightly. "You make it impossible for me to stay away from you."

"Why should you want to?" Held in his arms, revelling in the fact of his crumbling defences, in her ability to at last breach the barricade, the answer to that question was immaterial to Olivia.

But he gave her an answer anyway. "Because I am not used to being a slave to my wants. I am not used to being commanded."

She pulled back, wounded. "I have never commanded you!"

He kissed her mouth. "You command with every look, every touch, each time I think of you. You command when I am awake and trying to sleep and when I am asleep trying not to dream. You command," he ended savagely, "because I desire you more than any other woman I have known."

His resistance cracked; his arms tightened to crush her in an embrace that was harsh and violent and yet with the sweetness of honey. In the moist fullness of his lips there was anger, but to Olivia his kisses were touched with magic, the culmination of every dream she had ever dreamed about him, every fantasy she had ever played out with him in the secret niches of her mind. Extraordinary sensations, acute and piercing like shards of glass, chased each other around her body, awakening in it longings that might have been frightening had they not also been so exquisite. In his whispered endearments she heard not the hoarse confusion of sound in alien languages but the music of angels; in his trails of fiery kisses across her face, her neck, the dip between her breasts, she felt a flight of doves, soft and feathered with love. His fingers of darting quicksilver, inciting her nerve ends into flaring rebellion, covered her body with caresses such as she had never known.

"Olivia, Olivia . . ." His muffled groan was one of anguish. "What damnable tortures you are devising for me . . . !"

"Hush." She pressed his head between her breasts, spilling over with impossible joy. *"Hush . . . !"*

"Have you any idea, you callous sorceress, how *much* I desire you?" Buried in her bosom she could feel his teeth clench, his breath so hot that it seemed to burn craters in her flesh.

"Yes." In this moment of perfection there was nothing, nothing she could have denied him.

He raised his head to grip her shoulders with clawlike hands and nails that bit into her, making her wince. "Then why do you encourage me, you rash, foolish girl?" His eyes were wild and in his helplessness he shook her roughly. "Do you not know that men like me are animals who take their pleasures where they find them?"

The pressure of his nails brought tears to her eyes but she

held them back. "I love you, Jai." Gently, she wiped his forehead clear of moisture, looking into his wild, wonderful eyes without flinching. "Whatever I have is yours."

He held her stare, chest heaving rapidly as he struggled for control, and then his hands dropped. "Don't say that, Olivia," he said, wincing. "Don't ever say that again."

"It is the truth," she said simply.

"You make yourself into such an easy prey! Just as well I refuse to participate in your damned recklessness. If I did," he started to pace again, still agitated, "it would only make me hate myself more than I sometimes do now. And for that I would never forgive you." He paused to glower at her, bristling eyebrows locked together like warring caterpillars. "I have quite enough hate from others to last me through one lifetime!"

Olivia said nothing. She knew it was useless to argue. How quickly she was learning his chameleon colours, his fickle moods! Instead, she sat hugging her knees, watching him in silence, waiting for him to expel and expend the fearful energies that had blown him once more out of her reach. His kisses still clung to her skin like peach down, making it glow; what he had revealed of himself was like an oasis of hope in a desert of uncertainty. For the moment, it was enough for her.

Picking up stone after stone he flung them violently into the trees like trajectiles aimed at an invisible enemy. Excited by the game, both dogs pranced around yelping and dashing back and forth to hunt out the prizes from the undergrowth and fetch them back. It was only when the neat pile at his feet had grown substantially and the dogs, spent and panting, had flopped to the ground again that Raventhorne finally stopped. He was breathing hard from the exertions, and the fabric of his shirt clung wetly to his back, but whatever private demons had been haunting him had been cast out from his system. His expression was one of regained control.

"It is time you returned," he said, chastising his unruly hair with his fingers, "or your uncle will get Slocum to send a police posse after you."

Olivia didn't move for a moment. She filled with dread, for he said nothing more as he untied Jasmine's reins from a branch and held them out to her. Once again it seemed a dismissal, but now she was no longer willing to accept it without comment. Her eyes held challenge. "Will I see you again?"

He said nothing while he tightened the girth on her mare, then turned to search her face with sombre, speculative eyes. "Do you truly wish to?"

"Yes," Olivia said, pink faced and morose since it was she who had had the need to ask. "I truly wish to."

Lightly he trailed his fingers down her arm, his eyes cloudy and distant. "So be it," he sighed.

Olivia's colour deepened as she almost snatched Jasmine's reins out of his grasp. "If you believe it is *me* you are indulging—"

He cut her off with a snort. "If it were you I were indulging," he said irritably, "there would be no problem. Unfortunately, my gross selfishness allows me to think only of myself. I am angry because it is *not* you I am indulging!"

Olivia smiled again. "When?"

"Soon."

Already she trembled with mortifying impatience. "How soon?"

"Very soon."

"How will you know where I am?" she asked rapidly, feeling inept but unable to let go.

"I always know where you are," he said with a return of the gentleness that demanded she forgive him everything.

And she did. Instantly. However, his casualness, his ill-concealed reluctance, wounded her somewhat. In silence she mounted Jasmine but then once more he lifted the injury right out of her mind. "You can never know, Olivia," he murmured against the palm of her hand as he kissed it, "just how much I want to see you again."

Over the small kiss he folded her fingers, placed her hand back carefully in her lap and slapped Jasmine hard on the flank. Olivia knew that he stood and watched her ride away until she was lost to his sight.

She flew home on the wings of the wind, convinced that she could have done so even without a racing mount. She knew now that there could be no retraction from the path she had chosen. The obstacles, the hazards, the pitfalls and come what may Olivia brushed aside like inconsequential fruit flies. For this one love, this *only* love, she felt confident enough to take on the world.

In any case, she had long passed the point of return.

Sir Joshua was down with heat boils.

With Calcutta's mild winter approaching, it was cooler than in summer and the boils were less fierce than they might have been earlier. Even so, Dr. Humphries had confined Sir Joshua to his bed, which did little to improve his temper. He had insisted that papers and correspondence be sent home to him daily from his office. His two unfailing visitors on most days were Ransome and, much to Lady Bridget's chagrin, Kashinath Das. In between office papers and his two visitors, Sir Joshua spent much of his time exercising his temper on servants, members of the family and absent offenders. In fact, his generally foul mood created domestic havoc and reduced his wife's nerves to shreds. Not even Estelle was spared. Used to being spoilt by a father she usually twisted around her little finger to achieve her whims, Estelle was bewildered and desperately hurt by his sudden harshness.

"Papa doesn't love me anymore," she whispered miserably one morning when she had had a particularly stinging lash of his tongue over a footling crime. "He called me a . . . a s-selfish b-brat and said he'd bring his *c-crop* to me if I didn't l-listen to M-Mama!" Shattered, she burst into tears.

Even Olivia was shocked. That her impetuous cousin was both selfish and a brat she knew, but threatened with an unjust corporal punishment she had never had, Estelle was right to be outraged. Especially now with her newly acquired coming of age, the novelty of which still sat on her with excessive pride.

"He's very preoccupied with business problems, dear," Olivia nevertheless soothed. "And he feels his boils are not only undignified but an infernal interference with his badly needed presence in the office with that investigation still continuing. Of *course* he still loves you, silly!"

Estelle's interest in her father's business affairs was as cursory as her mother's. Her eyes glittered with malice. "I don't give a bloody tinker's *cuss* for his business problems," she stormed in high dudgeon. "I will *not* have anyone talking to me like that, not even Papa!" In a rare pet she stamped out of the room, calling back over her shoulder, "I'm not a *child,* you know. Papa might not appreciate that but *other* people do!"

Since Olivia appeared to be the only person in the family with whom Sir Joshua kept a reasonably civil tongue, it was she who was assigned much of his nursing. Lady Bridget wisely stayed in the wings issuing instructions out of his presence. Also wisely, Estelle took Olivia's advice to make herself as scarce as possible while her father's difficult mood lasted, particularly after his unfair threat.

"Where is that damn fool Munshi? Doesn't the ass know these have to return to Arthur this very instant?"

Olivia had completed her Hindustani lesson for the afternoon and, thinking that the pouch of documents was to stay with her uncle overnight, had sent Munshi Babu home. Sir Joshua's roar, which reverberated through the bungalow the moment she stepped into his sick-room, took her by surprise.

"I'm sorry, Uncle Josh," she said, contrite, "but I have already sent him back. I didn't realise that you still wanted him."

"Well, of *course* I still want him, dammit!" His face turned purple. "Arthur must have these today so that he can study them before he meets that ignorant oaf from Parliament first thing in the morning. How the hell is he going to put him in his place if he doesn't have the facts?"

Followed a colourful dissertation on members of Parliament from Westminster and their perpetual nose poking into colonial matters they knew nothing about since they lived in the clouds ten thousand bloody miles up and away and couldn't tell a tea-leaf from a stinging-nettle anyway. From that he progressed to the general idiocy of everyone about and in particular to that of "that butcher" Humphries, whose carbolic oil poultices stank of horse dung and even if the heat boils didn't kill him, those infernal devices surely would. Finally, having consigned everyone to an eternal fate of fire and brimstone, Sir Joshua stopped for sheer want of breath.

"Well, would you like me to take the papers to the office?" Olivia inquired, taking advantage of the hiatus. "It's quite easily done and the journey there and back shouldn't take long."

Deprived of the pleasure of further complaint, Sir Joshua grunted. Then, seeing no reason not to agree, he had the grace to look abashed. "You're a good girl, Olivia, saner and more responsible than most. I wish you'd give some of your good sense to your idle cousin. She sorely needs it, by Christ!"

It was quite the wrong time to mount any defence of his absent daughter. Olivia did not even try.

To any other pair of eyes Clive Street was an ordinary, mundane thoroughfare with little to distinguish it from other similar business centres in the city. To Olivia, however, Clive Street was positively touched with magic. As always, she craned her neck out of the window of the carriage as it passed by the Trident offices as if she would find suddenly revealed some little detail of significance she might have missed earlier. She had no idea when she would see Jai Raventhorne again; "soon" could mean a day or a decade, considering the man's contrariness. But now, just to be on the same street as he might be was enchantment. Even this solitary crumb of comfort she hugged close to her heart.

Arthur Ransome was delighted with both the papers and her

visit. "What a transformation the sight of a pretty face brings to our dull and dreary work place, Miss O'Rourke! And how very kind of you to bring these!"

The establishment he dismissed with such nonchalant modesty was in fact one of the better offices in town and the envy of many lesser merchants in Calcutta. It was elegant, capacious and finely appointed, for Sir Joshua's taste for good living was not to be denied even here. In its cool, high-ceilinged halls there seemed always a sense of urgency, as if great decisions were being made every minute of the day and fortunes bartered for commodities without which the world could not survive. It was an atmosphere Olivia found quite thrilling. As they settled down in Ransome's office for a few minutes of conversation, she decided to use the interlude to her best advantage.

"Uncle Josh told me all about the loss of the opium consignment," she began quite boldly. "Is Mr. Slocum's investigation going well?"

Knowing that his partner often confided in her, Ransome did not think to evade an answer. "It is going like all police investigations go when it comes to native involvement. In circles." He laughed grimly.

"They have not progressed much?"

"They have not progressed at all. Nor will they. When natives join forces against us they use two very effective weapons—convenient amnesia and a surfeit of witnesses all with contradictory accounts. What can poor Slocum do?"

"And Gupta still insists it was the thuggees?" Privately, Olivia was ashamed at how relieved she felt!

"Yes."

"You don't believe him either?"

Ransome snorted. "My dear Miss O'Rourke, when one has lived in this country as long as Josh and I have, one develops an instinct about these matters. No, I don't believe him either."

A peon, smartly uniformed in white with a red turban and cummerbund, entered bearing a tea tray with the solemnity of a priest making a sacred offering in a temple. He laid the tray on the table between them, poured out two cups of honey-coloured liquid, dropped a sliver of lemon in each with a silver toothpick, and withdrew. The cups, obviously Chinese and heavily ornamented with golden dragons, were as fragile as paper. Over the rim of hers, Olivia surveyed her host of the moment and decided to probe further. "Do you also consider that it was Kala Kanta who was responsible for the act of dacoity?"

Ransome looked briefly uneasy, then nodded.

"Will Slocum ever be able to prove it?"

"No." This time there was no hesitation. "Raventhorne has always had one prime advantage over us, one that we can never match. He has India on his side."

Something in his manner, calm and almost resigned, surprised Olivia. His acceptance of the situation seemed so different from her uncle's mercurial reaction. "Raventhorne's villainy doesn't incense you, Mr. Ransome? One way or another, I believe your losses threaten to be heavy."

He did not answer her immediately. Instead, for a moment he made a lengthy ritual of chasing a solitary tea-leaf around his cup with a spoon, then trapping it neatly and discarding it in the saucer. "Of course it incenses me," he finally said in a tone unusually quiet. "But it is, perhaps . . . understandable."

"Understandable?" She was quite astonished at an admission so unlikely and so generous. "How so? Certainly that is not a view Uncle Josh takes!"

"No." He turned thoughtful. "No. In his wrath, Josh is of course justified. Without doubt, Raventhorne is the most vindictive, vengeful bastard I have ever met . . ." He broke off with a look of remorse. "You must pardon my language, Miss O'Rourke, but Raventhorne is the kind of man who excites strong passions."

"Oh, I've heard far worse in our saloons, I assure you, Mr. Ransome!" Now highly intrigued, she bent forward to listen better. The opening that had chanced her way was too tempting not to explore. "But then, why do you feel that Raventhorne's crime is understandable?"

Ransome drained his cup and lit up one of his much-favoured cheroots. "Raventhorne has never made any secret of his loathing for the opium trade. To be quite frank, Miss O'Rourke," he inhaled deeply and then breathed out with deliberate slowness, "I myself have not much stomach for it anymore. During the so-called Opium War way back in thirty-nine, being a patriot loyal to my Queen and country, I fought as hard as the next Englishman, but I don't mind confessing that some of the sights I saw shamed and disgusted me. The yellow devils stood no chance against our superior fire power, naturally, but the physical condition of many, stupefied with the poppy, was shocking." He sighed heavily. "It was not a sight to be proud of, I can tell you that, Miss O'Rourke. Each time I go to Canton I am reviled by what is essentially our own handiwork. It is we who have made them slaves to this nefarious addiction from which there is no hope of respite." For a moment he looked deeply disturbed but then with an effort he smiled. "However, every good businessman knows that in the realm of hard commerce there is no place for sentiment. We sell to make profits, not necessarily to benefit mankind. It is the balance-sheet, not the conscience, that counts when it comes to the crunch." He had spoken with a smile but underneath there was bitterness.

Olivia sat up slowly and surveyed his face with renewed interest. Once again the sharp difference between the two partners and friends seemed greatly obvious. Contrasted to Sir Joshua's confidence and unvarying decisiveness, Ransome's sensitivity appeared very unusual. The qualms he felt about the opium trade, for instance, she could never think of ascribing to her uncle. She warmed to Ransome even more. Also, the novelty of being able to talk so freely about Jai Raventhorne was heady. "But when it comes to the crunch," she said, picking up the thread again, "doesn't this Kala Kanta also have a balance-sheet to consider? How can he afford a conscience when no one else can?"

"He has devised other means of making the sheet balance."

"But surely you are not the only merchants engaged in this opium-bullion-tea triangular trade. Does he also attack the others?"

"Certainly!" His tone went very dry. "In that respect, I assure you, Raventhorne is entirely impartial! During the Opium War, he aligned himself openly with the Chinese. In fact, he personally helped in the gutting of English factories in Canton, and assisted the Chinese commissioner in burning twelve hundred tons of opium—*twelve hundred tons!*—belonging to the English at the special pits dug for the purpose. That cost the community millions of taels, millions."

Despite the staggering figures, Olivia was not surprised; the act of defiance was certainly characteristic of Raventhorne's uncaring bravado. "Is that why there was a price on his head in India?"

"Yes." It didn't occur to him to question the source of her information. "Raventhorne has always sailed under an American flag. Since it was only British ships that were forbidden from entering the Pearl River during the hostilities, he and others were allowed free passage by our Royal Navy through their blockade at the mouth of the river. Many American and other captains acted willingly as our agents to carry our opium through with impunity—for handsome commissions, of course. Raventhorne never did. In fact, he blatantly attacked any ship he could that carried a cargo of opium even though America was not involved in the War. Can you blame us for baying for his blood?" For an instant he scowled and then, surprisingly, he broke into quiet chuckles. "Well, we didn't get it, not a lick, not a drop. Instead, we got the wily scoundrel as a competitor and a neighbour to continue making our lives a misery." His chuckles blossomed into hearty laughter. "Oh, I hate his guts just like everyone else, Miss O'Rourke, but I also have to give the devil his due. He might be as slippery as a cobra and just as venomous, but what he doesn't lack is gall. By heavens, he certainly doesn't lack that! And God knows he does have reason to hate the blasted poppy considering his . . ."

He stopped so suddenly that Olivia was startled. His laughter cut off as if sliced with a knife and his mouth snapped shut like a clam. Flushing a deep red, he stood up abruptly.

"Considering . . . what?" With her heartbeats thundering within her rib cage and her blood racing, Olivia stubbornly remained seated, refusing to accept this as the termination of their conversation. "Considering what, Mr. Ransome?"

But the moment had passed, the revelation—whatever it might have been—aborted. With a small, awkward laugh, Ransome shrugged and turned bland. "Considering his knowledge of Canton's opium dens," he said smoothly, then swiftly turned the topic around. "Josh tells me you yourself have had an encounter with Raventhorne."

"Yes." Inwardly Olivia sighed; she knew he would not now reveal to her what he almost had. She added quickly, too quickly, "The encounter was quite accidental."

"But of course!" He looked surprised at her explanation and she blushed. "What else could it have been? I hope there is no recurrence of the event, Miss O'Rourke." He looked stern. "Raventhorne is a most unsavoury character, *most* unsavoury."

It was a judicious moment to leave and, a little reluctantly, Olivia suggested that she do so. Outside it was dark and the street was crowded with home-going carriages. As Ransome courteously saw her to hers and bid her good night, he coughed and muttered, "I would be grateful if you would not repeat our conversation to Josh, Miss O'Rourke. As you know, his attitudes to some things vary greatly with mine."

"No, of course I will not," Olivia hastened to reassure him, smiling inwardly at the unlikelihood of such a dialogue with her uncle. Then, once again emboldened by the oblique reference to the subject of Raventhorne, she dared to inquire, "Has there been any further information from Kirtinagar about the coal proposal?"

"No. It seems that Arvind Singh is tempted but his friend remains adamant. Since the capital investment in the mine is mostly Raventhorne's, the matter appears to have reached an impasse. Our agent informs us that there is much friction already between the two."

"Friction?" Olivia tried not to show her dismay.

"So Das maintains. Now we have to wait and see which Arvind Singh values more, his irrigation project or his friendship with Jai."

Jai! Ransome's use of the first name went unnoticed by him, but it surprised Olivia. Indeed, it had risen to his lips with such naturalness that it confirmed a suspicion now taking firm root in her mind: Arthur Ransome knew more than he had chosen to reveal to her, *much* more! That undertone of sympathy, the lack of anger with which he appeared to accept Raventhorne's wrongdoings and now the slip with his first name—yes, they all added up to more than casual knowledge of the man.

But for the moment there was neither the time nor the opportunity to make further inquiries. In any case, Olivia was deeply distressed by the news that Raventhorne's friendship with Arvind Singh appeared to be in jeopardy. That the relationship was threatened because of the wretched coal, Olivia saw as a tragedy of even greater proportions. Love, trust, compassion, companionship—all these had been denied Jai Raventhorne, either by whimsical fate or by consequences of his own quirks of character. Could his stars now be so cruel as to also snatch away the one friend he had? And all because of a business dispute she saw as absurdly trivial?

Had Olivia been privileged to hear a discussion taking place between her uncle and Kashinath Das at precisely the time that she was with Ransome in his office, she would have perhaps had even greater cause for worry.

"But then, since the consortium is not willing to increase the offer, you wish to take your . . . other option?" Das was saying as he stared solemnly at his English patent-leather shoes. "It would be a simple matter to arrange."

Sitting on his bed propped up against a mountain of pillows that he pummelled frequently to lessen his discomfort, Sir Joshua muttered a curse. "Simple? Don't be an ass, Kashinath. Nothing you Indians arrange can ever be *simple!* Besides, we have yet to receive formal word from Arvind Singh of his refusal." Picking up the handbell from his bedside table, he rattled it vigorously.

Kashinath Das waited until Rehman had appeared, taken the order for two glasses of fresh lime sherbet and withdrawn before he spoke again. "You do not take me seriously, Sir Joshua, but I have considered all details very carefully." He raised his eyes without lifting his face, his expression smooth. "Two of the witnesses will be Englishmen." As Sir Joshua looked at him sharply, he added, "They will not be known in station. They will be brought from the mofussil. Neither Arvind Singh nor Slocum will question their credentials. Several birds can be successfully killed with the same stone."

"And one, of course, considerably fattened!" Sir Joshua said sarcastically as he plumped up another pillow, shifted position and winced at the effort.

"Ah, sir, you do this humble minion an injustice!" Das looked pained. "My modest commission will be a pittance compared to the benefits your consortium will derive from the coal." He paused, tilted his head and inquired slyly, "That is, of course, if you still wish to acquire the coal . . . ?"

Rehman knocked, entered and set the tray bearing the sherbet glasses by the bedside. Adding sugar from a bowl on the tray, Sir Joshua handed a glass to Das, then sat stirring his own thoughtfully. After Rehman had left he hardened. "Oh *yes,* I do still wish to acquire the coal! The option I mentioned to you earlier is not to be forgotten, by no means. But I am still hopeful that Arvind Singh's greed will prevail."

"It will not prevail," Das said sadly. "It will not be allowed to. Funds for the irrigation project will come from elsewhere."

Anger suffused Sir Joshua's cheeks as he stared into his sherbet. "From an Indian consortium? Mooljee, for instance?"

"And others, I hear. Kala Kanta's own resources are also considerable, let us not forget that." Inching forward, Kashinath Das boldly helped himself to another spoonful of sugar, sipped and nodded appreciatively. "For what you gain, Sir Joshua, should you decide on your remaining option, the risks will be minimal. You will sever the relationship forever, and the consortium will have the opening it seeks. Your plan will be welcom—"

"No!" Sir Joshua reacted sharply. "The consortium will not be involved in the details, the gutless bunch of pen pushers and clerks!" He snorted with disgust and shifted position again. "There is still a fatal flaw in the plan, Kashinath, as I told you. How—"

"Not *how,* Sir Joshua, but *when*—that is the very centre. It will be a matter of *timing* that removes the flaw." Sir Joshua narrowed his eyes in inquiry and Das smiled. With an informality few Indians would have dared in Sir Joshua's presence, he stretched out his stumpy legs, laid his head back and stared at the ceiling. "On the first night of the Dassera immersions every year, he is on the river. Alone. He will have no alibi."

Sir Joshua's heat boils, Estelle's brattish temper, Ransome's grim pronouncements and her own malaise—the following morning Olivia forgot them all. On a distant stretch of the river, she was once again surprised by Jai Raventhorne.

"I did promise we would meet again soon," he grumbled churlishly, "so why the surprise? Don't you trust me?"

"No!" She was ecstatic. "Not here, out in the open."

"What, cold feet already? I thought you considered me worth any fuss your uncle chose to make! One can either have one's cake or eat it." He signalled a waiting boatman, handed him the reins to their mounts and then propelled her towards a small craft. "Not even indomitable American ladies who let their hearts rule their heads can be allowed both!"

She didn't answer, too content for retaliation in the immense serenity of the early morning. Sitting opposite her, Raventhorne rowed in silence, his features sliding in and out of curling mists that still layered the waters. When they were midstream and shrouded entirely by patchy vapours, he rested his oars and sat back.

"Would you agree that we are satisfactorily cloistered now?"

Olivia knew that he was still mocking her but she didn't mind. "I guess so."

He extended his legs so that they stretched under the plank she sat on and crossed his hands behind his head. "How are the heat boils? Painful I hope?"

"No. As a matter of fact, getting better." She eyed him irritably. "Why do you need to be so childish. That remark was beneath contempt."

"Didn't Ransome enlighten you as to why? I saw your carriage on Clive Street yesterday."

A silly little thrill made her erupt in goose bumps. To think that he should have been so close without her knowing it! "Is there anything you don't know?"

"If there were, how would I keep you in such awe of my espionage system?" He swung forward to pick up the oars again. "I'm a survivor, remember? Knowledge is my weapon of survival."

They were moving again, threading through clouds of haze that loomed above them like transparent walls of some giant, secret palace inhabited by no one else. The muted splash of the oars resounded hollowly through their private world, glimpses of a salmon pink sky the only hint that they were in another world, too. Raventhorne's knees were so close to Olivia's that if she shifted position a little they would touch hers. She felt an urge to reach out and rest her cheek against the pocket beneath which his heart lay; she wanted to be assured that it was indeed keeping pace with her own, clattering like castanets with excitement. But she remained unmoving, satisfied to have him captive in her vision, satisfied to know that at least for the moment he was her prisoner to do with as she liked. Even in unspeaking silence these snatched moments were precious; rather than disturb it—and those delicate balances of his mind—Olivia held her peace.

The boat again came to a halt. With a sigh—which she chose to believe was one of shared contentment—Raventhorne lay back again and closed his eyes. "Why are you staring at me?" he asked after a moment.

With a jerk, she sat up and looked away. "Apart from your other evil powers, can you also see with your eyes shut?"

They opened again. "I don't need eyes to see you, Olivia." Sitting up, he took her hand and kissed each finger-tip in turn. "You could never hide yourself from my vision."

The hand that he retained in his trembled as their fingers entwined; threads of heat coursed through her veins. In that moment she loved him so completely that she almost cried out with the pain of it. *Who are you, what are you? Where did you come from and where will you go . . . ?* For an instant she was overwhelmed again with the yearning to know him truly, but she restrained herself. Instead, she asked casually, "Have you seen Kinjal recently? I dispatched a letter to her last week."

"Yes, she was pleased to receive it." He turned her hand over in his large, hardened palm and examined it closely, as if it were some rare object he could not translate into terms of understanding. "Kinjal is well. Busy with her children, who have returned to Kirtinagar."

Olivia chanced another question. "And . . . Arvind Singh?"

Carefully he returned her hand to her lap. "You have heard from Ransome that we are locked in battle—is that what you really want to know about?"

Olivia sighed. "I would hate to have you as an enemy, Jai. There is something about you that quite frightens me. Yes, that is what I really want to know about."

"Well, it is true." He seemed to take the question in his stride. "Arvind is tempted by Sir Joshua's dangling carrots; I am not. And Das, anxious to earn his commission, is making as much mischief as he can."

His unworried admission agitated her. "How can you allow a matter of mere business to disrupt a friendship of such affection and such long standing?" she cried. "Is it worth it?"

Raventhorne looked surprised. "It isn't. Business disagreements have nothing to do with our friendship. We have had plenty of differences before."

"But you said you were locked in battle . . . !"

He smiled with a sudden softening of the eyes. "I used a figure of speech not to be taken literally. When men have business disputes they can be fierce but they are seldom personal." His amusement deepened. "It is only women," he said witheringly, "who declare total war on each other when they fall out."

Olivia was amazed that he, of all people, should have the nerve to make such a remark, but she let it pass. "Then your friendship with Arvind Singh is not at stake?"

"No."

"But if his irrigation project suffers . . . ?"

"It will not. Indian merchants can be every bit as canny as boxwallahs." A smug little smile came and went and then the softness returned as he searched her anxious face. For a moment it seemed as if every nerve in his body was straining against some inner impulse he was determined to resist. Then, with a shrug he satisfied himself by pressing a finger-tip into the crease dividing Olivia's forehead and smoothing it out. "Don't be concerned for my sake," he said huskily, "if that is what troubles you."

"Yes, it does trouble me. I can't bear to think—" Olivia cut herself off, unable to tell him just how unendurable she found the prospect of his solitariness. It wounded her immeasurably that he should be deprived of his only friendship, of the only family he could almost call his own.

She had successfully contained the words, but what she could not contain was her expression of compassion. Like a trap springing shut, the grey eyes, melting only an instant ago, turned into stone. "I find your concern touching," he said with biting sarcasm, "but I can assure you it is not needed. Through whatever you've heard from Kinjal you have chosen to romanticize an image of what you think I am." Grabbing the oars, he thrust them again into the water and jolted the boat into action.

"I *did*n't—"

"Don't lie to me, Olivia. I can read you like a damned book."

"Just because I'm concerned—"

"Don't be. I am not used to anyone's concern. It makes me uneasy and suspicious of their motives."

"Suspicious?" Frustrated beyond measure by his sheer orneriness, she banged her fist on her wooden seat. "I *hate* it when you suddenly become irrational like this! I can't bear it when you choose to wound me with such lack of cause!"

He sneered at her and gave an ugly little laugh. "Can't you? I thought you were willing to accept anything I chose to be! Do I take it your courage doesn't measure up to your rather rash commitment?"

"No! But you persist in reading into simple words what there is not. You admit to regarding me with suspicion, with distrust. You conceal yourself from me with half truths and evasions and prevarications . . ." Her voice started to break but, gritting her teeth, she refused to cry. "I . . . love you, Jai," she whispered, miserable. "It is natural that I should want to understand you, know you, know about you . . ." She could not go on. Blinking rapidly, she turned her face away from him.

Anger spent, he was suddenly beside her, drawing her into the circle of his arms. "I have no idea what is or is not natural in your love, Olivia." He buried his face in her neck, stricken with remorse. "I have never been loved by a woman such as you. There is so much you need to teach me, so much patience you need to cultivate."

She filled with sweetness, the taste of sourness gone from her tongue as if it had never been there, her mind wiped clear of his taunts, his wounding barbs, his whimsicalities; in a single breath she had forgiven him everything. Pressing into the tense muscles of his back, she stroked the hardness out of them; with soothing sounds she solaced his inner torments and kissed away his ravaging turmoil until the crackling rasps of his breath settled again into cadences of calmness. The immense love she felt for him spilled over; in her limbs she felt the now familiar aches that arose whenever he was close. For a while he lay still in her arms, his fingers giving her the caresses her body was beginning to yearn, but hesitantly, cautiously, his restraint almost visibly tight. Then he raised his head and kissed her once, full on the mouth. "Don't encourage me, Olivia," he muttered gruffly, his face drawn with strain. "I am not easily frightened but you make me fear myself. It is an odd sensation."

He did not move from her side, yet in some subtle way he had withdrawn from her, once more coiled within that private shell she detested so much. Her hands balled with the effort not to touch him; she wanted to grab him, trap that elusive will-o'-the-wisp of his being and imprison it inside herself forever, but she knew it was not within her power. Not yet, perhaps not ever. Disconsolate, she allowed him his retreat without protest. "God knows it is not I either who has willed this, Jai."

"No." He moved away and retrieved his oars. "You asked me if there was anything I didn't know. There is. I don't know why you should want to love me."

Want to love? Did a choice exist? It was not a question to which he expected an answer and she gave him none. Glumly, she honoured his silent privacy but there was bitterness in her thoughts. Theirs was an extraordinary relationship, if it could even be called that! It was neither that of friends nor of lovers—neither flesh nor fowl. What she was giving him was a promise of abundant love, her everything; what he was giving her was words, a touch, a fleeting glance *almost* of love. Yet, how precious to her were becoming these random words and looks and casual caresses! Jai Raventhorne might be a shell, a husk, a phantom, and woundingly wayward, but it was this very outline of a man that she had sworn to love and accept as it was. Even as an outline, she would take him against all the other men in the world put together!

The mist had lifted completely. On the approaching bank the crouched boatman waited patiently for their return. There was no one on the embankment save for a dhobi and his wife beating their day's wash against a protruding stone. They paid no attention to them as the boat beached and, wordlessly, the boatman led up their horses.

Olivia mounted without breaking the silence. Raventhorne held on to her hand for a moment or two. "You know what it is that I dislike most about meeting you, Olivia?" She felt a rising tear and shook her head. Briefly, he laid her hand against his cheek. "It is that the time also comes when I must leave you."

She kept his diminishing form in her vision as long as she could before Shaitan vanished in a flurry of dust and kicking hooves. Her eyes welled; those last few words she secreted within her heart like gems in a meagre treasury. This time she had not asked when she would see him again, nor had he volunteered the information. But this time it was easy to be patient. She knew she would see him again. And again and again.

No force on earth could make it otherwise.

"You'll never guess what *I've* been doing!" For a change Estelle was in good humour. When Olivia came out of her bath, she was sitting on her bed munching an apple. "Well, aren't you going to ask what it is?"

"No." Olivia buried her head in her towel and vigorously rubbed her damp hair. "Because you're going to tell me anyway."

Estelle poked out her tongue but her eyes continued to sparkle. "I've been auditioning, that's what!"

Olivia stilled. "For the pantomime?"

"Yes." Estelle flicked the core of the apple out of the window. "Mr. Hicks thinks I dance very well."

For days now a battle royal had been raging between Estelle and her mother about that pantomime. A visiting stage company touring the country was planning to entertain Calcutta society over the festive season with a musical version of *Cinderella* at a local theatre. The main roles were to be performed by members of the troupe, but Mr. Hicks, the manager, was trying to assemble a chorus line from among Calcutta's young ladies. It was all really quite innocuous, but Lady Bridget objected to Estelle being one of the chosen for basically three reasons: Professional actors were all morally loose, the chorus girls would have to wear heavy paints on their faces and rather too light embellishments elsewhere, and the manager, Mr. Hicks, was a known personal "friend" of Mrs. Drummond.

Olivia regarded her cousin thoughtfully. "Does your mother know you've been auditioning?"

"No, but she will if I get the part."

"And *if* you get the part she's already said she won't allow you to take it." She began to comb out her long hair. "I'm not sure that Uncle Josh will either. Your Mr. Hicks certainly *looks* a card whether or not he is."

"He's not. He's really very nice, even though he does pick his nose in public." Delicately, she turned up her own. "I don't care what Mama has to say this time, Olivia, if Mr. Hicks thinks I'm suitable I'm going to do it. And Papa *won't* object because he doesn't know I even exist any more." Her lower lip stuck out defiantly. "Anyway, this Clarissa Rose showed Polly and me her gowns. She's played Ophelia at Windsor Castle, you know, before the Queen. And she goes to Covent Garden ever so often where the Queen has her own box and everyone has to stand up when she enters. They play the anthem and all the ladies curtsy. Isn't she *lucky?*"

"Who, the Queen?"

"No, silly, Clarissa Rose, this actress who's going to play Cinderella. Fancy going to Covent Garden!"

"I'm sure a lot of people go to Covent Garden."

"Well, *I* don't. I have to make do with that blasted Strand Road evening after evening!" She brooded for a while, then reassumed her good humour. "And she showed us something called dag . . . dag . . . ," she frowned, then shrugged, "anyway, it was a plate with an imprint on it of herself. She said it was the latest thing in England for portraits."

"Daguerreotype?"

"Yes, that was it, I think." Estelle struggled up excitedly. "She said the pictures were made with a box and you just sat in front of it with plenty of sunlight on your face. Miss Rose said it was a French invention. Have you ever heard of it?"

"Yes. I've never seen one but Papa has. They're using daguerrotyping to print pictures in the newspapers in America." She sat down on the bed next to Estelle. "You know the problem with you, Estelle? It's the same that Freddie has—you need more occupation. Why don't you ask Uncle Josh if you can help in his office? He'd really appreciate that, you know."

Estelle looked horrified. "Work in Papa's *office?* Ugh!" she shuddered. "I'd be bored to tears!"

"You're bored to tears now," Olivia pointed out. "At least you'd be doing something useful *and* pleasing your parents."

"I'm going to travel, Olivia. I'm going to do real things, meet real people." Estelle crushed her with a look and added loftily, "I'm going to be *independent.*"

"To be independent you have to earn your own living."

"You mean give piano lessons and take in sewing and read aloud to rich invalids and that sort of thing?" She was appalled. "I'd die, just *die* if I had to do all that!"

Olivia laughed. "Then how would you keep body and soul together in that wonderful state of independence—send your bills home to Papa? I don't call *that* being independent!"

"There are other ways, you know." Estelle's round, baby face assumed an expression of superiority.

"You mean marry John and let *him* foot your bills?" Olivia's eyes twinkled. "That isn't exactly independence in my book either."

Estelle gave her cousin a look of pity. "I could ingratiate myself with a rich old gent and get him to keep me in the style to which I am accustomed." She patted her hair and put her nose up in the air.

Olivia hooted. "Well, make sure he's rich enough to buy you all the chocolates you want so that you won't have to bribe the cook to steal them from the store-room!"

At this reminder of her secret pact with Babulal, Estelle muttered a proscribed oath, flung a pillow in Olivia's direction and, grumbling under her breath, flounced out of the room.

Jai Raventhorne did not surprise Olivia again until a whole week of leaden-footed days and nights full of tormented dreams had passed for Olivia. Sir Joshua recovered from his heat boils and resumed his hectic activity at the office, and Estelle's mood of rebelliousness kept getting steadily worse, with Estelle secure in the knowledge that since her father had little time to worry about domestic trivia it was only her mother she had to contend with, and that was done easily enough. And Olivia received her first letter from Greg. It was a warm, affectionate but thankfully unsentimental letter; the news it contained, however, worried her. There was a distant chance, he wrote, that her father would allow him to make an offer for the ranch. Greg had always wanted to become a homesteader himself, Olivia knew, but it came as a surprise that her father was thinking of selling out. Also, it hurt that he had not told her so himself. He had mentioned, of course, that he was considering buying land in Hawaii. Obviously, the two matters were connected, but what was making her father take such a drastic step? And in her absence? Anxiously, Olivia waited for another letter from her father that would perhaps explain everything, but in the meantime she felt depressed and again isolated from everything she held truly dear.

It was in a remote flower market veined with narrow lanes and gullies that Jai Raventhorne suddenly materialised at Olivia's elbow when she was least expecting him. She was standing in front of an open stall laden with marigolds, admiring their perfection of form and dazzle of colour when she heard his voice behind her.

"Do these flowers please you?"

Olivia almost fainted with shock as her hand flew to her throat and her head whirled with sudden dizziness. "You should have been an Irishman," she gasped, spinning on her heel to face him. "There is much that you share with the leprechauns!"

"I like to surprise you," he said, casually tucking a hand under her arm. "You look like a startled gazelle whose grazing has been rudely interrupted. And those eyes," he paused to stare into them, "I like to see them melt like molasses in the sun."

She felt weak with happiness. "For someone who doesn't much care for surprises," she murmured, already delirious, "you take some quite unforgivable liberties."

"But you will nevertheless forgive me?"

"Yes," she breathed fervently, "oh yes . . ."

The bazaar was a riot of colour and fragrances almost too overwhelming for the nostrils. Olivia's head swam even more as they walked leisurely among the tiered stalls heavy with zinnias, cocks-comb, heliotrope, phlox, larkspur, bunches of budding roses and the ubiquitous marigolds. They stopped before a stall that was vibrantly different from the others and Olivia gave a small cry. "Orchids?"

"Yes. Wild orchids."

The owner of the shop, a funny, shrivelled man with a skin like crushed brown paper, gave them a toothless smile and his eyes lit up. "Jai?" He peered closely, then half rose and caught both of Raventhorne's hands in his, shaking them vigorously. *"Tumi keneke asa, mor lora?"*

Raventhorne smiled, replied in a language Olivia could not understand but could tell was not Hindustani, and pointed to a trailing vine with exquisite, waxy mauve-blue blossoms and rich green leaves. "Do you like these?" he asked her, reverting to English.

"Yes, they're beautiful—what are they?"

"The blue Vanda. They grow wild up in the hills." He spoke again to the old man, who gleefully picked up an armful of the vines and started to tie them up in a length of jute sacking. "If you pack the roots with wet earth, then wrap them with the sacking around a branch in your garden, they will continue to grow and flower." He collected the bulky parcel and dug his hand into a pocket to pull out a fistful of coins, but the old man waved them away. Raventhorne cajoled him gently, pressing the coins into the man's hands. Finally, with a resigned shake of his head, the flower seller accepted. He glanced slyly at Olivia and made a remark at which Raventhorne laughed.

"What did he say about me?" Olivia asked as they walked away. She was still dazed not only by Raventhorne's presence but also by the accidental glimpse into his life. There was no doubt that the flower seller knew him well.

"He said you didn't look like a horse, like other European women he has seen."

"Oh." She giggled. "What was the language you spoke to him?"

"Assamese." It was said curtly, with reluctance.

Olivia knew better than to question further. They slipped into an easy silence, strolling idly through gnarled lanes knotted with people. Occasionally, low palanquins would brush past carried by coolies with jogging, measured steps that seldom faltered. Standing cheek by jowl with some of the thatched huts were one or two fine residences with grilled windows and ornate wrought-iron balconies. Under a thatched roof a stern Brahmin in a sugar white dhoti rocked back and forth chanting and conducting a class of young students who sat cross-legged on bamboo mats and chanted in unison. Walking with his hands clasped behind his back, Raventhorne answered her neutral questions willingly, his speech clear cut and economical, his explanations patient and precise.

"Calcutta might be a village but it is a village of palaces," Olivia remarked when they had passed by yet another lordly mansion, this one with a beautiful garden and cupolas on the roof. She felt a stab of apprehension. "Are these European homes?"

"Europeans do not live next to Indians, or vice versa. These belong to *zamindars,* or Indian merchants who have flourished in the wash of British success."

She threw him a sidelong glance. "Like you?"

"I suppose so," he conceded with surprising ease. "I have no qualms about making money out of the British—on the contrary. It's the only justification I can see of their presence here."

"But *you* have a home next to a European."

"A work place, not a home. I need to entertain business associates from overseas and to have a place to put them up. I suffer European neighbours for purely practical reasons." Perhaps in view of her outburst the last time they had met, he answered her questions readily enough, even with affability. Having vowed never to overstep her bounds again but emboldened by his amiability, she asked one more question.

"Then what to you is . . . home? Assam?" She had looked up the atlas to familiarise herself with its location north-east of Bengal toward the Himalayas.

They had left behind the congestion of the bazaar to arrive near a large, rectangular water tank on the banks of which women washed utensils and clothes and men performed morning ablutions. Raventhorne stopped, surveyed the scene seemingly without attention and kicked a small stone down the steps that surrounded the tank.

"They say home is where the heart is," he evaded.

"And where is your heart?"

He smiled. "At the moment, with you."

"At other moments?"

"Other moments." He turned the phrase under his breath as if tasting it. "There are no other moments. It seems you have appropriated for yourself far more than wisdom tells me to give."

The flicker of annoyance that crossed his eyes did not affect Olivia as, euphoric, she added another small gem to her treasure. Jai Raventhorne was becoming the nub around which her every moment, waking and sleeping, revolved; that she too had a place in his thoughts, in his heart, was a gift more blessed than any from heaven. And if her "appropriation" was causing him irritation—well, why should she be the only one to suffer?

At the moment of parting where they had left their horses in the charge of a disreputable-looking urchin who grinned cheekily as he accepted his rather handsome reward, Raventhorne asked her, "Do you still wish to see me again?" He did not touch her.

The traces of anxiety she sensed were to her balm for the soul. "Why do you ask me that each time we meet?" she countered, basking in the happiness nothing had marred this morning. "Do you truly believe me to be that fickle?"

"If only you *were* fickle," he grunted, thrusting his hands into his pockets as if to keep them well out of trouble, "I wouldn't have to make all these damnable decisions I'm having to now! It would settle the matter quite neatly."

She knew his restraint was deliberate, for she could almost feel the tightness with which he held himself back, but that too she acknowledged with tremors of excitement. It was enough that he desired her, that touching her gave him pleasure, that by forcibly denying himself he suffered a sense of loss, that merely by her presence she could provoke in him hungers duplicated within her own body. Even these minor triumphs Olivia was learning to cherish. Jai Raventhorne gave nothing of himself to anyone; at least he was giving her these.

With radiant eyes she bridged the distance between them. "When . . . ?" It was beyond her will-power not to ask that recurring question.

He sighed. "Tomorrow."

Tomorrow? Olivia was filled with rapture. He had never seen her two days running!

Mirage or man, shadow or substance; whatever the game, it was insanely exhilarating. It was as if Jai Raventhorne was devising for her some competition for stakes that he was mischievously keeping secret from her for the present. That the stakes might turn out to be exorbitantly high Olivia never even considered. Whatever the cost she was willing to pay it.

8

The game intensified.

True to his word, Jai Raventhorne met Olivia again the following morning, and then every morning after that. For her each day dawned with the promise of an uncut diamond waiting to be faceted into perfection. She never knew when he was going to appear, but like a shadow he always did. His instincts regarding her whereabouts were unerring; he seemed to know everything she did, everyone she met, almost every thought fermenting in her mind. Whether in person or not, she was always within his focus. Many times she tried to outwit him by hiding herself in unfrequented corners of the city, in little-known alleys and gullies, but she never succeeded. Home is where the heart is, he had said; and like a homing pigeon he always found his way to her, defeating and delighting her in the same moment.

Olivia began spending her nights in cursing the sun for not rising, and her days in counting the hours until dark. She lived only for those few speeding minutes of the lavender and saffron dawn when she would receive from him the elixir that would carry her through the rest of the hours when he was not with her. And until that magical instant when he actually did appear in her vision, not as a fantasy but as flesh and blood, Olivia died a thousand deaths of panic in case his unpredictability had finally taken him off elsewhere.

Patiently, she learned to recognise all his many moods. Her sixth sense about him honed itself to pick up every nuance from his extraordinary eyes, from the imperceptible movements of his muscles, from the merest droop of his lips. She became accustomed to not understanding some of the things he said, to not questioning when she sensed a retreat. Sometimes, ridden by his invisible demons, he was harsh; she accepted these moods meekly because there were others when he was as soft as the underwing of a dove. His hunger for her, Olivia knew, was immense, but he kept it securely trapped. Even this she accepted with joy, for she knew that one day, some day, when he gave himself rein it would be showering rainbows. On those enchanted mornings when she had her ear next to his heartbeat, it was enough to iron out every aching crease of her own heart and set it singing. Intoxicated, she met him again and again with a reckless abandon in which there was no place for guilt. For two cents, she would proclaim her love from the terraces of Calcutta, and some day soon she would.

Often, laughing within herself, she wondered why nobody noticed that when she walked her feet no longer touched the ground. Was it possible that such opalescent happiness as was hers could fill the world with so much light and still remain a secret? But, as it happened, the inner glow that radiated so fearlessly from her eyes now was by no means going unnoticed. Returning from church one Sunday when the girls had stayed behind with some of Estelle's friends, Lady Bridget remarked to her husband, "Isn't Olivia looking marvellously well these days, Josh? I do believe it is young Freddie's devotion that has effected the transformation. Don't you agree?"

Disgruntled at having been dragged to church again, an exercise he disliked intensely, Sir Joshua snorted. "I'm inclined to give the credit to his therapeutic absence from station," he commented drily.

"Don't be absurd, Josh! Olivia is extremely well disposed towards young Freddie. He's already written to her thrice from the plantation."

"That might prove *his* ardency," he was quick to point out; "it hardly proves hers. I doubt if Olivia has troubled to write back."

"Oh, I'm sure she has, dear! I shall have to ask Estelle—and speaking of Estelle," she frowned and drummed a tattoo with her fingers on the carriage window, "I'm really at my wit's end with that girl. You will have to make a strong stand with her, *very* strong."

Sir Joshua cursed under his breath. "God's blood, woman, don't you think I have enough to worry about? Manage as best you can but spare me these daily trials!" He knocked hard with his crop on the back of the coachman's seat as an instruction to go faster. "If she's frisky, then loosen the reins a little. It works with horses; there's no reason why it shouldn't with high-spirited fillies like Estelle."

"Loosen the reins enough to allow her to be in this wretched pantomime?" Lady Bridget cried. "Are you out of your mind, Josh?"

"Pantomime? What pantomime?"

But by the time Lady Bridget had finished telling her husband what she already had several times before, he was no longer listening.

A letter arrived for Olivia from Kinjal inviting her to Kirtinagar once again, this time for the Dassera celebrations. It was a tempting offer and Olivia was touched; she replied with equal warmth but made vague excuses for not accepting the invitation. To be away from Calcutta now, even for a day, for an hour, was to her intolerable; and Kinjal's well-meaning warnings would stand like a barrier between them. As for the dispute her uncle had engineered between Jai and the Maharaja, Olivia was no longer exercised by it. Raventhorne's shoulders were broad. God knew he was capable of resolving his own problems without her concern. Whatever burdens he had on his head had been there before she had come and no doubt would be there after she had gone.

After she had gone . . .

It was these four words that always brought Olivia's thoughts to a standstill and chilled her with apprehensions. Her future had become a cul-de-sac—unless Jai included her in his. Did he? She didn't know, he never said. Fiercely, she willed everything erased except for the present.

"Calcutta cannot be that much of a village if I can continue to meet you with such impunity!" Olivia could not help but jubilate at the persisting success of her subterfuges.

"*Is* it with impunity that you meet me?" Raventhorne asked.

She knew that it was not to the risk of exposure that he referred, deliberately twisting her question. Olivia's eyes blazed defiance; she hated it when he slipped into ambiguities such as this. "Yes!"

"Then you *are* less clever than I had thought!" His frame of mind this morning was cussed, there was no doubt about that. He was restless, refusing to sit still; his fingers were fidgety as they clasped and unclasped the holster he sometimes wore when he had what he called "serious" business to transact later. Olivia wondered about the reason for his mood when he abruptly asked, "Your Freddie returns shortly. Will you be seeing him again?"

"I can hardly avoid it." She spoke carefully, for the subject of poor Freddie Birkhurst was a prickly one with him. Secretly, however, Olivia was delighted that he should show signs of jealousy, an emotion so far removed from his usual confident self.

"Do you plan to marry him?" He sat down and glowered at her.

She was tempted to tease him but his humour was already so sour that she regretfully abandoned the thought. "No." She could not, however, resist exploiting her advantage to some extent. "Although it was you who recommended that I should. You said—"

"I know what I said!" He sprang up again, flicked his Colt out of its holster and fired at a *bel* tree, bringing a plump green fruit crashing to the ground, its bright pink pulp spilling in all directions. "I was angry then."

Olivia put her arms around her knees and rocked herself back and forth. "And you are angry again."

"I am *not* angry!" he shouted, balling a fist and hitting it against the palm of his other hand. Then his arms dropped. "Yes, I am angry," he muttered savagely. "I am angry because for the first time in my life I find that I am avaricious. I cannot let *go.*"

She got up and went to him. "Then indulge your greed," she dared to suggest, running her hand over his shirt sleeve. "Do not let go!"

He shook his head impatiently and moved away. "No, that must not be, cannot be." When he looked at her, his huge mother-of-pearl eyes were like distant moons covered in cloud. "You ask for the impossible!"

"But I love you, Jai," Olivia breathed for the hundredth, the thousandth time, pleading tacitly for a response that would not come. For all his moments of tenderness, his exasperated admissions, his cautious kisses and caresses, his ill-concealed desire for her, he had never said that he loved her and now she hungered to hear the words.

"You should not love a man such as me."

"You are the only man I *can* ever love!"

"Don't tempt your fates, Olivia. As it is you have produced turmoils in me that defeat me."

Then allow those turmoils to lead you to love me! Her passionate plea remained unsaid. Instead, the hurt she felt emerged as anger. "And you cannot tolerate to be defeated in anything, is that it?"

"I have never *been* defeated in anything." Supreme arrogance cemented the lines of his face into an aloof mould. "You ask for the impossible, Olivia," he repeated with a return to cold hostility.

She was unbearably wounded. "I have never asked you for anything," she cried, "except for crumbs of your precious time!"

"You ask without asking and I cannot refuse. It makes me angry that I should not be able to refuse even those crumbs."

"Then *don't* see me anymore!" she flung back in his face. "I can do without you, Jai Raventhorne, *believe* me I can!"

"In that case," he grated under his breath, "you *shall.*" He vaulted into Shaitan's saddle and thundered off in a cloud of dead leaves and dust, leaving her choked with unexpended fury.

Olivia cried silently all the way home. For three whole days after that, although she wandered the countryside far and wide in desperation and fear and bitter, bitter remorse, she did not see Jai Raventhorne. Her sense of loss was almost too much to bear.

Once more they had come full circle.

But then, on the fourth morning, he was with her again. Without a word he gathered her in his arms, crushing her to him as if he would never let her go again.

"Wipe out everything I said," he whispered huskily, covering her face with fierce kisses with lips that trembled. "Erase every damned word from your mind as if it had never been said. Forgive me, forgive me . . ."

She already had. With the magic wand of his touch the sorcerer had broken one spell and rapidly woven another to enmesh her once more in tangles of enchantment. She kissed away every line of unhappiness from his ivory face looking so wretched, to whisper back meaningless phrases of comfort.

"It is a novelty for me, this . . . relationship," he groaned, not letting her go, smoothing the hair back from her forehead. "Your love is like a mechanical toy for me. I see that it works but I am baffled at *how.* You should not make me angry like you do."

She laughed at his stern frown, his aggrieved expression. "*I* make you angry?" She kissed the corners of his mouth. "You do have such infernal gall, my darling!"

His sombre, worried grey eyes lit up in smiles. "Were it not for my infernal gall, would you love me at all?"

"Perhaps not," Olivia conceded, starting to purr like a kitten just surprised with a bowl of cream. "But a *little* less gall would make me love you so much more."

"Love me *more?*" She laughed delightedly at his alarm as he swore. "I cannot assimilate what you give me now. How can you punish me with even more?"

But she knew that he teased her, for in his eyes there was tenderness such as she had never seen before. He had brought her a gift, glass bangles in an iridescent display of startling colours that winked at her as they caught the early sun.

"Oh, Jai . . ." She was profoundly moved. "They're so lovely, I can't bear the thought of wearing them in case they break." Nevertheless, she allowed him to slip them over her wrist one by one, his huge brown hands clumsy in the unfamiliar effort.

"I have given you nothing," he lamented, once again unhappy, "*can* give you nothing to compare with what you give me. Tell me what would please you, anything at all—jewels, gold, beautiful clothes," he spread his hands helplessly, "*any*thing."

Give me part of yourself . . .

She held up her hand and turned it around slowly, thrilling to the gentle tinkles as the glass bracelets nudged each other. "What you give me now is enough. I have no need for jewels or clothes."

"But I thought all women liked jewels and pretty clothes."

She surveyed him coolly through narrowed eyes. "The kind of women *you* are used to no doubt do. I would be obliged if you would not include me among them."

"Christ!" He threw up his arms. "I thought I had learned everything that could be learned about women in my travels, but a sassy upstart from California now tells me that my education is incomplete! All right," he leaned and kissed the tip of her nose, "since I insist on giving you something in return at least for crumbs of *your* precious time, name it."

Olivia felt her throat tighten as she stared back into those bottomless dove grey pools of haunting tenderness that ravaged her dreams each night. *Just tell me once, only once, that you love me . . .*

She smiled. "I would like to know more about these travels on which you received such a comprehensive education in women," she suggested. "It might suffice to wipe out your crippling debt to me."

He laughed. It was one of those rare mornings when nothing disturbed the harmony of their communion, when he was willing to open up to her at least that part of his life that he considered dispensable. Gratified even to be admitted into the fringes of his carefully camouflaged world, Olivia listened entranced. With charm, with humour, he regaled her with anecdotes of his adventures in China, in America, in the Pacific, tantalising her with mention of women who had crossed his path but without ever elucidating, obviously pleased with her occasional displays of stabbing jealousy.

"You should be ashamed of making so many immoral admissions," she told him petulantly at one point.

"Would you be better pleased if I were celibate?"

"I don't think you could be, even if you tried!"

"Not so." Not even a dent showed in his complacency. "I could be anything if I tried."

"In that case, try not to be so conceited!" she snapped.

"You see? You *do* ask the impossible!"

It was a flawless morning. Olivia wanted it never to end, but then it did. He swept her up in his arms and held her close, that hated leash loosening in a rare moment of impulsiveness. His cheek against hers was stubbled but in that roughness there was such sensuality that Olivia felt almost giddy. "We might have been in the same town in America and not know it, do you realise that, Jai?"

"Unlikely. I would have known; the wind would have carried your scent to me."

She went weak with the feel of his flesh, with the caress of his groping fingers. "Even though I might have been in pigtails?"

"Even though you might have been unborn. Olivia, I . . ." The words stuck in his gullet like a fish bone that would not be expelled.

Say it, say it, please my darling one . . .

He could not. Instead, he smiled and shook his head and, one last time, kissed her with that fragile restraint hanging by a thread. And then he was gone. But with gratitude Olivia swept up the crumbs he had left behind; when starving, even a morsel or two helps.

Borne aloft on clouds of uncertain direction, in her linear preoccupations Olivia noticed little of what was happening in the house. She was vaguely aware that her aunt and Estelle barely spoke to each other and that her uncle was seldom home except at night. Therefore, it was with a considerable sense of shock that she returned from her ride one morning to find Lady Bridget crying. Olivia had never seen her aunt in tears. It was a sight that she found horribly distressing. She knelt and took her aunt in her arms, plunging straight into the heart of the matter. "Estelle?"

Lady Bridget nodded but it was some time before she could speak. "I don't know what to do with her, Olivia, I just do not know what to *do!*" Eyes streaming, she blew her nose and looked at her beseechingly. "He's a *frightful* man, Olivia, that Hicks. You've met him; you saw how he slurps his tea and drops his aitches. I couldn't understand anything he said! And Estelle seems *besotted* with him, at least with the idea of going on that stage . . ."

For all Olivia's sympathy for her aunt, it was difficult to know how to console her. Despite the unsavoury Mr. Hicks, whom she had met once when he came to tea, she couldn't help feeling it was all rather an overblown storm. Also, as she pointed out now to her aunt with as much diplomacy as she could muster, if most of her friends had been given roles in the pantomime, what was the harm if Estelle had too?

Lady Bridget smarted. "I'm *surprised* that Celia Cleghorne should allow Marie such licence! One could not, of course, expect any better from the Smitherses considering . . ." Her mouth tightened as she broke off.

"But Charlotte is a very good friend, Estelle says. Surely—"

"Good friend, my eye! She's meeting Clive behind my back, you know. Jane Watkins saw them on the river one evening. He was holding her hand."

Loyally, Olivia tried to salvage the situation. "Clive is a fine young man, Aunt Bridget. With his commission in the Navy he has a good future ahead of him."

"You don't understand, Olivia!" She looked aghast. "Herbert Smithers might be a big gun in the Company but it's no secret that his grandmother was the daughter of a native woman who kept boarders, one of whom happened to be a Smithers. Of course they deny it, but blood tells, you know. Sooner or later they'll have a tarred baby in that family, mark my words, and I'd rather *strangle* Estelle than risk her being its mother!" Suddenly her anger vanished and, with a quiet sob, she buried her face in her hands. "Oh God, oh *God,* how I wish we had never come to this bloody, benighted country!"

Olivia was taken aback by the obvious depth of her aunt's

unhappiness; she had never known Lady Bridget to curse before. "Estelle is going through a difficult transition," she said comfortingly. "It's a passing stage; she'll get over it soon. We all did, you know."

"*You* did?" Her aunt's puffy eyes welled again as she pressed her hand. "My dear, there was a time when I was concerned about your influence on Estelle, but I was wrong. You have come as a blessing for her. If she is refusing to benefit by your example, it is she who is to blame. How I wish Estelle had some of your moral strength!"

Olivia flushed and quietly left the room.

Driven by guilt at her thoughtless negligence and her aunt's painful sufferings, however trivial, Olivia determined to tackle Estelle without further delay. With her cousin's increasing absences from the house, the evening sorties along the Strand had become infrequent. Now, manipulating another carriage drive, Olivia plunged into her self-assigned duty with blunt lack of preamble. "Are you sincerely interested in Clive, Estelle, or is it just another frivolous flirtation?"

Estelle's smile was secretive. "Wouldn't you like to know!"

"Yes, I would! You're being dreadfully unfair to John, who isn't here, and you're making your mother very unhappy."

"Good! I'm sick of people taking me for granted."

"Nobody takes you for granted, Estelle. On the contrary—"

"Papa does! He doesn't even know whether I'm dead or alive."

"That's self-pitying nonsense! He's been very busy with all these problems at work. As for your mother—"

"I'm going to do that pantomime, Olivia," her cousin interrupted, her chin set with stubbornness. "Mama will not stop me *this* time! Hicks has agreed to all the costume changes Mama wanted, but you can't go on stage without these special cosmetics, Clarissa says . . . Oh, hell and damnation!" She slumped back angrily and crossed her arms. "I can't understand what all the blasted fuss is about."

As a matter of fact, neither could Olivia. "Well, it's not *me* you have to convince," she said, sighing wearily. "Why not put it to your father and get *him* on your side?"

"Papa?" Estelle's laugh was ugly. "Papa can't see beyond that precious coal of his. He certainly can't see *me* anymore!"

"But you know that coal is important to him, Estelle."

"Oh yes, I do know that—*far* more important than his daughter!"

Olivia searched her cousin's face, suddenly surprised to see in it signs she had not noticed before. There were dark smudges beneath her usually sparkling eyes, now dull and listless. Her childish features were drawn, her moon face somehow thinner. Unhappiness, tension—these were now writ large across her expression instead of mere brattish discontent. Estelle was obviously as unhappy as her mother: That she had not had the sensitivity to observe that before filled Olivia with renewed remorse. Quickly, she pulled her cousin into her arms.

"You must never, never think that your father doesn't love you anymore, darling," she said, now identifying the nub of Estelle's brooding misery. "You are dearer to Uncle Josh than anything else in his life, you must know that."

Slouched against her shoulder, Estelle's body trembled. "Not anymore, Olivia, not anymore." She began to sob.

"You silly goose. People who love you don't always *tell* you that they do, do they? The language of the heart is often silent, you know."

Estelle paused in her sobs. "It . . . is?"

"Of course. One just has to close one's eyes and listen."

"But that isn't *enough* . . . !"

The carriage was clip-clopping leisurely along the river front. Unconsciously, Olivia gazed over her cousin's shoulder to where the lofty multi-masts of Raventhorne's provocative clipper raked the low-slung clouds. "Sometimes one has to *make* it enough, Estelle . . ."

Sitting up to dry her eyes, Estelle seemed to accept Olivia's well-meaning platitudes. "Yes, I suppose you are right," she said with a long sigh that was wistful and resigned. "I too will try to make it enough for me."

Olivia shifted uneasily at the blithe facility of her clichés: Had *she* been able to make it enough for herself . . . ?

Without saying anything further to her woebegone cousin, Olivia decided to accost her uncle with his aberrations towards his daughter some day soon.

Jai Raventhorne did not appear by her side the next morning, nor the morning following that. Balanced precariously over an abyss of doubts and uncertainties, Olivia was devoured by conjectures and apprehensions. Was he ill? Merely too busy? Suddenly no longer caring . . . ? It was this last with which she punished herself into renewed fear and penitence. Had she offended him in any way, said something that had made an unwonted dent in that seemingly unbreakable carapace? Had he *tired* of her, perhaps?

Once more Olivia panicked. Jai Raventhorne to her now was like an addiction as deadly and as demanding as that of the opium he despised so passionately. She could no longer survive through the day without even those pathetically fleeting moments upon which hung her sanity. He had become her opiate, her daily ration of fulfilment both physical and mental. And in the realisation of her mortifying dependence on his whims, anger stirred and stayed. He had no business to subject her to such arbitrary and undeserved torture. She had every right to seek him out and demand some straight answers. She could not, *would* not, continue with these debasements—waiting upon his fancies, dancing to his tunes, sublimating her good sense in the erratic patterns of his perversities. She had forgiven him too often. She would not do so again.

Against all her better judgements, Olivia did something she had never done before. She rode out to Chitpur early one morning and banged resolutely on the large black gate. The man who irritably swung back the smaller inner opening was neither Bahadur nor any other of Raventhorne's staff she could recognise. "I wish to see the Sarkar." Spurred by the anger she no longer took trouble to conceal, Olivia spoke firmly in Hindustani and referred to Raventhorne as she had heard others of his staff do. But behind her haughty mask there was diffidence; was he perhaps still in bed? With Sujata . . . ?

"The Sarkar, I regret, is not at home." The man had obviously recognised her. A note of respect had replaced the earlier irritation.

She felt her spirits tumble and in her bitter disappointment Olivia became negligent of what this man might think of her probings. Was the Sarkar, perhaps, on the *Ganga?* The man thought it possible but he could not say for certain. When was he likely to return to the Chitpur house? He was unable to make a commitment, for the Sarkar had made none. She knew the man was stonewalling, and very possibly under instructions. It was only because of her galloping panic that Olivia lowered herself to ask the one question she had vowed not to.

"Is . . . ," what would it be appropriate to call her? ". . . the *lady* then at home, perhaps?"

There was no noticeable change in the man's expression. "No. The lady has gone away."

Panic surged again—gone away? *With* him? Why, it was cruel! How could she ever bear that? "Do you know where she has gone?"

A flicker appeared in the man's eyes. Amusement? He shook his head. "She has gone where she came from."

Olivia knew it was hopeless. She left without leaving a name, aware that she had made a fool of herself. Sitting desultorily by the riverside, alone and utterly wretched, she spent an hour cursing Jai Raventhorne for having reduced her to such a pitch of humiliation, then another hour cursing herself for allowing him to. And then she returned home to lock herself in her room to feign a migraine and to cry. Jai had turned her into a brainless puppet, a slave; she would not see him again. If it was the last thing she did, she would exorcise him from her heart, erase him from her mind, excise him forever from her life.

But in the morning, near the temple in Kalighat, Jai Raventhorne suddenly materialised beside her out of thin air. One moment she was riding through the street on her own and the next moment Shaitan was almost rubbing flanks with Jasmine who, out of surprise, nearly reared and threw her. Olivia gave a startled cry but Raventhorne had already galloped out of earshot with a careless look over his shoulder. Dazed into submission, Olivia followed him out of the bazaar. As soon as they were safely in the open, she flung herself off her mount and into his arms, shaking, sobbing, crippled with relief that he had not abandoned her after all.

He gentled her with loving hands and soothing words, surprised by the force of her passion. "Why were you looking for me yesterday?"

"Why?" Olivia wrenched herself free from his grasp and, reminded of her exploding rage, pummelled his chest with a shower of flailing fists. "How *dare* you ask me such a dumb, stupid, infantile question! It is an *eternity* since I have seen you!"

He manacled her wrists and forced them still. "It is exactly four days." He gave no explanations.

"Don't split hairs with me, you heartless . . . *monolith!*" she stormed. "I have not been able to think of anything except *you . . .*"

"You think too much about me."

". . . and you are hardly worthy of such dedicated concentration!"

"That is exactly what I have been trying to convince *you.*" He walked away to settle himself on a boulder. "I am not."

"You think it is *I* who have chosen this deplorable fate for myself? Do you believe I actually *enjoy* being tossed around like a damned skittle?" Outraged by his lack of reaction she flounced off to sit herself down on another boulder pointedly away from him.

With his riding crop he doodled idly on the ground, not looking at her. "You have another option. Take it."

Olivia clenched her teeth. "If you tell me *once* more that I should marry Freddie, I swear I'll put a hole through you with my derringer, and don't think I can't shoot straight!"

"I doubt if even a derringer could put a hole through a monolith."

She dragged in a deep breath and her eyes glittered. "By every normal standard of decency, Jai Raventhorne, I should hate you!"

He roused himself to look at her. "But you obviously don't," he provided flatly. "And therein, alas, lies the rub."

Her anger died; it seemed as pointless as it was self-defeating. "It is a rub I cannot help," she said dully. "Sometimes I feel I am truly diseased."

He was looking not at her now but behind her as if in the unremarkable scenery of untidy fields and clotted scrub he saw something he could not drag his eyes away from. "You love me too much, Olivia. Train yourself not to."

Olivia had seen many of his moods—of anger, of heaving restlessness, of suppurating frustrations and, yes, of immense tenderness trembling on the verge of something profound. She had known his moments of remorse, of self-flagellation, of raving dissatisfaction with himself when he had wounded her. What she saw now she had never seen before, and, suddenly, it terrified her because she recognised it for what it was: indifference. In loving him she had vowed to tolerate anything he chose to be, but among his choices she had not counted indifference. Olivia had started to include pain among her intimate and constant companions, but what she felt now, on the knife edge of his passionless apathy, was an incision in the core of her being and she almost cried out with the sharpness of it.

"You mean train myself as . . . you have? Fill myself with insidious poisons against the world? Sustain myself with hatred as you do?" Lacerated by his cold impersonality, she became uncaring of what she said, wanting only to provoke him into something, anything, so long as he discarded that hateful curtain of nothingness that veiled his face. "Should I also be frightened in case I mislead people into believing that I am human, of flesh and blood, like everyone else? Is that what you mean, Jai?"

Her spirited provocations achieved nothing; he merely shrugged and continued doodling. "If that is your interpretation, then yes."

Burning tears stung her eyelids but, determined not to lower herself further by crying, she dug her nails into her palms. "It's all a game to you, I know," she said miserably. "Nothing in life really holds any meaning for you, does it, Jai?"

He frowned and pondered for a while. "Yes, it is a game, I suppose." He sounded vaguely surprised, as if he had heard something new. "And no, nothing does hold much meaning for me." He leaned forward to balance his forearms on his knees and stared down at his boots. "I'm not sure anymore that the game is worth the candle, you know, Olivia . . ."

Her heart leapt; at last she had cracked that stony mould of indifference! His features had lengthened and in his voice there were uncharacteristic undertones of defeat. Olivia hastened to his side to kneel on the ground and rest her arms on his lap. "Then why do you continue to play it, Jai? Why?"

Her nearness seemed to please him, for raising a hand he allowed it to wander through her hair. A ghost of a smile, barely anything and yet to her so much, touched his mouth. "How can you put up with me, Olivia?"

She refused to be diverted. *"Why?"*

"Because if there is any meaning in my existence, however insubstantial, it is this game that I play."

Her throat tightened. "There can be other meanings—"

"Not now, not for me!" He became animated and restless. "What has been started must be finished. None of us can be spared, not me and not even . . . you, my innocent madonna . . ." In a burst of feeling he gripped her hand and pressed it between his palms until her bones ached, but she did not cry out, knowing, sensing, that he was at this moment closer to revealing himself than he had ever been before.

She trembled yet dared not make any other move that might snap that elusive filament of his thoughts. "I am not spared even now," she whispered, barely audible.

He dropped her hand. It felt numb. "I am helpless, Olivia."

His eyes stared at her, wild and unseeing. "And yes, I *am* insane . . ."

"Then let me share in that insanity, Jai," she implored, each nerve in her body straining to reach him. "Whatever its cause, your torment is half mine, yet you persistently keep me in the dark." Welling with love, she encircled his neck with her arms and pressed her lips into the hollow of his throat. "Give me a place in your life, Jai . . ."

There, it was out! She had at last vocalised her plaint. There could be no retreat now. Brazen or not, the words could not be unsaid.

He did not reply immediately, but he did not push her away. Instead, his fingers traced the line of her spine and in their tips Olivia felt the entire load of his longing. When he spoke it was with difficulty, as if he were having to prize every syllable out with a pair of forceps and it hurt him. "You have a place . . . in . . . my heart. You must know that . . . by now."

It was the closest he had ever come to telling her that he loved her. For a whole moment the world stopped. Nothing in it moved, not even a hint of life. Like a fossil destined to live forever in its stone grave, for her the instant petrified into immortality.

But then, impatiently, he stirred as if in annoyance with himself. "I must go."

In her daze Olivia was seized by terror. "Go? Go where?"

As always, he unlocked her fingers gently from behind his neck and, kissing each of her hands, stood up. "To the Customs house," he said with a lift of a quizzical smile at her stricken expression. "Donaldson is sending a consignment that will ensure your Freddie's continuing prosperity. I want to make certain it contains only what its documentation says it does."

She knew he mocked her extravagant reaction, but it didn't matter. Not today! He had not used the word *love,* but he had thought it. She had seen it in his mind as clearly as if it were emblazoned across his forehead! For all its inadequacies, this would still be the diadem in her treasury of jewelled moments.

"How suspicious you are of your clients!" she remarked, blissful again. "You know that Freddie's agency doesn't dabble in opium."

"At one time or another, they all dabble in opium."

"Even though it is a Company monopoly?"

"*Because* it is a Company monopoly! Those with monopolies have more to sell, and avarice feeds upon itself."

"You mean they allow opium to be smuggled out to Europe?"

"Some do. For a price."

"How?"

"Concealed in cargo, with couriers, through ships' crews—a thousand different ways. Europe too has its addicts, its stinking opium dens. Where do you think *they* get their supplies? There are no poppy plantations in England!"

"In that case, the traffic is enormous. Single-handedly you want to take on the whole world . . . ?" she cried in protest despite his darkening face.

Suddenly the clouds broke and a smile of genuine humour broke through like a hesitant ray of sunshine. "No, only *half* the whole world. For the present that is enough. Now come, or I shall miss my appointment, and possibly one more London den will have triumphed." Olivia did not argue; the idea of poor Willie Donaldson, a man of unimpeachable ethics and reputation, being an opium smuggler was laughable. But Raventhorne's obsession with the nefarious trade was not open to reason. She wondered briefly about that obsession. Could it be that opium was also smuggled out in tea chests and *that* was the source of his enmity with her uncle . . . ?

"The day after tomorrow are the immersions that mark the conclusion of the Durga festival." He spoke again with a switch of topics. "Would you like to see them?"

Olivia gave a small gasp of delight. "Yes, oh *yes!* Where are the images immersed?"

"Up and down the river at the various ghats. They take place mostly at night and are very colourful." He took her hand and held it for a while, his face solemn. "Can you get away without inconvenience?"

Inconvenience! Did he still not know that merely to be with him she would willingly walk through fire to the ends of the earth? "Yes. Inconvenient or not, I will get away."

"Very well. My carriage with Bahadur will await you on the night at the corner of your lane."

"At what time?"

"They will be there soon after dark. Come when you can."

Anxious that no detail be overlooked and the precious appointment missed by default, she asked, "Do you know my uncle's house?"

It was, Olivia realised instantly, an absurd question and

Raventhorne looked fractionally startled. Then he began to chuckle as he bent down to cup his palms into a foothold so that she could mount Jasmine. "Who in Calcutta does not know the house of Sir Joshua Templewood?" By the time she was in the saddle and the girth tightened to his satisfaction, once more his mood had changed. As he stood stroking Jasmine's neck absently, his pearl-sheened eyes had dimmed to move away from Olivia into some incalculable distance. If there was any identifiable emotion in his drawn features, it was sorrow. "You deserve so much better than I can ever give you, Olivia. I wish—"

"Don't!" She leaned over to place a finger across his lips. "Don't wish, it is bad luck. Let whatever comes, come. I can bear it."

He said something under his breath and turned away towards his own mount. It was only when she was half-way home that Olivia identified in a delayed reaction the few words he had mumbled. "I pray that I can too."

For the moment they made no sense. For the moment.

It was Dassera day.

Tomorrow the immersions would start. Scores of those exquisite images of the ten-armed goddess that Olivia had seen being lovingly fashioned in Kumartuli would be consigned to the river Hooghly, held in Bengal as sacred as the mighty Ganges. Today, in thousands of Hindu homes the final day of the ten-day celebrations would be dedicated to devout worship of Durga. There would be feasting and singing and chanting, and gifts would be exchanged, new clothes worn, alms distributed and maunds of sweets eaten. Even in the White Town there were reverberating sounds of revelry from the intermittent Indian dwelling-places: drum beats, cymbal clashes, chanting voices, tingling bells, the raucous laughter of children. In the Templewood house the enormous contingent of servants had constructed their own altar in their compound and installed in it an image of Durga.

"Oh, the noise, the *noise!*" Lady Bridget clamped her hands over her ears and shuddered. "I do wish they would keep their blasphemous heathen rites to themselves. Why should all of us be afflicted?"

"The festival comes only once a year, Aunt Bridget," Olivia

pointed out. "For them it is a great occasion and it means much."

"Thank the Lord it is only once a year! But if it's not one festival it's another. It's a wonder we're not all struck deaf."

Because of the holiday declared for the Indian staff, Sir Joshua had gone off with Arthur Ransome to pay Dassera visits to all their Hindu suppliers, agents, retailers and associates, as was the custom on this auspicious day. In exchange, baskets of fruit and sweets had been arriving at the house since the morning from those Hindu merchants of means with whom Templewood and Ransome did business. Estelle, as usual, was out. Olivia, tiring of her aunt's constant and tedious carping, took her book into the garden to read in peace, if that was the word that could be used considering the frantic impatience with which she awaited tomorrow night. The novel she was reading, *Wuthering Heights,* had been sent to her aunt from England by her Cousin Maude. It was, wrote Cousin Maude, creating a literary sensation in London. Although a poignant and daring love story, it had been written by an unknown spinster named Emily Brontë, the cloistered, unworldly daughter of an impecunious Yorkshire clergyman. Olivia's choice of reading was therefore fortunate; the book was so gripping, so moving and written with such beauty and passion that she could hardly bear to put it down.

She sat beneath a spreading acacia tree, to a branch of which she had tied her beautiful blue Vanda orchid. The creeper had now taken root in the bark to spill over with lovely cerulean blossoms framed by shining bottle green leafage. Suddenly, from the kitchen end of the garden, Babulal approached to shyly fold his hands in respect and then lay a marigold at her feet. Would the missy mem, he asked hesitantly, do them the great honour of participating in their worship rituals tonight after supper? It was the final and most auspicious day of the festival.

Olivia was touched. It was a simple request and came from the heart. She didn't even think to refuse it. Knowing that her aunt might make an unnecessary fuss if asked for permission, she decided to accept the invitation anyway and make her apologies later to her aunt should any be required. In her diffident but rapidly improving Hindustani, she accepted Babulal's invitation with pleasure.

Somehow, evening came, the creeping hours made less intolerable for Olivia by Emily Brontë's riveting story of love and despair and terrible tragedy. The cold supper of meats and salads served was well in tune with Lady Bridget's silent mood since neither Estelle nor Sir Joshua had returned in time for the meal.

As soon as it was over, Olivia set off as discreetly as she could to fulfil her promise to Babulal.

The sudden realisation that she had never yet set foot in the servants' compound came as a vague surprise to Olivia. Lady Bridget herself seemed to have a strange aversion to it; she neither spoke of it nor showed any concern over what might be its condition. To Olivia's knowledge, she certainly never visited it. Her own lapse made Olivia feel guilty; what little heed they all paid to those who worked hard to keep them in such comfort! Even though the compound was visible from the kitchen window, she was now astonished by its vastness. The compound was rectangular, lined on three sides by single-storied rooms, perhaps thirty altogether. At the far end was the washerman's house and behind that a water tank. Next to it stood the cow shed housing the milch cattle and the resident milk man who supplied their daily requirements. Olivia had often encountered the milk man at the pantry door making his morning deliveries. That the Templewood domestic staff was extensive Olivia already knew; what surprised her now as she was ceremonially escorted around the settlement was the number of women and children in the community.

Even in the modest environment, this evening there was gaiety and a blaze of light and colour. Everyone wore shining new clothes, no doubt those that Lady Bridget and Sir Joshua had distributed this morning as traditional baksheesh on Dassera day. Focus of all the jollifications was the altar, gaudy but cheerful, that had been constructed in the centre of the court-yard. The idol had been lavishly decorated with tinsel and bright silk vestments, a red sari and blouse and impromptu shining jewellery fashioned out of gold braid. Each of the ten arms of the goddess held a different item and one foot rested on a lion's head since the lion was her carrier according to mythology. Trays of flowers, sweets, fruits and nuts rested on the altar as offerings. Oil lamps and incense burners nestled in between. A Brahmin priest, hired for the night at considerable cost, it was proudly told to Olivia, sat singing vesper hymns and chanting *mantras.* Above the altar was an orange canopy on top of which had been fixed a metal trident.

Olivia was charmed. As guest of honour, she was given a chair, the only one in sight since everyone else squatted on the ground. Piety shone out of dark, glistening faces as the rituals proceeded, and there was a spontaneous, unspoken sense of joy that was very touching. Even though Dassera was a Hindu festival, all the Muslim servants on Sir Joshua's staff participated with equal enthusiasm. Rehman, the chief bearer, looked entirely strange in a checked shirt and bright green *lungi* as he happily stirred a gigantic cauldron on the verandah from which spicy aromas arose and wafted. Olivia barely recognized the normally impassive face and the stiff form that she was used to seeing only in characterless white uniform. The prayers concluded, a tray of sweets was passed around the congregation as a blessing from the goddess. Olivia took a piece of what looked like pistachio fudge and smiled to herself. She wondered how many of the ingredients for the feast being prepared tonight had been abstracted from her aunt's larder, but she could not help feeling satisfied that they had. Opening her purse she took out a handful of coins without counting them and placed them in the tray of sweets as her own contribution towards the modest but moving occasion.

By the time she returned to the main house, Sir Joshua had come back, eaten and closeted himself in his study. Lady Bridget had retired, perhaps to continue fretting about Estelle, who had not yet returned home from wherever her wilful wanderings had taken her today. After a moment's uncertainty, Olivia sought out her uncle in his study.

"There's something I'd like to talk to you about, Uncle Josh. It's about Estelle and I feel you should listen."

"Estelle?" Looking up from the figures he was scribbling, he seemed faintly alarmed, perhaps at the seriousness of Olivia's expression. "Why, is she ill?"

"No. She is in perfectly good health, at least physically." His stare became blank, indicating that he had no idea what she was talking about. Olivia grabbed his momentary attention and quickly continued. "I know and understand your recent preoccupations, Uncle Josh, but Estelle doesn't. Since she's had very little attention from you lately, she's convinced herself that you no longer love her."

"No longer love her? Bless my soul, what an extraordinary notion!" He looked vaguely unsettled.

"Well, of course it is, but Estelle doesn't see it that way." Olivia further pressed home her advantage. "And in her pique, she's taking it out on poor Aunt Bridget, who's at her wit's end. I think you should find some time to have a talk with her, Uncle Josh."

"Who, Bridget?"

"No, *Estelle.* She's set her heart on this pantomime, Uncle Josh. I know Aunt Bridget objects strenuously, but it's really quite innocuous. Maybe you could persuade Aunt Bridget to let Estelle have her way. You see," she hauled in a breath and plunged into a detailed description of the problem on both sides, noting that through her recital her uncle listened with undivided attention. She finished and then sat back to wait for his comments, since he appeared to be giving the matter some thought.

After a long while he looked up. "He's turned us down, you know," was all he said.

"What . . . ?" It took a moment for Olivia to understand the drift of his remark and realise that it had nothing to do with what she had said. She breathed in deeply and sighed. "Your proposal?"

"Yes. We got his formal refusal this morning."

So, Arvind Singh had not gone against his friend's wishes after all! "Does the consortium plan to better the offer?"

"The consortium!" He gave a snort of disgust. "A bunch of liver-faced goons scared of their own behinds! No, the consortium is not prepared to better the offer, but it no longer matters." He suddenly smiled. "There is more than one way of catching a monkey, my dear, *more* than one."

There was no point now in reviving the matter of Estelle and her pantomime. Sir Joshua's attention was no longer available, if it ever had been. She would have to wait for another opportune moment to broach the topic again. It was doubtful if in his present mood of rabid disappointment and anger he would consider favourably the idea of indulging his daughter's dramatic aspirations.

Without her knowledge, her deferment of the paltry matter was the second worst decision Olivia was to make in her life. The worst would come tomorrow.

At last, at last, it was the day of the immersions!

Estelle had returned scandalously late last night and a flaming row had ensued between mother and daughter at the breakfast table after Sir Joshua had left for work. Since, with deliberate disobedience, Estelle had stalked out of the house again today, no doubt another fireworks display would follow to enliven the dinner table tonight. Weighted down by her own anxieties and her almost intolerable feeling of suspense, Olivia no longer cared one way or the other. The morning had passed in completing

Wuthering Heights, and in the afternoon she had somehow forced herself to sleep, but once the nap was over and she had had tea with her aunt, after which Lady Bridget went visiting, the hours dragged by as if anchored down with millstones. For a while Olivia played with Clementine, a sadly neglected little pup these days, then she did some weeding in the garden and mentally plotted her escape route from the house for the hundredth time. Then, for no reason other than that her nerves screamed for relief and her mind for diversion, she wandered idly into the servants' compound. What she saw this time horrified her.

Under the cloak of darkness and the camouflage of the hectic gaiety and lights and colour last night, she had not noticed the squalor. What she observed now in daylight was the appalling deprivation and degradation that had lain beneath the veneer. Garbage heaps, scattered and putrefying, stank to high heaven. On either side of the court-yard there were open drains clogged with filthy slime and attracting a million flies and cockroaches. The quarters themselves were like ruins after a battle, with doors hanging loose and, in the walls, gaping holes that had been carelessly stuffed with gunny sacking and rags to keep out the rains. There were patches of green dampness everywhere and the stench was foul. The litter from last night had been swept aside but with enough apathy to leave plenty of residue. But what shocked Olivia most were the children, hordes of them, rummaging enthusiastically within the rot, their skinny limbs like sticks, their ribs showing in relief above their unhealthy pot-bellies, and their skin in some cases covered with open sores. How was it that she had never seen them, not one, out in the open before? Did they live hidden in the brickwork like the cockroaches . . . ?

Olivia felt sickened. And angry. Why were these people satisfied to live in such cesspools? If the Templewoods didn't give a jot for those who served them with diligence, could the servants not bestir themselves to improve their lot with their own hands? At home Olivia had seen plenty of squalor in the tenements of New York and Chicago, but it was understood that everyone worked hard to get out of that situation, to move on in the world, to do better and ever better for themselves and their families. Why, even the cattle at home had more decent accommodations! With the grim intention of collaring one of the sweepers, Olivia marched boldly into the quarter nearest to her, watched all around by silent, wondering eyes. The room into which she stepped was dark and reeked of dampness, for it was without even a window. Eventually her eyes discerned a huddled form lying on the bare brick floor riddled with rat burrows. Sitting beside the huddled form was a boy of about ten. As Olivia entered, the form stirred and tried to rise; she saw that it was an old woman.

"What is wrong with her?" Olivia asked in improvised Hindustani.

"She is sick."

"I can see that! Is she taking any medicines? Do you know what it is that ails her?"

The boy shrugged. "There is no point. She will be dead soon."

Shaking with frustration, Olivia was about to argue when she felt a presence behind her and, lightly, a hand touched her arm. It was Babulal. "Come, missy mem," he said solemnly, "this no place for you. Lady mem very angry, she no like you come here."

Olivia felt another surge of anger but couldn't find the words for it. In any case, Babulal had spoken in his pidgin English and, suddenly, it was like a snub, a slap in her face. What he was trying to tell her was that this was their world, not hers; and in it she was not welcome any more than they were in hers. Or, at least, that is how Olivia interpreted it in her silent rage. Without another word she turned and allowed him to lead her back to the garden. She felt suffocated and helpless—rage against whom? Against the Templewoods for being so uncaring? Against these wretched people for accepting these inequities without lifting either a voice or a finger? Against herself for never having even spared them a thought at all? It was all so hopeless anyway. For a while Olivia's depression persisted. Haunted by what she had seen in that miserable quarter, she brooded and tried to think of a solution. But only for a while. Then, as the clock ticked away the remainder of the evening, she remembered something her father had once told her: "The world is full of cruelty, injustice, tragedy. If you can do something about it, *do* it; if not, don't add insult to injury with armchair sympathy."

Pragmatism, or convenient amnesia? There was no time now for Olivia to philosophise. The clock that had been such a sluggard all day seemed now to positively race ahead as dinner came and went. Sir Joshua's meal, as had become the custom, was dispatched to his office in a tiffin box. Estelle did not appear at the dinner table, being not yet home, and Lady Bridget toyed with her food in grim silence as she ripened for another fight. As soon as she could excuse herself with decency, Olivia ran up to her room to prepare for her nocturnal adventure.

The hands of the clock finally showed half past eleven. Heart thundering against her ribs with sledge-hammer force, Olivia sat on her bed and waited. Dressed in practical outdoor clothes and boots, she tapped her foot impatiently on the floor, watching the clock face almost without blinking. Lady Bridget was by now hopefully fast asleep, having long given up waiting for either her daughter or her husband and having perforce to defer the battle royal till the morning. Suddenly on the staircase outside, a floor board creaked and then there was silence. Olivia exhaled with a relieved whoosh; evidently her cousin had finally decided to come home. Another fifteen minutes, she said to herself, to give Estelle time to settle in. Holding her breath, Olivia waited. Ten minutes to go, five . . .

The door of her room opened abruptly and Estelle walked in. "I'm glad you're still awake, Olivia. I must talk to you about something important." She walked to a chair by the window and sat down.

Olivia's thundering heart crashed into her sturdy outdoor boots as she tried desperately to fold her feet under the bed. Oh sweet heavens, not now, not *now* . . . ! Couldn't the selfish, thoughtless, irresponsible girl have returned earlier? All at once she was seized by a blind, unreasoning fury. "I'm sorry, Estelle," she ground out, not troubling to conceal her anger, "but I was just about to go to bed, and I'm extremely sleepy. Can't it wait until the morning?"

Estelle hesitated.

"Look, Estelle, if it's about the pantomime, I've already stirred the subject with Uncle Josh. He's . . . he's thinking about it, but tomorrow . . ."

"It's not about the pantomime."

Something in Estelle's tone silenced Olivia as she took note of the faded pallor, the swollen eyes and the rigid stance that made her back as stiff as a ramrod. Olivia felt another flash of irritation: Oh, damn! The silly girl had gone and done something really unmentionable with that Smithers boy . . .

But then the clock on the landing chimed. Midnight! Did the

immersions continue after midnight? What if Bahadur decided that she wasn't coming after all and left? What if Jai tired of the wait and decided likewise and she missed seeing him altogether? She panicked and, grabbing her cousin by the shoulders, urged her up from the chair.

"To tell you the truth, Estelle, my head is bursting with one of those wretched migraines or a cold or . . . or something. I can hardly keep my eyes open, see? If I don't go to sleep at once I fear I shall faint, collapse . . . and I won't be able to concentrate on what you're saying . . ." Incoherently, she babbled a string of excuses, the words tumbling out of her mouth in a jumble as she almost pushed Estelle towards the door. "Tomorrow, Estelle, tomorrow I promise. We'll talk all day if you like and all night too, I *promise . . .*"

For a moment Estelle stared at her in surprise and hurt, then she shrugged. "Very well. Tomorrow then. *Do* forgive me for having intruded on your time, my understanding Coz. Good night."

Estelle's sarcasm Olivia didn't even notice in her immense relief at her departure. She saw nothing else but the clock as she waited ten more interminable minutes; then she could wait no longer. She removed her shoes to hold them in a hand, locked the door of her room behind her as quietly as she could, tiptoed down the stairs praying that her uncle didn't choose that very moment to return home, and ran into the formal dining-room. Five minutes later—through the downstairs parlour, the billiards room and that back window she knew never did latch properly—she was flying down the vegetable garden path at the rear of the house, over the low wall and down the main road to the corner. Concealed by the dappled shadows of a giant peepul tree stood Jai Raventhorne's carriage. Next to it, patiently, waited Bahadur. With a small cry of relief, Olivia flung herself inside through the door Bahadur quickly opened for her and collapsed against the upholstery. She had already forgotten everything, everything else in the world that existed, save Jai Raventhorne.

Olivia did not think of Estelle again that night.

There was no way Olivia could have known then as the carriage sped away through the dark to meet the man who was her destiny that her summary dismissal of Estelle was the worst mistake she was ever to make in her life. And the price she was to pay for it was exorbitant, more exorbitant than she could ever have imagined.

9

Olivia could barely recognise him.

At the jetty to which the carriage bore her, the Dassera moon seemed to douse the world in its cold white light, making it eerily phosphorescent. Dancing silver shards slashed the black of the river; small breezes gusted like spurts from invisible bellows. Chained to a post of the wooden planked wharf awaited a longboat from the *Ganga,* identified by a winking metal trident on her prow. Beside it stood a strangely unfamiliar figure in cream silken dhoti and *kurta,* both edged finely with gold. A woollen shawl, embroidered and tasselled, was draped over one shoulder. Under a luminous moon his ebony hair glistened, smoothed back from his forehead with rare meekness to follow the curve of his arrogant head and curl upended at the nape. He was barefooted.

Tangled within her throat, Olivia's breath knotted further. In the delusion that she could recall every line and crease of his face, each contour of his sinewed body, she sometimes forgot just how compelling Jai Raventhorne's appearance could be. Tonight he looked patrician, a *zamindar,* scion of some aristocratic dynasty. Smiling a little, she told him so as, unspeaking, he helped her into the longboat. "A man of two worlds," she breathed, settling comfortably in a cushioned seat.

"Or of neither!"

Opposite her, his face was shadowed but she sensed that he did not smile. She was disappointed that they were not to be on their own. Somehow she had assumed it would be as always. But as the oarsmen started their smooth rhythms in the water and the longboat started to move to midstream, she discarded the small disappointment as ungracious. Jai Raventhorne sat no more than a foot or two away from her. She could taste him with her eyes, hear the muted undulations of his breath and the crisp rustle of his silk. Even untouching, she could feel his pulse as if it were her own beneath the warmth of a skin she almost shared with him. It was enough.

"Where are we going?"

"To Shiriti Ghat. The immersions are best seen from the river." He noticed the slight shiver she gave and frowned. "Why didn't you think to bring a shawl?"

Snugly clad in a thick tweed skirt and a long-sleeved woollen blouse, she had considered that she would be sufficiently warm, but the damp gusts decreed otherwise. "I did but I forgot when . . ." She stopped. Domestic problems would be of no interest to him and, in any case, they were not to be discussed with others. "When I left the house. I think I'd make a terrible burglar. I almost fainted with nervousness."

He made no return nor did he smile. He merely removed his shawl to arrange it carefully about her shoulders. In the shadows she searched for his eyes in a face that gleamed like bleached wood, but they told her nothing. She was touched suddenly by a vague unease; tonight she could not fathom his mood, for it seemed altogether unreadable. He was tense, this much she could discern, although his taciturnity was not motivated by indifference, she assessed. His invisible eyes, darting like fish, Olivia was certain, were missing nothing, not a single nuance of her own thoughts. Even so she felt warm in his vision, physically cosy in the embrace of a shawl that was of the softest *pashmina.* Against her cheek it was like a caress. Discarding her unease Olivia smiled.

"Do you perform the Durga rituals in your home?" However well read he might be in philosophy he had never struck her as a man of religion.

"Yes."

"Because of piety?" she asked, surprised.

"Because it is expected." By Sujata, she wondered? But then she remembered that Sujata no longer lived in his house. He sensed her question. "By my staff, those who crew the ships and work in my office, people of the neighbourhood too poor to raise their own altars." He shrugged. "Anyone else who wishes to worship." There was no mention of friends or family, but then he had none.

"The worship itself—does it mean anything to you?"

"No. I have neither a vote of thanks to offer the gods nor a shopping list for future favours. My destiny is my own."

As it always did, his cynicism wounded her. The isolation he cultivated so savagely made her heart ache, and once more she yearned to storm the citadels of his merciless privacy. In America she had sometimes met men who were also alone—drifters, lone riders, solitary homesteaders, ranchers in the remote wilderness who called no one family and no place truly home. Jai's isolation, however, was excessively cruel, for he lacked nothing that money could buy and everything that it could not. Who was the father who had abandoned him without leaving even a name? Had Jai ever sought him out, missed him, thirsted for that paternal affection that was every son's due? And his mother, that unfortunately ravished woman—had she never resented the child thrust into her womb by a fate that was callous? Was she really dead? That unknown father—was he dead? Or, perhaps, was he still living unconcerned in some distant land unaware that across the oceans existed a son who might bear his face even if he did not his name? And from which parent had *he* inherited his astonishing eyes?

"Don't dwell on irrelevancies, Olivia!" He burrowed inside her huddled thoughts as infallibly as ever. "Think of nothing except what you are about to see. There is a reason."

A reason! Unease, this time needle pointed, threaded through her veins. Her initial instinct had not been wrong; she knew now she had cause for that unease but could not decipher what, and she was frightened. Her ache, her acute need now to be held against that inaudible heart that seemed to beat so calmly within reach of her fingers, intensified into a torrent of longing, but she swallowed it. Even a foot away he was so far removed, so inexorably padlocked within the cavernous vaults of his unattainable mind, that she did not dare to intrude. Yet, Olivia knew that he felt everything she felt, breathed with the same breath as she, sensed accurately every one of her longings but deliberately without reaction.

"Observe," he said gently. That was all.

Like a wayward pup commanded to heel, she obeyed. And observed.

They had entered a stretch of the river where the bank to their right pulsated with life. Hundreds, perhaps thousands, thronged the shore, now so close to the longboat that Olivia could see their features clearly illuminated by the torches that flamed everywhere. Rumbling rolls of drums, regular and rhythmic, floated across the waters. Within their primitive cadences they seemed to carry esoteric messages decipherable only by the aware. The air around them reverberated with chants and wails, disembodied voices rising and falling like the tides of the sea under the baton of the winds. The longboat inched closer towards the undulating river bank, the sinuous movements of the oarsmen now as smooth as those of a serpent.

In rhythm with the drums, Olivia's heartbeats syncopated. She watched in awe-struck silence, prickles of fear playing her spine like a keyboard. They were now near enough to the river bank to be able to pick out details of the images being readied for immersion and extinction. The images were carried on platforms borne on men's shoulders, bare and black against the shining white of their long dhotis and short loin-cloths, an army of unearthly-looking creatures engaged in vital communal enterprise. Carefully, lovingly, the images were balanced between two boats waiting side by side in the water. Wading in waist deep, the men pushed the boats farther out into the mainstream with eager arms. A boatman with a long pole gently separated the boats from each other. For an instant, just an instant, the images teetered and seesawed, and then, as the boats sailed apart, they fell clumsily into the water. The ritual was repeated with the remaining images, and each time, a hushed wail of triumph stirred among the crowd and then died again. Having completed their duties, the waders returned to the bank.

Not one of them stopped to look back.

In silence Olivia and Jai sat and watched the final rituals of Dassera, the longboat still, the oarsmen immobile save for lips mouthing silent *mantras.* Olivia dragged away her spellbound eyes to look at Raventhorne and, in the glare of the torches, found his instantly, for they were riveted to her face. In the pearl grey depths there was now a question, a question apparently of such vital importance that she recoiled instinctively; Jai Raventhorne was waiting for her to say something of extraordinary significance. What?

Olivia swallowed and it was painful, for her throat felt dehydrated. "I have seen in Kumartuli the infinite care and devotion with which these images are fashioned." Was it this that he sought from her—approval and appreciation? "During the ten days that they are installed on altars, I know they are cherished and revered."

"Go on!" he whispered, not yet satisfied, wanting more.

Olivia licked her parched lips and stared, but all she could see on his face was a mask behind which there was another mask, behind which there was darkness. "Yet, when they discard the images they seem to do so carelessly, almost roughly, as if they meant nothing anymore. Not one of them looked back even once."

"Ah!"

He made a strange sound—part wail, part triumphal—something in between mortal torment and deliverance. At the same time his body, held in a frame of rigid tension, fell loose as if released from under some intolerable pressure. He moved, and with the shift in position his features blazed with the moonlight. A small cry arose in Olivia's throat but remained unborn as she congealed. His skin was suddenly like parchment, old and yellow, stretched across his cheek-bones in a lifeless expanse. But what produced in Olivia a new terror was the sight of his eyes, like empty sockets in a skull. For a moment she could only stare at the gaunt apparition who faced her, for it was that of a stranger she had never seen before.

When he spoke again he had moved, so that the illusion was gone and his voice once more was measured. "That is the lesson of the immersions. They teach to love but to remain detached, to renounce when necessary and never to look back with regret."

Olivia started to tremble. "But how can that be?" she breathed.

"It can be, it *must.* But because there is no regret does not mean there is no pain." He was again gentle. "Watch!"

Dutifully, her gaze pivoted back to the shore. Those who had completed their immersions—their renunciations!—had departed. The crowd had thinned considerably. But those who remained displayed expressions of racking grief, tears spilling down in glistening trails on dark cheeks, their eyes stricken with loss. Some cried quietly, their faces buried in their palms or in the shoulder of a companion; others mourned openly, their bodies contorted with anguish. The black waters of the Hooghly were now a battle-field littered with the remains of a hideous massacre. Arms, legs, painted and grinning faces floated past the longboat on their way to the eternity of the sea. Among the flotsam and jetsam were scraps of once beautiful clothing, tinsel crowns and armlets, glass bangles, beaded necklaces and, waving from guillotined heads, hanks of coarse black hair still entwined with flowers.

Dust to dust, clay to clay.

Olivia knew now beyond any reasonable doubt that something terrible was about to happen. In her stomach, tension knotted like a cramp and panic lay quivering just beneath the skin being warmed so efficiently by Jai's *pashmina* shawl of such exquisite artistry. Blinded by tears and the foreboding of tragedy, she asked, "Do you consider yourself a Hindu?" Aware of the futility of her question, she still refused to despair.

"As much as I consider myself anything, I suppose."

"And you too would be able to make such a renunciation without a backward glance?"

"Yes." There was not even hesitation.

"With no regrets?"

"None."

"Or . . . pain?"

This time there was hesitation but only fractional. "No."

Olivia's mind died. With each of his syllables she had hurtled farther and farther into an icy, airless space in which she was alone. The silence between them was sepulchral as, divided by their irreconcilable worlds, they drifted apart with not even the solace of a colliding glance. He stared through her and beyond her into vacancy; numbed by the enormity of what he had said, Olivia sat in glazed stupefaction. The polished disc of the moon was now behind the dipping fronds of the palm trees on its way below the horizon and toward other worlds. The longboat was again on the move on its return to the jetty. The shore receded behind them and with it the torches and the crowds and the chanting. Obeisance to the mother goddess Durga was over for another year and her devotees were dispersing. Olivia was not aware that with them she too was crying.

At the jetty Bahadur waited with the carriage. The rest of the street was deserted. In their homes people slept soundly, neither knowing nor caring that outside their pleasant dreams there were knells of doom sounding for some. The night that had brought sleep to many had brought for others a curse of eternal sleeplessness. They disembarked and, expressionless, Raventhorne held open the door of the carriage for Olivia. Just fleetingly his fingers brushed hers but neither lingered nor returned.

"I cannot see you again, Olivia."

It was what he had been saying to her all night. Long before the words were enunciated they resounded and reverberated in Olivia's head like an echo knocking against a bowl of mountains. She knew now that it was what he had been saying to her each time they had met, right from the beginning. Her paralysed mouth formed the word *why?* but no sound came. Like his sentence of death, it too remained only an echo in her mind. Then she was inside the carriage being jolted away into a night that did not include him. She looked back, unheeding of the rules of a renunciation that had not been hers, but he was only a speck in the distance. Then, rubbed out by the dark, he was not even that.

"Stop this carriage . . . !"

The thunder of hooves swallowed Olivia's belated cry as she returned to life, savaged by a despair that was a tangible entity. Unable to grasp or accept the finality of a sentence as cruel and as undeserved as this, her mind did not have the strength to rebel yet. Instead, like the images, she started to disintegrate within herself; like the images, something loved was being discarded and left to dissolve in some alien sea. The injustice of it crippled Olivia's thinking powers, save for that one recurring and unanswered question.

Why?

She thought she was dead, or would be soon.

There was a desert inside her mouth, arid and sandy. Her eyelids would not lift and when they did she was blinded by the dazzle. Within her head a maniac with a hammer drove nails into her skull. And there was fog, everywhere there was fog. Hidden in that fog there were voices, her aunt's, Estelle's, Dr. Humphries's. Some foul liquid was forced into her mouth; a cold compress was being pressed against her forehead and someone ordered her to sleep.

Olivia slept.

Weaving in and out of consciousness, she saw mirages—a play of colour and shape as in a kaleidoscope that made patterns and then fell apart to the roll of drums. There were also horrible nightmares, of graves and putrefying limbs and hideous painted faces, all skeletal in their finery, all with talons reaching out to trap her. Olivia screamed and thrashed to ward off the evil that was in the very air, and then out of the mist came a pearly cloak of security to enfold her in an embrace that was as soft as *pashmina.* She purred with contentment, nuzzling the warmth and the safety of arms. And then she slept again.

"Feeling better, dear?"

When she finally awakened to full consciousness, it was to a fine morning of milky autumn sunshine. Her aunt's face, creased with lines of worry, hovered above hers. The fever had broken. Olivia tried to sit up but, weakened beyond belief, she could not raise the effort. Her aunt's hand gently pushed her back among the pillows and made her sip warm milk through a spout.

"Thank goodness! Dr. Humphries said it was the ague compounded by a terrible chill." Lady Bridget dabbed her mouth with a napkin. "But the fever has run its course, praise be. We'll soon have you up and about again, you'll see. The secret is plenty of liquids, he said, *plenty.*"

Olivia nodded, sipped and felt marginally stronger. Behind her aunt Estelle hovered waiting for the empty invalid cup, her gaze circling the room as if to avoid her cousin's. Something tugged at the tails of Olivia's memory; she tried but she could not catch it. Like bricks, drowsiness pressed down over her eyelids. She could scarcely keep them open. Fatigue made it impossible to string together any intelligible thought except one.

She was not to see Jai Raventhorne again.

Her afternoon siesta was fitful but long. She opened her eyes to candle-light and the sounds of tinkling glass as the ayah rearranged the medicine table by the bed. More liquids followed, this time brought up by Sir Joshua, and the pleasing aroma of lemon-grass tea made a welcome change from that of chest liniments.

"Well, how do you feel, m'dear?" He settled down by the bed.

"Better, thank you." Olivia's voice, thin and reedy, seemed not her own. She struggled up against a supportive bank of pillows.

"Capital, capital! Humphries was right. This new bark from Malaya seems to be the answer. They call it cinchona—about damned time someone did something about this confounded ague." He patted her hand. "We had some anxious moments about you, my dear. It's good to see colour in those cheeks again." There seemed to be plenty of colour in Sir Joshua's own cheeks as he chatted amiably, temper bubbling and buoyant. Licking his whiskers like a cat after he had drained his own cup, he waggled a warning finger at her. "No more early morning rides for you, my girl. At least not until some of that strength is recovered." Whistling tunelessly, he sauntered out of the room.

No. No more early morning rides. There was no point in them now.

The next morning Olivia was declared well enough by Dr. Humphries to be sponged and given fresh clothing. The morning after that he even allowed her an hour in the garden, bundled like an Egyptian mummy in shawls and mitts and woollen stockings.

It surprised Olivia that her body could feel so strong again when her mind remained extinct. In a way she bitterly mourned the passing of her fever; while it had ravaged her body, there had been at least no need for thought.

With Olivia's recovery now confirmed, Lady Bridget decided to venture out for an afternoon to attend a furniture auction. "It's at the home of the Armenians, dear, who run the races every week. They're off to London and they do have some good saddles Josh wants me to look at. Also, some Chippendale chairs and almost new English curtains. I really must do something about Estelle's room. It looks deplorable."

Estelle! Olivia's memory clarified with a jolt and she filled with remorse. "Where *is* Estelle, Aunt Bridget? I haven't seen her around these past two days." How remiss of her to have forgotten her cousin so completely!

"She's gone to the Pringles' in Cossipore for a week. You remember that nice naval lieutenant at the Pennworthys? Well, his sister Anne is down from Lucknow with her two children. Estelle has taken quite a shine to her and I'm so relieved. Anne is just the right kind of friend for that girl." Lady Bridget looked anxious. "You don't mind Estelle having gone, dear, do you? You were so much better and Estelle has been such a little paragon lately that—"

"No, of course I don't mind . . . a *paragon,* did you say?" Olivia wondered if she had been hearing right.

Lady Bridget's smile was more expansive than Olivia had seen in weeks. "*Quite* a paragon, believe it or not! She even took Josh's dressing down about that ridiculous pantomime in her stride. As meek as a lamb, if you please. Not a word of protest."

"Uncle Josh refused his permission?"

"Well, of course he refused his permission!" Lady Bridget looked surprised. "Even if she hadn't caught him in the middle of this Kirtinagar business, Josh wouldn't have stood for it. But she's taken it well, astonishingly so. I can't say I'm not relieved the worst is over."

Olivia almost asked what "this Kirtinagar business" might be but then remembered the reality and didn't. "I'm relieved too," she said slowly, the image of Estelle's ravaged face rising in her mind's eye for a moment. "I'm glad Estelle has been civil to you for a change."

"She kissed me, you know." Lady Bridget's voice flickered. "She kissed me before she went off, the first time in weeks. And she said she was sorry for all the grief she had given me." She paused, then cleared her throat and composed herself again. "Incidentally, dear," she bent down to lift the shawl off a chair, "I do think this is quite lovely, quite the nicest one I've seen in a long time. I know Estelle would absolutely adore one for Christmas. When you're well again perhaps we can send for the pedlar from whom you bought it. It's not only *pashmina,* it's one of those *jam-e-wars* from Kashmir. Exquisite! Did it cost a fortune?"

Olivia pretended to be asleep.

Energies regrouped, cobwebs cleared from the walls of her mind and the fever did not recur. There was no way now that Olivia could escape from herself. There was not even Estelle's monotonous chatter to keep away the questions, the introspections, the puzzlement. And the pain. Why had Jai cast her off with such little warning?

Sitting for hours in the garden while her aunt was either busy or out visiting, Olivia remained balanced on the knife-edge of torment such as she had never known. The pain chipped constantly at her heart, paring it down to a knot that would not stop bleeding. Yet she recognised that in all and equal honesty, she had no excuse for surprise. Jai had never wanted her love; she had thrust it upon him regardless. He had often avoided meeting her; she had pursued him till he had capitulated. He had warned her frequently. It was she who had made light of it. Those few scraps of emotion he had tossed at her, those reluctant kisses and restrained caresses, it was she who had made into mountains what were essentially only pebbles. No, he had not discarded her; he had never accepted her at all!

But reasons and causes, however logical, do not lessen suffering. With each passing moment Olivia's anguish compounded. If there was any thread of light in the blackness of her despair, any hope in a jungle of hopelessness, it was one to which she clung tenaciously. Whatever Jai's motives, however bitter the taste of his renunciation, however small his capacity to receive and return love—he did love her. He could scorn and scoff and deny as much as he chose, but in some cloistered corner of that rock he had for a heart, Olivia was passionately convinced that he carried shared pain. And there was that affinity! *That* he could never refute, nor would she ever let him.

In the meanwhile, the pain had to be borne, the aching

separation tolerated, the sense of despair rebuffed. She knew she would see Jai Raventhorne again; no divinity fashioning their ends would dare deny her at least that.

The garden fragrances were strong and heady. Abstractedly, Olivia inhaled the scent of freshly mown grass, of river breezes, of the abundance of nature. With winter near, the garden exploded with new life and cold weather finery: double hibiscus, dahlias and chrysanthemums as large as fruit bowls; pink, white and magenta bougainvillea now returned to blossom after their heavy leafing from the rains; saffron marigolds, sweet peas, snapdragons and gladioli. Among the profusion a pair of bulbuls daintily gathered twigs with much debate; a wedge-shaped flight of parrots looped shrilly around a banana grove and a solitary kingfisher sat hunched on a pole, seeming to meditate. The blue Vanda orchid flourished. As it peeped at Olivia from behind a branch, it seemed to snigger with some private joke.

A carriage swept noisily through the gate and up the drive. Even before it reached the portico, Sir Joshua leapt forth from it. Waving extravagantly in Olivia's direction, he bounded across the lawn towards her.

"Koi hai?" His roar brought Rehman hurrying out of the kitchen house. "A drink, you moth-eaten rascal, a strong drink, *juldee, juldee,* or you'll have a taste of my crop across your idle backside, you black son of a whore!" He sat down heavily, almost upsetting the tea table in the act, and turned to Olivia. "As good as new I see, huh? *Shabash,* splendid! Now, that's what I like to see in you young chits, as many roses in the cheeks as in the garden, no?" He slashed recklessly at a nearby bush and guffawed.

Olivia stared at him in astonishment. His behaviour was extraordinary, so out of character! "Are you not feeling well, Uncle Josh? Somehow, you seem . . . not to be yourself today."

"Not myself today?" He grappled with the concept, then, unable to grasp it, shrugged and gave up the effort. Putting his head between his hands he groaned and cursed volubly. "The clap-riddled, horse dung–brained son of a two-anna harlot—I *told* the god-rotting jackass that nothing these bloody natives do is ever *simple . . . !"* His mouth dripped saliva and his speech was thickly slurred.

"Who, Uncle Josh, and do what?" Olivia was bewildered.

"Eh? Who . . . what?" Dazed again, he stared at her blankly. Then his face darkened again as he looked around for Rehman. "Where's my bloody drink, you misbegotten bastard? Can't you move your black butt faster?" Picking up a saucer he flung it at the terrified bearer as he approached. Rehman dumped the tray onto the table and fled. Sir Joshua half rose, as if to give chase, then slumped again cursing under his breath. "No risk, the man said, no bloody *risk . . . hah!*" Pouring himself a double measure, he downed it in a gargantuan gulp.

Sir Joshua was drunk!

Olivia had never seen her uncle in a state of such unmistakable intoxication. Indeed, his boast was that he could drink anyone under the table and still walk a straight line. Also, there was something in his disjointed ravings that was ominous—something to do with "that Kirtinagar business" . . . ?

"Risks *where,* Uncle Josh?" she asked urgently, forgetting that the matter, whatever it might be, should no longer be of interest to her.

He glared at her and through her, fuzzy eyed, unable to focus. "Slocum will earn his spurs this time," he muttered smugly. "*This* time he will not let go . . . *arrey, koi hai?*" He rapped the table with his crop and Rehman crept fearfully out from behind a flowering bush but poised for instant flight, if necessary. With unsteady hands Sir Joshua poured himself another drink, spilling much of it over the table-cloth. "Get some of that jam roly-poly Babulal made last night, the thieving swine. And if there's none left, tell him I'll string his black hide up the Ochterlony tower, *achcha?*" With a stricken nod, Rehman fled again.

"Not let go of *what,* Uncle Josh?" Olivia asked impatiently, her alarm rising for more than one reason. It was not his drunkenness as such that worried her. At home she had seen plenty of brawls in the saloons, even killings, when men had swigged with abandon, then drawn their guns at the turn of a card, the sound of a hasty word. Apart from the fact that something terrible had happened, she was nervous at Sir Joshua's belligerence where the servants were concerned. What if he exercised his wrath on them physically . . . ? He was a big man, well over six feet tall, with very solid strength in his muscled shoulders. She would not be able to restrain him, and for the servants to venture retaliation was, of course, unthinkable. Taking his arm firmly, she shook it. "Answer my questions, Uncle Josh!" Olivia commanded, not because she hoped to receive an explicit response but only to keep his attention diverted from the servants. "I want to know *exactly* what has happened." He did not reply, of course. Mouthing more graphic oaths, he merely laid his head down on the table.

Just then, a second carriage raced in through the gates, and

Olivia's heart sank. Her aunt? Home already from the church bazaar? But it was not Lady Bridget's carriage, nor did she emerge from it. The person who came flying out was Arthur Ransome. With a cry of relief, Olivia sprang up to hobble across the lawn as fast as her still-shaky legs would carry her. "Oh, dear God—thank *heavens* you've arrived! Uncle Josh is—"

"I know. That's why I'm here," Ransome said shortly, his face grim. "He's been in his cups all day at the office. Bridget home?" Olivia shook her head. "Well, bless the Lord for small mercies! She would have been even more disgusted than *I* am."

As he started to hurry across the lawn, Olivia stalled him with a hand. "Why has he been drinking all day? Something awful has happened, hasn't it?" He merely nodded, then left her standing where she was.

She was suddenly exhausted. She had not enjoyed the confusing interlude. Barnabus Slocum, the magistrate, was somehow involved in it and there was talk of "risks," which made it all the more disturbing. Olivia went up to her room and lay down to rest. It was not until Sir Joshua had been carried up to his bed with much heaving and huffing and cursing, and the tread of heavy footsteps had retreated down the stairs, that Olivia ventured out again. She found Arthur Ransome in the study.

"Is Uncle Josh asleep?"

"Out cold, thank God. The blithering idiot!" His face drawn with strain, Ransome sat down and pressed shut his eyes with his fingers.

Olivia held her questions for the moment. "Would *you* perhaps care to also have a drink, Mr. Ransome?"

"By gad, I *would,* thank you. It's been quite a day, one way or another. Haven't seen Josh hit the bottle so hard since one Christmas in Canton when he slung seven coolies overboard for having dropped a barrel of first flush tea in the briny. They didn't drown, of course, but we had to sail out fast or there would have been hell to pay. By the way, Miss O'Rourke, I hope that you are finally over your dreadful bout of ague?"

Over his whisky, which he drank in huge, thirsty gulps, Ransome made valiant conversation about the scourge that struck many in the tropics and the new miracle bark, the cinchona, that cured it, much to the wonder and relief of patients and medical community alike. It was only after neutral small talk was exhausted that Olivia asked, "Please tell me what exactly has been happening, Mr. Ransome."

He swilled his drink around the glass and evaded her eyes. "What did Josh say to you?" His voice was low and unsteady.

She sensed his caution. "Nothing coherent. However, I got the impression it was something to do with Kirtinagar."

"*Something* to do with Kirtinagar?" He looked astounded. "Then you haven't heard?" She shook her head as he walked to the desk and picked up the English language newspaper that did for the local community. He handed it to her. "Nothing I can say will be more explicit than this."

Not having seen a newspaper during her illness and not especially interested since, Olivia was startled by the bold banner headline: "Explosion in Kirtinagar coal-mine kills one." She read the rest at a glance. The explosion had occurred a few nights ago, collapsing the roof of the main shaft in the coal-pit and burying a night-watchman. By the time he could be extricated from the debris, he was dead. Sabotage was strongly suspected and the rubble left by the explosion was being investigated for remnants of dynamite. No one else was present at the mine site when the explosion took place, but several witnesses are said to have seen and recognised a certain person on horseback fleeing from the vicinity soon after the disaster. Since the man seen by the witnesses is a known resident of Calcutta and is now strongly suspect, Mr. Barnabus Slocum is in Kirtinagar requesting permission from His Highness Maharaja Arvind Singh to actively participate in the investigation. The newspaper quoted the magistrate as saying, "The prime suspect, unmistakably identified by five eyewitnesses, resides under the jurisdiction of the Calcutta police authorities. As such, it would be in the interests of the Maharaja to avail himself of our assistance and press charges without delay." The remainder of the story traced the history and development of the mine, repeated the importance of the coal find for British industry and related some cursory details about the State of Kirtinagar. These Olivia skimmed through; her throat felt tight, and within her was a feeling of distinct coldness.

"This Calcutta resident," she asked slowly, knowing already what the answer would be, "is said to be Raventhorne?"

"So the witnesses swear."

"Raventhorne would sabotage his own mine, kill his own man?"

Ransome's normally genial countenance was profoundly unhappy. "He has openly declared in the presence of many that he would rather see the mine closed than let a single lump of that coal fall into British hands. We know that there has been bitter dissension between him and Arvind Singh over the matter."

"But Arvind Singh has already rejected your proposal," Olivia said tiredly. God, how she was beginning to hate that damned coal and everything to do with it!

"Reading between the lines of his refusal, it is evident he might reconsider if the consortium agreed to make a higher offer," Ransome replied with dogged persistence.

"In that case, wouldn't Raventhorne have sabotaged it *then,* rather than destroy the mine before it was necessary?"

Ransome got up and turned away from her. "Raventhorne is known to be capricious, unpredictable, vengeful—especially when his hatred of the English is provoked. If he can also damage us, he would not hesitate to cut off his nose to spite his face. And with the mine destroyed, there is now no prospect of anyone getting that coal, at least not for months." Still not turning to face her, he quickly poured himself another drink.

His explanations rang hollow and Olivia's sense of dread compounded. "No!" she said angrily, throwing caution to the winds. "The rumour is that Raventhorne would have raised money for the irrigation project from the Indian money-market. Why needlessly ruin a valuable asset, and his friendship with Arvind Singh? Why execute the goose that would have laid golden eggs for both partners *and* Kirtinagar?"

"Perverse satisfaction!" Ransome cried, now distinctly agitated. "A means of extracting insurance money—who knows the mind of a madman?"

"Satisfaction also from killing a harmless watchman in his own employ?" Olivia asked with a caustic smile. "That makes the least sense." She ignored the possibility of an insurance fraud; it was too trivial to even consider.

"Ah!" At last Ransome turned towards her, trying hard to disguise his excitation with an unconvincing smile. "That appears to have been his miscalculation. He had obviously reckoned that on the first night of the immersions everyone, including the night-watch, would be out roistering with friends and family. Naturally, all the other men were. The watchman, however—"

"First night of the immersions?" Olivia had gone very still indeed. "Is that when the explosion took place?"

"So I read," Ransome muttered, pointing to the newspaper. "Five witnesses, unknown to each other and two of them Englishmen, profess to have recognised Raventhorne riding away from the mine site on that cursed black devil that he favours. All five have given sworn testimony."

Springing back to life, Olivia grabbed the newspaper to verify the date of the explosion. Then, hands shaking, she folded the paper neatly and replaced it on her uncle's desk. "They are lying," she said quietly. "Every one of them is lying."

Under the quietness there was such ferocity that, for a moment, Ransome stared. His complexion turned the colour of putty and his hand trembled so that he was forced to put his glass down on a table. "How can you say that with such conviction, Miss O'Rourke?" he cried as he went a shade paler. "Tell me, I beseech you—what did Josh blurt out to you during his drunken rambling? Please be frank, I would like to know everything."

Olivia was shocked at how ill he suddenly looked. And in his staring eyes she saw fear. Realising that she had been standing without having the need to and that her knees were threatening to buckle, she quickly sank down onto the couch. "Uncle Josh revealed nothing to me," she said, stone faced. "His babbling was quite incoherent. But tell me, with what is Raventhorne likely to be charged?"

In his own turmoil, Ransome had fortunately not noticed hers. "It is for Arvind Singh to prefer charges." Draining his glass, he tried to steady himself again as he wiped his glistening face with a handkerchief. "Even though Arvind Singh is a partner in the mine, if he chooses to do so, then sabotage will be the secondary charge. The prime charge will certainly be manslaughter."

"Will Arvind Singh prefer charges?" Mechanically, she rose to refresh his drink.

He placed his palm over the rim and shook his head. "No more, thank you. One of us needs to keep his wits about him." There was a touch of bitterness in his tone. "Slocum will certainly try to persuade Arvind Singh to prosecute, and make the charge stick to secure a stiff sentence. Slocum detests Raventhorne. With good reason, perhaps. His sister was once . . ." He stopped and flushed. "Yes, Slocum will not give up easily."

The aborted reference to Slocum's sister revived in Olivia's memory one of the many snippets of gossip Estelle had given her, but she did not pursue it. Instead she asked, hating herself for still wanting to know about the man whose name singed her lips each time she said it, "What has been Raventhorne's reaction to all this?"

"He has not chosen to make his reaction known."

"And he has made no effort to deny the fabrications?"

He remembered suddenly her previous vehemence and stared at her with renewed alertness. "What makes you believe so forcefully that they are fabrications, Miss O'Rourke?"

This time she was prepared. "Only what I am led to believe by rumours about the man. You yourself have insisted frequently that he is an uncommonly shrewd man, devious in the bargain. Given all this, can it be believed that if he did wish to play dog in the manger he would do so with such ham-fistedness? Or with a plot quite so transparently amateurish? Conveniently he is seen by five witnesses who identify easily not only the man but Raventhorne's unmistakable horse!"

"As I pointed out, Raventhorne is not beyond cutting off his nose merely to—"

"His nose, yes, but not his *head!*" Olivia knew she was teetering on perilously thin ice. At any moment Ransome might latch on to a reality that was, ironically enough, no longer a reality. Quickly regaining control, she assumed an air of nonchalance. "I am only stating the self-evident, Mr. Ransome, as even a simple-minded lawyer would do. But tell me, as a matter of mere curiosity, do *you* believe him to be guilty?" She did not look at him but instead made a ritual of playing with the tassels of her shawl.

His expression instantly closed. "It is unimportant what I believe, Miss O'Rourke," he said woodenly. "It is what Slocum believes, or is made to believe, that is material. Barney is as vindictive as Raventhorne, and he has many personal axes to grind." His shoulders sagged as a measure of his distress. "There is much evil afoot, I fear, Miss O'Rourke. I am gravely disturbed at the chain of events that has been set in motion, for it will now not be reversed. Slocum will go after Raventhorne whether he is guilty or not. No matter what the facts, they will be trimmed to fit the desired pattern. Public opinion, already violently against Jai—not without good reason, I daresay—will support Slocum, force his hand even further. I don't know where it will all end, or indeed if it will now ever end." As if unable to carry some unseen burden, his shoulders slumped further.

Again that unconscious use of the first name! Olivia sensed that Arthur Ransome concealed much from her, but she did not have the courage to question him further. Nor could she without exposing herself. Casual once more, she only asked, "Since Raventhorne does nothing to refute these charges, are there any rumours as to what his defence is likely to be?"

Ransome pulled a grim face. "Does a rabid dog run when it sees trouble coming? Does it turn tail against a mob armed with sticks? No, it bounds ahead joyously to meet the mob, and that is precisely what this damned fool appears bent on doing. He neither refutes the charges, nor does he hint at any means of self-defence. Holed up on that fancy clipper of his, in all probability he awaits Slocum's knock with impatience." He threw up his hands in a gesture of resignation. "As I've confessed to you, I am severely perturbed, *severely.* Not because I lose sleep over Jai's problems—God knows, he can look after himself!—but because bitter experience has taught me to fear his reprisals."

Lady Bridget's arrival put an end to any prospect of further discussion. Ransome hurried away to present loyal alibis for his friend's state of inebriation, and Olivia, restless and violently angry, returned upstairs to her room. They were preparing to lynch Jai Raventhorne for a crime he did not commit. And only she could prove that he was innocent!

Either Sir Joshua had no recollection of his behaviour the previous evening or he chose not to remember; in any case he offered Olivia no apologies. Whether or not he had apologised to Lady Bridget was difficult to tell. Marble faced and sullenly silent, she made no reference to the occasion, but judging from Sir Joshua's own grim expression, words had certainly been exchanged between them. Torn with her own anxieties, Olivia took only cursory notice of their friction. That Jai Raventhorne's life should be in jeopardy in so gross a miscarriage of justice was not something she could forget easily no matter what the circumstances between them. She faced a hideous dilemma; one way or the other it had to be resolved. Somehow she had to secure confirmation from Sir Joshua.

With no other option in sight, Olivia walked resolutely into his study that night. Engrossed in polishing his collection of Chou period bronze bells—a duty he always performed himself—he seemed nevertheless pleased to see her. "Still awake? Good. Come and sit with me while I get this done. See this?" He tapped the huge bronze before him with obvious pride. "Probably third-century *chung* from Shantung, part of a set. The *chih-chung,* hand-bells, are smaller, of course, like the harness jingles. A glass of Madeira, perhaps?"

Olivia shook her head, relieved that last night's episode was not to be mentioned. There were other matters she had to talk about. The opening she wanted lay on the desk before her. Picking up the newspaper, she asked boldly, "Who on earth could be responsible for this brutal vandalism? It's difficult to believe anyone could stoop so low."

His concentration remained focused on the bronze. "Obviously someone has, m'dear."

"This 'well-known Calcutta resident,'" she pretended to read, "has he been positively identified? They say he was actually seen leaving the mine site in a great hurry."

"Well, there are rumours, of course." For all the interest his expression showed, they could have been discussing the daily bazaar.

"Rumours? Surely more than that, considering five eyewitnesses!"

"Perhaps. It's up to Slocum to verify their accounts." He lifted the bronze to replace it in the glass-fronted cupboard and returned with another bell, a smaller one.

His reticence irked but did not deter Olivia. "In the dark, eyewitnesses can make mistakes. Or," she added pointedly, "they could have been drunk, considering the festivities."

His hand with the chamois-leather paused briefly. For the first time his impassive eyes showed expression, a glint. "The moon was almost full," he reminded her shortly. "Drunk or sober, a mistake seems unlikely."

Olivia felt her chest tighten in the effort to appear casual. "It says here that Mr. Slocum has gone to Kirtinagar. Has he discovered anything more of significance?"

"We will know tomorrow when he returns."

It was evident that her choice of subject displeased him, but if she were to take any action at all, she had to know everything. Ignoring his lack of encouragement, she recklessly probed further. "And the motive? I wonder what *that* could possibly have been—insurance fraud, perhaps, as some suggest?" By asking that, she subtly revealed that she knew the suspect was Raventhorne, but her uncle gave no reaction. She raised a light laugh and picked up one of the bronze bells as if to examine it carefully. "It's amazing what some businessmen will stoop to, isn't it? I know they do in America. My father has written about several cases of arson by small factory owners so as to collect insurance."

Her inane chatter brought no change to Sir Joshua's expression. "Yes. That might be a possibility."

"On the other hand, here the explosion killed a man. I guess that automatically means a charge of manslaughter?" She stopped and held her breath.

He folded the chamois-leather neatly and slipped it back into its pouch, then sat back to appraise her over his half-moon glasses. "I see that you have been giving the matter considerable thought, m'dear," he remarked with what Olivia knew was deceptive mildness.

Olivia shrugged. "No more than anyone else," she answered easily. "According to Mr. Ransome there is much conjecture and debate in station about the outcome of all this." She waved a hand across the newspaper. "Especially if the charge is manslaughter. A man could be put away for years for manslaughter, couldn't he?" Her heart throbbing painfully in her mouth, she waited for his response.

Almost imperceptibly, his face changed once again; it became very strange, very still. He moved his gaze away from her to fix it midair between the desk and the wall. Lost within himself, he fell into a deep silence. Watching the change in him, Olivia tried to discern its implications and couldn't; even in his silence there was menace. With an effort, Sir Joshua roused himself from his reverie. "Yes," he said, his face again hard, the moment of solitude over, "if Slocum so chooses. It would be no more than the man deserves."

"If Slocum chooses? Surely if Arvind Singh chooses to prosecute at all!"

"Arvind Singh will prosecute. Slocum will see to that."

"*See* to that? How?" She no longer cared what he might make of her questions, she *had* to have the answers!

"How? For an intelligent girl you're suddenly asking pretty daft questions!" As if to make amends for his reprimand, he smiled. "My dear, Kirtinagar might be politically independent, but economically it is far from so. There is no industry in the State worth mentioning and there is much Arvind Singh needs to buy from us for the subsistence of his people. That," he pointed out softly, "makes him highly susceptible to pressure."

Olivia started to feel sick. And frightened. What Ransome had said was true; whether or not the facts fit, they would be trimmed to the requisite size so that Raventhorne could be eliminated. "Then it is this Calcutta resident, Kala Kanta I hear, who will be deemed the guilty party?"

"He is the guilty party."

"And if he can present an acceptable defence for himself?"

"He can present none that Slocum will accept."

Who was her uncle to decide that? Olivia felt a stir of cold, consuming anger. But there was still one question, the most vital one, that remained unasked and unanswered. And it was on this answer that her entire life might depend.

Forcing herself to stay calm, she walked to the glass-fronted cupboard and set the last of the bronze bells in its place. "As I see it then, the success of the charge rests upon those five eyewitnesses. Supposing, just *supposing* as a hypothetical possibility, that this suspect could prove beyond all reasonable doubt that he was not in Kirtinagar that night, that he was elsewhere. What then?"

A flicker, a mere flicker, of uncertainty flashed in his eyes. She saw that this question had angered him more than any of her others. Even so, he remained in perfect control. "Hypothetically, such a contention, if proven, would invalidate the charge. Any fool can see that. But he was not elsewhere. Nor will he be able to prove that he was."

Yes, a lynching had been arranged. The tree had been selected, the rope was already in place, the mob screamingly impatient for the swinging. Olivia rose, her path now clear before her. "I see now exactly what you mean when you say there is more than one way of catching a monkey!"

If he noticed her contempt, he did not show it. Even if he had, it would no longer have mattered.

10

There was barely an apology of a moon, the thin sickle still weak and faint. In the flickering, filtered light of the stars the boatman rubbed the drowse from his eyes and peered at Olivia in astonishment. She opened her cloth pouch and laid some silver coins on the palm of her hand.

"Half of that now and the rest when you have brought back a reply for me." Her Hindustani was now reasonably clear and there was no ambiguity about the silver coins.

The man's eyes glistened as sleep vanished from them and he nodded with alacrity. *"Theek hai,* memsahib, very well. The letter?"

Olivia divided the coins in half, handed him his promised share and then an envelope. "Remember, I must have an answer."

"But if the Sarkar is not on board?"

"He will be," she said with more conviction than she felt. "The letter must be given only to him, no one else, *achcha?* Understood?"

The boatman yawned and nodded, shrugging away his amazement at having been shaken awake in the middle of the night by a solitary mem who had no business wandering the streets on her own. Her sudden presence convinced him once more of what he had long suspected—that all white people were vaguely mad.

The small rowing craft moved off on its journey across the river, leaving Olivia to the mercies of the cutting winds that seemed to pierce through flesh and bone to freeze the marrow. Pulling her heavy woollen cape more closely over her head, she placed Jasmine's night blanket on a dense knot of banyan roots and settled down to keep her vigil until the boatman returned. It was not yet ten o'clock but the streets were deserted, left to the scavenging mercies of stray dogs and huge bandicoots who scurried about making squeaking noises and rustling dead leaves. Occasionally there was a sharper squeal as some unwary smaller prey was undoubtedly caught and devoured on the spot.

Hugging her knees and gathering her skirts closer to her legs, Olivia shivered a little, her eyes fixed to a distant spot across the inky river where the *Ganga* was anchored. In spite of the blackness of the night she convinced herself that she could discern the ship's ghostly outlines, its blobs of diffused yellow lights on the deck, and she shivered again. Somewhere in that tent of dark was Jai, perhaps even at this moment reading the letter she had composed immediately after leaving her uncle to his brandy and his dreams of perverse triumph. Nobody had seen her creep out of the house (how expert she was now in the art of furtiveness!) or saddle Jasmine to the snores of the groom and his son up in the hayloft. But even if someone had, it was immaterial. By tomorrow, all of Calcutta would know the truth, and the prospect exhilarated her! She was done with deceit and subterfuge; tomorrow she would climb to the top of the Ochterlony monument and declare to the world her love for Jai Raventhorne.

A faint splash in the distance caught her attention and she was alert instantly; he was back already? With his reply? But when the boatman beached a few moments later and she ran down the slope to meet him, all he handed her was her own envelope. Unopened.

"The Sarkar is not on board," he said with obvious regret, wondering if the absence of a reply automatically deprived him of the rest of his payment.

Olivia's spirits crashed. "Who told you that? Who was it you saw on board?"

"Since the Sarkar was not on the ship it was not necessary for me to go up on board." He pressed his elbows and winced. "I am an old man. My joints are not what they—"

"Yes, yes, but whose voice was it that informed you he was not on the ship?" Olivia interrupted impatiently, almost crying in her disappointment. "Did you recognise it? Try to remember, did you?" There was only one slim hope left.

The man pondered. "Well, it's difficult to—"

"Was it Bahadur's?"

His face brightened. "Yes, yes, it was his. I'd know it anywhere because he has often hired—"

Olivia stopped him by opening her pouch and emptying whatever coins she had in it onto his palm. He gulped into silence, staring at the silver. She closed his trembling fingers around it. "All that is yours if you take me to the ship and wait there to bring me back."

Galvanised, the boatman leapt back into his craft, his grin of delight reaching from one ear to the other as he hastily tucked the coins into a twist of his *lungi.* Spirits soaring again, her face flushed and the fire of success racing through her veins, Olivia clambered into the *dhoolie.* She knew her instinct would be right; if Bahadur was on board it could only mean that Jai was too.

Hope, fear and mad longing washed over Olivia in successive waves as the little boat picked its way again across the river. Intermittently she felt anger. He had returned her letter without even wanting to know what she had to say! Did he think she was so foolhardy and with such little self-respect as to take this nocturnal risk without the greatest of urgency? But then, as the white hulk loomed ahead beneath the stars, Olivia's anger evaporated and her courage started to wane. Jai would be furious with her; he would refuse to see her. She closed her eyes in a moment of agony and, intimidated by the lunatic daring of her escapade, almost ordered the boat back.

But then she stabilised herself. And it was too late anyway; with a boom that sounded like the hollow beat of a giant drum in the silence of the still night, the *dhoolie* had slid alongside the *Ganga.* In the still silence it sounded like the hollow beat of a gigantic drum.

"Who goes there?" From above, the alert voice of the watch called.

The boatman looked over his shoulder questioningly at Olivia, then, upon her whispered instruction, shouted back, "A lady."

There was a startled pause. "What does the lady want?"

"To come aboard."

Another silence. "On what business?"

Olivia nodded at him and the boatman funnelled his hands around his mouth to be better heard. "On business with the Sarkar."

From above came sounds of whispered consultations, and her heart leapt—he *was* on board! Had he not been, the negative response would have been immediate. "The Sarkar does not wish to receive visitors."

Olivia's mouth set in a grim line. Even as the blood pounded at her temples, she again prompted the boatman. "The lady would like the Sarkar to be informed that if the ladder is not lowered within five minutes she intends to climb up the anchor chain." The boatman turned to look at Olivia with undisguised awe.

This time the confabulations were more prolonged and followed by the sounds of scurrying feet on deck. In the ensuing and seemingly endless silence, her heart sank with dismay on the chance he would decide to call her reckless bluff. But then the apprehension turned into triumph; the rope ladder snaked down the side, its wooden slats clattering noisily against the hull. A minute later she was being helped onto the deck.

Bahadur's inscrutable eyes widened briefly in surprise. Then, remembering his manners, he bowed and folded his hands in respectful greeting.

Nodding briskly, Olivia dusted her skirts. "Please inform the Sarkar that I would like to see him for a few moments." She spoke with the imperiousness expected of memsahibs in India.

Bahadur hesitated, bowed again, then walked away into the shadows through a doorway that led below. With shaking fingers Olivia wiped the dampness off her forehead, her breath exhaling in small puffs of mist. Oh God, how would he receive her? Would he receive her at *all?* She was alone on deck save for the watch, who stared at her open mouthed. Catching her eye, he hastily shut his mouth and turned away. Warm yellow light fell from swinging lanterns, making the polished brass rails gleam. The tops of the towering masts were buried within swirling night vapours that obliterated whatever stars might have been visible. Pale faced, Olivia waited. Her business tonight was formal. She was determined to make it also brief. But however briefly, however formally, she was to see Jai Raventhorne again.

Bahadur returned. As stone faced as she, he bowed again. "The Sarkar presents his compliments but regrets that he is not, at this moment, available." His eyes fell to the deck in embarrassment.

"In that case, would you please find out from the Sarkar at which precise moment he will be available? I am in no hurry." She smiled pleasantly enough as she added, "I will wait all night if necessary."

Bahadur bowed for the fourth time and returned to the doorway for an answer to this further inquiry. For a split second Olivia faltered; should she merely send in the letter and so eschew a doubtlessly unpleasant confrontation? But then she steeled herself again; to have come all this way and not see him? It was more than the weakness of her will would allow. Waiting only until Bahadur's form had melted once more into the shadows, she ran down the deck and slipped in after him. Keeping him within her sight, she followed him noiselessly down a familiar corridor, recognising it vaguely as the one leading to the main cabin. Bahadur halted at a door ahead but before he could raise a hand to knock, she had caught up to him, grabbed the knob and opened the door to plunge in. She heard him gasp behind her just as she shut the door in his face.

Raventhorne sat at his desk, writing. Disturbed by the noise, he glanced over his shoulder with a frown. Just for an instant their eyes met, then he turned back and continued writing. There had been no apparent change in his expression. Leaning back weakly against the door, Olivia watched him in a silence so complete that the scratch of his pen on paper was resounding. He sat with his sleeves rolled up to his elbows, one palm propped against the side of his head, his fingers splayed out in the untidy denseness of his hair. Under the desk his legs were stretched, the ankles crossed. His face in profile glowed in a pool of lamplight—the only light in the cabin—and was immobile in its concentration. Only his eyes moved as they followed the rapid progress of his pen across the paper.

For all her determination, all her anger, all her gnawing reservations at having undertaken this undoubtedly futile quest, Olivia became limp with love and longing. Everything within her melted and twisted like candle wax in a flame. But resolutely she discarded the clutching fingers of weakness and firmed her features into an impersonal expression. Boldly, she walked up to the desk. He still did not look up. And when he did finally deign to speak, it was without interrupting his labours.

"You should not have come, Olivia. You are making it very difficult for me."

Difficult for *him?* Her inadvertent softness vanished. "I don't think you could be fool enough to consider this a social call," she said coldly. "I have come only because—"

"I know why you have come. The noble gesture you feel constrained to make in my interest is not necessary."

"Feel *constrained* to make? Did you think I would sit silent under the circumstances?"

"If it is chivalry that has motivated this visit," a bare smile played on his mouth, "I am duly touched, especially in view of the illness from which I hear you have not fully recovered. You may now leave."

A curl of anger started to spiral upward. "Touched! You mean there is something that can touch you after all?" She laughed scornfully, but he neither looked at her nor responded to the taunt. Olivia's anger expanded. "You could at least do me the courtesy of looking at me when you speak, or are you afraid to?"

He completed what he was writing and, without hurry, laid down his pen. Then, leaning back, he stared at her expressionlessly. "No, I am not afraid. I am merely trying to indicate that although I appreciate your concern, I have nothing to say to you." He picked up the pen again and started to write. "Nor you to me."

It was not easy to sustain control but, with an effort, she did. Pulling up a chair she sat down and crossed one leg over the other. "Are you aware of what you are being accused?" It was a rhetorical question asked with more than a touch of sarcasm.

"I am constantly being accused of something. I'm not sure to which charge you refer."

"Don't be so damned flippant! They want to charge you with manslaughter, if not murder."

"Yes. I believe they do."

"You mean to do nothing to refute the patently false charge? Present no defence at all even though you have one that is cast iron?" In her lap her hands strained at each other in an effort to keep still.

Carefully, he blotted what he had just written and took a fresh sheet. "My defence is already taken care of. It does not include the shelter provided by your generous petticoats, which once before you accused me of misusing. Your reputation will remain unsullied."

"You think I care a *hang* about my reputation?" she cried in despair at his maddening obduracy. He gave no answer. "What . . . is your defence going to be? Please tell me, Jai!"

"Whatever it is, it shouldn't concern you." For the first time he showed a reaction but it was a flash of annoyance. "I meant it when I said I would not see you again, Olivia. I would be obliged if you would now leave me alone and *go.*"

The flow of ink, the rapid scribble and the infuriating scratch of the nib proceeded. Before Olivia's eyes descended a cloud of scarlet rage; already tightened to its limit, her temper snapped. Suddenly, she wanted to scream, to destroy and demolish this granite wall against which she was so needlessly banging her head. With a furious oath she sprang to her feet and snatched the pen from his hand. She flung it across the room with all the force she could summon. As it struck some unseen obstruction, it shattered with a metallic tinkle.

"I haven't come all this way at night to be dismissed like one of your goddamned doxies, Jai Raventhorne! Who the hell do you think I am to be sent off packing—some two-bit whore straight off the streets like your Sujata?" She swung an arm and swept all the papers off his desk; like a flurry of broken-winged birds they fluttered away to scatter on the floor. "How dare you treat me as if I were some dumb, common slut—how *dare* you!" Choking on her wrath she turned her back on him to hug her trembling body into stillness. "My God," she spat out viciously, "you *deserve* to be lynched!"

If he was intimidated by her outburst, he concealed the fact with admirable success. He got up, collected his papers from the floor and took his time rearranging them on the desk. "This is not your war, Olivia," he said quietly. "Don't get caught in the crossfire."

She shut her eyes in gathering anguish. "If it is your war, it is my war. I am already involved."

"I am giving you a chance to become *disinvolved.* Take it." Sitting down again he draped a casual arm over the back of the chair and faced her. "A few secret meetings, a few kisses exchanged . . ." He shrugged. "I can hardly believe those mean a lifetime commitment!"

Olivia had come prepared to be wounded afresh, prepared for salt on those wounds she already had, but the brutality of what he said now made her flinch. "Is that all our . . . relationship has meant to you, Jai?" There was an agony of disbelief in her whisper.

He stood up abruptly. "Olivia, don't make me say things that will hurt you more . . ." He did not look at her.

"Nothing you can say will hurt me more, *nothing!*" Stumbling forward, she confronted him with blazing eyes. "Do you have the courage to stare me straight in the face and answer my question—*do* you?"

Blank faced, he accepted her challenge. "Very well. If you insist. Yes, that is all our relationship has meant to me. You are nothing to me, Olivia, nothing at all."

Her bravado cracked. "I don't believe you, I will never believe you!" The pain suppurating beneath the façade exploded. "You're a lying, pernicious *bastard!*"

He laughed.

Olivia wasn't aware that she had struck him until the full force of her open palm connected with his cheek. It sounded like a crack of lightning. A glass bangle she wore—one he had bought!—shattered against his face; a turquoise-colored sliver embedded itself in his skin and drew a minuscule bubble of blood.

Raventhorne didn't move. Only the milky eyes flickered for an instant and then, slowly, his mouth curved into a mocking sickle. "So," he murmured under his breath, "the reckless American finds it difficult to honour her vow, does she?" He whipped the smile off his lips and his tone cemented. "If that is what I am, Olivia, then that is what I have chosen to be. Tolerate it if you can; if not, *get out!*"

Again her hand lashed out but this time he was prepared. She struggled briefly as he gripped her wrists but then, overcome by the hopelessness of her anger, she went flaccid and her body slumped. "I don't believe you," she said brokenly, "I don't believe you . . ."

He released her wrists with a jerk that wrenched her shoulders, and she almost cried out but didn't. Thunder faced and cursing under his breath, Raventhorne impatiently brushed the glass sliver from his cheek and started to pace with long, leonine strides as if stalking some unwary prey through a jungle.

"Who the hell do you think *I* am, Olivia? What gives you the right, the infernal daring, to poke and pry and intrude, yes, *intrude* into my affairs? I am tired of your invasions, Olivia, tired of your monstrous curiosities, your appalling presumptions, tired of *you!*" His eyes smouldered with malevolence. "You question me as if I owe you answers. I owe you nothing, *nothing,* do you hear me?" Briefly he stopped to glare, then, spinning on his heel, he started to pace again, hands clasping and unclasping behind his back as if unable to stay still. "I am beginning to hate you, Olivia. In your mind you have made me into a creature of your romantic imagination—a creature that doesn't exist, has never existed. What you think you love is an illusion, and the burden of living up to your illusion is not one I am willing to bear any longer." He halted again before her, expression venomous, voice dangerously low. "Get off my ship, Olivia, or I will have you forcibly removed."

Waves of pain rose within and crippled her. She was down to her last crumb of courage but she refused to let it go to waste.

Some remote sixth sense prodded her on and whipped her again into retaliation. Between them now was the moment of truth; it would not come again. She threw back her head and laughed.

"You are not only a liar, Jai, you are a coward. You cannot face the fact that, despite your cynical predictions, I *have* had the courage of my convictions after all. You may sneer at my alleged 'chivalry' in offering you an alibi for that night, but at the same time you feel small because I am willing to lay down my reputation not out of constraint but because my commitment to you *is* total." Her immense eyes flashed contempt in his face. "If you do not wish to use my evidence, I accept that. If you do not wish to see me or speak to me again, I accept that too, however wounding. What I will *not* accept, Jai, is the devaluation, the denial, of your feelings for me. You lie to hide your own delusions, not mine. You fabricate a hate that does not exist. You do love me, Jai . . ." A split second of anguish came and went. "As sure as the wind blows and I breathe, you love me, and before the sun rises tomorrow I will make you eat your words, Jai, every damned, lying one of them, I promise you that!"

"Get out!" His voice, tight in his throat, was strangled.

"I will, but not before you admit you have lied!"

The final thread of his control snapped. With a snarl he sprang at her and two enormous, powerful hands circled her neck. Distorted into a mask of virulence, his features turned maniacal, barely human. Thumbs pressed against her windpipe, he shook her with the fury of a mastiff gripping a rat between its teeth, all reason gone. Olivia battled to breathe, gasping for air but neither struggling nor feeling the faintest twinge of fear. A curtain of black started to descend over her eyes, but her last conscious emotion as darkness engulfed her was of triumph—she had broken through that shell! She felt herself slide and then go down, down, down, into some bottomless pit of blackness and silence. And then she felt nothing.

Time must have passed but Olivia was unaware of it. Laboriously, imperceptibly, she started to climb again, inch by inch, gasp by gasp. Air filtered through to her lungs and light into her eyes. She felt herself cushioned; against her cheek was warmth, and panting breath gushed into her ear. In the half haze of a mind not yet fully conscious, memory struggled and then broke through the mists. She smiled. Her mouth, buried deep against folds of musky, beloved flesh, formed a word. *Confess!* Even though no sound emerged, it was heard and it was understood.

"Why can't you leave me alone?" Against her cheek the

question sounded like a cry for help, a beseechment. "Why do you return to torture me like this?" Raventhorne raised his face and stared wildly into hers.

Ignoring the throbbing ache in her throat, Olivia clung to him. His breath scoured her skin like a rake; within her embrace his heavy frame twisted with spasms as he battled with his brutal inner devils. "Hush," Olivia murmured, cradling his head on her shoulder. "Hush, my darling one, *hush.*" Whispering comfort and love, she solaced him and waited, waited, waited patiently for the turbulence to subside, for the demons to retreat, for the body to still. Then she framed his tortured face between her palms and kissed him. Her eyes filled with tears. "Because I love you, Jai."

He shuddered. "Don't love me, Olivia." It was now no more than a weary, wasted refrain. His features contorted again. "My God, I could have killed you! What further proof can you want of my worthlessness?"

"It is also proof of what you deny. I see it in your eyes." She touched his lids with her finger-tips and smiled.

"You see too many damn things in my eyes that do not exist!" His fingers, clutching the rumpled confusion of her hair, tightened.

"They exist for me if not for you."

He groaned and his mouth on hers was punitive. It was a kiss not of love but of defeat and of rage at that defeat. "Go now, my golden-eyed innocent," he begged huskily. "Go, go, *go* before you commit yourself truly to a life of regrets."

Go? Go where? Olivia wondered. With her whole world held in her arms where was there left to go? "Regrets there will never be, Jai, that much I know. Whatever I am *is* yours."

He shook her in growing exasperation. "I can give you nothing in return, you foolish girl. I have nothing to offer you!"

"You give without knowing, Jai." Gently, she cleared his forehead of black strands heavy with perspiration. "And what you cannot offer is perhaps not worth having."

Hunger darting out from his eyes devoured her from only a whisper away. Hands, awkward and uncertain, fumbled within her cascade of hair as it spilled across the pillow on the four-poster where she lay. But with the hunger there remained stubborn incomprehension. "How can you still be so full of ideals, so blinded by unrewarding romanticism!" Even in his frustration he spoke with wonderment.

"The same way you can still be so full of senseless doubts!"

"I doubt because you commit without caution, tantalise

without apprehension, like a child ignorant of tomorrow—and I am only a man, damn you, as fallible as the next."

Olivia sighed, too overwhelmed for debate, too crippled by the burden of a love too long denied its natural fulfilment. She was no longer deceived by his assumed postures. What he refused to say in words he was saying to her with his eyes, with his hands, with every angry move of his body as it abrased against hers. "Then prove your fallibility," she murmured dreamily into his ear as she kissed it, "*prove* it, Jai Raventhorne!"

His response to her brazen challenge was savage. The last of his defences crumbled. Abandoning caution, he swept her into his arms, growling curses and hoarse imprecations as he tore at her clothing, wildly impatient with the buttons and bows and knotted laces. Assiduous in their fevered explorations, his hands wandered over her body leaving licks of fire wherever they touched her skin. Gone were the doubts, the indecisions and the uncertainties as he tossed aside each garment in a frenzy of haste. Then for an instant, one brief instant, his hands stilled. In smoky-eyed wonder he sat up on the bed to drink in the golden expanse of her body—long, tapering legs, generously moulded hips, the rose-tipped mounds of her breasts, the nipples already engorged and aching for his caress. Visibly awed, he skimmed their peaks with a trembling palm.

"My God, but you are exquisite . . . !"

The low, incredulous moan extinguished around the cinnamon dark of a nipple engulfed by his mouth. Wherever his eyes feasted, his lips followed, making her limp with love, weak with longing. At the havoc wreaked by his nibbling mouth, his flicking tongue, the inquisitive tips of his fingers, she cried out in agony. Ignorant of responses, she arched up against him, quivering like a leaf, ecstatic and yet astonished at the revelations of her body. She turned and buried her face in the pillow, covered in confusion. With a muted laugh, he drew out her face to smother it with kisses, his rampaging mouth unwilling to leave a single pore untasted, a solitary fibre unlearned. Holding her head steady, he explored the niches of her own mouth, his serpentine tongue drinking in her sweetness, making her drink in his. Olivia whimpered; there would be no turning back now. The appetite that belonged to them both with such impartiality demanded to be satisfied. She filled and overspilled with love, rejoicing in the abundant proof of his need for her, knowing that the words he had withheld for so long would also be part of their night.

He halted but only to cast off his remaining clothing, and she caught flashes of glistening nut brown flesh, hard and sinewed, sheened with damp. And then he was beside her again, the length of his body pressed close to hers, their legs entwined, their mouths inseparable with intermingling tongues and shared breath. Against the raven's-wing mesh of his chest, her cheek abraded into nettle stings, silken skin against stubbled maleness, and she melted into him. With their mouths locked, he traced the line of her spine to its base and pressed her—was it possible?—even closer into himself. Jerking into rebellion, Olivia burst into flame, savouring sensations as acute as pin points of fire. She cried out again and he stilled her protests with bruising kisses, drowning her whimpers with words that were alien. But the sounds of the words were primeval, universal, wild and wonderful because she knew they spoke of love. Like a musical instrument strummed for the first time, her nascent body leapt to life. Plucking, stroking, searing fingers made her vibrate with music such as she had never heard before. She knew not what further peaks were yet to be scaled on this her maiden voyage of divine discovery, but she sensed there were many. Velvet tipped intruders devised tantalising transgressions, with accuracy, with abandon, and Olivia convulsed into insanity.

"No more," she beseeched, crying out in a frenzy of unendurable rapture, "please, have mercy, my dearest one!"

For a fraction of a second his hand stayed. Glaze eyed with resurging uncertainty, he hesitated. Then, with a helpless groan, he buried his face in her shoulder. "There will be pain, my angel. How can I spare you that?" He was again ravaged with doubts.

She circled his neck with her arms and held him secure. "I love you, Jai, I love you more than my *life!*" Her whisper was fierce with emotion, thick with feeling. "It is not pain that I will feel, I promise you. Whatever else, it will not be pain."

The pain came but once, like the nick of a knife tip, the flick of a whip, forgotten even before it had passed, for with it Olivia swept on the crest of an incredible flood into womanhood. Past and future were obliterated; there was only the here and now of each moment stretching into an eternity of timelessness. Their bodies melded and merged and swayed into oneness, moving into rhythms as old and as enduring as time itself. His love-making was violent, his need for possession compulsive. Olivia jubilated in the possession, revelling in it, responding to it, reacting to her joy with delirium. When her moans became too fevered, he soothed them with kisses; when she could tolerate the exquisite torture no longer, he gentled her with sudden flashes of tenderness. And when his own fulfilment was imminent and he teetered on another perilous precipice of doubt, she locked her legs around his and tacitly forbade him to leave.

Give me something, something of yourself at least, now . . . !

The sheer magnitude of her surrender defeated him; not even he was man enough or perhaps too much a man to deny her silent supplication. In a cascade, his essence, the life force of his manhood, coursed into her, flooding and filling and fulfilling every last fragment of her body. Olivia gasped with happiness, then convulsed again and again, then catapulted like a trajectile into realms beyond reality. Suspended high in time and spaces unknown, she was blinded by the matchless perfection of the moment. And then slowly, softly, delicately, trembling in the folds of a nameless oblivion, a little death, she floated down again along slopes of a magnificent contentment into a dreamless valley that is the ultimate resting place of fulfilled love.

Even before their bodies drew apart, she was asleep.

A minute passed, or maybe an hour or a day. When Olivia opened her eyes again, dazed and drowsy, Jai was lying next to her on his stomach, his cheek cushioned on his arm, his face averted. Her throat constricted with emotion and her eyes melted. Across the hardened ridges of his bare shoulders she ran a hand, loving him, cherishing him, in silence. She laid her cheek on his back and whispered, "I love you."

He stirred, then turned and gathered her again in his arms, cradling her so that her lips nuzzled the base of his throat. In its hollow, she dropped a kiss and fingered the silver pendant he wore around his neck. She had never known such peace, such perfect serenity. Lightly, he kissed the top of her head. "You love me too much." In his tone there was fatigue and an immense unhappiness. "I have wronged you."

Olivia struggled up so that she could look into his face. "You have made me complete," she protested, searching for his eyes.

He looked away. "It was not meant to be like this. It was never meant to be like this."

She cupped his face and forced his eyes back to her. "It was always meant to be like this, always! From the very first moment we met that night on the river. It was *fated* to be like this!"

He exhaled a long, boundless breath, anxiety etched into every tired line of his face. "It is dangerous to love too much, Olivia."

"It is the only way I can love."

Gently he kissed the hurt away from her eyes and shook his

head. "You should not have come, Olivia. You will regret the commitment you have made tonight. I should not have allowed you to. It is I who am to blame, it is I."

The commitment *you* have made . . . ? Was it not shared? A question trembled on the tip of her tongue but she swallowed it; to ask it would be to break faith with herself. "Whatever the commitment, I have made it voluntarily. I do love you so very much, Jai."

He sighed and ruffled her hair but he did not smile. "It is not a love that will bring you worthwhile compensation."

"It already has," she said bravely. "If it brings nothing else, there will always be this."

"I am the wrong man for you, Olivia—you have chosen to love the wrong man." His inner storms would not subside.

"You are the only man for me, Jai," she explained patiently, despairing of ever breaking the vicious circle but not wanting to tempt the fates again with a futile argument. "Don't spoil my moment of happiness, Jai," she implored. "I refuse to let you." She hugged him close and, caressing his chest, deftly changed the subject. "How did you get this scar?"

With a sigh he surrendered. "In a fight."

She followed the livid line from shoulder to hip with a finger-tip. "From a sword?"

"No." He hesitated. "From a whip."

With a small cry of horror she bent down and kissed the scar from one end to the other. "Oh, how I wish I could erase all your scars with my kisses!"

He looked amused. "You think love is a universal panacea, do you?"

"Yes. If one allows oneself to be loved." She scanned his face for hints of his private thoughts. "Why don't you, Jai? Why are you afraid to be loved?"

He laid his head back and stared at the ceiling. "Because love such as you give me humbles me. It reduces me to something despicable in my own eyes. It diverts me. I feel threatened." He gave a hollow laugh. "Perhaps I am not used to being humbled."

"Then humble me too!" she whispered, hating the subtly increasing distance between them. "Reduce me too, divert me, threaten me, do with me as you wish—but don't stop me from loving you!"

His eyes liquefied, their corners suddenly bright. He pulled her close to him and rocked her back and forth like a child and his voice became thick with feeling. "Yours is an extraordinary love, Olivia, pure and undemanding, unselfish and, alas, unrewarding. I have never known anything like it; it baffles me, strikes wonder in me, decimates me." Lifting her hand, he kissed it almost with reverence. "Yes, I lied to you. What you have come into my life as is . . . a miracle. You have washed away so much of its ugliness, so much. In return you have asked for nothing, and I have given you even less than that." He lowered his head onto hers and his arms tightened. "You can never know what you have meant to me."

She squeezed her eyes shut. "Then tell me."

"I don't have the words. Perhaps there are none."

"There are, oh there are!" Every little muscle in her body tensed as she waited. "Just tell me once, only once, that you love me . . ."

He seemed astonished. "You still need it to be said?"

"Yes. I still need it to be said."

"To prove that you have won your challenge?" he teased but with involuntary annoyance. "To ensure that you have indeed made me eat my words?"

"No. The challenge was won even before I threw it!" She sat back smugly and defied him to deny it.

"In that case, why? They would be only words, what would you do with them after I have said them?"

A moist film removed him briefly from her vision. Why was he mocking her? "I will let them console and comfort me when I am not with you. They will sustain me, nourish me, keep me alive and breathing until I am again where I am now. Why else?"

"No. That is what you must not let them do. You must merely listen and forget them." There were strange shadows in the depths of his eyes, still unhappy and profoundly troubled. "You have a death wish, Olivia. And you are naive, exasperating, incorrigible, persistent and outrageously wilful." He paused to lay the back of his hand on her cheek and there was in the gesture entrancing tenderness. "But yes, I do love you . . ."

He had said it. At last it was hers, *at last!*

The words dropped, one by one, into the stunned quiet of her mind to take root, to grow, to flower like the waxen orchids that clung to the acacia tree in her uncle's garden. In time, like the orchids, the words now echoing endlessly through the silence of her mind would blossom further, remain perennially radiant and fresh. Olivia had never known a moment of such unadulterated happiness. In just a single instant her life seemed enriched beyond measure. She wanted to cry.

He did not break the silence between them. Instead, he filled it with unspoken things, sharing with her the joy he had evoked with such an effortless triviality. With his eyes, full of softness and unfettered love, he touched and caressed her body still flushed pink with the residual effects of love-making. The swell of her breasts, nipples once more taut and engorged; the dip of her waist as it curved and flared into rounded hips; the shapely legs threaded through his; the perfectly fashioned toes that idly stroked the side of his calf. He left nothing untouched. Olivia's amber eyes, mellow with happiness and the aches of love given and received, watched him as he watched her, the communion between them as perfect as a rainbow, a summer rose, a drop of dew. He took her face in his hands and kissed the corners of her tranquil smile. Pulled up close against him, she felt the stir of renewed yearnings.

"Teach me how to love you, Jai," she whispered. "Teach me everything." With the tip of her tongue she reached up to remove the tiny dot of dried blood that still clung to his cheek. He shivered with pleasure. Without fear or inhibition, she ran the flat of her hand down the expanse of his skin in a caress that brought a gasp of delight to his lips. He had given her the right to love him; to exercise it she now knew there was no bound she would be unwilling to break.

He made love to her again, with passion but with a tenderness that went far, far beyond the demands of mere physical hunger. Dictated by love, his whispered commands were still hesitant; intoxicated with success, Olivia hastened to obey them. An apt pupil, a swift learner, she abandoned restraint without qualms. Coached by a masterly lover, she teased and tantalised and tasted him as fully as he had done her, eager to give as much pleasure as she had been given. Startled but enchanted by her unlimited offerings, he tutored her shyly, guiding her hands when they faltered, wincing in savage rapture when they didn't, increasingly enflamed when she surprised him with some erotic innovation of her own. Her success in rousing him to such extreme pitches of pleasure flushed her with triumph. She matched him kiss for kiss, caress for caress, exploiting at random the wonderful freedom he gave her of his body. He took her again, with gentleness, and this time his rhythms were leisured and languid, a celebration that was mutual, a revelation that was to be savoured slowly. So skillfully and unerringly did he guide her and with such compelling subtlety that when she reached the crest, Olivia's senses deserted her. She flailed the air, cried out his name and clawed at his flesh in a crescendo of sensation. In her ear he laughed, even more abandoned. Ruthless now in his perpetration of delicious torment, he captured her mouth to silence her; within her head a galaxy of suns exploded, blinding her with their dazzle. The cataracts of sensation became impossible and, driven beyond the pale of tolerance, she burst into tears.

He was frantic with anxiety. "What did I do? Did I hurt you? Was I rough, brutal? Oh God, I am an animal!" Maddened with remorse, he showered her with kisses, wrapped her in his arms and rocked her. "Don't cry, for pity's sake, don't cry. I can't bear it."

Weakly, drenched in sweat, exhausted, Olivia shook her head. Still muttering self-imprecations, he crushed her to him and cocooned her in his love, unspoken but oh so eloquent! Gradually her breath quietened; peace returned to her body and with it an enormous contentment. Her life was now truly complete; she wanted nothing more from it, nothing. Wordlessly she rested her head on his shoulder. A moment of silence expanded into an eternity of jewelled perfection. Then he released her to lie back, lace his fingers beneath his head and close his eyes. Cushioned against the gleaming damp of his shoulder, watching the once-again calm rise and fall of his chest, Olivia drew languorous patterns above his heart, smiling to herself. Suddenly, her hazy thoughts crystallised into a tangible question. She frowned but did not speak.

"Ask it."

She started. "I forgot that you see with your eyes closed," she complained, piqued at having been caught.

"I don't need eyes to read your mind."

The finger-tip doodling across his heart stopped. Her gaze dropped and she blushed. "How many others have lain with you on this bed?"

"Why? Does it bother you?"

Animated again, her finger-tip drummed a grim tattoo. "Yes, it bothers me."

He laughed, slid up against the bank of pillows and took her up with him. "I warned you, I am not exactly a *brahmachari.*"

"What is a *brahmachari?*"

"What you said I could never be even if I tried." He cupped a breast in his palm and kissed its tip. "Hasn't it pleased you that I am not?"

Blushing deeper, she hid her face from him, suddenly shy. "Then why have you sent Sujata away?"

"Is there no stone of my life you would leave unturned? I sent her away because I no longer needed her."

Olivia recoiled. "And is that what you will do when you no longer need me?"

He became motionless, staring through her as if she was suddenly no longer there. "It is you who will cease to need me, Olivia," he said quietly. Taking off his silver pendant threaded through a fine chain, he slipped it over her head. "I have never given you anything because I cannot give you what I don't value myself, and I value nothing. Except this." His face was again haunted. "It belonged to my . . . mother."

A hard knot formed in Olivia's stomach. He had never before spoken of his mother! The significance of the gift, the enormity of his sacrifice in making it, the subsumed sanctity of the moment reduced her to silence. Lifting the pendant, she kissed it and then held it against her cheek, too moved to speak. It was in the shape of a box, heavy but obviously hollow. Along three sides was a hair-line crack. She started to run a finger-nail in it but, with a quick gesture, he stopped her.

"It was my mother's. It must not be opened, not even by you." He spoke with great agitation in short, gasping phrases. "Promise me that."

She nodded. Questions flocked to her mind but she did not ask them. What she had received from him tonight was a treasure chest of joy; she would not be greedy for more. She craned her neck to kiss both his eyes, his nose, the curve of his mouth, still too full for words. He had allowed her a glimpse into his private world; for the moment, it would suffice. And she had his love. Sweet Lord, how *much* she had of his love!

He swung his legs off the bed and stood up. One by one he picked up his scattered clothes and slipped into them carelessly. Then, with care, he gathered her garments, shook each one out and folded it, then laid them in a neat pile beside her. For a moment longer he stood feasting his eyes on the unashamed length of her body. Something flickered in the greyness, a momentary ache, a rippling sorrow. He bent down to brush his lips over the flatness of her stomach within which, somewhere—everywhere!—she held the cherished proof of his love. He turned away to stand at a window, looking out, one hand absently stroking the back of his neck.

Whoever and whatever Jai Raventhorne was in his innermost self, Olivia knew their communion was over. Once more he had carried himself away and beyond her reach.

With a sigh, she stretched her limbs and yawned, her body throbbing with the sweetest pain she had ever known. Humming under her breath, she got up and dressed herself. In a nearby drawer of a mirrored dresser, she found a comb and ran it through her disarrayed hair. The dark patch at the window through which he stared with such intensity was starting to tinge with an icy blue. Olivia was surprised—had any night ever flown by on such lightning wings? Watching the rigid back turned on her as if in denial of the intimacy they had shared only a few moments ago, Olivia coiled her hair into a chignon. Inadvertently, her thoughts began to race again and, as always, he sensed them.

"You are still concerned about my defence." It was not a question but a statement, uninflected and matter of fact.

She saw no point in denying it. "Yes."

He walked to his desk, picked up a sheaf of papers and tossed them in her direction. They fell onto the bed. "Read them. You might find what they say of interest." He returned to his abstractions near the window. For all his impersonality indicated, they might never have shared a glance let alone a bed of such consuming passion.

The top sheet of the sheaf, stiff and formal, was a legal document. It was brief and to the point and Olivia read it quickly. Then, more carefully, she read it again. The remaining papers she had no need to go through; the top sheet had said it all. Stunned, she sank down on the bed.

"Well?" It was Raventhorne who spoke first. "Would you consider that an adequate defence?" His eyes were like flint, untouched by his amused smile.

"This . . . can't be true!" Olivia breathed as her colour drained.

"It is."

"Das signed this willingly?"

"Hardly!"

A cold hand wrapped itself around her heart. "There must be some mistake, some hideous misunderstanding . . ."

"The mistakes and hideous misunderstandings are not mine, I assure you," he informed her drily.

"But . . . why *Das?*"

"He was the one most easily bought by them to engineer the farcical plot."

The cold turned to ice in her veins. "Was?"

"Yes."

She knuckled a hand against her mouth. "You . . . killed him?"

"Yes."

She was aghast at the unconcern with which he made the admission. "But why? *Why* when you already had his signed confession?"

He regarded her coldly. "Dead men can neither tell tales nor deny signed and sworn testimony. Das was scum. He deserved what he got."

That he had killed a man did not shock Olivia; she could well believe that Raventhorne had killed before. And she had been brought up with sudden death in environments of violence where a man could be drinking at a bar one moment and dead the next, driving a coach on a highway and ambushed into a ditch before he could turn around. What terrified her was Jai's added vulnerability.

"They'll never let you go, Jai. They'll hound you until they get you one way or another!"

"I'm used to being hounded. They will not find Das's body until it . . . no longer matters." Something amused him about that and he smiled.

Olivia fought back the biting fear that brought beads of moisture to her forehead, and brushed an unsteady hand across her eyes, trying to think clearly. "With Das . . . missing they'll say this confession is a forgery."

He shrugged. "Perhaps. It doesn't matter."

"What will you do with his statement?"

He raised a quizzical eyebrow. "What do you think?"

Olivia swallowed. "Make it public?"

"Don't you agree that I should? Don't you believe they deserve to be exposed?" For the first time he indicated anger. "I say *they,* but you know as well as I do that only one of them is twisted enough to concoct such a devilish plan. Ransome is a loyal stooge but he is not evil."

"And if you do make this public, will my uncle be the one charged?" The new situation added further dimensions to her horror. "It's unthinkable, monstrous!"

Raventhorne laughed. "You have much to learn, my naive American, about the workings of blind justice in India! Criminal offences can be tried only by English judges, and no Englishman—policeman or magistrate—would ever allow such an impertinence against a member of his club. Slocum will have the earnest endeavours of the entire community to discreetly whitewash the façades. The main consideration will be to avoid a public scandal, and your uncle will enjoy unanimous sympathy among those who matter. If need be, the Governor General will be asked to intervene. Justice will not be miscarried; it will merely be gently diverted into channels more acceptable to the community. Das's confession will be scoffed at, pronounced a fake and finally buried. Everyone will contend that Kashinath Das was, after all, only a dirty, native turncoat and liar, that he was forced by me to make the confession and to bite the hand that had fed him for so long, and that Calcutta is well rid of his kind anyway. And when and *if* his body is ever found, Calcutta will secretly heave a sigh of relief and sleep better that night, for not even dirty, native turncoats and liars are wily enough to speak from the grave. Far from being hounded, I might even be discreetly praised for having killed Das. 'At last that infernal bastard Kala Kanta has done something to justify his misbegotten existence,' the English will say in careful whispers over their evening brandies and cigars. 'Let's drink to the half-breed just this once, even if he has grown too big for his boots.' " He paused to take a breath and rested his head back against the chair, suddenly spent. Fatigued, he shut his eyes. "You need not be concerned for your uncle. No, I will not make Das's confession public."

It was the first time he had spoken to her at such length, and so openly. Tears swelled in Olivia's eyes at the extent of his bitterness, at the depth of his cynicism. But she could think of nothing to say, no words with which to contradict his dismal predictions. Restless again, he walked up and down and she watched him in helpless silence, herself torn between divided loyalties to kith and kin and to this haunted man to whom she had committed her all.

"Arvind is the only one I care about." Face cracking with strain, Raventhorne spoke again. "He knows the truth, of course. As for the rest of the bunch, Slocum already has a copy of this; so do Ransome and your uncle. Whatever their public postures, in private they will sweat, for among them only Arvind knows that Das is dead and can no longer bear witness one way or the other."

"And those witnesses under lock and key?" Olivia asked dully, filled with love for this maligned man already so burdened with undeserved ill repute. "What about them?"

A touch of humour relieved the strain on his face. "They are no longer under lock and key, I presume." He paused to flick a careless finger through the sheaf of papers on the bed. "If there is anything a money-lender has reverence for, it is accounting. And, of course, receipts. The 'witnesses' were handsomely paid with Templewood money. As his natural instincts dictated, Kashinath made them all sign receipts." Contemptuously he tossed aside the sheaf. "Not even Barnabus Slocum can produce a smell of roses out of this stench!"

It was difficult not to share in his contempt, not to participate in his anger at the infamy, but part of Olivia still held back. "That poor old man's death was an accident, Jai, it was not intended—"

"Not man, Olivia, *native!* Any European will tell you that with so many about, one more or less makes little difference. None at all when an aristocratic English skin is at stake." Once more his bitterness bubbled. "Kashinath Das was filth. The world *is* perhaps a better place without him. But our innocent watchman, Haveli Ram, was a harmless soul devoted to us and to his gods. We have broken bread with him, Arvind and I; we know his wife, his sons, his grandchildren. He trusted us, served us diligently and with loyalty—until one white man's greed snuffed out his life just like *that!*" He snapped his fingers, lips twisted with hate. "Does it make it easier for his family that his death was an *accident?*"

Olivia longed to go to him, to hold him, to love him again and somehow use her love to cleanse his festering wounds, but she knew that he would not now allow himself to be reached. "What my uncle did was wrong, hideously wrong. I know that." She spoke with despair, seeing the futility of words to repair the damage but unable to leave thoughts unsaid. "You don't see this, Jai, but in many ways he is as blind, as obsessed as *you.* He too has a canker in his soul. It forces his hand, clouds his judgement, induces strange madnesses . . ." In her anxiety to touch some chord somewhere, she ran to him and held his hand. "For what he has done he will be accountable one day to *God!*"

He shook off her hand and started to laugh. "God has an eternity at his disposal; I am somewhat less patient. Besides, I do not believe in divine justice. My means of retribution are less ethereal, more earthy." He laughed again as if at a jest she had made.

But Olivia saw that the pewter eyes were unamused, alien. The look in them could have come from the dead; it was lifeless. Suddenly frightened, she took his hand again and would not let it go. "No more killing, Jai, *please . . . !*"

He shook his head. "No. No more killing. There will be no

need. As the uncle on whose behalf you supplicate so laudably is fond of saying—there is, after all, more than one way to catch a monkey." He kissed her hand, disengaged his and was once more empty of everything, even hate. "A longboat awaits you below. As always, I trust Bahadur to reach you back safely." He walked to the door and opened it for her.

She was once more excluded from his mind. Morosely, Olivia followed him up onto the deck, where the freshness of dawn stung her cheeks and chill breezes whipped her skin into blushes. Spectral vapours lay on the waters but the river was beginning to stir into daily life. The reviving breezes cleared Olivia's head of its encroaching fatigue but she walked in a daze, unable to assimilate reality. So much had happened in this one night, too much! She felt sad and happy and confused with a mind like jelly and a body still marvellously enriched by the intoxicating passions of the night that had fulfilled her as a woman. Savouring the delicious languors weighing down her limbs, she stretched with feline pleasure. Sheer force of habit brought an eternal question to her lips but, with a smile, she bit it back; she knew, as always, that she would see Jai Raventhorne again, albeit in his own time, at his own choosing. In the meantime she was content to wait. Content? No, not content! But she would wait. If it took the rest of her life, she would wait. There was nothing better she would want to do with it anyway.

"Take care of your health. The ague can be notoriously persistent; it will weaken you further."

The return of his concern for her, the gentle worry in his face, suffused Olivia with warmth. For a fleeting second she clung to him on the deserted deck. "I love you, Jai. I love you with all my heart."

"Yes. I know." Just that, no more.

Against all good judgement, the eternal question erupted. "When . . . ?"

He put a finger across her lips. It felt cold. And in the coppery dawn light, his pallor was bloodless. "I have loved you neither wisely nor well, Olivia, but I have loved you. Can you remember only that?"

"How can I not, oh how can I not?" Torn with longing, she surrounded him with her arms and held him close.

"Then will you trust me, Olivia, *trust* me?"

"Yes!"

"Promise me that you will."

"I promise, I promise." Anxiously she searched his face for

a motive for his urgency, but she could identify none. He was still unsmiling, his skin still pallid white. "Of course I trust you, Jai!"

Briefly, a strange smile touched his mouth. "Then, perhaps, you will find the humanity to also forgive me."

"There is nothing to forgive." Aching to dally, to stay with him longer, she curbed her yearning to raise a matching smile. "I have loved you wisely, well and willingly, Jai—how can you still not know *how* willingly?"

He merely shook his head. "Then make haste and go. Soon it will be bright and you must not be seen." He did not kiss her.

From the longboat below, Olivia shaded her eyes and squinted up for a last look at his beloved face. The *dhoolie* she had retained had obviously long since been dismissed, for it was nowhere to be seen. With neither fear nor embarrassment, she waved. Standing motionless at the deck rails, he did not wave back. His concern for her reputation moved and amused her; by tomorrow there would be no more need for deceit. She was proud, yes *proud,* of her chosen destiny. And by tomorrow all Calcutta would know it too! With a light laugh she looked up again, savouring a last glimpse. He stood in the same spot, straight and immobile. The wind blew his jet black hair into a cloud around his face; his eyes, Olivia knew, were upon her. In the rapidly lightening morning a shaft of early sun caught and held his features. Something glistened; Olivia's waving hand stilled and on her lips her smile died.

In Jai Raventhorne's eyes there were tears.

"They're having such a lovely summer in Norfolk, Cousin Maude writes. The Broads are chock-a-block with boats and the banks are very lively with Sunday picnickers." Lady Bridget heaved a wistful little sigh. "Maude says she went to Kew for a friend's wedding and the Gardens were bursting, simply bursting, with summer flowers."

Picking at a piece of toast and scrambled eggs, Olivia said nothing.

Lady Bridget lowered the letter she was reading. "I wish you hadn't missed luncheon, my dear. You do look, well, feverish. Are you sure you are well enough to be out of bed?"

"Yes, of course." Olivia smiled. "I'm just a little tired."

"Even with all that sleep? Perhaps it's that draught you took.

They do tend to deplete the energy entirely." She returned to her letter.

It was almost four in the afternoon. Nine hours of sleep following her furtive return from the *Ganga* had not refreshed Olivia. Her body felt languid and ached in secret places, a throbbing reminder of the night that had unfolded for her the meaning of love. The memory flooded her cheeks with crimson; in her eyes there were far-away, vacant glints that made her stare without seeing anything.

But yes, I do love you . . .

Olivia stirred; the secret she had concealed in her bosom for so long no longer needed to be hidden. "Aunt Bridget, there is something I feel I must tell you . . ."

Her aunt looked up. "Yes dear?"

"There is someone I . . . I have become . . . attached to." She swallowed and steadied her voice. Beneath the table her nails cut half moons into her palms. A trickle of sweat dripped between her breasts. It felt strangely cold. "I . . . have not been as . . . as honest with you as . . ." She swallowed hard again and stopped, her courage so strong only a moment ago suddenly ebbing. Help me, God, *help* me!

Lady Bridget leaned forward and covered her hand with her own. Oddly enough, she was smiling. "I know, darling," she breathed. "I know. You don't have to spell it out for me—I'm not exactly *blind!* Just the other day I was telling Josh how strongly I *sensed* something in the air. Otherwise why on earth should the dear boy be sending you all those letters?" She laughed happily and squeezed Olivia's hand hard. "Take your time, dear, take all the time in the world. You can tell me when you're good and ready. I've waited so long, I can wait a little longer." Her eyes suddenly shone with tears and, filled with emotion, her voice quavered. "You have no idea, my child, no idea at all how much what you have to say will mean to me, oh how *much!*" She sniffed damply, dabbed her eyes with a hanky and, lips trembling, returned to her letter.

Olivia stared at her aunt, bewildered; she could not imagine what she could possibly be talking about. But then the penny dropped—Freddie Birkhurst! Olivia almost laughed out her incredulity; her aunt actually believed it was to *Freddie* she was referring? On the strength of those tiresome letters he had been sending and which she had been consigning to the waste-paper bin unopened? Why, it was laughable! But laughable or not, the inadvertent touch of farce had provided a note of anticlimax and, already ebbing, her courage deserted her altogether. For the first time Olivia was struck forcefully by the sheer enormity of the announcement she had been about to make, and by the grim seriousness of the consequences it would no doubt have on her family.

They had to be told, of course, and soon, very soon. She could no longer continue to live under conditions of such gross duplicity. But the words with which she dropped her indubitable bomb-shell had to be carefully chosen. Tact would be needed to soften what would certainly be a blow of monumental cruelty to them. There would be scenes, terrible scenes, with melodrama and fainting fits and tearful vituperations. Olivia's heart dipped, but at the same time her intentions hardened; whatever the consequences, they had to be faced, if not today then tomorrow. Naturally, there would be a scandal. Oh, how Calcutta would love that scandal! And, also naturally, she would have to move out of the Templewood home. Where would Jai take her—to the Chitpur house? The *Ganga?* Wherever it was, he would want her to be with him. Limp with renewed longing, Olivia shivered with happiness thinking of those telltale tears at the moment of parting, that desperately anxious promise he had extracted. *But yes, I do love you . . .* Her throat went tight; yes, whatever the consequences, however bitter and insufferable, she would not be able to hold on to her beloved secret much longer.

". . . would you, dear?"

Her aunt, still suffused with happy anticipation, had asked a question, which she had missed.

"I was wondering, dear, if you would take a cup of tea to Josh," Lady Bridget repeated with a smile of knowing indulgence. "He's been so dreadfully preoccupied all day."

Olivia came back into unpleasant reality with a jolt. Uncle Josh! She shot with involuntary anger at the mere mention of his name. With Das's sworn deposition in his possession, of course he was "dreadfully preoccupied"!

Bearing a teacup and a sour taste in her mouth, Olivia finally tracked him down in the rose garden, where he was busy at work, pruning. She stared in suspicious surprise; if Sir Joshua's interest in his home was cursory, in his opulent gardens it was nonexistent. They were, to him, his wife's preserve and responsibility. The sourness in her mouth increased; it was his machinations that had brought death to two men, and a third, wholly innocent, had been almost tarred, feathered and lynched in the frame-up, yet he could sit there casually trimming rose-bushes?

"Aunt Bridget has sent you some tea," she announced coldly.

Sir Joshua waved aside the tea and bent to pat Clementine's head as she blissfully trapped an earth-worm. "Did you know, m'dear, that roses existed twenty million years ago?"

"No." Olivia handed the unwanted teacup to one of the attendant gardeners and ordered that it be returned to the pantry. Had he been drinking again?

"See this?" He seemed not to notice her coldness. "Bridget imported these last year from France. The *Rosa multiflora*—floribunda to us. Some call it primrose. Spectacular, eh?"

Olivia made no response, surprised even more by his horticultural knowledge than by his sudden inclination to share it with her.

Sir Joshua stalked down the path towards a riot of blood red flowers. "The *Rosa chinensis,* m'dear. I brought this from Canton years ago. Oddly enough, they now call it the Bengal rose. I understand they're growing it in Europe with considerable success." In gathering bafflement Olivia trailed after him, certain that he had indeed been at the bottle again. He went down on a knee to gingerly part two branches of a bush heavily studded with thorns. "The *Prunus spinosa.* In other words," his oblique glance at her was strangely sly, "the black thorn. You see, Olivia, in strict botanical terms, thorns are only modified branches. The sharp point at the end pricks, of course, and often its poisons can be lethal . . . ," he jabbed one hard into the ball of his thumb and a pin-point of blood bubbled up, ". . . but it is also easy to remove, see?" With a finger-nail he scraped the thorn clean off the stem. "Of course, it does attempt to leave a scar, but that heals remarkably fast, with surprising efficiency." He stood up, wiped his hands on a handkerchief and smiled. "So you see, m'dear, nature poses problems sometimes, but then she also readily provides the answers."

Olivia decided that he *had* been drinking, but at the same time her pulse skipped a beat: He was trying to tell her something! What? Renewed fear assailed her; could he be up to some fresh trickery? Boldly she asked, "I hear that Mr. Slocum has returned from Kirtinagar—has there been any further news from there?"

"Only what was expected. Arvind Singh will not press charges." He shrugged. "That is his privilege, of course."

His volte-face alarmed her even more. And why was he not

concerned about Das's damning deposition? "In that case, the prime suspect will go free? He will not be charged?" Her heart beat hard in painful hope.

"He will not be charged, no." He bent down to lift a fat, furry caterpillar off a leaf and tossed it aside. "But he will not go free."

"Oh?" Her stomach gave a sickening lurch; she studied his determined face. His mouth was set and he breathed heavily, as if with unusual effort. Uncaring of how odd he might consider her questions, she followed close on his heels as he strode into his study. "So, there *have* been some unexpected new developments, have there?" Oh God, she had to know!

He lifted his coat off the back of a chair and started to thread his long arms through the sleeves. "New, yes. Unexpected? No, I would not say so." He fell silent. For a long, agonising moment Olivia despaired of him telling her more, but then, all at once and abruptly, he did. "Remember that fellow Das whom your aunt cannot abide?"

Her heart stopped. "Yes?"

"Well, I'm told he's missing."

"Missing?" Her tongue, dry and sluggish, could hardly move. "Is that of any . . . significance?"

Carefully, Sir Joshua unfolded his silken cravat, walked towards the mirror hanging over a tallboy and started to arrange the tie meticulously around his neck. "No, except that he isn't missing. He's dead." Cravat draped to his satisfaction, he patted it firmly into place.

Olivia almost stopped breathing. "Dead? How do you know?"

"Instinct. Pure and simple intuition." He turned, smiled vaguely and pinched one of her cheeks. His fingers were like ice; she was faintly startled to note that they also trembled. "You see, my dear, Raventhorne has killed him. I would have been surprised if he hadn't."

This time her breathing did stop. "Why?" she whispered, shocked at his apparent unguardedness, the fluency with which he spoke of matters that he, more than anyone else, must want to keep secret. In her mounting trepidation she suddenly saw that today his mood was also utterly alien. The faint whiffs of alcohol her nostrils picked up were hardly enough to warrant such recklessness.

"You see, Olivia," he said in a tone pleasantly conversational, ignoring her question, "he has killed Das and concealed the body. Slocum will not find it in a thousand years." His stare bored through her like a drill; mesmerized, she could not pull her eyes away. What he insinuated was clear, horribly clear.

"And . . . you can?"

"Oh yes," he said softly, "oh *yes.* I know the native mind down to its last trick, m'dear. And Raventhorne's mind . . . ," he smiled, ". . . I know it as if it were my very own."

Frozen, Olivia asked mechanically, "What will happen then, when you find the body?"

He stood absolutely still for a space, lost to her, blind and deaf to the world. "Then," he said, squaring his shoulders, "Raventhorne will hang." He walked to the door and called out to her as he left, "Tell your aunt I will not be home for dinner." Disconsolate at being abandoned, Estelle's puppy sat and whined at the door he closed behind him. Olivia did not hear it; she remained where she was, impaled with dread. Her uncle knew more than Jai suspected!

Lady Bridget sat in the verandah, still happily immersed in her mail packet. Behind her the gardeners hand-sprinkled water over huge chrysanthemums that looked like floor mops, and sugar candy–pink clouds sailed across the sunset. In the driveway Sir Joshua was dismissing his carriage and asking for his giant bay gelding to be saddled instead, chop, chop! Slipping quietly into the chair opposite her aunt, Olivia stared blindly at nothing.

"Flora Langham writes of her holiday in Brighton, where she says she met this most *gifted* man," Lady Bridget's face was serene with contentment. "Apparently, he plays the piano like a dream—she does too, you know—and he paints wild flowers. I sense a little romance brewing there and oh, I *am* pleased! Flora was quite the nicest, most devoted governess Estelle had, not at *all* like that silly Perkins woman who just would *not* learn to do the ringlets right . . ."

Olivia heard nothing. Her mind was frantic with conjecture, her thoughts chasing each other in endless circles. She must do something, but what? And *how?* It was not yet dark, and the servants would see her if she went over the wall behind the vegetable plot. She had to warn Jai without delay, but her uncle already had a headstart. Oh God, oh *God . . . !*

". . . to the flour mill. Sarah, as wilful as her daughter was to be later," still lost in her nostalgia, Lady Bridget laughed, "refused to give heed to Croakie's warnings—she was our nanny, you know, dear, *dear* Miss Croker. Well, of course Sarah lost her footing and of course she went crashing down into the vat, our

Sarah did, all arms and legs and flapping pigtails!" She laughed again at the cherished memory. "And, my goodness, she did look like a ghost, quite a *hoot!* It took poor Croakie hours, simply *hours,* to scrub it all off. Father roared with laughter but Mother was very cross indeed. She always was a tomboy, you know, your mother. If the stork hadn't blundered, Father always said, Sarah would have been born a boy. Always up to mischief, like the time when . . ."

Olivia had heard the stories before. Normally, she loved listening to anecdotes about her mother's childhood and early life in England, but today, with frustration and fear raging, she could scarcely keep still. Finally, almost cutting her aunt off in mid sentence, she muttered some inane excuse and fled. Upstairs in her room she sat down to compose a message. Her hand shook badly and it took several attempts to make her handwriting legible and the message adequately clear. It was more than likely, of course, that Jai already knew everything, but she could not take that chance. Better to be teased later for needless panic than to court a lifetime of regrets.

For one silver rupee, the stable-boy assured her rapturously when she sought him out at the water trough, that he would not only deliver her note to the boatman of her choice, he would also sell her his soul if she so desired. She gave him another rupee for the boatman, instructed him carefully, made him repeat all her instructions twice and then, with a warning not to dawdle, sent him packing. He grinned cheekily, leapt over the back wall with the nimbleness of a squirrel and, without the *malis* having noticed, sped away into the dusk. Olivia almost collapsed with a relief that could only be meagre, for the note might well arrive too late to be of use. Still horribly agitated, she returned to the verandah.

It was almost dark. Lady Bridget was sitting quite still and in her hand she held a letter. Olivia slipped back into her seat and observed idly that the handwriting on the envelope that lay on the table face up was that of Estelle. Her aunt had been expecting a note from her seeking permission to extend her stay with the Pringles, of which Lady Bridget quite approved. Hunched tiredly in her chair, Olivia leaned her head back against the wall and closed her eyes. It was when she reopened them that she noticed something odd about her aunt's figure, still in exactly the same position. Her hand, up in the air, held onto the letter but she neither moved nor appeared to be reading it. In fact, her eyes seemed to be fixed unblinkingly on some spot on the wall. When, after a moment or two, Olivia could perceive no movement in her aunt, she quickly rose and bent over her.

"Aunt Bridget?" Lightly, she touched her on a shoulder. "Are you feeling all right?"

There was no response. Indeed, Lady Bridget seemed unaware of her touch as well as her presence. The face, mobile and happy only a short while ago, was white and waxen; her cornflower blue eyes remained glassily riveted to the same spot and showed no signs of life. She appeared to be not even breathing! Greatly alarmed, Olivia shook her aunt by the shoulder. "Please say something, Aunt Bridget, look at me! Is something wrong? Are you ill?"

She still received no reply, but, with the shake of her shoulder, the letter fell from her aunt's fingers and fluttered into a flowerbed below the verandah. The hand that had held it remained in mid air, the fingers curved in the same position as before. With a cry of fear Olivia leapt after the paper and retrieved it. It was indeed a message from Estelle but hardly the note her aunt had been expecting. Small, cramped writing filled every available space on both sides of the foolscap sheet. What the main body of the letter had to say Olivia had neither the time nor the need to pursue. The first two sentences said it all.

Jai Raventhorne had sailed on the *Ganga* with the afternoon tide. And her cousin, Estelle Templewood, had sailed with him.

11

There was much to be done.

In a state of unconsciousness Lady Bridget was carried upstairs and put to bed with hot-water bottles. The coachman was dispatched in a carriage to summon Dr. Humphries. Rehman hurried off with a note to Sir Joshua at Barnabus Slocum's headquarters in Lal Bazaar. Olivia had kept the message deliberately unspecific: *Please return immediately. Aunt Bridget has taken ill.* It was a mastery of understatement, considering the truth of the matter, strong enough to fetch Sir Joshua yet adequately obtuse to avoid instant panic. There would be enough of that in due course.

Issuing brisk orders, conducting herself calmly and with competence, Olivia bustled about with the mechanical efficiency of a puppet responding to the deft dictates of a hidden string. Her mind was blank; only one corner of it, inexplicably, was alive and crystal clear, setting her in a dreamscape outside of herself from where she viewed the scene with detachment. It was this corner that warned her of the need for action in many directions. She did not falter in her rapid assessments, nor was it necessary for her to think. In any case, there was no time for thought.

Mercifully.

The first to answer her summons was Dr. Humphries. Bounding up the stairs with an agility that belied his sixty-odd years and was the constant envy of his peers, he huffed into the master bedroom and snapped open the black satchel that was one of the most comforting sights in station. Taking out his pocket-watch he examined Lady Bridget's pulse as her unconsciousness started to lift.

"Nothing much wrong there," he said, opening each eyelid

in turn and peering under it closely. "What appears to have caused her to faint? Some kind of shock?"

Olivia nodded. "She was reading a letter from her cousin in England. It contained news of the death of a very old and dear friend." It was the first of many plausible lies that she was to tell, more than even Olivia could have divined at that particular moment.

"Sentimental rot!" Dr. Humphries snorted. "We've all got to go sometime, but don't worry," he patted her arm heartily, "it isn't your aunt's turn yet, not by a long-shot. Bridget has the constitution of a dray-horse. She'll be back in harness soon enough. Got any laudanum in stock?" Olivia nodded, went to fetch it, then listened attentively to his instructions, which amounted to nothing more than practical common sense. Finally, sipping with appreciation a bowl of chicken broth she offered him in the downstairs parlour, he asked, "And how are you, young lady? As good as new again, I trust? You look well enough I must say."

"I am. Thank you."

"Good, but don't overdo things yet. We don't want a relapse, do we?" He whipped out his pocket-watch again and clucked. "No peace for the wicked. Some perverse woman has decided to have her baby two weeks ahead of schedule, no doubt with the specific intention of ruining my billiards evening." He gave a fog-horn of a laugh and it sounded so out of place that Olivia almost winced. "Josh still at work?"

"Yes, but he should be home shortly. I've sent him a message."

"Well, tell him not to worry unduly about the mem. She'll outlive him yet, especially if he doesn't stop hitting that bottle like a shippie in port, the silly ass." Flying down the last few steps in the portico, he tossed his satchel through the door of the carriage. "And where is my little monkey brat? Titivating herself for the panto, no doubt, like the rest of her empty-headed bunch?"

Few European children who had passed through Calcutta during the past thirty years had not been delivered by Dr. Humphries, and Estelle was a particular favourite. "No, Estelle is not taking part in the pantomime. She is spending the weekend with friends." The ease with which she could answer his inquiry surprised Olivia, as did her instinctive cunning in withholding the Pringles' name. There were not many Europeans with whom Dr. Humphries was not personally acquainted.

After seeing the kindly physician off, Olivia sat down to a hot cup of tea thoughtfully provided by Rehman and considered the immediate future in cold-blooded dispassion. More lies had to be devised to explain her aunt's collapse; those that needed to be forged to account for Estelle's disappearance from station would come later. In between, there would be Sir Joshua's imminent nightmare to be considered. In her own mind there was no hint of a reaction; it appeared that her capacity to feel had ceased to exist.

Sir Joshua's mood, when he returned half an hour later, was partly of alarm but mostly of extreme annoyance. "What the devil is wrong with Bridget? She was perfectly healthy when I left the house. Has Humphries been here?" He could barely contain his impatience.

"Yes. He said to tell you not to worry. It's nothing serious. She's fast asleep at the moment."

"Nothing serious?" He went cold with anger and his voice rose. "In that case, why was I summoned? Are you aware of the business your untimely message interrupted?"

"Yes, but the message was sent before Dr. Humphries arrived." His anger suddenly seemed pathetic to Olivia. It was unlikely he had not heard of the departure of the *Ganga* but obvious that he had no idea of the extra passenger she carried. "In any case, it is not the matter of Aunt Bridget's illness that is serious."

They were standing outside the bedroom door as they talked. In the act of turning to go down the stairs again, Sir Joshua stopped. There was no change in his expression—arrogant, inflexible and incensed—but an eyebrow lifted in impatient inquiry. He showed no sign of presentiment, no inkling of the whirring wings of disaster. Olivia felt a stab of pity. Wordlessly, she handed him the envelope containing Estelle's letter and slipped into her aunt's room.

The hooves of the bay gelding were not heard again on the gravelled drive outside. Sir Joshua Templewood was not to leave his house again that evening. Or for many more evenings to come.

Drawing the curtains against the night, Olivia sent the ayah off for her meal and positioned herself on a stool to resume her vigil. Lady Bridget slept on, protected for the moment by the blessed waters of Lethe, but for how long, how long? A paraffin lamp burned low on the chest of drawers, and around it, bent on apparent self-destruction, fluttered a large fawn-coloured moth with scarlet-tipped wings. Finally, as it deserved to for its foolhardiness, it dropped to the floor, twitched its shredded wings a few times and died. Olivia watched it without compassion.

Jai and Estelle . . .

The night wore on. The majolica clock on the wall ticked away the leaden moments. Sir Joshua did not come up the stairs again. On the bed, snoring slightly, Lady Bridget slept on. The ayah, propped awkwardly against a wall, dozed fitfully. Outside, the noises of the night came and went: the discordant chorus of cicadas, the rustling symphonies of leaves, the intermittent calls of the watchman on duty warning away intruders. The lamp, starved of paraffin, spluttered and fizzled out, but Olivia didn't notice the added dark. Disjointed fragments waltzed across her mind's eye carrying images and imaginings, reveries and revocations that came and went at random. They left behind no impression; it was as if she was watching the passing parades of quite another life. Alien to her, they bounced off her deadened mind like raindrops off an impervious surface. Only the stubborn beats of her heart, even and steady, told her that she was still alive. All else was an unreality of shadows and silences and the smell of impending death.

Jai and *Estelle . . . ?*

Charitable mists of sleep provided occasional oblivion, but when they dissipated they left behind deeper unrealities, greater disorientation. Suspended upside down like a bat, she hovered between dream-worlds that gave her no clue as to where she was, who she was, *why* she was at all. And then, suddenly, night was done. The slits between the curtains became slices of light; the chatter of early birds in the garden revived. Perched on a ledge a crow cawed out his lungs as if delivering a message of vital importance that simply could not wait. Olivia rose, stretched her numb limbs and shooed him off, irritated by his noisy persistence. Mouth agape, one arm flung over the side of the bed, Lady Bridget breathed evenly in her sleep. The ayah, untidily heaped on a rush mat outside on the landing, stirred, then went back to sleep. Olivia did not waken her. Instead, she washed in cuttingly cold water, combed out her hair and wove it into a plait, and went downstairs.

Another dawn, another day. Another age. Everything was different and yet the same. Even the thirst for morning tea.

Sir Joshua was not in his study. Olivia found him in the back garden hunched over on the wall, sitting and hugging his knees against the late autumn cold. She set the tea-tray down beside him, went inside to fetch his woollen cape and draped it about his shoulders. He turned and her breath caught. During the night, strands of his hair had streaked with grey. His eyes looked like pools of stagnant water; they had sunk into his skull, creating black hollows of his sockets. In the unearthly light his skin looked crackling dry, stretched taut and yellowing over angular cheek-bones that Olivia could have sworn were not visible yesterday. What seemed to have gone during the night was the substance of the man, like a snake that sheds its skin, leaving behind an empty husk. Her uncle had aged ten years in as many hours.

She said nothing; there was nothing to say. Even "good morning" would have been a travesty for them both. In silence, divided by their separate thoughts, they sipped hot tea with funereal solemnity. Then Sir Joshua sighed, and a spasm rippled through the frame of what was once a man. He said nothing, but a tear trickled unnoticed down his face. Olivia gathered up the tea things and walked back to the house, leaving him to his grief. They all, each one of them, needed their own private space to lick their wounds in solitude. They could all cry for themselves; who would cry for her?

The household was stirring. In the pantry, Rehman was washing apples preparatory to slicing them for breakfast. The milk, gathered each morning by the resident *gwala* from the two cows tethered in the shed behind the servants' compound, was already on the boil. The second bearer was stacking cutlery and crockery to lay the breakfast table in the back verandah, where the meal was taken in winter. Outside the pantry door, Babulal waited for orders and money to do the daily bazaar. The *jamadar,* the coachman, the gardeners, the day-watchman—all stood in line outside, sombre faced and unspeaking, because everyone knew something bad had happened. The stable-boy was the only one who spoke. Sidling up to Olivia, he followed her into the dining-room with the sotto voce information that the *Ganga* had already left anchorage when he reached the river bank. He waited with some anxiety for her to demand back the rupee she had given him for the boatman. But Olivia had already forgotten about it. Taking the envelope he held out, she tore it into small pieces and tossed them in the waste-paper basket.

"Yes, I know."

One by one she dealt with the servants. Devising a menu for the day she dispatched Babulal to the market, ordered oatmeal porridge and fruit juice for her aunt and uncle and returned upstairs to rouse the ayah. Lady Bridget was starting to toss restlessly. Her forehead felt warm to Olivia's touch, so she moistened a towel, doused it with eau-de-Cologne and pressed it against her aunt's face.

"Estelle . . . ?" Lady Bridget's eyes flew open.

"No, dear. It is I, Olivia."

Lady Bridget gave a little moan. The effect of the sleeping draught was still strong with her and her senses were scattered. Olivia spoon-fed her the two other mixtures Dr. Humphries had prescribed, then went to her own room for a bath and change.

Estelle and *Jai?*

Oh sweet mother of God, there was still so much to be done! She sat down to write an urgent note to Arthur Ransome.

"Mrs. Drummond?"

Polly's mother's yawn as she opened her front door turned into a round-mouthed "oh" of surprise. It was almost nine o'clock but signs of a hasty departure from bed at the ring of the doorbell were obvious. Her Chinese kimono was only partially on, barely covering her undergarments, and her eyes, full of drowse and smudged kohl, were still half shut.

"Why, *Olivia!* What a surprise!" She was flustered and not entirely pleased, her eyes suddenly alert and darting inward towards the room behind. Patting her dishevelled henna-dyed hair that framed her face like a bizarre haystack, she quickly rearranged her kimono and opened the door wide. "Come in, dearie, do. What brings you our way so early this fine sunny morning?"

Olivia followed her into a large, untidy front room with shabby, chintz-covered furniture and the smell of stale cigar smoke. The debris of some past conviviality was strewn everywhere—dirty glasses and plates, overflowing ash-trays and a pair of gentleman's boots, which, with a deft kick, Mrs. Drummond sent sliding behind a settee. Sitting down on the lumpy sofa with bulging springs into which she was waved, Olivia flushed as she heard the sound of a door being shut firmly somewhere behind her.

"I'm sorry to be disturbing you so early in the morning, Mrs. Drummond, but I wonder if I could have a word with Polly. Is she back yet from Chandernagore?"

Mrs. Drummond's wide mouth, smeared with the remnants of very bright lip salve, twitched in a smile as she cast another sidelong glance in the direction from which the sound of the door had come. "Er . . . Polly? No, I'm afraid she's not back yet but due any day." She ran hasty fingers through her mass of hair. "You must forgive the mess, love. I was . . . entertaining last night, you see." Her smile was apologetic. "I haven't had a moment to clean up—not that *I* have to. I do have servants, you know, for what they're worth, which isn't much." In an affected, high-pitched accent she subjected Olivia to a lengthy homily about her woes with her domestic complement before returning to the subject at hand. "What she's still doing in Chandernagore goodness knows, with rehearsals for the panto due to start soon and Hicks yelling bloody murder—but didn't Estelle tell you she's not back yet?"

It was the opening Olivia was waiting for—hoping for, rather. She smiled and leaned back, then quickly shot forward again as a spring bit sharply into her spine. "Actually, no, Mrs. Drummond. You see," she conjured up a small laugh, "Estelle was in such a state of high excitement before she left, as you can well imagine, she didn't have time to tell anyone anything! And I do so want to borrow those new music sheets Polly told me she had sent out from England. With Christmas so—"

"Before she left?" Mrs. Drummond stopped fussing with an array of glasses on the piano lid and frowned. "Left for where? I didn't know Estelle was going anywhere. I thought she was going to be in the panto."

Olivia feigned surprise. "You mean Estelle didn't even tell *you* she was sailing for England yesterday? How terribly remiss of her!"

Slowly Mrs. Drummond folded onto the piano stool, her face a picture of amazement. "Sailing for *England?* Estelle . . . ?" Her black-rimmed eyes widened in disbelief. "Well, bless my soul! No, she never breathed a word to me, not a *word,* and I saw her only the other day buying ribbons in Whiteaways!" She looked very put out. "Fancy that! Fancy going off without even a hint to anyone, *fancy!*" She picked up a palm leaf fan and waved it briskly in front of her face, her untidy eyes not only envious but also suspicious. "But I thought her father absolutely refused to let her go home until after she was married—at least, that's what Estelle has always said."

"Oh, that's quite true, Mrs. Drummond. Uncle Josh has always been adamant about that. As you know, he couldn't bear to be parted with his daughter even to send her to school at home. It was all very sudden, you see. Not so long ago he happened to meet this ship's captain who was voyaging with his sister on board. Aunt Bridget took quite a shine to the sister and, when Estelle pleaded with her mother to let her accompany them since such a worthy chaperone was available, my aunt managed to persuade her husband to relent. It all happened almost overnight, I'm afraid." She added with a pointed smile, "The fact that John Sturges is also in England, as you are aware, no doubt had something to do with Uncle Josh's change of heart."

"I . . . see." Suspicion still lurked in Mrs. Drummond's shrewd little eyes as she appraised Olivia thoroughly. "Which ship did you say she sailed on?"

Olivia was prepared for that, knowing only too well how many seagoing captains, naval officers and personnel from the port Mrs. Drummond counted among her friends. "I'm not very certain, Mrs. Drummond. It was all arranged when I was ill, you see. I had very little to do with Estelle's preparations." That, at least, she thought grimly, was perfectly true! "I think it was a Dutch ship, or maybe Swedish. In any case, I'm almost sure it was European, although it might have been English."

The palm leaf fan again started to wave briskly. "Well, you can knock me over with a feather, ducky, really you can!" At last she seemed reasonably satisfied. "Polly will be green, absolutely *green* when she hears, not that I'm not." She gave a shrill, discontented little laugh. "Of course, I could get up and go anytime I wished, anytime. But then a girl does have to be careful with *whom*, doesn't she?"

Hastily, Olivia got to her feet. It surprised her that her mission had been accomplished with such relative ease. She had established that Estelle had taken neither the Drummond daughter nor the mother into her confidence. Also, with Mrs. Drummond's propensity for spreading gossip, the doctored version of Estelle's departure would soon be open knowledge. There would be talk, naturally, but at least a scandal of monumental dimensions had been averted for the moment. Or so Olivia hoped. There were other investigations to be made, of course, other leaks to be plugged. And many more lies to be told. First and foremost she had to find out just which one of her friends Estelle *had* taken as a conspirator.

The answer, when it came to her, arrived like a thunderbolt. For a moment Olivia stood rooted to the middle of the narrow, crowded lane outside Mrs. Drummond's house. Of course! How could she have missed the obvious? Whatever else Jai Raventhorne might be, he was not a fool. If there was one thing he must have learned about Estelle in a hurry, it was undoubtedly that she was a compulsive blabbermouth. Whatever plot had been concocted, he must have made damn certain that Estelle knew none of the details, and what better place to ensure her silence than the house in Chitpur? The use of the Pringles' name had been wise since they lived too far away for immediate enquiries to be conducted. And, come to think of it, could there be a better reason for getting Sujata out of the way during these vital past few days?

Which meant that while she herself was on the *Ganga* in Jai Raventhorne's bed and arms, committing to him her body, her soul and her life, Estelle was in the Chitpur house awaiting his summons to come on board and take her place in both his arms and his bed!

Within Olivia cold fury stirred, but she strangled it at birth. The luxury of emotion was not yet to be hers; there was still so much, so *much,* left undone! At the Templewood bungalow an answer awaited her from Arthur Ransome—true, loyal friend that he was—promising his presence as soon as he had completed some urgent paperwork at the office, and expressing concern at the sudden "indispositions" of both Sir Joshua and his wife. Knowing that Ransome would read between the lines and realise the urgency of the situation even without knowing it fully, Olivia had refrained from elaborate explanations. But Arthur Ransome was the only one who could, and must, be taken wholly into her confidence. With Estelle's parents both stricken and disabled, she desperately needed an ally or she would go insane. She could not bear the burden alone.

Dear Lord, would she be able to bear it at all?

Just before luncheon, Dr. Humphries called again. After he had once more examined his sleeping patient—unaware of the crumbling world around her—Olivia took him downstairs into the parlour and dutifully repeated the story she had concocted for general consumption. Millie Humphries was as avid a gossip as Mrs. Drummond; between them, the plausible fabrication would have as wide a distribution as possible. The doctor himself, Olivia realised with a sinking heart, would have to be given if not the entire truth then a diluted version of it. As family physician and long-standing friend of the Templewoods, he could probably not be fobbed off with less for long. For the moment, however, the chain of falsehoods already forged would suffice to ensure a brief breathing space.

Dr. Humphries was astounded. "Great balls of fire, so Josh finally relented, did he? Well, I'll be damned!" He accepted the story without question. "I'm glad for your little cousin, my dear. India is no place for skittish young things out to have fun. So, *that's* the reason Bridget has taken to her bed, is it?" He nodded sagely. "She'll miss her, you know. No matter how hot their battles, that girl is the apple of her mother's eye. Well, I hope Josh knows what he's doing. Young Sturges is away on furlough, isn't he? I suppose that has something to do with it. By the way, is Josh in? I didn't see his carriage outside his office this morning when I passed."

"Yes, he is in but he's . . . asleep. In his study." Olivia gave the doctor a look that he interpreted as she had meant him to.

"Again?" He tsk-tsked and frowned. "You tell Josh from me that if he doesn't let up he's going to be in very deep waters pretty soon, although," he paused and picked up his bag, "in a way I don't blame him. He's been under great strain just lately. Mind you, it's nobody's doing but his own, the stubborn fool. He's got that blasted coal on his brain, to say nothing of his obsession with that half-breed scoundrel. Tell him from me it's got to stop, will you?"

Olivia smiled. "Don't worry, Dr. Humphries, I think he knows that already."

It astonished her vaguely that she could still smile, talk normally, plan, devise and improvise. And yet feel nothing.

The answer to her second note that morning arrived soon after the luncheon hour, not that there were any appetites to be satisfied. The tray that had been sent in to Sir Joshua had been removed, untouched, by Rehman an hour later. Olivia fed the heavily drugged Lady Bridget a few spoonfuls of soup but it was a wasted exercise and she soon abandoned it. She herself felt sick at the thought of food and contented herself with yet another cup of strong black coffee. Charlotte Smithers's reply to her note brought further relief. No, she had not borrowed Estelle's box of water-colours, Charlotte wrote. Estelle had obviously made a mistake if she thought she had. And while they were on the subject of borrowings, could Estelle please be reminded to return her silver sandals since she needed them for the panto rehearsals. No, Olivia concluded, Charlotte knew nothing either.

Another hurdle cleared. And another brick placed in position in the edifice of illusion behind which the Templewoods could shelter themselves briefly in peace. Peace? She almost laughed at her strange choice of words; would there ever be peace again in this house for any of them?

"Oh, *Christ . . . !*"

Before Olivia's eyes, Arthur Ransome shrivelled. His colour turned puce and, unable to breathe momentarily, he opened and shut his mouth like a fish out of water. Bubbles of cold sweat speckled his forehead and his expression was horrified. It was only after he had gulped down two pills from a bottle in his pocket that he seemed able to speak again.

"Why didn't you summon me earlier?" With a shaking hand he returned Estelle's letter to her. "I had no idea, no idea at all . . ."

They were in the garden sitting on an iron bench by the embankment wall, away from the house. "I didn't want to alarm you any more than you would be later anyway. I know you had urgent business to attend to, with Uncle Josh incapacitated."

He groaned and covered his face with his hands. "Poor Josh, poor Bridget . . . oh God! How will they ever be able to survive this?"

Olivia's expression remained stony. "Before you see them I think you must know everything I have been doing. That is why I brought you out here so that we could talk in private away from the servants."

With clinical precision, Olivia proceeded to give him a blow-by-blow account of her activities that morning. She presented her account with neither ornamentation nor any comment of her own. Ransome heard her through without interruption, looking increasingly ill as the sordid saga of lies and deception continued and he realised all the ramifications of what had transpired. "We will have to discover which ship sailed for Europe yesterday," she concluded. Yesterday? Was it only twenty-four hours since the world had come to an end? How extraordinary! "I hope there is one or we will have to concoct fresh explanations."

In spite of his daze Ransome nodded, having taken her point with alacrity. "Yes. I will see to that. One of our consignments was billed aboard a Danish schooner. It *was* due to sail yesterday. But is it certain that Estelle wasn't seen by anyone before she sailed?"

"I'm sure she wasn't," Olivia said calmly. "I think Raventhorne must have covered all her tracks well." With what admirable sang-froid she had said his name!

The full horror of their situation finally began to dawn on Ransome. "That Jai, even Jai, could have perpetrated such an evil, such an obscenity . . . !" His features contorted with repugnance.

"He could because he was driven into a corner. Both you and Uncle Josh know it better than anyone else." Olivia was astonished at what she had said—she could still find words in his defence? For a moment she seriously doubted her sanity.

Ransome's shoulders sagged. "Yes. He was driven. He has always been driven. Retaliation, heaven knows, is justified, but not like this, not like *this!*"

"There are no rules in wars of attrition, Mr. Ransome," she said with disdain. "If you do not bar holds, then why should you expect your adversaries to?"

"I don't know," he muttered unhappily. "Perhaps I didn't expect them to. God knows there is enough blood on everyone's hands already."

"Yet some of the guilty will remain unpunished!"

"No," he said forcefully shaking his head. "No! Can you envisage a punishment worse than this for us?"

"Perhaps not," Olivia said evenly. "Nor for the innocent."

He looked even more wretched. "The innocent! Yes, it is foolish, innocent Estelle and her mother who will suffer the most."

She let it pass, too spent and weary for verbal fencing. It was too early for anger. Or, maybe, too late.

"I must go to Josh and Bridget." With painful slowness Ransome rose to his feet. He looked dreadfully ill. "I have no words for their comfort, only meaningless platitudes, but I must make the motions." He paused to take her hand and press it. "It is you who are a pillar of strength to us all, my dear child. May the good Lord bless you for bearing with such sanity a cross not of your own making."

Olivia smiled.

Evening came and went. Arthur Ransome remained closeted in the study with his friend, solacing perhaps only by his presence. Olivia did not join them. Instead, she sat patiently by Lady Bridget's bed, knowing that her aunt's time for awareness was fast approaching. Her consciousness could no longer be kept deadened with sleeping draughts. Reality, however harsh, could not be held at bay for very much longer. Estelle had gone, possibly forever. Her mother and father had to learn to live with that. However deep the submerged grief, it had to be brought to the surface, allowed full play and then controlled so that the healing process could start. The "healing" process! Olivia considered that with amusement; after an amputation, was anyone really whole ever again?

Lady Bridget moaned, softly at first then with gathering strength. Now and then she thrashed her head from side to side, fingers clawing at the air, lips forming and unforming jumbles of sound as her drugged brain groped for reason. Disfigured and puffy, her face looked like that of a stranger. Her condition was pitiable, her immediate future would be even more so, but Olivia watched with impassivity, wanting only for the crisis to come and then go.

And when it did come, she was ready for it. As if with the release of an invisible spring, Lady Bridget suddenly shot into a sitting position and screamed. Gripping her shoulders on either side, Olivia pushed her down again and held her there. "Hush, dear, hush. I'm right here beside you."

With enormous force Lady Bridget flung off the repressive hands and screamed again. "My baby, oh my little baby . . . !" Sobbing hysterically, she sat up again and, rocking herself back and forth, relapsed into incoherent animal-like whimpers, her face between her hands.

Forcing steel into her heart, Olivia retreated to sit down again. It had to come; however cruel, it had to. Nothing could be more brutal than to deny her this, her legitimate grief. Lady Bridget screamed again and there was something maniacal in the sound. Olivia felt her skin erupt in goose pimples and her hair stood on end, but she didn't move from her seat. The door opened suddenly and, wild faced, Ransome and Sir Joshua stood framed in the doorway with a whole tribe of servants behind them.

"Bring her back to me, Josh, bring my baby back . . . have pity, oh have pity . . . !" Lady Bridget held out her arms beseechingly towards her husband, tears pouring out of her demented eyes.

Sir Joshua stood still for a moment, then went and sat down on the bed and took her hands in his. "Bridget . . ." He could say nothing more.

Behind him Ransome shut the bedroom door, then limped to the window and stood silently in front of it. Lady Bridget's pleadings turned into incoherent gibberish as she threw herself back on her pillow and started to pummel it savagely. It was not a pretty sight; Sir Joshua merely sat and stared at her in stupefied silence as if he could not fully understand what was happening. Ransome, unable to bear her agony, made a move towards the bed but Olivia stopped him. "Leave her be, Mr. Ransome. Let her expend whatever must be expended. It is the only way she will accept it later."

Ransome's hands dropped. Features twisted in shared pain, eyes glistening and dim, he nodded and then returned to the window. On the bed Lady Bridget's intolerable convulsions continued, her sobs huge and turning hoarse. Olivia felt her own eyelids smart with the tears she knew she must not shed yet. The effort to hold them back burned her throat, and sharp finger-nails cut deep cracks in the palms of her clenched fists, but her iron control remained intact. Like a man in a dream, Sir Joshua blinked in bafflement, as if uncertain who the woman he faced was. He again groped for her hand. "Bridget . . . ?"

She recoiled as if stung. Hysterical and crazed, she cowered back into the bed-clothes and, without warning, started to scream. "Don't you come near me, do you hear? Don't ever come near me again, Josh! It's you, *you,* I hold accountable; it's *you* who has invited this . . . this *putrescence* on my baby, you and your—"

"Be quiet!" In his lightning return to sanity he straightened and towered above her, vicious and ugly in his own unleashed rage. "There will be no more accusations hurled, Bridget, *not one word more!"*

Next to Olivia, Ransome went rigid, even his breath forgotten. In great, gusty heaves Lady Bridget fought for air, silenced by the whip-lash command but only for a fraction of a second. The venom in her eyes, which never left her husband's face, matched the venom in his. Between them, all at once, there was such abhorrence that Olivia was stunned. With slow, deliberate movements Lady Bridget sat up again. "No, Josh," she hissed, lips pulled back in a snarl, "I will not be quiet! Not now, not anymore." Each word she spoke was spiked with poison, her eyes wild with hate. "You think I can ever forget what I saw in you that day? That look that bore the seed of this evil, this . . . *malignancy?* I *know* why your hand stayed! I saw everything that day, Josh, *everything."* The pupils of her eyes dilated and sparkled. "You cheated me out of my *life,* Josh. Can I ever forgive—"

The sound of the flat of his palm against her cheek was as sharp as a rifle shot. Balanced on the edge of her bed, Lady Bridget fell back with a gasp and the unspoken words rattled and then died in her throat. For a split second no one moved or could move. Then, with a shocked oath, Ransome forgot his affliction and hurled himself at Sir Joshua. "For Christ's sake, man, have you gone clean out of your flaming mind?" He gripped both arms and tried to pinion them to Sir Joshua's sides.

With effortless ease Sir Joshua shook off Ransome's hold. He advanced a step, hand still stretched out, as if to repeat the blow. Insane wrath was creased into every line of his face as he stood and stared at his cringing wife nursing her cheek with a palm. Suddenly his shoulders slumped; his trembling torso stilled and his face crumpled. Visibly he receded into himself, his colour fled and he lowered his eyes. "I'm . . . sorry. Forgive me . . ." Dazed again and once more swaying on his feet, he awkwardly shambled out of the room. Lady Bridget moaned, pressed her face into her pillow and quietly started to weep.

It had been a scene of harrowing rawness, its ugliness never to be forgotten. Olivia felt physically sick. What animals Jai Raventhorne had made of them all! And how flimsy were their veils of pretence!

Gratefully, Olivia accepted Arthur Ransome's offer to stay another night. In his level-headedness, his sense of perspective and proportion, she saw the sane balance that she herself needed so desperately to sustain. Also, his presence was vital for other selfish reasons; how long before her own pretences shredded in their flimsiness? His presence was a barricade between two parts of herself—one thinking and feeling, the other mechanical. Soon, the dividing line between them would start to dissolve; she would begin to feel again, and the prospect filled her with dread. Therefore, like a child dragging its feet on its way to school, she welcomed even a brief span of remission.

After a meagre meal of soup and Welsh rarebit, they sat in the formal drawing-room by a blazing log fire while Rehman, an expert masseur, pressed comfort into Ransome's gout-ridden legs. Lady Bridget had refused even a mouthful and, once more mildly sedated, lay alone in her room flitting in and out of her solitary nightmares. Sir Joshua remained in his study, drinking. But tonight not even his staunchest friend and supporter had the heart to protest. "Let him drown in it as best he can," Ransome said with sad resignation. "He will never need it as much as he does now, poor devil."

For a while they talked only of trivialities as a means of keeping away the yawning silences during which insidious little thoughts pounced. It was after Olivia had sent Rehman off to prepare the bed in the downstairs guest-room that the subject could no longer be ignored. "He is using that misguided child as a means of reprisal," Ransome said in a voice still quivering with shock. "It is an abomination he has perpetrated, Olivia, an abomination!"

"Estelle is no longer a child. She knew what she was doing."

She said it but despised herself for it. Her cousin's pinched, achingly unhappy face swam before her eyes; Estelle had desperately wanted to talk to her. It was she who had turned her away. Estelle had pleaded silently for her help; it was she who had been unwilling to provide it when most needed. Would their fates have been any different had she listened to Estelle? Now she would never know and it was the not knowing that would be the most difficult to live with. If she had persisted with her uncle and persuaded him to let her do that wretched panto, would Estelle have taken a step of such extreme rebellion? If, if, *if!* Angrily, Olivia snapped the serpentine line of her unwanted conjectures—what did if's and but's matter now when he was gone, gone, *gone!*

She got up. "I think I will go to bed now, Uncle Arthur. Perhaps you should too. It has been a . . . strange day."

Drawn together by a shared affliction, they had unconsciously slipped into a less formal mode of mutual address. The "Uncle Arthur" brought a flush of pleasure to his cheeks. "Yes, that it has, that it has. The day has revived too many memories for me, opened too many wounds for me to entertain thoughts of sleep. But by all means go to bed, my dear. I'll sit here for a while."

Olivia's eyes stung with fatigue but the prospect of closing them and letting loose the menagerie of her own fearsome memories was suddenly terrifying. She sat down again. With no awareness of having solicited any inquiry at all, she asked, "What did Aunt Bridget mean by saying, 'I know why your hand stayed'? Stayed against whom?"

Ransome closed his eyes. "It is old history, Olivia, let it lie."

She felt a stab of anger. "If it is old history, then why is it not dead? Why is it allowed to desecrate lives even today?"

He pondered that for a while, then nodded. "Perhaps you are right. Too much has lain hibernating for too long." He placed another log on the fire and waited for it to catch. "There was a time when Josh could have whipped Jai to death, but he stayed his hand. You see, Olivia, Jai was only eight years old then."

Olivia sat very still. "You . . . knew him as a child?"

"Yes. I knew him as a child." There was an odd flatness in the way he said it. "We were all there that day—Josh, his mother, Bridget, myself. Something happened. Josh took out his hunting crop and gave the child a lash, just one. Then his rage lifted and he stopped. He realised what he was doing." Ransome shook his head sadly. "Now I too find myself wishing he had not stayed his hand . . ."

That scar. Against her cold, stiff lips Olivia once more felt the toughened ridges along which she had laid a hundred kisses, wanting to erase them with her love. The slicing pain of the moment returned, but only for an instant; biting her lip until she felt the salt of her blood, she extinguished the emotion. Raven-thorne's warts and weals and scars were no longer any part of her life. That hibernating history, whatever it might have been, must not be revived. But then she heard a voice say, "Tell me how it happened." Was the voice hers? She couldn't tell.

"We would have all perhaps been better off with Jai dead," Ransome said heavily, "but . . ." He fell silent and looked away.

"But?" Wildly she thought, why am I encouraging this, *why?*

"But . . . he was wronged. However soulless, however cursed, however misbegotten, Jai Raventhorne was wronged." He laughed mirthlessly. "But then, Jai Raventhorne has always been wronged. He is one of those creatures of warped destiny who will always be wronged." He stared deeply into the blazing fire. "You see, Olivia, Jai was born in my house."

Whatever it was she had expected to hear, however little she wanted to hear it, it was not that. For a moment she could only stare at Ransome in incredulity. Despite the heat of the fire, her extremities felt cold.

"He was born in the servants' quarters at the back. His mother was a young tribal girl from the hills. One day my bearer found her near my gate on the verge of collapse. She was destitute and hungry and in an advanced state of," he coughed, "impend-ing motherhood. With my permission the servants gave her shel-ter, and the child, an obvious half-caste, was born that very night. I remember it was raining. It was the monsoon season, you see." With fumbling fingers he pulled out a cheroot from his pocket and lit it. "Later, when she recovered, I let her stay on with her child. I don't know why I did that. Perhaps it was to salve my own conscience at what had been perpetrated upon her by one of my own kind. In any case, she worked for her keep in the gardens. She was good with her hands, I remember, good with plants and growing things, with whittling wood, toys and ships' mascots and things. I recall we bought a mascot from her once." Realising he was digressing, he stopped and coughed again. "The servants told me she never revealed her name. They used to call her *malan,* gardener's wife."

Unaware, Olivia's hand crept up to touch the chain around her neck. Jai Raventhorne had uttered his first cry, drawn his first breath, opened those grey eyes to first light—in a servants' quarter? Like the one in which she had seen that emaciated old woman coughing her life away? Had she died after all? She should have returned to help, but she never had. She had forgotten all about her. Was that how Jai's nameless mother had also died?

Steeped in his own bygone world, Ransome noticed neither Olivia's silence nor the whiteness of her face. "I didn't like him, you know. Even as a child there was something . . . menacing about him. He seemed to have some inner, arcane device to look inside one's mind, and it was most disquieting. Indeed, Jai never really was a child. From the day he was born he was like a . . . *man.* It was weird, eerie." He shivered a little as if someone had just walked over his grave. "He never spoke to me, never smiled. He only stared—accusing, resentful, simmering always with some hidden anger. I hated that stare, hated it. It made me uneasy. Finally I forbade his mother to let him near the main house when I was at home."

Olivia roused herself to ask, "And the whipping . . . ?"

"Oh yes, the whipping." Ransome had been speaking rapidly, compulsively, as if relieved to be jettisoning an obstruction in his gullet, but now he quietened down and spoke slowly. "Josh, Lady Templewood and Bridget had come to dinner. There were just the four of us. After the meal Bridget happened to go into the pantry to fetch something or call someone, I forget which, and came face to face with the boy. He was in the act of stealing a plate of food. Bridget was startled. When she rebuked him, he called her a vile name. Bridget slapped him and, like an animal, he went berserk. He leapt at her and dug his teeth into her hand, drawing blood. Bridget screamed. We all ran into the pantry and as Josh did so he grabbed his hunting crop. He saw the blood on his wife's hand and went blind with rage. He lashed at the boy and at the boy's mother, who had run to shield him.

He cut them both badly. There was blood everywhere." Ransome was again agitated, his staring eyes witnessing the entire scene in his mind.

"Of course, the boy fought back like a rabid dog—teeth bared, throat growling, nails scratching. Hearing the commotion the other servants came running, trying to take the boy away. His mother pleaded with her son to stop, sobbing and protecting him from a second blow. Josh had raised his crop again but then, suddenly, his hand remained where it was above his head and his enraged vision seemed to clear. Poised to strike again, he hesitated, uncertain. Bridget stood in a corner crying quietly. Josh's mother, Lady Stella Templewood, leaned against the dresser observing the scene in silence. As Josh stilled his crop, she raised an eyebrow and commanded imperiously, 'Kill him, Josh. A gentleman hunter does not leave wounded prey.' She spoke as she always did, precisely, dispassionately, and with the same decisiveness with which she had fashioned her son's career and moulded his remorseless ambition into a scourge. I'll never forget that moment, Olivia, never. Or her expression. She was the most cold-blooded, self-seeking, determined and dominating woman I have ever known." He inhaled deeply and wiped his damp face with his handkerchief. "It was a moment of madness. I had to stop it. She controlled Josh totally, you know. In his daze he might have obeyed instinctively, as he always did, but I sprang up to restrain him. Was I right to do so?" He grimaced. "Today, I wonder."

He rose to stretch his legs and poured himself a drink from the decanter Rehman had thoughtfully left on a table. He cocked an inquiring eyebrow in Olivia's direction but she shook her head.

"That night mother and son both disappeared." Ransome sat down again and continued. "I had sent for a doctor. Regardless of anything else, the boy and his mother were badly cut; the wounds had to be treated. But they left before the doctor could arrive. The servants formed search-parties and braved the storm, but they could find no trace of them. Later," he shrugged, "nobody bothered very much. I must confess that I was not unrelieved. The boy was trouble right from the start; he stole, told lies, was insolent and ill behaved. I was glad to be finally rid of him. Besides, these people are tough. They are used to living violently. They run the streets in packs, biting and scratching their way through life, licking each other's wounds when the need arises. I had no doubt they would survive." He raised a weak little smile and gulped down the rest of his drink. "It seemed of no great importance at the time one way or another."

Olivia got up to douse the fire, now only smouldering embers. Carefully she put the fire-guard in place, returned the poker to its container and swept up the ashes that had spilled out onto the carpet. Ransome watched her in silence, taking in the unhurried way in which she moved, the competence with which she brought order to the hearth. "Josh and Bridget are fortunate to have you with them in their darkest hour of need, my dear," he remarked, feelingly. "In all this miasma it is only you who remains calm and eminently resourceful."

Olivia laughed. It was the first time she had done so in a seeming eternity. The sound, even though soft, grated on her ears and appeared hideously out of place. She suppressed her laugh to contain her misplaced amusement in a smile. "But then that's understandable, isn't it?" she remarked lightly. "After all, it seems it is only I who have no axes to grind with Mr. Raventhorne, isn't that right?"

"No, it is not!" he protested. "You have had your holiday ruined through no fault of your own. Jai has not been fair to you either."

"Perhaps you are right, Uncle Arthur," Olivia agreed with a shrug. "In which case he has been *most* fair—he has left equal portions of misery for us all."

Finally, she was alone again in her room. Sheer exhaustion made her feel light-headed. She welcomed her crushing fatigue because it promised a sleep that would be dreamless. Sharp little thoughts, evoked by Arthur Ransome's reminiscences, were starting to scratch again for entry into her mind, but she did not let them in. Not yet, she whispered fiercely into her pillow, *not yet!* There was still work to be done, little chinks to be cemented with more fabrications, holes to be plugged, the world to be faced.

And, intent on further self-flagellation, she had to talk to Arthur Ransome again. But that night her sleep was not dreamless.

Even husks of human beings, after all the substance has been removed from within, make demands. They have to be washed and clothed and fed regardless of circumstances. The pursuit of survival is as shameless as it is persistent. Time moves, the earth spins, the sun rises and sets; the home might be a ruin but the household still has to run. And for this small blessing, Olivia was grateful. With Lady Bridget confined to her room and still compressed within her solitary self, unspeaking and uncaring, the duties of maintaining a semblance of domestic normalcy naturally fell on Olivia's shoulders. Like a sinking man chancing upon a piece of drift-wood, she grabbed the opportunity with both hands.

News of Estelle's hasty departure for England and of Lady Bridget's sudden "illness" spread rapidly. Inevitably, a steady stream of daily visitors followed. Early each morning Ransome arrived to whisk Sir Joshua off to his own home, where he would be away from prying eyes, for his condition was still pathetic. Since his presence at home during the day was not expected anyway, no questions were asked about his absence. Lady Bridget, on the other hand, was simply not allowed visitors yet, everyone was told. What alibis Arthur Ransome presented at the office Olivia didn't know, but they seemed to be adequate for the moment. For the moment. Those three words set the tone of the household now, and what was most important for the moment was to avoid a scandal that would surely take Lady Bridget to an early grave even if she survived her daughter's monstrous elopement. The daily visitors with their probing questions, their sly little observations, their expressions of deceptive innocence—all these Olivia managed, if not with ease then certainly without overt unease. Dr. Humphries, however, came under a different category altogether. Arthur Ransome agreed with Olivia that they would have to take him into their partial confidence.

There is very little in life that can shock a family physician, especially one as experienced and canny as Dr. Humphries. After Olivia had completed her recital, he merely harrumphed and remained silent for a while. A bristly red eyebrow rose minimally and he scratched his large sponge of a nose with the tip of a finger-nail. "So that's what it's all been about, is it? Well, I've had my suspicions, I can tell you that. I can't see Bridget in such a state only because of the death of some old biddy of a friend or Estelle's departure on a normal holiday." He frowned thoughtfully. "And you have no idea who the man might be?"

"No, none. Estelle doesn't seem to have confided in anyone, certainly not me. She knew I would have tried to stop her. They obviously planned the elopement with great secrecy to ensure its success."

Not for a moment did the doctor doubt Olivia's sincerity. He merely tsk-tsked in detached disapproval. "Silly, straw-headed lass! She'll regret it, of course. They all do. But often, the leisure to repent comes too late to prevent a bun in the oven—if you'll excuse my frankness—and nine out of ten times without benefit of clergy." He shook his head and pulled in a breath. "How has Josh taken it? I can see what it's done to her poor mother."

"Very badly. He's been drinking steadily. One more thing, Dr. Humphries . . ." She coloured slightly. "As you can see now, there is a desperate need for total discretion on our part. For Aunt Bridget, especially, a scandal must be avoided at all costs. Even the whisper of a rumour at the moment could be added disaster for her."

He smiled a little, catching the point immediately. "My dear, doctors these days might not know much about the practice of medicine," he said drily, "but not one that I know is idiot enough to share such a confidence with his wife. Of course, how long you can keep this kind of thing under covers I'm not sure. In India, if you happen to sneeze in Peshawar, everyone hears it right down to Cape Comorin. But don't worry," his eyes twinkled, "if Millie ever learns about this, it won't be from me."

He refused bluntly to propagate the canard that Lady Bridget had been struck down by some rare, mysterious tropical fever that might be contagious, but agreed to help as far as not denying the rumour if someone else started it. He promised, however, that he would confirm that he had forbidden her visitors for the present. Well, so much for Lady Bridget's enforced withdrawal from the world, Olivia thought, envying her bitterly; Sir Joshua's, on the other hand, was easier to explain. His recent business troubles had taken a heavy toll on his health, and now added to that was his wife's serious condition. That he was also pining secretly for the beloved daughter who had never before left his side was also natural. If he was drinking heavily, well, it was small wonder. In his shoes, any man would.

Her own situation Olivia had no time to consider, or made sure she had no time to consider. As she went through her onerous daily chores—making as much work for herself as she could—she charmed visitors, parried questions and devised new lies and excuses. Always smiling till her jaws felt numb, she observed herself in wonder. She should be sick of being a pillar of strength, of being noble and virtuous and selfless and resourceful, as everyone never tired of telling her. After all, she too had been bereaved; she too had been abandoned, deceived and discarded. Behind her patently cultivated façades too lay a living hell that should be charring her to ashes. She should be sick of pretending to be invisible.

She should be crying. Oh dear God, how very much she needed that!

But no tears came. Within her she was a desert, vast and empty and parched, devoid of any but the most elementary signs of life. Inside she seemed to have almost withered and died. What she should be feeling was grief, anger, bitterness and hate, but all she felt was fatigue. One small blessing kept her away from rank insanity: the steady flow of mail packets from her father, from Sally and her boys, from Greg—from all those who held meaning in a life that was remote but not wholly forgotten. The letters became the pivot of her days, securing her tenuous hold on reality, reassuring her that apart from this world there was another to which she would return one day when all this was over.

Over? No, that was the wrong word; it would never be over. The escape vital to her salvation was not from this world of her doom but from herself, and that would never be. In the meantime, in one of his letters her father wrote, "By the way, you mention that you have not met any young man so far who has impressed you. It is possible that this is no longer so, and I await your response anxiously."

The bitter irony of the inquiry should have made Olivia weep. It didn't. Instead, it left no impression whatsoever.

The laughable charade being played for the benefit of the society that Lady Bridget feared so much could hardly continue indefinitely. But to flee suddenly into some distant oblivion was impossible, for it would merely set wagging those very tongues that Olivia was trying so frantically to still. But ten days after Estelle's elopement, when the travesty of their lives had stretched their nerves to the breaking point, Arthur Ransome decided that the need to escape was now acute.

"To hell with them all," he said in a rare burst of temper. "I will make arrangements to spend a few days in the Barrackpore house. We can leave early next week as soon as I have tied up some loose ends at the office."

Olivia guessed what those "loose ends" might be but she

didn't ask any questions; she no longer cared one way or the other. "Yes. That would be fine. For what it might be worth, we do need to get away."

Physically, Lady Bridget had recovered but her mind still seemed to be a blank. She spoke little and cried not at all, at least not in anyone's presence. Refusing to leave her room, she sat brooding for hours, eating only what was absolutely essential for survival and responding to no stimuli that Olivia could produce by way of conversation. Clearly but gently, Olivia explained to her the cruel facts of their subterfuge and what had been told to Dr. Humphries. Lady Bridget listened with an appearance of intentness, but since she made no comment it was difficult to tell how much she had assimilated. She never mentioned Estelle, and showed no reaction when her name was spoken. Neither did she ever mention her husband. Outwardly she seemed serene but her eyes remained vacant, as if not in the same dimension as the rest of her body. Only her hands moved constantly, nagging at each other in her lap in some nervous frenzy of inner restlessness.

On Dr. Humphries's advice, Sir Joshua's articles of daily use had been removed from the master bedroom into the second downstairs guest-room. "Both he and Bridget need privacy from each other at the moment," Dr. Humphries had said. "In any case Bridget hates the smell of liquor and I don't want my patient asphyxiated with those damned fumes Josh carries around with him like a perambulating distillery."

Of course, Dr. Humphries did not know that since that first night, Sir Joshua had not climbed the stairs even once. When he was at home he remained incarcerated in his study, where only Rehman and Arthur Ransome ventured. Lost on either side of a wordless world of bitterness, Sir Joshua Templewood and Lady Bridget had ceased to acknowledge each other's existence.

The decision to temporarily move to Barrackpore seemed to put Arthur Ransome in a better frame of mind and his expression brightened. "I myself could do with a fishing holiday," he muttered. "And the Barrackpore place is very comfortable although Josh and Bridget hardly use it." Ransome and Olivia were sitting by the cheerful fire sharing idle chatter after the day's work was done. Sipping a mug of hot milk Olivia examined him with compassion; if the past few days had been hard on her, they had not been easy on him either. He looked worn and at the end of his tether. He spoke again. "Slocum is prepared to bury the whole tedious business," he said abruptly. "With the bird having flown, there's not much point in keeping the cage."

They had not touched on the subject for days. The distance it had acquired in Olivia's thoughts obviated the need for caution. "But they have not found Das's body yet, have they?"

The look he gave her was sharp. "He may not be dead."

"Uncle Josh seems certain that he is. For my uncle's sake—yours too, perhaps—I hope he is right. Alive, Kashinath Das could be a further embarrassment to you both, considering that explicit confession." She said it all with admirable lack of inhibition. With no more sides to take, she could afford to be blunt.

He didn't insult her intelligence by denying it. "Yes," he conceded, "he would. Where did you read the document?"

"Uncle Josh has a copy."

He did not question the plausible explanation. "So does Slocum," he said sourly. He cogitated a moment, then nodded. "Yes, Josh is right, Jai has killed Das. In view of his damning testimony, his part in this . . . this tragic misadventure, it is unlikely that he could have escaped." He lowered his eyes, depressed by the admission.

"And the body will now never be found," Olivia commented.

"No. It will never be found. You see, it has sailed with Raventhorne on the *Ganga.*" A small sense of shock stirred in Olivia—that last night in port he had had a *cadaver* aboard? While she was with him? "Josh guessed that, of course, but Slocum could not have. He issued warrants for several other places to be searched."

"And Uncle Josh did not enlighten him?" she asked with a touch of sarcasm, recalling her uncle's odd behaviour that evening. "Surely he would not have missed such a golden chance to see his hated adversary hanged, would he?"

"No, but then you sent for him," Ransome reminded her. "After that it was too late anyway. Even if a steam packet had pursued the *Ganga* down river with a warrant to board her, it would have been futile. Raventhorne would have already been past the estuary and in the open sea."

"On the other hand, Uncle Arthur," Olivia commented acidly, "how fortunate for everyone concerned! Now everything can be safely blamed on Das, if not Raventhorne. Slocum will say that Das, crushed by his sense of guilt, absconded after a clumsy attempt to involve both of you in that confession of his. The confession, therefore worthless, can be burned and forgotten. Even the handful who know the truth will conceal it willingly in the larger interests of the community. What would be the gain in another pointless scandal, anyway? So you see, this way nobody loses out, do they?" It was all exactly as Jai had predicted. At another time, under other circumstances, Olivia might have been incensed. But now she was merely amused.

Ransome flushed. "I wish I could refute your allegations, Olivia, but I cannot," he muttered unhappily. "It was a vile, immoral and ungodly scheme. I did not learn of it until it was too late, but I can by no means abrogate culpability. In Josh's defence I can say nothing except that, like Raventhorne, he despises the very idea of being a loser. The China Coast trade teaches you to fight back when threatened, to neither give nor take quarter. Deaf to common sense, Josh wanted to destroy Raventhorne's friendship with Arvind Singh and Arvind Singh's trust in his friend so that the consortium could neatly step into the breach and triumphantly take over the devastated mine, and Arvind Singh would then jump at the existing offer, eagerly and gratefully. Raventhorne would be persona non grata in Kirtinagar forever—and, of course, also behind bars. In fairness to Josh, that was the extent of his plotting. He certainly never intended that a man should die."

"Not a man," Olivia murmured absently, only half listening, "just a native . . ."

Genuinely distressed, Ransome did not hear her. "Estelle's elopement has destroyed the balance of Josh's mind, but my moral responsibility remains, Olivia. I will go to Kirtinagar before we leave for Barrackpore. If Arvind Singh is generous enough to receive me, I will plead for forgiveness, I will humble myself willingly. And reparation must be made, substantial financial reparation, for all the mindless destruction."

Lost within herself, Olivia did not concentrate on what Ransome was saying; the matter had ceased to exercise her. But mention of Kirtinagar had brought back graphic memories of Kinjal. Clear as a bell, she heard Kinjal's voice in her mind: *I fear for you.* A twinge, a tiny twinge of emotion, nudged her heart—with what face could she ever look at Kinjal again? "If Uncle Josh had obeyed his mother, then none of this would have happened."

Olivia was not aware of having mused aloud until Ransome answered. "No." He grimaced. "I know of no other man so many have wished dead! But then, Jai is like the phoenix. He survives, he endures, he rises again and again from the ashes. And he returns to our lives, as he will return once more, God damn his soul!"

The tiny twinge that had informed Olivia that she was, after all, alive, became more persistent; it would not be ignored. If only as an exercise in futility, she had to know it all.

"When did you see him again?"

She had no need to remind Ransome of the context. It was still alive and vibrant in his mind. "When?" He squinted his eyes in thought. "I'd say about six years or so later. One morning Josh found him standing at his gate. Just like that—Lazarus risen from the dead!"

In a reflex action, Olivia's eyes flew to the window beyond which stretched the driveway to the gate, almost as if he might still be there. Her mind raced with silent calculation; eight and six, fourteen—he must have still been at the tavern. How ironic that those dark areas of his life that she had once yearned so passionately to enter should be suddenly available to her now when she had no further use for them! Somewhere in the arid wastes within her, she felt another throb of life, a tremor—a mere tremor, but oh, so welcome!

"What was he doing at the gate?"

Ransome made a gesture of puzzlement. "Nothing. Just standing and staring. As Josh's carriage passed on its way to work, Jai merely looked at him, hard and long. He didn't say anything. Josh ignored the boy, but then Jai took to coming and standing at the gate every morning with that same unblinking stare as Josh passed. He never spoke, never made any sign, just *stared.* After three or four days of this curious and apparently senseless exercise, Josh began to be rattled. There was in the boy's stare such menace—loathing, Josh called it—that he was very close to again losing his temper. At first, he ignored the boy . . ." Ransome broke off. "You know, even though he lived in my compound for eight years, oddly enough I never cared to find out his name. To me he was always 'the boy' or 'that damned boy.' It was only after he had gone I discovered from the servants that his mother had named him Jai."

"I'm told it means *victory,*" Olivia provided. How appropriate!

"Yes, I believe it does," Ransome nodded. "Anyway, to return to that ruthless morning vigil—Josh was furious about it. He threatened to take his crop again to the boy, but I calmed him and advised him against precipitous action. After all, the boy wasn't doing any harm and he never ventured beyond the gate onto Josh's property. Why not, I suggested, continue to ignore him until he himself tired of his silly little game? For another few days Josh did that. Then, one morning, purely out of impulse, he threw him a fistful of coins as the carriage passed the spot where he stood. The boy did not even look at the money, but instead he leapt onto the step of the carriage and spoke for the first time. In halting English he enunciated his words slowly and with effort as if they had been carefully rehearsed many times over. 'There is nothing you can *give* me, Sir Joshua Templewood. But one day I will *take* from you everything—your money, your business, your reputation and all else you hold dear in your life.' With that he jumped off and scampered away. Josh didn't see him again."

"Until another six years later."

If Ransome was surprised at her information, he gave no evidence of it, too engrossed in ravelling the tangled skeins of his own suppurating guilt. Or, perhaps, her interruption escaped his notice. "Yes. And when he resurfaced this time, it was a very different personality that he had assumed. In fact, the picture he presented was quite startling. Without waiting to be announced, he walked straight into Josh's office—unrecognisable save for two things: that damnable arrogance and those frozen, lifeless silver-fish eyes that still stared devilishly. But now, his eyes no longer spewed childish hatred. Instead, they spilled over with icy cold confidence and an assurance with which he appeared over-endowed. He was totally in control of himself, polished in his manner and faultlessly dressed in an expensive, stylish three-piece suit, high leather boots and silken cravat. He clicked his heels smartly, bowed with a flourish and put an insolent hand on a hip. He spoke only to Josh, and what he said was in perfect, well-modulated English—and a fluent repetition of what he had threatened six years ago. He added, 'I have come to remind you that I am still alive, Sir Joshua, and that as elephants are reputed not to, I too never forget.' He laughed, bowed again and turned and walked out."

In the middle of his account, Ransome had got up and started to pace in halting but measured steps, leaning heavily on his stick. He now went to the window, threw it open—for the room had become close—and swallowed several lungfuls of the sharp wind that gusted in.

"I am not a nervous man, Olivia, and Josh certainly isn't. But that day, I can tell you quite honestly, we were shaken. The sudden, unexpected resurrection, the incredible metamorphosis from worm to butterfly, the fearless mockery, the confident threat—these were bad enough, but what was haunting was the aura the man seemed to carry. There was something inhuman about him, a smell of something . . . *unholy.*" He stopped and gave a modest, apologetic laugh. "You might think me unduly melodramatic, Olivia, but neither Josh nor I is given to flights of fancy and we were truly shaken. That I did not like him, I already knew; that day I also learned to fear him. We later came to know that he now called himself Raventhorne."

Through the open window a fire-fly floated in and twinkled its way across the room. Olivia followed its flight thinking how pretty it looked against the massed shadows. "So then he *has* finally fulfilled that long-pending destiny of his."

Ransome caught her murmur and frowned. "A curious way of putting it! Whatever his cursed destiny might be, he has certainly fulfilled his threat." The corners of his mouth turned down in a gesture of repugnance. "What we must mourn now is the undeserved destiny of that innocent, gullible child."

The plucking aches, the wavelets of resurgent emotion, grew into a flood of resentment. And who will mourn for *my* destiny, Olivia cried within the confines of her mind, I who have also, in my gullibility, lost my all? Who will shed tears over the passing of *my* innocence? But her cries of inner anger remained, as always, unvoiced.

She knew, however, that Arthur Ransome had not been entirely honest with her; he had not yet told her everything.

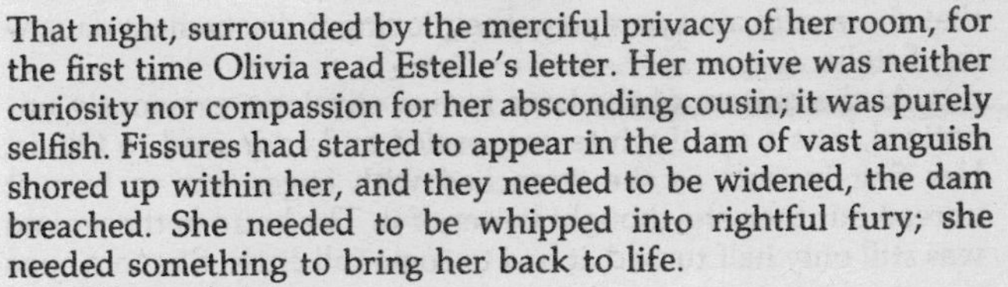

That night, surrounded by the merciful privacy of her room, for the first time Olivia read Estelle's letter. Her motive was neither curiosity nor compassion for her absconding cousin; it was purely selfish. Fissures had started to appear in the dam of vast anguish shored up within her, and they needed to be widened, the dam breached. She needed to be whipped into rightful fury; she needed something to bring her back to life.

She needed to cry.

Olivia read:

> My darling Mama and Papa,
>
> By the time you receive this letter I will be on the *Ganga* sailing towards the Bay of Bengal and America with Jai Raventhorne . . .

Olivia skimmed the following two paragraphs containing vehement protestations of remorse for the pain she was causing and of "understanding" what they must be suffering. She assured them that, when she was not deliriously happy, she too was suffering with them, sharing their grief, but that she found she could not ignore the passionate dictates of her heart no matter how strong her reason. The reasons she gave for having taken what she called "this irreversible step" were the humiliations she had undergone as a "bird in a gilded cage" with no liberties befitting her state of adulthood, and her overpowering love for a man they had hated and maligned with such rampant injustice.

The next page, seething with emotionalism, was in defence of Jai Raventhorne, a scapegoat of society whose fineness, whose innate decency and gentleness, strength of character and endurance they had never taken into account when passing sentence on him. He had shown her nothing but courtesy and, of course, such selfless love as she had never considered possible.

> I am not ashamed of my love for Jai. On the contrary, I am proud, *proud,* of it! I have entrusted my life to him because my faith in him is unshakable. For the first time in my eighteen years I am truly, truly happy.

The letter ended with more pleas for forgiveness and with impassioned exhortations that they too should share in her happiness if they really did love her. She concluded by assuring them that she would always remain their loving if disobedient daughter, Estelle.

At the bottom of the large brown envelope, previously unnoticed, was a small white one, sealed and addressed to Olivia. Her first instinct as she wrenched with anger was to burn it unread but then she thought better of it. The knife in the wound was still only half turned; it had to come full circle. She tore open the envelope and started to read:

> My dear, darling Coz, my only friend—
>
> There are no words with which I can express my gratitude to you. It is you who showed me the way to this wonderful, wonderful fulfilment, to the love of my life, my only love. It was you who triggered my interest in the man you met once so casually—and it was

you who taught me how to see him in a light so different from that in which others saw him. Instead of contempt and hate, you unknowingly showed me how to regard him with compassion—the one feeling he has always been denied by everyone. Once we were not allowed to mention his name in our house; now his name resounds in my heart with its every beat and it fills me with a joy that I can never hope to put into words.

I wanted *so much* to tell you everything, dearest Coz. I felt you were the one person in the whole wide world who would truly understand what I felt. Alas, you fell ill and I couldn't. Perhaps just as well! Knowing your high ideals, your sense of duty, the honesty with which you conduct yourself always—knowing all these I have no doubt you would have tried to dissuade me. Would you have succeeded? Who can tell! Not because I love Jai less but because your logic is so hideously persuasive.

I write this from Chitpur, from one of Jai's quaint and quite amusing homes. In an hour—sixty minutes!—he will send for me. I am to be summoned aboard the *Ganga*—remember that beautiful clipper we admired one day from the Strand? How I would love you to see it, my darling Coz! It is in this graceful machine that we are to explore the seven seas, Jai has told me. Oh, I can scarcely wait! At last, Olivia, the wide, wide world and its secrets are to be mine. No, *ours!*

Whether you believe this or not, the pain I have in my heart for my beloved Mama and Papa is acute, the only cloud in an otherwise clear sky. I know that in your immense wisdom, in the sympathy and love that you have for me, you will solace them and at the same time assuage my own crime by pleading forgiveness for me. You will be to them, I know, a far, far better daughter than I ever was. They will need you—and you will fulfil that need just as you have always fulfilled those of your own father. But in your anger with me, my darling Coz, promise me that you will never, never stop loving your incorrigible brat of a cousin, for my love for you is deep and abiding. I have told Jai so much about you, so much! God willing, one day you too will know him as I do and learn to love him as I have.

And now I must fly. Jai's man waits at the gate with a carriage. The *Ganga* must not miss the tide or Jai will be livid. Adieu, sweet Coz, adieu—but not farewell. For everything you have given me and taught me, I am grateful, forever in your debt. I will try to emulate your fineness always, for it illuminates my life like a beacon guiding me to a destiny that will not be diverted. If not now, as you read this, one day you will consider me worthy of your love, but for the moment I remain your worthless, selfish cousin, Estelle.

There was a postscript:

Did you really believe it was *Clive Smithers* who had bewitched me? Ugh!

And another:

When you clear my room—as Mama will not want to wait to do!—please return Charlotte's silver sandals to her. Also Polly's music sheets, which are in my bureau. I can never forgive Papa for all the nasty things he said, nor Mama for her instigations, but despite their little love for me I have preserved such secrecy that you, especially, would be proud of your chatterbox cousin! I have told no one of my plans, not even Charlotte. Mama will be content that she may have lost a daughter but not her reputation. If there is a scandal, that, at least, will not be of my doing. E.

With the letter in her hand, Olivia sat motionless. Everything within her had come to a standstill. She was in the eye of a cyclone; the world still swirled but inside there was only eerie calm. Then she lay down on her bed and closed her eyes. Behind the darkness of her lids, those visions kept locked in frozen seclusion for so long slunk out one by one to parade in gleeful abandon. Spectres lurking in crevices unknown scuttled out to mock with no further constraints. The cyclone spun like a top; the vortex that had given her brief sanctuary moved on. Suddenly something struck with the force of a sledge-hammer.

She doubled over with pain.

All night long the storm raged. Honed knives scythed her flesh, slashing and shredding till it parted in ribbons. Memories, acid edged, cut into her mind, spreading their poison so impartially that nothing was left uncontaminated. The agony became fierce; to stop herself from giving it voice, Olivia stuffed bedclothes in her mouth but in the knowledge that the agony would cease only when her breath did. Her pain poured out spasm by spasm and yet more remained to be excavated. The more she expunged, the more her body generated. Like an open-ended cataract, her torment was eternal.

She wanted to die.

But death is no easy benefactor to be invoked lightly. In her body, her energies remained tireless, marvellously resourceful in their infinite variety. She was not to be allowed facile escape from the whispered echoes of love, the melancholy beckoning of ashen eyes deceptively tipped with tears, the scoring sensations of caresses given by the man who had known her but whom she had not known at all. Bewilderment, bitterness, futile fury—like grinning ghouls they lingered and waned and then waxed again reminding her of her helplessness. And in the twisted conjurings of an imagination run wild, she saw hallucinations. Estelle delightedly exploring the quaint house that amused her so; Estelle clambering up the rope ladder to receive the hand of love from above; Estelle with her flaxen curls spread across the fat bolsters and pillows of the four-poster bed. And Estelle in that same embrace, incited into a passion that would carry her too into triumphal womanhood . . .

Trust me.

Forgive me.

But yes, I do love you . . .

Lies, lies, lies, all lies! The extent and finality of her betrayal were so gross, so grotesque, that Olivia could not yet assimilate them. *Victim!* Enmeshed in an unending skein of tangles, she could not unravel any conclusions. Which one of them was the victim, she or Estelle? Or both? The longest night of her life brought neither answers nor relief. And when the dawn finally pinked the east, all it provided was the promise of another day in hell, and beyond it another and another.

At last she laid her head on the window-sill and wept. Who for? She could not tell. All she knew from her tears was that her body lived even though nothing else within her ever would again.

12

The Danish Settlement at Serampore was a pretty, whitewashed town, which, from the Templewoods' Barrackpore bungalow on the opposite bank of the Hooghly, appeared even more European than Calcutta. It was from here that the Baptist Mission published their quasi-religious periodical, *The Friend of India,* under the inspired guidance of the celebrated Dr. Marshman, a liberal and widely respected missionary. Barrackpore, which Olivia liked, was on the other hand a military establishment, which accounted for its equally neat and orderly appearance with its cool green forests, its lovely stretches of well-tended park land and its air of quiet efficiency. They had journeyed up the river in a convoy of boats laden with baggage and servants, between banks ablaze with red, white and purple balsam, bright blue convolvulus, white datura bells and myriad creepers that festooned thick fences of aloe. Coconut and date palms, thickets of bamboo, and fernlike grasses stood tall against the clear periwinkle skies washed with winter sunshine.

The five weeks since Estelle's flight had dulled the cutting edges of pain but had brought little other comfort. They each still remained steeped in their separate silences nursing separate wounds with whatever pitifully inadequate therapies they could devise for themselves. The once-compelling merchant prince remained a vacant-eyed husk, his mind closed to reality, a seeming stranger to the body he inhabited without awareness; Lady Bridget had plunged herself into religion, her twitching hands forever clasped around a Bible from which her glazed eyes seemed not to read a word. Olivia courted fatigue as her only salvation, her own despair buried under pretences of frantic activity. Like one's travelling possessions, what is locked inside the heart must also be transported when seeking escape through a change of scenery.

The single decision that sustained Olivia now was that as soon as she could, she would return to her father in Hawaii.

"I wish Bridget and Josh would join us in our evening strolls," Arthur Ransome said one day when they had been in Barrackpore a week. "An occasional outing might help divert their grief."

They were walking around the parade ground watching the energetic manoeuvres of a group of soldiers. To one side of the ground stood high-roofed stalls in which some sturdy elephants were being fed on leaves and branches while the sepoys went through their daily drill with meticulous precision. "People tend to be jealously possessive of their grief," Olivia replied. Estelle's little spaniel, as abandoned as they, whined and tugged at the leash she held, so she bent down and released it. "And like everything else, grief has to be lived through before time heals it, whether one wants to be healed or not. Sooner or later, they will come to terms with their loss." How brittle she sounded, how pedantic! Would she ever come to terms with her loss?

"I daresay they will," Ransome agreed. "But what pains me most is their seeming loss of each other."

What he said was true. Tragedies usually served to draw families together. Estelle's desertion, however, appeared to be forcing the Templewoods apart with a vengeance. Between them now hovered constantly simmering resentments, unspoken accusations, a waste land of dead considerations and an aversion to each other's company. They rarely spoke, each confined to spaces that were mutually exclusive. It was tragic, yes, but for Olivia it was also worrisome for other reasons. In their growing distance from each other, it was to her that they both now turned for emotional strength. *How* could she leave them now when they both needed her so desperately?

It was the last week of December. Christmas Day came and went, barely noticed. A luncheon invitation from the Baptist Mission was declined, as was one from the army commandant. It was left to Babulal to commemorate the occasion with a roasted guinea fowl and some hot mince pies baked with marvellous ingenuity in a makeshift oven. There were no gifts exchanged, no carols sung, no tree adorned, no indications at all of the *burra din,* big day, being celebrated elsewhere by enthusiastic Christian groups. Despite Lady Bridget's newly generated religious fervour, she recoiled at the idea of attending a local service where others would be present. Nobody even thought to make the suggestion to Sir Joshua.

If the prospect of merry-making on Christmas Day was preposterous, New Year's Day was not remembered at all until the following morning. A messenger arrived from Calcutta bearing greetings from Freddie Birkhurst and his mother, reminding them that sometime during their nightmares 1848 had quietly slipped away and a new year arrived. In a separate letter to Olivia, Freddie mourned her absence from station and begged to be allowed to call on her the very instant she returned to town.

Freddie! In the past weeks, Olivia had barely thought of him! But now, of course, she would have to. He would have to be given his answer soon. There was no ambiguity about Olivia's answer, but the prospect of comforting him with pointless platitudes, of listening to his stricken bleatings and perhaps prolonged persuasions, was unbearable. She had intended to request Arthur Ransome to book a passage for her as soon as they returned to Calcutta. Faced with Freddie's ardent letter, she decided to broach the subject to Ransome immediately. To soften her request, she compiled a litany of excuses—her father's asthma was flaring up again, he had written for urgent help with a new book, he had bought land in Hawaii and to toil on it alone would be an intolerable strain . . . Feeding this kind, sincere friend with yet another tissue of lies made Olivia feel soiled and ashamed. But despair had dulled the edges of her conscience, and a fresh storm, more relentless than any other she had known, was about to break over her head. Already the swiftly advancing gusts of panic threatened to blow her away.

"Of course, my dear." Struggling manfully to conceal his disappointment, Ransome accepted her prevarications without question. "It is unforgivably selfish of us to want to keep you here for our own ends when you are so vitally needed elsewhere. Certainly I will do the necessary as soon as we are back in station. You can depend on me." Visibly saddened, he said no more about the matter but turned quickly to another. He started to talk to her about his visit to Kirtinagar.

Olivia had forgotten that he intended to seek an audience with Arvind Singh. In fact, the matter of the ill-fated coal and all the misery it had caused had become anathema to her. If she listened now with concentration it was only because Kinjal had lately been in her thoughts a great deal, even more than usual.

Arvind Singh, Ransome informed her, had received him after all but with an anger that was as obvious as it was, in Ransome's opinion, justified. But at the same time the Maharaja had made it clear that he had no desire to create a continuing scandal. Since the insurance company was being obstreperous and trying to find flaws in their claim, it was up to Templewood and Ransome to make immediate compensation for the repairs of the mine as well as for the bereft family of the unfortunate watchman. Naturally, Ransome said, he had agreed. "There can be no further denial of justice even though our damages will be crippling. We might as well shut up shop," he concluded dismally. "In any case, I have lost the taste for commerce and Josh has lost his mind. By the time everything is paid off, there will be little liquidity left. And I am too old and disheartened to start all over again. After the *Sea Siren* went, I knew we could not rally."

Even in her apathy, Olivia was vaguely surprised. "But surely your funds cannot be that low—what about reserves?"

"Reserves are what we are living on now. Few are willing to trade with us for fear of being blacklisted by Trident. Nobody wants to endanger his investments by risking Raventhorne's wrath when he returns." He smiled. "My dear, if the East can make men monarchs overnight, it can also turn them bankrupt just as fast."

When he returns . . . !

Olivia heard the phrase but it was too grotesque, too unreal, to leave any mark on the surface of her consciousness. Instead she was overcome with renewed anger at the sheer waste of it all. So much heart-break, so much destruction, so many lives laid in ruins. In fulfilling his own misbegotten destiny, Jai Raventhorne had ensured that no strand of their existences should be left unbroken.

It is not your war, Olivia. Don't get caught in the cross-fire.

That night Olivia cried again. She cried quietly, seeing for the first time how neatly and methodically she had devised her own perdition. She had heard warning bells; she had not listened. She had seen signs and omens and portents; she had not recognised them. She had instead hurtled headlong towards a disaster she had not tried to divert but he had. No, neither Jai nor Estelle was her true betrayer. She had betrayed herself. And in doing so she had denied herself even the solace of having someone else to blame. Time—she needed time, or did she? Ironically, what was rumoured to be a healer for everyone else was for her a fraudulent quack, for it would bring her no curative balms, this Olivia now knew with growing certainty. Just as Jai Raventhorne had, time too was preparing to abandon her totally.

Since she had learned the shameless truth, Olivia had avoided her uncle. The compassion she felt for him was minimal and she found it difficult to camouflage her contempt. But whatever her personal feelings, courtesy demanded that she make known to him her decision to leave his home and hospitality. Lady Bridget, she decided, could be informed later, when her frame of mind improved sufficiently to allow her to receive the news with coherence.

Olivia's chance to talk to Sir Joshua came one afternoon when he surprised them all by announcing his decision to go fishing. Since Arthur Ransome's legs were again painful, it was Olivia who offered to accompany her uncle to the fishing grounds on an upper reach of the Hooghly where *bhetki* and *rahu* fish abounded. The path led through a forest of sal, and the region was known for its prolific spotted deer and bison. With his rifle tucked under an arm and his deerstalker snug over his head and ears, Sir Joshua silently navigated the long march ahead of Olivia. Behind them, with the equipment, came Rehman and two other servants. As she walked, enjoying the quiet and the scenery, Olivia formulated in her mind the conversation to come. She would, of course, be blunt; there was no point in shilly-shallying. And no matter what her uncle said, she would not be dissuaded from her decision to leave.

Oddly enough, it was Sir Joshua who provided her with an opening. As he started to assemble his fishing-rod on a low promontory that was their destination, he spoke without looking at her. "I am glad that you decided to accompany me, m'dear. I have been meaning to express my gratitude for everything you have done for us. I have not been unaware of your selfless efforts in that direction."

His speech was slightly slurred and his voice sounded strained, but apart from that he appeared unusually normal. "The misfortune that has befallen us belongs to us all," Olivia responded stiffly. "I deserve no special gratitude."

He shook his head. "Arthur tells me that it is entirely due to your resourcefulness that we have been spared a scandal. Bridget," he paused to swallow, "would not have been able to survive that."

"Would you have?" she asked with an edge of sarcasm.

Carefully, he slid the bait up the hook. "In India one learns to improvise one's own means of survival." He stood up, circled the line about his head and cast expertly in midstream. "I have. Bridget has not."

Puzzled, Olivia was on the point of asking a question but then she stopped. Whatever the import of his mysterious pronouncement, it was now outside her interest. Firmly, she returned to the purpose of her excursion with him but worked her way up to it with tact. "You say you are grateful for what you consider I have done for you. In that case, would you see your way to some repayment?"

He looked surprised but nodded. "If it is within my power, you shall have it."

"It is well within your power. I would consider your gratitude genuine if you would make your peace with Aunt Bridget. That would be more than adequate repayment for me."

Sir Joshua went still. For a while he sat motionless, then his chin slumped to his chest and he shook his head. "What you ask is not within my power," he muttered. "Had you asked for the moon I would have given it more easily."

Olivia regarded him with anger—was there no end to his obduracy? "I don't pretend to understand the complexities that are between you, Uncle Josh, nor would I consider it my position to ask. But surely the time for false pride and petty grievances has passed? It would please Aunt Bridget if you—"

"You are mistaken, Olivia," he cut in harshly. "Nothing will please her anymore. I must now do what I have to do."

That pronouncement Olivia did not even try to understand. Each one of them had to lead his or her own life; it was not for her to rush in where she was not required. Frustrated, she dropped the subject. "I wanted to tell you, Uncle Josh," she said instead in a flat monotone, "that I would now like to return to my father. He has written that he has need of me in Honolulu."

Briefly, his hands trembled around the handle of the rod, but he said nothing. A little ashamed at the brusqueness with which she had made her announcement, Olivia plunged hastily into the fabrications she had already given to Arthur Ransome. He listened in silence, his staring eyes glued to the spot where his still-slack line pierced the water. "Would it be easy," Olivia concluded with some gentleness, "to book passage on a boat sailing to the Pacific?"

He looked vague again. "The Pacific? I should imagine so. Arthur would be able to answer that better." He frowned, then said suddenly, "She has not said so but Bridget wants to return to England. I can sense it. Could I impose on you one more time to ask you to wait and accompany her to England? I would arrange for you to proceed home from there, although the route would be circuitous." His expression was anxious, the half smile apologetic. Olivia's colour drained, and inadvertently her expression became one of horror. To wait? Why, that was impossible! Observing her reaction, Sir Joshua's shoulders drooped. "Yes, I know it is an imposition," he muttered. "You have already given us so much of yourself. I should not have asked."

Inwardly, Olivia dissolved with sudden shame. They did still need her—how could she turn her back on them now like the daughter they once had? But she had to, she must! How ironic that had her uncle also asked for the moon she could have given that more easily! Panic trickled through her veins in icy little dribbles. Which way was she to turn? The storm she had sensed brewing was now a reality—a grim, living reality.

In her womb she was carrying Jai Raventhorne's child.

The mail packets that awaited Olivia from Hawaii on their return to Calcutta were gratifyingly bulky. Apart from letters, they also contained generous gifts for everyone to mark the Christmas season. Impatient for news of home, Olivia quickly disbursed the presents, then withdrew to her room to read the letters. Astonishingly, together with her father's, there were also letters from Sally and her boys. They too were in Hawaii . . . ?

Skimming over the main body of her father's letter, Olivia reached the concluding page knowing instinctively that this was where the crux of his news would be. *I know it will not surprise you,* he wrote finally in his firm, unhurried handwriting so reminiscent of the man himself,

> that Sally and I have finally decided to marry. I am sure you have long suspected that one day we might, and our mutual decision has been made in the secure knowledge that you will approve and be happy for us. The boys, bless their cotton socks, are delighted. I have been as much a father to them since Scot died as Sally has been a mother to you. You must know, my darling daughter, that your mother's place in my heart

> is secure and always will be so. Nobody can ever take that away from me. But you know, my sweet, there comes a time in a man's life when the sight of a cold stove, a darkened house and one pillow on the bed starts to hurt like a knife wound. The heart yearns for joys shared, for . . .

Olivia's eyes brimmed and her heart filled with happiness. Yes, she had known that one day Sally and her father would marry, and she could not envisage a more perfect arrangement for any of them. She loved Sally dearly, and Dane and Dirk were already as brothers to her. Brushing aside her tears, she read on.

> . . . sorrows divided and the warmth of mundane companionship. I don't want you to feel, as you do now, that your own life must stop so that you can take care of your lonely, aging Dad. I want you too to marry, to set up a home, to have children, to travel and grow and develop in your own way at your own pace. It is what I have always wanted for you, to be independent, to be your own person, to fear nothing, to experiment boldly and always to be true to yourself. Perhaps you have already met a man you consider worthy of your love, that man you wrote you had met and whom you wanted to meet again, for instance . . .

She could not go on. Crushing the pain that shafted through her, Olivia gritted her teeth and thought only of her father and Sally and of the quiet contentment that reached out to her between the lines. They would be a family again. Perhaps there would be a farm in some idyllic Hawaiian valley, maybe a whitewashed farm-house full of the fragrances of freshly baked bread and cinnamon-smothered doughnuts and the ocean right outside the window. There would be chickens and pigs, a horse or two, a swing in the garden, a sugar white beach for the children to play on . . .

For the first time in weeks, Olivia felt her pall of endless gloom lift. Suddenly, life didn't seem totally hopeless after all.

More than ever now she longed to be up and away, and in her bounding exhilaration she found the courage to break the news of her intended departure to her aunt. Since their return to Calcutta, Lady Bridget had improved perceptibly. There was again colour in her cheeks, firmness in her step. Only this morning she had caught Babulal with two cucumbers concealed under his turban and had been animated enough to scold him severely. This portent alone, Olivia decided, was enough to indicate that the worst was over for Lady Bridget.

Sitting in the garden with her ever-present Bible resting in her lap, Lady Bridget heard Olivia out with surprising calm. When the announcement had been delivered and the explanations were over, Olivia hugged her aunt. "You have been so good to me, Aunt Bridget," she whispered with a catch in her voice, "and I have been happy with you, truly I have, but now I must return to my father."

"Yes, I know, my dear, I know." Absently, her aunt kissed her on the cheek.

"And you will soon be leaving for London," Olivia hurtled on so as not to lose her advantage. "Perhaps Uncle Josh can be persuaded to go with you. You have always wanted that, haven't you? You could be in Norfolk for the spring and the daffodils, with the Broads again alive with Sunday picnickers." Emboldened by her aunt's look of frowning concentration, Olivia ventured further. "You and Uncle Josh have only each other now; both of you have suffered equally. Can you not bring yourself to forgive him?"

She shook her head vigorously. "It is for the good Lord to decide that. The vengeance is only his."

Vengeance? Olivia suppressed a stab of irritation. "What is done cannot be undone now, Aunt Bridget; it can only be accepted. You will have to someday accept Estelle's elopement, however obnoxious you might find it." Her tone hardened. "And someday, maybe, Estelle will return to you—"

"Return?" Lady Bridget half rose to her feet. "Do you think I could ever accept her back after this? *After this . . . ?"*

Her vehemence, the ugly distortion of her features, her whole demeanour, startled Olivia. Even now, when they were tasting the dregs of a common despair, when so much had already been lost and so little was left, her aunt could still pronounce moral judgements? "Everyone deserves forgiveness for one mistake in life," she persisted earnestly. "Surely you must now find it in your heart to forgive Estelle too." The gallantry with which she was defending someone who had helped to destroy her own life brought a sour smile to Olivia's lips. How open ended was her pious selflessness!

Lady Bridget retrieved her fallen Bible and rose to her feet. "You are a noble girl, Olivia, but you have understood nothing, *nothing.*" Tucking the Good Book under her arm she walked away, her expression one of utter contempt.

Olivia started to pack.

In her own desperate need to be gone, she closed her mind to all other thoughts and considerations. Yes, she felt deeply for her aunt and uncle, but each of them had come into this world with a separately predestined burden of woes graphed individually on a chart of fate. She could not now afford to consider any burden save her own, the burden that she carried within the confines of her body. She hardened herself against even those thoughts of Jai Raventhorne that arrived uninvited in various unexplored recesses of her mind. He was gone. She would never see him again, nor did she especially want to. That fragment of her life he had taken with him would not be missed much longer; she would make it dispensable. For the moment all she wanted was to flee, to escape to where her home truly was, and to cast herself and her sorry load into the arms of her beloved Sally. Her situation frightened Olivia—oh God, how terribly it frightened her!

An Australian ship that had recently arrived in port for repairs was moving on soon to the Pacific and would most certainly call at Honolulu. Arthur Ransome had spoken to the captain, who had agreed to take on a single lady passenger from Calcutta provided she could be ready to sail at short notice. Delirious, Olivia plunged into a flurry of preparations with renewed vigour for more than one reason; Freddie Birkhurst was deluging her with frantic letters beseeching her to see him. Olivia knew that she would have to, of course, but not until the very last moment when nothing, nothing, could go wrong with her plans.

To provide salve for a badly scarred conscience, Olivia convinced herself that the Templewood household and its inmates were now securely on the path to normalcy, or at least an acceptable form of it. Sir Joshua was still a shockingly diminished man with prolonged spells of vagueness, but Ransome had persuaded him to attend the office for short periods each day and the enforced mental exercise appeared to be therapeutic. Lady Bridget had started supervising the gardeners again and her daily arguments with the cook were heartening. All in all, she seemed to have accepted Olivia's imminent departure without excessive reaction. At least, since that day in the garden when the initial announcement was made, she had not referred to the subject.

Among the letters Olivia wrote prior to the sailing date was one to Kinjal. It was not an easy letter to write. Kinjal must know, of course, that Raventhorne had sailed away. Whether she also knew of the extra passenger he carried was impossible to ascertain, but as a point of honour Olivia felt that Kinjal must be told everything. In the end she wrote asking only if she could come and spend a day or two in Kirtinagar before her ship sailed. Kinjal's response was immediate. She was heart-broken, she answered, that her dear American friend was to desert them all so soon, but with her usual discretion she neither commented on nor questioned Olivia's decision. A carriage would arrive from Kirtinagar to fetch Olivia on the following Saturday, which, the Maharani hoped, would be convenient.

As it happened, it was not only convenient, it was desperately necessary. On Wednesday, a week prior to Olivia's sailing date, Lady Bridget locked herself inside her bath-room and tried to kill herself.

"What the hell have you been thinking about, Josh? Can't you see, man, she has to be taken away from this infernal country?"

Exhausted, sweating profusely and livid with anger, Dr. Humphries sat slumped in a chair downing a stiff whisky. Nobody could think of voicing an answer as they all sat white faced and shaken in the Templewood parlour. Hands clasped tightly in his lap, Sir Joshua stared stolidly at the carpet.

"You can't keep her here anymore, Josh." Anger removed, the doctor's tone was now emphatic. "That was as close a shave as any I've seen. It was only because her hands shook badly that she couldn't entirely sever the blood vessel, and if Olivia hadn't chanced to hear the crash of Bridget's fall in the bath-room it might have been a very different tale indeed. As it is she's lost a dangerous quantity of blood."

Sir Joshua still said nothing but Ransome shook himself out

of his stunned torpor. "Yes, of course Bridget must go home and Josh must be the man to take her. I've been telling Josh that for weeks."

Dr. Humphries rose, walked to where Sir Joshua sat and put a hand on his shoulder. "She'll try again, you know," he said bluntly. "They always do."

He went but left behind a chill, sinister silence that no one had the courage to break. Standing by the window staring out blindly, Olivia remained numb. What if she had not heard that crash? What if nobody had? What if her aunt did try again? The ayah, taking her afternoon siesta on the landing, had remained dead to the world. A dozen more maidservants would be a dozen times more useless. Lady Bridget, now more than ever, needed constant attendance. Would the hired nurse Dr. Humphries had promised be adequately vigilant? Within herself Olivia screamed with anguished protest: *It's not my responsibility, it's not my problem! God knows I have my own . . .*

Nobody heard her screams. Like all her others, these too were destined to remain buried in silence.

"If Bridget wishes to return to England," Sir Joshua finally offered a comment, "I have never indicated any objections."

"But you can't stay here on your own, man! You couldn't manage a *day* without Bridget." Ransome sounded utterly fed up with him.

Sir Joshua pierced him with a look. "I *intend* to stay on! I am perfectly capable of managing my own affairs. Besides," his voice fell into a mumble, "I have things to do here; Bridget knows that."

"Don't talk rot, Josh! There is nothing you have to do here, absolutely nothing." Ransome's rebuke was unduly sharp. "You know I can deal with whatever is left of the business." Without replying, Sir Joshua got up clumsily and shuffled out of the room. Ransome tossed up his arms in despair. "What is one to do? What *is* one to do? He won't listen to anyone, the stubborn fool!" Then he brushed the subject aside and attempted a smile. "And you, my dear? Are you all packed and ready for next Wednesday?"

"Yes." Olivia did not turn to face him.

"Is there any way in which I can be of service?"

"Thank you, no. You have already been most kind."

"I am arranging dry provisions and some comfortable furniture for your voyage. The conveniences on board are, I regret, woefully inadequate, as you know."

Again Olivia murmured her thanks, fighting off surging tides of claustrophobia. Slowly, she was being lowered alive into a coffin. One by one the nails were being hammered in. It was dark and dank and she could scarcely breathe. From all around forces were converging and conniving to trap her within that coffin and then leave her to suffocate. "What will happen to them when I'm gone?"

Ransome shrugged. "I will be as persuasive as I can with Josh, and hope for the best. The nurse, Humphries assures me, is sane, responsible and alert, so we must keep our faith in that. And in God. But if Bridget does stupidly try to harm herself again . . ." He trailed into silence, unwilling to complete the sentence.

Olivia allowed the silence to expand before she could bring herself to ask dully, "After this Australian ship sails, when might be the next departure for the Pacific?"

He could not conceal the spark of hope that leapt into his eyes. "There are many sailings from here to San Francisco via Honolulu. I could try for something suitable in, say, a month or two."

A spasm rippled through Olivia's body. A month or two! No, that was utterly out of the question! Already the flatness of her stomach was being rounded into a telltale mound. Come what may she *had* to leave next Wednesday. She made no further offers; an unkept promise was more cruel than no promise at all. Quietly, she slunk out of the room.

With her poor, damaged wrists heavily medicated and bandaged, the colour of her skin deathly pale, Lady Bridget lay unmoving on her bed. Her eyes were open but they were unseeing. Next to the bed sat Mary Ling, the half Chinese nurse Dr. Humphries had summoned and briefed without delay. She was a bright young thing no more than twenty-four or -five but, according to the physician, highly competent. And, he further assured them grimly, the girl knew how to keep her mouth shut. Dismissing the nurse from the room for the moment, Olivia sat down on her aunt's bed. "How do you feel, Aunt Bridget? Is there anything you would like me to fetch you?"

Lady Bridget gave no response, her sightless eyes fixed to the ceiling. But then she moaned and tears started to trickle down the side of her cheeks. "I have failed you; I have failed Sarah. I am sending you back as denuded as you came . . ."

The voice was whispered, an effort, but the words were clear enough. Olivia trembled with renewed shock. "You have not failed either of us," she whispered back passionately. "And you are not *sending* me back. I return of my own free will because I must, Aunt Bridget, I *must* . . ."

"But then how will I ever atone?" She became agitated. "A promise to the dead is sacred and I have achieved nothing, *nothing!* Sarah will never forgive me. I have a duty to her." Her voice had risen, the words tumbling out in a frantic rush.

"You have duties to the living, Aunt Bridget, not the dead!" Olivia held her down gently as she tried to sit up. "To Estelle, when she returns, and to Uncle Josh. They—"

"Estelle is dead too." Her throat rattled with an unpleasant sound. "As for Josh, it is too late for him. It is too late for everything."

"That is not true!" Olivia cried, struggling between impatience and panic. "When you are both in England you can—"

"I will never see England again. I can face nobody." The voice dropped and she started to sob quietly again. "My life is both finished and unfinished. There is nothing left."

She was being blackmailed! Olivia knew she was being held ransom for someone else's guilt, someone else's omissions and commissions! Well, she would not stand for it. How dare her aunt force her into corners, impose her will on her, cut off her sole avenue of escape? "Your life is neither finished nor unfinished," she grated harshly, almost shaking her aunt with the violence of her resentment. "You have no cause to seek forgiveness for imagined offences of yester-years, but if it is forgiveness you want, then as my mother's proxy I forgive you a hundred times, a thousand if you wish."

Lady Bridget fell silent. For a while she said nothing, but then she spoke again, quietly and calmly. "Very well, Olivia. I accept your forgiveness on your mother's behalf. But no one can force me to live if I don't wish to."

The final nail was hammered into the coffin. Fate had defeated Olivia after all. The diabolic melodrama that had begun that long-ago night on those steps by the river was approaching its climax and she, for her sins, was its leading performer. The time for indecisions was over.

Therefore, when Olivia stepped into the splendid Kirtinagar coach on Saturday, it was with a resolve that was as cold-blooded as it was inevitable.

"Are you certain this is what you really wish, Olivia?"

If Kinjal felt any sense of shock at what had been asked of

her, she did not show it. Indeed, the cool eyes appraising Olivia showed only concern.

In the warm welcome that had greeted her in Kirtinagar, Olivia had found no recriminations, no complacency, no unspoken moral judgements. There had been no need even for words as Olivia had flung herself into Kinjal's arms and burst into a storm of tears against the comforting shoulder. "I should have paid more heed to your warnings," Olivia had sobbed brokenly. "I am sick, Kinjal, more sick than you can suspect. Unfortunately, my sickness is not one that guarantees death."

"My goodness, how defeated you sound!" Kinjal had exclaimed in an effort to conceal her anxiety under a spark of humour. "What has happened to all that fiery American spirit?"

"No longer fiery but crushed." The wan smile Olivia allowed herself had soon dropped. "I need your strength, Kinjal. It is only to you that I can reveal my weakness, for I have nowhere else to turn. And I am tired, so *tired* of being silent and noble and a pillar of courage and forever resourceful. I too want time to mourn, to indulge my sorrow, to consider my loss, to wallow in self-pity if need be, to return myself to myself . . ."

They had sat on the terrace of the Maharani's palace from which the view was magnificent. Under a lather of roseate clouds the sun was slipping into the lake; the scents of the evening were intoxicating. For Olivia, the return to Kirtinagar was wounding—but then no more so than anything else in her life, she reminded herself bitterly. Her need to talk was all-consuming.

"My husband has taken the children for a picnic," Kinjal had said. "They plan to camp near the mine where the debris is being cleared and to hunt for deer in the forest. We will not be disturbed for a day or two. You can talk to your heart's content."

The source of Olivia's anguish was, of course, already known to Kinjal. Only the details needed to be filled in. And oh, what bliss it had been for Olivia to at last shed pride and pretences and to deliver the truth, the whole truth. In her account she had omitted nothing, revealed everything, castigating herself with an honesty that was almost masochistic. Kinjal had listened with patience and with tacit understanding, her reactions devoid of anything but compassion. It was only when Olivia had concluded and blurted out her eventual request that the Maharani started to ask questions.

"Have you thought about it carefully, my dear friend? Kinjal repeated. "Is this truly what you want?" For the first time the serene eyes turned reproachful.

Olivia's mouth set. "Yes. I need help to forget Jai Raventhorne," she said stonily. "The memories in my mind are hidden and with time they will fade. What can no longer be concealed in my body needs to be excised and discarded."

The sloe eyes, shrewd and reflective, surveyed Olivia carefully. "And you assure me that you have thought about it well?"

"I have thought of little else these past few days."

"Then you have decided not to return to your father for the time being?"

"It appears to have been decided for me," Olivia said bitterly. "If my aunt destroys herself, no matter how insane her reasons, how will I ever be able to live with myself again clear of conscience? And I do love her, Kinjal. She is my own flesh and blood. To abandon her now might be to sign her death warrant." With a sob, she covered her face with her hands. "Oh, it is all so unfair, all so cruel and iniquitous! If I stay on as I am, she will die, not by her own hand but by the scandal of this noxious tumour in my womb. If I go, then she will try again what she tried on Wednesday and, perhaps, with greater success. What am I to do? What options do I have?"

Kinjal took her hands and pulled them gently away from her face. "I can listen to you, Olivia, talk to you, share in your sorrow and perhaps even lighten it momentarily. What I cannot do is make your decisions. Those must be yours and yours alone."

Olivia's face again set. "I have already decided. Whatever my other options, I will not nurture Jai Raventhorne's child in my womb."

"You would knowingly destroy something that one day will have a life of its own?"

"Yes."

"You would cast aside the consideration that this is a child conceived in what was once love?"

"Not love, self-delusion! Love is not a word Jai Raventhorne includes in his vocabulary, as you yourself impressed upon me not so long ago."

"But *you* include it in yours, Olivia. Can you forget that?"

"Yes. But to forget it I must first exorcise him entirely from both body and mind." Her voice broke. "I am shackled, Kinjal, within and without, physically and mentally. At least this one shackle I can shake off to make my burden more tolerable."

Kinjal's gaze remained stern and unwavering. "You have never been a mother, Olivia. You have never brought into this world a handful of flesh that is of your own. Once gone, that handful will never be again—you have considered the irreversible finality of your decision?"

"That handful will be flesh from two bodies, not one. To rid myself of its other component I willingly make the sacrifice, if indeed it is one!"

"One final question, then." A crease in the Maharani's forehead neatly divided into two the vermilion spot she always wore. "Is it fear of public censure that also motivates you? The shame that society can heap on unwed mothers and their children?"

For the first time Olivia pondered. "The answer to that question," she then said, "would vary with the geography of my situation. In America, I would not give a damn about public opinion and neither would my father or Sally. But here," her expression filled with slow horror, "here in India, I would rather kill the child than subject it to the unholy mercies of Calcutta's social vultures ready to pick at any carrion that will provide a tidbit of gossip. And they will pick clean whatever remains on the bones of my poor, miserable aunt and uncle should I have my baby here. For myself I can perhaps fight back, bite as hard as these harpies can, but would it be worth it?" She swallowed her anger and balled her fists. "No, no, *no!* As Jai once said to me in another context, the game is not worth the candle. And in any case I have no great desire to bring to life the bastard of a *bastard.*"

There was nothing left to be said.

After a moment of silence, Kinjal smiled. "You are a brave woman, Olivia. Perhaps you are right. Perhaps the past can be forgotten only if excised. It is the future we must think of now. To wipe a dirty slate clean and start afresh might be a sensible new beginning."

She rose, beckoned a maidservant and proceeded to dispense rapid instructions.

The old woman was like a crow, hunchbacked with age, and with long, hooked fingers that felt like talons. As she poked and pried under the bed-clothes, Olivia watched with nervous fascination the single large tooth that was contained in the floppy, cackling mouth. Around them, maidservants hurried about on velvet feet carrying brass vessels of hot water, banana leaves, bundles of twigs and other leaves, hairlike roots with bulbous endings, bottles of coloured liquid, and crude, hideous implements. A live rooster, his scarlet cocks-comb looking as though it bristled with indignation, was securely trussed inside a basket. Near it rested an ominous-looking knife with a curved blade. In a corner of the chamber a paraffin stove bubbled like a witches' cauldron with a viscous concoction the colour of ebony. In the general gloam, even Kinjal appeared to have taken on an unfamiliar, sinister appearance.

"What is to be done now?" Olivia asked, running a dry tongue over her parched lips.

"Whatever is required to fulfil your wishes," Kinjal replied, her tone sombre. "The old woman is knowledgeable and experienced. She says yours is an easy case. She guarantees success. Can you give her the approximate time of conception?"

Approximate? Olivia almost laughed as, through a knot of sourness in her throat, she voiced the time exactly down to the last minute. And as she did so, the languid, lazy arabesques of their love-making leapt into the forefront of her mind, her memory relentless in its clarity. In searing detail the images of those once-precious moments started to dance before her eyes, every nuance vivid. It was not Jai who had wanted to implant that devil's seed she was now cursing, it was *she.* It was to pleasure her, to indulge her erotic whims, to sharpen her own sensual gratification that he had let his essence flow into her unimpeded. She had, she knew, conceived his child at that precise moment because, passionately and unequivocally, that was what she had wanted.

Give me a part of yourself . . . !

In sudden despair, Olivia clung to Kinjal's hand. "Stay with me, stay with me please—I cannot bear it alone."

Cool fingers soothed her drenched forehead. "Yes, I will stay with you. The woman asks if she should begin." Despite the physical contact, Kinjal seemed detached and far away.

The despair receded; Olivia ossified again. "Yes. She can begin."

Against a hum of incantations and chanting, Olivia sat up to drink a dark-coloured potion offered to her in a silver glass. Its effect was instant. A heavy lethargy pervaded her limbs and body as she sank back against the pillow and shut her eyes. She seemed to be floating away from herself to stand apart and watch the old woman sway from side to side, her hooked fingers flying over packets and bottles to mix and match and pick and reject with an expertise handed down through the centuries. Drowsily, Olivia blanked out of her mind the ugly present. She thought instead of beautiful dawns, of strutting peacocks resplendent in their brilliant mantles, of roses and horses and cottonwood trees and butterflies in the paddock flitting over carpets of green grass. A hot, sweet fragrance wafted about her nose and filled her head. The chanting became louder, the rooster flapped angrily somewhere in the distance, and then silence, followed by Kinjal's quiet command as something was pressed to Olivia's lips.

"Drink this."

In a twilight sleep, Olivia drank. The liquid was warm and quick-flowing and red. Like blood. But before she could retch, she was asleep. The final words she heard were Kinjal's. "There. It is finished and done with. By morning it will be as if it has never been . . ."

Finished and done with.

In her sleep, dreams and fantasies crawled through Olivia's mind like rain insects, nimble legged and fluttering. Unaware and uncommanded, her hand groped for and found the locket she wore around her neck. Tactile memory brought with it a succession of others: satin finger-tips on her cheeks, a silken mouth moistening her breast, fragile kisses across her lips. Pools of smoky grey doused her with their pain, and in her ear a mist, a shadow of a voice murmured, *but yes, I do love you . . .*

She slept on and on. When she woke again it was to find that her cheeks were bathed with damp. Trapped between her chin and an arm, the locket felt as cold as ice, its chain cutting into her flesh like an accusation. Her eyes flew open to see Kinjal's face, bathed in sunlight, staring down at her with a smile of satisfaction.

"There! By tonight your unwanted appendage will wash away in a flow of your normal menstrual cycle. You will be forever rid of that noxious tumour that threatens your sanity. Aren't you relieved?"

Unable to speak, Olivia turned her head to the wall and shut her eyes tight. What had she done? Dear God, *what had she done . . . ?* Wilfully she had destroyed the only part of himself Jai had ever given her! Flesh of his flesh, blood of his blood—whatever little love he had had for her, even that was gone. Sick at heart, Olivia clasped the locket tightly within a palm, kissed it and started to weep softly.

Bending over her, Kinjal peered closely into her face. "Tears?" she exclaimed in some surprise. "Only of relief, I hope?" When Olivia did not reply but only drew up her legs beneath her chin and buried her face in her sheet, Kinjal pinched her cheeks between her fingers and forced Olivia to look at her. "I suspect that you are unhappy, my dear—can it be that you regret yesterday's decision? Come on, Olivia, tell me truly, do you?"

"What does it matter now?" Olivia turned her face away again. "It's finished, isn't it? Done with."

"But isn't that what you wanted?" The voice, usually so soft, so gentle, was harsh. "You are crying over spilt milk, Olivia. Something created in love has been extinguished in anger. What should have been considered profoundly as a matter of life and death has been subjected to reckless whim. I cannot undo what has been done, Olivia. You will have to live with it now."

"I know, oh I *know!*" Wounded by the verbal lashing, Olivia dug her face into her pillow and exploded into tears. "If you despise me now, I accept that, for I despise myself. I too am not fit to live . . ."

This time Kinjal offered no sympathy, no words of comfort. Instead she sat in grim silence listening to Olivia's self-abuse with impassivity. It was only after the storm of tears had spent itself and Olivia once more lay submerged in her silent wretchedness that Kinjal chose to speak. "You do still have love left for Jai, haven't you?"

A spasm ripped through Olivia's body. "How can I not, Kinjal?" she cried, "How can I *not?* He is part of me, in me, all around me everywhere, all the time. And when he is not, it will be because I too am dead like his child that I have slaughtered so callously."

Kinjal changed position to sit down on the bed, and her tone softened. "You still love Jai enough to want to bear his child?" Olivia did not answer but her stricken expression was response enough. "But is your love adequate to bear also the ignominy of bearing the bastard of a bastard?"

Olivia recoiled at the words, recognising them as her own. "I don't know, I don't know . . ." Dropping her face into her palms, she sat up and rocked back and forth.

"But then, you must find out, my dear, and soon! Jai has treated you abominably. Can you be big enough to not only bear his child but also to love and cherish it when you cannot forgive Jai's betrayal of you?"

Goaded into response, Olivia flared. "I promised to tolerate anything Jai chose to be, I gave him my word. I wish to God I could truly blame him, but in all honesty I can't. He is what he is; he never pretended otherwise. Yes, I can be big enough to love his child if only because as much as it is possible for Jai to love any woman, that night he did love me . . ." Her voice broke; she could tear herself apart no more.

Without another word, Kinjal rose and took her into her arms to hug her, her own throat tight. "Yes. In his own strange way, Jai did return your love. This much I am certain of. But Jai is unlike other men. He is a creature of circumstance; like the wind, like running water, he cannot be possessed. Fulfil that promise you made to him that night; *trust* him. However galling, have faith. Wherever you are, some day he will come to you. This much belief I have in a man I have called my brother."

"And in the meanwhile," Olivia asked with scathing sarcasm, "what is it that I do with my own life?"

"Wait," Kinjal said quietly. "And think. However much you might dislike the word, you are resourceful. I have faith in you, too; a solution will appear."

"It is too late now for votes of confidence, Kinjal!" She felt another surge of bitterness and her face crumpled. "All that remains for me now is to wither away like that noxious tumour. I deserve no better."

Under her breath, Kinjal laughed. "It is not too late. You silly, headstrong girl—did you really believe that I would permit you to make such a rash decision without protest?" Gently, she kissed Olivia on the forehead. "My dear friend, what I put you through was merely an absurd charade devised to frighten you into your senses again. I wanted only to test the strength of your decision, and I'm happy, so happy, that I did." She pointed to the scattered remains of the old woman's ministrations. "What she gave you was only a harmless mixture to make you sleep. Rest assured, my dear confused American hothead, what is within your womb remains safe and secure for the present."

Dumbstruck, Olivia could only stare.

Once more Kinjal became grave. "The old woman says we still have time on our side. During that time, think well and dispassionately and thoroughly, Olivia. I know that it is a cleft stick that you ride; either way your decision will bring torment." Placing a palm on Olivia's stomach, she stroked it. "What lives in here is still no larger than a mango seed. But it grows by the day, by the hour, each time you take a breath. After four weeks it will no longer be safe to remove. Whichever path you choose, there will be pain—but either way I want you to know that you will have my support and help." For the first time, the Maharani's eyes filled with tears. "If you are still in India, I will wait to hear

from you. If not, I will miss you with all my heart and pray that God will always watch over you in your travails."

Olivia was too overwhelmed to speak.

Her visit to Kirtinagar, accepted as one of farewell, raised no questions at home, which was a relief. But now, with time running out, Olivia could no longer postpone that which she never wanted to do again—*think.* She had not only to think, she had to calculate and consider, balance and weigh, assess and examine. Make decisions. Momentarily lulled into hibernation, her conscience once more became a prowling menace that refused to be silenced. At these the most vital cross-roads of her life, her conscience taunted and teased and tossed down a gauntlet it challenged her to ignore. And in her nostrils, whichever way she turned, she smelled only defeat.

Be true to yourself.

Her father's advice now sounded hollow, irrelevant. She no longer knew who she was. That "true self" her father held so dear seemed forever obscured. All night Olivia paced, trying hard to gouge out from her memory the sight of her aunt on the bathroom floor, her lacerated wrists gushing blood like a fountain. There was still some blood on the hemline of her own dress, which she had not been able to wash out, and when she had touched her aunt more blood had smeared her palms. Angrily, Olivia brushed aside sentiment in an effort to reduce her options into terms of cut and dried reality. She could return to Kinjal during the month and overnight flush away that loved-hated mango seed that was at the core of her misfortunes. Or she could stay on in India and bear her child despite the scandal, despite the slings and arrows of an unforgiving society. Or she could flout the pernicious demands of her conscience to march up that gangplank next Wednesday, and to hell with all other problems!

Two other options remained. She could throw herself into the Hooghly and thus find instant salvation. No more thought, no more pain, no more decision making! This, of all her options, was to Olivia the most tempting, the simplest, the easiest. But then—what would that do to her father? She would destroy herself yes, but she would also destroy him, not only because he had lost her but because she had died a coward.

There was only one choice left. Ironically, it was the option that repulsed her the most. But it was the one that presented the fewest complications. It too called for destruction, but only her own. It was a straw, the final one, but the sole straw within her reach. If it saved her from drowning it also condemned her to a living death. On the other hand, what was her life worth anyway?

All night long Olivia paced, thinking, thinking, thinking! By dawn, with her hated resourcefulness stretched to its limit and every consideration exploited to the full, she arrived at a decision. It was a decision that was like a cyclonic gust of wind, extinguishing her spirit and withering away her heart. But it was the only decision that was available to her.

And with the coming of that decision Olivia felt the first stirrings of an emotion she would have considered impossible only a few weeks ago. It was hate for Jai Raventhorne.

13

Freddie Birkhurst was stunned, so much so that he could not speak. For a moment Olivia thought he might faint.

"I mean it, Freddie," she repeated. "If you still want me for a wife, I accept your offer."

It was early morning. The haze had not yet lifted off the river. They sat in the same clearing in the Botanical Gardens where, ironically, Freddie had stammered out his proposal. Now, pressing unsteady fingers to his eyes as if to dispel a dream, he gulped and his Adam's apple bobbed up and down like a child's yo-yo. "My God . . . ," he breathed finally, "I can't believe it, it can't be true . . . !"

"It is true." Olivia's amber eyes, vacant and lifeless, stared nowhere in particular. "Does your offer still hold good, Freddie?"

He sprang up, galvanised. "Of course it still holds good! Dammit, what kind of a cad do you take me to be?" He bristled with hurt.

"In that case," evading his arms, she moved away, "would you agree to an early marriage?"

"Early marriage?" Disbelief turned into rapture. "How early—tomorrow? *Today,* if it suits you better!" He could barely stay still.

"Don't be silly, Freddie. Next week will do just fine. I want no fuss. A simple, private ceremony with just the families." She spoke with a curious calm, a sense of purpose that was nerveless, as if she had died and emerged elsewhere, evacuated of all feeling.

"An elopement, dear heart, if you wish! Only the two of us—"

"What would be your mother's reaction to a quick wedding?" she cut in impatiently, dismissing his suggestion with a gesture.

"Oh, you can leave the mater safely to me." In a burst of confidence, his chest expanded. "She'll damn well do as I ask."

Again Olivia dodged his arms. "Wait, I haven't finished yet! You must hear me out. I have a condition." Trying not to give in to the revulsion that lay just beneath the hard outer skin, she sounded brisk.

"A condition? Only one?" He laughed with abandon, one hand flat against his heart. "Well, lay it down, my darling—lay them *all* down. I accept with no questions. You think I give a damn when—"

"Freddie, please *stop!*" Cracks threatened the surface of her iron control. "My condition is not an ordinary one. You must listen to it very carefully and then give me your answer. It is possible that you might wish to retract your offer."

He paled. "Retract? Christ, I know I'm an idiot, Olivia, but I'm not certifiably insane! If you think—"

"It is for *you* to think, Freddie, profoundly and seriously," she cried, pushing him away as he leapt at her. "The reason I accept your offer is—"

"I don't give a bloody hoot for the reason!"

". . . purely selfish. In fact, despicably so. First, I have to make it clear to you that I do not love you."

He looked relieved. "Oh. Is that all? Well, I already know that! I can hardly expect someone as perfect, as intelligent, as—"

"No, that is not all! Freddie, please *listen*—you have no idea how difficult it is for me to say what I'm trying to." Chastened, he finally took note of her chalk-faced anxiety and sobered. Olivia pulled in a long, hard breath. "I am carrying another man's child. I need to marry because I do not wish it to be born out of wedlock." She removed her eyes from his, dying a thousand invisible deaths.

This time Freddie remained still, very still. Even the rolling, protuberant eyes froze. Then he swallowed. "Another man's child? Ah, whose . . . ?"

"That is not important. What you must understand fully is why I must now acquire a husband." Crushed by her inner shame, her voice dulled. "You have been kind enough to offer me your name. I want that name to be shared by my unfortunate unborn."

Stupefied, Freddie said nothing as he sat with eyes lowered, grappling with his inadequate comprehension.

"Having said all that," Olivia continued doggedly, "I want you to appreciate that if you now wish to withdraw your offer,

I will not in any way think less of you, however low you might consider the woman you have mistakenly held in high enough esteem to want to make your wife." Watching his baffled, bewildered face, she filled with pity. "I will still regard you always as the kindest, most decent man I have ever met."

Olivia wondered anew at her gall, her unspeakable insolence, in matching his mother's impious proposition with one of her own! What she had dared to suggest in her search for cheap respectability was an affront to a man and his manhood, even to one as self-effacing as Freddie. If he now sent her packing, it would be what she so richly deserved. Perversely, she almost prayed that he would.

But Freddie did not send her packing. With a supreme effort he pulled himself together and mopped his brow. "This . . . man, he will not marry you?"

"No."

"Ah, why not?" His brow darkened.

"He has gone away."

"Where?"

"It doesn't matter. He will not return."

"And it is this man that you love?" He turned wistful.

"No. He took me . . . by force." The first of the many lies she was to evolve now for the benefit of this essentially good man had been uttered. She felt no special stings of remorse. How thick one's skin turns in the pursuit of self-interest!

Freddie jumped up with an angry oath, his expression murderous. "Give me the name of the swine and, by *gad,* I'll horsewhip him within an inch of his rotten life wherever he skulks!"

Sadly, Olivia smiled—a mouse aspiring to be a giant killer! "He is not worthy of your effort, Freddie. But we stray from the point. My question remains unanswered—are you still prepared to marry me?"

He gulped again convulsively, his expression aggrieved. "Good God, Olivia, what do you think I am—one of those bloody weathercocks that swings with the wind? Of *course* I'm still prepared to marry you!"

"And declare a child not your own as yours?"

"Yes, dash it, yes!" He knelt before her to capture her hands and kiss them frantically. "Do you imagine that I would ever abandon you in this condition under any circumstances—*do* you?"

Olivia's throat tightened. Freddie's clear blue eyes, his unquestioning faith in her, his naive love—all were so guileless, so childlike. She knew that he had not yet assimilated the awesome finality of his commitment, nor the potentially terrible conflicts it might engender in him. Irrationally, she filled with resentment; why did he not reject her out of hand and force her to thus abandon this most obscene of options? Impulsively, she reached out to smooth his thinning, straw-coloured hair, ashamed of her gracelessness. "Think well, Freddie dear," she said huskily, "would you truly accept me in such scandalous circumstances?"

"I would accept you in any circumstances," he said simply. "You see, I love you . . ."

She fell silent, hushed by the innate goodness of a man who asked for so little. There was in his unambiguous nobility a selflessness that reduced her to ashes. He could not see that she was exploiting him, taking ruthless advantage of his innocence, using him. Feeling squalid and soiled but helpless in her despair, Olivia hid her burning face in her shawl. She did not repulse him this time when he took her in his arms. Instead, she laid her forehead against his shoulder and wept. "One promise, Freddie, my dear—after my child is born, if you so wish I will take it and disappear out of your life forever. Your obligation to me will be over. I want nothing from you or your family."

"You know that I can never wish that, my darling. My obligations to you and to your child will be for life. Honour will not allow me to have it any other way." His arms about her tightened protectively.

Jai Raventhorne had once complained that her love humbled him. It was now her destiny to be given a taste of the same medicine by Freddie. How black was the sense of humour of the divinities!

"No, Aunt Bridget, your ears have not deceived you," Olivia assured her incredulous aunt wearily. "I have accepted Freddie's offer of marriage."

If there were any rewards to be had for Olivia, they were all contained in her aunt's joyous face. After the anticipated fury of tears and copious expressions of gratitude to the Lord for having answered her prayers, Lady Bridget lost no time in getting down to business.

"Of course you will wear white. Sateen? No, maybe Chinese

silk with pink rosettes. Josh's mother was a magpie with lace; there's yards still in the second store-room." Alive and animated, she grabbed a pencil and settled down at her bureau, her wrists still bandaged and her skin not yet restored to its normal hue. "Naturally, a layered petticoat with a band of blue ribbon. We'll have to order a veil, a long one. I like regal trains, don't you? Now, what was it that Jane Watkins said about . . . ?"

Too sick at heart to interrupt, Olivia allowed her aunt her say for a moment or two, then added as gently as she could bring herself to, "We both want a private ceremony, Aunt Bridget. You are not fully recovered and a grand affair will tax your strength. Besides, people will ask questions about Estelle . . ." Lady Bridget stilled and Olivia pressed on. "In any case, there is now no time for lavish arrangements at St. John's or elsewhere. We plan to be married next week."

"Next w—?" Words failed Lady Bridget and her eyes dilated. But reminded of the harsh realities prevailing, her face fell.

"The longer the notice, the more time to ask questions. You will have callers pouring in, cats with their claws unsheathed and waiting to scratch. Do you have the confidence to field taunts from any of them about Estelle's absence?" If she sounded heartless, it was deliberately so; to stem her aunt's enthusiasm might be cruel but it was also necessary.

Lady Bridget slumped back in her chair, the tears again starting to roll down her cheeks. "But I wanted to give you a memorable wedding-day, one that you would never forget," she whispered. "It is the least that is owed to you."

Olivia smiled. "Whatever the arrangements, for me my wedding-day will be memorable, one I am not likely ever to forget. That much I promise."

If Lady Bridget heard the bitterness in her niece's tone, she did not recognise it as such. Too euphoric to quibble about details, she dabbed her eyes dry, blew her nose and raised a beatific smile. "I *told* Josh long ago that one day you would marry Freddie of your own free will!"

But if manipulating her aunt had been easy enough for Olivia, the audience with Lady Birkhurst was an ordeal. "There is no need to worry about Mother," Freddie had pronounced airily. "Whatever has passed between us will remain our secret." Would it? Olivia had merely smiled and let it pass.

"A private wedding *next week?*"

Sitting in the formal Birkhurst drawing-room impaled again by those gimlet eyes that missed nothing, Olivia stared demurely at her feet. Freddie, however, bore the prolonged inspection through the all-seeing lorgnette with unexpected courage. "Yes, Mother," he said firmly, clearing his throat. "Lady Bridget's delicate state of health precludes anything more ambitious, and since that is so, why, ah, wait?" Red faced with effort, he inserted a finger in his collar and loosened it.

"I . . . see." The lorgnette swung around in Olivia's direction. "Whether these are my son's wishes or not, I take it that they are certainly yours?" How subtly she had made her point!

"Yes, they are, Lady Birkhurst."

Behind her veneer of radiant happiness and serene composure, Olivia shivered a little. However controlled Lady Birkhurst's reaction, she knew that under those tight little white curls was a shrewd brain churning away like a paddleboat wheel. No doubt the questions being tossed about in the whirlpools would be made known to her in the not too distant future, and she would have to supply the answers. It was not a confrontation Olivia considered with any enthusiasm.

Lady Birkhurst thoughtfully sucked on a jujube. "And how is Lady Bridget's mysterious tropical fever? I would have called had not Millie Humphries warned me of her husband's ban on visitors."

"My aunt is much better now, thank you," Olivia replied, grateful to be on relatively safer ground, although this too was not without pitfalls since rumours about Lady Bridget's attempt at suicide might well be about by now. "In fact she is well enough to formally call on you in a day or two in order to finalise . . . arrangements." *Finalise*—how sinister was the ring to that word!

"And your cousin Estelle, I understand, is en route to England?"

"Yes."

Whether privy to town gossip or not, Lady Birkhurst made no further mention of either Lady Bridget or her daughter. "Well, you may inform your aunt that I look forward to receiving her. I am relieved that she is once more on her feet. And Freddie, I presume, will soon seek an audience with Sir Joshua to ask for his formal permission?" As usual, she referred to her son in the third person.

"Freddie has an appointment with my uncle this afternoon." It was Olivia who answered. "Isn't that right, d-dear?"

Freddie beamed. "Oh, rather! Absolutely."

For a long while Lady Birkhurst stared at her finger-nails as if suddenly realising for the first time that she possessed them.

Then she inched her vast bulk back against the cushions and nodded. "Well, as long as Sir Joshua and Lady Bridget have no objections, especially to the undue . . . *haste,*" she paused and filled the significant gap by reaching for her filigreed ivory fan, "you both have my approval. I must confess, a wedding congregation of twittering old biddies matching bonnets and blouses while sacred vows are exchanged nauseates me." She smiled blandly in Olivia's direction. "I am enormously relieved, my dear, that you have finally decided to put my son out of his misery. His tiresome, hang-dog looks were beginning to quite ruin my digestive processes. I see no reason why *he* should pine and *I* should be the one to bear the consequences. I happily give both of you my blessings." A handkerchief was patted over each eye in turn and then a flabby cheek was raised upward to receive their salutations. "We will, of course," this to Olivia, "have occasion to talk at greater length later."

Olivia had absolutely no doubt that they would.

That night Olivia sat down to write to Kinjal.

> You were, as always, right—a solution has been found and that handful of flesh is not, after all, to be terminated. I am tempted to plead humanity, but I cannot lie; for whatever it might be worth, my mango seed is the only proof I will ever have that, if only for one night, I was loved by Jai Raventhorne.
>
> And to preserve that proof I am now in the process of perpetrating a vile fraud on a man who least deserves it. For the dubious, hollow privilege of having me for a wife, he is giving me his name. The wedding-ring that comes with the name will give me a pretence of that very respectability I have always boastingly despised. He asks for nothing in return. I will give him even less.

On a crisp, late-January morning, when the sky was of sapphire and the sun a brassy gold, Olivia Siobhan O'Rourke promised to love, cherish and obey the man standing by her side till death did them part, and so became the Honourable Mrs. Frederick James Alistair Birkhurst in the eyes of man and God. The brief, austere ceremony was held in the Templewood home and presided over by a cherubic young chaplain from the Church of St. John's. The bride was given away by her uncle; the best man was Peter Barstow. There were no bridesmaids and only a handful of guests.

For Olivia her wedding-day was also the day of her death. She felt nothing. The dull rhythmic thumps of her heart indicated that she was alive, but to her they held no credibility. Nevertheless, as is the bounden duty of every bride, she looked radiant. The white organza hastily rustled up by Jane Watkins was of lovely design (with side seams secretly let out during the night) over a full, layered petticoat. The late dowager Lady Templewood's Brussels lace had been fashioned into an exquisite train with diamanté and a deluge of pink satin rosettes. The bride's jewellery, much admired by all, was of diamonds: tiara, three-strand necklace of graded marquis-cut brilliant whites, Christmas tree earrings and a bracelet. A walnut-sized solitaire, a wedding gift from the besotted groom, was on the third finger of Olivia's left hand just above the narrow gold band for which she had sold her soul. The solitaire was only a small part of what lay stored in endless velvet-lined boxes in the Birkhurst mansion strong-room, the collection of pigeon blood Burmese rubies alone alleged to be worth a king's ransom.

None of Olivia's new possessions brought her any pleasure or pride. She was an impostor, a confidence trickster who was extracting bounty under false pretences. Even her magnificent dowry from her aunt, which included her own mother's rejected share, Olivia could not look upon without shame and embarrassment. Apart from the cascade of ornaments, she was also to have a sizable bank balance with Lloyd's of London. She was overwhelmed, but her aunt had cut off her protests with passionate determination.

"I have waited twenty-four years for this moment, Olivia, *twenty-four years*—I will not *allow* you to spurn this as your mother did! This is my bridge to Sarah, my atonement for what she suffered. Are you going to deny me her forgiveness when there are no other means by which I can obtain it?"

"No, Aunt Bridget, but—"

"It was *I* who forced Father to disinherit Sarah when she ran away with Sean. It was *I* who forced her to live in America where deprivation and penury ate into her health so that she died while bearing that still-born son she wanted so much." Her face twisted with anguish and her eyes turned wild. "I *killed* her, Olivia, can't you see that? As sure as I know my own name, I killed Sarah!"

Shaken by the raw agony on Lady Bridget's face, Olivia did not have the heart to protest more. For the first time, she saw the depths of her aunt's long suffering, the incisiveness of her continuing guilt. Lady Bridget was a proud, intractable woman; it could not have been easy for her to say all this now. Without a word, Olivia capitulated. Drying her tears and regaining control of herself, Lady Bridget now handed Olivia a black tin box together with its keys. "And this," she said, again composed, "was to have been Estelle's. This too I give you now." Like a clean slate, her face was wiped of all emotion.

But this Olivia could not let pass unchallenged. "I will not touch Estelle's portion, Aunt Bridget," she said evenly. "It is unfair of you to offer it to me. One day when Estelle returns—"

"She will not return. Estelle no longer exists." It was said very calmly, with no sign of the passion that had convulsed her only a moment ago.

Neither do I exist! Olivia wanted to shout, *but no one seems to have noticed!* Somehow she restrained herself. In any case, she was too dejected to do more battle. Silently, she took charge of Estelle's dowry, privately appointing herself merely its caretaker. Her own mother might have turned her back on her portion, but Olivia could hardly see Estelle allowing her pride to deprive herself of such bounty!

The wedding breakfast, over which a transformed Lady Bridget presided with a return of some of her erstwhile spirit, was as lavish as the ceremony itself had been meagre. Encased in a stiff morning suit two sizes too large, Sir Joshua perambulated among his guests in a daze that gave him the fortuitous defence of absent-minded dignity. Ransome never left his friend's side, quick to step in when a lapse of memory or an unwitting gaffe occurred. The handful of guests included Willie Donaldson—Freddie's agency manager—and his wife, Cornelia, and the Humphrieses, the Pennworthys, Peter Barstow, Hugh Yarrow, senior accountant at Templewood, and Ransome, whose wife was away in England. The exclusivity of the occasion had already caused much gossip in station and the Spin, for one, had been heard sniffing, "Mark my words, there's something fishy going on there. I can *smell* it."

And then, of course, there was Lady Birkhurst. Enthroned on the largest chair in the room, quite spectacular in her steel grey satin and ostrich feathers, she sat in silence observing the proceedings with regal detachment. During the ceremony she had shed a discreet tear or two—whereas Lady Bridget had wept openly—but afterwards, dry eyed and hawkishly attentive, she had kept Olivia constantly in her vision, watching, watching, watching. Olivia's perpetual smile ran stakes through her jaws, her throat undulated with her ever-present nausea and her eyes were glassed over with the shine forced into them, but not for an instant did she dare let her façade slip.

In the moment of parting, Olivia clung to her aunt in sudden despair. The journey that loomed ahead was terrifying, and she stood alone, absolutely alone, now part of a chain of events that could never be reversed. Today was her wedding-day—and her father and Sally, from whom she had never concealed anything before, were not even aware of it! Nothing else identified for Olivia with more sinister accuracy the underlying evil of this masquerade upon which she was so firmly embarked.

She had believed that she could feel no passion more violent than the love that she had borne Jai Raventhorne. She recognised now that she had underestimated her capacity for emotion. And overestimated her ability to forgive.

Olivia was sick from the moment she boarded the *Seagull.* With each heave of the ship in the swells and troughs of the Bay of Bengal, her stomach lurched in harmony. She had agreed to a honeymoon in Madras mainly because she didn't care one way or the other. But now, sprawled permanently on the canopied four-poster in the owner's stateroom, since the vessel belonged to the Birkhursts, she cursed herself. Waves of nausea sloshed around her body; once horizontal, she despaired of ever becoming vertical again. It was common knowledge that Freddie often used the ship to take his favourite doxies to Burma or Siam or Malaya. How fervently Olivia wished it could have been one of them in her place now as she was being buffeted so mercilessly to death!

Freddie's ministrations were copious. "But you must *eat,* my darling," he insisted with the best intentions in the world on their first evening at sea. "Shall I fetch you some fish curry with coconut?"

She turned over on her side to reach for the slop bowl and pleaded to be left alone for a while. To her relief, Freddie quietly crept out of the cabin and thankfully she slipped into sleep. Her last waking thought was—Olivia Siobhan O'Rourke has ceased to exist, both in name and in person.

It was much later that, deep in exhausted slumber, Olivia felt a crushing embrace choke out her breath. She woke with a cry, but it was drowned in the rasps of Freddie's noisy breathing laden with the unmistakable fumes of alcohol as he covered her mouth with wet, drooling kisses. Olivia went cold. "Freddie, *please . . . !*" Retching, she struggled violently to wriggle out of his grip.

"Please . . . what?" Through a foul-smelling mouth he laughed, his hands on her body everywhere at once. "My God, you looked delicious in all those yards 'n yards of . . . ," he hiccupped, "whatever. Nearly killed me to hold myself back . . ." His mouth clamped down on hers so swiftly that she couldn't stop his tongue snaking down her throat.

She retched again, fought like a wildcat and, taking advantage of the slack in his arms as he cursed, broke loose to slide away from him. "Freddie, you're *drunk!* And you smell *revolting . . .*" Panting with fear, she crouched on the farthest corner of the bed.

"Course I'm drunk!" With a lunge he grabbed her again and dragged her back. "You think any damn fool would be sober on his *wedding* night, you saucy little tease? Stop *wriggling,* blast you!" Huge hands, possessed suddenly with more strength than Olivia could have imagined, clutched at her breasts beneath her nightgown and squeezed hard.

Shooting with pain, Olivia screamed but his ravaging mouth was tight on hers, biting and nibbling and devouring horribly. Blind with panic, Olivia pushed hard. "Freddie, not now, I beg you! I'm not well, I'm terribly ill, but tomorrow . . . I promise, I give you my word . . ." Disgust and humiliation made her sob.

He swore richly, raised his face from hers enough for her to see that he was furious. "What are you frightened of, eh?" he hissed between clenched teeth. "I'm not going to hurt you—and it's not as if it's the first time you've had a man between your legs, now is it, precious?"

Even in her state of abject fear, Olivia's shock was so profound that, without realising it, she stilled. This was *Freddie* speaking, *Freddie?* The nicest, kindest, most decent man she had ever known?

There was no time for further wonder. He cursed again and pounced unerringly on a body made even more vulnerable by shock. Olivia used all her ebbing strength to fight, to escape his marauding mouth and hard, plucking hands, to plead for mercy; but he was past reason and in his drunkenness his strength was prodigious. Past words, past coherence, past any semblance of tenderness, he set out to systematically and single-mindedly defile her body in every way that he could. The flimsy night-gown ("Why, pink for the honeymoon, of course!" her aunt had insisted coyly) lay on the floor in shredded pieces, wrenched off her with scant regard for its finery. Rough hands abrased her skin into stinging fire, pinching and pummelling and almost tearing it off her bones. His breath, rancid and hot, spurted dribble everywhere. With the brute force of his kisses, her lips felt crushed and her cheeks and breasts were raw. Her revulsion almost suffocated her but, powerless, she could do nothing to divert his repeated violations. And when he finally possessed her, his brutalisation almost cleaved her apart and Olivia cried out in pain. It was an assault, an act of degradation, but in her despair and helplessness Olivia protested no more. To whom? And with what validity?

The vandal making free with her body was her legally wedded husband. She had married him not only willingly but eagerly. The ravishment was part of his conjugal rights. And the sweet Lord knew he would be getting little enough out of this farcical marriage anyway.

Clenching her eyes shut to blot out the nightmare of Freddie's love-making, Olivia trapped her screams of outrage within her throat. Searing tears burnt holes behind her eyelids, but she willed them not to fall. On her tongue was the taste of salt as her teeth dug into her lips and drew blood. In her physical capitulation, she uttered no more sounds but, slowly, she died again within herself. The husk of her being could be used and abused but it could not be obliterated; what could be cancelled out was her mind. Blinding herself resolutely to the present ugliness, Olivia quietly transmigrated into the past. Like a homing bird, her mind took wing to fly back over forbidden memory to another world she had once inhabited. She was held in different arms, being kissed with feather-tipped lips, in love, in tenderness and in a passion that dazzled with its purity. Drugged with the past, she forced herself to forget the present.

But yes, I do love you . . .

The fibres of her skin turned into glowing repositories of memories, golden and guarded, unforgettable and eternal. One by one she savoured them again, turning them over on her tongue like drops of an elixir too precious to be swallowed. *Where are you Jai, my love, my life, my everything?* The silent echoes in her heart reverberated hollowly. *Why have you abandoned me to this, to this . . . ?* There were, of course, no answers. But then there would never be.

Floating within her trance into a realm that was hers and hers alone, Olivia barely noticed that Freddie's appetite was satisfied. Drained and replete, he now lay snoring by her side dead to the world. Olivia struggled up, stumbled to the bath-room and was heavingly sick. Then she scrubbed herself clean, changed into a fresh night-gown and returned to the cabin overwhelmed with defeat and abandonment. Her head swirled, her body felt sore and bruised, but sleep was impossible. For the rest of the night she sat crouched on a stool gazing out of a porthole. Her eyes were dry, but everything else inside her wept, mourning for something that would now never be hers again.

Her hand strayed unconsciously to the gentle mound of her stomach. It felt warm and alive. A strange emotion, unfamiliar and potent, stole across her heart. She filled with revelation, a sense of something miraculous. She was not alone after all. She would never be alone again.

The odium of the night washed away. She could bear it.

"Morning, dear heart, I've brought you some hot milk. Feeling better today?"

Olivia awoke with a start and recoiled. Freddie was leaning over her and there were still whiffs of alcohol on his breath, but his expression was open, anxiety writ all over his face. Eyes wide with nervous tension, Olivia merely turned away.

Freddie flushed, his pink skin turning even blotchier. "I know I, ah, drank rather too much last night. Stupidly, I let the captain talk me into a, ah, few." He laughed sheepishly. "I wasn't too, ah, rough with you last night . . . ah, was I?" He crimsoned further and lowered his eyes.

Rough? Slowly Olivia sat up, took the cup he offered and started to sip with her face still averted. "Why, don't you remember?" she asked with bitter sarcasm.

"Well, actually, no." He grinned quite cheerfully. "Never can, you know. Dashed waste and all that—especially on a chap's wedding night." He frowned and looked dreadfully cross with himself.

Concealing her astonishment but still wary, Olivia scanned

his face closely. There were no indications of subterfuge, of shame or cunning; as always, he shone with earnestness and a sort of inane innocence that had always been his hallmarks. She was bewildered—could it be that he was telling the truth? But her suspicious disbelief lingered. "You really have no recollection of . . . last night?"

He was instantly stricken. Grabbing her hand, he covered it with kisses. "Then I *was* rough! Forgive me, forgive me, my beautiful, perfect, mistreated darling—I would rather blow out my brains than hurt one single hair of your exquisite head. I am an oaf; no, worse, a *cad.* I don't deserve the honour you have done me by becoming my wife. I—"

"No, you weren't rough." Quietly she cut him off. "You were most considerate." Heat flooded Olivia's cheeks and she again turned away.

He let go of her hand to crush her in a clumsy embrace, laying frantic kisses all over her face. "If in my sottish stupor I did or said anything to offend you, my sweet, I beseech pardon, I did so unknowingly." His voice quivered. "I do love you with all my heart, Olivia, you must believe me, you must."

She almost retched afresh with the foul fumes of his breath but, gritting her teeth, she somehow managed a smile. "No, you did and said nothing to offend me. You worry unnecessarily."

His relief was pitiable as, with reverence, he kissed her hand again. "Does it make you unhappy when I drink?"

"Yes. Very unhappy. It is stupid to indulge to the extent that all memory is wiped out."

"All right, in that case I won't." His chest filled out with manly pride. "Not one drop from now on. It won't be easy, dash it, but if it will make you happy, so be it."

She didn't believe him, of course. "If that is a promise, Freddie," she said, trying inwardly to equate this disarming, utterly simple and likeable man with the crude, brutal animal of last night, and not succeeding, "I assure you it is worth more than all the diamonds you could possibly give me."

"Of course it's a promise! I'm a man of my word, dear wife, haven't I proved that already?"

Throughout that day Freddie remained Olivia's ardent slave. Every wish of hers became his command, her comfort his only consideration. In an infinite number of ways he waited on her hand and foot, talking when she wanted conversation, falling obediently silent when she didn't. By evening Olivia was convinced that his lapses of memory were genuine, and the realisation filled her with sadness. Poor Freddie! Underneath that veneer of infallible good humour and self-effacement lurked resentments. Sober, he could sublimate them, perhaps was not even aware of them, but when loosened with drink, they erupted over his tongue with all the viciousness so carefully suppressed under unconscious pretences. How would he be able to survive a lifetime of this duality?

How would she?

Stone cold sober that night, he lay with her again but with trembling, almost reverent awe. For Olivia it was still unmitigated torture, but, grateful for minimal crumbs of mercy, with the force of her sheer will-power she endured his clumsy gropings, his stuttering declarations of love and his constant pleas for responses. Somehow she quelled her nausea, allowing only one thought to dominate others: A bargain was a bargain. Whatever the cost it had to be paid. Freddie had fulfilled his part of the deal; on hers she could not and would not renege.

Olivia hated Madras.

Only ten degrees north of the equator, Madras—unlike Calcutta—had no winter. It was hot and humid all year round, its atmosphere soaking up all her strength like a carnivorous sponge. They stayed in a tidy little whitewashed bungalow belonging to friends of the Birkhursts who were away, and like all European habitations, this too was comfortable and well staffed. If the bamboo blinds were lowered early enough in the morning, the stone interiors remained reasonably cool throughout the muggy day. But forevermore, Madras for Olivia became a station associated with disgusting sickness. Nausea now was her constant companion; she could not keep down even the tiniest morsel of food. Sometimes she was laid low for hours with not even the energy to curse. Had it not been for Freddie's unfailing devotion and understanding, she felt she would have gone mad.

The choice of Madras for a honeymoon had been dictated by a polo tournament now being held at the local army establishment, Fort St. George. Freddie had been looking forward to the games with tremendous enthusiasm. "Will you come to the match this afternoon?" he inquired anxiously two days after their arrival.

With a shudder, Olivia clamped a handkerchief to her

mouth, waiting for the spasm to subside. "I will not be able to sit through it, Freddie, and if I were to be sick I would be an embarrassment to you."

"Oh." He looked crestfallen. "How much longer does this, er, sickness persist?" he asked, suddenly awkward.

"A month or so, I guess." Then, because he asked so little of her and his demands were so few, Olivia felt ashamed. "If I rest all morning, perhaps I will feel sufficiently recovered to sit through the match. I've never seen you play before. I think I'd like to."

If she had given him the moon on a plate, he could not have been more ecstatic. "Capital, capital! The chaps all want to meet you, especially their lady mems. I say, after the game I'd like to ask them for supper and maybe a glass of beer," he said, avoiding her eyes. "Can you manage something at home or shall we stay on at the Fort?"

It was such a trivial request that she did not have the heart to refuse. "Of course I can manage something here. The servants are well enough trained. All I have to do is give the orders."

Overjoyed, he crushed her in an embrace. "My God, I want everyone, the whole world, to see just how lucky I have been in my choice of a wife."

Olivia wanted to cry. Was he trying to convince her—or himself?

As socially desirable to the "Mulls" as to the "Ditchers," the Birkhurst newlyweds were suitably lionised by Madras society. At the game that afternoon, Olivia made a concerted effort for Freddie's sake to be sociable, although she was bored to tears. The women fussed and flattered but she knew inwardly that they had already dubbed her a gold-digging hussy who had used her American forwardness to snare the Birkhurst heir. The men, as usual, were more forgiving; indeed, they seemed enchanted by the new Mrs. Birkhurst's charm and intelligence. She was, they decided privately behind the backs of their wives and daughters, far too good for that idiot Birkhurst. But then they asked each other, come to think of it who wasn't?

Generously unconcerned that his lovely wife outshone him in company, Freddie rejoiced in her success. "You know, I still can't believe it!" he whispered to her during the carriage ride back. "I keep thinking you'll turn back into a pumpkin or something at midnight and fade away."

"No, I won't fade away, Freddie dear," Olivia responded

with caustic humour, "but yes, I certainly am turning into a pumpkin!"

He coloured and fell silent. If there was one topic that made him visibly uncomfortable, it was her pregnancy.

Their first *burra khana* that evening turned out to be an unqualified success. Olivia had taken endless trouble over the buffet menu and in some odd way it gave her pleasure to do so. She had laden the table with a considerable variety of well-prepared food and, with grave apprehensions, had also ordered an extravagant quantity of beer and liquor. Whatever her qualms, she felt she could not shame Freddie before his friends by appearing niggardly. She went out of her way to make the raucous polo crowd welcome but, since there were no ladies in the party, retired to her room early. As the hours ticked by and the jollifications became noisier and more uninhibited, she started to fill with dread. With enough alcohol on the premises to launch a ship, what would be Freddie's condition when the party eventually concluded?

It wasn't until four in the morning that he finally crept into the bedroom. Shaken out of her restless doze, Olivia stiffened. He leaned over her quietly and kissed her on the forehead. As discreetly as she could, Olivia sniffed at the air around him. He chuckled. "Sniff away, dear wife, sniff away to your heart's content—you won't sniff a whiff tonight, not one damned *whiff!*" Chortling proudly, he opened his mouth wide and panted rapidly for her benefit.

With a small cry, Olivia sat up. "Oh, Freddie—you didn't drink at all this evening?"

"Not a sip, not one blasted swallow! See, my love? Tonight I smell of roses. Huge, horrible, god-rotting roses." He groaned.

"Oh, Freddie dear . . . !" It was all Olivia could say in her relief. Impulsively, she pulled down his head and kissed him.

Slowly, his eyes filled with tears. "You know, that is the first time, the very first time, you've kissed me of your own volition."

Gritting her teeth, she forced herself to kiss him again. "For keeping your promise you deserve more, much more. If it were within my power to give it, I would gladly."

"Whatever you give, my sweet, is gratefully accepted," he breathed thickly. "I want nothing more." Slipping into bed beside her, he fell asleep with his head on her shoulder.

But someday you will . . .

If there was anything Olivia found entrancing in Madras, it

was the beach along which their bungalow stood. She had not been by the sea since she had left California. Now, walking along the white sands barefooted every morning, she felt achingly close to home, once more overwhelmed with nostalgia. She would never see her beloved country again, never. She was caught in a trap, this silken trap that was India. She would never be free again. Fanned by the saltiness of the sea breezes, she walked miles each day fluttering helplessly within her solitary cage of despair and loneliness. The endless expanses of the ocean brought with them other heartaches; it was somewhere on this very water that Jai Raventhorne sailed on his *Ganga*.

She forced herself to abandon the thought and harden. The involuntary weakness of her wedding night would cripple her mental processes no more; with each passing day, her hate for Jai Raventhorne was turning stronger. She would make it sustain her, nourish her. She would not allow it to lapse again.

The dreaded summons for Olivia came three days after their return from Madras.

In their absence, an independent apartment had been fashioned for them on the first floor of the Birkhurst mansion on the Esplanade. It had two connecting bedroom suites, a sitting-room and dining-room, a study, a pantry and a scullery. If the Templewoods lived in style, the luxury of the Birkhurst home spoke of far greater wealth and taste for good living. In its Gobelin tapestries, its scintillating crystal chandeliers, Belgian gilt mirrors, Meissen and Ming porcelain, clocks, oil paintings, French furniture with brocade upholstery and its series of well-stocked strong-rooms lay the accumulated treasure of family money as well as that earned through trading endeavours in India. The triple-storied house also boasted gun and games rooms, a music room, a library, a formal study, reception-rooms of which one was a full-sized ballroom with a dais for orchestra, guest suites, a portrait gallery and several porticoed verandahs opening out onto flawless gardens maintained by an army of gardeners. Behind the vegetable gardens were the stables, coach-houses, kitchens, store-rooms and servants' quarters and compound. Lady Birkhurst's apartment, to which Olivia had now been summoned, was on the ground floor adjoining the glass-roofed arboretum.

Olivia was awed by the splendour of the manse, more so

since, upon her return, her mother-in-law had consigned to her charge the hundreds of neatly labelled keys of the household. In the tacit abdication of authority were symbolised Olivia's new role as mistress of the house and the expectation that it would be discharged with responsibility.

"I think, my dear, that it is time for our private little tête-à-tête." Lady Bridget sat in the sunny morning-room in which she spent much of her day. "You and I have promised to be frank with each other, have we not?"

Olivia moistened her lips and nodded.

"Then you must now tell me the true reason why you suddenly decided to accept my son for a husband." The grim solemnity of the occasion was such that a bowl of bonbons before Lady Birkhurst lay untouched. "I was given to understand that you were . . . romantically inclined towards some other person."

"Yes." She swallowed hard.

"The attachment did not develop as you had hoped?"

This time Olivia smiled inadvertently. How had she hoped the attachment to "develop"? "No." Her chin rose a fraction. "I do not love Freddie. He is aware of that. But then, love was not one of your conditions, was it? You wanted someone who would accept him for what he is, to forgive his excesses and to take care of him well. I think I fulfil all these conditions."

Lady Birkhurst nodded. "Yes. I did mean every word I said, Olivia. My opinion of you as the perfect wife for my son has not changed an iota, nor will it no matter what you reveal to me. You are honest and honourable and you have courage. Also, the very fact that Freddie no longer drinks is a testimony to your success as his wife. What Freddie does with his soul is God's business. As a mother, I am interested only in ensuring his physical salvation, and in this my gratitude to you is immense. But, whatever your virtues, Olivia," her tone sharpened, "you are not a crusader. It is not for my son's benefit that you have opted to become his wife. I now want the real reason, Olivia—the truth."

Against her ribs Olivia's heart thudded compulsively and the sweat on her clasped palms felt cold. But, in a way, it was almost a relief to be rid of at least one pretence. "I am pregnant. The child is not Freddie's."

With a sharp sibilance Lady Birkhurst sucked in her breath. The expression on her face, however, changed only inasmuch as her beady eyes became even more alert. For a while she sat immobile; then she sighed.

"Freddie knows the truth, naturally," Olivia proceeded with

as much calmness as she could muster. "There was never any question of not telling him. I know that few men, if any, would have accepted me as I am. My debt to Freddie is not one I can ever repay."

All of a sudden, Lady Birkhurst laughed. "I had assured you that as Freddie's wife you would have a certain moral . . . independence. I had not thought that you would have taken my words *quite* so literally or, indeed, with such dispatch!" Just as suddenly she sobered. "Why didn't you tell me about your condition earlier?"

It was Olivia's turn for amusement. "If I had, would you have allowed the marriage at all?"

"No. I would have certainly tried to dissuade my son from exercising his gallantry with such careless bravado! But not for the reasons you might think, Olivia." Heavily she sat back. "I am a woman of the world. Nothing shocks me anymore. My regard for you is no less because you have, perhaps, loved unwisely and consorted with a man not your husband. Believe me, I've seen worse." She snorted. "My goodness, half the crowned heads of Europe would be hard pressed to name their real fathers! No, Olivia, my objections are purely pragmatic. You see, your marriage to my son rather *muddies* the future for us." Her eyes narrowed. "Who is the father of your child?"

Olivia's chin firmed. "I'm sorry, that I am not prepared to reveal. I have told Freddie that once my baby is born, if he so wishes I will go away. Whatever waivers or legal documents need to be signed to renounce all claims to money and title I will sign willingly. There will be no question of inheritance."

In Lady Birkhurst's spontaneous chuckle there was humour. "Oh dear, how dreadfully naive you Americans are! Do you really think that is *all* there is to the matter? If your child is a male, he will certainly stand to inherit the title."

"But I do not want any part of all that!" Olivia cried. "You are free to disinherit, disclaim, declare dead both me and my child if you wish. All I want for the present is for my child to be born with a name."

"You are still missing the point, Olivia," Lady Birkhurst sighed. "In any case, English titles cannot be renounced just because someone feels like it. The point I am trying to make is that unless you die, Freddie cannot marry again, which means that the direct Birkhurst line would die with him." For the first time she showed signs of agitation. "That is unthinkable! The next incumbent would be a loathsome cousin with pigeon-toes and bad breath whose wife is too stupid to be an English barmaid let alone an English baroness! To see them installed at Farrowsham would be an abomination to me, even in my grave."

Overwhelmed by these complexities to which she had not given any thought at all, Olivia looked bewildered. "But then . . . what is to be done? Is there a solution?"

Lady Birkhurst pyramided her fingers and sank her several chins into her chest. "Yes, there is a solution. I have no objections to your child bearing our name for the present. Later on, we can arrange for him—if it is a male—to disappear and be declared dead. Fortunately, there is enough corruption in England to manage that somehow. If your child is a female the matter becomes much easier. Do I make myself clear?" Olivia nodded and the baroness's expression changed perceptibly. "Now we come to the crux. *Whatever* the sex of the child you bear, you will have to also produce a male child from Freddie's loins to preserve the direct line of his family."

The bottom seemed to fall out of Olivia's world at this thunderbolt. She could only stare at her mother-in-law's determined face in appalled disbelief. But of course Lady Birkhurst was serious. It was an aspect of the matter that had not even occurred to Olivia. In resolving her dilemma, she had thought to satisfy only her own need.

"You mentioned a debt, Olivia." The sonorous tone was now relentless. "And yes, no man would have agreed to what my son has, but then we both know that he is a fool. I do not expect you, an American, to be aware of the intricacies of British inheritance laws, but Freddie certainly should have known better. *Now* do you see the cause of my distress?"

Unhappily, Olivia nodded.

"If you do wish to repay your debt to Freddie, then there is only one way in which to do it. You have no legal need to do so, of course. Your obligation is entirely moral. I have always known that you are a young woman of rare spirit. I now realise that you have even more courage than I had initially assessed." She paused to allow her words to sink in. "Tell me, does your courage allow itself to be stretched even further?"

The cost of her shoddy, opportune grab at respectability was to be higher, far higher, than she had ever imagined! But with so much already lost, so much more committed, the dye was set with indelible fastness. How could the bargain now not be concluded?

"No, my courage does not allow it," she said, trammelled with despair. "But given time, somehow I will expand it. I cannot let Freddie's family be the losers." Unconsciously, she straightened her back to sit up. "If God makes it within my power to so ensure, I will not let your direct line be extinguished."

Unexpectedly, Lady Birkhurst's stern face puckered and her lips trembled. She reached out to take Olivia's hand in hers. "You are a remarkable young woman, my dear. The decisions you have had to make in your short life have been horrendous. I do not envy you them." Her voice rang with genuine feeling. "However bizarre your circumstances, I still consider that my son is blessed to have you by his side. Don't desert him now, Olivia; that is all I ask." She dropped Olivia's hand to wipe her eyes dry, then asked with a return of composure, "Tell me, what would you have done if my son had refused you? Would you have returned to America?"

America!

In searing anguish, Olivia shut her eyes. From where she was now, sinking steadily into a vast bog of inescapable sludge, America might well be on another planet! "Yes, I guess so," she lied dully. "With my aunt eventually returning to England, as she is now contemplating, there would have been no point in staying."

"I take it that they are not aware of your condition? No, of course you did right in keeping it from them." She dismissed the subject to state abruptly, "You must not think of having your baby in Calcutta."

Olivia frowned. "Why not?"

"Think of the consequences, my dear! That wily old fox Humphries will not be fooled for a moment that the child is before its time. More to the point, neither will Millie and we all know how *she* can talk! Everyone will whip out their calendars to make secret calculations. At best, you and Freddie will be laughing-stocks; at worst, he will be dubbed a cuckold. Not even he deserves that."

Once again, Olivia was caught unawares; this too was not an aspect of the situation she had considered. But, as always, Lady Birkhurst's wisdom was unquestionable. Had she not been so totally desolate, Olivia might have seen the droll humour in discussing such a subject with a woman who was her husband's mother. But then, she was beginning to realise, this was an extraordinary woman indeed, so out of the norm as to be unique. "But then, what would you suggest I do?"

Lady Birkhurst pondered. "I suggest you arrange for the birth elsewhere with an unknown doctor in attendance. Return to Calcutta after six weeks, by which time it will not occur to anyone to ask discomfiting questions."

More lies, more pretences, more webs of deceit and delusion! Dear God, would there ever be an end? With an effort, Olivia pulled herself together. "I would rather Freddie did not know that we have spoken about all this. I cannot bear to wound him more than I already have."

"No, we will not reveal our agreement to him." Lady Birkhurst's face softened. "Tell me one more thing that troubles me. This man," she fixed Olivia with her rapier stare, "is he likely to enter your life again at some future date?"

"No."

"He does not know about the child?"

"He neither knows nor cares."

"And you? Do you still care for him?"

Olivia returned her probing look squarely. "No. My single act of madness was no more than just that. For that insanity, I blame only myself."

Lady Birkhurst asked no more questions.

Later, in the solitude of her own room, Olivia exploded with resentment. *No, the blame for the insanity was not only hers!* She rebelled against bearing the intolerable burden alone, rebelled against being noble and logical and forgiving. For her unspeakable situation Jai Raventhorne was as culpable as she—more so. He knew that she was an innocent, reckless and a blind slave to her emotions. He recognised her lack of comprehension of his twisted mind, his perverted idiom. That she had been unable to understand his enigmatic hints, his bewildering warnings, was no secret to him. He had talked in riddles to which she could not possibly have put any answers. She had sought him out, yes—but he had not lacked in reciprocation! He knew that she was bewitched, *besotted.* And knowing that he had led her on, only to betray her.

The nebulous memory she was left with of a transient, illusory paradise, Olivia dismissed; even that would evaporate soon. What would linger was the defilement of every area of her life, of her future. Not even her unborn child, already entangled in impostures and deceit, was to be spared. He had abandoned her to a quagmire; the more she struggled for release, the deeper she was being sucked in. Yes, perhaps during that one night Jai Raventhorne had loved her, but it wasn't enough.

It was not enough!

14

If it was impossible to give Freddie love, Olivia compensated by giving him dedicated service. In a hundred, a thousand different ways each day she devised reparations for the one thing he could never have from her in order to correct the yawning imbalances of their oddly mismatched lives. She threw open her house for his friends, keeping what soon became known as the finest table in town. She gladly suffered *burra khanas* and polo matches and brunch sessions at the Tolly Club, spending hours on the screamingly tedious social circuit listening to fatuous, frivolous talk. Gracefully she tolerated Freddie's idiocies, tended his clothes, kept him ungrudging company and never complained of the ludicrous hours he kept. In the process, she suppressed all her own desires, because the rewards of her labour were great. Despite her constant worry, Freddie remained true to his word. Since that impulsive vow on the *Seagull,* he had not touched a drop of liquor.

Two months after the wedding, when neither full skirts nor loose, waistless dresses could help, the fact of Olivia's pregnancy was admitted publicly by Lady Birkhurst. Of course the news spread in the station like wildfire and, inevitably, Freddie came in for much risqué ribbing. For the most part, he took the banter in his stride with his usual good humour, but Olivia could tell that sometimes, just sometimes, he hated every minute of it. Once, in answer to a particularly ribald remark, he actually snapped back and sparks of anger glowed in his normally placid eyes.

"Hark, the worm turneth!" Peter Barstow drawled with an arched eyebrow. "What's been getting into you lately, old chap—losing your sense of humour?" He looked squarely at Olivia and the look was questioning and sly.

Poor Freddie!

That evening he looked so thoroughly woebegone that Olivia could not help asking, "Tell me truthfully, Freddie, have you ever regretted marrying me?"

His denial was instant. "No! Dammit, a chap doesn't make a lifelong commitment one day and take it back the next! You think I'm that *low?* Dash it all, I *love* you!"

Olivia sighed. "I know you do, Freddie dear, and I'm so grateful . . ."

"I don't want your gratitude," he protested morosely, suddenly even more desolate. "All I want is your love. Not much," he was quick to add, "just a little, a very little."

"I do love you in my own way, Freddie! I . . . I'm extremely *fond* of you . . ." She trailed off and bit her lip.

"You still love this . . . man, don't you?" With a clenched fist he expended his uncharacteristic frustration on a table top. "My God, it's driving me potty just thinking about it!"

"No, Freddie." Olivia forced herself to sound casual, offhanded. "I don't and I never did. I've already told you—"

"If only I knew who he was," too engulfed in his own jealousies, he was uninterested in her denials, "I swear I'd *kill* him!"

She smiled acidly. "You would be in excellent company, my dear. You are by no means the only one who wishes him dead."

But once more she filled with compassion for Freddie.

Since her return Olivia had tried to visit her aunt and uncle as often as possible. Sir Joshua refused to go to England and Lady Bridget refused to stay, so her aunt was to leave alone, and her departure was imminent. As such, there was a great deal to be done about the house. Some of the rooms had to be locked, dust sheets fitted over furniture, store-rooms cleared of accumulated clutter, silver packed and put away in the strong-rooms and a good home found for Clementine, Estelle's little dog. It was a lifetime that Lady Bridget was leaving behind, and lifetimes are not easy to shed either mentally or physically.

Most worrisome was that copious means had to be devised for the continuing care of Sir Joshua, who was still refusing to entertain thoughts of a country where the sun never shone and, as he said with contempt, people ate hog slop and stewed dish rags. Olivia's marriage to Freddie had made little impact on him save to elicit one cryptic comment, "Teach him to at least pass out on his own doorstep next time." For the rest, he seemed to recede each day farther into himself. He spent hours pruning the roses or just sitting on an upturned flowerpot staring into space. For a man who had once prided himself on his sartorial elegance, his attire was careless enough to seem sloppy. And he had no interest in what he ate. Even though the indifference persisted between him and his wife, Olivia had secretly hoped that her aunt would be concerned about him, but there seemed no signs of a thaw; quite the contrary, in fact. Whatever resentments Olivia had once had against Sir Joshua had long since faded. In their own divergent ways they were all cogs in the same wheel. Who was she to allocate guilt?

After all efforts to persuade him to accompany his wife back to England had failed, Olivia tried another ploy. "All right then, come and live with us," she pleaded. "I hate the idea of you remaining here all on your own."

"You may not appreciate it, Olivia, but I have a great deal to think about," he snapped irritably. "Do you believe that any man could think clearly with that Birkhurst biddy about? No disrespect intended."

What he had to think about nobody could tell, but he sometimes sat up all night scribbling in his diary. "What Josh thinks about is between him and his Maker," Ransome remarked when questioned. "Neither of them has seen fit to make *me* privy to their deliberations! But don't worry about Josh," he added. "I have decided to sell my house and move in with him after Bridget goes. It is the height of absurdity for two lonely men to each rattle about in separate establishments. And, of course, the financial savings would be considerable."

When Lady Bridget heard the news of Olivia's impending motherhood from Lady Birkhurst, she wept with joy, but she also began to have second thoughts about her departure. "I feel that Sarah would have wanted me to be here, by your side," she wailed tearfully. "I feel you will need me."

Alarmed, Olivia hastily conjured up passionate reassurances. Her aunt's presence at the birth of her child would be cataclysmic! "Freddie's mother is very much here, Aunt Bridget, and I shall be very well taken care of between her and Dr. Humphries. I promise you there is absolutely no need for you to change your plans. I know how desperately you want to be away."

Torn between guilt and relief, Lady Bridget muttered, "Well, you must write to me in detail, every single detail, of how you are progressing. And, of course, when the baby comes I will want to know *everything.*" She eyed Olivia's stomach with a frown. "You do seem unusually large for your time. Get Dr. Humphries to give you a thorough examination soon."

Hastily Olivia diverted her attention. "Would you like me to also go through Estelle's room and tidy her possessions?" Since Estelle had left, Lady Bridget had refused to step foot inside the room. Olivia had been in on occasion and the *jamadar* was let in daily for the sweeping and swabbing, but for the rest of the time the room was kept locked. It was as if, with a padlock on the door, Lady Bridget had also obliterated from view part of her own life.

Her aunt's expression closed. "No. Leave it for the moment. You can give her things away to charity later."

Having once given Olivia the responsibility of the household, Lady Birkhurst never interfered with her running of it. Nor did she ever question Olivia's expenditure, not even when, almost as a first compulsion, Olivia ordered a complete restructuring and repair of the servants' quarters and compound. Freddie, of course, was generosity itself, delighted at any cost to be rid of the tedium of housekeeping and its finances. Despite the crippling burden that Lady Birkhurst had laid on her conscience, Olivia thought of her warmly—and gratefully—as a friend, an ally. Her mother-in-law's mere presence in the house gave Olivia comfort, for, apart from Kinjal, it was only she who shared her monstrous secret. Therefore, one morning when she received another summons, Olivia had no idea that what awaited her was yet another blow. The conversation started lightly enough with a suggestion that was extremely welcome.

"You are active and intelligent, Olivia—does the prospect of working for part of the day at our Agency House appeal to you? After all, we don't want you dying of boredom, do we?"

Olivia was delighted by the suggestion. "Indeed it does! I have thought of asking you myself but hesitated in case you disapproved."

"My dear, I have already approved of so much," Lady Birkhurst said drily, "and this would be trivial, an act of sheer self-preservation. I shall have a word with Willie about it. He'll hate the idea, of course. The very thought of a skirt flapping around his precious domain will drive the grumpy old Mother Hubbard daft, but there's no one who knows more about trade in the East than Willie, although he'll reduce you to tears in five minutes." She laughed. "I shall see to it before I leave."

"Before you leave?" Olivia paled. "Leave for where?"

Heaving a tired sigh, Lady Birkhurst reached for a letter lying on the table at her elbow. "This has come from our estate manager at Farrowsham. Caleb is dreadfully unwell. He urges that I catch the next ship home." While Olivia sat shaken by the news, deep lines of strain appeared on her mother-in-law's face. "You see, Olivia, unlike his son whose ill health stems from indolence and indulgence, Caleb's ailments come from overwork and self-negligence. He is passionately involved in the estate, which is vast, and he takes his attendance in the House more seriously than most other peers of the realm, pompous idlers that many of them are. Caleb's body is now starting to rebel, and no one ever gets any younger, do they?" She tapped the letter with a fingernail. "This is already three months old. It will be another three before I reach home."

"You are considering departing immediately?" Olivia was dismayed. Without the compassionate support of this infinitely pragmatic woman, how would she tolerate the frightening trial that loomed ahead?

"I must, dear," Lady Birkhurst said gently. "Caleb needs me now more than ever. I have therefore decided to sail with Lady Bridget. We will be good company for each other."

"But that is next week!"

"Yes." For a moment she fell silent. "I would have wanted to participate in your coming ordeal, my dear. Sadly, I will not be able to. Have you decided upon some satisfactory plan of action?"

"I will leave for Kirtinagar a month before my child is due," Olivia answered morosely. "The Maharani welcomes the idea. I will place myself entirely in her capable hands."

"Excellent, my dear, excellent! I am relieved that you will be with friends. I would be beside myself with worry otherwise."

A lump rose in Olivia's throat. "Thank you for your concern. You can never know what your understanding has meant to me. I shall miss you."

"And I you, dear child." Equally moved, she reached out to squeeze Olivia's hand, her eyes moist. "But I leave in the conviction, yes conviction, that you will do your duty by my son. Had you been a lesser person, I would have had my doubts. I have none."

The avowal of faith was intended to comfort and solace Olivia; the words had been spoken out of kindness. How could Lady Birkhurst have known the even blacker depression into which that very kindness served to plunge Olivia?

The parting from both her aunt and her mother-in-law a week later was for Olivia inordinately painful. Once more she felt abandoned. It was as though they were also taking part of herself with them. Imprisoned by her circumstances, she could do nothing. Her destiny had slipped out of her hands, if indeed it had ever been in them at all!

"Listen to your wife," was Lady Birkhurst's parting command to her son. "She has more sense than you ever will." To Olivia, as she clasped her to her bosom, she whispered, "Write to me often, child. Remember, wherever I am, I am a friend. But I fear we might not meet again . . ." Olivia cried.

Sir Joshua was not among that vast throng that saw the ladies off at wharfside. "Look after him, Olivia," Lady Bridget blurted out impulsively as she was about to embark. "Protect him, do not let him be hurt more. I fear that when . . . when *that* man returns . . ." She stopped and said no more, but the fear remained in her eyes as, with supreme dignity, she turned to negotiate the gangplank.

When that man returns . . . !

The Farrowsham Agency House, started by Caleb Birkhurst in 1815—two years after Parliament revised the Company's charter to abolish all monopolies save that of tea—was a thriving concern. It was run by Willie Donaldson, a tall, angular Scotsman spare of both flesh and words, who had been with it since its inception. He had come to manage Farrowsham by dint of hard work, honesty and canny business sense; he ruled with an iron hand and remained fiercely protective of the Agency's interests and reputation. Freddie's disinterest Donaldson saw as a boon and, by similar token, received Olivia's induction into the firm with something less than enthusiasm. Two weeks after she had joined, however, he grudgingly revised his estimation. He saw that she had potential, and in recognition of it he appointed one of his most experienced and trusted Indian employees, Bimal Babu, as her aide.

Olivia was, Donaldson conceded to his wife, Cornelia, very

different from what he had expected of a young mem. She didn't gossip or chatter idly, she was singularly well informed about some commercial matters and unashamed to profess ignorance of others and seek guidance. Most gratifying, she didn't volunteer daft opinions or throw her weight about as one might expect of an owner's wife, and she was a rapid learner. "She's na anybody's fool, my love," he told his wife. "And she's na a silly little chit with oats instead of brains. Aye, she's a bonny lass too. Of course she's American but that's na the puir lassie's fault. What I canna figger's, *hoo* she came to settle for our Freddie, by God I canna."

For her part, Olivia took to Willie Donaldson instantly. He was gruff, sometimes blunt to the point of rudeness and swore like a whore, but he was bright as a new penny and one always knew where one stood with him. Eager to be tutored, she started to learn much from him.

Farrowsham did not involve itself in the China Coast trade and had never touched opium, for Caleb Birkhurst was a man of stern Christian principles where drugs were concerned. What he had built his fortune on was plain and simple salesmanship. If Britain's industrial revolution had left her hungry for markets overseas, then this was where expertise was needed. In this he was not alone, of course, but he was certainly one of the most successful. Exported out by the profitable shipload was the endless wealth of the Orient: cotton, jute, shellac, spices, oils and essences for the European perfume industry, furs, gems, wool and a dozen other cargoes, and, of course, indigo from Farrowsham's own spreading plantations. The export figures for indigo in that year, Donaldson told Olivia, totalled about ten million pounds, and a healthy proportion of that could be attributed to Farrowsham's production. Returning shiploads brought British goods that filled the coffers even faster with imports of agricultural machinery, printing shop equipment from inks to paper, hand tools, books, medical materials, a host of sophisticated consumer goods and, most important of all, cloth from Lancashire's textile mills. There was no way in which Indian hand looms could compete with the prolific might of Britain's machine-made fabrics. To crush the indigenous industry further and make vaster markets for manufactured cloth, a duty had been imposed on hand-loom products with the result that imports from Britain sold for less in the shops. Soon, save for the very poor, everyone in India was wearing British cloth, dooming local production, even the exquisite muslins of Dacca, to obscurity. In addition, Farrowsham also invested money for Company employees since they were forbidden direct involvement in commerce. "Farrowsham was one of the first to mop up savings of Company blokes," Donaldson said. "Nae a man alive could juggle borrowing and lending rates like old Caleb, the old buzzard, may God bless the man." He chuckled. "I was a mere wee lad then but, God's truth, it was bliss to watch him rake in the shekels. Farrowsham stood firm even during the upheavals of the Thirties. By God, we made it faster than anyone, save of course Trident." He made a sour face. "But then that devil's pup Raventhorne has feet in both camps, dinna he?"

Mention of Raventhorne and his agency brought no change to Olivia's expression. "Do you have many dealings with Trident?" she asked casually.

"Oh, aye. We lease their warehooses, book all our cargo in those bloody clippers of his since they're the fastest there are. He's a thieving cutthroat with rates but he delivers on the damned nose, I canna deny that." He paused and scowled. "For what he's done to your uncle and Ransome, I'd horsewhip the skin off his bloody butt, and I reck'n someone will some day. I hold no brief for that Lucifer's seed, but with us he's been a man of his word. Noo," he shuffled his papers and returned to immediate business, "like I was saying, Caleb bought the hinterland properties in thirty-eight. Before then, a daft Company rule forbade Europeans to buy land in India. Since then . . ."

The matter of Jai Raventhorne was laid aside for the moment.

Since Freddie usually slept until noon, Olivia sometimes lunched with her uncle and spent time ensuring that the household ran well under Rehman's devoted supervision. With the Templewood and Ransome offices not far from the Agency on Old Court House Street, she also contrived frequent visits to Arthur Ransome. She was astonished to learn from him one day that he was having difficulty selling his house.

"But why? Surely the property is on prime land and valuable?"

He gave her a curious look. "Templewood and Ransome have become pariahs, my dear. People fear that anyone who trades with us or helps us in our travails will be punished by Trident, as I had explained to you once earlier."

Olivia now recalled a brief conversation she had had with Ransome in Barrackpore to which she had then paid scant attention. "But that is absurd!" she exclaimed indignantly. "What more can he possibly want from you? Has he not done enough harm already?"

"There is still something he wants." Ransome spoke without anger. "Our name plate. He will not rest until we are driven into the bankruptcy courts. That he has avowed."

"Raventhorne wants to drive you out onto the *streets?*" She was appalled that this evil man's vindictiveness should be so total.

"Yes," Ransome said simply. "Oh yes. He wants us to end where he himself began, you see. I suppose you might call that poetic justice." He laughed a little. "And it appears that he will succeed. With Josh now incapable of business, our credit is no longer considered good. Even Pennworthy's bank will not discount our bills since there is no incoming. Besides, Trident banks with Pennworthy and he too has to guard his interests. In the meanwhile, one errant consignment of our tea lies rotting. It arrived here in Calcutta instead of going directly to London from Canton, due to a shipping error. Nobody now is willing to transport it to London for fear of reprisals when Raventhorne comes back, and neither will the domestic wholesalers touch it."

When Raventhorne comes back. How Olivia was beginning to detest that ever-recurring phrase!

"I had no idea things were so dismal for you," she said slowly, greatly upset by the extent of his dejection. Her own spirits plummeted. "Can you think of no solution to your troubles?"

He shrugged. "Perhaps there are ways out, Olivia. Ten, even five years ago, I would have fought tooth and nail but now I no longer have the energy. Or the will. I'm beginning to feel my age, and that's no help." He got up to stretch his stiffening legs. "We've had a damn fine life, Josh and I, and I have no regrets. We've made enormous sums of money and we've spent enormous sums of money. Now perhaps it is time to pack it in. There are younger men, better men, coming into the tea trade. Indian tea will some day prosper and there will be no need for the China Coast. Gone will be the excitement, the adventure, the thrilling sense of conquest. Tea will become just another crop, and I don't much fancy being a farmer. Maybe Josh is right, maybe steamships will be de rigueur soon and the sailing vessels will vanish. Life will become routine, humdrum, and I for one want no part of it. Frankly, it appalls me . . ."

Olivia's own depression turned into flaming anger. There was nothing Raventhorne had left untainted, undiseased, in his masterly plan of wholesale destruction. For the first time she truly appreciated the aptness of his accursed symbol; he had indeed done the Lord Shiva proud!

Over the following weeks Olivia saw in the city how ubiquitous were the reminders of Jai Raventhorne. Reminders, that is, quite apart from the one within her that supped on her blood and lived off the very breath of her lungs. Almost daily she passed the Trident offices with their blank façade and mocking windows. One day, she again saw Raventhorne's dun gelding with white stockings being ridden by one of his minions across Tank Square. Farrowsham's own ledgers abounded with mention of Trident, and bills and receipts bearing Raventhorne's sprawling, arrogant signature were plentiful. In Raventhorne's absence, Trident was managed by his trusted and loyal lieutenant, a Bengali called Ranjan Moitra, a dapper young man always immaculate in white dhoti, shirt and shawl, with open sandals on neatly kept feet. Moitra visited the Farrowsham offices regularly. Olivia had yet to speak to him but he never failed to bow low to her whenever their paths did cross.

One morning when Olivia was on her way to John Company's offices in Writers' Building to obtain some information for Donaldson, a beautifully ornamented palanquin passed by her. Fleetingly, through a break in the curtain covering the doorway, a face peeped out and Olivia halted in her tracks; it was Sujata's! For an instant their eyes locked. Then Sujata's kohl-laden gaze dropped to the slight mound of Olivia's stomach and remained there. The ruby red lips curved in a derisive smile and across her face flashed a look of such venomous dislike that Olivia stood transfixed. The palanquin passed on but that smile—so ugly and so knowing—troubled Olivia through the rest of the day.

If her work at the Farrowsham Agency provided Olivia with much needed mental stimulation, it seemed to upset Freddie increasingly. "What do I do with myself while you're gone?" he grumbled churlishly at dinner one night. "I miss you when you're not here."

"But I'm gone only while you're asleep, dear," Olivia pointed out with patience. "More or less. I like to keep Uncle Josh company occasionally or he lunches alone."

"Well, I lunch alone too!"

"Not often, Freddie. And I'm always at home in the evenings."

"Even so, I do miss you," he insisted stubbornly, then turned wistful. "Do you ever miss me, Olivia? Tell me truthfully, do you?"

She spent the next half hour assuring him that she did, and the better part of the night trying to prove it. Freddie's sexual appetite, Olivia had discovered, was prodigious. Many of his demands when locked in passion revolted her, but with grim stoicism she fulfilled them through the simple expedient of divorcing her mind from her body. She trained herself to pretend she was someone else and thought of the act of copulation only as a street bitch might do, forcing herself to turn as promiscuous, as wanton, as her husband demanded. The growing round of her stomach made the act even more distasteful, but she performed it dutifully, like a penance. With many protestations of love Freddie always declared himself satisfied, but Olivia knew that he pretended, too, and that the gathering dissatisfactions festering unknown to him within his body would not remain unexpressed for long.

On nights like these Olivia felt she would gladly sell her soul to be able to love Freddie even half as much as she had once loved Jai Raventhorne.

Those leisurely drives down the Strand were still something Olivia enjoyed occasionally. Sometimes Freddie accompanied her; at other times when he was out with his friends, she went alone. Calcutta's riverine port always bustled with excitement and activity, especially when new arrivals were scheduled. Watching the hurry and scurry, breathing in the heady tang of salt, reading the boldly displayed labels on crates of cargo, Olivia somehow felt alive again. Instead of a castaway marooned forever in an insular wilderness, she felt that she was again part of the real world somewhere within which there was still America.

One evening she was taken unawares by an alarming sight: a three-master painted white, flying a familiar saffron flag with a black motif! Her stomach, never stable these days, heaved. Was it, could it be, the *Ganga?* Memory flew back eight months to Estelle and her opera-glasses; only eight months had elapsed since that day so clearly etched in her memory, but it seemed as if in another lifetime, another age altogether. In a trance, Olivia stopped her carriage and stepped down. There was chaos and confusion everywhere, but suddenly through a gap in the crowd she spied Ranjan Moitra, Trident's manager. With a sheaf of documents in his hand he was arguing vociferously with a Customs official. On an insane impulse, Olivia picked her way through the throng towards him. Moitra saw her immediately and, surprised, stopped in midsentence to bow with elaborate deference.

"Please to come this side, Madam," he said, hurrying towards her, then guiding her away with the stiff, traditional courtesy Bengalis always showed to women. "These coolies are uncouth louts with no manners."

What Olivia planned to say she had no idea but, urged on by some force beyond her comprehension, she smiled and allowed herself to be escorted away. "Thank you, Mr. Moitra. I notice that one of your ships has arrived today," she said casually, her breath shallow.

"Indeed it has, Madam." His chest puffed out with pride. "It is from Boston that it comes, *your* Boston," as if there might be a hundred others, "and it brings cotton gins and tobacco leaf." Emboldened by Olivia's flattering interest, he waxed eloquent about excise officials, his opinion of whom was the same as Donaldson's although he expressed it in less colourful terms.

"Well, let me see," Olivia murmured after Moitra had said his piece, "that is a clipper, is it not?"

His chest expanded further. "Yes, oh yes. Only Trident sails American clippers out of Indian ports."

"Of course." Her heartbeats accelerated madly. "And this one is called the . . . *Ganga,* if I am not mistaken?" To stop herself from fainting, she clutched at the iron rail behind her back.

"No, this is the other one, the *Jamuna,*" he clarified. "We have many American clippers, Madam Birkhurst. As Madam might recall, the *Ganga* has a steam engine. That vessel remains in New York."

"And the owner . . . ?" Throwing caution to the winds, in her lingering dread Olivia turned reckless.

"Also. The Sarkar—that is, my employer—remains with the vessel, I believe." He patted a plump mail parcel in his hand. "In New York our packet teas are selling like your cakes that are very hot." He allowed himself a small laugh in his pride of achievement.

Olivia's gaze was riveted to the parcel in Moitra's hand. For a mad moment she was certain she would snatch it away from him, tear it open on the spot and devour its contents. But then, aghast, she stifled the lunatic impulse and recollected her balance. She recalled that for all she cared, Jai Raventhorne could be at the bottom of the Hudson River. "Indeed!" Her voice chilled as she punished Moitra for her own insanity. "I am pleased that Trident goes from strength to strength, Mr. Moitra, but you can hardly expect *me* to jubilate with you." With a freezing smile, she walked away.

Still annoyed with herself for having solicited the pointless conversation, Olivia nevertheless derived some comfort from one small discovery: Not even Ranjan Moitra, trusted confidant of his employer, knew of her cousin Estelle's presence on board the *Ganga.* From a purely selfish standpoint, this was good news indeed. Obviously, if one were clever enough, secrets could be kept even in a village such as Calcutta!

Early the next morning, as Olivia was preparing to leave for the Agency, a visitor was announced. According to the card the bearer brought, it was a Captain Mathieson Z. Tucker, master of the Lone Star line vessel *Maid of Galveston* out of Texas. He had, he wrote on the card, brought for her gifts and messages from Mr. Sean O'Rourke in Hawaii.

Wild with excitement, Olivia flew down the stairs to greet Captain Tucker. "How very kind of you to call personally!" She gripped his huge hand and clung to it. "Do I understand that you have actually seen and talked to my father?"

"Sure thing, m'am. And that ain't all, Mrs. ah, Brixton . . . ?"

"Birkhurst."

"Pardon, Mrs. Birkhurst . . . I was there, right there m'am, at his weddin'. And a mighty fine weddin' too, as is only fitten for a fine gent such as yer Paw." He squeezed her hand and shook it so hard that her knuckles cracked, his bright red hair bobbing up and down at the same time. "As to yer own weddin', m'am, yer Paw said nothing. T'was to the Templewood house I went lookin' for yerself this mornin'."

"Yes, well, the news could not have reached Papa yet when you left him, Captain Tucker." Eagerly she led him into the dining-room, where she had ordered an elegant table laid for breakfast. "Oh, I'm so impatient to hear all the news you bring, Captain!"

Over a gargantuan meal to which the Captain did full justice, Olivia listened in enthralled silence as he gave her a detailed account of the great event. The ceremony itself, he said, took place in a wooden shack of a church built entirely out of sandalwood, for which the islands of Hawaii were famous. Sally had worn a dress of shell pink and in her hair she had tucked a red double hibiscus in deference to the native custom. The groom had been in a morning suit (How he must have hated that! Olivia chuckled inwardly) and so had Sally's boys. Dane, the younger, had been best man and Dirk had given his mother away. Later, they had celebrated with a luau on the beach with spit-roasted suckling pig, taro bread, sweet potatoes, sand-baked fish and " 'Nuff danged coconut wine to float my goddam ship, beggin' yer pardon, m'am." They had sung and danced till dawn. It had been, he concluded fervently, the best goddam wedding he had ever been to, including his own. Shaking his head, he thrust another vast spoonful of scrambled eggs through the shock of red whiskers that all but concealed his mouth.

For more than two hours over endless cups of good, strong Brazilian coffee, a gift from the Captain, Olivia plied him with questions about all those thousands of details that could never be put into a letter. Hawaii, he said, like America was becoming an amazing melting-pot of folks from everywhere because the islands were heavenly. "Many Americans too, m'am, like yer Paw, runnin' away from California, where the gold scramble's bringin' every kinda scalawag there is. There's not a crooked son of a sea cook who ain't headin' West for the loot, m'am. And," he wagged a stern finger, "there's other rumblin's. In the South, I've even heard talk of open defiance by the slaves."

"And the house Sally and my father live in?" Olivia asked, eager for more personal news. "What is that like?"

Captain Tucker chuckled. "Houses on the islands ain't always like in America, m'am. This one's of grass, tapa cloth and blocks of coral." He told her that in the yard Sally had planted bread-fruit, taro and such vegetables as would grow on the islands' generally poor soil. They were lucky to have fresh water on their land and the fishing was good. When not at the missionary school or being tutored by her father, the boys were learning woodcraft, goat hunting and shearing and skinning, as well as marine engineering down at the shipyard. When they were old enough, her father planned to send them to Yale on America's

East Coast. " 'Tis a fine sight to see those lads on a surfin' board, m'am. Brown as berries they are, and happy as bloody sandpipers." Captain Tucker's sigh was deep and hearty. "A few more voyages, a few more shekels and, by Christ, I'm ready for the fragrant isles m'self."

Olivia's eyes, far-away and wistful, filled with longing. *So was she, oh God; ready but unable!*

Captain Tucker pointed to the large parcel he had brought. "If it's more news yer after, 'tis all in there, I guess."

"Yes, I suppose it is." Loath to let him go, she forced another cup of coffee on him. "You bring with you sights and sounds of an outside I had almost forgotten is still there, Captain Tucker. I am very grateful for your time and trouble. Do you plan to stay awhile in port?"

"Alas, no. We only stop long 'nuff to collect cargo, m'am, a day or so at most."

"What cargoes have you been carrying so far?" she asked only to prolong the conversation a few more minutes.

"Mostly goat skins from Hawaii to Canton, bolts of silk now from China to Europe and America. And some of that carv'd, curlicu'd furn'ture the Chinks make. Too fancy for my likes but," he grimaced, "goes like free booze to the thirsty for them that has the cash in the West."

"Does it?" Olivia's eyes had suddenly turned thoughtful. "Did you say you plan to touch England too, Captain Tucker?"

"Aye, m'am. Southampton."

"In that case," she said crisply, "would you be so kind as to give me another few minutes of your time? There is a small matter I would like to discuss."

Arthur Ransome stared. "Yarrow has just returned from the docks. The *Maid of Galveston* can carry no more cargo. Her holds are full."

"If Mr. Yarrow goes again and meets Captain Tucker personally, he will find that the situation has changed." Olivia explained her fortuitous encounter with her father's friend. "He is willing to oblige on the basis of his friendship with Papa. He tells me he has good contacts in Southampton. He will sell your tea locally and," she leaned forward and smiled, "I will purchase your consignment before dispatch so that you can receive payment immediately."

Ransome's eyes widened. "Good God, my dear, Willie would have a fit! To involve Farrowsham in this—"

"The involvement is not Farrowsham's, it is mine."

"But I cannot allow Birkhurst money to—"

"It is not Birkhurst money, Uncle Arthur. It belongs to me, personally." Her tone turned persuasive. "If you miss this opportunity, Uncle Arthur, that tea will deteriorate further and become unsalable. I assure you that the money I offer is mine to do with as I wish without consulting either Freddie or Willie Donaldson. I consider my investment safe since I am not looking for profit. If I break even in Southampton, I will be satisfied."

Deeply moved, Ransome fell silent. Then, noisily, he cleared his throat. "Your offer is generous enough to render me speechless, but . . . ," he shook his head uncertainly, "but you make yourself vulnerable and, through you, Farrowsham."

"Farrowsham is big enough to take care of itself. As for me, I neither fear nor care a crooked cent for your Mr. Raventhorne's reaction. In fact, I dare him to do his worst!" She flung the challenge with supreme confidence. For her, Raventhorne's worst had already been done.

Eventually, albeit reluctantly, Ransome capitulated, abandoning foolish pride to accept a golden chance that might never again come. The other project Olivia had envisaged for Ransom's benefit, while chatting with the obliging Captain, she decided to reserve for later, following further investigations.

If Arthur Ransome had been at a loss for words, no such reticence afflicted Willie Donaldson the next morning when news of the impromptu sale and dispatch of the moribund tea chests became known to the business district. "You should na have done that, lass," he exclaimed heatedly. "By Christ, it ain't *our* business what bad blood exists twixt Trident and anybody else!"

"It still isn't Farrowsham's business," Olivia reminded him, unruffled. "And it isn't a matter of 'anybody else'; it's a matter of my uncle's firm. Besides, there is no need for the Agency to be involved."

"There's na need but it *might.* Because we dinna ever touch the damned poppy trade, the cursed madman leaves us alone. To interfere noo with his affairs is foolhardy. It canna but invite trouble." He was extremely put out.

"Trouble!" Olivia's lips curled. "Why is everyone so damned

scared of trouble from Raventhorne? He's a bully, not some magical genie with supernatural powers!"

"He's na genie but he *is* vicious and vindictive. What he's done to your uncle—"

"What he's done to my uncle he's done because everyone was too lily-livered to stop him! Well, in my book he's just a cocky, self-opinionated smartass who's sledge-hammered his way to the top because no one has had the guts to settle his hash. Well, *I* have, Mr. Donaldson, I surely have!" Furious, she stood up and glared down at him with flashing eyes. "And if in the process I wish to help my kith and kin with my own money, I will damn well do so, and to *hell* with every one of Calcutta's whey-faced, yellow-bellied merchants!" Violently angry, she flounced out of his room.

Open mouthed with astonishment, Donaldson gaped after her for a moment, then slowly sat back and took a deep breath. He remained awhile rubbing his chin and pondering and suddenly he broke out into quiet cackles. "Well, bless my soul, bless my *soul!* For a wee lass na yet dry behind the ears, she na runs short on bloody gall!" He roared and slapped his thigh. "But by *God* it's a grand pleasure to put one over the satchel-arsed bastard!"

Olivia spent an evening of undiluted delight with the packages Captain Tucker had delivered. She read all the letters contained in them over and over again. How different they were in tone from her own blatantly fabricated, insincere bulletins! Besides the letters with their welcome news, there were gifts galore: carved sandalwood figurines and animals from Dane, similarly crafted book ends from Dirk, clothes hand stitched by Sally, books, newspapers and magazines from her father, cans of coffee-beans, coral jewellery and a goat-skin jacket specially made for her birthday. Her birthday! Lost in her fragile, perilous world so far away from reality, Olivia had forgotten even that!

But if the generous parcel from Hawaii filled her heart with sweet and sour aches, the memory of another parcel from a different part of the world made Olivia's heart burn with persistent curiosity. Try as she might, she could not forget the sight of that fat brown bundle clutched in Ranjan Moitra's hand at the docks! It was not idle news about Raventhorne that she craved. Only one devouring question dampened her forehead with cold sweat and brought a sick, hollow feeling to her stomach: *Was he intending to return soon to Calcutta . . . ?*

As it happened, no great deviousness was required to trap Moitra into somehow releasing the information; two days after the encounter at the docks, he simply walked into the office and requested an audience with her. Olivia's pulse skipped—why the sudden call? "Yes, Mr. Moitra. What can I do for you?" A few minutes later when he was settled opposite her in her room, the front she presented to him was businesslike and composed.

He coughed and looked unhappy. "Please to forgive the intrusion, Madam, but it is to beg Madam's forgiveness that I have come. I offended Madam the other evening." Olivia looked blank, so he continued ruefully. "I should not have mentioned Trident's successes in your country. It was—how to say it?—a foot in my mouth, a gross error. Naturally Madam cannot jubilate with us, naturally! As the esteemed daughter of Sir Joshua's esteemed lady memsahib's sister, it would be unthinkable. Please to pardon this humble, mannerless idiot." The corners of his mouth drooped in abject penitence.

Olivia was tempted to smile but, of course, didn't. "There is no need for an apology, Mr. Moitra. You are, after all, a loyal Trident employee. Your pride in your employer's achievements is understandable."

He was even more overcome by the gracious concession. "Madam is too kind, too kind," he murmured, then sat toying with a thought for a while before blurting it out. "Madam is also a fine, dutiful lady who is doing much to aid her family. I was personally very happy to learn that Mr. Ransome has been able to dispatch his tea to England." He turned earnest, his expression intent. "The Sarkar is my revered friend and mentor, but I do not approve of some of his methods. It is not with disloyalty that I speak, for the Sarkar is well aware of my opinion."

Olivia was surprised and touched by this unexpected sympathy. Also, it provided her with a tailor-made opening to probe. "Thank you, Mr. Moitra. Your words are greatly appreciated. Now, would you care to join me in a cup of cardamom tea? There is a certain matter I wish to bring to your notice."

In no way suspicious of her motives, he nodded shyly. When the tea-tray was delivered a moment later, Olivia opened a ledger sitting on her desk. "On going through this, Mr. Moitra, I notice that your cargo rates are higher than everyone else's." Aware that Willie was fortuitously out of the office, she spoke with confidence. "The consignment of shellac you carried on the *Tapti,* for instance, cost us twice as much as it would have on another vessel."

Moitra looked considerably surprised. "It is well known, Madam, that our rates are higher because our clippers are the fastest vessels available from Calcutta."

"That is not entirely true, Mr. Moitra. Other lines, foreign ones, use clippers as well. Lone Star, for instance. Captain Tucker charged us far less for that tea than what we pay Trident."

"But Lone Star ships do not call here regularly," Moitra protested. "Our sailings are like the workings of clocks. Besides, our contracts are all long term . . ."

Moitra was beginning to look puzzled. He knew, of course, that this sharp American lady whose brain was like a man's was now holding top position at Farrowsham, but why had Mr. Donaldson not brought up this question before? Olivia had expected resistance but she persisted. "What I would like to know is—would you be willing to re-negotiate lower terms with us, Mr. Moitra?"

"Oh no, Madam." His reaction was immediate, as she knew it would be. "That is entirely beyond my authority. Only the Sarkar can make changes." His smile was profoundly apologetic. "I fear that Madam will have to wait for the Sarkar's return to re-negotiate the contract."

"Oh, I see. In that case, have you any idea when that is likely to be?" It was tossed out so lightly, so casually, that Moitra's response came without hesitation.

"The Sarkar's plans are always not to be predicted, Madam." He shrugged. "He has travelled much in England and in Europe. Three months back he was in his rented London residence. It would be best to await his return."

"Fine. I will take the matter up with Mr. Donaldson." A residence? For Estelle and himself . . . ? Nevertheless she felt enormous relief. Moitra's next remark, however, startled her.

"Do not be misled, Madam," he said, suddenly on the defensive, "For one with so deprived a childhood, the Sarkar has no yearnings for material possessions. He acquires residences only for business reasons."

Concealing her surprise, Olivia regarded him thoughtfully over the rim of her cup. "You were acquainted with him in childhood?"

"Indeed! Had my father not found the Sarkar lying badly wounded in the gutter, he would not have lived. The Sarkar was only eight years old at that time. It was a white man who had beaten him, although he would not say who. The Sarkar's hatred for your race is therefore not entirely unjustified, Madam." Still on the defensive, he spoke with feeling.

Another piece of the jigsaw puzzle! "Oh, really?" she murmured.

"Yes, Madam. My father was a renowned *ayurved,* an herbalist. He cured the Sarkar's wounds and made him live with us for two years since he had neither home nor family." Reticence forgotten, Moitra now wanted only to present his beloved Sarkar in as favourable a light as he could. His efforts to make reparation on behalf of his employer were vaguely touching.

No family? What about his mother? For a split second Olivia's thoughts flashed to a drawer somewhere in the house where the forgotten locket lay, but then she dismissed the memory. How ironic that all this information should suddenly arrive on her desk unsolicited! But old habits die hard and she heard herself asking, "He left after two years?"

Moitra smiled sadly. "Yes. We never knew for where. My mother was very upset. But," his smile widened, "the Sarkar had not forgotten us, Madam, not for one moment! Twelve years afterwards, he came back to us. We could not recognise him. Now he had become a man, a *gentleman!* Since then, his generosity to my family has been boundless. To me he gave a job in his new company. I have been with him ever since." He cleared his throat and added quietly, "Your dislike of the Sarkar, Madam, I understand, for he has ruined your esteemed uncle. I beg of you now to understand also my love for him."

He rose, gave a jerky little bow, and left.

By pumping Ranjan Moitra, Olivia had got the information she wanted—that Jai Raventhorne was unlikely to return in a hurry. The rest of the information had come gratis. Olivia was astonished, and pleased, at how little it had affected her. Where once it would have whipped her emotions into an inferno, it now left her with no reaction at all. It was a small triumph but it was significant; truly, she had dismissed Jai Raventhorne from her life forever.

15

Once more the rains came.

And again the leaden skies swung low, obliterating the sun but soaking up the intolerable humidity like a sponge. The heat was crippling. For Olivia the punishment of the oppressive weather became a penance. The weight of her belly pushed down into her sensible shoes, making her ankles bloat, and every effort seemed too much. It was no longer possible to go out in public even in carefully designed clothes; she had to stop work. Also, it was time to escape to Kirtinagar.

"But why Kirtinagar?" Freddie asked, dismayed. "I don't trust those native quacks. Surely Dr. Humphries should be in attendance."

When Olivia explained to him the reason, he fell silent. Then, with a curt nod, he walked out of the room. Olivia's eyes brimmed. Whether or not her sins would some day be visited upon her child, they were destined certainly to be visited upon her blameless husband.

"Don't worry about Josh," Ransome assured her when she expressed concern about him. "I shall be with him. But tell me, my dear, is it necessary to undertake this trip now? Would it not be better to leave it until after your child is safely born?"

"I am in excellent health, Uncle Arthur," she reassured him gently. "The journey will in no way endanger me. You see, the Maharani is keen to hear all about the first women's rights convention held last year in Seneca Falls in America. My father has sent me copies of the speeches made by Lucretia Mott and Elizabeth Cady Stanton, which the Maharani anxiously awaits and wishes to discuss. Also," she smiled at his perplexity at the elaborate lie, "I need to be away for a while. Calcutta sometimes depresses me."

He seemed surprised. "But why? God has given you a good life, my dear child; be happy in it. It is time you stopped carrying burdens not your own. Suffering by proxy is noble, but your own life beckons. But yes, if you need a respite then of course you must go."

Her own life! It seemed that she had almost none left and whatever little there was had long since ceased to make sense.

To which sentiment Kinjal reacted strongly when Olivia repeated it to her a few days later. "Your life makes perfectly good sense to *me,*" she scolded, very cross. "What makes even better sense is for you to now be serene, to rest mind and body so that your baby is born happy. Whatever remains of your term is to be used as you wish. You have no obligations to anyone here, only to yourself."

It was good to be back in Kirtinagar. The place made no demands, called for no pretences, required no alibis to be manufactured. Here, at last, she could be free—free even from herself.

The weeks that followed were for Olivia sublimely blissful. If her mind flowered in the freedom given her of thought and action, so did her body. With the simple yoga exercises that Kinjal taught her, her physical aches and pains diminished. The tensions melted away and, gradually, she began to feel marvellously well. With the library once more at her disposal, Olivia spent long, carefree hours reading about Hindu philosophy and the astonishing knowledge of the ages that was part of India's complex heritage. No one, not even Kinjal, busy with her own affairs and with her two children, intruded on her privacy. Arvind Singh, now totally immersed in the repairs to his mine, was as discreet, as unquestioning, as his wife. If he was aware of Estelle's elopement with his friend, he never mentioned it. In any case, for herself Olivia had stopped caring; it was all dead history and, like all things dead, worthy only of burial.

What Olivia enjoyed greatly were the hours spent with Kinjal's son and daughter. Tarun, twelve, was a serious, sombre-eyed lad whose education as heir apparent was the consuming passion of his parents' life. Tara, the girl, was nine. Cheerfully extroverted, she lacked any trait that could even remotely be called serious, although she too was subject to an education schedule as arduous as her brother's. All in all there was a normalcy, a cleanness, about Kinjal's household that made Olivia's days idyllic. For the first time since she had come to India, she could do what she had done so rarely: laugh. With all restrictions removed, she could roam freely, absorbing the flavours of a rural India of which she knew little. She walked miles, watching farmers and fishermen and weavers toil at their labours, and was once more struck by the harmony of an environment that was true to itself. Life here was like an ocean; waves rose and waves fell, but none disturbed the oneness of the larger space to which they all belonged.

If only she could live on like this, free and unfettered! She had seldom been so content even in America. Tomorrow existed only when it arrived and, for the moment at least, there were no hard realities. She wished it could go on forever but, of course, it could not.

Olivia's baby was born at midnight.

Outside the elements were wild. The monsoon storm roared through the trees, flattening them like blades of grass. Inside, there was the fury of another storm as whipping pains marked the end of Olivia's transient paradise, gained only to be lost again in the imminent creation of another life. The waves of pain, cutting in their sharpness, struck in rhythms, ever-accelerating rhythms, that crushed her mind to pulp and shredded her body into ribbons. Something living tore and clawed and punished her flesh in tempestuous temper, determined not to leave a single fibre of her being undestroyed. Repeatedly Olivia screamed, and repeatedly it was Kinjal's soothing voice that reached out to her midstream in the river of her torrential pain.

"Hush, *hush* . . . it will not be long now. Breathe deeply, push hard, *harder* . . ."

The savage hammer blows continued. Swimming in and out of blood red mists, Olivia pushed harder and ever harder, gasping with agony and liquefying into sobs. Cool hands swabbed the sweat slicks off her face; expert fingers poked and pried and pulled. Around her there were sounds that melted and merged into a symphony of whispers, of sloshing water, of confabulations clothed in urgency.

"One last time, Olivia dearest . . . *push* now as hard as you can. It is almost over, almost over . . ."

One last time Olivia pushed, and one last time she screamed. She felt as though the slicing edge of a knife cleaved her lengthwise into two as something punishing and pitiless exploded out of her body. She had no more strength left even to breathe. With a small gasp, mauled and battered beyond the limits of endurance, Olivia slipped into unconsciousness, her energy drained. After twenty hours of torment, she finally slept. It was the sleep of the dreamless dead. And in it she was unaware that she had, at last, given birth to Jai Raventhorne's son.

Many hours later Olivia woke to brilliant sunshine and fragrances of jasmine and sandalwood and gentle herbal potions being prepared for the restoration of her lacerated body. In a dim blur she saw the midwife, the experienced herbalist, the maidservants, setting about their business with a calmness that astonished Olivia. But then, they had seen birth and death a thousand times over; both were part of the cycle of life and scarcely novelties. Deft hands changed bloodied bed sheets, salved gaping cuts and removed all vestiges of the long battle that had ended in an act of miraculous creation. The tempest had petered out, and there was no more pain.

"Is it over . . . ?" Olivia breathed with no strength to ask more.

Something cool and delicious touched her lips and she drank in great, thirsty gulps.

"Yes, it is over." Kinjal's face resolved in Olivia's vision and her eyes were filled with tears. "And it is also beginning. You have a beautiful son."

A strange feeling crept through Olivia. It was not pain, yet it was not far from it. Kinjal laid a small bundle beside her on the bed. Ignoring the searing spasm that was her reward for the effort, Olivia turned on a side and gazed down curiously for the first time on the countenance of her baby. It was ugly and crumpled, still not recovered from its nine-month-long compression, but when she hesitantly touched its cheek with a finger, it felt as soft as the underwing of a dove. The midwife waddled forward, adjusted the front of Olivia's robe and nodded. Shyly, uncertainly, Olivia guided her breast, heavy with milk and ache, towards the tiny orifice. Instantly, the puckered lips opened and clamped firmly around her nipple. Olivia gasped; the sucking movement that commenced immediately gave her the most incredibly sweet sensation she had ever known. She was suffused with a joy so novel, so overwhelming, that she could not hold back a sob. Tenderly, she brushed her son's hair away from his forehead. Decimated with love, she pressed him closer to her, unable to remove her wonder-struck gaze from his face. His eyes were opalescent, ebony fringed. Wild and profuse, his hair was jet black.

Some day he would be the image of Jai Raventhorne.

When his feeding was finished, Kinjal removed the bundle from the bed and secured the shawl around the baby's head. "Wipe your eyes. Your husband awaits in the antechamber; you must not cry before him." Olivia did as told, not aware that she had been crying. Fifteen minutes later, when Freddie tiptoed nervously into the chamber, she was sitting propped up by pillows, her hair neatly coiled into a chignon.

For a while Freddie stood staring down at the crib in which the baby lay. Then, pale faced, he bent down and kissed Olivia formally on the cheek. "Was it very . . . bad?" His voice shook and his lips had felt stiff and cold on her skin.

"No. No more than is normal." Impetuously, she took his hands in hers. "Thank you for coming, Freddie dear . . ."

He flushed. "Oh, I couldn't have, ah, stayed away. Came as soon as I got the message." He released his hands and forced his glance in the direction of the crib. "Ah, jolly little beggar, isn't he . . . ?" He turned to leave.

His stricken face twisted Olivia with pity—what could her transient pains be worth compared to his lifelong yoke? "Please stay a few days, Freddie," she begged. "The Maharaja would be delighted. There is good duck shooting on the lake and plenty of billiards."

He refused to meet her eyes. "I'd like that, truly, but Peter and some of the chaps plan something by way of . . . celebration. They would be awfully offended if, ah, I were absent . . ." He threw her a wan smile.

Olivia could imagine the ordeal for him of that "celebration"—coarse quips about having sired a "son and heir," much back slapping and winks and loud guffaws. She cringed and felt her throat constrict. "Freddie, I'm sorry . . ."

He turned and fled.

Quietly, with her face hidden in her shawl, Olivia wept. Her child had been conceived in reckless passion and nurtured through nine long months in frequent resentment. What did she feel for him now that the abstraction had become a reality? She did not know yet but she understood what Kinjal had meant: One intolerable chapter had ended but another, as intolerable, had begun. For all her lies, all her humiliating alibis, for this monstrous marriage, she had gained nothing; in the very face of her son lived the unmistakable identity of his father. How ironic remained the divinities and how cruel their sense of humour! If the mills of God ground fine, then truly the mills of Jai Raven-thorne ground even finer.

Olivia wept for her innocent son, for herself, for the ominous future. But most of all, she wept for her husband. For the moment her baby's eyes were closed and his telltale black hair was concealed by a shawl, but for how long, *how long?*

It was time for more lies.

With Freddie Olivia dispatched a letter to Dr. Humphries informing him of an unfortunate fall in Kirtinagar that had precipitated the premature birth of her baby. By the grace of God, she wrote, the Maharani's personal physician and an experienced midwife were at hand. The baby had been delivered safely and they were both now well. However, she had been advised to remain in Kirtinagar for a month so that her child, naturally born small, could gain weight. Olivia also sent letters to Arthur Ransome, Sir Joshua, Lady Bridget and her mother-in-law. The letter she composed for dispatch to her family was long, effusive in tone and filled with mendacious detail, which she knew would be avidly consumed. Of all the lies she was forced to tell, those that she was transmitting home were to Olivia the most sinful, for they trusted her implicitly.

Her brief, serene idyll was now over. Ahead, the future towered with sinister intent, alleviated only by her unalloyed wonder as she gazed for hours upon her son. That such a small sample of perfection could have been fashioned inside her body without her conscious participation was to Olivia a miracle. But that he should visually give so little credit to the mother who had borne him was something she resented bitterly. "Why should my precious little one be made to bear a cross not of his making?" she asked Kinjal repeatedly.

"It might not be a cross," Kinjal comforted. "Many of your race have grey eyes and black hair. Nobody else is likely to make the connection between him and Jai."

"Freddie will," Olivia said, unconsoled. "Whatever little is left unbroken in him will then shatter."

For which not even Kinjal—angelic, caring Kinjal—could offer any reassurances.

It was about ten days after the birth that Arvind Singh

requested permission to visit Olivia in her apartment and give the child his blessings. During her stay in the palace complex, the Maharaja had been a frequent companion to her and the Maharani, for they dined together often in the zenana. Olivia had enjoyed talking politics with him, giving him information about Hawaii and America, and eagerly absorbing the intricacies of Indian rulership. Though between them there existed a formality, the friendship had developed well, but not enough to be able to talk about the sordid mine disaster and her uncle's complicity in it. Even so, Raventhorne's name cropped up often, for the Maharaja knew nothing of her involvement with him.

I hope you never have occasion to regret your visit to Kirtinagar. Did Arvind Singh recall his distant warning uttered with such foresight? Awaiting his arrival in her apartment, Olivia wondered.

"I understand from my wife that your son is quite the most beautiful baby ever born." Settling himself down in her verandah, Arvind Singh appeared his usual charming self. "My children both agree with her."

"Well, you must see for yourself," Olivia responded with a calm smile. "In the meantime, may I offer you some Brazilian coffee?"

Over cups of the aromatic brew they talked again about her work at the Farrowsham Agency. The Maharaja reiterated his admiration for her ability to hold her own in a world so preponderantly male. "I understand," he suddenly remarked, "that you have also been assisting Templewood and Ransome in their difficulties."

He referred, Olivia knew, to the recent dispatch of their tea consignment. She was not surprised that he had heard about it; his information regarding Calcutta's day-to-day corporate affairs was remarkably thorough. "Yes. But what I have done is negligible. The difficulties they face are not."

An attendant delivered the Maharaja's hookah, which he arranged on the floor at his master's feet. Arvind Singh puffed contentedly for a moment or two, then observed, "Unfortunately, those difficulties they have brought upon themselves. Forgive me if I am blunt, Mrs. Birkhurst, but Sir Joshua is lucky that a major scandal was averted." He smiled drily. "The English are, after all, adept at dividing others while remaining united themselves."

It was the first time he had brought up the topic with such directness. Olivia was startled, but because she now had so little interest in the matter, she could take it in her stride. "Yes. My uncle was misguided, tragically so. But I must say in his defence that he was also provoked beyond the limits of endurance."

"One could say the same for Jai. He is not an ordinary man; he cannot be measured by ordinary standards."

"However extraordinary," she said with an edge, "surely all men need to conform to some basic norms of decency?"

Arvind Singh abandoned his hookah for the moment to stir his coffee. "Jai is driven by forces that are difficult to comprehend at the best of times—"

"On the contrary, he is driven by forces that are very easy to understand!" she retorted, not letting him finish. "Every one of them is identifiable as perversity, a need to destroy."

"True. But there is hate on both sides. Sir Joshua—and the English—cannot stomach that the son of a servant woman, a native tribal, has risen to beat them at their own game."

"But there are many others who have similarly risen from humble homes to be accepted. Why generous allowances for your friend and none for the English? Surely such wholesale condemnation comes from prejudice?"

Arvind Singh laughed. "I had forgotten how difficult it is to win an argument with you, Mrs. Birkhurst! The truth is that both Jai and your uncle are extreme men. Their collisions tend to be explosive and the detritus widely scattered." He stared reflectively at his cup. "Forgive me if I am wrong, Mrs. Birkhurst, but at one time I was under the impression that you had some . . . admiration for Jai. Certainly, he had a great deal for you." It was an indication of their friendship that he could make such a comment without embarrassment.

"If I did have 'admiration,' as you put it," Olivia countered lightly, marvelling at how well Kinjal had guarded her secrets, "then it was misplaced. One way or another he has caused the disintegration of my uncle and his family." Of her own disintegration, she said nothing. He would see for himself in a moment.

He spread his hands in a gesture of resignation. "Well, let us just put it all down to the misfortune of an alien presence in our country. It has produced tensions that frequently detonate, that are like lava fighting to burst through our soil. Sooner or later, the volcano will erupt."

On the whole, Olivia was relieved by the switch to impersonalities. "You mean a revolt? By the Indians?"

"Yes. The revolt will have small beginnings, but the eventual conflagration will send the entire country up in flames."

She remained sceptical. "The English presence is too strong

to be dislodged like a pebble. To be successful, a revolutionary needs fire power, not mere numerical superiority."

"Suppressed anger and frustration are sometimes stronger than fire power, my dear Mrs. Birkhurst, as the French proved with their bloody revolution, to say nothing of your own country's battle for independence. Bondage, whether alien or indigenous, political or economic, benign or malicious, goes against the nature of man everywhere. But," he broke off with a laugh, "the argument is endless. Perhaps we will continue it later when my wife too is free to join in. And now," he rose, "may I be allowed to offer my blessings to the infant Birkhurst son and heir?"

"Yes, of course." Smiling steadily, Olivia signalled to the ayah to bring in the child.

"I know it is difficult to tell at this age—I never could with my own children—but which handsome parent does the boy resemble?"

"No, it is not difficult," she contradicted. "My son is the exact replica of his father."

As the nurse approached, Olivia positioned herself in a far corner of the verandah to watch from a distance, her face expressionless. Sounds emerging from the bundle in the nurse's arms told her that her son was awake and that his eyes were open. The bonnet used to cover his head had been removed according to her instructions. With an unsuspecting, benign smile the Maharaja took the child into his arms. For an instant Olivia saw him stare. His smile froze, then faltered and then faded away altogether. She turned away to gaze vacantly into the garden.

For an inordinate while there was silence, broken only by the raucous cries of the peacocks in the garden, an ugly call considering the beauty of their appearance. Out of the corner of her eye Olivia saw that Arvind Singh still held the child, his gaze incredulous and his complexion pale with shock. Then he bent his head, kissed the baby's forehead and returned him to his nurse. From his pocket he withdrew a red velvet pouch similar to the one Kinjal had given, containing the traditional gold coins offered in blessing to a new-born. Carefully he placed it inside the child's blanket. As he did so, his hands shook.

"My wife has often told me that you are a courageous woman, Olivia." He walked over to her, his agitation so great that he did not notice the informality of her first name. "I had underestimated the extent of that courage. I pray that God may forever be with you and your son." He spoke with difficulty.

Olivia's smile was metallic. "Do you consider that we will be in need of divine assistance?"

"Oh yes." He sat down heavily. "Oh *yes,* you will indeed! As for my own participation in the matter, what I will need is divine forgiveness . . ." There was deep distress in his face.

Proudly, her chin thrust forward. "No one's participation can be given credit, Your Highness. I have been very independent in plotting my own destiny."

He accepted the cynicism with a rueful shake of his head. "Jai will not stay away forever."

"So I am assured by many, but his return does not frighten me," she retorted with slicing disdain. "Your friend cannot reach me again, Your Highness." She paused and hesitated; well, why not say it? "You might or might not be aware that he has taken my cousin, Estelle Templewood, with him."

Arvind Singh coloured and his eyes fell. "Yes, I am aware of it. Neither Kinjal nor I were part of those nefarious plans, I assure you. Jai's act of revenge was loathsome, unforgivable—but, as we both know, he is a man obsessed to the point of madness."

"He is indeed fortunate to have a friend such as yourself," Olivia commented with inadvertent scorn, "who can provide him with such stout defences!"

He rose again to come to where she stood and touched her hand. "I am also your friend, Olivia," he said gently. "Now more than ever."

She was instantly ashamed of her show of brittleness. "Yes, I know. Without you and Kinjal I would have crumbled. Or died." In her sudden emotion, her composure wavered. How she wished the name of Jai Raventhorne had not been invoked between them!

"You must leave India."

He said it so abruptly that Olivia was taken by surprise. "There is nothing I would like better but it is impossible at present. Why do you say that?"

"When Jai returns it will be . . . unsafe for you here."

"Unsafe?" His choice of word amused her. "Why? He can do me no further harm, I promise!"

Arvind Singh regarded her with sudden pity. "Oh, but he can." His face was deadly serious. "Jai will not allow his son to be brought up a Birkhurst. He will leave no stone unturned to take him away from you."

Freddie was not at home when Olivia returned from Kirtinagar. Instead, she was dutifully awaited by Mary Ling, the nurse Olivia had engaged on high recommendation from her aunt prior to her departure for Kirtinagar. Mary was competent, cheerful and discreet. She also had a good singing voice and played well on the piano. To assist her, Olivia had hired Lady Bridget's old ayah, a lazy woman but experienced and pleasant enough. One of the guest suites on the second floor had been prepared as a nursery, with nanny's quarters and pantry attached.

Olivia decided to name her son Amos.

Before her talk with Arvind Singh, Olivia had merely hated Jai Raventhorne; the unexpected warning was now teaching her to also fear him. Arvind Singh's words had struck terror in Olivia's heart. The need to escape this benighted city became paramount in her mind. The question was how, how, *how . . . ?*

When Freddie returned home it was midnight and he was drunk. He weaved his way awkwardly between pieces of furniture, then sat down, legs askew, and belched. "Welcome home, dearest wife," he slurred, squinting bloodshot eyes in Olivia's direction. "And how is my son and heir getting along, eh?" He guffawed.

Sitting up in bed reading, Olivia hid her apprehensions behind a smile. She had not seen him drunk since that awful night on the ship; she now felt a rush of bitter guilt because this was proof not of his failure but of hers. "He is getting along very well, thank you."

"And what is my son and heir to be christened, dear heart?" He tried to stand up, failed and folded back with an oath. "Not after me, I take it, his one and only father?"

She winced at the cruel taunt. "I thought we might christen him Amos James Sean, if that is acceptable to you."

"Amos, eh? Well, I'll be damned—the bearer of burdens!" He chuckled and Olivia realised he was not as drunk as he pretended. "In that case I'd better have another dekko at the little . . . ," he hiccupped, apologised and hiccupped again, ". . . *b-bastard . . . !*"

She was flooded with pain, her own and his. "He is asleep now. Of course you will see him in the morning if you wish."

He groaned, clutched his temples, staggered to the bed and

fell heavily onto her lap. "Oh, 'livia, 'livia—do you know what agony it is to love and not be loved . . . ?" Laying his head against her breast he groaned again and passed out.

Yes, I know, Freddie dear, I know. I wish I could make it better for you but I can't, I can't . . .

Gently, she disentangled herself, fetched a damp cloth with which to wipe his face, changed him into his pyjamas and tucked him into bed. She lay down next to him and cradled him in her arms like a child, his head cushioned on her shoulder. Later, still not sober, he woke to claim her with that same mindless fierceness he had shown on their wedding night, thrusting into her brutally and repeatedly, threatening to tear her apart with his frustrated passion. She neither refused him nor did she complain. Not yet fully healed after the birth of her child, her body revolted and exploded in pain, but she did not cry out. Fists and teeth clenched, she suffered the assaults wordlessly. He too, after all, had demons riding his back; who better to help him expel them than she?

When he was finally done and had fallen again into snoring slumber, she rose quietly. She had begun to bleed. Doubling over with the pain, she hobbled to the bath-room to wash and medicate herself. She crept back into bed and gave in to exhausted sleep.

When she woke in the morning she was alone. She got up, quickly removed the blood-stained bed sheet so that he would not see it and went in for a prolonged bath. When she returned to her bedchamber, Freddie was sitting by the window. On the table before him were a tea-tray and a folded newspaper. Neither had been touched.

Concerned at the blankness of his expression, Olivia asked quickly, "Freddie? Are you not feeling well?"

His pale, washed-out blue eyes swivelled in her direction. They were still shot with tiny red veins, and his skin looked horribly pasty. "I went up to see the baby. He reminds me of someone." His tone was as flat as his expression. "Tell me now who his father is."

"No! It is no longer of importance, Freddie. I—"

"It is of importance to me." With a shudder, he buried his face in his hands. "I cannot forget that you have lain with another man, Olivia, and that the living, breathing proof is now here, in my house, a constant reminder of that act!"

His muffled words sounded like the cries of a wounded animal. In an effort to lessen his anguish, she knelt down and put her arms about him. "I have never lied to you, Freddie; I never deceived you. I told you the truth, Freddie, and I gave you the freedom to refuse me . . ."

"I have never had the freedom to refuse you, Olivia!" Huge, grotesque tears spilled down his hollow cheeks. "My love for you has never permitted that." He refused to be consoled and shook her off roughly. "I know nothing of babies, dammit! It was all so . . . unreal, so far away, but now," a spasm tore through his hunched body, "now, it's suddenly *here,* in front of my eyes. It mocks me, taunts me, forbids me to forget that you have borne the fruit of another's loins . . ."

The scope of his hopelessness defeated her, as did the awareness of her own inability to redeem it even marginally. She was struck again by the enormity of his sacrifice, the injustice of her demands on him. In fierce remorse, she grabbed his hands and kissed them. "I can't bear to see you like this, Freddie! What is done cannot be undone, but I would do anything, anything, to help reduce your torment. I can never forget your kindness, your—"

"Kindness!" Wrenching his hands free, he exploded. "Kindness, fondness, friendship, gratitude . . . ! It is not *kindness* that I have given; it is my heart, my love, my *life.* In return what you give me at best is gratitude, at worst . . . *pity.* No, don't deny it, I have seen it in your eyes. You feel you owe me, it is a debt you repay, which is why you tolerate my presence in your bed. I repel you, Olivia, admit it!" He halted his feverish pacings and, as she opened her mouth to protest, held up a hand. "No, don't lie, Olivia. Don't pretend with me anymore. A chap senses these things—a gesture, a grimace, a frown here, an unaware expression there . . ." He broke off to slump again in a chair, his face once more dull with despair. "He didn't take you by force, did he? You gave yourself willingly because you loved him, still love him."

It was the end of his innocence, an innocence *she* had snatched away from him. "I do not love him, Freddie, have never loved him, never, I swear to you." Frantic to salvage at least some of his broken illusions, she showered him with scraps of solace. "And I do *care* for you, deeply and sincerely. Oh, if only I could cut open my heart and prove to you how bitterly I regret that one transgression . . . !" Choked and ashamed, she could not go on.

For a moment Freddie stared down at her upturned face and into her stricken eyes filled with tears of supplication. Then, taking both her hands, he raised her and kissed her lightly on a cheek. "In many ways, Olivia, I am a fool, I admit it. But, my dear, the heart has an intelligence of its own. With the very best will in the world, I do not believe you." Smiling strangely, he turned to go. "I do not believe you."

After that day Freddie never returned home sober. Nor did he ever go up again to see Amos.

Sublimely unaware of the eye of the storm into which he had been born, Amos flourished. Happily, the world and its sorrows were not yet upon him, his limited universe beginning and ending with his four hourly pleasures at his mother's breast. Full of energy and fierce of temper when crossed, Amos continued to grow bigger and more delightful with each passing day. His large grey eyes, alive with curiosity, were never still; when amused, his laughter rang out with lusty vigour to fill the cavernous Birkhurst mansion with good cheer. For Olivia, he was the focus of her existence, her very reason for it. He was flesh of her flesh, her life's blood, her everything.

"He gets his unusual colouring from my Irish grandmother," Olivia explained to Mary Ling. "She too had mother-of-pearl eyes and ebony hair—isn't that something?"

With time the glib lies became easier, except that Mary Ling was somewhat more gullible than the daily stream of callers who came bearing gifts and piercing, inquisitive glances. But this situation too Olivia resolved with the same resourcefulness (deviousness!) that was now second nature to her. Awake, Amos was not presented for inspection under the excuse of tetchiness or stomach disorder; when asleep, he was shown off from a safe distance, his hair secured under a close-fitting bonnet. If a tendril or two did manage to escape, the Irish grandmother never failed to come in handy. On the whole the charade came off well enough. It was only when Dr. Humphries made his unavoidable professional call that Olivia panicked and did something that later disgusted her. She drugged Amos with a tiny lick of opium. "Hmmm! Healthy little blighter, isn't he?" was the doctor's sole comment as he threw a few perfunctory glances at the bonneted child, apparently satisfied. Olivia prayed fervently that Amos would never need Dr. Humphries in an unguarded emergency.

She despised herself for her shoddy little subterfuges, appalled at the moral weakness that forced her to indulge in them.

But then, with poor Freddie's reputation hanging by a thread anyway, she knew that she dared not experiment with whatever radical ideas she might have once had. And now with Arvind Singh's unexpected warning striking further terror in her heart, bravado was out of the question.

Olivia's most frequent and most welcome visitor was, of course, Arthur Ransome, delighted when asked to be Amos's godfather. "Bless my soul!" he exclaimed the first time he saw the child. "Never thought he would be quite so small!"

"Babies usually are, Uncle Arthur." Retrieving Amos with a laugh, she was vastly relieved that he, who had known Raventhorne so well, had noticed nothing. The suspense, however, with which she had awaited her uncle's comments as he had peered and poked at her sleeping son (once more dosed with opium and securely bonneted despite Olivia's revulsion of the ploy) had been acute. Notwithstanding his air of vagueness, there were times when Sir Joshua's perceptions seemed alarmingly lucid. But his interest in Amos was mercifully minimal and his observation offhand. "Very fine, very fine. Bridget will be delighted," was all he said.

It was from Ransome that Olivia heard of Freddie's renewed acquaintanceship with the Golden Hind. The news was distressing but hardly a surprise; Freddie's daily drunkenness, his ghastly pallor and his long absences from home each day were testimony enough. Genuinely concerned, Olivia tackled him firmly one morning. "You promised me you wouldn't, Freddie, you gave me your *word* . . ."

He groaned and cradled his head. "It's too early, dash it, for—"

"It's not too early. It's almost noon. In any case, this is the only time I can see you during the day." She softened her tone. "Freddie, what are you trying to do to yourself—to us?"

"I am trying to forget something I need *not* to remember!" He emphasized each word as if speaking to a backward child.

Olivia stared, attempting to equate him with the man he once was and twisting with familiar angst. "You need only to accept, Freddie," she said, again miserable, "to trust, to believe me and *in* me."

He shrugged. "I cannot force myself to accept or trust or whatever, any more than you can force yourself to love." He held his head again and winced. "I told you it was too early for an argument! I think I'll go back to bed." He walked unsteadily out of the room.

Whatever her other considerations, Olivia's alarm was primarily for Freddie's health. It was already fragile and she had made a promise to his mother, a promise that she was being prevented from keeping. In her anxiety Olivia spoke to Peter Barstow. It was a mistake.

"Stop old Fred hitting the juice?" he drawled, even more bored and supercilious than before. "My dear Olivia, that's the duty of a loving wife! Now, if he were getting at home what he gets in abundance at the Behind, he wouldn't have the *need* to drink, would he?" His thin smile was insultingly suggestive.

She wanted to slap his grinning mouth but, with surprising control, desisted. "Get out!" she snapped instead, cold with disgust. "I think you must be the most despicable man I have ever known."

"Despicable but honest, you'll grant me that at least." He again wore that shrewd, speculative look Olivia knew and hated. "You're too intelligent to have married Freddie for love, Olivia, too independent to have married for money, and not snobbish enough to have married for a title." He cocked his head to a side and smiled. "So, why *did* you marry Freddie? You know, I've been wondering about that a good deal . . ."

Her heart gave a lurch of alarm; she could no longer dismiss these barbed innuendoes with the contempt they deserved. Not after Arvind Singh's warning. If Peter Barstow had been wondering, perhaps so had others. *Would Raventhorne . . . ?*

"Yes, yes," Sir Joshua muttered testily, "of course you must have the christening here. Bridget will be livid if you don't."

It was in answer to a question Olivia had asked several days ago. "Thank you, Uncle Josh. I . . . we've asked Uncle Arthur to be Amos's godfather."

"That's all he's good for now, since he won't get off his butt and go to Canton!" He scowled, lost again in the mists of his mind. "It is this fellow Birkhurst you said you were marrying, isn't it?"

"Yes, Uncle Josh."

"And it's his mother who grazes like a cow in pasture, I believe?"

She had to smile. "Yes, Uncle Josh."

"And Birkhurst himself tends to pass out in strange gardens?"

"Sometimes, Uncle Josh."

He looked very grave. "Olivia, are you *sure* you know what you are doing?"

"No, Uncle Josh," she said sadly, "I'm not sure that I do."

"Well, if I've told Bridget once, I've told her a dozen times—little Estelle goes to boarding-school over my dead body. And if that imbecile woman with bad teeth and dandruff isn't the nanny Est—" Waggling a stern finger in the air, he shuffled off muttering to himself.

Following with her eyes the bent, carpet-slippered body of this caricature of a man as he floated away in his lonely bubble, Olivia filled with rage. Estelle had been gone almost a year—and still not a word from her to the doting father she had turned into a travesty! Ensconced in that luxurious London residence with her indulgent paramour, was she too besotted to spare even a thought for her aging, ailing parent? Corroding with wrath—a wrath she seldom gave free rein to now—Olivia strode into the pantry to arrange a light luncheon for her poor uncle—a quarter boiled egg, some buttered toast and Babulal's much favoured jam roly-poly. Seething within, she laid out a neat tray while giving brisk orders to the ever-attentive Rehman. The modest meal ready, she picked up the tray and went into the dining-room to collect the cruet stand from the table.

A fine layer of dust covered all the surfaces in this elegant room that had once seen so many splendid *burra khanas,* so much gaiety. There were cobwebs in every corner, the majestic chandelier no longer glittered and the large oil paintings on the walls hung awry under coatings of dull grime. Leaving the tray on the table, Olivia picked up a feather duster as a natural reflex and brushed off a pile of stray fluff from the cushion of a chair. Then, balancing on a stool, she straightened all the pictures on the walls. In the alcove, away from the other paintings, hung the portrait of the haughty and perpetually disapproving Lady Stella Templewood. It looked even more woebegone than the rest. In deference to her uncle's sentiments, Olivia picked up a dusting cloth and carefully wiped the surface of the painting, which had obviously not been cleaned in years. Standing on the stool, for the first time Olivia found herself at eye level with the imperious face of Sir Joshua's mother. She frowned and observed the face closely. Her hand stilled; for a long moment she remained entirely motionless, staring.

Then, one by one, a million goose pimples started to erupt over her body; her skin chilled. The blood in her face drained, leaving it deathly. Within her grew a vast silence; her heart faltered, then leapt, then stopped altogether. In a daze she somehow stumbled down from her perch, unaware that she had done so. In order not to faint, she clutched the back of a chair, too stunned to think of sitting down. She did not notice when Rehman retrieved the tray and carried it out of the dining-room into Sir Joshua's study. She forgot that she had promised to sit with him while he ate. She forgot everything.

Except for that portrait. And the shock of what the dead had just revealed to her.

But when Olivia reached home, even that shock was wiped clear from her mind; Willie Donaldson awaited with grave news. A messenger had disembarked from an English vessel not an hour ago with word that Lord Birkhurst had passed away at his home in Suffolk. Freddie had been summoned home by his mother with the utmost urgency to take charge of his estate and its administration. The news, vital in all its implications, was already three months old.

An escape!

Keeping her sudden hope securely anchored behind a solemn front in view of Donaldson's grief at having lost a friend, mentor and employer, Olivia set about doing what Donaldson had tearfully requested, help him in locating Freddie. Unaware of his father's death, Freddie had not been found in any of his usual haunts or with any of his regular cronies. Quickly Olivia scribbled an address on a slip of paper; it was of her husband's most recent doxy on Armenian Street. Apart from a dark flush, Donaldson showed no reaction as he hurried away to do what was needed. Half an hour later he returned bearing Freddie in his carriage with all the blinds discreetly lowered. Snoring blissfully in his intoxicated stupor, Freddie was not to know until the following morning that three months ago he had become Baron Birkhurst of Farrowsham, eighth holder of the title, and one of the wealthiest men in Britain.

The passing away of his father, for whom he had little love, left Freddie unimpressed. Over breakfast the next morning, his eyes blinked rapidly in an effort to focus on the voluminous mail packet the messenger had brought from his mother. Olivia's own letter from her mother-in-law had been warm, her concern evident in her oft-repeated hope that Olivia's child had been born safely. She looked forward, she wrote, to receiving them both at Farrowsham with Freddie.

"Yes," Freddie muttered, trying to suppress a yawn, "I'd better leave right away. Has Willie reserved passage aboard a vessel sailing soon?" If anything, the prospect of a return to England cheered him considerably.

I'd better leave . . . ? "I believe he has. The *Queen of Norway* sails on the afternoon tide the day after tomorrow." Heavy with anticipation, Olivia's heart skipped several beats but she made no other comment.

"Good." He got up, yawned again and went in to bathe.

So much now needed to be done, as Olivia set about preparing Freddie's trunks for his long journey home, that there was little time to brood. Even so, her thoughts and conjectures raced. Would Freddie want to take her with him? Should she go if he did? Yes, oh God, *yes!* She had the second part of her bargain to fulfil; it might not be legally binding but as a moral obligation it was as shackling as an iron chain. Also, once in England only one ocean would separate her from America.

For the first time in months, Freddie was forced to attend to his office. Matters concerning the plantation had to be given formal approval, legal papers had to be signed, dispatches had to be prepared to carry to London. To see to more mundane matters, Olivia remained at home, and read for the umpteenth time the letter from her mother-in-law. Nowhere did Lady Birkhurst remind her of her promise, but it was in the final sentences that her inviolate faith in Olivia's honesty lay concealed. "I look forward immensely to your arrival (and that of your child) at Farrowsham. You will be good for me in my grief, good for Farrowsham and, most of all, good for my son. It is my hope, nay *conviction,* that you will never disappoint me."

On the eve of his departure, Freddie returned home early from the office. For the first time in weeks they sat down to dinner together, and for the first time in weeks he was stone cold sober. Between them as they ate hung a pall of tensions that could not be pierced by meaningless conversational shafts. Like a caterpillar, Freddie had woven a cocoon around himself; he had excluded her from himself and it pained Olivia deeply. How much Freddie had changed! That the change had not been for the better, Olivia realised sadly, was a consequence of her wretched circumstances, not his. Like her, Freddie also was a victim, a bystander caught in the cross-fire of somebody else's war.

"I will not be returning to India." The meal was over, the

staff dismissed for the night. Both of them knew that whatever needed to be said could no longer be postponed, for there was no more time.

"Yes." Composed outwardly, Olivia sat with her hands clasped in her lap.

"Will you join me in England later?"

Her heart leapt but she remained cautious. "Would you want me to?"

"Yes, I would want you to. You know that I love you. As my wife, your place will always be at my side."

To leave India, never again to face or fear Jai Raventhorne, to someday secure Amos even more completely in Hawaii . . . ! "My promise to leave you whenever you wish still holds good, Freddie." She restrained soaring optimism to stay practical.

"Whenever *I* wish? How neatly you throw the ball back into my court, my love!" He smiled but he looked tired and ill and, as he spoke, did not meet her eyes. Instinctively Olivia knew that there was more to come, much more. Even before he said it, her heart had already heard what it was. "If you join me in England, Olivia, then it must be . . . alone." He stood up and walked away from her.

"Alone?" she echoed, not surprised and yet stunned.

He could not turn around to face her. "I know who your son reminds me of." Well, it had come, as she had always known it would one day. In some odd little way, it was to her a relief. Freddie whirled around, his face a mask of horror. "How could you, Olivia, how could you! My God, the man's not even *white!* The child you asked me to give my name to, the child you expect me to rear as my own, is *one quarter native . . . !*" Suffocating on his own passion, he started to splutter.

Within Olivia something more withered and died. There was no longer any point in denials. Engulfed in her dull despair, she did not even feel pain anymore. "I cannot abandon my child, Freddie. You know that whatever he is, he is mine. You might not be his father but I am his mother. What you ask of me is impossible."

"Don't I know that I am not his father!" he spat out, now furious. "Raventhorne is. *Raventhorne*—a half-caste gutter-snipe bastard! Holy mother of God—could you find no other man to open your legs to in this entire cursed city? Was there no pure-bred Englishman left in Calcutta on whom to bestow your generous favours?" Gripping her shoulders he shook her with a savagery of which she could never have thought him capable.

"Why, you rotten *slut . . . !*" Demented, he scarcely knew what he was doing as he pushed her away so that she fell back onto the couch.

Wearily, she lay back and made no effort to rise again. "For me Jai Raventhorne is dead, Freddie," she intoned mechanically out of habit. "And if he is not, then I pray that he soon will be. He no longer means anything to me."

But crushed by his own misery, Freddie was beyond listening. With an anguished cry he collapsed into a chair and noisy, dry sobs racked his body. "Raventhorne possesses the only thing that I have ever wanted in my life. *Christ,* it's evil, malignant!" He was inconsolable. "I am not the man I thought I was, Olivia. I beg you to release me from my promise. I am not equipped to fulfil it. I do not have the moral strength, or the capacity to forget. Forgive me, Olivia, forgive me . . ."

From a distance, separated from him by a space too vast to negotiate, Olivia watched his world crumble. They had all changed, or been changed, reduced to their basic components like Humpty-Dumpty, impossible to put together again. She rose to sit on the arm of his chair and stroke his neck, gently but with deadened impersonality, as if he were only an acquaintance. "I release you, Freddie dear, of course I do. You were good to me when I needed goodness most, I can never forget that. Whatever happens, I will never think less of you. It is my strength that lacks, not yours—my equipment that is inadequate. You see, my dear," she said bitterly, "not one of us is the person we thought, not one."

He did not hear a word. Instead, he turned and grabbed both her hands. "I'll find a good home for the boy, Olivia, decent foster parents. I promise he will be well looked after, that he will lack nothing. You will be free to return here to visit him whenever you wish, for as long as you wish. I swear it, Olivia, you have my word!"

Sorrowfully she shook her head. "I cannot do that, Freddie. Without Amos I would die. He is my life, my reason for living. You are asking me to cut out my heart and survive without it." Gritting her teeth, she made one final appeal, thinking only of the vow to which she was shackled. "If you let me take Amos with me, I promise he will never intrude in your life. You will not even be aware that he *exists . . .*"

"He exists in my mind, *here.*" He tapped his forehead, laid his head back and closed his eyes. "Excise him from my mind, erase my memory, drug forever my consciousness, and I will agree." The grim silence between them filled suddenly with his laugh, a macabre rattle. "A bastard of a bastard, a touch of the tar-brush, and heir apparent to the barony of Farrowsham—Lord, what a joke!"

"Amos will never be your heir! If you take us to England, I will give you a son of your own, I swear it!" Recklessly, she lowered herself even further, seeking escape, any escape.

He shook his head. "Each time we lie together it will be with *his* bastard in between, a reminder that someone has already poached my preserve, or is it the other way around?" His disillusion was heart-breaking. "It is more than my weak flesh can bear, dear heart. Don't ask me to perpetuate the agony. I cannot."

"It is my duty to provide you with an heir." Dull with failure, she spoke without emotion. "You cannot marry again."

"I would not wish to marry again. For me there can never be any woman but you, Olivia."

Despite her numbness, her eyes filled. "Bury the past, Freddie," she implored one last time. "Raventhorne means nothing to me, even *less!*"

"Then give up his son."

He waited for an answer. A seeming eternity passed without it coming. But then, they both knew that it never would, for it had already been delivered. Freddie rose, went to the door and opened it.

"I have instructed Willie to provide you with anything, everything, that you might need by way of funds. As for the Agency, the plantation and the other Indian assets, you may utilise them with total freedom as you wish. Should you leave Calcutta, my instructions remain. I am making lifelong provision for you wherever you might choose to live. As for your son," a cloud flitted over his face, "he will, of course, remain my financial responsibility throughout his life. That obligation, at least, I am man enough to honour."

"I want nothing from you, Freddie, not a penny!"

He did not even hear her. "I would have taken anyone else's child, Olivia, anyone but a miscegene. I would like to make that clear." His shoulders sagged again. "If ever you can find it in your heart to do so, forgive me." He closed the door very softly behind him.

It was the end of their life together. Such as it had been.

The next morning, early, Willie Donaldson arrived to collect Freddie's baggage, all neatly packed and labelled, standing in readiness in the hallway. Freddie himself was not at home, having gone out again last night without returning. At noon, Donaldson came back to report that His Lordship had been found once more on Armenian Street and had had to be carried aboard the *Queen of Norway,* which was now away down the river towards the estuary. Unknown to Freddie, Olivia had slipped a letter inside his portmanteau for his mother. *Dear Lady Birkhurst,* she had written formally,

> It is with regret I inform you that my debt of honour to your family is destined to remain unrepaid. I have also failed to bring your son the salvation that you had so generously expected, and I so unthinkingly promised . . .

It was not until much later that Olivia recalled another little irony. Now, it was *she* who was Lady Birkhurst.

16

There was now nothing more to keep her in India.

Thrusting aside her failures, Olivia resolutely vowed to look only ahead. She had tried—God, how she had tried!—but no one could fight so perverse a configuration of their stars and win. Her fate, Freddie's fate and their combined limitations had all conspired against them. But until now her life in India had been like that banyan tree forest with serpentine tendrils transfixing her to the ground. Suddenly and miraculously, she was free, at liberty to choose her own destiny. She could return home whenever she pleased! Dazed by this unsolicited and undreamed-of freedom, she was buoyant and light-hearted again, done once and for all with regrets and remorse and guilt. All at once she saw Freddie's departure in an entirely new light and with such relief that she could not help feeling almost ashamed. Ruthlessly she brushed away the past; not even the shock of what she had learned at her uncle's house that day disturbed her anymore. She no longer cared. It was not her secret to worry over unduly; let those whose it was be concerned!

Letting only the bare minimum of a decent interval elapse, Olivia requested Willie Donaldson to make arrangements for her passage to Hawaii.

In the meantime news of Freddie's precipitous departure and the reason for it brought the inevitable torrent of callers. Amusingly enough, the gentlemen all came with sincere condolences, but the ladies, green eyed with envy, concealed their chagrin beneath crocodile tears.

"What a tragic loss, my dear Olivia!" Mrs. Smithers, once with high ambitions for her Charlotte as the future Lady Birkhurst, could barely control her vexation. "But then, we must look on the bright side, mustn't we? *Some*body has to die before a title can be passed down, mustn't they?"

"Oh quite!" Mrs. Cleghorne, with similar aspirations for her Marie, agreed heartily as she dabbed her eyes. "And how fortunate to be able to enjoy a title while still so young! My sister-in-law was fifty before *her* father-in-law even sneezed and fifty-*seven* when he actually died. My dear, they almost landed in the poor-house by the time he deigned to breathe his last."

"Well, there never was any danger of the poor-house for dear, dear Olivia, was there?" Millie Humphries privately compared her present opulent surroundings with her own rather shabby medical officer's bungalow, and burned with jealousy.

"The poor-house for Olivia?" the Spin exclaimed with a malicious smile. "Why should the dear girl have crossed the ocean at all if that was the fate she envisaged for herself? What a hoot!"

Smiling graciously as she dispensed the endless tea and cakes and sandwiches, Olivia remained the perfect hostess, wondering if they realized just how little she was touched by their chatter.

"Dinna listen to these cats, lassie. They na ken nothing but to mock and mewl." When everybody was gone, Cornelia Donaldson squeezed her hand in sympathy.

Olivia shrugged them all off with a laugh. "Oh, they don't worry me, the poor dears. Since Freddie expects us to join him in England by next year, I shall be gone soon anyway."

Cornelia Donaldson looked genuinely saddened. "My Willie will miss you, lassie. He might na say it, the sore-headed bear, but he'll miss you soondly aroond the office."

Olivia was moved. "Oh, but some day of course we'll be back," she lied. "In the meantime, you both will come to the christening, won't you? Freddie had wanted a grand affair at St. John's, but now, under the circumstances . . ." She left the rest unsaid with a gesture of helplessness.

"Oh aye, lass, to be sure," Mrs. Donaldson agreed solemnly. "A grand affair would na be fitting noo, would it?"

It was the last of the lies she would have to tell, Olivia thought in relief. Once the shores of India were behind her, so would also be the need for demeaning deceptions.

It was after the simple christening was over that Arthur Ransome handed Olivia a mail packet, which had arrived for Sir Joshua that morning. It was from London, and it was from Estelle!

Drugged into deep slumber (for the last time, Olivia vowed ferociously) and with his hair shorn down to the skull as the only measure that would ensure safety under the circumstances, her son had been officially named Amos James Sean Birkhurst, the ninth heir apparent to the barony of Farrowsham. There had been only six witnesses present at the Templewood home: Sir Joshua, Arthur Ransome, the Donaldsons, Mary Ling and Olivia herself. The same cherubic chaplain from St. John's who had officiated at the wedding had performed the honours. Tea was served to the guests after the ceremony, sweets and cash were distributed to the staff at both houses and then it had all been over, easily and painlessly.

Now, at the sight of her cousin's familiar but forgotten flowery handwriting on the large brown envelope, Olivia went rigid. It was as if, magically, the clock had whirled back a year and in the process whipped away every anaesthetic benefit time had given. The envelope, she noticed, had been opened by Ransome. "I considered it wise to vet the contents," he explained in a fluster, "in case the silly girl had more shocks planned for her father."

"And has she?" Olivia pulled herself together and returned the envelope to him without making any move to read the contents. For all her assumed offhandedness, she could not help a shudder of revulsion in the light of what she now knew.

"Yes. In a manner of speaking. But, for a change, the shocks are not unpleasant." He withdrew a sheet from the envelope and scanned it again. "Estelle is in England. Apparently, she has been there now for six months. Three months ago, just before this was dispatched, she was married to John Sturges." He could hardly keep the astonishment from his face. "John has since been posted to Cawnpore. They should both be arriving in Calcutta forthwith." Succumbing to his incredulity, he sat down quickly and swallowed some tablets from a bottle that had lately become an inseparable companion. His expression was one of perplexity; he kept staring at the letter as if to convince himself that his eyes did not deceive him. "She mentions nothing about . . . the rest, not a word. Perhaps she gives more information to you, Olivia." He withdrew a square, sealed envelope from within the packet and handed it to her.

"Yes, perhaps." Olivia thrust Estelle's letter into her purse without reading it. Later, she intended to burn the envelope unopened.

There was no letter from Lady Bridget, and one from her Cousin Maude to Sir Joshua gave only expected news. Ransome read it with care in case there was in it something that might agitate his friend further. "Maude writes that Bridget's religious zeal continues," he said for Olivia's benefit. "She spends hours with her Bible and her rosary, Maude says, and appears to think or talk of little else but sin and absolution. But, Maude feels, Bridget has yet to find peace." Fingering his chin, Ransome saddened. "Maude makes no mention of Estelle except to say that she has seen her. I fear that it is not all sunshine and light, as Estelle would have us, particularly her father, believe." He scanned Olivia's ungiving face, then asked with a trace of anxiety, "Would you ever be able to make your wayward cousin welcome, my dear?"

"Why ever should I not?" Olivia countered. "Whether or not she has been forgiven by her mother and father, who am I to sustain grudges? I have no axes to grind, remember? As a matter of fact, on reflection, Estelle's return will be a boon. I will shortly be gone and she can start discharging some of those filial duties that have been neglected for so long. *And* damn well start clearing up some of those sorry messes that she left behind."

Not for the first time Ransome sensed Olivia's bitterness—that steady, all-pervasive anger that seemed to lie so close under the skin and seep through once in a while like a festering sore. Goodness knows, she had just cause for resentment; had it not been for the girl's quick thinking and determined labour, the scandal would have blown their world even higher. That he understood well, yet there was much that baffled him about her. But, silent in his discretion, he did not question her.

Olivia knew that her glib assurance to Ransome was false; under no possible circumstances could she ever make Estelle welcome again. For more than one reason, her cousin's return filled her with dread.

"An earlier sailing, Your Ladyship?" The next morning Willie Donaldson received her request with astonishment. "Any special reason for the sudden change of plan?"

"No. It's just that the sooner we are away, the sooner we join His Lordship in London."

That Donaldson appreciated and understood. "Och, aye. I reckon'd that. Well, I'll make inquiries but I doot if an earlier sailing can be arranged." He shook his craggy head. "I hear Miss

Templewood returns shortly from England as Mrs. John Sturges. Och, that should gladden Your Ladyship's heart for shure!"

It did not surprise Olivia in the least that the news had spread so fast. Knowing Estelle's expertise in disseminating information, she had no doubt her cousin had already written to all and sundry. She marvelled anew at her brazenness, not in what she had probably written but in what she positively had not! "Yes, it surely does," she replied with a grim nod. "And now, tell me Mr. Donaldson, have you made any progress with this American who is considering leasing my house?"

Donaldson's face fell. "Och aye," he said glumly. "His agent here tells me the man's keen on the place and a five-year lease would suit him well." He struggled for a moment, then added warmly, "But is it wise to give up the manse to this unknown cotton farmer, probably a bloody uncouth boor who canna tell glass from crystal? Na disrespect to your country, lass." In his distress he dropped his formalities. "After all, the valuables in the house will belong to the bairn some day and he may wish to make his life in India."

The prospect of drastic changes in a household that he had served so diligently for decades was causing Willie Donaldson untold grief, Olivia realised. For a moment she did not know how to respond, saddened that even this blameless man should not be left unhurt one way or another. "Nothing of value will remain unlocked in our absence, Mr. Donaldson," she soothed him gently. "I am storing everything in the strong-rooms, for which you will retain the keys until such time as our . . . future plans can be formulated." She was lulling this good man with false hopes; neither she nor Freddie nor Amos—especially not Amos!—would ever return to India to live in that mansion again. "In the meanwhile, please finalise the details of the lease with this man's agent."

They went on to discuss other matters needing attention before her departure. She would have to leave on the *Lulubelle* if an earlier sailing was unavailable. (Oh, how she prayed that it would not be!) Freddie's generosity to her was lavish, as was evident in all the copious arrangements he had made for her continued support. Olivia had no intention of accepting any part of the Birkhurst bounty, but she made no mention of that to Donaldson. He would not understand and there was no point in upsetting him further. It was as she was leaving the office that he suddenly broached quite another subject after much hemming and hawing.

"I gather from, ah, bazaar talk that Your Ladyship has been, ah, advancing funds to Templewood and Ransome?"

"Yes, that is correct." She continued to fill her portmanteau with papers that she was taking home for perusal.

"I also learned something I canna believe, I just canna: To raise the loan Your Ladyship pawned a diamond bracelet with that stenchified bloody crook Mooljee?" His sallow cheeks showed two high spots of bright red.

"You can believe it, Mr. Donaldson," she replied, unperturbed. "It is quite true. He gave me the best terms. My funds from Lloyd's of London have not yet arrived; when they do, I will retrieve my bracelet."

He was aghast at the easy admission. "But to pawn Birkhurst jewels—it's the talk of the bloody town! If Lady Birkhurst heard, she'd be scandalised, bloody *scandalised!* In all my years with Farrow . . . why you dinna ask *me* for . . . ," he spluttered into shocked silence.

She showed no sign of remorse. "First of all, Mr. Donaldson, it isn't Birkhurst jewellery; it is mine from my mother's portion. Talk of the town or not, I can do with it what I wish. Secondly, you know that I will not touch Farrowsham's funds to help my uncle's firm. And thirdly," she pointed out not unkindly, "are you forgetting that now *I* am Lady Birkhurst?"

That night Olivia sat down to write a letter to Kinjal.

> Estelle will be back shortly! Her return terrifies me for reasons I can tell you and only you—she will want to see Amos and she cannot, she *must not!* Therefore, once again I turn to you for help, my dearest, truest friend. I beg you to take care of my son for as long as my cousin chooses to remain in Calcutta—or until I sail, whichever is expedient. I will send Amos to you as soon as I receive your answer.

But even before receiving Kinjal's answer, Olivia knew what it would be. With no questions asked, no explanations demanded, no conditions stipulated, Kinjal wrote only one sentence. *Send Amos whenever you wish.*

There were no sailings to the Pacific prior to that of the *Lulubelle,* and three days after Amos had been fortuitously dispatched to Kirtinagar with Mary Ling and the ayah, Estelle returned to Calcutta.

Already desolate at being without her son, Olivia received the news in abject depression. The ship had docked in the early morning. By afternoon, while she was at the Agency, Olivia had received a note from her cousin asking, imploring, her to come immediately. "I am dying, just *dying,* to see you again, my beloved Coz. Fly here the instant you see this." Olivia's anger revived; she did not grace the note with a written answer. Instead she merely asked the Templewood coachman who had brought the letter to inform missy memsahib that she would come as soon as her day's work at the Agency was done.

Of course there was no way that a meeting with Estelle could be avoided altogether, but by the time Olivia forced herself to face the prospect, it was well into the evening. She had used the intervening hours well. Ironing out all the sharp-edged creases in her emotions, she had come to a pragmatic conclusion. She had survived the past agonising months somehow; she would also survive Estelle's return.

The moment the carriage rumbled up to the Templewood porch, Estelle came flying down the portico steps. Throwing herself into Olivia's arms, she exploded with noisy tears. "Oh, Olivia, my darling, darling Coz . . . *how* I have missed you!"

Olivia detached herself from the suffocating embrace. "Have you? Well, welcome home, Estelle. And my congratulations. Where is your John?" She felt proud of the ease with which she could actually smile.

"In Madras with his parents," Estelle gulped, still tearful. "They disembarked en route to see an ailing relative . . . oh, Olivia, there were times I thought I would *die* without you to talk to . . ."

"But you obviously didn't." Olivia removed Estelle's restraining hand from her arm. "Where is Uncle Josh?"

"In the back garden with Uncle Arthur." Saucer eyes swimming, Estelle again grabbed Olivia's hand. "How *awful* Papa looks! I couldn't believe it, he's lost *pounds* and *pounds* . . ."

"Weight isn't all that he's lost, Estelle." Olivia surveyed her coldly. "Come on. Let's go and join them in the garden." Without giving her cousin another chance to protest, she walked away.

Sir Joshua and Ransome sat on either side of a wrought iron table sipping iced beer and gazing silently in opposite directions.

As Olivia and Estelle joined them, they rose. Ransome muttered some monosyllabic inaudibilities in greeting and Sir Joshua nodded as Olivia kissed him on a cheek. She seated herself next to Estelle and wondered what might be considered appropriate topics of conversation at a family reunion as unwanted and as bizarre as this! Had any dialogue already taken place between father and daughter? Certainly there was no way of telling from her uncle's facial blankness, the vacancy of his eyes and the customary slouch of his shoulders. As usual, he sat immersed in silence, making no contribution to the conversation. Sombre faced and shifty eyed, Ransome merely fidgeted with a key chain, saying little and looking extremely ill at ease.

As it happened, nobody's conversational expertise was unduly needed to fill what might have been hideously gaping silences. Estelle took the lead in keeping the small talk flowing smoothly. "You could have knocked me over with a feather, darling, when I heard you had actually *agreed* to marry Freddie!" She laughed a shade too loudly. "But then, I always did maintain that you would, you know, Coz—truly I did. And my, my—Lady Birkhurst *already!* Oh, it's all turned out so . . . so *perfect,* hasn't it?" She clasped her hands and beamed.

"Yes. Perfect." Olivia said.

"And oh, Olivia . . . *why* did you not bring Amos with you? Could we fetch him now, this very instant? I don't think I could *bear* to wait until tomorrow." She pouted appealingly. Despite the coat of cosmetics, she looked again like a little girl, but now not innocent—merely indecent.

"Amos is away. He is with friends."

"Away?" Estelle's face fell. "But you *knew* I was returning; could you not have kept him back at least awhile?"

"I'm sorry, the arrangements were made before we learned about your return," Olivia lied with practiced ease. "But I will try to bring him back before you leave for Cawnpore. How long do you propose to stay?"

"John has to report for his new duties in a month. He refuses to consider staying longer." She gave a very wifely sigh. "Oh, *husbands!*"

A month! She would have to be without Amos for a whole month! Olivia filled with dismay. Somehow, she forced herself not to react and asked instead, "And how is Aunt Bridget? Well, I hope? You bring no letters from her?"

For the first time ripples appeared in Estelle's smooth façade. Her eyes dropped, as did her smile, and she looked fractionally uncertain. Then, she nodded. "Yes, Mama is well." She said no more.

During the banal exchange, neither Sir Joshua nor Arthur Ransome had offered any comments. But now, all of a sudden, Sir Joshua chose to speak. "So you see, Arthur, how the divinities mock the hand that stayed?" He threw back his head and roared with laughter. There was in his non sequitur and his merriment something grotesque, and jarring; embarrassed, they all stared. Still chuckling, he got up and wove his way back into the house. Ransome's eyes followed him until his ungainly form in its ill-fitting clothes disappeared from view; there was compassion and misery in those eyes.

"What an odd thing to say!" Estelle exclaimed with an unsure laugh. "Whatever could Papa be thinking of?" Without waiting for anyone to vouchsafe an answer, she plunged into a voluble account of her explorations in London, garnished lavishly with characteristic emphases and superlatives.

A creeping sense of unreality started to disorient Olivia. She had the odd feeling that they were all on a stage mouthing fictional dialogue in a mystery thriller; the surprise ending would suddenly burst upon them and it would bear no relation to what they were saying. Or, they were involved in a party guessing game in which there were too many red herrings to find the true answers. Listening to her cousin's inconsequential chatter, Olivia felt an overwhelming sense of déjà vu; the clock again moved back and she was once more perched on Estelle's bed munching ginger biscuits and sharing fantasies. It seemed incredible to her that they could all be sitting here, in the Templewood garden, pretending that nothing had changed, that their lives were still intact, that there had been no shattering diversions of their desired destinies. They were pretending that they were whole people again.

Almost whole, but not quite.

Estelle's exuberance was forced, a camouflage for twisting turbulences underneath. Her voice was too shrill, her laughter too affected, her gestures laden with artifice. Below the caked black kohl streaked with dried tears, her eyes shone with too bright a sparkle. The stylish fuchsia velvet gown with its daringly dipped neckline provided a veneer of chic, but the sophistication she tried so hard to project could not conceal the nervousness she was not yet clever enough to suppress. The truth was that Estelle was profoundly unhappy.

And so she damn well deserved to be! For Olivia it was impossible to evoke even a fragment of sympathy.

Dreaded as the prospect was, it was inevitable that at some point during the evening Olivia would find herself alone with her cousin. As soon as supper was over—a false, brittle affair dominated by Estelle's still pointless prattle—Olivia found herself finally cornered. "I know how angry you are with me, Olivia, but it is imperative that I talk to you."

"Talk? You've been doing nothing *but* talk, my dear!"

Pretences exhausted, Estelle ignored the taunt. "You cannot deny me the opportunity to make explanations."

"If explanations are due, they are to your father. You owe me none."

A sob caught in Estelle's throat. "I have tried to talk to Papa but he does not respond. He merely listens; he says nothing. I can't seem to reach him anymore." She looked bereft. *"Please,* Olivia, don't turn me away!"

Heaving a resigned sigh, Olivia shrugged. None of it mattered now, after all. If Estelle could not reach her father, neither would she be able to ever reach *her* again! Grudgingly, she followed Estelle up the stairs. In spite of her aunt's offhand instructions, Olivia had chosen to leave Estelle's room as it was, thus depriving some deserving charity of no doubt much useful bounty. As a consequence, the sense of déjà vu was again overwhelming. All of her cousin's gewgaws were exactly as they had always been, but, grimly, Olivia hardened herself against the onslaught of nostalgia. No matter how manipulative or crafty her cousin's devices this time, she would not allow herself to be fooled again. To each his own mess; whatever Estelle's might have been, she was not about to make it her own.

Estelle flung herself onto the bed, and her unhappiness erupted. "I cannot *bear* what has happened to Papa! Oh God, how he must have suffered!"

Olivia avoided the enforced intimacy of the bed and positioned herself in a chair by the window. "And that surprises you?"

Estelle lay back and stared at the ceiling. "No, it does not surprise me. Not now, not anymore," she said dully. "A year ago it would have. I knew he would be livid, mad with frustrated fury and bitterly disappointed in me. I thought he would cut me off with the proverbial farthing, command that I never darken his door again, rant and rave and do all the things outraged fathers do in those dreadful novels. And Mama," she threw her hands up in the air, "would swoon and rush for her smelling-salts and moan interminably about the scandal and what all her friends would say behind her back." She sat up and her eyes widened with horror. "I never *dreamed* that they would just . . . *disintegrate.* I swear I didn't, Olivia! How could I have, how *could* I have? I didn't know the truth, no one *told* me . . ." She broke off as if uncertain how much more to say, unsure of the extent of Olivia's knowledge. Staring out of the window, Olivia volunteered no comment. "Oh God, oh God . . . no, it has *not* turned out perfectly, has it?" She flung herself down on her pillow and started to flail it with angry fists. "It's all gone so wrong, so *wrong!* I meant it only as an escapade to . . . to teach them a *lesson . . . !*"

Escapade! Olivia went numb with fury. Did this spoilt, stupid *bitch* have any idea how much she was repulsed—yes, *repulsed!*—by her? "Oh, I'd say you taught them a lesson all right! I do not doubt they have profited greatly from your tutelage."

"Don't mock me, Olivia, I beg you! You are the only sane and true friend I can turn to now when it's all become such a confounded . . . *pickle.*" She turned her face to the wall and began to sob quietly. "I lied to you and Papa in my letter, Olivia—Mama refused to see me in Norfolk. Through Aunt Maude she said that for her I was dead. She th-threatened to throw herself into the Broads if Aunt Maude gave me shelter." The memory made her shudder. "If it hadn't been for John, I would have gone out of my mind. His parents don't know . . . everything, but John does. I kept nothing from him." She had the decency to at least lower her eyes. "We had a quiet wedding at his home in Liverpool. I forged a letter from Mama to his parents pleading an indisposition too severe to permit travel." Covering her face, she swayed back and forth moaning to herself. "Oh, Olivia, there is so much, so *much,* I did not know . . ."

But you do now, don't you, precious! Watching expressionlessly, Olivia remained silent.

"Only my John, my beloved John, has seen fit to forgive me. He . . . understands." Noting Olivia's arched eyebrow, she pushed her chin out in a familiar gesture of defiance. "Yes, he does, and I do love John! He does not find it unacceptable that I should also love Jai, no matter how misguided my running away with him."

Olivia started to freeze; this was the line beyond which she could never permit Estelle to venture, *never.* How dare the brazen hussy flaunt her misbegotten love in front of *her* face! "No! That is your business, not mine," she said sharply. "Keep it to yourself."

"But, Olivia, I've been waiting *months* to talk to you . . . !"

Estelle was dismayed. "I tried to write but I couldn't—it was all so complex, so damnably confused. You must listen to me, Olivia, you *must* . . . !"

"This might be a surprise to you, Estelle, but there is now absolutely nothing in my life I *must* do unless I wish to. I am no longer interested in your affairs." She walked to the door and opened it.

"You have a right to be angry with me," Estelle cried, leaping off the bed and running to cling to Olivia, "my God, I do know that! Uncle Arthur told me of the burden you carried alone, of your resourcefulness, of your nobi—"

"I only did what needed to be done," Olivia said, each syllable icy. "Now, please let me go."

"But I want to know everything that happened *here!*" Estelle tightened her grip. "Can't you see how much needs to be aired and repaired? I *cannot* do it without your support, my eminently sensible cousin."

"What happened is no longer relevant; it's what *will* happen—to your father, for instance—that matters. The responsibility of looking after him can no longer be that of Uncle Arthur, have you thought of that? And you do know that I leave soon for Hawaii?"

"Yes." Her underlip started to quiver again. "Of course I will look after Papa, who else is there? I will make him come to Cawnpore with us. But before that something else must be remedied. Jai has been wronged, Olivia. You were so correct in your—"

"I told you, I'm not interested in hearing about Jai Raventhorne!" Outraged, she wrenched her hand free. "I do not wish to hear either his name or his alleged persecutions or, indeed, how you propose to remedy whatever it is that you do wish to remedy. I no longer want to be *involved!*"

Estelle stared in surprise, then, slowly, her expression changed. "How droll, how very droll, considering it was *you* who objected most to his name being forbidden in our house! It was *you* who insisted he shouldn't be treated like a pariah, it was *you* who—"

"*Stop* it, Estelle!" Trying to leash her rage, Olivia crossed her arms against her chest but her eyes glittered. "Don't try to force any more issues. What you have already forced will do us for a lifetime."

With equal belligerence Estelle spun around to confront her enraged cousin. "Isn't it time somebody *did* force some more issues? I'm *sick* of talking in hushed whispers behind locked doors about issues that are being swept under the carpet, issues that are never held up to light, issues that are neither explained nor understood. What is everyone so frightened of—what are *you* so frightened of, Olivia? Gossip? Poison tongues and scandal? Well, the pox on all that, I say, the *pox!*" Breathing hard, she put her hands on her hips, and the corners of her mouth drooped in a sneer. "You are the person I admired most in the world, Olivia, because I thought you were fair and just and liberal and independent. Was that all a sham, then?"

"*Yes,* it was all a sham! I am not the person you thought I was, nor the person *I* thought I was. Satisfied? Now, please get out of my way and allow me to leave."

Estelle did not move. Instead, her lip curled further. "Isn't it strange, Olivia, that now *I* should be the one with courage? Well, I *do* love Jai Raventhorne, and I don't care who knows it. At one time you too had some empathy for him, some curiosity about him. You made a thousand excuses for him, gave him the benefit of so many doubts. And now, like the rest of them, you hang him without even a trial? Or could it be that," she turned skittishly sly, "what suddenly motivates you is *jealousy,* darling Coz! I seem to remember—"

Before she could complete her sentence, Olivia's palm had flattened to slap Estelle hard, so hard that she stumbled back and almost fell. In the hushed silence that followed, Estelle cowered against the wall, nursing a face distorted with horror. For a while neither of them spoke, their sense of shock mutual. Olivia recovered first. Sick at herself, she stepped forward to place a frigid little kiss on her cousin's forehead. "I'm sorry. I should not have done that." Her voice was low but she showed no other sign of repentance.

With a whimper, Estelle slunk past her to fold limply onto her bed. "You've changed, Olivia," she whispered. "You've changed so . . . dreadfully."

"Changed? Who, I?" Olivia started to laugh. "It's only your imagination, dear cousin. I haven't changed at all. I'm exactly the same as when you left on your little—what was it you called it? Oh yes, escapade. *Exactly* the same."

Still laughing, she turned and walked out of the room.

Inevitably, many aspects of Olivia's daily life altered with her cousin's return. For instance, her onerous duties in the Templewood house were considerably reduced. It was impossible to avoid Estelle entirely, but she became adept at visiting Sir Joshua when her cousin was out, as she frequently was. When they did have an encounter, Olivia made certain that it was brief and passably amiable. That she had lost her control so completely as to strike out at her cousin, Olivia regretted deeply—although by no means out of sympathy for Estelle; for daring to make her impertinent suggestion she deserved to be punished. What Olivia, in all her innate honesty, was beginning to wonder about were her own motivations, and her self-doubts were starting to turn troublesome.

Estelle did not mention Jai Raventhorne to her again.

The aspect of Estelle's return that Olivia resented most was that she was forced to be without her beloved son. She missed Amos desperately, yearned to hold and cuddle him again, to listen to his marvellously eloquent babblings, to bask in the dazzle of his smiles. She missed watching his day-to-day development that she had made a habit of observing so meticulously. Kinjal wrote that Amos had started an upper tooth, and Olivia was inconsolable; oh, to be forcibly denied such a momentous event! Amos was now sitting up with confidence, Kinjal informed her, and was surely attempting his first intelligible word, *Mama.* Over that, Olivia cried, longing to fly like a bird to Kirtinagar, where her child was learning to call out to her. The information Kinjal dispatched every second day by her personal courier was received joyously by Olivia, but with each delivery her bitterness against her prodigal cousin turned more and more unforgiving.

However, personal and private animosities apart, appearances still had to be maintained within the suffocating surrounds of the society that Lady Bridget and her peers held in such reverence, especially in Lady Bridget's absence. Not without considerable sourness Olivia recognised that it was only proper that she arrange some kind of social reception for Estelle and her husband. It was what Calcutta's society would expect, and not to fulfil the mandatory obligation would further encourage already busy tongues. However facile the explanations she had improvised for Estelle's abrupt departure from station, there had been plenty of whispered innuendo about it at the time. Arthur Ransome, Olivia was aware, had sternly warned Estelle against either elaborating on the alibis already propagated or inventing new ones. However, if whatever rumours that persisted were to be laid to rest once and for all, then Estelle and her husband had to be formally introduced into the station's society as a respectably and happily united man and wife.

When Olivia mentioned her proposal to Arthur Ransome, he was instantly approving and endorsed the idea heartily. Her added suggestion that, in the absence of Freddie, he could perhaps assume the duties of host he also accepted with alacrity although with many protestations of inadequacy and many modest blushes. If not for herself, Olivia was pleased for Ransome. There was so little in his life these days apart from endless bills and creditors and headaches that even one evening of light revelry would be worth-while. And, after all, this was the last service she would ever need to perform for her cousin Estelle.

"Would it not be proper to send the invitations out in the name of Uncle Josh?" Olivia asked in order to clarify a point of social rectitude.

"No." Ransome was firm in his disagreement. "Indeed, it might even be wise to keep Josh right out of the picture. Although," he stopped and pondered a minute with half closed eyes, "I strongly suspect that Josh *does* comprehend more than he would have us believe."

"Oh? What makes you think so?"

"I will show you in a moment. Did you say you had matters to discuss with Estelle? She's upstairs in her room. I will wait for you in your uncle's study."

Estelle was indeed up in her room writing letters. At Olivia's sudden appearance, her face lit up. It was the first time since their ugly confrontation that Olivia had been in the room. Pecking her cousin impersonally on the cheek, Olivia placed on the desk two cloth-wrapped packages. "When Aunt Bridget left she gave me this to keep for you," she said indicating one of the parcels. "I now ask you to take charge of it."

At the formality of Olivia's approach, Estelle's smile dropped. "What is it?"

"Your portion. And this," from the second package she withdrew a crimson velvet case, "is with our good wishes, Freddie's and mine, for a fulfilling married life. We hope John and you will share many joys."

Estelle opened the box eagerly. Inside, on a bed of white satin, rested an exquisite diamond necklace with earrings to match. *"Oh!"* For a moment she was speechless. About to give vent to her rapture with customary effusiveness, she hesitated and turned sedate. "This is so . . . so generous. I hardly know what to say. Thank you, thank you b-both." She swallowed hard and fell into an awkward silence.

Impassively, Olivia informed her cousin about the reception she planned as soon as John and his parents arrived from Madras. Estelle's egg-shell thin sedateness cracked; she was openly thrilled. "Oh, that would be *wonderful!* How very kind of you to even consider such a lavish gesture, Olivia."

"Good. I'm glad the idea appeals to you. I shall start to compose the invitations tomorrow morning."

"Do let me help, *do*—I would so love to!" Estelle begged.

"Oh, that won't be necessary." Olivia forced a pleasant smile. "I have plenty of experienced staff who can manage well." At the palpable disappointment in Estelle's face, Olivia relented. "What you could do," she amended quickly, "is to compile your own guest list. I will place no restrictions; you can invite whom you wish."

It was a small joke, a reminder of the clashes between mother and daughter at her coming-of-age ball, and Estelle laughed. Encouraged by her cousin's apparent softening, Estelle might have said something more had Olivia allowed her a chance, but she didn't. Using Arthur Ransome's wait for her in the study as an excuse, Olivia quickly left the room.

Sir Joshua had not yet returned from his daily evening walk along the embankment and Ransome was alone in the study. As Olivia went in, he hurried to the desk and, signalling her to shut the door behind her, he unlocked a bottom drawer. From it he extracted a large leather-bound diary. "Have a look at this quickly before Josh returns."

Olivia hesitated. "Oh, but should we . . . ?"

"Yes, we should! It is the reason why Josh refuses to go to England. And the reason why, more than any other, we must persuade him to go to Cawnpore with his daughter."

Intrigued by his tone of urgency, Olivia opened the diary. The top of each page was neatly dated, the last entry being that of yesterday. Like a child's exercise book with the same line repeated as a punishment, the diary was filled from cover to cover with a recurring sentence: *The time has come; the hand can no longer be stayed.*

Olivia looked puzzled. "What does it mean?"

"It means that when Jai returns Josh intends to kill him." He pulled open two adjoining drawers of the desk. They were packed tight with similar diaries. "All the entries are the same. You see?"

"No, I'm sorry, I don't."

Ransome shut the drawers and relocked them. "The initial entry in the first of these is dated a week after Estelle's elopement."

Despite his intenseness, Olivia could not resist an acid little smile. "And that surprises you? Uncle Josh would have helped him hang long ago had Raventhorne not pulled the rug first!"

Ransome gave her a strange look. "It is not as it seems, Olivia," he said quietly. "Josh needs to be protected."

With Estelle's entry into the room, the subject was not pursued, but Olivia was not alarmed, neither for her uncle nor for herself. What a lot of fuss about nothing! She trusted Ranjan Moitra's information. If and when Raventhorne did return, it would certainly not be before Sir Joshua had been borne to safety by his daughter, and she herself—with Amos!—had sailed away on the *Lulubelle.* Staunch friend that he was, Arthur Ransome worried unduly.

By the time Olivia had arrived home she had forgotten the matter—and another letter awaited from Kinjal. Her son was now reaching for objects with discrimination, his favourite being his silver rattle. His grip was firm and his determination to guard his precious possessions even more so. Kinjal's children were teaching him to sing, convinced that his tuneless responses were proof of potential musical genius. Over that Olivia cried again, then proceeded to compose a pleading reply to the letter.

> The day following the ball that has been arranged for my cousin and her husband, they depart finally for Cawnpore. Please, please send my darling boy home to me that very day, my dearest Kinjal, that *very* day! Each moment without him now is torture.

Light-hearted once more, Olivia coasted happily through her day at the Agency, humming as she worked. On the way home she called again at the Templewood home. Whether or not her uncle was fit enough, courtesy demanded that he be informed of the upcoming occasion. Estelle was out visiting and Ransome had not yet returned from his office. As always, she found her uncle in the study at his desk. As she entered, he gave a start and hastily concealed something beneath a square of blue velvet. "Don't you believe in knocking before you come in?" he grumbled as Olivia bent down to kiss him in greeting.

She smiled at his bad temper, murmured a hasty apology and

proceeded to give him the news of the forthcoming event. He made no response except to grunt and wave aside the information without the slightest indication of interest. Olivia peered at him with a frown. Today his eyes were far from vacant; instead, they seemed unusually alert, even shrewd. "What is it that you're hiding under there, Uncle Josh? May I see it?"

"Certainly. If you insist—not that it's anyone's business." Apart from his irritability, he showed no other reaction to her request. He pulled aside the cloth to reveal a pair of brand-new American Colts, no doubt part of his extensive collection of firearms mounted on handsome mahogany racks in the billiards room. He had obviously been polishing the revolvers, for they were both burnished to a rare shine. Ignoring her, he persisted with his labours.

Olivia sat down to watch as his fingers flew over the weapons with confident, practiced expertise. Yes, there *was* something quite different about him today! His shoulders, for instance, were squared back, the stoop forgotten; the eyes that peered into the barrels were clear, steady. There was no tremble in his fingers. And the voice with which she had been reproved had been strong and authoritative. Something sharp caught in Olivia's throat. "Why are you cleaning these weapons?"

"For the same reason that anyone cleans weapons. To have them in perfect firing condition."

"Why should you suddenly want them in perfect firing condition?"

"Because I wish to fire them." He laid down the Colt he held and subjected her to a stern stare. "Now, do you have any more silly questions, or can I be left in peace to get on with my work?"

As he again reached for the Colt, Olivia caught his hand and stopped it. "Whom do you wish to fire them at, Uncle Josh?" Her voice was level but the catch in it made her sound breathless.

"Ah!" He sat back, his hand still in Olivia's grip.

She shook his hand hard. *"Tell* me, Uncle Josh! Whom do you plan to kill with these weapons?"

He swung forward again, released his fingers one by one and resumed his labours. "I plan to kill Jai Raventhorne."

She was convinced that his mind, already teetering at the brink, had finally snapped. "But Jai Raventhorne isn't *here,* Uncle Josh!" Olivia cried. "You know that as well as everyone."

"He will be. Soon."

"Soon? What do you mean, *soon?"* She could barely speak.

"Who's been telling you all these lies? Tell me, *who . . . ?*" In her panic she gripped his hands again and held them fast, shaking them back and forth with punitive force.

Carefully, almost delicately, he pried her fingers apart, released his hands and returned to what he was doing. "They are not lies. The *Ganga* has been sighted in the Palk Straits west of Ceylon. She was heading north."

Olivia regained consciousness to the feel of her own bed at home and the sight of Dr. Humphries's face bending over hers with some seriousness. Behind him, trying hard to minimise her presence but also anxious, stood Estelle. Olivia struggled up on an elbow, dazed. "What happened . . . ?"

"You don't remember?" Dr. Humphries inquired. Olivia shook her head, lay back again and closed her eyes. "Apparently you fainted, but with enough good sense to wait until you reached your own threshold. The servants went to fetch me and I sent for your cousin." Putting a hand behind her head he raised it and poured a dose of foul-smelling liquid down her throat. Olivia retched. "Tsk, tsk! No nonsense now, my girl! Drink it all up. You'll be right as rain in the morning."

Memory returned in a cascade and Olivia fell back to bury her face in her pillow. "I'm as right as rain now. There's nothing wrong with me."

"Temper, temper!" he reproved cheerfully. "I never said there was anything *wrong* with you. In fact, quite the contrary." He snapped his black bag shut and beamed. "I'll be sending you a mixture that will steady your tum. Three times a day before meals. Estelle will see that you rest and behave yourself, won't you, you saucy little monkey?" He pinched Estelle fondly on a cheek.

"I don't have *time* to rest," Olivia cried, praying that Estelle would just go away. She wanted to be alone—God, how she wanted to be alone! "I have *thousands* of things to do before I leave."

"All in good time, all in good time." Using the indulgent tone all doctors used with their patients invariably assumed to be half-witted, he laughed. "Well, seeing as you are an old customer and entitled to your little tantrums, I'll give you the good news anyway." He patted her hand and held it. "Then you must sleep. I forbid you to wake up before morning. My dear, you are going to be a mother again."

Without assimilating the momentous information, Olivia sank into sleep.

Her sedated slumber was long, restful and reviving. She awoke, just as dawn filtered through the bedroom drapes, to the sound of bird song. In a corner with her hands crossed in her lap, Estelle sat on a chair dozing. Hearing the rustle of bed-clothes she sat up with a start. For an instant she looked flustered, as if caught doing something she shouldn't. "I'll go down and ask for some tea, shall I?"

"Have you been here all night?" Olivia spoke with her eyes closed.

"Yes. I thought you might need something."

"You shouldn't have sat up. Salim would have prepared a bed for you in one of the guest-rooms."

He is on his way back!

Olivia could think of nothing else as she hid her waves of crashing panic from Estelle behind tightly shut eyelids. Did Estelle know? But of course she must! Who else would conspire to devise his premature return but her shameless cousin? And what about Amos . . . ? With a cry, Olivia leapt out of bed, forgetting even Estelle. She had to write to Kinjal immediately; Amos must not return before she was absolutely ready to sail! If Raventhorne were to hear of her child . . . oh, sweet Lord, she had to get rid of Estelle! To even have her in the same room now seemed an abomination.

"You must rest, Olivia," Estelle was pleading. "Dr. Humphries has insisted on it. You must avoid over-strain for the sake of the baby."

The baby . . . ?

Olivia's memory flickered; *the baby!* Dr. Humphries had said she was to be a mother again! She was going to have another baby, Freddie's baby. A *Birkhurst* baby. Her mind, still foggy with panic, could not yet absorb the total significance of so unexpected a happening. Still in a daze, she crawled back into bed and lay again with her eyes closed. The sheer force of her colliding emotions drained away her strength and, perhaps, she slept. When she eventually surfaced Estelle was no longer in the room.

Later, much later, Olivia steeled herself to think again of Jai Raventhorne's imminent return, and of his renewed physical presence in the city. But that too was a reality that her brain could not yet fully accept. She had lived with the fear for so long, had watched it weave in and out of her nightmares with such persistent regularity, that now it eluded her comprehension. Incoherently, she sensed his presence everywhere; like a wraith, sinuous and elusive, he was still all pervasive—as if he had never gone away at all! She knew that her mind was playing tricks, but as her carefully erected mental barricades crumbled one by one, she felt defenceless, exposed. At the same time she recognised that now, at this crucial juncture in her bizarre life, more than ever she needed to retain her equilibrium. She had to sustain her sense of perspective; she must not let go of her most valuable defence against Jai Raventhorne—the determination that he would never touch her life again.

"Is it true?" It was the first question Olivia asked Arthur Ransome when he called to inquire after her well-being that evening.

"Yes, it is true." Instinct told him to what she referred.

Olivia quelled her resurgent alarm at the unambiguous confirmation; she had to know more. "How did Uncle Josh happen to hear the news before any of us did?"

Ransome gave an indulgent laugh. "Oh, Josh is a crafty old fox not yet gone to earth, as he sometimes pretends. He still has his sources, especially where information about Raventhorne is concerned. In any case," he sat back, brow furrowed in thought, "rumour also has it that Raventhorne will travel directly up to Assam."

Olivia's heart leapt as a faint spark of hope rekindled. "And this rumour is accurate, you think?"

He spread his hands. "As accurate as any rumour about Raventhorne."

With that, for the moment, she had to be satisfied. "The alleged intention to kill Raventhorne," Olivia asked now, "is Uncle Josh serious about it? I can hardly believe that he is!"

"He appears to be serious."

"But Raventhorne will kill *him!* Surely Uncle Josh realises he will be a sitting duck for Raventhorne if he forces this ludicrous confrontation?"

"He feels he must, Olivia. He believes he has a moral debt to discharge to Bridget."

"And you will do nothing to prevent this . . . murder?" It astonished her that this eminently balanced man could approve of such foolhardiness.

"My own reactions are immaterial," Ransome hedged. "But

I have long accepted that a confrontation is inevitable. Sooner or later it will come and one of them will be eliminated. There is neither space on earth nor air in the heavens for both."

Olivia opened her mouth to indignantly dispute his limp acceptance of what to her would be an act of suicide, but then she shut it again. *It is not as it seems,* Ransome had said once in another context. Now she got the feeling that it was what he was saying to her again. And who was she to argue, or to air secrets not her own? If she had been unable to divert the course of her own fate, it was unlikely that she could that of another.

After Ransome had left Olivia forced her scattered faculties to regroup and sat down to recapitulate logically. John Sturges planned to depart for Cawnpore with Estelle, his parents and Sir Joshua on the afternoon of next Sunday, the day after her reception for the newly-weds. No more than a week later the *Lulubelle,* already in port and being provisioned, would sail for the Pacific. Even if the *Ganga* were to dock in the interim, bazaar gossip—often gratifyingly accurate—had it that Raventhorne would not linger in station. The probability of any confrontation, either with Sir Joshua or herself, simply did not exist.

God willing, it would all work out, it *must.* She would yet beat Jai Raventhorne to the draw!

17

Whether or not Olivia paid any heed to the social snobberies of Calcutta, the wife of a newly titled baron—and rich, too—was of consuming interest to the community. In the aristocratic pecking order a barony was not as elevated as, say, a dukedom, and titles were by no means exceptional in the general administration, but it was the combination that the new Lady Birkhurst presented that was irresistible. She was young, uncommonly easy to look at, wealthy in her own right and possessed an unusually hard head for business that put to shame many of the foppish popinjays who masqueraded around Tank Square in the guise of merchants. That she was also American had long ago been condoned; after all, nobody was perfect! It was a matter of universal regret, that the baroness no longer gave or attended *burra khanas* in the absence of her husband but, on the other hand, that very exclusivity set her apart and made her even more socially desirable.

Therefore, when Olivia's gold-crested, exquisitely penned invitations to her banquet in honour of Major and Mrs. John Sturges were received by prospective guests, there were few refusals. It was an occasion, everyone felt, that would be socially memorable. Just how memorable, however, not even Olivia could have foretold with any degree of accuracy.

As a gregarious young blade in Calcutta, Caleb Birkhurst had loved parties, which accounted for the copious and complex paraphernalia required for wining and dining that reposed in the mansion's well-stocked strong-rooms. There was delicate Irish linen napery, England's finest Wedgwood crockery, China's most translucent egg-shell porcelain, Belgian crystal, innumerable chests of monogrammed silver, Czechoslovakian cut-glass goblets and decanters, Russian caviar bowls, gold-plated serving dishes, platters and salvers galore. The dowager Lady Birkhurst had obviously been a painstaking hostess to whom dinner dances for a hundred and more were all in the day's work. As a consequence, there was hardly anything Olivia needed to supplement her requirements for the ambitious festivities she had planned.

Under her assiduous supervision, teams of servants leapt into action with days of polishing and scrubbing. The rooms were all opened, swept, swabbed and dusted till marble floors shone like mirrors and window panes turned invisible. The chandeliers sparkled, brassware glinted, Persian carpets were aired and brushed into renewed life and the velvet draperies almost purred under energetic strokings. Olivia diligently unpacked many of the crates she had stored away in preparation for her departure, sparing neither effort nor expense. If not to Estelle, she owed at least that to her absent aunt. After this final celebration, they would all disperse to different parts of the world, each to their separate futures. They would probably not see each other again. For Olivia, therefore, the way to her duty lay clear; also, it was essential that she should be able to depart with a conscience unblemished by regrets. Her cousin's repeated pleas to be allowed to help she fielded politely but firmly. "I have plenty of help, thank you. Let the evening come as a surprise for you and John."

"But Dr. Humphries has forbidden you undue exertions," Estelle protested. "We must consider only the baby."

"I will have no opportunity for exertions on board the ship. There will be nothing to do but rest." She smiled. "And I assure you I do consider the baby."

If only Estelle knew how much!

"All this for . . . *us?*" John Sturges was thunderstruck at the opulence that greeted them. Estelle, equally speechless, only formed a silent Oh! with her lips.

"Why not? Estelle is the only cousin I have and you the only cousin-in-law." Congratulating John on his recent promotion to the rank of major, Olivia kissed them both in welcome. Noticing the quiver in her cousin's vulnerable underlip, she added, not unkindly, "Don't cry, Estelle. You don't want black all over your face, do you?"

This evening, Olivia had promised herself, she would be kind to Estelle no matter how sharp the provocation. She could afford to be generous now. In a day, Estelle would be out of her life forever. In little more than a week, she herself would be aboard the *Lulubelle* with Amos, and en route to her father. The ignominy of an unpaid debt of honour was almost behind her (entirely, if she could give Freddie a son) thanks to this unexpected little mango seed that now rested in her womb. God willing, soon she would be released from all moral bondage. And from the hovering spectre of Jai Raventhorne.

Yes, this evening would mark the last of her penances, the last!

In sudden elation she put an arm fondly around Estelle's shoulders. "Tonight will be your night. Enjoy yourself as you will. I make no demands nor lay down restrictions."

In black tailcoat, striped trousers and white starched shirt with a carnation in his lapel, Arthur Ransome obviously intended to take his duties as host most seriously. "It's a little tight," he muttered, patting his convex stomach with a blush. "Haven't worn it in years, not even for your wedding if you recall. Smells of moth-balls, I'm afraid."

"You look *splendid.* The Spin certainly won't be able to resist you this evening!" Olivia laughed and squeezed his arm. "Uncle Josh definitely isn't coming then?"

"No. Leave him be. He's better off at home."

"Well, if you say so, but I will miss him."

Standing next to her cousin in the receiving line as the guests started to arrive, Estelle could hardly contain her delight at being centre stage for the whole evening. Her fashionable gown, of peach velour and ermine, looked *vraiment parisienne* in cut and style, its bodice—*très, très* daring!—covered with Japanese seed-pearls. Uncaring of the mismatch, she displayed in her cleavage the elaborate diamond necklace that was Olivia's gift. "You don't think I'm going to miss showing *this* off tonight, do you?" she had replied smugly to Olivia's eyebrow arched in questioning amusement.

No, Estelle had not changed much, Olivia concluded to herself. In those round blue porcelain eyes the underlying shrewdness, the calculation and the cunning were the same. If there were changes at all they were physical, in the greater roundness of her cheeks and figure, in her air of insouciant confidence. As she observed Estelle laughing and bantering and flirting with such bounce, Olivia could not help feeling a stab of envy. Estelle had a capacity for fun that had been denied to *her;* she had the gift of carrying her cares lightly. Whatever scandalous secrets

Estelle concealed in her heart never seemed to interfere with her appetite for extravagant enjoyment. And in that knowledge, Olivia sighed; what a gift it might have been for her, too—that talent to bear burdens with such nonchalance!

"Give nobody's heart pain so long as thou canst avoid it, for one sigh may set a whole world into a flame . . ."

Olivia spun around to face Peter Barstow.

"I was only remarking," he explained, "on that profound sigh you heaved. The wisdom, alas, is not mine. It comes from Sa'di's poem *Gulistan.* I read it in translation, of course, but you see, I'm not as illiterate as you think."

She had not wanted to invite Barstow but had capitulated finally to the dictates of social convention. He had, after all, been Freddie's best friend. "I sighed because I was wondering if the pomfret galantine would be enough to go round twice," she answered coldly.

"Indeed! No sighs then for the absent spouse sorrowfully adrift?"

"Plenty, but not necessarily as an exercise in public. And he's not 'adrift'; he's on a ship. Excuse me." Barstow's barbs made no dents in Olivia's composure as she walked away to mingle with her other guests. In any case, they were no different from the conjectures of others in Calcutta.

The reception-rooms were ablaze with light from the many multi-tiered chandeliers, and conversations hummed with liveliness. Olivia was aware that in the medley of accents there were some that would have never got past the doorman of an aristocratic home in England. Indian colonial stations remained loyal to social hierarchies, but since the English here were in a minority, they had the wisdom not to be picky. In India, it was the native who was considered the outsider; snobberies tended to be more of colour than of class. Crisis conditions called for a united front in which it was expedient to hold rank superior to pedigree.

Because the late November chill in the air that marked the start of Calcutta's short winter was noticeable, and because huge log fires looked so pretty, Olivia had ordered them to be lit in the marble fireplaces. Now, to counteract their rather excessive heat in a roomful of people, she asked for all the French windows to be opened. Immediately, the luxurious fragrance of the Queen of the Night wafted pleasantly across the two main reception-rooms. In between, she had arranged a bar counter that shimmered with bottles of iced champagne, French wines, whiskies, brandies, beer, port and sherry, and post-prandial liqueurs. An

English barman with two assistants had been hired for the evening from the Bengal Club and drinks were being dispensed hand over fist to loosen tongues and induce conviviality. An army of bearers passed around sherbets and cordials. If there was anything Olivia disliked, it was the English custom of using the need to smoke as an excuse for sexual segregation after dinner. To ensure against the ladies being abandoned for shop talk behind closed doors, she had given permission to the gents to light up if they wished, and Dutch cheroots were being passed around, only the Havana cigars and the blocks of pipe tobacco being kept for after dinner.

Estelle's friends, of course, were all out in force this evening. Over the past months Olivia had avoided meeting them; the need to answer awkward questions about her cousin's abrupt withdrawal from Calcutta was one she was determined not to burden herself with. But whatever alibis Estelle herself had made to them were obviously adequate, for there appeared to be no signs of strain anywhere. The camaraderie and bantering sounded perfectly normal.

"Oh my, motherhood does suit you, Olivia!" Polly Drummond's envious gaze alternated between Olivia's royal blue gown of Kashmiri *pashmina* wool embroidered in gold thread with the traditional paisley motif, and the sapphire jewellery she had worn as a concession to the occasion. "And marriage, too—you look divine! Obviously, both are to be recommended?"

"If that's a hint, my sweet, I'd better strike while the iron's hot." Polly's beau, a curly-haired, dimple-cheeked young clerk with the Company, fell to his knees amidst much giggling. "To press my suit, I—"

"Press yours by all means, but don't ruin *mine,* dash it!" someone else groaned as his action sent a beer glass flying.

"And *mine!* Ooh, I've got sherbet all over my dress and it's *new.*"

"Is it? I say, I'm dashed sorry. Here, I'll fetch some water—"

"Don't be daft, Howard, georgette *shrinks* . . ."

"Does it? Well, *that's* quite a prospect!"

"Oh Lord, I can't take him anywhere!" Polly choked with laughter.

Amidst the renewed giggles, Estelle sidled up to Olivia. "You *do* look divine, you know, Coz. I wish I could be as slender, and I'm not pregnant even with a first baby let alone a *second.*"

"Oh, Oddivia, oh you sdy puss!" Lily Horniman, the girl with enlarged adenoids, squealed at Estelle's stage whisper.

"How marveddous to be—" Aware suddenly of the intimate nature of the remark she was about to make, Lily stopped and went scarlet.

But it was too late. Not many had missed Estelle's stage whisper. Hastily, the men all looked away and the girls, oohing and aahing under their breaths, dragged Olivia aside for excited questioning. Annoyed, Olivia clung tenaciously to her vow to forgive Estelle her silly excesses at least for this evening. By the time she had extricated herself from the melee, she had decided—not for the first time—that it was in the company of men that she felt more comfortable by far, and purposefully turned towards the bar counter. Between her own guest list and Estelle's, most Europeans of consequence had been invited, including two visiting directors of the Company from London. Because of John's connection with the army, there were plenty of uniforms to be seen among the crowd of merchants, bankers, civil servants, Company officials, chandlers and stevedores, and three American medical missionaries from Bombay brought by Dr. Humphries. Much against his wishes, Willie Donaldson had been prevailed upon to bring the cotton man from Mississippi, Hiram Arrowsmith Lubbock ("Jes Hal to mah fray'nds, my'am"), who was interested in leasing the Birkhurst mansion, and was introducing him around the bar with an expression of unconcealed disgust.

"Sir Joshua still under the weather, Your Ladyship?" The tactful inquiry was from a tall, uniformed brigadier with a medal-encrusted chest who had recently been appointed an aide-de-camp to the Governor-General, Lord Dalhousie. Being family friends of the Birkhursts, the Governor-General and his lady had been invited, of course, but Olivia had been much relieved when they had sent their regrets due to a prearranged absence in the mofussil. The stiff protocol that surrounded the Queen's premier officer in India was tiresome. Whatever prestige Their Excellencies' presence brought to a gathering, it also brought yawning dullness.

"My uncle recovers well, thank you, but his lingering weakness precludes the exertions of *burra khanas.*" Olivia's reply was equally tactful.

"And what precludes Your Ladyship's attendance of *burra khanas,* may I ask? I was most disappointed to receive your own regrets to our invitation for His Excellency's ball this year. So were Their Excellencies."

"With His Lordship in England, I shy away from parties,

especially formal ones," Olivia explained smoothly. "But I'm certainly enjoying my own. I hope you are too, Brigadier."

"Oh, *rather!* Quite the most splendid jollification we've seen in a long while. A great pity His Lordship cannot enjoy it with us."

"Yes, isn't it?"

At the bar over fast-flowing champagne, Calcutta's latest scandal was being debated hotly. It involved, Olivia gathered as she joined the men, the new Resident of Murshidabad. He had, it was believed, paid the astronomical sum of twenty thousand pounds to the incumbent as an inducement to early retirement from a post said to be the most lucrative in the service. Even Lord Clive had once made the observation that there was more gold in Murshidabad with the Nawabs than in the whole of London. Such job "purchases," Olivia had heard, were not uncommon. What gave the present debate its heat was the fact that the new Resident had also "gone native" and had established for himself in Murshidabad a sizable harem of nautch girls.

"A swine, sir, a disgrace to the community!" Barnabus Slocum huffed.

"Well, what can one expect?" someone else remarked. "His father was a Covent Garden lute maker."

"Aye, and known in the trade as *Disso*lute Dave, to boot!" There were guffaws all around, the loudest from Mrs. Drummond, who was thoughtfully eyeing the medal-studded chest of the brigadier aide-de-camp.

"Shocking, sah, shocking! Deserves a taste of the horsewhip." Henry Cleghorne bristled with moral outrage.

"Heah, heah," Smithers murmured in that affected accent he always used to divert attention from his own social inadequacies.

"Och laddie—you would na be a wee bit jealous, noo would you?" Willie Donaldson gave Smithers a sly wink. "Noo, if it's skeletons we're rattling, let him with none in *his* cupboard risk the first rattle!"

Smithers flushed and there was a short, awkward lull during which only Hal Lubbock had the gall to roar with laughter. "Waal, like mah Aunt Jemimah might say, boys will be boys—and a *dy'am* good thing too, eh pal?" He guffawed again and landed a hearty slap on Smithers's back, which made him splutter and nearly choke on his drink.

Willie Donaldson winced audibly and everyone else froze as they instantly closed ranks against the mannerless American upstart. Who the hell was he to make free with one of *their* scandals? Olivia felt a stab of compassion for the haplessly vulgar Lubbock, who stuck out like a sore thumb in a manicure parlour. Wrenching herself away from the earnest nostalgia of a desperately homesick young Company Bahadur recruit fresh from their training establishment at Haileybury in England, she impulsively and pointedly guided Lubbock towards the ballroom, where Estelle had chosen to start the dancing before dinner. The parquet floor was already crowded. On the side lines sat those waiting to be whirled off by beaux, and fond Mamas shrewdly sizing up eligible prospects before they could be grabbed by unwanted competitors. Quickly introducing Lubbock to two young ladies obviously waiting for an invitation to dance, Olivia set off in search of Arthur Ransome.

She found him in a far corner hopelessly trapped by the Spin and looking decidedly hunted. "May I please have a word with you, Uncle Arthur?"

Gout forgotten, he almost flew out of his seat like a wild bird suddenly finding its cage door open. "Dreadful woman, dreadful!" He mopped the sweat off his brow. "You saved her life, my dear, to say nothing of mine. I would have strangled her in a moment."

"Or proposed to her, I daresay!" Olivia laughed and Ransome cursed under his breath. "What I wanted to ask you is—do you consider it too early to serve dinner? The dancing has only just started and the men still drink. I don't want Estelle to feel I'm trying to short-change her guests with the liquor."

Excited by his role as host, Ransome consulted his watch. "No, that wouldn't do at all. We can't have them thinking we're cutting down on their spirits, ha, ha. Perhaps we might give them another half hour or so?"

"Fine. As long as the soufflés don't collapse. Rashid Ali would never forgive me. In the meantime, I'll send round some more canapés. The prawns seemed especially popular. Or we could . . ."

Olivia stopped, for Ransome was no longer listening. His gaze seemed riveted to something behind her. Casually she turned to cast a glance across her shoulder. At the door of the room a new arrival had been announced. He was being warmly welcomed by her cousin, Estelle.

It was Jai Raventhorne.

He smiled. He took Estelle's hand in his, bent over and kissed it lightly. John Sturges appeared next to his wife. The two men shook hands, exchanged a smile of greeting. Across the room, all at once engulfed in a deathly hush, a fragment of laughter floated, then another. All talk forgotten, everyone stared avidly at the scene contained in the doorway. In the unearthly silence a burning log fell from the grate with a hiss. Nobody thought to replace it. Then, face aglow, step firm and purposeful, Estelle led a path through the forest of motionless figures to guide Raventhorne down the length of the room towards their host and hostess.

"Olivia dear, may I present Mr. Jai Raventhorne? I believe that you have met once. Jai, I think you must remember my cousin, Lady Birkhurst." In her voice there was not even a tremor and her unwavering blue eyes were crystal clear.

Olivia had no awareness of having extended a hand, but then it was being held in his. The flesh against hers felt cold, the lips that skimmed her skin even more so. Did she speak? She couldn't tell. But then he did. "Indeed! Yes, we did meet once. Perhaps it has slipped Lady Birkhurst's memory. How kind of you to offer me your hospitality tonight!"

They passed on. Hands were shaken with Arthur Ransome, a few words exchanged, and another nervous guffaw of laughter cut across the silence. White faced, Ransome asked somewhere in the vast, echoing distances of Olivia's mind, "What may I offer you to drink, Jai? If I recall rightly, two fingers of Scotch on ice is what you are partial to."

"Thank you. That would be perfect."

For the moment, no more formalities were called for. There were few present to whom Raventhorne was not already known. In a recovery little short of miraculous, Ransome led his unexpected guest towards the bar chatting with admirable amiability. Behind her, Olivia heard some woman's sharp intake of breath, "Oh my sainted aunt, it's not possible, it *can't* be . . . !

The silence cloaking the room lingered a moment or two longer. Then, like an incoming tide, the murmurs crept back and accelerated. Beneath the hum, however, remained a hint of subdued excitement, a frisson of breathless suspense—what was the notorious Kala Kanta doing in an Englishman's drawing-room, and that too at the invitation of Joshua Templewood's daughter? Amidst astonished whispers and covert glances exchanged over rims of glasses, conjectures and questions criss-crossed the room like firework rockets. But then, gradually, normalcy returned. In a flurry, bearers again zigzagged through the crowds bearing trays of fresh drinks and canapés, and suppressed laughs burgeoned once more into hearty roars. A resonant roll of drums sounded to announce the start of a waltz. Whatever tensions remained were soon dispelled by the energetic endeavours of the army band.

Only Olivia remained rooted. A dreamlike mist, vaporous but determined, obliterated the present. *But yes,* a voice rose from some mouldy sepulchre to echo in a corner of her mind, *I do love you . . .*

She turned and fled upstairs.

Estelle has gone mad, Estelle has gone mad . . . Crumpled in a trembling heap on her bed, Olivia could think of no other explanation for the horror being visited upon them all. Like a moth fluttering for release from its cocoon, her panic-stricken brain thrashed helplessly inside the walls of her skull. Once again her cousin had trapped her in a situation not of her own making, but this time she had no more resources to manipulate an escape. Oh God, oh God—what was she to do . . . ?

The door opened and, noiselessly, Estelle slipped in. "I know that you are furious with me, but I had to do it. I'm sorry. I could think of no other . . . method." Speaking from the doorway as if afraid to step inside, she faltered.

Olivia sat up slowly, loath, even in her state of panic, to expose herself to her obnoxious cousin. She pressed shaking finger-tips to her temples, but not even closed eyes could blot out the vision of those mutually warm looks, that welcoming smile, the unspoken rapport to which Raventhorne had subscribed so openly. Behind shuttered eyes Olivia's hate swilled and spilled over and she contorted with rage. "How dare you, Estelle! How *dare* you use my hearth and home for your shameless exhibitions!"

Quietly, Estelle entered and closed the door behind her. "You said I could ask anyone I wished to. You made no demands, placed no restrictions—did you not mean that, Olivia? Was that too a hypocrisy?" She was pale but in her attitude there was only defiance.

"Anyone, yes, but not . . ." She could not speak the name. "I meant what I said because not even I could have guessed the extent of your immodesty. In flaunting your . . . relationship with that man, you feel no sense of . . . of defilement? No *contamination . . . ?*"

Estelle flinched but held her ground. "No. I am proud of my relationship with Jai. I want everyone to know about it, to *accept* it. And one day, I promise, they *will.*"

Her own words of so long ago! Olivia flew off the bed, grabbed her cousin's shoulders and shook her in a fury no longer containable. "And does your husband know and accept it too? You have no guilt about thrusting your . . . your *lover,*" she spat out the word in Estelle's face, "down *his* throat—forget mine and everyone else's!"

Estelle wrenched herself away and, all at once, her face puckered. "John understands," she whispered, her tone suddenly weighted down with misery. "Perhaps you would too if—"

"I have no more understanding to spare. Keep your squalid alibis to yourself, Estelle." To hide the shaking of her hands she tucked them out of sight under her arms and walked away to stand at a window. Breathing in great lungfuls of cool night air, she forced her anger back under a cover of brittle control. "After tonight, Estelle, I never wish to see you again. I want you out of my life forever. Frankly, I don't care a ha'pence what you do with your life and with whom. I am not your keeper; you owe me no excuses. But yes, in one matter I have erred—I did say you could have anyone here you wished to with neither demands nor restrictions. I shall not go back on my word. Now please leave me alone and go down to rejoin your guests."

For just another moment Estelle hesitated, her face cracking with unhappiness. "Very well. If that is what you wish," she said quietly. "But please be polite to him, Olivia. You have no idea how difficult it was to fetch him here. He . . ." She stopped, the despair in her voice compounding. Then her expression firmed again. "But what must be done, must be done." She turned and walked out.

Behind her Olivia locked the door. Going into Freddie's adjoining bedroom, she opened his bureau to take out a half-finished bottle of sherry. Without bothering about a glass, she downed several gulps. The burning liquid brought tears to her eyes and made her stomach scream in protest, but, resolutely, she downed several more. For a moment her head spun but then her nerves responded and she steadied. Five more minutes before the mirror brought vibrant colour back to her cheeks and a gloss to her lips. Whatever flickers of fear were left, she crushed them ruthlessly beneath the heel of her will-power. Amos was safely away and Jai Raventhorne was to her now a meaningless quantity. Whatever suspicions he might have about her son were mere suspicions; she would manage them. His effrontery and Estelle's brazenness could not be matched with wilting weakness and hysteria. If they could display hides of leather with such inglorious abandon, then—hell's bells and damnation!—so bloody well would *she!*

Head held high, cheeks again aglow with confident colour, she swept imperiously down the marble staircase.

Pausing minimally to take stock of the scene below, Olivia was amazed at how normal everything seemed. Through the archway to the ball-room she could see feet twirling unconcernedly to some strange Latin rhythm that was quite the rage, she had been informed, in London. Directly ahead was the bar counter. Mellow eyed, indulgent, the men still lounged and drank and squinted cordially at each other through the thick spirals of smoke. Raventhorne leaned against the counter, composed and entirely at ease, talking to John Sturges, Clarence Pennworthy, an Indian army colonel with a wooden leg and, of all people, the police chief Barnabus Slocum. There appeared to be nothing untoward in anyone's manner and if there was hostility, none was apparent. What they said was lost in the distance and the general hum of conversation, but it was obviously cordial enough to provoke some stiffly polite laughter.

A paragon of unlikely European elegance, Jai Raventhorne was formally and impeccably dressed. His suit, English and three piece, was of dark burgundy and fashionably cut. A cream silk shirt, ruffled down the front, was framed by black velvet lapels. The black cummerbund circling his slim waist was pleated with precision. As his ankles, crossed casually, moved, the gold buckles on his black patent leather shoes caught the light of a chandelier and twinkled. Gone was the riotous ebony hair; trimmed and brushed scrupulously back, it had been tamed into uncharacteristic submission. The picture he presented was of a high-born English gentleman supremely at home in his natural habitat, an elegant drawing-room. A forgotten vision flashed across Olivia's mind as she observed the scene—that of a dirty dish-washer by the well of a roadside tavern. But this time, she did not discard the vision out of hand. Instead, she scrutinised it from afar, with detachment. She discovered that her scrutiny brought no sudden twists of the heart, no involuntary wrenches. All it brought was cold anger. Impatiently, she cleansed her mind of the past, consigning again to oblivion that which oblivion deserved. She had a need to survive this evening, and survive it with triumph. That need would not go abegging. Jai Raventhorne would never be allowed to touch her again.

Holding her head even higher, she nimbly ran down the remaining stairs.

"Did you invite him?" As soon as she descended, Arthur Ransome cornered her. He looked far from easy.

"No. Estelle did."

"She had no damn business to, not without at least forewarning us. He docked last night, I learn. Tomorrow he goes to Assam."

Raventhorne had not glanced at her even once but Olivia knew instinctively that with some invisible, inner stare, he had her skewered in his vision. For all his offhandedness, she could almost physically feel that hateful pewter gaze dissecting her as if with a scalpel bent on merciless surgery. With an effort, she pried her own eyes away from the bar. "Why has he come?" she demanded in a fierce whisper.

"I have no idea." Ransome shrugged but his frown deepened. "There is some motive behind it, there must be. I don't mind confessing that I am distinctly worried."

"Estelle's liaison with him might not be common knowledge, but your enmity is. Surely he would not—"

"Oh, I'm not concerned about the enmity. Not here anyway." He grimaced. "The world of commerce is pragmatic, Olivia. If all those who hate each other's guts in office rooms ceased to drink together, there would never be another social occasion shared in station! No, it's not as simple as that, my dear. There is something else, I fear, that does not smell quite right."

"Perhaps." She gave a vinegary smile. "After all, whatever the assumed civilities, Raventhorne can hardly be called the most popular man in town!"

"On the contrary," Ransome returned drily, "I would say that with at least half your guests, Raventhorne is extremely popular."

He referred, of course, to the ladies. Giggling, fluttering eyelashes and simpering coyly, many hovered close to the bar counter, making no secret of their hopes of earning some attention. The displays of coquetry disgusted Olivia. She made a gesture of contemptuous dismissal. "Oh, I don't mean them, they are immaterial. I mean the men."

"I do not exclude the men either. Personal grudges are all very well, my dear, but business is business—never forget that. There's not a man here who does not, however indirectly, have dealings with Raventhorne's Trident. Kala Kanta puts many shekels into many coffers when he wants to. No, however great the private temptations, I daresay he is unlikely to be murdered publicly on your priceless Persian carpets." But despite his laugh, he continued to look worried.

Olivia could no longer avoid circulating. Moving away, she

walked towards the group farthest from him and the bar counter. But each step she took was like treading on knives: Even with her back to Raventhorne, she could feel his eyes—Amos's eyes!—follow her like a tail attached to her body. Between his stare and that of Estelle (watching warily from a safe distance), Olivia began to feel impaled, her flesh singed and branded. Her nerves started to falter. Recklessly, she downed two more glasses of sherry.

She started to float. Once again the feeling of fantasy was strong, a bubble enclosing her in the dreamy ether of unreality. Was it true that this was happening, or was it an illusion, a mirage, a nightmare merely come alive? She was actually in the same room again with Jai Raventhorne. To touch him with her eyes all she had to do was turn. If she traversed the length of the room, she could reach for his hand. At one time she had sold her soul to do both; now she did neither. Instead, she called for some more sherry, demolished another glassful and asked for dinner to be announced.

And inwardly she laughed. To think she had presumed that Estelle could not keep her secrets well!

Savagely, Olivia took hold of her mind again and latched it on trivialities. Had the cruet stands been refilled with fresh mustard? Were the flowers wilting because the fires were too hot? *Should* she risk sending the pomfret galantine around twice; was the French cheese too ripe, the English Stilton not ripe enough? The boom of the silver dinner gong rumbled funereally through the reception rooms, the band struck a last chord and, eagerly, two by two everyone streamed into the dining hall resplendent with candelabras and silver and crackling crisp white napery. The repast that Olivia had arranged was quite splendid, with game soup, chicken curry in coconut milk, black mushroom pilaf, sheeps' trotters with chick-peas, toad in the hole, hams, sides of roast beef, salted venison, roast duck, mounds of delicately steamed vegetables, compotes and pies, lemon meringues, American chocolate cake with clotted cream and deep sprinklings of nuts. There were compliments galore as everyone ate and drank heartily. Everyone, that is, except Estelle and Jai Raventhorne.

Ensconced in an alcove, they conversed with apparent unconcern. Estelle's cheeks were high with colour, her eyes alive with sparkles. Raventhorne's gaze was glued to Estelle's face as he sat cradling a brandy between his palms, but Olivia was not fooled. She knew by the crawl of her flesh that she was still tightly encapsulated in that damnable vision, held ruthlessly within those pupils that saw without watching. *I don't need eyes to see you . . .*

I must not let go, I must not let go!

No, *this* excess she would not forgive Estelle, not ever!

"What a superlative evening, Olivia!" Across her overflowing plate, Betty Pennworthy leaned forward to gush. She dropped her voice. "And, my dear, what a *coup* to have enticed our reclusive neighbour into coming! Just as well Josh—"

"Betty!" Her husband cautioned her with a frown. "It is not for us to comment upon what is not our business." To underline his point he thrust his empty plate forward, tacitly demanding a second helping.

"Doesn't he want to talk with anyone except Estelle?" Susan Bradshaw wailed. "All he does is drink—what a waste! Can you not persuade your prize guest to be kind to us too?"

"Mr. Raventhorne is the guest of John and Estelle. It is to them that you must direct your appeal," Olivia answered with a flinty smile. "My own influence in the matter is minimal."

"Oh, *look!*" The Hendersons' recently arrived daughter gave a little cry. "He's drained his glass. I *do* believe he means to head our way at last! Oh, do you think I dare?" she asked no one in particular. "Yes. I do. Coming, Polly?"

Even the very superior Charlotte seemed flustered. "Oh dear. My hair, it's in such a mess! I wonder if I should . . . ?" Muttering to herself, she hurried off in another direction.

A tall freckled girl with ginger-coloured hair and a green bow in it sighed. "Isn't he quite the best-looking man at the party, Clive?" she asked her escort with supreme lack of tact. "I don't believe he has a *trace* of native blood in him, truly I don't."

"Well he has," Clive Smithers snapped. "Besides, he's a cad, a thorough swine. I can't imagine what Estelle and John are up to. Come away, Hattie, before you make a fool of yourself." Considering the gossip about the Smithers's own ancestry, the remark was amusing. But then, such precisely were the ironies rampant in Calcutta's social self-delusions.

Wherever Olivia moved, she heard and overheard comments about Raventhorne—some malicious, others gleeful, but all charged with excitement. Why *had* this arrogant half-caste bastard suddenly decided to grace the English drawing-room in which he had sworn not to be caught dead? The endlessly repeated question that worried Ransome was beginning to worry Olivia too. Yes, why?

Whirling around the dance floor in the arms of a deferential young Port Trust official whose name she could not recall, Olivia wanted to plug her ears to stop the snatches of conversation that wafted past.

"... dare to show his face? Poor Oli—"

"... hardened rogue, my love, *hardened* ..."

"Oh Ted, you're *jealous! You* couldn't fit a cummerbund over ... now then, could you?" Giggle, giggle.

"Everyone's saying [whisper, whisper] isn't it *awful?*"

"—erican, after all. So *uncaring* of scan—"

"Really, Archie! To hell with the half-caste when he has such ..."

By the time she could escape onto the verandah and be alone, Olivia was limp. Weakly she leaned against a pillar, shivering but not entirely with the cold. Whatever the circumstances, she had not been prepared for the shock of this evening, for the defeat of not being able to beat Raventhorne to the draw. Taken by surprise and lulled into a fool's paradise, she had not bothered to retain her defences, to predetermine reactions, to make herself totally immune to his presence. This Olivia now admitted to herself. To hate was not enough, not nearly so! By natural progression, that hate had to evolve into indifference, and she was not yet entirely indifferent to him. Both love and hate meant an expenditure of energy, of time and thought. She resented that expenditure, even during the hour or two more that she would have to spend with him under the same roof.

From behind the pillar Olivia had a partial view of the dance floor. Raventhorne was now dancing—dancing!—with Estelle in his arms. Olivia had rarely seen him smile with such ease. Or such warmth. Barely reaching his shoulder, Estelle gazed up at him with her heart pouring out of her eyes. Olivia felt sickened with the obscenity of it all. Her stomach heaved and she could not contain it. Holding her mouth, she ran silently into the garden to be ill behind a bush bursting with white winter blossoms. Skirting the house, she then ran to the kitchen to rinse out her mouth and lubricate her ragged throat with a drink of water, watched by her astonished staff. By the same route she returned to the verandah.

Where Jai Raventhorne awaited her.

"Why does the refined Baroness Birkhurst need to be sick in her garden?" he asked with cloying softness.

Olivia froze. She had not envisaged so private an encounter away from the insulating presence of others. For an instant she lost contact with her mental moorings, but only for an instant.

"Perhaps because," she replied in a lightning recovery, "some of her guests reduce her to it." She moved to walk past him but he had her by the arm.

"Even though she had pledged to accept them for what they were?"

He had the nerve to resurrect *that?* Olivia wrenched her arm free to stand and survey him through narrowed eyes. Her punctilious investigation was a therapy; it gave her time to recover more fully. She had never before seen him so formally dressed. She was glad she had done so now; the paragon of sartorial perfection wiped out forever that haunting vision of a deprived menial so callously defrauded by fate. And in the act of their flesh touching, even minimally, she felt a revived sense of outrage. And courage. Staring contemptuously into the mother-of-pearl eyes that were his accursed legacy to her son, she asked, "Why have you come?"

"Why? I could not refuse Estelle."

"Estelle is a conniving minx!" She hadn't meant to say that but it was out and irretractable.

"Most women are. Some are conniving sluts." Olivia stiffened, but he manacled her wrist so that she could not walk away. "Which is the second reason why I am here. I couldn't resist the temptation to see Lady Birkhurst in the luxurious habitat she had long selected for herself with such relentless duplicity. How diligently you set your sights on Freddie Birkhurst, with what accuracy and how swiftly!"

She had tasted his gall many times before; its flavour was sharp in her tongue's memory. Even so, the magnitude of his insolence and the inequity of his presumptions swept her with blind fury. But, with miraculous calm, she caught the tail of her rage before it could flare. If she had to pay him back at all, it was in his own currency. *And he had not yet mentioned Amos!* "Supposing I were to say that a choice between decency and degradation, if offered, is not to be spurned?" she inquired with scathing sarcasm.

"You had already chosen to tolerate what you call degradation, and chosen freely."

"Free choices operate in both selection and rejection!" She could scarcely believe that even with his nerve *he* could flaunt recriminations. "And a few kisses here and there hardly constitute a lifetime commitment, do they?"

His own words of so very long ago thrown back in his face elicited no overt reaction. "I left a letter for you. It could not be delivered. The man died of cholera. By the time it was relocated, it no longer mattered. Now I see that it would not have mattered anyway."

A letter? Olivia stared at him dumbfounded. *A letter . . . ?* And that was all he had considered necessary to obliterate an act of callous betrayal? To repair the cavernous breaches in her life, to replace a future he had stolen and carried away with him? She went rigid with renewed fury.

"And what was it that you wrote in that conveniently lost letter, Jai? With what euphemisms did you inform me that as your mistress you had replaced me with an equally willing cousin?"

She had the vicious pleasure of seeing him flush, and the taste of first blood was uncommonly sweet. "By marrying your pet loon you have lost the right to the contents of that letter. It was not addressed to Lady Birkhurst."

"Ah, but you see, idle curiosity is still my predominating vice!" she tossed off with a light laugh. "Surely it deserves to be indulged one last time for past services rendered so well and so willingly?"

In her mockery, his flush deepened. "You disgust me, Olivia!" he breathed, icy with anger.

"I?" she mocked further, sickened by his fulsome lies, his alibis and excuses. Anything in that undelivered letter would have been too little, too late. In any case, she didn't believe that it existed. *"I?* Who have so devoutly sanctified your insanities and obsessions, treated as holy ground all those dark areas I once longed to illuminate? Why, *surely* you do me an injustice!" Filled with aversion, she hid behind the device of another laugh.

Below his temple a wayward pulse throbbed. "You also once promised to trust me, Olivia."

For a moment she was stunned; even he in his arrogance couldn't mean that! Between them the words hung in the air as if a phrase of the music inside had somehow detached itself to float out into the verandah. Then they fell with a crash into her consciousness and she jolted back to life. She wondered wrathfully if he toyed with her, taunted her. Yes, she had promised to trust him once. And she had! She had trusted him totally, with everything, her all—had he *forgotten?* Had he any conception of where she would have been now with the hollow rewards of that misplaced trust? She almost blurted out the question but then choked it back; obviously he hadn't, and for that she must remain forever grateful. For if he knew the answer to that, then he would also know about Amos—*and that he must not ever!* In her fragile imbalances she sought refuge in more flippancy. "Did I? I don't remember. Just as well. In any case, cast-off mistresses are known to be notoriously fickle."

"So I have come to learn!" He was tight with leashed rage. "How else would you have netted that prize buffoon with such admirable dispatch and celebrated instant motherhood?"

Her pulse skipped. "Well, maybe better a prize buffoon than a prize profligate!" she threw back with gathering breathlessness. "You cannot deny that a bird in the net is a more attractive bargain than some perverted prospect frolicking out of reach in far-away bushes." With a coy smile she added, "And you *did* recommend Freddie highly to me once, remember?"

"And now that that bird is no longer in the net," he sneered, the cracks in his composure widening, "no doubt the vacancy in your bed has been filled by other willing surrogates?"

"Why not?" Brazening her way further she turned the knife a little more. "Once a slut, I guess always a slut!" How amusing that both her husband and her child's father had chosen the same word with which to condemn her! But the insults no longer stung; she had passed beyond them. Frantic to steer him away from even a suggestion of Amos, she did not care how rashly she vilified herself, or allowed him to.

In the semi-dark of the verandah his eyes smouldered, but before he could spit out a retort a small group wandered out through a French window amidst much laughter and gaiety. For a moment they stood chattering within earshot before moving away into the garden, but that moment was all Raventhorne needed to repair the damage to his control. "It is considered good etiquette in your elevated circles," he said then with a return to arctic formality, "to dance at least once with one's hostess before leaving a party." Expression once more cemented, he held out a hand.

Olivia shied back, taken by surprise. Dance? With Jai Raventhorne? Oh no, *no!* "I'm sorry. I have promised this dance to—"

"Whoever he is he won't mind."

"But I *do* mind . . . ," she started furiously, only to be sliced off by his ruthless grasp of her elbow. Ignoring her comment, he propelled her firmly but subtly back into the ballroom and, aghast, she had no option but to submit. To protest within earshot of others was, of course, unthinkable. As it was, their re-entry was greeted with looks of unabashed curiosity. A pressure around her waist informed Olivia that his arm had been positioned, and that too securely. Their fingers touched, his breath brushed her ear in a closeness that to her was intolerable, and then he was guiding her smoothly across the flagged marble in a catchy waltz. In a breathless daze, Olivia marvelled with irrelevant surprise—who would have believed that Kala Kanta could be so competently versed in such palpably European frivolity as dancing? Deprived of even the will to protest further, Olivia surrendered herself to the inescapable and briefly closed her eyes. Her head swam. The feet tapping in rhythm to her madly pulsating temples seemed to have a will of their own. Behind closed lids she struggled for control and, when she opened her eyes, her breath was again even. Her gaze was level with the nut brown column of the neck she had kissed so often that she could almost taste it, but forcibly she concentrated her attention on his cravat, silken and fringed, and his coat buttons of beaten gold fashioned into seashells. What she could not ignore, however, was the deep, evocative muskiness of his skin. It was so intensely familiar that she thought she would faint. Against him she stumbled.

"My fault," he murmured, the metallic hardness of his eyes belying the perfunctory gallantry. "But if you find the music too fast for comfort, I would be only too relieved to stop—etiquette having been sufficiently satisfied for the benefit of your guests."

With supreme courage Olivia tacitly shook her head, loath to allow him even this minute victory. Everywhere eyes watched, tongues whispered, mouths drooled waiting for an excuse for salacious comment. In a corner Estelle stood with her gaze riveted and watchful. The exchanges with Jai Raventhorne, acrid, vitriolic and so totally fruitless, had eroded Olivia's Dutch courage and left her limp with revived injury. It seemed obscene to her that they could be dancing, casting pleasant smiles around, talking against a background of music about something that had laid so many lives in ruin. And at any moment he might mention that one subject she dreaded more than any other: her son! Against his shoulder her fingers clenched. "Why, *why* in the name of heaven," she whispered fiercely, "have you chosen to come here tonight, Jai . . . ?"

"I have given you two reasons, I will give you a third." He had conquered his anger, his tone was conversational. For all it indicated, he might have been complimenting her on the lush display of her flower arrangements. "In marrying Freddie you have allowed him to appropriate something that I considered to be mine." He smiled pleasantly and matched her own flippancy.

"For that act of stealth the Birkhursts owe me at least a drink in reparation." The music stopped. He stepped back and bowed.

Amos! Panic flared, blinding her to all other interpretations of his flippancy. With his unerring instincts about her, he had found out about Amos. Any moment now he would announce his intention to claim him, take him away from her. He had been to Kirtinagar and of course he had seen him . . . Wild conjectures chased each other around her mind stupid with terror. White faced, she stood transfixed before him on the rapidly emptying dance floor.

He was speaking again, still pleasantly smiling, still impeccably courteous of tone. "You are a whore, Olivia. I should have recognised that earlier." Fleetingly he took her hand again to skim icy lips over it. "We will not meet again. As the wife of an Englishman and the mother of a Birkhurst brat, you repel me." Throughout his few sentences, his smile never faltered, nor did the level of his tone.

A Birkhurst brat!

In a chest dangerously close to exploding, Olivia's breath gushed back into her lungs and she gasped. The sudden inhalation made her head whirl and it was with an effort that she steadied herself. But the relief at what he had just said brought the colour back into her cheeks and made her eyes sparkle with a vivacity she no longer needed to simulate. She laughed lightly as they walked side by side off the dance floor. "Oh, there will be *two* Birkhurst brats soon," she retorted in a rash whisper loud enough only for him to hear. "I can then repel you *twice* as much as I do now, and with even greater justification!"

He gave her the parting gift of a flinch, and Olivia jubilated. It was a crumb, a mere crumb, but oh, the satisfaction! "In that case, my congratulations." His recovery was swift. "Once again I thank you for your excellent hospitality, Lady Birkhurst. I wish you good night and a safe journey to your father in Hawaii."

For the second time in her life, Jai Raventhorne turned to walk out of it.

It had been an excruciating and demanding charade for Olivia and it had taken its toll on her. Her throat felt so parched that it pained her to swallow; her knees, as soft as water, were threatening to buckle under her. She longed to escape out of the room into some dark corner, but she dared not—she was still the cynosure of a hundred pairs of eyes. Underneath her exhaustion, however, lay a soaring sense of triumph, a bounding and unashamed elation. She had survived the acid test! She had lived through her most persistent nightmare and emerged on the other side with only minor scratches. Her will-power had endured; she had not disintegrated. Whereas Jai Raventhorne had lost forever the capacity to wound her, *she* could still make him flinch! It was another crumb, poor compensation for a crushed life, for the humiliating farce of her marriage, for a betrayal too vile to ever forgive, but it was better than nothing.

And he had not the whiff of a suspicion about Amos! The rest was worthless, immaterial, a mere flea bite. She would think about it tomorrow. Or not at all. The dreaded interlude had come and gone. It was over. She would never have to see Jai Raventhorne again.

Gaily, with rejuvenated enthusiasm, Olivia allowed her hostess mind to once again take over.

Now the fires did need to be doused; the rooms were turning uncomfortably close. To chase the smoke haze out of the room she sent instructions to the punkahwallahs to accelerate their efforts with the swinging overhead cloth fans. Some of the ladies were dabbing their foreheads with hankies soaked in cooling eau-de-Cologne and others were vigorously flicking their painted ivory and sandalwood hand fans across their faces. The musicians had finally gone to eat. As Olivia crossed the deserted dance floor, she caught the unexpected sight of a burgundy-clad back still standing erect and motionless next to Ransome. Loath to encounter him again, she was about to change direction when a corner of her mind picked up an odd observation. For some reason, everyone had suddenly gone very still and quiet. The flowing banter, the sound of conversation in the main salon—loud and lusty only a moment ago—seemed to be fading into untidy silences. Half-completed sentences dangled in the air; laughter, so boisterous until now, was petering out and melting into a sporadic murmur. Soon, even the murmurs were gone. A hush, thick and tangible, was suddenly upon them like a shroud. Puzzled, Olivia walked through a doorway, craned her neck for a better view of the room—and then very slowly turned into stone.

In the entrance now clearly in her vision was Sir Joshua Templewood. Next to him was her cousin. Across the deathly quiet room Olivia's gaze collided with Estelle's and held it for a moment. In the depths of Estelle's baby blue eyes was defiance, a challenging innocence, that seemed to dare Olivia to do her worst. It was evident that whatever little games her enterprising cousin had devised for the evening's entertainment were by no means played out. There were more yet to come.

Sir Joshua was in formal evening dress, perhaps still a size too big but worn with the same casual elegance that had always characterised him in happier times. A naturally large-boned man, at his peak he had towered over most. Now, once again his shoulders were squared and thrown back proudly and his head, greyer than it had been thirteen months ago, was held customarily high. There seemed to be no sign of the stoop that had so diminished his ramrod spine in recent months. Only in the oversize of his greatcoat was noticeable the loss of flesh from his body. For the rest, although his usual ruddiness had paled and the hollows of his sockets deepened, the sheer force of his personality still arrested the attention and held it without effort. He was again as he had been before, and for those who had believed him to be on his deathbed, the vision was a revelation.

Carefully now Sir Joshua unwound the rich silk cravat from his neck and handed it imperiously to John Sturges, who was standing behind him and looking desperately ill at ease. Then, with similar concentration, he worked his fingers out of his gloves one by one and neatly put the gloves in a pocket of his greatcoat, which he chose not to remove for the moment. The precise little gestures, the placid expression, the astonishing steadiness of his hands, the compelling, commanding air of confidence—all were astounding to those who had known him intimately during the preceding months.

Having completed his small duties, Sir Joshua advanced towards Olivia, who now stood rooted to a spot next to Arthur Ransome. Looking neither left nor right, he strolled casually down the centre of the room as if he were alone, as if the gaping throng on either side of him were nonexistent. Sir Joshua's steps were measured, unhurried, his expression one of supreme composure. For the very good reason that something in his eyes forbade it, nobody ventured to utter even a word of greeting. He stopped in front of Olivia, held out his arms and placed a hand on each of her shoulders. He smiled and kissed her warmly on both cheeks. "Forgive me if I have surprised you, my dear, but Estelle insisted that I make an appearance." He nodded approvingly. "You look very fetching in that blue, my dear, very fetching indeed."

Somehow Olivia found a voice. "I . . . I'm delighted that you have decided to come, Uncle Josh. We . . ." Her voice trembled and died and her frightened eyes flitted helplessly between Arthur Ransome and Jai Raventhorne, both motionless and without expression, not far from each other. Formally, Sir Joshua shook Ransome's hand. Neither man spoke, at least not in words. What passed between them otherwise could be anybody's guess. Ransome's face, as wooden as Raventhorne's, revealed nothing. The immediate formalities completed, Sir Joshua turned on his heel to walk briskly and directly up to Jai Raventhorne. He thrust out his right hand.

"Good evening, Jai."

"Good evening, Sir Joshua."

The hush in the room deepened perceptibly, like a fog, all-encompassing and impenetrable. There had never been a single occasion when the two men had come face to face, at least in public, and the effect of the confrontation now was electrifying. Nothing in Raventhorne's body seemed to be moving, not even his breath. Only a small muscle beneath his right temple twitched; the pale, staring discs of his eyes were blank as if they perceived nothing. He neither looked down at the hand proffered nor made any attempt to take it. For a few more terrible seconds Sir Joshua's hand remained suspended, unacknowledged and disdained. It was only when, with an indifferent shrug and no noticeable loss of confidence, he dropped it finally to his side that Raventhorne spoke again. He used the same tight tones as he had done before, but now he spoke quietly. "I think you must know, Sir Joshua, that what is between us cannot be redeemed by a handshake."

Sir Joshua appeared to consider that with singular concentration, then he nodded. "No. It cannot," he agreed. "Not now. Particularly not now, but then Estelle does not see that."

Had Olivia not been standing close behind her uncle, she would not have heard the exchange made in almost inaudible undertones. Something at last flickered in Jai Raventhorne's soulless eyes, a spark of amusement, a flash of contempt. In her peripheral vision, Olivia saw Estelle recoil and nervously reach out for her husband's hand. Abandoning his casual, almost cordial manner, Sir Joshua suddenly turned businesslike, a man of purpose. Removing one of his gloves from the pocket of the greatcoat he still wore, he flicked it swiftly across Raventhorne's face.

"Tomorrow morning at the Ochterlony tower. Promptly at six. Ransome and Sturges will be my seconds. Choose whatever weapons you wish."

From the riveted crowd there was a collective gasp, undoubtedly of delight. It had been many months since Calcutta had witnessed a duel that promised to be as worth-while as this. Worth-while? Why, this one promised to be sensational! Suddenly, detaching herself from her husband, Estelle ran to her father and flung herself at him. "*No!* Papa, you swore that you believed me!" Her anguished whisper was fierce as she clutched both his lapels in her trembling hands, her face horror-struck. "You *swore* that you did, you gave me your *word!*"

"Take her away, John." Save for a curt glance and an effort to detach himself from Estelle's grasp, Sir Joshua paid her scant heed.

"But *sir . . . !*" Shocked, his son-in-law made no move to comply, unsure as to how serious was his father-in-law's command or, indeed, the rest.

"Take her away, John!" Sir Joshua did not raise his voice but there was a hard glint in his eye and there was no mistaking the ring of authority in his command. With the trained reflexes of a soldier used to obedience without question, John firmly grabbed his wife by her arms.

Estelle resisted violently and promptly burst into tears. "You lied to me, Papa, you *lied* to me! You *know* I told you the truth, you *know* I could never fabricate—"

"Let go, Estelle!" John interrupted sharply, speaking for the first time. "Do as your father says."

Estelle let go and turned her tear-stained, despairing face to Olivia. "*Stop* him, Olivia, he mustn't . . ." The rest of her sentence dissolved in a fresh burst of sobs and then John, looking perfectly wretched, was marshalling her away hurriedly through the nearest exit.

No one else dared to intervene. If the frightened and fascinated onlookers had understood little of Estelle's confused exhortations to her father, what they did understand was that high drama was about to be enacted and they were damned if they were going to miss any of it. The compacted excitement in the room was intense, bouncing back and forth, up and down, against the walls and ceiling like water sloshing around an inadequate container. Through the flurry of Estelle's enforced removal, Raventhorne had remained silent. But now, as everyone's attention focused on him, and Sir Joshua's challenge awaited a response, he became mobile again. Casually he turned and strolled back to the fireplace. Balancing an elbow on the mantelpiece, he crossed his ankles in a stance of intended insolence. The curve that slashed his hard mouth open did not even pretend to be a smile, but it was audacious.

"No."

The single syllable was said mildly, even amiably, and Sir Joshua stiffened. "You refuse to offer me satisfaction, sir?"

"Oh, absolutely!" Under his breath he made a sound that might have been a laugh. "That, as you might recall, Sir Joshua, has always been the single purpose of my life."

Nobody even tittered. Closed into thin slits, Sir Joshua's shining brown eyes registered no reaction to the taunt. He shrugged and, with continuing calm, dug his hand into the pocket of his greatcoat and extracted a blue velvet packet. "Very well. In that case, we might just as well settle the matter here. We have enough witnesses." Swiftly he removed his coat, tossed it back into Ransome's arms and started to unroll the blue velvet.

Raventhorne's expression turned watchful, but he did not alter his posture. "Here?"

"Why not? As good a place as any other, wouldn't you say?"

Slate grey in their wariness, Raventhorne's eyes moved down to stare hard at the careful, loving delicacy with which Sir Joshua's adroit fingers unwrapped his possession. The palms of both hands now cradled the glinting metal of his twin Colts. Tossing the velvet wrapping over his shoulder, he half smiled, but it was Raventhorne who spoke. "I do not usually come to dinner-parties equipped to duel, Sir Joshua. Had I been forewarned," he shifted the weight of one foot onto the other and laced the fingers of his hands, "I would certainly have dressed with greater care."

Taking no cognisance of the mockery, Sir Joshua nodded. "Oh, I appreciate that. Therefore I have come equipped for both." He went down on a knee and slid one of the revolvers along the carpet. It spun with the accuracy of a well-aimed missile to stop just a fraction before the toe of Raventhorne's shining black shoe. "You may verify, or have verified by your chosen second, that it is loaded in all chambers and is in perfect firing condition. If you wish, you can test it yourself."

The tremor that swept across the room was undulant, like an earthquake. Fevered murmurs hummed in the air like swarms of bees. Huddled against each other in a corner, a group of ladies stuffed dainty lace handkerchiefs in their mouths, almost fainting with anticipation. Only one, however, had the gumption to actually do so. Tight lipped, her husband looked the other way and it was left to two young cavaliers to leap forward and hurriedly carry her out of the room. The call of chivalry completed, they returned equally hurriedly without any loss of entertainment. If there was to be bloodshed, nobody wanted to miss it, no *sah!* The remaining ladies valiantly sniffed courage out of their ammonia vials and silently vowed not to swoon, at least not until it was all over.

The revolver, in the meantime, continued to lie at Raventhorne's feet. He had not given it the courtesy of even a glance.

"Well?" Sir Joshua's whip-lash query rang with impatience.

"No, Sir Joshua. I commend your thoughtfulness, but I do not fight with borrowed weapons." His expression was alert, but his manner was still casual, as if in his offensiveness he merely played a game.

"Pick it up, Raventhorne," Sir Joshua commanded evenly.

"No. I do not fight with broken-down old crocks either!"

Nothing changed in Sir Joshua's face. The ruthless self-discipline of decades appeared to make him impervious to Raventhorne's continued barbs and taunts. Under the circumstances, his control was admirable. "Whether you do or not, I intend to kill you, Raventhorne. I hope that much, at least, is clear to you."

"By all means try." Raventhorne's lip thinned in a sneer. "*If* you have the accuracy left. And the guts."

"Oh, I have both the accuracy and the guts!"

Raventhorne laughed. It was a strange sound, neither full throated nor a chuckle, more an expression of continuing scepticism. "You know as well as I do, Sir Joshua," he said softly, "that you have never had the guts to kill me. Nor *will* you ever have. Not even now."

Sir Joshua frowned. "You are wrong, Jai," he said, enunciating with great care. "It is not the guts that have been lacking. But whatever the lack, it cannot prevail now. That you must already know." He inhaled; it was almost like a sigh. "Very well, then. If this is the way you choose to die, so be it. To give you a fighting chance, I will count up to three—"

"For God's sake, man!" A figure leapt out of the hypnotised audience to position himself between the two adversaries. It was Barnabus Slocum. His forehead dripped sweat and his pendulous jowls quivered with pious indignation. "You can't shoot an unarmed man in cold blood, Josh! Have you taken leave of your senses? Dammit, sir, it . . . it's *illegal!*"

"Shut up, Barney." There was no heat in Sir Joshua's order, only irritation. "Stay well out of this."

"Stay out?" Slocum went scarlet and started to splutter. "Now, look here, Josh, enough is en—"

"If you don't step aside, Barney, I promise you will get hurt."

"Good God, man, this is a civilised gathering. You can't carry on here like some blasted highway hooligan!" The bright red face turned purple. "As an officer of the law, in the name of Her Gracious Majesty, I forbid it, I absolutely and categorically forb—"

"Do stop blithering, Barney! This is not your business, even less Her Gracious Majesty's." He raised the barrel of the Colt and aimed it squarely at Slocum's bulging paunch. "Now get out of the way unless you want to be rid of that beer belly in a hurry."

A shrill, nervous giggle sounded in some far corner but was instantly throttled. Already red veined with an excess of champagne, Slocum's eyes shot open wide in alarm. He blinked, gulped a few times with an astonished orifice opening and shutting like that of a gasping fish, then hastily opted for discretion over valour. Cursing under his breath, he retreated and melted once more into the crowd, duty done. Nobody else even considered intervention, and with good reason. If Raventhorne was damn fool enough to meet his Maker with such arrogant dispatch, then who were they to stop him? In any case, it couldn't happen to a more deserving man.

"One."

Rumbling comments sliced off sharply as Sir Joshua began his count. Paralysed into immobility, Olivia finally stirred but as if in a dream. She felt she was under water, her limbs pressing down with heaviness as she floated in and out of herself far away from her coherent mind. "Stop him, please . . ." The mouth that moved was hers but the voice was somebody else's.

"No." Ransome's skin was ash grey, but there was no hesitation in his response. "It must come. Let it."

"But Raventhorne will die!" Her words echoed and re-echoed in the hollow that was her brain; her tongue was like lead in her mouth, each movement of it an effort. With supreme courage she started to walk towards her uncle, to stop the senseless slaughter from happening, to do something, anything! But before she had even taken a step, Ransome had her arm in a vice grip.

"*No,* Olivia!" His whisper was uncommonly harsh. "One of them *must* be eliminated today! *Leave them be.*"

Standing next to Olivia, John Sturges shuddered and looked ill as he repeatedly rubbed his eyes with the back of his hand. He muttered something to Ransome but received no reply. Eyes riveted, face bloodless, Ransome only watched. And waited.

"Two . . ."

With the lazy grace of a fawn taking its ease, Raventhorne raised a hand to brush a slick of hair off his forehead. In his expression there was neither fear nor, indeed, hostility. Only an oddly amused curiosity—and that enduring contempt. Within the empty caverns of Olivia's mind arose a recurring refrain: *Jai Raventhorne is going to die, Jai Raventhorne is going to die.* Did she care? she wondered idly. She could not tell. From behind, someone took her hand and pressed it as if in support. She turned to look and saw that it was Willie Donaldson. He shook his grizzled grey head in a cautionary gesture, a tacit reference to her abortive attempt at intervention. "You canna do aught, lassie, not in your condition." She smiled without having heard anything.

"Three!"

In the sepulchral silence, hushed as in a tomb, nothing moved; there was not a breath, not a whisper. Then Raventhorne laughed. "What's the matter, Sir Joshua? Running short of courage *again?*"

The cutting barb preceded by a minim three simultaneous happenings: Sir Joshua's revolver blazed, Raventhorne sidestepped—in a lightning reflex—and behind his shoulder an exquisite gilt-framed Belgian mirror of handsome dimensions exploded in a firework display of tinkling glass. Extensive as it was, the room reverberated with the shot as if it had been cannon fire. Women screamed, there was pandemonium all around and the noise of human voices was ear shattering. No one was certain as to what exactly had happened and in precisely what sequence. In the babble there were hoarse oaths, incoherent expostulations and a few hysterical giggles. Then, gradually, the smoke started to clear; the confusion spent itself and receded. What emerged from both was the form of Jai Raventhorne still standing erect and once more in the same place and the same derisive posture as before the shot. The room froze. Once more everyone fell silent. Could it be that the best of the evening's entertainment was still to come?

"Try again, Sir Joshua!" Raventhorne's taunt was soft but incisive. In it now was a ring of confidence. "Aim three inches lower this time. My heart still beats."

There was a ripple of disappointment around the room. Dammit, not a drop of blood shed yet? What the deuce could Josh be thinking of! Slowly and very deliberately, Sir Joshua's right hand rose again. As he took aim, his facial muscles were taut with concentration, his dark brown eyes hooded into slits and unmoving. Once more curled around the hairspring trigger, his index finger was as steady as the rock out of which his huge body seemed to be hewn. It seemed impossible that he could miss again. In desperation, Olivia swivelled her head to look imploringly at Arthur Ransome, her own limbs petrified into immobility, her senses skittered. But Ransome neither felt her look nor returned it. He stood as if in a trance, motionless, staring. The suspense of the moment was excruciating. Eyes boggled, mouths gaped and foreheads dripped with sweat, but not a hand rose to dab them dry. Everyone waited for that second shot with which the life of Jai Raventhorne would be ended. To even blink might deny them the thrill of a lifetime, the culmination of a strange vendetta such as they had not seen before nor, probably, ever would again.

An eternity passed. But Sir Joshua's second shot did not come. Time pulsed by in tick-tock rhythm as a dozen clocks marked collective heartbeats. Patiently everyone waited, breath bottled tightly, eyes still wide and unblinking. The seconds passed, and then a minute—and still there was no second shot. Sir Joshua's index finger hugging the trigger, caressing it, trembled once, and then it trembled again. Nothing in his face changed, not even the fixedness of the eyes boring into those of his intended victim. But slowly his firing arm descended until it was once more hanging loose and vertical by his side. For a moment longer the two men held each other's gaze, one challenging and derisive, the other ungiving and unreadable. Swinging lazily, the Colt dangled from Sir Joshua's forefinger, then with a soft plop fell onto the carpet. In the electrifying silence it could have been a clangor. Sir Joshua did not pick it up again. What he picked up instead was his greatcoat draped over Ransome's arm, behind him.

Very briefly, his expression casual and untroubled, Sir Joshua smiled, first at Ransome, then at Olivia. He arranged the coat in careful folds over his own arm, turned on his heel and started to walk out of the room. Despite the universal puzzlement, no one stopped him; no one uttered a word in question or comment. Parting, like the Red Sea before Moses, the crowd merely gaped, the mystification unsaid. As when he had entered, Sir Joshua's steps were firm, his towering figure stately and imperious. In no more than a quarter of a minute, he had traversed the length of the room and passed through its doorway.

Puzzlement became shock, and shock, indignation—and then all was bedlam. There were incensed opinions being voiced everywhere, all at once. What the *devil* did Josh think he was up to, dash it . . . ? How dare he, an Englishman and a gentleman, lose his nerve in the midst of his own challenge? Why, it was outrageous! Worse, in scandalous poor taste, scandalous! The man had proved a disgrace to decent colonial society, to say nothing of to his Club. The consensus having been arrived at with her own shrill participation, the Spin decided to finally swoon. Vociferous in their disappointment at having been short changed in their expectations, everyone decided it was time to go home.

Only Barnabus Slocum heaved a long-suffering sigh of private relief as he swabbed the pouring perspiration from his face. Had that damn fool Josh actually killed the half-caste bastard (as Slocum had secretly hoped), he, personally, would have been in a pretty pickle as the station's chief law officer. It would have been a clear case of murder. He would have had to go through the tedious procedures of arresting and charging Josh publicly. Of course, subsequently a case would be devised somehow or other for self-defence, but with so many blasted witnesses it would have been sticky, to say the least—*damn* sticky! Josh would have had to be given at least simple imprisonment for three years. The native community would have howled, naturally, and there would have been hot, embarrassing exchanges with London. Just as well the man had not only missed the first time around but then also turned yellow. Slocum was damned if he understood *how,* but then he wasn't about to probe further. As for that bloody, trouble-making sod, Raventhorne . . .

Slocum looked around, as everyone else appeared to be doing, with perplexity, but there was no sign in the room of the man whose life had missed being extinguished by a whisker. Sometime during the melee he too had slipped out, leaving behind even more unanswered questions. Grudgingly, another consensus of opinion was conceded. A dashed shame, of course, that Josh *had* unaccountably misfired, but neither could it be gainsaid that Kala Kanta himself had displayed exemplary courage. Not every man—not even a pure-blooded Englishman!—could have flirted with death with quite such panache. And that too unarmed and in confrontation with a crack marksman of proven mettle. It hurt to admit it, naturally, but British fair play decreed that even the devil, when deserving of it, be given his just due.

Suffocated by the warmth of a pressing crowd, all talking at once in their expressions of polite thanks and good nights, Olivia finally capitulated. Someone, perhaps Willie Donaldson or the doctor, she could not tell which, steadied her with an arm and then lowered her into a chair. In her hazy vision she saw Lubbock approach, his face alight with pleasure at having seen this dreary town redeem itself with *some* goddam action. His grinning lips moved but she did not hear a word. Mrs. Sturges, John's mother, placed a handkerchief soaked in eau-de-Cologne on her forehead; a familiar voice—Estelle's?—murmured soothing words and John Sturges's strong hand vigorously fanned her face to produce cooling breezes. Olivia closed her eyes in transient relief, but she knew that she was going to faint. Before she actually did so a second later, a wild thought streaked through her mind, almost reducing her to hysterical laughter.

Now she had one more score to settle with Jai Raventhorne. Not content with having ruined her life, he had also damn near ruined her party.

18

Whether ruined or not, Olivia's extraordinarily suspenseful *burra khana* was the talk of the station everywhere on the following day. Little else was considered worthy of dissection at the Tolly's Sunday brunch, on the cricket pitches and in private homes, both European and native. Nor was the matter likely to be laid to rest through many more days and weeks to come. It was, everyone agreed without reservation, the most conversationally productive event in the town since 'Forty-five, when Charlie Bagshott-Brown had decamped with his wife's jewellery, his employer's petty cash and his daughter's piano teacher, and Prudence Bagshott-Brown had retaliated by inviting her friends to a public bonfire of her husband's remaining possessions on the Maidan. That Olivia's lavish dinner-party would have been even more conversationally fertile had Sir Joshua not made such a spectacle of himself by turning his back on his challenge was a matter of collective regret. But few denied that whatever the quantum of unplanned entertainment generated, it had been worth every minute of the evening.

Olivia spent the morning in bed. Her physical and emotional stamina was exhausted. And once more she was a victim of that convulsing nausea that was an inevitable symptom of her condition. Honed into a habit, her selective memory resolutely pushed aside for the time being the more devastating aspects of the evening: Raventhorne's diabolical return, the crippling suspense, her uncle's unforgivable melodramatics, Estelle's unspeakable duplicity in inviting both Raventhorne and her father, and Sir Joshua's strange wilfulness in inviting public scorn. Was she relieved that it had been so, that Raventhorne still lived? Olivia chose not to think about that at all. What she filled her mind and heart with instead was an overwhelming prayer of gratitude; Jai

Raventhorne had no suspicions about Amos. *She and her son were safe!* And now with both Raventhorne and her cousin out of her life forever as of today, the path was clear for the return of her darling son from Kirtinagar.

For the moment nothing else mattered.

At tea time Arthur Ransome called, hunched with unhappiness, drawn and suddenly aged, and sunk in mute depression. Making inquiries about her health and being reassured by Olivia, he then relapsed into silence and sat sipping his tea with no further attempt at conversation. What had happened last night was harrowing enough; it was not easy for him to listen to the harsh mockeries and ridicule now being heaped openly on a friend with whom he had shared almost all his life. But what appeared to be weighting him down now went far beyond the reach of mere public displeasure. Something pressed on his mind that could not be explained by the debacle of last evening. Olivia's heart went out to Ransome, but she had no words with which to solace him. Rather than insult him with platitudes, she chose to merely sit, sharing his silence. In the face of his loss of spirit, she even felt involuntary pangs of sympathy for her uncle. If she had had to make self-destroying decisions in her life, so perhaps had Sir Joshua. As ordained by circumstances, the blueprint of his life too was perhaps as tragic in all its compulsions as that of the rest of them. Even as tragic perhaps as the life of the man he had tried to destroy last night.

That morning, early, a letter had been delivered to Olivia from John Sturges. He had begged to be received, even briefly, one last time before their departure for Cawnpore. Not unkindly, for she had nothing against Estelle's husband, whom she liked without qualification, Olivia had used her fatigue and indisposition as an excuse for her inability to receive any visitors. In a separate envelope, there was also a letter from Estelle. That Olivia had returned unopened.

As far as she was concerned, Estelle was dead. As dead as Estelle's own mother still considered her, never to be accepted back into her life.

And then, the following morning, Amos was returned!

Fatigue forgotten, Olivia was delirious with joy. The child's howl of indignation as she strangled him with a hug and covered his face with kisses was music to her ears, starved for so long of the sound. She could not stop touching him, caressing him, savouring him like a hungry man suddenly presented a feast. He had grown considerably even during that one month, and now actually had a tooth showing. Mary Ling displayed the fine line of white in his gums as proudly as if it had been her very own achievement.

Throughout the day Olivia did nothing save sit and devour her son with her eyes. One by one, she celebrated each of his new, unfamiliar aspects—the rounder plumpness of his cheeks, the growing inquisitiveness in his darting grey eyes as they perceived and appraised everything in the nursery, his denser riot of silken black hair, the newly acquired sounds and gestures and little mannerisms. With all their trials behind them—almost, almost!—she swore silently that they would never again be parted, not for a moment, not if it was within her power to prevent it.

But in the meanwhile, there still remained a great deal to do. Infused with renewed energy, Olivia settled down to prepare in earnest for her imminent departure.

Crates reopened for the ball had to be packed and sealed again, the contents listed for Donaldson's benefit. Unwanted bric-a-brac had to be given away to charity, the staff's wages and baksheesh computed, gifts purchased for home, cupboards and writing desks cleared, bills paid, office matters settled and, of course, the house lease finalised with Lubbock. Mary's boisterous songs and Amos's amusing responses up in the nursery as she worked greatly relieved the tedium of Olivia's chores, and as she laboured she smiled almost in contentment. If life gave her nothing else but her son and a return to her father, it would have still given her enough.

The pile of thank-you notes that were being delivered in a steady flow Olivia discarded unread in her waste-paper basket. She had no wish to be reminded of an evening that had brought nothing but all-around agony. One by one she went through the compartments of her desk, throwing away without remorse the accumulated impedimenta of months. It was as she shook out the final drawer that something fell onto her desk flap with a metallic tinkle. For an instant Olivia's breath caught; she had no recollection of having stored the silver locket here. But then, ruthlessly, she swept that too into her waste-paper basket. The past was finished, forgotten. She had no more need of its tawdry souvenirs.

But that night, irritatingly, she could not sleep. An odd little prickle kept gnawing away at her mind, refusing to let it rest. Finally, with a mild oath of exasperation, she rose and walked towards what she knew to be at the core of her problem: the waste-paper basket. Cursing both her compulsion and her weakness in indulging it, she retrieved the locket and held it for a moment in the palm of her hand. Against her pink skin it looked tarnished, even shoddy. Returning to her bed she sat down, sighed heavily and, with her thoughts again rampaging, started to polish it absently with a corner of her bed sheet.

In marrying Freddie you have allowed him to appropriate something that I considered to be mine.

It was not, of course, to Amos that he had referred. It was to her! There was a time when she would have been flattered by the conceit, but now it merely helped to incense her further. Once, her affliction had been gullibility. It was not that now, nor would it ever be again. *Mine!* With what infernal presumptuousness he had staked a claim to what he himself had abandoned with such irreversibility! And he had had the nerve to fabricate the existence of a mythical letter, proud that he had written away her life and appended it with his signature. How conveniently he had hidden behind silence rather than explain that ultimate abomination, his shameless relationship with her cousin! Mine? No, he had never accepted her as his, never, not for an instant, even during that much flaunted affinity. Now, as smooth as cream, he had twisted the facts to brand *her* as the villain. Perhaps not even Estelle in her bovine stupidity was to blame. Perhaps. The culpability was totally his, his, *his.*

And he had called her a whore.

Olivia recognised her rising fury for what it was, a weakness. A chink. A lacuna in her character. No, she was not yet indifferent to Jai Raventhorne. The testimony of the tremble in her hands, the smouldering embers of anger so ready to flare, the intensity of her reaction to the sight of that damned locket—all these were proof of her failure. Callously, Olivia tossed the locket into a corner of her almirah, vowing to discard it later. But the embers continued to smoulder; Jai Raventhorne had called her a whore. And he had not thought to ask her, not once, *why* she had married Freddie!

Ironically, that was the one question from Jai Raventhorne that Olivia still feared the most!

"Any further instructions for furniture and suchlike?" Willie Donaldson asked. "Ships' rations are bloody near inedible. I've made arrangements for plenty of dry stores and for two milking goats for the bairn."

Willie's grave concern for her, and his obvious grief at her abandonment of Calcutta, again touched Olivia. "No, Mr. Donaldson," she said gently, with affection, "you have done more than enough as it is."

Gruffly, he waved aside her gratitude. "Noo, aboot funds for the journey and after . . ."

"I have enough, thank you," she said and quickly steered him toward another matter. "About Hal Lubbock—have you been in touch with him again?"

He turned even more glum. "Aye. The danged dandiprat canna wait to move in," he muttered sourly. "Her Ladyship would faint at the very idea of that ill-mannered oaf loose aboot the manse." He brooded for a moment on that, then sighed. "That loan Your Ladyship has made to Ransome . . ."

"Yes? What about it?"

"Would there be more loans being planned?"

"If necessary. Why?"

As an indication of his disapproval he tapped the point of his pencil against his front tooth. "I would na advise it. Certainly na after what happened at the manse that night." To Donaldson the Birkhurst house was always *the* manse as if none other existed.

"Oh? I'm sorry, but I don't see the connection."

He bristled. "The connection is that Josh might be finished but the Templewood and Ransome name plate still remains. The bastard's na going to rest till he puts them right *oot* of business. He's going to hit oot in any direction, and I happen to believe we should na be giving him provocation by trying to salvage a sinking ship."

"*We* are not, Mr. Donaldson, *I* am. And you already know my views on that. In any case," she retrieved some papers off his desk and rose, "I will not be here when Mr. Raventhorne returns from Assam. Therefore his future designs, evil or otherwise, are immaterial to me."

She left Donaldson dissatisfied and still glowering at his feet, but by the time she had reached home, Olivia had forgotten the conversation. It was Amos's supper-time. As always, she liked to feed him his evening meal because he gobbled it up with such amusing relish. With a sprightliness that would have surely earned a sharp rebuke from Dr. Humphries, she ran up the stairs to the top floor and flung open the door of the nursery. But then she skidded to an abrupt halt.

Sitting cross-legged on the floor and feeding her son out of his little silver bowl as he sat on her lap was her cousin Estelle.

Estelle? *Estelle . . . ?* For a moment Olivia thought she was hallucinating. Why, Estelle was well on her way to Cawnpore! Surely this was some horrible trick being played on her by a hyperactive imagination?

But then Estelle confirmed her flesh and blood manifestation and spoke. "Can you believe it? The little imp actually *bit* me! Who would think that one half of one tiny tooth could inflict such damage?" She laughed and wryly held up a finger.

It was the laugh that, like a splash of ice water, jolted Olivia back into reality. Weak with shock, she clung trembling to the door-post. "What are you doing here . . . ?" she whispered, deathly white.

"I came to see you." Estelle showed no sign of embarrassment. "I was waiting downstairs when Amos started to cry. Naturally I had no idea that he was here, so I ran up to see him. Mary was about to give him his supper. I took charge of that and sent her and the ayah off for their meal." She looked mildly accusing. "I persuaded John to postpone our going so that I could see you." She chuckled the child under the chin and he gurgled.

"Get out." Olivia's eyes were stricken and, try as she might, she could not raise her voice above a whisper. The familiar fingers of fear played havoc with her spine—*Estelle would know, Estelle already knew!* With a single blow she had made a mockery of all her precautions, all her lies and her plottings and her manifold deceptions. She ran forward and wrenched her son off her cousin's lap. *"Get out!"* she screamed. "If you dare touch my son again I . . . I'll *kill* you!"

Slowly Estelle stood up, her face as chalky as her cousin's. "It's no use, Olivia," she said, starting to tremble. "It's too late—you see, I know that Jai is your son's father. Now give him back to me, can't you see he's still hungry?" As if to confirm her observation, Amos emitted a furious wail and started to struggle in Olivia's arms. Estelle calmly reached out to retrieve him, then sat him up in his crib and began to feed him again.

Numb with despair, Olivia had no strength to resist her. Slowly her rage dissolved into an overwhelming sense of defeat. She had lost. She had been a blind fool to even consider that she would not. There were too many variables against her, there always had been. Sick with hopelessness, she slunk to the nearest chair and slumped into it. "Why did you not go to Cawnpore?" she asked dully.

"Because *John* felt that I should meet you and apologise in person." Estelle's tone was flinty. "Whatever explanations I had wanted to make to you earlier, explanations you would not hear, I felt you had forfeited the right to have. I came here today only to please John. What I had not bargained for was . . . ," she faltered and her tone changed, "Amos." Unbidden, a sob sounded in her throat and she could not suppress it. "I know now why you have hated me so much . . ."

Wearily Olivia dragged the back of her hand across her eyes, the fight flowing out of her. "I don't hate you, Estelle. I just want you to go and leave me alone. Please, Estelle, just . . . *go!*"

Engrossed in feeding the child, Estelle made no move to comply. "Jai does not know that he has a son, does he." It was a statement, not a question.

Olivia shuddered but could make no response. Too broken even for anger, she merely sat with her chin lowered against her chest.

"That is why you had to marry Freddie. I know now about Mama's attempt to kill herself; I forced Uncle Arthur to tell me everything." The last of Amos's supper gone, she wiped his mouth with a napkin and handed him a toy. "By leaving Mama you risked having her make another attempt, as she had threatened to. By staying, you risked a scandal even more horrendous, considering who Amos's father is." Her voice cracked and her china blue eyes suddenly welled. "Yes, you do have cause to hate me. Your hate is entirely justified, Olivia. Oh God, *how* justified!"

"Estelle, please . . ."

Embarked at last on her voyages of belated discovery, Estelle could not be stopped. "*I* was the ill-starred, ill-fated weapon Jai used to destroy your life, and I never even suspected it!"

"The time for penitence and recriminations has passed, Estelle!" Loathing the prospect of post mortems, Olivia harshly scythed through her remorse. "Explanations are now irrelevant. Can't you see it's too late for all that?"

"For you, maybe," Estelle cried, her tone equally resolute, "but not for *me.* Can't *you* see that now more than ever I must convince you that Jai has never been my lover?"

More tricks? Dear God, no more! Olivia prayed in silent despair.

"It's true, Olivia, I *swear* it." Her eyes dropped and she flushed scarlet. "I give you my word that Jai has never, never laid a hand on me. How could he have when . . . ?" She choked and turned her face away.

"No?" Olivia's laugh held a vicious touch of humour. "My dear, *dear* Coz, you wrote me a letter, remember?" Did the brainless girl really expect her to believe her barefaced lies?

"Yes, I remember." With an effort Estelle retrieved her composure. "I don't deny that I was dazzled by Jai. The . . . elopement was his idea, but I did agree to it with alacrity, with enthusiasm. That much is true. I genuinely believed that he returned my . . . feelings, although he never said so, not once, with words. Oh, he spun me plenty of fairytales, insinuated many promises, blinded me with glorious visions of London and New York and the wide, wide world outside that I longed to see." She stopped to glare defiantly. "*You* must know better than anyone else, after all, how plausible that silver-tongued charm of his can be!"

Anger stirred but Olivia refused to dignify it with a reaction.

"I was bewitched by Jai." Calm again, Estelle continued. "Like a mindless puppet, I followed him onto his *Ganga,* filled with inane dreams of eternal rapture. But once the *Ganga* sailed, everything changed. Jai changed . . ." Her voice hushed; her expression stilled. "That first night, intoxicated with my silly dreams, I lay preening myself on the four-poster in my new georgette négligé waiting for—"

"Stop it!" Outraged, Olivia leapt to her feet, unable to tolerate more. "I don't want to hear any of this! A few days ago you called it an *escapade,* a trifling adventure to teach—"

"Whether you want to or not, my precious cousin, you *will* hear it! You will hear every damn word I am about to tell you." Estelle ran to the door, slammed it shut, turned the key in the lock and rammed it down the front of her bodice. "Sit down, Olivia. All these days you have denied me a hearing. Even if I have to tie you down in that chair, you will not deny me one now, you *can't* deny me one now!"

Faced with her cousin's blazing eyes, cheeks flaming with hot anger, Olivia felt her own will falter. "You can't force me to listen . . . ," she began weakly. Regardless of the protest, Estelle forged on.

"When Jai finally came into the master cabin, he had turned into someone I barely recognised. He looked demented, so ravaged by restless energy that he could scarcely stay still. He tore down a curtain from a porthole and flung it at me, commanding me to cover myself unless I wanted to have my backside tanned with a hairbrush." Even to that, Olivia made no sarcastic comment. If nothing else, it might be interesting to see just how far Estelle was prepared to go with her ludicrous fabrications. "Then he sat down and informed me that, as a woman, I offended the man in him. In fact," Estelle quivered, "he said he despised me because I was a selfish, cosseted, English brat who sickened him with her blatant immodesty. His intentions towards me were simple: He would take me to England and dump me with either my mother or with John Sturges. He looked at me very strangely, *cruelly,* and added, 'whichever of the two is prepared to accept you.' " Estelle paled at the memory, her face almost translucent in its loss of colour. "I didn't understand what he meant. At least not then . . ."

"Oh, is that so?" Wildly sceptical, Olivia finally sought refuge in sarcasm. "Hence all this sudden affection? These glowing character certificates? To say nothing of that impertinent invitation to *my* house!"

Estelle laughed, a pathetic little sound full of sadness. "Oh, Olivia, Olivia—my poor, dear, ill-used cousin! I never thought I would see the day when *you,* so infinitely superior to me, would turn jealous. No, *please* don't flare up again, I haven't quite finished." Amos whimpered. Ignoring Olivia's angry expletive, she walked to the crib and handed him his silver rattle. Then she went to stand by the window with her back to the room. "I was livid with him, of course, shocked by his callousness and mortally offended. I tried to argue, to fight, to demand explanations, but he would neither listen nor answer any questions. Instead, he locked me up in the cabin, vowing to keep me there until we docked at Southampton." She turned, empty faced, to look at Olivia. "All those days that I remained locked up, I fumed and fretted and cried, not understanding anything about his sadistic motivations, unable to see *why* he had humiliated me with such callousness. Then, when we reached Cape Town, he suddenly relented and removed the lock from the cabin door." She stopped to refresh her throat with a drink of cold water from the carafe that stood on a table. Then, running the tip of her finger around the rim of the glass, she stood lost in thought for a moment. "It was in Cape Town," she said eventually, her tone deathly hushed, "that Jai told me the truth. Everything. I now know that he held back nothing. I asked Uncle Arthur to corroborate it. He did." Her hands were shaking so much that the glass almost fell, so she replaced it on the table.

So, Estelle also knew! Then why had the unthinking, foolish girl risked that confrontation between Raventhorne and her father at the ball? Pulling in a crisp breath, Olivia chose not to make any comment just yet. There was more to come and Estelle would not now be thwarted.

"Why Jai decided to suddenly inflict the truth upon me, I had no idea—except to ensure that it would double my suffering, perhaps. I was appalled, Olivia, decimated—I couldn't *believe* it!" Softly, she started to weep. "Later, I began to recall things—snatches from the past, fragments of overheard conversations, furtive whispers between Mama and Papa, terrible rows behind closed doors. And I remembered something else: that portrait of Grandmama in our dining-room. Then, everything started to fall into place. I was astonished that I had not made the deduction before. Grandmama's eyes had stared down at me all my life, Olivia." Her own eyes rounded with renewed horror. "Amos's eyes. *Jai's* eyes . . ."

Estelle's voice trickled away. Between them, covering the room like a dense fog, a silence fell. It was thick and it was chilly. In the lull Amos dropped his rattle and they both started. Mechanically Olivia rose, picked up the rattle and handed it back to the child.

"Yes," Olivia said calmly, cracking the silence first, "I know the truth. I know that Uncle Josh is Jai Raventhorne's father."

It was out. For the first time the secret behind the enigma had been spoken aloud. Even though she had known the truth for some time and now it was she who had voiced it, Olivia felt a frisson of shock run through her and she shivered.

With a cry, Estelle covered her face with her hands. "You are clever and perceptive and far too astute not to have guessed, Olivia, but to me Jai's revelation came with the force of a thunderbolt. I could not believe that such a hideous thing could be true!"

As Estelle surrendered herself to emotions raked into rawness, and huge, rasping sobs rocked her shoulders, Olivia was suddenly beset with confusion. Watching Estelle, she felt the first stirrings of uncertainty. Could it be that her cousin's absurdly improbable farrago was *true . . . ?*

Estelle wiped her eyes and noisily blew her nose. It looked as red as a boiled lobster. Fighting for control, she swallowed hard. The effort to continue did not come easily. "I saw then why Jai had persuaded me to run away with him," she said wretchedly. "Jai had vowed to destroy us all. He knew nothing could be more thorough a weapon than the stench of . . . of . . ." Stuck in her throat, the word took time to dislodge, "of . . . *incest.* It was he who suggested that I write that letter to Papa and Mama, that letter that would not leave any doubts in their minds as to his intentions. They had never told me the truth. They knew I could not have possibly suspected that Jai was my half brother, that we shared a father. Jai didn't care a damn about a public scandal. If it came, well and good; if it didn't, it wouldn't matter. As long as my *parents* believed me to be defiled, contaminated, forever a pariah, it was enough for his purposes. They would never recover from the shock; they would always remain trapped in the secret hell of that knowledge they could not share with anyone. However much I protested my innocence, no one would believe me." For the first time Estelle sounded bitter and, in her bitterness, angry. "And no one does. No one except my darling, sweet, trusting John. And, perhaps, Uncle Arthur." She gave a despairing little laugh. "You don't believe me either, do you, Olivia? Isn't that why you have found me . . . repugnant?"

It was an accusation Olivia was not yet prepared to deny. Boiling with doubts, her mind bubbled like a cauldron about to overflow. There was in Estelle's voice something she could no longer dismiss: the unmistakable ring of truth. But a hundred mushrooming questions still remained unanswered. Loose ends dangled, puzzles still cried out to be solved, paradoxes abounded. And, in the ultimate analyses, no matter how startling her cousin's confessions, nothing she had said reduced the enormity of her own betrayal by Jai Raventhorne.

Estelle misinterpreted her silence and stiffened. "I know you still don't believe me, but it doesn't matter. Had I not learned about Amos, I would not have wasted so much of your time. It is because of him that I felt you earned the right to know the truth." Softening, she walked to the crib where the child had finally dropped off to sleep, gently smoothed his hair and draped a sheet over his exposed legs. "You must have loved very deeply to have risked so much, Olivia." Her voice was husky.

Olivia stared at her glacially. "One way or another, it no longer is relevant. I am the wife of another man. I might not love him, but I cannot forget his goodness to me." The cold eyes turned empty. "My son's name is *Birkhurst*—make no mistake about that ever, Estelle! My once-upon-a-time motives are forgotten. After I have gone away, they will cease to have even existed." She held out a hand. "Now, may I please have back that key?"

Estelle searched her expression. Finding no encouragement in it, she shrugged. "By all means." She dug into her bodice and tossed the key to Olivia. "Two more explanations whether you like them or not. Yes, it was insane of me to ask Papa to come that night, but it was a justifiable delusion. When I returned, I told Papa the absolute truth, as I have told it to you now. He pretended to believe me. Or, because I so desperately wanted his love and trust again, I convinced myself that he did believe me. But Papa lied to me. In my naive faith, in my innocence, I did not see his lie. Not for a moment did he deviate from his intent to kill Jai. Laughably, I thought the public gesture of a simple handshake would suffice as a first step to a reconcilation even after a lifetime of such profound hatred." Her bitterness erupted again, making her distort her mouth as if the taste offended it. "As for Jai, he—"

"Doesn't much like surprises?" Olivia provided with a derisive laugh. "Yes, I know. And you omitted to tell him in advance of your game plan for a family reunion!"

Estelle flushed. "If I had, he wouldn't have come," she said simply.

"And that astonishes you? You expected a man who had vowed to destroy every one of your family to suddenly accept olive branches in public? Yes, Estelle, you *must* have been mad to hope for such consideration!"

"That is not *all* there is to Jai!" Estelle cried. "You don't know everything yet, Olivia."

"Nor wish to, dear Coz! All your many whys and wherefores of whatever happened or did not happen are not part of my life anymore. Had your father been able to pull that trigger, my reactions would have been no different."

With an unhappy nod, Estelle conceded the point. "Yes, I can understand your hatred for Jai, but he is my half brother, Olivia. There are many things about him that I have truly learned to love. At present he is furious with me, I know, but his anger will pass. He will forgive me because he will see that I meant well—and because he too cares for me as a sister. All these months that we were together . . ." She stopped. Taking note of Olivia's stubborn lack of response, she stood chewing uncertainly on her lip and refrained from saying more.

"I rejoice that you have found a brother, Estelle, and I wish you good luck in your relationship." Olivia unlocked the door and held it open for her cousin to leave, a pointed reminder that the debate was now over. "I take it that you start on your journey to Cawnpore tomorrow? I hope you have safe passage and contentment in your new home. My love to you both and to Uncle Josh."

Estelle's mouth curved in a scornful little crescent. "Yes, I see why you went to such inordinate lengths to keep me from Amos. You fear that Jai will learn of his son and want to take him away, and naturally you believe that the one to inform him will be me!"

It was a doubt that had been haunting Olivia from the moment she had seen her cousin in the nursery. She battled not to voice it but her anxiety flared and she could not stop herself. "And will you?"

A great sorrow settled over Estelle. "You are justified in your distrust, I know that. It is *I* who helped to deform your life, albeit unwittingly. To even ask for forgiveness now is an insult. I accept that you can never forgive me. But, for whatever you consider it's worth, I promise that I will not be the one to inform Jai about his son." Wistfully, she smiled. "Believe it or not, you are still the paragon I admire most. I could never harm you knowingly. So, go to your father in peace, Olivia. Your secret is safe with me."

She fell silent and waited in hope for some sign of friendship, some final word of affection as they parted for the last time. None came. Granite faced and unforgiving, Olivia returned her pleading look with matching silence.

"Well, farewell then, my heartless Coz." Disappointed, Estelle made a hollow attempt at lightness. "I wish you two a safe journey home with much happiness in Hawaii." Formally they kissed each other on the cheek. Casting a loving glance at the sleeping child, Estelle suddenly laughed. "Isn't it ironical, Olivia, that without even knowing of each other's existence or destiny, both Jai and his son will have lived deprived of their fathers?" With that final thought, she left.

The irony of the thought, however, stretched even further. When she voiced it Estelle was not to know that such a deprivation was not to be that of only Jai Raventhorne and his son.

Three days after they had departed for Cawnpore, a messenger brought for Olivia a letter from John Sturges. Sir Joshua Templewood was dead. Sometime during their first night away, as they camped in the compound of a dak bungalow near Burdwan, he had walked out into the dense forest that surrounded the region.

There, in solitary communion with nature and her prowling denizens, he had placed the barrel of his revolver in his mouth, pointed it upward and shot himself through the head. The act had been committed lying full length on a grassy verge with a cushion carefully arranged beneath his head. Consequently, whatever mess was made by his blood and brains had been efficiently absorbed by the cushion. The attention to detail was not surprising; as everyone knew, Sir Joshua was in essence an extremely neat man, fastidious almost to a fault in his personal habits.

A *chowkidar,* keeping watch over the sleeping travellers, had heard the shot and, fearing dacoits, had immediately alerted the party. It was as the men were hastily taking up their weapons to repulse a possible attack that Sir Joshua's absence was noticed. A search-party was mounted bearing guns and lanterns. Deep in the bowels of the jungle in the direction from which the shot had been heard, Sir Joshua's body was found, with the back of his head and half his face missing. He had left no note to explain his act of self-destruction. Perhaps he had recognised in his infallible perceptions that none would be necessary.

It was not until morning, John wrote, that a village carpenter could be located to fashion a crude coffin, and a priest disturbed from his early duties at a Burdwan mission and persuaded to administer the rites required for a burial. Reluctant to sanctify a suicide, the priest had protested violently. He had to be taken to the site by force and the simple and hasty interment conducted at gun point. The grave had been dug deep because predators were forever on the hunt for handy cadavers, and it was unmarked, save for a rough cross. The ceremony concluded, the party had to hurry away by a different route to avoid trouble with the local authorities and District Collector. Subsequently, two witnesses had been bribed to swear to a more socially acceptable cause of death, and a vaguely worded death certificate extracted from a drunken medical officer in the mofussil in exchange for seven rupees and three bottles of army grog. Estelle had not taken her father's death at all well . . .

John had sent his message from their next stopping post. A similar letter had been dispatched to Arthur Ransome. Should an obituary notice be placed in the Calcutta newspaper? John left that, and its wording, for Ransome to decide.

Olivia was horrorstruck by the news, then bereft and riddled with remorse. Buried in the turmoil of her own situation, she had selfishly not even bid her uncle farewell before he departed on his fateful journey! She had profoundly resented much that Sir

Joshua had perpetrated upon them all in his arrogant intractability. But now that he was gone she knew that she would miss him sorely, miss the many fulfilling hours they had spent together. She had learned much from him; she would always be grateful for his many kindnesses, his abundant generosity to her, and would always mourn him. In the aftermath of the shock of his death by his own hand, when her tears had been shed and the sorrow subsumed, Olivia had an inadvertent thought: Lady Bridget would have approved of at least this, his final thoughtfulness in avoiding a scandal by blowing out his brains away from Calcutta.

Without further delay Olivia hurried over to the Templewood house to be with Arthur Ransome in his moments of ultimate grief. The house and servants were shrouded in a pall of gloom, and poor Rehman and Babulal were inconsolable. Ransome, however, was not at home. Aware that as soon as the terrible news became public hordes of visitors would descend to unwittingly desecrate his solitude, he had probably retired to some secluded corner elsewhere to grapple with his irredeemable loss and shed his tears in privacy.

It was a loss, Olivia saw now, that Arthur Ransome had expected for a very long time. And he had been accurate in his calculated prediction: Of the two men, one had to be eliminated; and now one had. Another victim? No, not this time. A casualty, yes, but never a victim. Sir Joshua Templewood's pride would not have ever allowed such an indignity.

Olivia returned home and sat down immediately to write a letter to her cousin Estelle.

It was during the next night that the bleeding started.

"Not a healthy sign, my girl, not healthy at all." Summoned in the small hours of the morning, Dr. Humphries looked concerned.

"Could it be something serious?" A chill hand wrapped itself around Olivia's heart. "Could there be any danger of . . . losing the baby?"

His expression mellowed. "No, no, nothing like that. At least, not at the moment. We'll have the haemorrhage checked in no time, but no more *burra khana* jollifications and suchlike." He frowned his displeasure. "What you will have to do now is *rest.*"

"Rest?" She struggled up on an elbow. "For how long?"

"Oh, not long. I'd say about a month." Whistling, no doubt to introduce some note of good cheer, he set about preparing his medications.

"A month!" Olivia blanched. "But I sail within a *week!*"

"So I hear. And right sorry we'll be too to lose you, my dear. But Hawaii or Timbuktu or, for that matter, capers around that blasted Agency—they're all out of the question. That is," he peered at her from beneath bristling eyebrows, "if you don't want to risk losing the child. Do you?"

"No, of course not." Miserably, Olivia laid back her head again. "But I must also *leave* . . ."

"You will, m'dear, you will." He patted her hand. "One month here or there won't make all that much difference."

"I can rest on the ship!" She grabbed his hand beseechingly. "I could stay in bed every day, *all* the way to Honolulu. Mary will take good care of me, you know that."

He sat down and looked solemn. "There are storms in the Pacific, dreadful storms, Olivia. I know, I've been in some. The buffeting is fierce. Not even those in strong condition can withstand it. Few of the ships carry adequate medical supplies, surgical equipment in case of emergency, if they carry doctors at all. Willing to chance all that, my girl? If you are, then by all means sail. With my blessings."

Olivia was crippled with despair. "But if I delay now, it will be too *late!*"

"Too late?" Not knowing the problem, he looked puzzled. "Well then, just have your baby here! It isn't the end of the world, you know. I may be a grizzled old goat with rude bedside manners, but I've brought more confounded little blighters into this station's bloody confusions than you memsahibs have had hot breakfasts! Why all the silly fuss? Don't work up a lather for nothing; it's bad for the liver." He dismissed the matter with a cluck and began rattling off instructions to Mary. Then, having sent her off to the kitchen on some errand, he sat down and yawned away his drowsiness. "Incidentally, that tamasha of yours—damn fine bash, you know. Millie hasn't stopped talking about it." He removed his glasses to polish them. "Wouldn't have expected a tough old buzzard like Josh to turn chicken. But perhaps just as well. Not every hostess wants murder on her menu, eh?" The news of Sir Joshua's death had evidently not yet become common knowledge, although it soon would. In the kindly doctor's seeming insensitivity, however, Olivia felt a stab of pain. She closed her eyes and turned her face away. "It was all that Wild West stuff that brought on this little drama, wasn't it?"

"No," Olivia said bitterly, the sorrow cleaving her heart many pronged and many sided. "But I see now that I've been living in a soap bubble. I should have had the sense to see that it could not last forever."

"Soap bubble?" Used to the babblings of patients, he paid scant heed to hers and, as Mary returned, became busy again. Olivia submitted to his ministrations without protest, barely conscious of them. It was as he was leaving that Dr. Humphries sought to offer more salutary advice. "If I were you, I'd send again for that giddy cousin of yours. I hear they're not long gone and are probably still within reach of a swift horse and courier. *She'll* cheer you up pretty fast, I wager!"

Olivia gave an unhearing nod, but as soon as he left she succumbed to a despair so violent, so fathomless and unrestrained, that it seemed to devour her. Stifling her voice with a pillow, she started to scream. And continued to scream until her bones ached and her throat rebelled and dried up in defeat.

Of course, as always, nobody heard her.

She had no more resources left.

Within Olivia's grasp now lay no more devices with which to divert the flow of a fortune so single-mindedly malignant in its intent. Exploiting her weakened condition were other searing anxieties. Raventhorne suspected nothing yet, but for how long? Olivia cursed the waywardness of her body that had again made her a prisoner constantly awaiting the call of a hangman, forgetting what gifts that body had given.

To secrete Amos once more in Kirtinagar was impossible; Raventhorne was a frequent visitor to the palace. No matter how total her faith in Kinjal and Arvind Singh, royal courts were rife with intrigue, with invisible spies. And servants talked. To rent a house in some distant mofussil and remain there with Amos until her baby was born and then swiftly leave for Hawaii was to invite even more attention. Why, pendulating tongues would ask, should Lady Birkhurst choose to have *both* her children away from station? It was not the gossip that deterred Olivia; it was the shrewd interpretations Raventhorne would put on it. Amos could, of course, be dispatched to Hawaii in advance with Mary

Ling, but that option Olivia could not bear to consider seriously. To be deprived now, at this lowest of low ebbs, of her only emotional support would be an intolerable act of self-cruelty. She needed Amos for her survival, to be able to face whatever else was yet to come. The thought of Cawnpore flashed through her mind too and then lingered. Olivia recognised that this was, perhaps, also Estelle's lowest ebb, her most crying hour of need. The loss of her father would have brought crushing anguish—and, unavoidably, it would have also brought lashings of renewed guilt. To try to resolve now who had started what, when and where was futile; but the toxic little seed that Estelle had helped to sow, from which had sprouted so much of their collective present misery, would now inevitably infuse even more poison in her unfortunate cousin's mind. Nevertheless, however much she might want to provide solace to Estelle, Olivia had of necessity to abandon any such project. Dr. Humphries would never allow her to travel by coach on rough roads in her present condition. And, for the moment, nothing was as vital in her life as the precious "mango seed" that had arrived in her womb with so little warning.

That Jai Raventhorne might be delayed in his return from Assam and that she would have time to escape after all, Olivia did not even consider. With the configurations of her stars so relentlessly inimical, not even by divine oversight could such a miracle be possible.

Sunk as he still was in his own morass of dejection, Arthur Ransome—again a daily visitor—was even more depressed by her all-pervasive air of hopelessness. He disapproved of the reclusivity on which Olivia insisted. Many kind sympathisers called and left their cards—especially now since the news of Sir Joshua's ghastly death "in the jaws of a man-eating tiger near Burdwan" had shocked the city out of its wits—but Olivia would see only Ransome, the Donaldsons and Dr. Humphries. As he was in the habit of doing lately, Ransome came armed with the station's newspapers, both English and vernacular, in which glowing tributes were being paid every day to an erstwhile merchant prince who, despite his recent reverses, had left an indelible mark on the corporate life of the city. There were, of course, many veiled and hostile references to Raventhorne, but none at all to that memorable evening that had started the process of Sir Joshua's demise long before he placed the revolver barrel in his mouth. By dying, it seemed, Sir Joshua had earned the station's forgiveness for an act at first believed to be cowardice but now talked of as one of honourable mercy toward an unarmed opponent. The papers were full of the early history of Templewood and Ransome, spiced liberally with anecdotes of their Canton days. Clinging to his nostalgia, Ransome relived their lives vicariously through the newspaper articles, reading them aloud to Olivia, enjoying again the company of a friend forever lost. And as a last act of loyalty he had concealed the true cause of death in the obituary.

One day, emotionally drained by his second-hand existence through written words—and perhaps prompted by the good doctor—Ransome hesitantly suggested that Olivia send for Estelle from Cawnpore. "You must forgive her now, Olivia; the poor child has lost both her parents," he said heavily, unaware of what had passed between them already. "Just as there are comedies of error, we must now think of our mishaps as tragedies of circumstances even now not totally irredeemable. Whatever is left to end will perhaps still end well for us." He shuddered with the force of a sigh. "Those of us who remain, that is."

Olivia looked away. How was he to know, this most gentle, most sincere of all the dramatis personae in those "tragedies of circumstances even now not totally irredeemable," just how far it still was for her from ending? Laden with her own sorrows, she did not reply to his suggestion. She knew, however, in her unfailing self-honesty that she had been harsh with her cousin, unduly so. Whatever Estelle's delusions about Raventhorne, in Olivia's mind now there was no doubt that her cousin had told her the truth. But for the moment, she decided, she didn't want to talk about it. Instead, she stirred a new topic. "I've been meaning to ask you for some time, Uncle Arthur, about the sale of your house. Have you had any luck yet?"

Ransome made a wry face. "With Raventhorne back? There will be no luck with any buyers, my dear. He will see to that."

She couldn't believe what she had heard! "Even *now?* Even after Uncle Josh is dead and buried . . . ?" She was incredulous.

"But *I'm* not."

"He can have nothing against you!" Olivia said warmly, her indignation so sharp that it shook her out of her torpor. "I have an idea—since Lubbock cannot now have my house, shall I ask if he might consider yours? I understand he's impatient to settle down as soon as possible."

"Lubbock will not consider mine. He too deals with Trident."

Even in her residual apathy, she felt a stab of irritation.

"Well, we'll never know unless we *ask,* will we? Hal Lubbock is an American, a roughneck, a born and bred fighter. He's not scared of bullies!"

Ransome still looked dubious. "But why should Lubbock want to *buy* unnecessary trouble?"

"He's a maverick; he doesn't give a damn about trouble. Perhaps he'll even thrive on it! I feel it truly is worth at least a *try.*"

Ransome scanned her face, his own uneasy. The colour had risen in her cheeks and her expression was suddenly animated. "Now, now—you're not going to appropriate for yourself more of my problems, are you, dear? I would much rather your prime duty remained to your health and to your unborn child."

"Yes, of course it will," Olivia murmured. But for the rest of the evening she remained abstracted, lost once more in her own thoughts.

They ate a simple supper of mulligatawny soup with warm, crusty rolls, and later played a few desultory games of backgammon. Neither was inclined to make idle small talk, both steeped in their separate ruminations and both sipping rather more glasses of claret than they had intended.

"He couldn't fight it, you know. And it finally killed him."

"What?" Olivia was startled by Ransome's sudden remark just as she had asked for the decanter to be refilled. It seemed apropos of nothing.

He stirred out of his brooding study of the opposite wall and sighed. "Jai was right to mock that night, Olivia. When it came to the crunch, face to face, Josh didn't have the guts to pull the trigger on his son . . ." He broke off, confused. "You . . . er, do know, I think, that Josh is . . . was Jai's father . . . ?" Never having said it before, he coloured.

"Yes."

He was full of remorse. "Forgive me, my dear, if there are matters that I have concealed from you, but there are areas of their lives, Josh and Bridget's lives, that I did not feel morally competent to discuss with anyone. Now that it is all over . . . ," perturbed again, he hung his head low, "yes, all over, there is no more need of shameful fabrications. I can now tell you everything, even my own part in the sordid saga. It will be a relief for me to unburden myself fully, that is," momentarily, he looked uncertain, "if the nostalgic ramblings of a bereft old man will not bore you out of your mind."

The burning anticipation, the insatiable hunger with which

Olivia had once waited for revelations about Jai Raventhorne's life had long been dissipated. Now if she shook her head in denial of Ransome's hesitation, it was for her own selfish reasons. Foreknowledge, she saw, was ammunition. Should it be her misfortune to ever confront Raventhorne again, she would need adequate weaponry. Mere hatred would not be enough. She leaned forward with interest and asked, "What was it that stopped him from pulling that trigger? I can hardly believe it was *compassion!*"

"Compassion?" Ransome laid his head back and looked up at the ceiling. "No. Not compassion. Something less tangible, more abstract. I wish I could find a name for it but I cannot." They had not yet talked of that strange evening, or of its traumatic and far-reaching consequences. Olivia saw that it was there that his thoughts now dwelt. "You see, my dear, *I* believe in Estelle's innocence, but Josh never did. Despite all her protestations, he was convinced that Jai had desecrated her—and he was insane with shame, with fury. They were both his children, after all. That there should be such . . . contamination between them lodged like a burning coal in his gullet. He knew he now *had* to kill Raventhorne. He had no other option left."

Involuntarily, Olivia smiled, not without some scepticism. Ransome had put it rather curiously, considering that was what her uncle had been trying to do for years!

He caught her thought and was again confused. "Yes, I know what you are thinking, but there were factors, other factors . . ." He tossed up his hands in apology. "I see that I must start at the beginning if I expect to make sense of this. And the beginning, I suppose, is when Josh first met Jai's mother up in Assam." His eyes crinkled at the corners in the effort to recall a history more than three decades old. "Much of this is already known to Estelle. Had she been told earlier, Josh might still be alive." With unsteady hands he lit a much favoured cheroot and watched closely as a perfect smoke ring shivered away into nothingness. "Anyway, Josh had gone up into those hills to see for himself the recently discovered giant tea trees, which everyone was talking about. He was very young then, newly wed in England and awaiting the arrival of his bride. Our partnership had started to prosper with regular China Coast runs, his mother had recently selected a handsome residence for him—the present bungalow—and Josh himself was as carefree as a lark." Visualising the past, his face seemed to come alive in the recreation of that contentment. "But in those godforsaken mountains, Olivia, strange things happen to men's minds, especially to those of white men unused to the jungles. She was, Josh said, a mere slip of a girl, innocent and untouched like a naiad, a magical sprite spun out of moonbeams on a midsummer's night . . ." He stopped and blushed. "At least, that's how Josh described her. Of course he was instantly smitten. *Bewitched* was the word he used later. Like many hill people unsullied by civilisation—or what we believe to be civilised—she was a child of nature, free as a mountain stream, delicate as a petal. Josh had never seen anything like her and, well, he lost his head. He forgot everything, past and future. Only the present mattered—and this ethereal nymph sent by the gods to guide him through the portals of paradise." He coughed and added quickly, "Josh's words again. Anyway, he eventually had to return home, still befuddled with euphoria. But then Bridget arrived and, within a week of their rapturous reunion, Josh had forgotten Assam as easily as if it had been a dream. Perhaps to him a dream was all it had ever been."

Olivia pulled her shawl closer about her shoulders. It was suddenly eerie talking before flickering fire-light about a dead woman whose silver locket she had once worn around her neck. She wished she had not agreed to listen with quite such willingness; she wished she had not drunk so much wine either, but it was too late. Drowned in his tumbling reminiscences, eager to shed their ancient load, Ransome would be hurt if silenced.

"Unfortunately for both Josh and the girl, she happened to be the only and much cherished daughter of a tribal chief. Her involvement with a white man was a disgrace for her people, especially when her condition became evident. Tribal laws are rigid, the same for all. By consensus of the elders, she was expelled from tribal country and told never to return. She had some silver jewellery. She sold it and fled to the plains in search of the sahib she knew only as Josh. It took her months to complete the journey, further weeks to locate the house. By the time she arrived at the gate she was in a state of collapse and her child was almost due."

A detail flapped loose in Olivia's memory. "So, it was to the Templewood house that she went, not to yours. And it was in those servants' quarters that her child was born."

It was not said as a reminder of his earlier lie, but he was again instantly apologetic. "Yes. I did not tell you the whole truth then, Olivia, but from what you hear now nothing has been omitted. Yes, it was Josh's staff that gave her shelter and it was through them that her story, or part of it, was pieced together. By now Josh had only a hazy memory of the girl, but when it sharpened, he was appalled. It was a Sunday morning, I recall. Both Bridget and Josh's mother were at church. Nevertheless he panicked and came running for my assistance. Of course I agreed immediately to house the girl in my servants' quarters, but before the transfer could be effected, Bridget and his mother returned. The girl's presence was hastily explained with the alibi that she was the younger gardener's wife. Neither of the ladies was particularly interested. The lie was accepted at face value and the girl's transfer to my house deferred. But then that night, Josh's luck ran out further. Around midnight, amidst a fearful monsoon storm, the girl was delivered of her son, Josh's son, with the dhobi's wife and daughter acting as midwives. And with that deliverance, unknowingly and innocently, the poor girl diverted the course of all our histories forever."

He stopped to pluck an orange from a fruit bowl resting between them and to peel it with singular concentration. It was only after they had shared its juicy segments in mutual silence that he again picked up his narrative.

"Imagine the nymph, Olivia, that unfettered creature, imprisoned in a dark cell like a butterfly pinned under glass. It was pathetic, dreadful—but she, poor child, never had any thoughts of revenge against the man who had reduced her to this abysmal situation. It was the gods themselves who decided to come to her aid and rectify some of the imbalance in her young life without her intervention. Her mixed-blood son was born nameless but bearing ample proof of his parentage in his eyes. The connection was not difficult to make."

"Who first made it, Aunt Bridget?" Olivia asked.

"Good heavens, no! Almost fresh out of a convent school with a prim, proper upbringing that taught her that even to *think* of sin was a sin, such a prospect never even occurred to poor Bridget. But to Lady Templewood it did, when she marched into the quarter to see the newborn, as she had done with every new addition on the premises. She knew instantly and she was livid. With no second thought, she commanded Josh to have mother and child removed immediately from the house, before Bridget too could make the connection. But you know something, Olivia?" Rubbing his chin as his memories jostled, Ransome paused. "Josh refused. For the first time that I can recall, he openly defied his mother. Finally, after much heated and surreptitious debate, Josh forced her to compromise. It was decided that they could stay, provided the girl never allowed the child to stray out of the servants' compound."

Momentarily Olivia was astonished. How could such an arrangement have been successful and for so long? But then she recalled her own visit to the Templewood staff quarters behind the kitchen house. There had been hordes of children about whom she had neither seen nor whose existence she had even suspected. She remained silent.

"The night after Jai's birth, Josh and I stole into the quadrangle to have a look at the infant he had so unfortunately sired. When he saw him, Josh was paralysed with shock. Then he was so overcome with feeling that his eyes filled. He realised that it was upon the face of his first-born, his son, that he gazed and he was speechless with awe. He was still appalled, disgusted, at what he had done, but at the same time he was fascinated, in some inexplicable way almost *thrilled.* And you know something else, Olivia?" The energy drained out of him and he seemed to wilt. "It has always been these two diametrically opposite emotions, emotions one would consider mutually exclusive, that have controlled Josh's relationship with his son since that first time he held him in his arms. If the paradox puzzled me, it absolutely bewildered Josh. That he should be horrified at having sunk low enough to have spawned a half-caste bastard, Josh understood. It was the other half of the paradox that confounded him, at times incensed him. To him it was a flaw in himself, a weakness—and Josh despised sentimental weakness, human fallibility. But that first night he was torn, utterly torn, and the illogicality in himself defeated him."

"I don't suppose Uncle Josh ever considered actually *acknowledging* the relationship, did he?" This Olivia asked out of curiosity; she was now deeply intrigued.

"Oh no." Ransome's denial was categorical. "No. There was never any question of that, never. Above all, Josh was fiercely jealous of his position in society. His driving power was ambition, pure and simple. Oh, he took pride in defying some minor social norms, but privately he retained a healthy respect for public opinion. He could not risk public condemnation in a matter of such grave moral laxity, and that too with a native woman. Hundreds of Englishmen before and since have fathered bastards, many of them half castes, but for Josh to invite open censure was tantamount to professional suicide. Besides, his was a happy, harmonious marriage. He had no wish to disturb it and invite more trouble."

Olivia stretched out her legs to make herself more comfortable. It was late, but she felt not a hint of tiredness. "And through all those eight years Aunt Bridget did not have even a glimpse of the boy?"

"Oh, she probably did have glimpses, but then, as you know, poor Bridget always despised native servants. She never had any interest in them as people, as individuals. To her they were all the same, thieves, cheats and liars to be suffered through necessity. Even if she did see the boy, she would have paid him scant attention."

Without realising it, Ransome spoke also of Lady Bridget in the past tense. It was a small but significant lapse; it filled Olivia with melancholy—and with reinforced resoluteness. The fulfilment of Jai Raventhorne's twisted destiny might have destroyed others. She would not let it destroy either her or her son!

"I think I told you earlier that the boy had this irritating habit of staring. It was, of course, at Josh that he used to stare, sometimes for hours, hiding in the bushes outside his study. Occasionally, Josh exploded with temper, but then, at other times, he tried to be kind and offered the boy sweets. Perhaps out of nervousness, perhaps because he was naturally resentful, sullen, the boy never responded. Once, when the boy ran away from Josh, he slipped and grazed his knee. Not realising that I was watching, Josh took out his handkerchief, brushed the graze, then tied the cloth round the injury with infinite gentleness. When he suddenly spied me, he pushed the boy away and stalked off in a huff, angry that I had caught him indulging that weakness he detested in himself. He never admitted it, you see, never. Not even to me. Maybe not to himself either."

"But surely Raventhorne knew by the time he was eight that Uncle Josh was his father?" It seemed strange to Olivia that a child so aware of so many things would not.

"Only God and Raventhorne know the answer to that. It is a possibility, certainly, but I doubt it."

"Why?" Olivia persisted. "Didn't his mother ever tell him? Or, perhaps, one of the servants? Some of them must have at least suspected the truth."

Her persistence seemed to disturb Ransome. He merely shook his head and said nothing. Still wondering, Olivia let the subject lapse. It was past midnight and the lamps burned low.

Olivia rose to summon Salim to replenish their fuel and to order two glasses of hot milk and a plate of biscuits from the pantry. Then, avoiding the question that had worried him, she asked Ransome another. "All right, I accept that in those early years Uncle Josh did have some feelings, however secret, for his son. But then, why the savage change of later years? Why the bitter hatred?"

"Ah!" Ransome exclaimed, raising a finger at her. "Ah—that was the essence, Olivia, the essence." He puffed vigorously at his cheroot, coughed and thumped his chest. He threw a rueful glance at the pile of stubs in the ash-tray and shook his head in self-reproach. "If it doesn't make sense, so much else in a mind divided against itself doesn't also, you know. Given a basically insoluble dilemma, it develops aspects and facets continually in collision with each other. So much so that in Josh's case, even Bridget became uneasy. What suspicions were building up in her mind we will never know now, but that night when she suddenly came face to face with the boy in the pantry, in a flash of insight she *knew,* perhaps because inwardly she was preparing for it. For her it was a shattering blow. Even more shattering was the look on Josh's face as he raised his crop again and then stilled his hand."

You think I can ever forget what I saw in you that day? In the still of the night Lady Bridget's cry of despair rang in Olivia's ears with the clarity of a bell. She could now guess the context of that cry but she waited for Ransome to vocalise it.

Forgetting his self-reproach of only a moment ago, he reached out for another cheroot and lit it. "Josh recognised the boy, you see, and could not lash him again. For a moment he could only stand and stare. It was only for a moment, but it was enough for Bridget. The emotion in Josh's expression was fleeting, but it was eloquent. And irreversible." He closed his eyes. "So much was destroyed that night, Olivia, so much! If Jai's birth in his father's house distorted our destinies, then this night in the pantry confirmed the mutilations. Bridget might conceivably have, in time, forgiven Josh his infidelity, the social crime of having lain with a native woman, the subsequent shame of a half-caste bastard, even his deceit in harbouring them in her house without her knowledge. What she could never forgive was his tacit, unguarded admission—to her, in her piety and propriety, a shameless admission—of also having *feelings* for the abomination of a half-caste bastard conceived in sin. She was ravaged with jealousy, heart-broken, bitter and disillusioned. In her sense of betrayal, of defilement of her sacred marriage vows, she collapsed and remained bed-ridden for months. Bridget never again lived without fear, nor Josh without guilt towards her for his deceit. Many years later Raventhorne was to return to her life. Mercifully, this was knowledge from which she was spared at that time, but fear of his return some day remained her most persistent trauma." Lifting the glass of forgotten and now cold milk from where Salim had placed it silently, Ransome drank in noisy gulps, greedily, as if to slake an unquenchable thirst.

"Bridget was terrified that if Raventhorne returned, his presence would revive those earlier emotions in her husband, that in his impetuosity Josh would be driven to acknowledge him publicly as his son, that out of sheer vindictiveness, Jai himself would talk. Because she was always a proud woman, Bridget bore her cross with dignity, but within herself she never ceased to suffer. And then, of course, Raventhorne did return." He levelled into a monotone. "The rest you know. I need hardly repeat it. All I see now is that whatever the reality, whatever the truth, however innocent Estelle may be, Bridget will not receive her daughter again. Will she ever forgive Josh now that he is gone? I don't know." He sat shaking his head, reliving his pain. "I don't know. I've written to her, of course. Possibly, she will not reply. If she grieves at all, she will do so quietly, secretly. If she doesn't, that too will be her privilege, not unjustified. Josh did cheat her out of her rightful life, Olivia. It was he who launched the irreversible chain of events, after all. It was his obsessions, his hate, that brought the abhorrent word *incest* into Bridget's chaste world—a word she would never have allowed in her mind, let alone through her lips. As Jai had vowed when he was fourteen, he did take everything away from them, especially the *other* family . . . oh! Did I ever tell you about that or did I omit it?" He frowned, then nodded. "Yes, of course I omitted it, but you shall have it now. Among everything that Jai said he would take from Josh was 'your other family.' Those were the three words he used, your *other* family. Recalling that Estelle had just been born then, the event that took place eighteen years later assumes a frightening significance, does it not?"

Olivia sat motionless. Jai had already decided *then* to include Estelle somehow in his plan of general destruction? Yes, there was something frightening about such invidious planning. She shivered a little, then remembered that this very arch plotter might one day be her own adversary—and she shivered again.

"You asked me a question about Josh. I will now answer it.

Had Jai returned to Calcutta with appropriate servility, with deference, begging assistance from a benevolent father, Josh might have been magnanimous, his reactions to him might have been different. But Jai did not return as a minion or an obsequious mendicant. He returned as a *competitor,* a rival in the tea trade, a challenger—this bastard son of his from the wrong side of the blanket who had been born in his *servants'* quarters! I had never seen Josh as staggered, as shocked, as outraged as he was on that day of Jai's impromptu visit to our office to announce his return. Then came further effrontery, even more galling than his visit. Jai's rise in the commercial world was meteoric. You must appreciate, Olivia, that in our colonial society, alas, Eurasians are considered the lowest on the social scale by both the Europeans and the Indians. Raventhorne, however, traded shrewdly and successfully with both and with equal facility. Perhaps because he was vociferous about his dislike of the British, he earned the trust of the growing Indian merchant community. His dealings with them paid rich dividends, which we could not match. And over the years he made it such that the Europeans could not do without his clippers, his warehouses and all the efficient benefits he provided."

Olivia nodded. "Yes, I do see all that but about my question . . ."

"I'm coming to that, I coming to it." Animated, Ransome inched forward in his seat as if to emphasise the importance of what he was about to say. "Everything Josh had dreamed of achieving, you see, Jai seemed to achieve first: sizable tea exports to America despite those Tea Parties, the innovation of individual tea packets for the retail trade, the fastest fleet of seagoing vessels out of Indian ports—and Josh's ultimate dream, steam navigation. Josh had seen those giant tea trees up in Assam. Anyone who could cultivate indigenous tea would be forever free of the bondage of China, of opium. Thanks to his tribal heritage, Raventhorne did and was. Whereas European experimental tea gardens struggled with labour problems, rising costs, poor quality crops, Raventhorne's tribal kinsmen used their traditional expertise, and his gardens thrived.

"Riddled with envy and corrosive jealousies, Josh began to feel dangerously threatened. And don't forget those acts of ruthless sabotage whereby our opium consignments were consistently pillaged and our teas to London adulterated. Our reputation was crumbling, our credibility was on the chopping block, the roots of our very endeavours were being eroded—and

Raventhorne still flourished. The man was a maniac. He had to be stopped somehow."

"And so," Olivia mused aloud, "a lynching was arranged . . ." Remembering her own glass of milk, she started to sip. Despite Ransome's passionate efforts, somehow none of the dramatis personae in his story seemed real to her anymore. From a distance, they all looked faded, like flowers pressed between the pages of a book and forgotten.

"Yes." He did not deny the charge. "The night-watchman's death was not part of the plot, but everything else was. Thwarted in his ambitions, Josh forgot that Jai was his son, forgot those early years, forgot all the indecisions and contradictions, remembered only that the labours of his whole life were at stake. He . . . I too, of course, how can I deny that? . . . wanted Raventhorne dishonoured, publicly disgraced, thrown out of Kirtinagar, barred from commercial practice—"

"Hanged!"

He was startled by her caustic interjection. "Yes," he conceded. "Even that. And Raventhorne would have hanged, make no mistake about that, had Josh revealed to Slocum the whereabouts of Das's body."

Olivia sat up and looked openly sceptical. "Are you trying to tell me that he didn't?"

Carefully, Ransome reclined again. "I don't know. I wasn't with Josh that night. He *said* he did, but that Slocum dithered. By the time Slocum decided to move, the *Ganga* was out of reach anyway."

"He *said* he did? You don't believe that?"

"At that time I didn't know *what* to believe!" He spread his hands. "When I questioned Josh later outside Slocum's office, he flew into a temper and shouted at me, railing obscenities. 'How dare you question my motives, Arthur?' he yelled, apoplectic with rage. 'Don't you think I *want* to see the bastard swing?' Well, I believed him then. But now I wonder again, Olivia, I wonder again. I suppose I will always have to wonder now." The deeply etched lines of sorrow were once more upon his face. "Had Josh known that his daughter too had sailed with the *Ganga,* there would have been no need to wonder."

Briefly, the faded flowers pressed between the pages of memory burst into full blossom, their colours alive and vibrant. The evening of her party leapt into Olivia's inner vision as clear as crystal. "It was on this tenuous chance, this whimsical fragment, that Raventhorne staked his life that day?" Like the flowers, her incredulity revived. "He could court certain death merely in the *hope* that his father would not be able to kill him? Because of some vague childhood memory . . . ?"

"Again, I don't know. I simply do not know." He shook his head. "Unless Raventhorne chooses to confide in us," he laughed at the absurdity, "that too we will never know. But Raventhorne is canny, unnaturally perceptive. And he has, as he warned us, a long memory. He remembers details, has an arcane ability to reach into people's minds—as I once told you. Even as a child, he was disquietingly intuitive. Perhaps there is some other-world language he shares with his father; perhaps it told him something in those few minutes. Or, perhaps, it was just his good luck. Besides, he had no choice *but* to face Josh's challenge."

"Of course he had a choice!" Olivia scoffed. "He could have picked up the Colt and shot his father instead. He *was* facing a challenge. It would have been an act of self-defence."

"Yes. He could have. And it would have been justified. I know a great deal, Olivia, some of it admittedly conjecture, but I don't know everything. I certainly don't know Jai anymore. Sometimes I feel I didn't even know Josh as well as I had thought. What I *do* know with certainty, however, is that with his despised weakness publicly exposed, Josh would not be able to live with himself. He believed fervently that his son *had* desecrated his daughter, he believed that he *should* be killed, he believed that he *would* be the one to do it. But when the time came, he could not look into his son's eyes and wilfully destroy him. It was a moment of bitter self-knowledge for Josh. He was fallible like other human beings—and in that fallibility, he had let Raventhorne snatch victory away from him. No—that he could never have lived with."

This time as he relapsed into silence and the quiet expanded into ticking minutes, Olivia presumed that he was finally finished, and she rose. If, by breaking the seal of confession with such brutal frankness, Ransome had expunged much from his conscience, he had also exhausted himself completely. But he still made no move to rise with Olivia. Obviously, there was more he had to say. His gaze, open and steady until now, dropped towards his toes as if the weight of his eyelids prevented him from meeting her patiently questioning eyes.

"You asked me something earlier that I was not ready to reveal to you then, not because I intended to withhold it but because I am covered with shame at what else was perpetrated. Yes, Jai has a great deal against me too! This, you see, has to do with his mother." Alert again, Olivia shook off her drowse and reseated herself. "Once more we have to go back three decades, to when Josh saw that forgotten naiad again. What he felt for her now was not passion but pity. Removed from her pastoral utopia, she had become ordinary in his eyes, merely another native woman like one of the ayahs. In his persisting guilt he was still kind to her, but throughout those eight years of her stay in his house he was terrified that one day she would, perhaps unwittingly, reveal her secret. And his!"

"And she never did? She never confided in anyone, even the other servants?" This was another aspect that Olivia's rational mind could not accept. "Knowing servants and their penchant for gossip, surely they did at least talk amongst themselves about their suspicions?"

He nodded, but a trifle impatiently. "It is precisely this that I am about to explain. As for Jai's mother, no, she didn't confide in anyone, perhaps not even in her son. Josh had forbidden her to, you see. For her that was enough. She loved him, you know. Right until the end, she loved Josh without seeming qualification. If the servants did gossip among themselves, well, half-breeds were no longer a novelty. Many sahibs kept Indian mistresses, some of whom might be good-looking domestics from their own households. It is an iniquitous sign of our times, Olivia, that to some Englishmen such arrangements are included in their rights as rulers. And many Indians—curse their submissive fatalism!—meekly accept that right without question, some even with pride." For a moment he forgot his indignation to glower at the fire-red tip of yet another cheroot. Then he recollected the thread of his intended revelation and shook off the momentary deviation. "Nor should you find it surprising, Olivia, that in later years no one in station has made the connection between Lady Stella Templewood and Jai. She died even before Estelle was born. Jai did not return to make his splash until many years after even that. Apart from myself and maybe one or two oldtimers, no one remembers the *colour* of Lady Templewood's unusual eyes!"

But Olivia was no longer interested in that obscure phenomenon; what gripped her mind now with curious tenacity was that blameless waif and her blind devotion to one who so little deserved it. It was about her that she wanted to learn more. "But did the girl never want justice for herself? For her child? Uncle Josh's one callous command was enough to keep her quiet?"

"Yes, it was enough. For her, it was enough. But it was not enough for the rest of us. To ensure that she did not break her silence, we initiated other precautions. We kept the girl quiet on opium." His eyes again dropped to his toes, his deliberate monotone more expressive than any emotion. "The idea originated with Lady Templewood, but we both, Josh and I, endorsed it with enthusiasm. And it was those lethal little pellets that put the unbreakable seal on her tongue. They made her a slave to our will. They drove her and kept her chained to that dream-world where there is no inconvenient reality, no escape. By the time Jai was eight, she could not survive a day without those pellets. She was a hopeless addict and, of course, no longer a threat to our respectability."

From Olivia no comment was required, nor was any offered. But even though the fire glow was warm, she felt her extremities tingle with cold. Haunted by his relentlessly resurrected private ghosts, Ransome shuddered. Wordlessly he rose now, glanced at his pocket watch through obscuring tears, then nodded, as if really aware of the time it told him, and picked his coat off the back of a chair. He started to put it on in front of the long mirror, fastening each button with meticulous intent.

"So you see, my dear, between us we destroyed Jai's young mother." His air of calm was a façade; inwardly he was trampled by guilt. "We sacrificed her without a care in the good cause of preserving our pristine reputations. Oh yes—Jai Raventhorne has plenty against me still, plenty!" He thrust his hands deep into his pockets and a bitter little smile sat on his mouth. "What he has been seeking to redeem over these many years is merely this infamous disparity in the scales of justice. All things considered, would you not say we have been entirely deserving of his vengeance?"

Mumbling apologies for having ruined her rightful hours of sleep with his pointless remembrances, expressing gratitude to her for having listened to them with such patience, he quietly walked out the door. Still shaken by his final confession, Olivia watched him go in silence.

It was almost three o'clock in the morning. They had talked for hours, scratched many surfaces beneath which wounds still throbbed. By all considerations Olivia should have been exhausted, her debilitated body screaming for slumber. But in the aftermath of Ransome's pitiless self-recriminations she felt wide awake, strangely re-energised. All at once her thoughts raced on several levels, her mental revival as therapeutic as Dr. Humphries's copious medications. For one, talk of Hal Lubbock, even in passing, had jarred her into a much needed reminder. She too was an American, a born and bred fighter! All her life she had lived with the glowing example of a father who never conceded defeat even when defeat was a foregone conclusion. He had taught her to detest moral cowards, to despise those who would not fight, who surrendered without even attempting battle. She had suffered a setback, true, but—as Dr. Humphries had pointed out—it was not the end of the world. Why should she hide in corners from Jai Raventhorne? What would her father have to say now if he could see her crippled with anxiety, wallowing in self-pity? His advice to her, were it available now, would be to *let* Jai Raventhorne return and do his worst! If circumstances ordained that she had to stay, had to fight, then she would stay and accept his challenges as they came. And if he ever dared to claim her son and try and remove him from her, she would not make the mistake her uncle had: She would aim straight for Jai Raventhorne's heart. And she would not miss.

The complex, cathartic narration with which Arthur Ransome had sought to relieve his long-fermenting transgressions had melded in Olivia's mind the past with the present in odd, patchwork patterns. Her heart ached for him; he had not spared himself even though his was not the major part in the conspiracy. In his generous loyalty to his dead friend, he nonetheless appropriated half the blame. This other level on which Olivia's thoughts raced produced inner turmoils of a different nature, guilt in another direction. As much as Ransome had been able to, as much as he would ever be able to, he had cast off some of the ballast weighting down his conscience. It was perhaps time she too did the same.

Ignoring the dawn of another day and the fact that she had not slept at all, Olivia sat down at her desk to write another, longer, letter to her cousin Estelle.

19

It was the season of Christmas.

In the cosy downstairs parlour of the Birkhurst residence, the least formal of the reception-rooms, a tall conifer stood in a wooden tub, and it was splendidly decorated with coloured streamers, glass baubles, silver fairies in twinkling tinsel, gold stars, snowy white cotton wool, a cardboard Santa Claus and his reindeer, and banks of mistletoe and holly purchased with scandalous extravagance from Whiteaways. The house was filled with music and song and seldom heard gales of laughter. On Christmas Day the Donaldsons, the Humphrieses and, of course, Arthur Ransome had been guests at a veritable feast of traditional fare produced with uncanny skill by Rashid Ali and the specially summoned Babulal. There had been gaily wrapped gifts for everyone, including the servants and their families, particularly the children. There had also been crackers and fireworks, boisterous carol singing and generally uninhibited revelry such as had not been witnessed in years at the austere, under-inhabited mansion.

It was Olivia's second Christmas in India. And so different in spirit from that miserable occasion of twelve months ago in Barrackpore, which no one now could rustle up the courage to remember!

But if it was different in spirit, the credit for making it so, Olivia conceded readily, went entirely to her cousin Estelle. Her response to Olivia's letter had been warm and pathetically eager, and her return to Calcutta gratifyingly prompt. Olivia was shocked to see the change in her cousin. In her consuming sense of loss she had shed weight, the abundant vitality subdued and the sparkle sadly diminished. In the week Estelle had been here she had seldom talked of her father. It was only when she had first arrived that she had not been able to control her grief; she had thrown herself into her cousin's arms, clung to her like a limpet and wept like a frightened child suddenly finding itself lost and alone at a fairground. But then, after that, she had resolutely cast her own feelings aside to cater to those of her ailing cousin. That she cried privately in the solitude of her room, Olivia knew; sorrow was never far from her eyes, but she kept it hidden. In her palpitating and durable guilt at having contributed so heavily to Olivia's misfortunes, Estelle spared no effort to make reparation in a hundred different ways. She waited on Olivia hand and foot, anxious to please and to earn that forgiveness she despaired of. And with the grim determination of a bulldog she had set about bringing good cheer to a house that so badly needed it.

The Christmas festivities and frivolities had been her idea. "A *quiet* Christmas?" She had echoed Olivia's desultory suggestion with horror. "Why, Amos will never forgive us that! If only for *his* sake, we must make it as merry as we can no matter what our own feelings." Olivia could not deny that she had been touched.

In fact, Olivia could not deny that it was Estelle's effort and initiative that had brought about their rapprochement with such painless ease. If during the first day or two there had been stiffness between them, it had by now melted considerably. Estelle forcibly suppressed her own depression to work hard at lightening Olivia's; whatever the cost to herself, it must have been heavy. The smoothness with which their badly jarred relationship was being patched up was a relief to Olivia. She had not been entirely fair to Estelle, and her cousin's inability to sustain grudges made it easier for her own conscience. Besides, with this truce there was at least one less tension in their lives. Also, Estelle had been spending long hours with Arthur Ransome; therefore, by now there was no doubt that she too knew everything, and it was another relief not to have to pretend with her.

The tedium of Olivia's enforced convalescence weighed heavily on her. Estelle's high spirits and spilling vivacity, however forced they might be, made her an amusing companion, and the confinement to barracks less difficult to bear. In her year away, and with the gruesome tragedies and traumas she had had to bear, Estelle had matured. Outgrown largely were the compulsive flow of trivialities, the irritating prattle that centered forever around herself, the torrent of gossip about Calcutta's tiresome follies and frolics. Now there was restraint in her conversation; finally, Estelle had attained that adulthood she had always craved. But what an exorbitant price she—and others—had had to pay for it!

"Tell me about your father's death," Olivia said one evening after Christmas was over and the year 1850 ushered in with due aplomb.

"No!" Estelle shrank back in horror, all her hidden sorrow contained in the force of that negative. "I can't . . . talk about it. Not yet."

"But you must, my dear," Olivia insisted gently. "It is only talking about it that will make you accept it and set your mind at rest. To keep it imprisoned like this will only delay the healing."

But Estelle buried her face in her hands and shook her head. Taking pity on her acute distress, Olivia dropped the subject.

If, however, Estelle had her own reasons to cover her pain about her father's death, about her experience with Jai Raventhorne she had equally strong reasons to wish to reveal all. At first, refraining scrupulously from again risking her cousin's wrath, she made no mention of him. But then one day, inevitably, the name cropped up between them. Now it was Olivia's turn to recoil, but she didn't. As she had been steeling herself to ever since Estelle had arrived, Olivia showed no reaction save for cultivated indifference.

"I only mentioned Jai because . . . because you said he didn't matter to you anymore," Estelle said uncertainly, again nervous.

"He doesn't," Olivia assured her. "As far as I am concerned, feel free to talk about whomever you wish."

Estelle was not to know that behind the generous invitation lay a motive, the same motive that had made Olivia such a willing listener to Ransome. To her, the past was not relevant anymore; it was the future. Soon Raventhorne would return from Assam. Working in the same business district, with an agency that dealt frequently with Trident, Olivia knew she would not be able to avoid encounters with him, even confrontations. It was not she who intended to incite those confrontations, but Raventhorne certainly would! He had already branded her the betrayer, stigmatised her motives, demeaned and abused her. He hunted for palliatives for a sorely damaged ego, and his vindictiveness, as she now knew, was even more open ended than she had imagined. She had to learn to fight him—and fight him well, to a standstill!—or else, in his uncanny perceptions and intuitions, he would somehow, from somewhere, drag out the truth about Amos.

But to learn to fight such a man, Olivia realised, she needed more equipment, any instrument that might somehow help. Her armoury was slowly filling, but it was still woefully inadequate. During Estelle's one year with Jai, she had become close to him, won him over, as he had her. Estelle had seen him in unguarded moments, with defences down, in situations of revealing informality, when he had perhaps exposed himself without even realising that he had done so. Raventhorne had alienated Estelle's mother from her, been the catalyst for her father's death, almost succeeded in ruining *her* life—as he had planned to all along. What Olivia now burned with eagerness to learn was by what subtle processes Raventhorne's mind and intentions had changed. And how, with all his criminality, had Estelle come to actually accept and love him as a brother? Instinct told Olivia that the seeds of her own strategy would lie somewhere in Estelle's garrulous outpourings; she would have to listen very carefully and then do what Lady Birkhurst had once told her she had learned to do with consummate skill—separate the wheat from the chaff. Hardening herself to all other considerations, Olivia swallowed her distaste and encouraged her cousin's volubility.

For her part, Estelle accepted the encouragement humbly, with gratitude, taking it as another sign of her cousin's generous forgiveness. So far, understandably, she had not had occasion to share her confidences fully with anyone. And to whom else but her beloved Olivia could she possibly strip her heart bare as frankly as she longed to?

In Olivia's forced willingness to receive Estelle's confidences, there was also initial wariness. She remained alert for the offensive phrase, the subtle innuendo, the concealed sneer—but none came. Estelle showed neither slyness nor embarrassment in unveiling what she had once called her "escapade," only a passionate desire to withhold nothing from her tragically wronged cousin. Olivia had always envied Estelle's talent for taking even life's most deceitful manoeuvres in her stride. It now astonished her to see with what pragmatism and lack of ambiguity Estelle had assimilated her experience into the fabric of her thinking. It now appeared that in inverse ratio to her reluctance to talk about her father's suicide was her eagerness to tell Olivia all that she had experienced with Jai Raventhorne.

Once she had learned to live with what he had revealed to her with such unfeeling bluntness, Estelle said, she had rallied fast. The hideous implications of their situation—which Raventhorne had not spelt out but which she understood fully—she accepted also, although with boiling anger. After he had released her from the master cabin, they again had ferocious rows, violent arguments. "I told him I was sick of his silly temper," Estelle said, incensed even by the memory of those humiliating days. "What had happened had happened. If all he said was true—and I knew that he had not lied at least about that—then it was time we learned to endure each other and *he* learned to treat me like a sister. Well, he was shocked. The word *sister* had not even occurred to him, you see. And then he was furious again, so I gave him an ultimatum—either that, or I would go on a hunger strike and starve myself to death. He laughed. He said he didn't give a broken farthing *what* I did with myself. For all he cared, I could jump ship and get lost on the African continent. As far as he was concerned, his purpose had been achieved."

If parts of Estelle's reminiscences were undoubtedly hurtful to her, then there were some that she enlivened with her gifted sense of humour. This one brought an involuntary half smile to Olivia's lips. "*You* go on a hunger strike? That I would have to see to believe!"

"Oh, I didn't really." The brief return of adolescent complacency in a face so drawn with unhappiness was somehow appealing. "I saw no reason to suffer because of *his* cussedness. I persuaded Bahadur—you know, his inseparable factotum—to bring me up dry rations that I could hide under the bed."

This time Olivia was forced to laugh.

"Jai didn't know that, of course. When he thought I had eaten nothing for four days, he was worried. Supposing I did die and he was lumbered with my body? At least, that's how *he* explained it when he himself brought me up a tray and thrust it under my nose. He pulled out his gun and held it to my head, tight with anger. 'Now *eat!*' he said through clenched teeth. 'If you don't, I swear I'll blow your brains out, whatever little you have of them.' Well, I ate of course. My goodness, how I ate! He hadn't needed to brandish that gun, but I didn't tell him that, naturally. In fact, I told him that I was not prepared to be treated like an encumbrance anymore. If he didn't keep me in the style to which I was accustomed, I would go on *another* hunger strike!" She smiled in remembered triumph. "That really alarmed him, you know. At first he raved and ranted and again threatened to spank me, but then suddenly he threw up his arms in surrender and sat down to roar with laughter." That recollection made her laugh too; then she turned wistful. "After that, Olivia, he became quite another person again. He was incredibly kind. I would not have believed him capable of such consideration, but he was. In time, he started to trust me, perhaps not entirely, but somewhat. He began to talk to me, loosen, ask me many questions, listen carefully to my answers, tell me things about himself."

"With all that kindness and consideration," Olivia said with an inadvertent return of resentment, "did it not occur to you to write at least a few lines home?"

Estelle's mood of brief abandon faded. Once more her face became pinched. "I tried to, Olivia. I tried several times, I *swear,* but I couldn't find the words. What explanations could I possibly give? How could I say in cold black and white everything that needed to be said? Besides, if I had to account for my behavior, then they too, Papa and Mama both, had to account for *theirs.*" Her cheeks showed red with the force of her anger. "They had concealed the truth from me, such a *vital* truth. Had I known it earlier, would all this have ever happened . . . ?" Her anger collapsed as fast as it had arisen; she remembered that the people on whom she expended it were no longer in a position to repent. The effort to regain control was punitive, but somehow she managed. "Those mutual explanations could only be made face to face. Since Jai promised a return in six months, if I wished to return after I married John, I decided to let the matter rest until—"

"What?" Olivia's exclamation of surprise slipped out before she could stop it.

Equally startled, Estelle snapped out of her ruminations. "I only said, since Jai intended to return to Calcutta within six months with a swift turnaround from England . . ." She faltered, again nervous. "D-did I say something wrong . . . ?"

With a low, mumbled incoherency, Olivia shook her head and buried her attention again in the crochet bonnet she was making for Amos. Six months! A drop in the ocean of time, and yet an eternity! How had he presumed that she *did* have six months to spare? That his offhand, unilateral decision would dovetail neatly into her own compulsions? And, having abandoned her without a word of explanation, did he really believe in his arrogance that she would *still* be waiting for him like a bonded slave purchased by some feudal plantation owner? Olivia curdled with fury, with bitterness, but no change was noticeable in the resolute serenity of her face.

Nevertheless, she gathered up her sewing materials and replaced them in her wicker-work basket. She was, she decided, tiring of Estelle's recollections, tiring of the sound of Jai Raventhorne's name and of all the virtues Estelle had suddenly discovered in him. However profound her compassion for her bereaved cousin, that name buzzed in Olivia's ears like a poisonous insect with sting upraised. It threatened her mental equilibrium, infected her reason and, in the final analysis, it was offensive to her self-respect as a woman.

"You look tired, Estelle," she said as lightly as she could so as not to wound her feelings. "And you distress yourself even more with all these heart searchings. We have all the time we want at our disposal—why don't we leave the rest for another day?"

Anxious to please in any way she could, Estelle accepted her dictum at face value and with meekness.

The days of mandatory rest, of enforced idleness, infused new strength into Olivia's mind and body. Eventually, even Dr. Humphries declared himself satisfied with her progress. What he categorically refused to even consider, however, was her tentative question about the possibility of sailing. She was certainly not well enough for *that,* he growled—but, if she insisted, he would allow her a few hours a day at the Agency. "Provided," he warned, "there are no more high jinks around town! We still have to be cautious. On the other hand, we don't want you to atrophy into a cabbage, do we?"

Olivia bowed to his judgement with resignation. It would be self-destructive not to when she was bearing a child who depended on her own health, when that child would some day mean so much to so many. And then, even brief visits to the Agency were better than mental stagnation at home. Olivia realised that in elitist colonial society it was considered scandalously immodest for a pregnant woman to be seen in public. She had flouted the norm once and had received harsh criticism for her defiance. To do so again would be deemed tantamount to open rebellion—not that she gave a damn about that.

"Oh, fiddlesticks!" It was Estelle who supported Dr. Humphries's suggestion with the most enthusiasm. "To hell with so-called propriety! No matter what one does here, *someone* always has *something* to say about it, so why worry? Besides, by going to the Agency you won't have to suffer all those who still call every day to give me their condolences."

All of which was true. Estelle's daily visitors were a penance for Olivia although she had taken great care not to show that, especially never to her cousin. That Estelle should have noticed it anyway and endorsed the remedy touched Olivia, and she said so. Estelle went crimson with pleasure; even this scrap of approval she received with boundless gratification. Emboldened perhaps by Olivia's few words of praise, she ventured a step on territory she had never dared to invade before.

"You're not ever going to join Freddie in England, are you?"

The sudden inquiry jolted Olivia but she saw no cause for concealment. "No."

"He knows the identity of Amos's father?"

"Yes."

"Is it because of that that he will not accept him?"

It was an astute deduction, another sign of her maturity. "Yes."

Olivia's intention had not been to give another turn to the knife already buried deep in Estelle's conscience, but her cousin was crushed with remorse. "For me, who deserves it so little," she whispered, "something at least has turned out well. But for you, with no crime, no blame, nothing has gone right. Oh, if only we could somehow go back in time and live it all again!"

"If we could live it all again, nothing would be different," Olivia commented. "What the past teaches us is that the past teaches us nothing. Given second chances, we would all make precisely the same mistakes."

Even though Estelle was by now used to her cousin's cynicism, the frequently acerbic remarks with which she spiced her conversation, she winced. How much Olivia had changed! Nothing truly touched her anymore. Like a land struck with drought, she had withered. So little took root in that infertile region of a heart once lush with plenitude. And how vitriolic her tongue, even when cruelty was unintended! This feral arrow, Estelle knew, was not aimed at her alone, but finding a vulnerable opening it entered and pierced deep.

"Don't destroy all my illusions; leave me some to survive on!" The lid flew off Estelle's trapped sorrow; she cried out in anguished protest. "I want to believe that if I *did* live again, I would cherish Mama, inundate her with a love she could not deny, beg forgiveness for every harsh word I ever spoke. I would *will* them, Mama and Papa, to abandon their secret, and so avert all our wasteful tragedies. In this second incarnation I would be spared the knowledge that I took your life away, condemned my mother to an eternal limbo. I would not have as a companion as chronic as my breath the awareness that . . . that I *conspired* to kill my father!"

Olivia was taken aback by the ferocity of the sudden eruption. "The blame is not only yours, Estelle, we all—"

"Yes, we all contributed, I know—but that no longer consoles. It makes it even more painful. I have lost Papa and Mama, both of whom I did love to distraction but, shamefully, with them my resentments have not been lost. They lied to me, goaded Jai into terrible things, incited me to rebellion uncaring that I was a fool, a pampered child engrossed only in herself. And then they questioned my innocence. Papa looked at me like . . . like high-caste Hindus look at sweepers, as if I were *untouchable.* What a legacy he left me, Olivia! I can *never* forgive him that."

Still startled by her cousin's bitterness, her burning sense of injury, Olivia allowed Estelle her say without comment. It had to be aired sometime; better now than to let it corrode her forever. All she ventured, mildly, was, "The brother you have found is also part of that legacy, Estelle. At least *that* you consider as a gain."

"Yes—a brother hated by everyone, even you! Hated for many faults that were part of *his* legacy from his father. They shared the same moral contamination, hated the same weaknesses, turned sentiment into a crime. When I pointed that out to Papa, he merely hid behind that stubborn silence, but I know now that my defence of Jai enraged him more, reinforced his determination to kill him, convinced him finally that I *was* guilty. Oh, what a mess, what a *mess* we helped each other make of everything, Olivia . . . !"

A mess. Yes, that it was. But what would Estelle have to say, Olivia wondered, if she could surmise how much more mess was now waiting to be added?

Willie Donaldson was overjoyed to have Olivia back at the Agency, but he would have died rather than confess just how much he had missed her these past weeks of her indisposition. He already knew that she had no plans to leave station in the immediate future and this too delighted him. The incidental benefit of her decision to stay he was unlikely to miss either: The sacrosanct manse was not to be defiled by an alien presence after all! But once the formalities were over and he had finished bringing Olivia up to date with current developments, Donaldson revived a subject that was uppermost in his mind. The subject now not only disturbed him, it was beginning to alarm him seriously: her continuing loans to Arthur Ransome.

"I appreciate, Your Ladyship, that personal considerations have much to do with your generosity." He was formal in the extreme. "No doot, poor Josh's untimely accident has added to Your Ladyship's sentiments. But," he loaded the qualification with meaning, *"but,* Your Ladyship must see that in my own sentiment for Caleb's Agency, I *canna* allow Farrowsham to become a target for *any* bloody lunatic in a danged fight that's not even ours. To me, such intervention is oot*rag*eous!" He calmed down to turn earnestly persuasive. "Templewood and Ransome are finished. With Josh gone, irredeemably. We canna breathe life into a corpse, Your Ladyship, certainly na at the cost of ending in the mortuary ourselves."

"They are not yet in the bankruptcy courts, Mr. Donaldson," Olivia reminded him, annoyed. "They still do have assets left. I mean to see that they get a square deal when they sell them."

"Ransome is na exactly incapable, Your Ladyship! He's as old a hand at the bleeding game as any of us."

"I know, but in his present frame of mind he's disinclined to fight. He'll make distress sales and lose the value of even those assets he has left. I merely loan him the wherewithal to survive until he can regain his equilibrium."

"Assets, *hah!*" Donaldson snorted, as unconvinced as ever. "A hoose in Barrackpore falling to ruin, Ransome's bungalow for which na offer is likely to be received, likewise the Templewood hoose. The *Sea Siren*'s already gone for scrap to Banaji's shipyard in Kidderpore, but even Banaji won't touch the *Daffodil* . . ."

"Well, I happen to disagree, Mr. Donaldson. Those houses are still good, solid real estate properties and the *Daffodil* might be a wreck but she's far from done. Refurbished, she could still give yeoman service to some less affluent merchant."

"You reck'n any sane sailing man would look twice at that toothless, worm-eaten old hag?" He made another sound indicating disgust. "Bar Raventhorne, of course. Na that anyone with his marbles intact would call *that* eccentric bastard *sane!*"

"Raventhorne?" Olivia stared at him blankly. "He's back from Assam?"

"Aye. Gossip is he's putting oot feelers for a purchase."

For weeks now Olivia had been preparing herself for the

moment of Raventhorne's return to Calcutta. She had managed to even persuade herself that she was absolutely ready for the eventuality. But now, she was aghast at the swiftness with which Donaldson's brief syllable of confirmation had reinvoked her heavy sense of dread. Somehow she hid her apprehension behind seeming unconcern and stilled her hands fidgeting nervously in her lap. Donaldson's other bit of news, momentarily forgotten, now leapt to mind and she looked surprised, certain that she had misheard him.

"For a purchase of the *Daffodil,* did you say?"

"Aye. So the rumour goes."

"But why . . . ?" Olivia was bewildered. "Trident uses only clippers. As she is now, the *Daffodil* isn't remotely seaworthy. What would Trident want with a wreck like that?"

Not particularly interested, Donaldson shrugged. "He could use her for firewood, I reck'n. *When* Ransome's price dips to a penny and a half." Reopening his ledgers, he proceeded to other matters.

But throughout the day, Olivia's own conjectures proliferated. They all centered around the curious question, why should Jai Raventhorne, of all people, want to buy the *Daffodil,* of all ships! To take advantage of Ransome's state of depression, then make profits on a resale? No, that was palpably absurd. Subsequent profits, if any, would be a pittance; for all his faults, Raventhorne didn't scrounge for petty gain. That much Olivia did know as a certainty. Something about the snippet dropped so casually by Donaldson excited Olivia. Raventhorne did nothing without good reason. Instinct warned her that if the gossip was correct, behind his interest in a junk vessel belonging to a company whose very name plate was anathema to him must lie a *very* good reason indeed. But what?

The answer, when it finally came, was from an expected source: Estelle. But it was not an answer Olivia would have ever deduced for herself without her cousin's unknowing help.

It was the day before Estelle's return to Cawnpore.

John had been generous in allowing his wife a longer stay in Calcutta than he had originally intended. But, in his level-headedness, he hoped that for the cousins to spend time together would prove therapeutic for both. Having met and talked at length with Raventhorne in England, John now knew a great deal more than he had before. About Olivia's unhappy circumstances he had heard everything from his wife. Between them the cousins had many misunderstandings to settle, much rancor to dispel. And Estelle needed badly to unbottle her manifold guilt and smouldering anger. In his warm letter to Olivia, John tactfully said only that he hoped his wife's company had not been too much of a strain and that it had proved mutually beneficial.

Yes, Olivia conceded to herself, the interlude with Estelle had been mutually beneficial. It had released them both from some tensions at least, and had provided occasional light-heartedness. Olivia was genuinely glad that in her spontaneous outburst Estelle had pin-pointed verbally that inner sore that was causing her the most suffering. It was disappointing, of course, that from her compulsive outpourings about Raventhorne, Olivia had not gleaned as much "wheat" as she had hoped, but every little bit helped. If not dramatically revelatory, the outpourings had given her many further insights into the cracks and crevices of the man, many little sidelights that might someday prove useful. He had talked, for instance, about Sujata to her cousin, perhaps because Estelle had bluntly asked him about her. That little fragment Olivia stored away carefully in her arsenal; discarded mistresses, especially when disgruntled, were weighty cannon-fodder, after all!

On Estelle's last evening in Calcutta, the cousins strolled the embankment after supper, as had become their custom. The January night was bracingly chilly. It made a pleasant change from the cloying humidity of the still, warm days with their brassy sunshine. There were spectral mists on the river, enclosing them as they ambled leisurely in a cool, dark tent of privacy peppered above with stars.

"I went to see Jai this morning." With Raventhorne back from Assam this too was inevitable; even so, Olivia felt a mild sense of shock. She received the information in silence. "He's still in a vile temper with me," Estelle continued with a sigh. "He hasn't forgiven me for that evening. We had another flaming row. He was insufferably callous about what happened to Papa." Even in the dark Olivia could sense the quiver of her lips.

Only because of her own inner turbulence, Olivia blurted out, "Did he by any chance mention Amos?"

Estelle looked surprised. "No. Why should he?"

"Did you?"

She regretted the question instantly, but it was out. "No, of *course* not!" Estelle was immeasurably wounded. "Can you still not bring yourself to have at least *some* faith in me and the promise I have made?" Contrite, Olivia touched her arm but she pulled back. "If you only knew how *sick* I am of all these stupid acrimonies and animosities! My father, the cause of them, is dead, dead, *dead!* Can't we *now* think of repairing the damage instead of perpetuating it?"

"Uncle Joshua's death, much as I mourn it, has nothing to do with my own 'acrimony,' as you call it," Olivia pointed out a trifle coldly.

"Yes, I know." Deflated again, Estelle sat down on a boulder and stared at the river. "But all that's behind you, Olivia. If you . . . *we* made an effort to forget, wouldn't our lives be less complicated?"

"By forgetting, do you think those lives would be instantly refashioned into little idylls of contentment?"

"They could. If we *wanted* them to be!"

"And how willing is your allegedly maligned *brother* to forget!"

Estelle shook her head in despair. "He's as bad as . . . as everyone else. Pigheaded and self-destructive! I know he too has a lot to forget, to forgive, but had he seen my poor father with his head blown away . . ." She stopped, unable to dispel the vision, and shut her eyes tight.

There was something heart-wrenching in Estelle's simplistic, artless blueprint for universal regeneration and, impulsively, Olivia sat down beside her and laced her arm through hers. "Then why not give up and leave us to our continuing perversities to wallow in as we see fit?"

"No! You can scoff as much as you like, dear Coz, but you will never convince me that *you* are perverse." Resolutely, Estelle abandoned her grief. "Nor, despite all his infuriating antics, *Jai.* Don't forget, now I know him better than even . . . better than anybody else. He has hidden depths, Olivia, depths in which there is such softness that you would be *astonished.*"

"Yes," Olivia agreed lightly, "I surely would!"

Estelle clutched at the arm laced through hers. "No, *listen,* Olivia—what I was trying to tell you the other day isn't a fabrication. When I mentioned the word *sister* to him, it angered him, yes, but it also utterly bewildered him. The concept of any relative, apart from his mother and her people, was so alien to him that he was staggered. Initially, he rejected it with contempt. He took to glaring at me by the hour, nervous and suspicious, as if

I might suddenly spring up and bite him. But then, the thought of having me as a sister intrigued him. Once and for all it cleared the air between us of all that silly romantic rubbish," she had the grace to lower her eyes and blush, "and paved the way for quite another relationship. I began to fascinate him, I could see that. He began to actually *enjoy* the prospect of being an older brother, solicitous and protective. And, of course, authoritarian." With another remnant from earlier days, Estelle giggled, a forgotten sparkle returning to her brilliant blue eyes. "It was then that he started to mellow, to talk with relaxed restraint, to regret his unkindness to me—although he never said so with words—and to arrive at the decision to meet John, make frank explanations and then persuade him to still marry me. But then, all at once," Estelle stopped, again uncertain as she cast an oblique glance at her impassive cousin, "Jai changed again. It was very sudden and it was after we touched some other port in Africa. He locked himself in his cabin, refused to see me. He took to pacing the decks at night, obviously in the grip of some terrible torment that threatened his sanity."

Remembering those nights, Estelle was again stepped in melancholy. "I longed to reach out to him, help him, comfort him, assure him of at least *my* love, for he had no other. But he wouldn't let me come near. I have never known any man, Olivia, so alone, so much in need of *someone.* In that stony citadel there are cracks, Olivia," speaking with passion, she got up to walk about restlessly, "gaping holes, soft spots easily penetrated. One I know is his mother. The other, which I did not know then but do know now, is *you.*"

Olivia congealed. *None of this means anything to me now. I don't want to hear it!* Gritting her teeth, she continued to show indifference and, in fact, raised a hand to her mouth to hide an extravagant yawn.

"Oh, I know you're bored, I know you find this tedious—but tell you I must!" However much she wanted to earn Olivia's total forgiveness, Estelle was not prepared to abandon her defence of her brother. "I didn't notice it then, but Jai talked—railed, rather!—about Papa, about Mama, about *Grandmama.* On occasion, when he couldn't avoid it, he even talked about his mother, although never in any detail. The one person he never mentioned, never even referred to in passing, Olivia, was *you.* But when *I* spoke about you, which was constantly, Jai would listen with the attention of one in a trance, his eyes fixed, unwavering. Hindsight tells me that he was memorising every word about you, every syllable, hoarding it away like a squirrel gathering nuts for winter."

Frantic to halt the flow, Olivia opened her mouth to lodge an indignant protest, but Estelle would not have any of it. She silenced her with an aggressive gesture.

"All this I *have* to tell you before I leave, Olivia!" Fearful of being blocked, her gushing cataract of words gathered momentum. "But that transformation in him, that sudden agony—it was only when I returned here and saw *Amos* that the cause of it became clear. In that African port there were other ships from Calcutta. The captains of the vessels were known to Jai; he spent time with them. And it must have been then that he learned of your marriage to Freddie Birkhurst. I can't see any other reason for his physical and mental collapse." She paused to let that sink in, then leashed her belligerence, content that she had made the point she sought to. "Anyway, we proceeded to England. Embittered as Jai was, he made tremendous efforts to win John's confidence, and eventually did. It was Jai who made arrangements for the wedding, paid for it, bought me an elaborate trousseau, lavished gifts on us and then, as a 'family friend,' gave me away. John's parents were not told the entire story. They are simple people; they would not have been able to understand or accept the whole truth. But, won over by Jai's silver tongue, his inimitable courtesy and generosity, they asked no questions." In the argentine dark, her eyes shone with tears. "If Jai once sought to break my life, then it is he who also made it, Olivia. He *is* capable of reparation, he *does* have a conscience. Mama's rejection of me, Papa's too, has made him angry again, frustrated him, for he knows it was he who instigated it. He will not forgive them ever, for that and for everything else, but he knows now that *I* at least am on his side. With you also gone, Olivia, as you will be one day, I have only Jai left whose veins share my blood." Having said so much, she could not leave the vital rest unsaid. "If I can forgive Jai, Olivia, then can you also not bring yourself to?"

Estelle's bold question, the question to which she had been building right from the beginning of her visit, wafted away on the wind. She waited with trepidation for an answer. It came and it was what she had, unhappily, expected. "No." Just that one syllable of finality, nothing more. Saddened by her failure, Estelle fell silent. And in her disappointment she saw that whatever had been between Jai and her cousin was not available to her, perhaps never would be. Nor was it, sadly, any of her business. Olivia yawned, this time with genuine fatigue. "If you have nothing more to say, then can we think of returning so that we can both go to sleep? You have a long journey ahead of you tomorrow."

"There is something more I have to say, another small example of—"

"No, Estelle! Maybe tomorrow morning." Her effort at pretences had worn her out; she could not take anymore, not tonight!

"Now, Olivia! Tomorrow there will be no time." In her final bid to move her unyielding cousin, Estelle too was determined. She put a restraining hand on Olivia's arm to stop her from leaving. "During those days of my imprisonment in the master cabin, I discovered something. As you must know, Jai has no interest in possessions. Like his Chitpur house, the cabin was bare save for essentials. What I found hidden in a bottom drawer under a pile of old sea maps was a cloth bundle. A square of red velvet with some oddments within. Jai had humiliated me and I was livid; I unwrapped the bundle without any qualms of conscience." Because it was her last opportunity to say all this, Estelle spoke very fast, breathless in her eagerness. "There was a bizarre assortment inside—that is, bizarre to me at the time. Silver bangles, nose and toe rings such as Indian women wear, a pair of rope slippers, some wooden animals, chiselled toys in various shapes, one—a female figure—that reminded me of a ship's mascot, a gauze veil, two faded cotton blouses, a skirt with braid edging and," she swallowed and hushed her voice, "a small pellet of opium."

A silver locket.

Olivia fought back the image. A night hawk shrieked and zigzagged across their path in its eternal hunt for prey. They both started. Its cry was piercingly shrill and jolted the quietness of the night.

"These were his mother's meagre belongings, but I didn't know that then. Foolishly, I later asked him about the curious bundle. The effect of my question was electric. Jai first went chalky white, then absolutely *berserk* with temper. He called me vile names, raged like a maniac, accused me of every criminal vice he could think of, said I was a true daughter of my parents. I was terrified; I had made a gaffe, but I didn't know what. Jai didn't relent for days. During that time I vowed never to mention that bundle again, either to him or to anyone else. And I haven't. I tell you now only to *prove* that, like Papa, Jai also *pretends* to be above the human weakness of possessing normal feelings, but he does have them."

A captive audience, Olivia had listened to Estelle in stoic

silence. But, as Estelle now saw, she was not touched by anything she had heard. Indeed, she was irritated. "Save your breath and your recommendations for someone to whom they will mean something, Estelle. Although," she camouflaged her reaction with a smile that tried to be light but succeeded only in seeming false, "they tempt me to also say something I have been intending to for some time. Once, I blamed you for the wreck that is now my life. I don't anymore. Like me, you were a victim; unlike me, you have survived. I don't begrudge you that, Estelle, believe me. I rejoice in your marriage, rejoice that you have formed new relationships that have brought you satisfaction. In your crusade to regenerate lives, I admire your zeal, because it is noble. However," she dropped her pretence of a smile, "in healing everyone's scars you mustn't begrudge me mine. Nor my crusades, whether you consider them noble or not. If Jai Raventhorne now exists for me at all, it is as a threat to my son."

"Amos is also Jai's son!"

"No, oh *no,*" Olivia breathed softly. "Were it only biology that made fathers and sons, why the need for noble crusades? No, I *don't* accept him as the father of my son! Amos is a Birkhurst, as I warned you never to forget. To secure him that name, I have on my conscience another broken life, that of the decent man whose only fault was that he married me for love. Until Freddie decrees otherwise, Amos will remain a Birkhurst. But when the time comes to choose another name, that of your brother will not be a contender."

Despairing at a bitterness that could be so enduring, Estelle again tried to plead. "But Jai has no inkling of the truth! Is it fair to condemn him regardless?"

"He has never made any effort to discover the truth."

"But you don't *want* him to! You ask to have it both ways, Olivia, and that isn't fair either."

"To be contrary with impunity is a rule *he* has devised. Besides, he once advised me never to consider him fair. And only those capable of giving justice are fit to receive it."

It was hopeless!

Bitter and blinding herself to the truth, her cousin had passed beyond all rational limits. To argue further, Estelle saw, would be futile. "Olivia, *tell* Jai about his son," she suggested once more in weary defeat. "*I* will ensure that Amos remains in your custody. It isn't right to deprive a child of his father."

"No. And if *you* ever tell him," the smile was back but there was an ominous glint in her eye, "you will have made yourself an enemy for life."

Estelle had neither the courage nor the energy for further confrontation.

As for Olivia, she was suddenly relieved that her cousin's visit was at an end. A hundred hammers resounded within her head; every bone in her body ached, her feet were swollen, her brain clogged with useless clutter. So much talk, so many debates, such strong emotions! What had they all achieved for either, except less peace of mind? Yes, Estelle's company had been amusing in many ways, but now she was glad that Estelle was going.

It was only after Estelle had finally departed that Olivia suddenly pinned down the microscopic speck abrading the back of her mind. Something Estelle had said had struck a chord somewhere; in the wake of her departure, Olivia identified it. The sudden flash of inspiration first startled, then excited her enormously. It took her breath away and instantly dispelled all her weariness. No, Estelle's lengthy discourses had not been entirely unproductive; they *had* achieved something! If and when Jai Raventhorne chose to open hostilities, she would be ready. Her armoury now boasted that one possible weapon to which he would not have an answer.

As it happened, Olivia did not have long to wait. Raventhorne fired his first salvo a week after his return.

"I did tell Your Ladyship that Kala Kanta is back, dinna I?" Willie Donaldson asked her the moment she stepped into her office.

"Yes. Why?" From his very tone she suspected that it was not an idle inquiry. It wasn't.

"Trident has cancelled our credit facilities. The letter from Moitra is on Your Ladyship's table. What they demand now is payment in full in advance of all consignments the clippers carry for us." His words didn't say so but the spaces in between them were rife with accusation. "And I reck'n that's only the start. I can give it in bloody writing." He put his head between his hands and stared at a fly trying to settle on the rim of his teacup on the desk.

Olivia refrained from comment, but her spirits sank. Raventhorne *had* chosen to declare open hostilities after all! What he had fired as an opening shot was not a broadside, not yet. But the denial of the customary credit upon which all large business houses operated and based their finance management would be a drastic set-back. It would mean total reorganisation of their budget, possible losses in their investments and, for them all, an irritating state of confusion in the office at least for a while. Moreover, privately Olivia agreed with Donaldson although she did not depress him further by saying so—yes, this was only the start. More would certainly follow. Willie Donaldson knew Raventhorne's methods well; what he did not know, of course, was the reason for his sudden wrath. Or, indeed, his target! As with all of Raventhorne's battles, it seemed, innocents were to be slaughtered again; and this time it was Farrowsham's bad luck to be the ones caught in the cross-fire. It was not she who had asked for the fight. But if Raventhorne was determined to incite one, then so be it; he would get one worthy of whatever her capacities.

All this Olivia pondered quietly as she watched poor Willie sit and wallow in his self-righteous gloom. That not even this loyal, devoted, blameless man was to be spared filled her with anger. But the face she presented to him as he finally looked up was clean of everything she felt inside.

"Well, if that is what they want, I suppose we have no option but to comply," she said with an assumed air of resignation. "It's a damned nuisance, of course, but we do have the liquidity to pay in advance."

Donaldson swore with more colourful abandon than usual before regaining normal speech. "It's na only a matter of bloody *liquidity;* of *course* we have that! Who better than us?" His chest expanded with pride as a reflex. "The point is I dinna *want* to tangle with the son of a whore! Why should we? *We* have na god-rotting bones to pick; it's *Ransome's* pile of dung, let *him* clean it up." He breathed noisily through flaring nostrils as if about to spit fire.

It hurt her to hear poor Arthur Ransome maligned with such little justification. But, of course, Donaldson could not know how reluctant Ransome was to accept her continuing help. Nor could Olivia enlighten Donaldson as to the real reason for Raventhorne's fury against her. Donaldson would continue to curse Ransome, and his interpretation would be the one universally accepted by everyone in the business community. "Well, it would seem that it no longer is only Mr. Ransome's pile of dung," she said lightly. "But I see no cause for undue alarm. If we have to pay in advance, well, we'll have to, won't we?" She paused to smile. "That is, of course, for the time being."

He stared, shocked by her offhandedness. "For the time b—?" Words failed him. "And how do we restrict it to the *time being,* may I inquire?"

Olivia ignored his caustic tone. "Oh, don't worry, Mr. Donaldson. I guess we'll think of some way as we go along."

The airiness with which she had evaded Donaldson was not in evidence when Olivia went to see Arthur Ransome in his office later in the day. Indeed, Donaldson might have derived some satisfaction from how worried she herself looked. She wasted no time in the usual formalities. Abruptly she asked, "Has Raventhorne made you a bid for the *Daffodil?*"

He was not surprised that she already had the information. During the past year and a half he had developed a healthy respect for her skill at gleaning and gathering news around the commercial district. He made a face. "If you can call it a bid. An insult might be a better word. Why?"

"Can you think of any reason why he should make a bid at all?"

"Perhaps he can think of some use for her. I cannot."

"And do you intend to take the offer?"

Ransome shrugged. "Why not? So much has already gone, Olivia. The *Daffodil* is a white elephant, of no use to anyone. She'll probably never sail again, certainly never for me. And the days of the tea wagons are over. Now everyone dreams of sailing these clippers, which even Clydeside is building. Very soon the tea wagons will go for scrap anyway. Yes, I'm inclined to accept Jai's offer for whatever it is worth."

Olivia sat back and drummed a tattoo on his desk, her face thoughtful. "Would you say that the Burma teak, the mahogany and the brass fittings on the *Daffodil* would collectively fetch more?"

"You mean if she were dismembered?" He looked taken aback. "Well . . . I daresay they would." He sat back and, briefly, his expression turned dreamy. "The *Daffodil* was our first ship, you know, the first to carry our flag and to take us to Canton, the first to bring back tea chests for Templewood and Ransome. The others came later, but none of them meant to us what the *Daffodil* did. In any case, they've all gone too." He sighed. "No, I don't know why Jai would want the *Daffodil.* Perhaps, as the rumour goes, he does intend to make firewood out of her. To be frank, it no longer matters. What he does with it will be his business."

"I have someone in mind who might pay better for her components, Uncle Arthur." Her eyes showed a glint. "If it's all the same to you, would you let me approach him first?"

He searched her face with a frown, then smiled a little uncertainly. "Ah, I can almost hear those tireless little wheels spinning away inside that indefatigable brain! What are you thinking of this time, my dear—pulling another wee rabbit out of that magic hat of yours?"

"No," Olivia answered with perfect truth, "what I am thinking of this time is Captain Mathieson Z. Tucker. And something he once told me."

If there was much about Hiram Arrowsmith Lubbock that bewildered Calcutta's well-ordered, neatly defined society, the feisty southerner returned the compliment with hearty feeling. A prime exporter of best quality long-staple American cotton from Mississippi to Europe and England, Lubbock had arrived in station at the invitation of some conscientious officers of John Company. Bengal's cotton industry, which produced only short-staple cotton unsuitable for Lancashire's textile mills, was flagging; it was believed that an American expert might well help to revive it. Lubbock, on his part, had come to the Orient—as he had no qualms about informing all and sundry with what was considered vulgar openness—to make his second fortune in life. He had heard, he told anyone who cared to listen, that the streets of Calcutta were paved with gold. But from what he had observed so far (as he also informed all and sundry), if the streets *were* paved with anything, it was "what oxen perdoos jes' as waal in Calhoun as in Calcutta." And he was fed up to the teeth with his woeful lack of business activity. All he had done since he had arrived was to distribute a few ploughs, some hundred or so bushels of cotton seed and a negligible number of cotton gins. The men he dealt with in Writers' Building, Lubbock maintained, were indolent, ignorant and pompous, and couldn't tell cotton from candy-floss anyway. Now he was rapidly coming to the conclusion that the Orient was strictly for the birds. It was bad enough having to speak a foreign language (since he couldn't understand a word anyone said and vice versa), but from the time he had left the American ship that had brought him to India, he had not even had a decent drink of bourbon. And that, to Hal Lubbock, was the bottom line.

Which was why it was only after he had consumed several glasses of his favourite brand that Olivia eventually decided to get down to business with him. The mandatory small talk had been dispensed with, a mutual sizing up concluded; now it was time for brass tacks. "I have a deal to suggest to you, Mr. Lubbock," Olivia began. "From what you have told me about yourself, I feel you will be interested."

"A deal?" He looked somewhat taken aback. "What kinda deal, my'am?"

"One that will, if tackled with imagination, fetch you top dollar, Mr. Lubbock. What I am about to suggest, however, might be a little out of your line."

He stared into his drink with a frown, then inched forward in his chair. "For top dollah, my'am," he said simply, "there ain't nothin' that's outta mah lahn."

Whatever his battles with the Queen's English, "top dollar" and "a deal" were part of a vocabulary Lubbock understood perfectly. Deals and top dollar were what he had been making all his life. Indeed, to him they *were* what life was all about. For the first time since he had arrived in this goddamn country, he was being served a man's drink, talked to in a language that restored his faith in the human condition and entertained charmingly by a true-blue American gal from Sacramento. For the moment Hal Lubbock asked for nothing more. He listened entranced. When Olivia had concluded her detailed explanations, he sat back and mulled over what he had heard.

"Furniture?" he asked, more than a little puzzled. "Yuh mean, *chairs* and things?"

"Yes, precisely, Mr. Lubbock. Chairs and things. Lots of things."

He scratched his abundantly brilliantined head for a moment, then laughed. "Waal, ah'll be god*damned!*"

Olivia decided in that instant that she liked Hiram Arrowsmith Lubbock. He was a huge, bull-necked man with a quick smile full of gold teeth, and his clothes were shockingly loud. But like all self-made men he was tough, shrewd, blunt and practical. It was a combination Olivia knew and trusted. The fact that he stood out in India like a mocking-bird among peacocks didn't bother her. Whatever his social inadequacies, for her immediate purpose she needed Lubbock badly.

"Come, Mr. Lubbock." She turned brisk as soon as he had finished his fourth drink. "Let me show you exactly what I have in mind."

The next hour was spent with obvious profit for, at the end of it, Hal Lubbock's expression of puzzlement had translated into positive interest. "Top dollah, eh?" He stroked his chin and reflected.

"So I have been assured, Mr. Lubbock. Naturally you will wish to conduct your own investigations through your agents abroad."

"Uh-huh." He was already busy scribbling rough calculations. "And yuh think this could be stahted raht away?"

"Yes. Right away." He nodded, his eyes crinkled and shrewd. Olivia explained further. "So far, Mr. Lubbock, it seems no one has attempted such an export from here on any sizable scale. My informant has made a few sales himself and he sees an enormous potential in Europe and America. The markets might be restricted but I'm told the profits are not. Those who can afford it will pay generous money."

Lubbock nodded again. "Wall, why not?" His golden smile twinkled in the lights of the chandeliers. "Ah'm as game for a good deal as the next man, my'am, and ah've nevah knocked a challenge. Besides, this sure tickles mah fancy, my'am, by God it does!"

"Excellent." Olivia dazzled him with one of her own smiles. "But now I must mention a condition, one that goes with the deal. I hope you can consider it favourably."

Confronted with a fresh bottle of bourbon, bought off an American ship at absurd cost purely for Lubbock's benefit, he beamed and turned expansive. "For top dollah, my'am, there ain't nothin' I cahn't consider favourably. Jes' lay it on the lahn, Yer Ladyship, jes' lay it on the lahn."

"*Furniture?*" Arthur Ransome looked even more blank than Lubbock initially had. "Good grief, girl, what do I know about *furniture . . . ?*"

"You don't need to know anything, Uncle Arthur," Olivia assured him. "Lubbock will manage everything. You will merely be a sleeping partner—and, of course, an equal sharer of the profits."

"But Lubbock is a cotton man! Why on earth should he want to start exporting Chinese furniture?"

"Well, for two reasons. Primarily, he's a businessman. He'll put his hand to anything that promises good returns, and this does. And, the prospect of doing something nobody else has yet appeals to his sense of adventure. Captain Tucker told me that abroad elaborately carved Chinese furniture is considered exotic and a status symbol. All we have to do is supply the wood."

"You mean, he plans to make the furniture here? In Calcutta?"

"Yes. Mary Ling's father and brothers are professional carpenters. They trained in Shanghai and they're confident they can copy exactly the pieces that I have at home as well as those at the Templewood house. They even have the original Chinese lacquers and a source for future supplies."

"By George!" Ransome gasped weakly. "You *have* been busy, haven't you! I hardly know what to say."

"Just say yes. Lubbock will do the rest."

Ransome relapsed into thought. With his shoulders increasingly stooped, his cherubic face now pinched and sallow, his eyes tired, he looked as desolate as the once bustling offices in which they sat. Most of the staff had been disbanded. Only Hugh Yarrow, Munshi Babu and one or two peons remained. The Canton establishment had already been closed. With no incomings, the heavy compensations being paid for the mine disaster had sucked their savings dry. Their only daily visitors were now incensed and impatient creditors. Even the Parsi landlord who owned the premises had given them notice to vacate. Very soon, Raventhorne's last wish would also be fulfilled; there would be no Templewood and Ransome name plate on the door.

But, as he introspected, it was not on these familiar problems that Ransome's thoughts dwelt. Olivia's project, although for his benefit, worried him for reasons he could not pin-point. "This wood you want me to supply, I presume it is from the *Daffodil?*"

"No, Uncle Arthur. It will be from the timber market. The *Daffodil* will be sold to Jai Raventhorne as she is, but only after he has doubled his offer." He sat up with a jolt and Olivia's eyes twinkled. "Or, possibly trebled it. We only have to maintain the myth of the ship's dismemberment for a while. In the meantime, Lubbock plans to make contact with you presently." As she got up, something kicked hard inside her stomach and she winced, but then the pang passed. Olivia smiled. It was an internal activity that never failed to give her encouragement. "Oh, by the way,

Lubbock is willing to purchase your property. He feels the servants' compound and quarters would be ideal for a workshop. The house, of course, he plans to live in."

Ransome gave a sharp intake of breath. "You used that as a condition for helping him set up this project?"

"No."

Ransome received her lie in silence but he did not challenge it. The bright gleam of triumph in her beautiful amber eyes, the small smile of complacency, the grooves of determination on either side of her mouth—all these again filled him with unease. He loved the girl dearly; he knew he could trust her with his life. In all their travails she had remained steadfast by their side, loyal and loving. But now he was worried, truly worried. Something other than what he had been told was brewing in that unusually sharp brain of hers. And right at that moment Ransome would have given a great deal to know what it was.

Had he been in a position to know, he would have been even more disturbed. What was brewing in Olivia's brain at that moment was that it was now time to pay a visit to Jai Raventhorne.

Willie Donaldson was aghast. "You canna go visiting a scoundrel such as Jai Raventhorne, Your Ladyship! Why, it's . . . it's na *decent!*"

"Why not?" Olivia inquired, wide eyed with innocence. "Mr. Raventhorne is a business associate. He has been to my house socially and very formally introduced to me by my cousin. I shall be calling on him at his office during business hours, Mr. Donaldson. I can't imagine anything more decent than that!"

He pinked. "I dinna mean . . ." He hid his embarrassment behind a cough. "Anyway, what might be the purpose of this sudden decision, if I may be bold enough to inquire?" By God, the American lassie was beginning to sorely try his patience!

"I'm going to request Mr. Raventhorne to restore our credit."

His jaw swung loose, exposing the wad of shag that was a permanent resident within. "*Just* like that?"

"Yes. Just like that."

There were times when Donaldson admired and respected his owner's wife enormously, but this was not one of them. Now he was in serious doubt of her sanity, and even more appalled. "He'll insult you, he'll . . . he'll show you the door! You've na experience of his tongue but, by *Christ,* I *have.* He's a right mean son of a bloody sea cook, lass, and that's a fact." As always when agitated, he dropped his formalities.

"Show me the door? Oh, surely not, Mr. Donaldson!" Olivia looked shocked. "Why, he was charming with me at my party, *charming.*"

"I'm na talking of bloody parties," Donaldson raged, chomping furiously on his tobacco. "I'm talking of business, *hard* business. We *know* why he cancelled our credit—he's na going to restore it *just like that!*"

"Oh, I don't know. He might. In my experience Mr. Raventhorne can be very reasonable when approached politely. What I intend to do is to appeal to his sense of fair play."

"Fair p—?" Willie Donaldson turned speechless.

"It's worth a try. If he refuses, well, we're no worse off than we are now, are we?"

"It's the *manner* in which he will refuse—and he damn well will—that sticks in my craw, lass. For a Baroness of Farrowsham to be shown discourtesy by that uncouth, ill-bred—"

"He will not show me any discourtesy, Mr. Donaldson. That much I assure you. Believe me, our Kala Kanta is not entirely without social graces."

He gave up and, rigid with disapproval, shrugged. "As Your Ladyship deems best. My humble duty is but to advise as I consider fit."

That night when Willie Donaldson related the day's events to his wife, as he always did each evening, he made no bones about his perturbation. "She's up to something devious again, my love. I'd give my last poond of haggis to know what it damn well *is.*"

"Och, the puir wee lass, Will," Cornelia Donaldson chided with a frown. "All alone at the mercy of that savage hellion—imagine!"

Over the rim of his glasses and from behind his four-month-old copy of *The Scotsman,* her husband withered her with a look. "You dinna see that bloody glint in the lass's eyes, love. I did. If it's sympathy you want to dispense, I suggest you keep it for the savage hellion."

"The Sarkar . . . ?"

Ranjan Moitra blinked owlishly behind his neat, gold-framed spectacles, unable to believe the evidence before his eyes.

A lady in the Trident offices, a white mem? And that too, *this* mem . . . ? Oh, great mother Kali—it was unthinkable!

"If you please, Mr. Moitra. I need to see Mr. Raventhorne for a few moments." She opened her purse and, smiling cordially, handed him an exquisite ivory and gilt visiting-card. "I have already established that he is in his office."

Ranjan Moitra swallowed hard. "Yes . . . no, er, I shall see . . ." Holding the card gingerly by a corner, he hurried away.

Mesmerised by the splendid vision Olivia presented, the uniformed doorman seemed awestruck by her finery. He was not to know, of course, with what effort she sustained her assumed hauteur, or at what absurd speed her heartbeats galloped beneath the bodice of her cool, leaf green linen dress cut with such perfection. Outwardly she radiated confidence, the elegance of her appearance positively regal to those unused to such sophistication. Osprey feathers cascaded down from the crown of her wide-brimmed green suède hat raffishly tilted over one eye. A fine black veil obscured her features but not enough to conceal the arrogance in them. Even though it was the middle of the morning, discreet diamonds glinted around her neck and on her ears, reinforcing the imperiousness. Had it not been for the billowing folds of a very full skirt, the doorman would have certainly noticed that her legs shook badly and occasionally her knees knocked against each other.

Moitra returned. "I regret, Your Ladyship, that the Sarkar is unavailable." He looked desperately unhappy. "He presents sincere apologies but is unable to see you this morning." His manner was deferential and suitably rueful but he could not meet her eyes. "Perhaps another time given prior intimation . . ."

"Given prior intimation, Mr. Moitra," Olivia pointed out pleasantly, "I have no doubt your Sarkar would have arranged to be out. I require very little of his time and I'm afraid I cannot wait." Brushing past him, she walked out of the antechamber in which they stood and, giving him no further opportunity to protest, marched into the main offices beyond.

"Your Ladyship . . . !" He hurried in after her looking hapless, trickles of perspiration starting to trail down his temples. "The Sarkar is truly engrossed at the moment. He cannot be disturbed, I assure—"

"Engrossed or not, Mr. Moitra, he will have to spare me some time. My business is urgent." Halting in her majestic sweep down the central aisle of what was the clerks' room, she retained her pleasant smile but her voice rang with authority. "I too have other matters to attend to. Would you therefore be so kind as to announce me?"

A hush had settled over the room as serried rows of clerical staff laid down their quills and sat back to listen with interest, all eyes on the extraordinary sight of Ranjan Moitra in confrontation with a white-skinned mem. For him, second only to the Sarkar in the Trident hierarchy, it was an impossible situation. He gulped again and mopped his dripping brow. "Perhaps tomorrow morning?"

"No, Mr. Moitra, *now.*"

A ripple of astonishment floated across the staff sitting cross-legged on white floor cushions before the traditional Indian knee-high desks. Moitra flushed. It was unthinkable for him to lose face before his subordinates at the hands of a woman. "Very well," he said stiffly, pulling himself up and assuming an air of control, "I will again make a request to the Sarkar for—"

"That will not be necessary, Ranjan." The quiet, measured tones came from an archway at the far end of the room. "I will see Lady Birkhurst. Would you kindly show her into my office?"

Their encounter at her party had come as a surprise to Olivia. This one, however, she had planned carefully. Even so, she felt her audacity waver in the rush of blood that flooded her temples, and her hands turned clammy. "Thank you."

As Raventhorne turned and vanished from view, she started to follow Ranjan Moitra in the path he had vacated, keeping her thoughts deliberately on the trivialities around her.

For all its commercial prosperity, the Trident office was Spartan, like every other environment Jai Raventhorne inhabited. There were no outward indications of the power it enjoyed in the corporate structure of the city, no signs of that opulence so beloved of others who had made their mark in Calcutta's mercantile achievements. The accommodation was extensive, airy and immaculately clean, but arranged solely for function. The walls were whitewashed, the floors plain, uncarpeted and of sombre marble. The staff was all male and dressed like Moitra, in traditional dhoti and *kurta,* for it was well known that Raventhorne employed no Europeans on his immediate staff as a matter of hubristic policy. Raventhorne's personal office, into which Moitra ushered her now with due ceremony, was not appreciably different in character. There were no deep-pile Persian carpets, no triumphant trophies from conquests in other lands, no jade and porcelain antiques, no proud evidence of marksmanship mounted on the walls. Only in one corner was there a westernised seating arrangement of three chairs and a low table, perhaps as a concession to European visitors. And under domed glass were exquisitely fabricated scale models of Trident's fleet of clippers.

As Olivia entered, Raventhorne rose briefly. It was, she deduced with some amusement, only as a concession to Moitra's presence. He did not extend his hand, nor did she offer hers. Politely, Moitra pulled out a chair for her so that she could sit facing Raventhorne at his desk. "Thank you, Mr. Moitra." She smiled her gratitude. "I find it difficult to stand for any length of time these days."

So far, Raventhorne had suffered her presence impassively, with no identifiable expression to give away his thoughts. The deliberate reference to her pregnancy brought a slow flush creeping across his face. Catching it in her peripheral vision as she sat down, Olivia smiled to herself; behind that mask of studied offhandedness, Raventhorne was desperately uneasy! Apart from the flamboyance with which she displayed Birkhurst jewellery and the sartorial finery she could now well afford, what made him uncomfortable was the fact of her condition. A slow, acid anger built up inside Olivia. How easily he had absolved himself of all responsibility!

"Well?"

The offensively brusque question came as soon as Moitra had left the room. Olivia ignored it to make a small ceremony of lifting the veil off her face with unhurried deliberation. Having completed the task, through which Raventhorne sat with ill-concealed impatience, she turned her attention briefly to the chair upon which she sat. "Chippendale?" she asked, tapping a fingernail on the arm. "I'm surprised you didn't prefer something less European."

His expression chilled further. "I can hardly believe this brazen expedition is merely to discuss furniture with me!" The hooded gaze flicked across her diamond necklace and his jaw tightened. "What is it that you want?"

Olivia pondered. What was it that she wanted from Jai Raventhorne—apart from her life back? The anger expanded but she continued to smile cordially at him across the unfathomable abyss of hostility that divided them forever. "What I want is very simple. I want you to restore Farrowsham's credit."

Astonishment flickered in the eyes Olivia would have given almost anything never to have had the misfortune to look into. It was evident that whatever else he might have expected, it was not such bald effrontery. He laughed. "And is that all?"

"For the moment, yes."

The smile snapped off his mouth as he glared at the ivory visiting-card that lay on the desk before him. "Well, that's settled easily enough—the answer is *no.* In spite of your newly acquired authority in your husband's Agency, there is a great deal you still need to learn about business methods, especially mine. Donaldson should have known better than to depute you as his emissary." He sat back and scowled.

"Appealing to your finer instincts was my idea, not Donaldson's." She kept the mockery out of her tone, but that which was subsumed in the remark itself brought another flush to his face. "Donaldson doesn't believe that you have any. Finer instincts, that is."

He raised a caustic eyebrow. "And you do?"

"Well, we shall see. The fact is that you took the decision against Farrowsham out of petty pique. To penalise Freddie's Agency for no fault of theirs is iniquitous. I felt that, perhaps, if I appealed to you with due—what is the word I want? Ah yes, due *humility*—you might be reasonable enough to reverse your decision."

She heard his indrawn breath, although it was very soft, and he started to look faintly, almost imperceptibly, puzzled as if suddenly out of his depth. Pleasant and noncommittal, she made sure that her own expression gave away nothing. Secretly, she exhilarated in his discomfiture. Within him somewhere—everywhere!—she could feel his creases of anger. He could not tell the direction in which she was going, but he knew that she continued to mock him.

"I do not reverse decisions once taken." The clipped dismissal came with finality, but the puzzlement was replaced by a certain circumspection. "You should have had sense enough to be guided by Donaldson."

"Then you are determined not to be fair?" She sighed, as if in disappointment. "And I had come here this morning with *such* high hopes!"

In the tautness of his jawline was the indication of a temper being stretched to perilous limits. His eyes narrowed. "I'm not sure what little game you happen to be playing, Olivia, but I find it singularly unamusing. I told you once not to make the mistake of believing me to be *fair.* I am not. Nor do I intend to be for your personal benefit."

"Yes, I do remember. In fact, I have not forgotten anything that you *once* told me, Jai." She matched both his purring silkiness and the sarcasm. "But your self-assessment is unduly harsh. You have always done yourself the injustice of underestimating your considerable virtues." She sat back to enjoy a fresh rise in his colour and a return of the perplexity. "I, personally, have never had any doubts that you can be both fair and reasonable," she paused to shift position, "given the right combination of circumstances, of course." She changed position again to lean an elbow on his desk and clasp her fingers. "I understand you have made an offer for the *Daffodil?*"

Her abrupt question threw him momentarily off balance, which is what Olivia had intended. Normally, she knew, he would not have given her an answer at all but, already out of kilter, he voiced a terse "Yes."

"What could the only man to sail clippers out of Calcutta want with a wreck like the *Daffodil?*" she inquired softly.

He stiffened and stood up with such force that the ink-wells on his desk rocked and a quill fell to the floor. He did not pick it up. "Whether it is your habitual scourge of idle curiosity or whether Ransome has asked you to play broker, it isn't any of your damned business. Now, if you will please excuse me, I find I have no more time to waste."

"I only ask the question all of Calcutta is asking." Olivia shrugged and made no move to get up. "But you're right, of course. It isn't any of my business." His show of anger didn't fool her. She knew she had hit a nerve end and that it was raw. He was entirely taken by surprise. "As it happens, neither is it yours anymore. It now lies between Arthur Ransome and Lubbock."

"Lubbock?" He was startled by what she had said and then angry that he had shown it, but it was too late to take back. From behind lowered lashes Olivia studied the nuances that chased each other across his face, and once again she exulted. No, her estimates had not been wrong; that nerve end was even rawer than she had hoped! Savouring triumph, she quickly pressed home her advantage.

"Yes, Hiram Arrowsmith Lubbock—Hal to his friends. He's the cotton man from the Deep South who boasts a camel might die of thirst crossing his plantation. He—"

"I know who Lubbock is! Considering you've persuaded him to buy Ransome's property, I take it he is also a surrogate for that bird that is no longer in the net?"

The slur incensed Olivia but, keeping her mind only on the main objective of her visit, she somehow smiled. "If that is what you choose to believe—not that *that* is any damned business of *yours.* However, since you like to know about everything in station, I must also tell you that the price Lubbock offers for the *Daffodil* is far, far in excess of yours."

"Lubbock is not a shipping man," he said contemptuously. "If this is a wily trick to force me to offer more, you can tell Ransome that it will not work. Now, get out of my office."

"Oh, he doesn't want to *sail* the *Daffodil!*" Olivia laughed, still showing no signs of wanting to leave. "He only wants her for the wood. To make this Chinese furniture he plans to export. He says he's going to dismantle every *bit* of the ship to ensure him a year's supply of teak and mahogany. Somebody seems to have convinced him that there is a good market abroad. Hal is remarkably enterprising, you know. He's not just *any* old cotton man!"

Through the explanation, Raventhorne had remained silent and unmoving, but beneath its coppery veneer his skin had turned a shade paler. No longer were the eyes distant and contemptuous; there was in them now a strangeness, a measure of emotion, that he could not quite succeed in concealing. The emotion was pain, just a streak, a shadow, but for Olivia it was enough. She had worked hard for that pain and God knows it was her due. In her body every fibre began to tingle; *quid pro quo, Jai Raventhorne, now it is my turn!* Callously, she turned the knife again, digging deeper.

"There's a figure-head on the prow of the *Daffodil*—perhaps you might not be familiar with it—that Lubbock believes will fetch a good price as a carriage mascot in Jackson. Or, perhaps, as a roof-top ornament for some rich Southerner with a craving for English maritime gewgaws. Lubbock says it's amazing what some Americans will pay for junk these days."

Raventhorne had walked away to stand by the open window that overlooked the river. A squat little schooner, Olivia could see, was offloading bales of something. One had fallen into the water and a sharp altercation was in progress. It was at this scene that Raventhorne seemed to stare fixedly, but Olivia could sense that he saw none of it. The arrogant profile, moulded in stone now, was motionless against the white of a far wall. With one hand he held the back of his neck; the other was gripped tight around the window-sill. He seemed no longer aware of her presence in the room.

There was about the hushed moment a déjà vu and unconsciously Olivia's memory quickened. With awesome diligence it raced back in time to when she had driven herself to learn every shade, every whisper, of his changing moods. She remembered the despair when she failed or miscalculated, the absurd raptures when she did not, the bounding joys of discovery with which she collected pieces of his life and painstakingly joined them together to make pictures that would please her or wrench her apart. She remembered the aches, the yearnings, the pitiable little cache she treasured of half endearments given grudgingly with half love. And she remembered the fulfillment. The memories, so long muzzled, frightened her and caught her unaware. She was horrified at the knowledge that, cruelly, they still clung to her brain like bubbles of air trapped forever in water. Shaken out of her complacency, she felt disoriented, betrayed all over again.

Why was my love never enough to heal you . . . ?

"Get out of my office." He did not turn to look at her. "I have no more time to waste on you, Lady Birkhurst."

Slowly, one by one, the bubbles of memory floated away, leaving her brain once more unencumbered. The thin, wasted thread that had bound her momentarily to the past snapped and freed her again from her bondage. She despised herself for even that one instant of slavery. "With pleasure, Mr. Raventhorne. My business with you is over. Thank you for seeing me, even though I have been, alas, unsuccessful in my mission." This last she added with just enough regret to make it an insult. She had not been unsuccessful. And Jai Raventhorne knew it.

Still standing at the window, he made no move to escort her to the door. "I had hoped not to find you here on my return from Assam. Don't make a fool of yourself again by seeking me out on flimsy pretexts." A cool river breeze blew through the room but his white mull shirt clung to his back in damp patches. He was perspiring freely, nevertheless he had enough control to keep his voice uninflected.

"Why? Does seeing me make you nervous?"

"No, it makes me sick. And now you even look like a whore."

"Oh? Because I wear Freddie's jewels, bear his title and carry his child?" She laughed. "Surely by now you are used to the perquisites that whoredom can bring."

"Yes. I am. But I have known many whores who do not disgust me." It was now with extreme effort that he was keeping himself in check. "I give you fair warning, Olivia: Don't take upon yourself tasks that are beyond your tawdry skills. And don't play silly games when you have no idea of the means to win them."

At last she stood up. "If you penalise Farrowsham, then I will retaliate with whatever means my 'tawdry skills' dictate. Your threats no longer intimidate me, Jai Raventhorne. Don't make the mistake of believing that they will." She crossed the room and halted by the door with a hand on the door knob. "Oh, I almost forgot!" So as not to leave any doubt about her mission, she now spelt it out. "You see, I *do* know what it is that you want from the *Daffodil.* And I guarantee that you will never get it, except on *my* terms. Who knows? Maybe I too have a damned destiny of one kind or another to fulfil."

She walked out, slamming the door hard behind her. There could not have been anyone in the Trident offices who did not hear it. Her last look at his face was the most rewarding, for he evidently hadn't expected her to glance back over her shoulder; his face looked stricken. She was satisfied with her day's work.

It was in this lingering mood of belligerence that Olivia received her first mail packet from Freddie. But reading his letter, short and pointedly impersonal in its news, her mood changed to one of despondency. She was not deluded by Freddie's curtness; behind the trivia, the awkward phrases and, indeed, in the spaces between the lines, the letter throbbed with unexpressed pain. It was as if instead of ink, Freddie had dipped his quill into his heart and written in blood. In the last few sentences his anguish exploded. "I dream that some morning when I am least expecting it, I will open my eyes from sleep to the sight of you standing beside my bed holding a cup of tea. I dream, Olivia, I hope incessantly and I pray, but in my heart of hearts I know that you will not come . . ."

He made no mention of Amos.

Olivia cried. Sharing his anguish across the oceans and continents, she cursed again her inability to help him. There was also a letter from his mother.

> Freddie tells me nothing, but I fear he has lost you and I am heart-broken. You write that you have failed me. Perhaps it is a failure to be commonly shared. My disappointment is acute, but I am woman enough to understand that your fate has not been in your hands. I am now resigned to having that odious cousin some

day appropriate Farrowsham and the title. The prospect is ghastly and still wounds me, especially since the eventuality might arrive sooner than I had anticipated. Freddie drinks incessantly.

Cradling her head, Olivia surrendered herself to her grief. She had not informed Freddie or his mother about her pregnancy. With her stars, disaster lurked eternally around every corner; she could not raise their hopes only to dash them again. It was possible that someone had written to them already; there was no shortage of busy-bodies in town. And Peter Barstow too had sailed for England only recently. In due course he would certainly convey the news to the Birkhursts. Even so, Olivia prayed fervently that somehow they might not come to know until there was no risk of a bitter disappointment.

Prayed!

While abhorring rigid beliefs and bigoted superstitions, her father had nevertheless inculcated in her a strong faith in the essential benevolence of some force that controlled their destinies. He had spurned the hypocrisy of mandatory Sunday church-going. Although Olivia had accompanied her aunt willingly enough in this weekly duty, to her, true belief remained something less overt, more profoundly individual. That she could no longer accept that mysterious force as benign, Olivia felt her father would forgive were he to be privy to the maleficent mutilations of her life. But now, with Freddie's tortured words again burning holes in her conscience, Olivia abandoned her unbending postures to turn in desperate selfishness to the God she no longer trusted. She prayed for Freddie to be granted a son.

In the meantime, the days swept by. There was only silence from Jai Raventhorne.

With the mild, all too brief winter over, Calcutta was again turning piercingly hot. In homes and offices, overhead fan pullers doubled their efforts and slogged in relays, but the air, humid and heavy, merely moved around in turgid circles. Even the city's proliferating flies seemed struck with lethargy, easy prey to desultory swatters. Only the mosquitoes were fewer, as always, chased away by the crippling heat.

With even the weather hostile, Olivia became horribly dispirited. For all her bravado, in retrospect her visit to Raventhorne's office was a wasted effort. Perhaps he was right; she had only made a fool of herself. Looking back, her petty little verbal triumphs had been meaningless. They would add up to naught. Raventhorne (as she herself had once assured him!) was a monolith hewn out of rock. Toughened by the buffetings of his lifelong fate, he was impervious to silly darts, unlikely to be even dented by her own childish little feints. Her rash adventure had brought her nothing save even more humiliation from a man she had recklessly challenged to turn adversary. Had he ever been anything else, she wondered? She had once confessed to him, half in jest, that she would hate to have him as an enemy—but that precisely was what she had dared him to become! She had misjudged his vulnerability and, in her miscalculations, she had exposed her own. He would hit even harder at Farrowsham and, thinking of poor Willie and his justified apprehensions, she filled with shame. Still sullen and horribly distressed, Willie had never questioned her about her encounter in the Trident office. Nor, with pointed disapproval, had Arthur Ransome. Both these omissions Olivia took to be what they were intended as—tacit reproaches for her unseemly boldness. To make some reparation, at least, she worked hard at launching the furniture project.

Never one for wasting time once a deal was struck, Hal Lubbock was now satisfactorily installed in Ransome's house. The huge property was again a hive of activity. Hired draughtsmen already laboured over drawings of Chinese furniture at the Templewood house, and the Ling boys with their father had set up a carpentry workshop in the servants' quarters. Now wildly enthusiastic, Lubbock set about milking the last drop that promised profit. If the whirlwind methods of his partner made Ransome nervous and sometimes shocked his neat accountant's mind, they also impressed him. "There ain't no flahs on yours truly, pard," Lubbock assured Ransome. "Ah promised yuh top dollah, and that's what ah aim tuh delivah." Fascinated, Ransome nodded without having understood a word.

Some of Lubbock's wheelings and dealings positively scintillated with ingenuity. Since furniture on board ships was sparse, passengers usually purchased cheap movables for their long voyages to make do. Arrangements were generally made through Company clerks, who earned handsome commissions as middlemen. Lubbock struck private deals with these clerks whereby he would pay well if allowed to supply the furniture, Chinese and exquisitely elegant, free to all passengers. All they had to do was to relinquish the furniture on disembarkation in Europe to Lubbock's waiting agents. The risk of loss or damage promised to be more than compensated for by the savings in packaging and freight.

"By Jove, the chap's a genius!" Ransome was overwhelmed by the brilliance of the simple scheme. "I must confess, much to my astonishment, his enthusiasm puts new life in these old bones I considered dead."

That the highly unlikely partnership was beginning to blossom brought great pleasure to Olivia. Not even the prospect of sharing his Englishman's castle with the brash Southerner seemed to faze Ransome anymore. All that remained for the venture to start functioning was to procure a stock of suitable teak and mahogany. Still no further offer had been received from Raventhorne for the derelict *Daffodil!*

"I am inclined to let Hal start carving her up, Olivia. To wallow in sentimentality is foolish. Indeed, I am at a loss to understand why you persist in hoping that Jai will make another offer. Why should he?"

They were seated in the Templewood garden over afternoon tea. The rambling, oversized bungalow presented a dismal appearance. When Ransome shortly vacated the two ground-floor rooms he occupied and moved into his erstwhile home with Lubbock, these too would be locked and the furniture dust sheeted. In the peeling yellow walls, shuttered windows stared blindly like sightless eyes. The scarlet bougainvillea over the portico, with no one to prune it, ran wild; the rose garden had long since withered. In the once immaculate flowerbeds where butterflies feasted now there were only weeds. Only the orchid gave a brazen splash of colour and still flourished untended, as if a living mockery mounted only for Olivia's benefit. She hated the sight of it, had often wanted to tear it down from its stubborn roots, but could never remember to do so when there was the opportunity. It was well that Estelle, shrinking from memories that her old home held for her, had finally decided to sell the bungalow, if some intrepid buyer could be found. Even if John were ever transferred back to duties at Fort William, Estelle would not be able to bear living here again.

"No." Picking up the thread of their conversation, Olivia shook her head. "The *Daffodil* will remain as she is. Raventhorne *will* make another offer. I know it." The tenacity of her conviction surprised her. So far, the bait she had cast had not even been nibbled at. Her reason told her that Raventhorne would not budge; his pride would not allow him to. Yet, however strong her logic it was her instinct that seemed determined to prevail.

The tube of ash at the end of Ransome's cheroot quivered, then dropped onto the white table-cloth. Carefully he brushed it onto his palm and discarded it on the ground. "Why did you go to see Jai?" he asked with no warning. He had not stirred the topic before. "Was it anything to do with the *Daffodil?*"

"No."

"You know that Jai is livid about the sale of my house to Lubbock?"

"Yes. I daresay he is."

"And about your own participation in the affair?"

"Yes."

Ransome sighed. "My dear child, I am neither noble nor am I pleased to be a martyr, but I have always recognised that Jai's vengeance against us is inevitable, even justified. You, on the other hand, have no personal enmity with the man. It disturbs me greatly that you choose to suffer on *our* behalf. I wish you would not. He will harm Farrowsham further."

Olivia shrugged. "Perhaps. But he can also be made to undo that harm." She saw no reason to tell him it was no longer *his* battle!

"*Made* to?" He couldn't help a laugh. "No one has ever made Jai do what he has determined not to, or undo what he already has done. On what premise do you base your extraordinary assumption?"

Olivia looked away, momentarily uncertain. "Not having a more rational explanation for you at the moment, I can only put it down to a . . . hunch. Trust me a while longer, Uncle Arthur. I promise I will clarify everything in due course. In the meantime, let us not make any hasty decisions."

And with that he had to be satisfied.

That night, alone and armed with a lantern, Olivia went down into one of her basement strong-rooms and unlocked a sizable tin trunk. From it she hauled out—glad that Dr. Humphries was not there to rebuke her!—a large object wrapped in gunny sacking and tied with rope. She undid the wrapping and laid the object on the floor. Then, sitting on a stool and wiping away the fine mist of sweat that covered her forehead, she examined the object with single-minded closeness. She again took note of every detail, marvelling anew at its simple beauty, the innocent grace of its lines, the spirit it seemed to embody of something earthy, something free and altogether natural. *Had* she been right in her conjectures? *Was* she reading too much into the few words her cousin and Ransome had let drop so casually? *Could* it be that she was depending unduly on that "instinct" and had miscalculated badly?

But then she remembered her final look at that shocked, stricken face as she had left Jai Raventhorne's office, and her spirits started to revive again. No, she was not wrong in her conjectures; the nerve end he had exposed in his confusion was not a figment of her imagination. She was certain that Jai Raventhorne *would* make another bid for the *Daffodil!*

It was time to precipitate the issue.

"I fear that I have been wrong in my hopes," Olivia remarked to Arthur Ransome the next morning in his office. "It seems stupid to waste time waiting for something that might never come. If you so wish, let Hal Lubbock commence with the dismemberment of the ship."

If Ransome was astonished at her sudden reversal, he was gentleman enough not to show it. Neither did he indicate to her his increasing suspicions about her motives. He felt he no longer had the competence to understand Olivia's curious methods, but he had promised to trust her. What he found himself unable to trust with gathering disquiet was the direction in which her strange compulsions appeared to be driving her. He did not approve of it any more than he could understand it. But, of course, he still asked no questions. Instead, he quietly accepted her suggestion and issued the requisite order.

By six o'clock the following morning, Lubbock's team of carpenters was ready to start the massive task of taking apart the *Daffodil.* The abandoned ship lay beached on an upper stretch of the Hooghly, a sadly decaying reminder of the proud flagship she once was. Clad in dungarees and shirtless, Lubbock supervised the operations with exasperated gestures, irritated barks and many highly graphic expletives, which, fortunately, his workers failed to understand. A small crowd had collected to watch, since free entertainment of any sort was not to be scorned and the dismantling of a tea wagon didn't happen every day. Despite the two watchmen Ransome had hired to prevent arrant vandalism, much had already been pilfered from the vessel. Even now, a cheeky gang of urchins was having a field-day trying to snatch whatever was loose and salable, and having their ears frequently boxed for their boldness. But for all her diminished prestige, the *Daffodil* was made of stern stuff. She had been built to withstand the cataclysmic typhoons of the South China Sea; the punishment she received from the carpenters and their axes she accepted with hardly a dent in her hide. Lubbock jumped around like an excited kangaroo, swearing volubly at the slow progress but achieving little. The *Daffodil* groaned and creaked and her timbers shivered, but even by noon not much headway had been made.

Ransome squatted on a nearby outcrop of rocks, huddled in studied silence. Some distance away Olivia paced impatiently under the pleasantly cool shade of a spreading banyan tree. Her face showed no anxiety but the suspense within her was acute. Was she to be bitterly disappointed after all . . . ?

She was not.

Shortly after two o'clock in the afternoon, Ranjan Moitra was seen hurrying onto the scene bearing a letter. It was addressed to Arthur Ransome and it was from his Sarkar. It was brief and to the point and its tone was unmistakably offensive. But the message it carried was clear enough: If dismemberment of the *Daffodil* could be halted, then Raventhorne was willing to negotiate better terms for the vessel.

Ransome and Moira stared at each other in absolute silence. It was difficult to say which of the two was the more astonished.

20

News of the eleventh-hour and totally inexplicable reprieve of the *Daffodil* swept Calcutta like the bubonic plague. It was alleged that Kala Kanta had paid an absurdly large price for the wreck—more gleeful grist for the gossip mills. If there was considerable perplexity in town, there was also much jubilation among the European community. Jai Raventhorne had publicly eaten crow! Why, it was not important to know; it was the how—and how thoroughly!—that needed to be remembered. Arthur Ransome was congratulated very soundly but also with low-voiced caution; it was true that the bastard's wings had been clipped but there was still plenty of beak and claw left to be considered.

Two Europeans did not rejoice with the community. One of them was Willie Donaldson. "Why should he pay anything at all for the god-rotting wreck, let alone a small fortune? And that too after putting Ransome as close to the bankruptcy courts as any man can get?"

Olivia sat examining some bills of lading in which her aide, Bimal Babu, had pointed out errors. "I'm afraid I have no idea, Mr. Donaldson. I'm as mystified as everybody else."

Every hair of his bushy eyebrows quivered with scepticism. "Well, *I* have a wee idea it's something to do with Your Ladyship's visit to Trident. *And,* there's na a damned mother's son in town who does na believe it."

"Really?" She spent a moment explaining the error to Bimal Babu and then dismissed him with the bills. "I can't help what people choose to believe, Mr. Donaldson. That's their business."

He was not to be put off. "Rumor is, someone forced Raventhorne's hand. *Rumour* is."

"I shouldn't imagine anyone *could* force Mr. Raventhorne's

hand! At least, that is what you yourself have given me to understand. What possible pressure could I have brought to bear? I scarcely know the man. My visit was only to ask about our credit facilities."

"Which," he pointed out with some perverse satisfaction, "are *yet* to be restored, I notice!" He scanned her impassive face through slitted eyes. Gad, she was a rum 'un, a real *rum* 'un! He would dearly like to know how she had swung it, and swung it she bloody had! He'd wager his best tartan socks on that, he would.

Frowning, Olivia tapped a front tooth with the end of her pen. "No, they have not been restored yet," she admitted, then started to write again. "But they will, Mr. Donaldson. I assure you they will."

He snorted. "*Just* because he's laid doon good shekels for a sieve na worth a row of beans?"

"No. Because what Mr. Raventhorne has done, he's done out of the goodness of his heart," Olivia said with perfect seriousness. "Which goes to show that he does have one, after all." She dabbed what she had written with a blotter and blinded him with a smile.

Donaldson wasn't sure whether he should laugh or go up in smoke. He settled for further sarcasm. "*If* he has a heart then it sure ain't like any *I've* known—unless our definitions differ."

"In that case, maybe he's decided to repent." She smiled at the sarcasm but otherwise ignored it. "Let's just be grateful for the salvation."

"It's *Ransome* that's benefitted from this miraculous salvation, na Farrowsham! You truly believe he's planning to let the Agency off the hook?" He expressed his disgust with a hoot.

No, Olivia did not believe that, not for a moment. But she didn't have the heart to confirm his justified trepidation. "Let's not be unduly pessimistic, Mr. Donaldson," she comforted instead. "The worst may never happen."

But they both knew that it would. When Donaldson related to his wife the day's events that evening, he described at some length a curious weapon called the boomerang, which was used by aborigines in Australia, he had heard. He had always been intrigued to learn how it worked. He had a horrible suspicion, he told Cornelia, that he was about to find out for himself in the very near future.

In spite of his open relief and astonishment, neither did Arthur Ransome rejoice. Immediately he had no time to unravel his confusions or ask for explanations, for Hal Lubbock was hopping mad. In retaliation for being deprived of his timber he was threatening to storm Raventhorne's office with the specific intention of "re'rangin' his goddam nose on his goddam face," and it was with great difficulty that Ransome restrained him. It was only after fresh supplies had been secured from the timber market and several bottles of bourbon begged and borrowed from various quarters that Lubbock quieted and Ransome could sit down and ponder.

That evening, filled with rare resolve, Ransome called again upon Olivia. "I think the time has come, my dear," he said decisively, "when I must be told what went on behind the sale of the *Daffodil.* Why does Raventhorne want the ship so badly as to offer such an unrealistically high price for it?"

"He doesn't want the ship. He never has. He has no use for it. What he wants badly is something that was mounted on it."

"Mounted on it?" Ransome looked blank. "What?"

"The figure-head on the prow. Am I right in presuming that it was his mother who had chiselled it? At least, that's what you yourself once told me. Don't you remember?"

He obviously didn't, for he continued to look utterly at sea. "*I* told you? When?"

"A very long time ago. You said that she was good with her hands—she carved wooden toys and you bought some from her once, also a ship's mascot. At that time you had only one vessel, the *Daffodil.* If you had mounted it at all, it had to be on the *Daffodil.*" From the crystal decanter on the sideboard, Olivia poured two glasses of Madeira and gave him one. "When I learned of this sudden bid for the ship, I recalled what you had told me. Without your permission, I'm afraid," she smiled an apology, "I went to see the ship for myself. The figure-head on the prow was obviously the work of an enthusiastic amateur, but it was very beautiful. It had a startling spontaneity about it. I could see that it had been executed with great feeling. And the figure itself, a female with her hands stretched above her head as if reaching out for something unattainable, was that of a young girl draped in a deerskin. Don't some tribal women cover themselves with animal pelts?"

Listening with undivided attention, Ransome nodded but vaguely as his memory started to uncloud. "Now that you mention it, yes, I do recall saying something of the sort. And yes, I recall that it was Jai's mother who had carved that figure-head. She was sitting in the garden one day, Josh said, chiselling it when he saw her and, on an impulse, bought it for the *Daffodil.* We did mount it on the prow, come to think of it, but good grief—you came to deduce all that *just* from the few words I had let drop?"

"No. In fact, I had forgotten about them. It was something Estelle later mentioned that brought them back to mind. In Raventhorne's house, she said, she had seen a few of those wooden toys his mother was fond of making, although at the time Estelle had no idea who the artist was. One of the toys, she told me casually, was in the shape of a female figure that reminded her of a ship's mascot. Her comment meant nothing to me at the time, but later, when I heard that Raventhorne had made an offer for the *Daffodil,* I suddenly remembered that, curiously enough, both you and Estelle had used the words *ship's mascot.* What Estelle of course was thinking of was the *Daffodil,* where she had seen the figure-head. Raventhorne obviously still retained a miniature replica, possibly a sort of draft design for the larger model." Having suitably doctored the story for Ransome's benefit, she added carefully, "Raventhorne, Estelle felt, was very . . . particular about his mother's little souvenirs."

"Yes, I daresay he was," Ransome said absently, still not able to shed his bafflement. "But if he wanted only the figure-head, why in God's name did he have to pay for the whole ship? Had I known, I would have been pleased to let him have that figure-head with my compliments!"

"He paid for the whole ship because there was no other way he *could* have procured that figure-head. Certainly, he would never have *asked* you for it!"

"Well, he could have just . . . just taken it! The ship was lying out in the open. Two meagre watchmen were not enough to stop *other* vandals."

"He didn't consider it worth the trouble. He was so sure of getting the *Daffodil* for next to nothing. By the time he must have realised that it wouldn't be quite that easy, it was too late to remove the figure-head." She smiled in renewed apology. "You see, I already had."

"God bless my soul!" Ransome exclaimed. "You removed it? How . . . ?"

"I took one of Mary Ling's brothers to saw it off the prow. On the day Raventhorne made you payment in full, I retrieved it from my basement store-room where I had hidden it and had it delivered to Raventhorne's house."

Amazed, Ransome said nothing for a while. Then he asked slowly, "Who told Raventhorne that his bid for the *Daffodil* wouldn't be considered unless he raised it—was it you? Is that why you went to see him?"

"I went to see him to request him to restore our credit facilities. In passing, I might have mentioned something about the *Daffodil.*"

He lowered his eyes towards his drink and kept them there. "You have taken a great deal of trouble on our behalf, Olivia," he said, uneasy. "Are you sure that was wise?"

Olivia shrugged. "Wise or not, Raventhorne has paid you a fair price for what he wanted. That's all that matters."

"Is it? He has lost face, Olivia. He does not forgive easily. However grateful I might be for your extraordinary endeavours, and I am, believe me, it is Farrowsham that must be considered. Raventhorne will harass you mercilessly, and do God knows what other damage."

"Yes, I am not unaware of that possibility, Uncle Arthur. We will just have to tackle each harassment as it comes." She quickly reassured him with a gesture. "What you must forgive me for are all the liberties I have taken, unbidden. I have done things behind your back, lied to you, been far from straightforward . . ."

He dismissed her apologies with a wave, but he could not shake off his visible distress with the valiant smile he attempted. Like Willie Donaldson, Ransome knew that the sale of the *Daffodil* was by no means the end of the matter.

As, of course, it was not.

Three days later Raventhorne struck again. Farrowsham's most recent consignment of indigo intended for London, packed and ready for loading at the wharf, was refused space aboard Trident's clipper scheduled to sail the following day on the morning tide. The consignment had been paid for in full as per the new requirements, and the bills of lading were all in order, as was the clearance from the Customs. No reason was specified for the refusal to accept the cargo. Moitra's businesslike letter only stated bluntly Trident's inability to oblige. It also added that no guarantee could be given for hold space for future cargo from Farrowsham in any of the company's clippers. Enclosed with the letter was a banker's draft for the sum paid in advance for freight.

After Donaldson had expended his rage and much of his choice verbiage on Trident's hapless messenger boy, his own nervous staff and the world in general, he sat slumped over his desk sunk in gloom blacker than any he had ever known before. "I knew it would come to this, I *knew* it!" was what he kept muttering to himself over and over again, now with no pious glow of perverse satisfaction at having been proved right. He had passed beyond that. All he could think of was that Farrowsham, *his* Farrowsham, held in sacred trust by him for the soul of Caleb Birkhurst and the comfortable profit of his son, had become the ham in a sandwich neither to his taste nor of his making. Without a sin to its fair name, Farrowsham was being pilloried, put in the stocks.

Privately, not even Olivia could deny that she was shaken. Trident's blanket ban on their cargo was indeed a severe broadside, and she could not insult Donaldson's intelligence by trying to minimise it. Their profitability would be badly hurt, for in the export-import business, as in any other, time translated automatically into money. It was not that there were no other clippers available; American lines sent plenty of vessels, but they called irregularly and their schedules were erratic. Raventhorne guaranteed sailings as regular as clockwork; the speed and accuracy with which his ships delivered goods to their destinations were admirable. Which, of course, was the reason for his considerable success as a shipowner. To secure other hold space now in outgoing vessels, Farrowsham would have to pay through its nose and bribe Company officials and captains heavily. It would mean stealing cargo space booked by others, which would, understandably, create dissension and bad blood in the business community—something Donaldson had always avoided with his scrupulous code of ethics. In any case, only Indiamen were available and these took double the time Trident's clippers did. Not to be overlooked were the gleeful gains of competitors, already at wharfside scrambling furiously for the hold space vacated by Farrowsham in the *Jamuna,* as well as for future bookings.

Ensconced in her own office, Olivia sat thinking hard. The summer's heat in the middle of the day was punitive. The humidity was making it even more difficult to bear. Even her light calico dress was soaked through with perspiration and clung uncomfortably to her damp petticoats. From the large clay pot balanced on an iron stand in a corner of her room, she poured herself another glass of cool water, drank it thirstily and then sent for Willie Donaldson.

"We have an annual contract with Trident. If they flout it, can we appeal to the Chamber for redress?"

"The Chamber!" In short, succinct words, Donaldson proceeded to tell her exactly what he thought of the Chamber of Commerce and then, despondent again, shook his head. "Na we can't. A clause in the contract warns that if our indigo stains any part of the hold, Trident will hold us responsible for heavy damages. That last consignment, if you recall, was imperfectly packed," he paused to heap liberal curses on the absent warehouse manager, "and it made a god-awful mess. Raventhorne will cite that as justification for cancelling the contract altogether."

"But supposing we agreed to pay damages and dispatched only," she riffled through a ledger, "saltpetre, camphor, salt, timber and that Dacca muslin that is on order?"

He gave a bark of a derisive laugh. "What he's telling us, plain as plain can be, is that he's *na* going to lift our cargo again, *any* cargo. You can see what he thinks of that damned contract." He dug in his pocket and strewed her table top with scraps of paper. "These also came with Moitra's letter."

Understanding his anger, all his resentments and his unspoken accusations, Olivia made no attempt to comfort him. For a while she merely stood at her window peering through the bamboo slats of the *chik* that did nothing to keep out the searing midday heat. Picking up a palm leaf fan, she waved it across her face, her mind now racing along quite another track.

"The Trident clipper that sails next month is the *Tapti,* isn't it?"

"Aye." His eyebrows locked horns like battling bulls. "What of it?"

"Well, since it appears that we cannot avail ourselves of the *Jamuna,* we will just have to wait for the *Tapti* to sail. Or, maybe, the clipper after that. This much delay we can easily afford. In the meantime, we'd better get that indigo back from the wharves for repacking. If there's a nor-wester storm in the offing and the river turns blue, we'll have every dhobi on the Hooghly panting for our blood."

Slowly Donaldson sat up straight and stared. "Perhaps Your Ladyship has na yet fully understood the import of *this!*" He waved Moitra's letter in the air. "Moitra says—"

"I know what Moitra says," she interrupted gently. "What I am trying to convey to you, Mr. Donaldson, is that when the *Tapti* or the next clipper sails, Farrowsham's cargo *will* be on board despite Moitra's letter, as it will be on board every Trident clipper sailing thereafter." She swept up the pieces of the torn contract and put them inside an envelope. "In the meanwhile, why don't we get that nice young Sol Abrahams to stick these together again?"

Jesus! That glint is back in her eyes, so help me God! thought Donaldson. He swallowed hard. "We'll na need them again . . . ," he began weakly.

"Yes, you're right. We won't." She tossed the envelope carelessly into her waste bin. "We will get Trident to draw up a fresh contract with more reasonable freight rates. Double duties for foreign shipping were abolished two years ago and they can well afford to reduce their charges. In fact, I have been meaning to talk to you about this for some time, Mr. Donaldson."

Wildly, his eyes flew to the liquor cabinet where Olivia kept her supplies to entertain business visitors. God's nails—she'd been at it herself, she bloody had! Olivia caught his glance and her eyes twinkled. "Seriously, Mr. Donaldson, do you know what I think Farrowsham needs to do now?"

He saw that she had intercepted his glance and, only to hide his embarrassment, growled, "Na, what?"

"I think Farrowsham needs to diversify. There's something very sordid about being held for ransom, don't you think?" Dreamily, she again gazed out of the window.

"Diversify?" He now had no doubts about her insobriety. "Farrowsham does na *need* any bleeding diversifications! We have more damn business than we can reck'n what to do with!"

"Oh, I disagree entirely, Mr. Donaldson." She picked up a pencil and started to doodle. "In America we believe there is *always* room for expansion. For instance, Mr. Donaldson, how does the idea strike you of acquiring a Farrowsham hotel?"

The idea struck Willie Donaldson forcefully. In fact, it struck him dumb.

Almost a century had passed since 1756 when Siraj-ud-Daula, Nawab of Bengal, had marched from Murshidabad to attack and capture Calcutta. It had been a fearsome, uneven battle and at least part of the blame for it (for the consequent rout of the Company's garrison at Fort William and even for the hideous deaths of one hundred twenty-three British prisoners from suffocation in the notorious Black Hole) many still ascribed indirectly to the evil machinations of one Amin Chand, a Hindu money-lender of alleged ill repute. It was this man that Ram Chand Mooljee proudly counted among his forbears.

Like his ancestor, Ram Chand was a money-lender by profession, a manipulator by inclination and a crook by sheer natural instinct. If Clarence Pennworthy's Imperial East India Bank was the conduit between the Company Bahadur and its masters on London's Leadenhall Street—as it was between most respectable merchants—it was Ram Chand who was the pipeline in every clandestine, illicit but lucrative financial transaction in town. Also like his ancestor, he had amassed a considerable sterling fortune to become one of the richest Hindu merchants in Bengal. He, like Amin Chand, boasted a privileged residence in Calcutta's White Town—not surprising, since it was his money that had financed the construction of several European homes.

Unlike his forbear, however, Ram Chand despised politics. Money, he often said, remained money regardless of political affiliations, and to its pursuit he dedicated his life. As the fiscal conscience of many—black, white, brown and yellow—Ram Chand thrived on financial adventurism. He had learned through his exploits that nothing denuded a man's soul as much as the lure of lucre. Consequently, nothing surprised him, for in satisfying everyone's greed—and, indeed, using it to his own profit—he had become a canny calculator of human nature. It was his boast that to him what was unexpected was the expected.

But now, as he sat facing the white mem called Lady Birkhurst, on one of the extremely rare occasions of his life Ram Chand found himself taken by surprise. "A loan?" he murmured slowly to give himself time to think. Why should she, with all those Farrowsham funds, need to ask him for another loan? The first, he knew, was for Ransome sahib, but now . . . ? He concealed his surprise behind an obsequious smile and declared himself a humble servant whose command was her wish, then said, "Yes, certainly a loan can be arranged, even though what little this miserable slave has could not be more than a pittance compared to your esteemed lord and husband's—"

"It is in my personal capacity again that I wish to take the loan," Olivia interrupted, answering the convoluted question he slyly asked. "I do not wish it to involve either the Agency or my husband."

"Ah, I understand perfectly, perfectly." The oily folds of his fleshy face lifted in a smile, but his eyes remained cool and appraising. "It takes time, I know, for money to arrive from

Lloyd's in your Blighty—whereby, of course, this honour for your unworthy servant."

Olivia was not surprised at his information. In her one previous dealing with him, she had learned to regard his espionage system with the same awe that she regarded Jai Raventhorne's. "Yes, precisely. I need the money immediately to cover a certain transaction I wish to make."

"A private transaction, no doubt."

Since Ram Chand disliked having to ask questions, this too was inflected as a statement. "Not at all," Olivia smiled. "It will be quite public. I intend to acquire a property with a view to starting a top-grade hotel. As you know, Mr. Mooljee, there is only Spence's, which is inadequate. We could well do with another. I consider this to be a sound business proposition."

"A hotel?" He could not have been more taken aback, and he was peeved. All this was being planned and he had not an inkling? He decided to instantly dismiss his informer on Old Court House Street and replace him with a more competent man. "A hotel owned by your noble self?" he was forced to ask.

"At the outset, yes. Then I might lease it to Farrowsham. Or, perhaps, offer shares to investors."

Ram Chand forgot his chagrin in order to ponder. It was indeed an inspired project. Not that he would ever consider losing caste by patronising such a place, but it was true that decent lodging houses in the city were sadly lacking. Those that did exist were ill kept and dirty, with atrocious food, he had been told, and worse services. Usually friends and family offered hospitality to visitors, but should a top-grade hotel become available, he had no doubt it would attract excellent custom. And he, of course, could make a killing on those "shares" she had mentioned . . . But, the lady mem in the *hotel* business? Why, her people would never stand for it! It would be worse than shopkeeping, and he had learned enough about *firanghi* prejudices to know how that was despised! However, Ram Chand took care not to reveal any of his reactions.

"Yes, it could be a viable proposition," he said, looking dubious, but then he turned expansive. "However, first we must have refreshments. Forgive this coarse animal for having the manners of a donkey. It is deplorable!"

He clapped and half a dozen minions appeared. Berating them soundly for not having thought of it themselves, he ordered spiced tea and English biscuits. Olivia watched, amused. In spite of his wealth, she knew Ram Chand deliberately maintained this mean little office in a crowded bazaar not far from, appropriately enough, the Royal Mint. Many of his clients were rich and politically powerful, but his bread and butter (and jam!) came from hundreds of modest salaried employees of Company Bahadur for whom he performed financial services forbidden by the rules of employment. For a fee (high but never too high), he invested their funds in buying commodities in Calcutta to sell in the hinterland. He loaned them money at murderous interest rates to cover their various short term embarrassments, such as imprudent gambling debts. Without the knowledge of either Pennworthy or other bankers, he arranged to remit illegally acquired funds to England, earning not only undying gratitude but generous commissions. With at least two Company Directors as his clients, he was in a position to extract various favours for his Indian patrons in exchange for handsome "gifts." He advanced to impecunious young civil and military English gentlemen passage money to send for lovelorn fiancées and pining wives, was willing to keep in hock even the meanest of mean household articles and propped up limping commercial ventures with transfusions that ensured worth-while returns later. It was rumoured that he could mate and match supply and demand with such skill that he could name his own fee in the middle and frequently did. In the burgeoning middle class of Calcutta's Indian businessmen, Ram Chand Mooljee was an undoubted pioneer.

His duties as host discharged, Mooljee returned to business, his pudgy fingers once more interlocked across his paunch. "The site for this hotel—I take it that has already been decided?"

"Yes. The site is the residence of my late uncle, Sir Joshua Templewood. I intend to purchase the property."

Mooljee was even more put out. But then he knew that lately there had been some very curious goings-on in the city: Ransome's arrangement with the vulgar American, the lady mem's extraordinary *burra khana,* that business with the ship and now Kala Kanta's sudden aversion to Farrowsham. It was believed that the common factor in all these was this mannish, free-minded lady mem who had beauty and far too many brains but little modesty. *How* she was the common factor Mooljee could not fathom and this irked him too. And now with this projected sale, his nose smelt both trouble and profit. Would the Eurasian allow it? The sahib might be dead but the missy mem was not! Nonetheless, Mooljee's interest quickened further; that Templewood property was, after all, prime land.

"Ah yes, what a sad loss has been the untimely demise of your dear uncle—a fine gentleman, very fine indeed." He paused for a decent interval, wiped an imaginary tear, heaved a sigh of grief, then became brisk again. "The lady memsahib's plan is ambitious and also long term. Do I take it that she will then not be deserting us—leaving us utterly bereft—and going to lord sahib in London?" Unafflicted by codes of ethics, Mooljee had no qualms about asking openly what others wondered only in private.

"Yes, it is ambitious and long term." Olivia knew the reason for his concern and, side-stepping a complete answer, produced a purple satin–covered box from her purse. "This is my collateral against the loan. An authorised valuation is in the lining, but you are free to make your own if you wish. You will find this covers my loan very adequately. And my funds will not be long in arriving from England."

He made vehement protestations that he cared nothing for collateral. Indeed, if her honourable family's solvency could be questioned, then what was *he* save a miserable worm, a penniless pauper. "For Ram Chand Mooljee," he thundered, "the lady memsahib's word is enough, *enough!*" Nevertheless he opened the box to cast a careless glance within. He recognised the tiara immediately, for he never forgot gem stones he had once seen. It was part of a collection he had evaluated for Lady Bridget years ago and its diamonds were flawless, worth far more than the sum of the loan requested. There was no change in his remorseful expression as he snapped the box shut. "The money will be delivered to your residence in the morning." He scribbled out a quick receipt. "Will that be convenient?"

"Perfectly. Thank you."

Business satisfactorily concluded, Mooljee allowed the corners of his mouth to sag a little. "It has pained me greatly to learn of the honourable Agency's troubles with Kala Kanta. The man is a menace. I have always believed these Eurasians cannot be trusted."

She almost smiled; Mooljee, she knew, was one of Raventhorne's most loyal supporters. She got up to leave. "Problems come and go, Mr. Mooljee. One learns to keep them in proper perspective."

The money-lender's shifty little eyes gleamed with admiration. What a woman! Naturally, it was she who was at the eye of all the problems, but to be so daring as to mock the Kala Kanta himself! It was foolish, of course, but it was also worthy of applause. "I take it as said that Mr. Ransome and the charming Mrs. Sturges are fully in favour of the sale?"

"Oh yes. Fully."

It was a slight variation of the truth. Ransome, in fact, was dead against it. If he had eventually succumbed to Olivia's pleas, it was only because his great affection for her prevented him from refusing her anything. Estelle had agreed to a sale; the details she had no need of yet. She would bow meekly to Arthur Ransome's decisions. But all this was unnecessary for Mooljee to know.

"And it is the main house itself that the lady memsahib intends to convert into this hotel?"

A small smile touched the corners of Olivia's lips. "No. That would hardly be adequate. To house the hotel I have other plans."

The spate of letters arriving daily from Estelle, and Olivia's own persuasions, finally convinced Arthur Ransome to agree to a holiday in Cawnpore. Truly, there was now no reason for him to remain in Calcutta. Having found his footing, Lubbock no longer needed assistance; neither the fabrication of the furniture nor finances presented any more problems. All things considered, Ransome should have been a man satisfied with at least this aspect of his life. He was not. On the contrary, he was still eaten away with anxieties. Try as he might, he could not rid himself of the suspicion that everything he had been watching had been a cleverly stage-managed shadow play, that the reality behind the screen was entirely different. He had, reluctantly and against his better judgement, accepted Olivia's offer for the Templewood house as part of Farrowsham's diversification plans, but he was not satisfied with her explanations, however plausible. It was not the commercial viability of the scheme that worried him. The market was already humming with interest; even the Company's top echelons were putting out feelers. Ransome's worry stemmed from a more personal cause and, eventually, he could not hold his tongue any longer.

"You have made a great deal of work for yourself with this hotel project of yours, Olivia. I wish I could believe your intentions of actually seeing it through."

It was the night before his departure for Cawnpore. They were in the Templewood dining-room sharing Babulal's final offering of an aromatic stew, more Indian than Irish but still very tasty. Tomorrow there would be padlocks on all the doors and, save two watchmen and a part-time sweeper, no servants would remain. Ransome would hand over possession to Olivia and that would be that. Another chapter of his life was concluding and the thought was making him melancholy.

Recognising his sentiments, Olivia pressed his hand fondly. "Don't *worry,* Uncle Arthur! Everything will turn out for the best, you'll see."

The vague reassurance did not address the point he was trying to make. He knew she had deliberately evaded it. "Olivia, before I leave I feel it is my duty to say what I am about to." He couldn't accept any more prevarications. "I hope you will take it well, for I speak as one to whom your welfare is of utmost concern. You are a woman of grit, of exceptional resilience and competence. The reputation that you have earned for yourself as an astute businesswoman is really quite enviable and I, as do many others, respect it—indeed, I more than anyone. I personally am beholden to you for life. No, don't dismiss that!" He aborted her move to protest. "To our beleaguered firm you have been a selfless supporter. But," he paused, looking for words, "you are still a woman, a wife and a mother. The world of commerce is unparalleled in its excitement, I grant you, but it is also a world of cutthroats, dirty dealings, graft, corruption and gutter moralities, to say nothing of often gutter mentalities. Of course it's much the same anywhere in the world where there are such rich pickings, but this, Olivia, is not the world for you. Your life and that of your child," he said with solemn earnestness, "must be with your husband. It is to England that you must now look for your future. Leave Willie to tackle Raventhorne as best he can. Left on his own, he will conjure up some adequately crafty devices and compromises."

It was the most frankly personal advice he had ever ventured to give her. Listening to it, Olivia filled with sadness. No longer could she keep at least part of the truth from this man she had learned to love and regard as a father. "I will not be joining Freddie in England," she said quietly. "There are too many irreconcilable differences between us to ever consider being together again."

Hearing the town's gossip confirmed so bluntly, Arthur Ransome's warm, kindly eyes dimmed. When he spoke, his throat was thick with feeling. "But there must be some grounds for a rapprochement at least for Amos's sake!" He was, of course, unaware of the supreme irony of that remark. "And also for the sake of the little one that is to be. What on earth can Freddie be thinking of! *Two* fatherless infants—how will you manage?"

"It is not Freddie who is to blame," she muttered inaudibly, almost blurting out the rest of the truth but then realising just how foolish that would be. It would only shatter all the rest of his illusions and cause him even more sorrow. A ribbon of pain threaded through the unguarded crevices of her mind. "Oh, I will manage. As you yourself said, I am resilient."

"But my dear child . . . !" Once again unembarrassed to display emotion, he could not hold back his grief. "The load of your responsibility, the moral stresses—have you considered those? I need hardly add that, for what it is worth, you can always depend on me for any assistance, *any.*" Overcome, he stopped. Then, in quite a different tone, he added, "I know that in our lives we must each do what we think is right. But, Olivia, I beg you, in your . . . crusade against Jai, do not lose sight of the forest for the trees." For all his confirmed bachelorhood, his lack of experience with women, Arthur Ransome was no fool. He had long sensed that there were in Olivia's life vast tracts that were hidden, tracts where trespassers would not be welcome. So far he had made his observations in silence. Even now he treaded warily, for the ground was largely unfamiliar. "Don't drive Jai too far, Olivia. Cornered, he can be uncompromisingly vicious—as I scarcely need to remind you. Jai never forgives, never forgets."

Olivia broke the uncomfortable tension of the moment with a light laugh and a shrug. "In that case, we are certainly well matched. You see, Uncle Arthur, neither do I."

It was June again. For the third time since Olivia had been in India, the monsoon clouds started to gather.

Though satisfied with her general health, Dr. Humphries passed severe strictures on Olivia's continuing attendance at the office and what he called her game of ducks and drakes with the collective nerves of the city. "I appreciate your efforts to bring me patients, my girl, but with your Willie as a charge I might as well take to the asylum myself! What are you trying to do, take over the blasted Empire? For heaven's sake, woman, at least for the time being leave the acrobatics to the men!"

"But I enjoy my work," Olivia protested. "What would I do at home all day? I'd be bored stupid."

"Do? Good God, do what other women do when they're about to deliver babies. Make booties and bonnets and jams and lace doilies, *that's* what! Incidentally, didn't you tell me that Estelle plans to return in time for your confinement?"

"Yes. She insists on it."

"And a damn good thing too! If nothing else chains you to the hearth, I'm sure your determined cousin will. By all means return to do battle—but *after* your child is born."

It was, of course, salutary advice. Wisely Olivia resigned herself to it, knowing that in order to "do battle" her presence wasn't really necessary at the Agency. The front that she had now opened was located elsewhere. Also, the enforced inactivity allowed her to spend longer hours with her son. It broke Olivia's heart that, save for the servants' children, Amos did not have any little playmates. She was aware that the strange seclusion in which she kept her child was the subject of avid gossip in station. Since the time of his birth Amos had never been seen either in the park or at other children's birthday parties or, indeed, in the carriage driving out with his mother. Not even the good doctor—as Millie Humphries frequently pointed out to her friends—had ever set eyes on Amos Birkhurst's little face, except just after he was born when he had been displayed briefly to callers. Some whispered knowingly that the boy was deformed, so hideously in fact that his mother dared not reveal his person for fear of open ridicule. Others, less imaginative, put it down baldly to Olivia's intolerably hoity-toity airs. The schemingly acquired title and riches had turned her head, and her victories over *that man,* paltry business successes and importance in her husband's Agency even more so. The truth was, the majority averred, that milady considered her precious son too good for the likes of *their* modest, middle-class progeny. In that case, la-di-da—see if *they* cared!

Aware of the rumours, Olivia was more wounded than she was willing to admit. Within her own premises also, she lived in perennial fear. Mary Ling was a simple, trusting girl, but she too was Eurasian. How soon would she start to wonder about the child's resemblance to Raventhorne? And the rest of her staff who had seen him in such memorable circumstances at her cousin's reception, how soon would *they* start talking—or did they do so already? All this frightened and hurt Olivia, but she was helpless; now more than ever she simply could not afford to take risks. But once disentangled from the pernicious threads of this giant silken cobweb, she vowed to herself she would spend every moment compensating Amos for his present cruel deprivations.

To avoid the inevitable spate of morning callers, Olivia started to pass the hours before luncheon at the Templewood bungalow with Amos and Mary. She felt she could not face those who indubitably came with gossip in mind, to sniff and smell out juicy snippets of information that could then be scattered around at *burra khanas* to add to the spicy offerings. Others would come with possibly kinder intentions, but in her present mood of restiveness, Olivia felt she could not stomach them either. Besides, some preliminary activity had already commenced at the Templewood bungalow. A firm of surveyors had been called in to accurately measure the land, some uneven ground at the back was being levelled and a suitably qualified architect was in the process of being selected to design the Farrowsham hotel on the lines of the most modern establishments in America. Olivia had also made known her need for an experienced, possibly retired, hotelier of repute who would be competent to act as her adviser. There was no doubt that the project was gathering momentum. The interest it was generating among potential investors was prompting a daily deluge of inquiries at the Agency. If Donaldson was gratified by this favourable reaction he did not show it; dour and unbending, he remained as suspicious as ever.

But from Jai Raventhorne there was only silence.

One of the few callers Olivia genuinely welcomed was Hal Lubbock, fast developing into an India hand of confidence. For Olivia, even his unbridled vulgarity came as a touch of the home that was now only a mirage, and she found it vastly refreshing. One morning he arrived with a not unexpected tidbit of news. "This gah Raventhorne, ah'd shure lahk to know what makes him tick. Heard what he's doin' with that old shipwreck?" Olivia told him that she had not heard. "Nuttin'. Would yuh b'lieve it? *Nuttin'!*" Added to that, he proceeded to tell her with much astonishment, he had removed the guards from the site and made it known that anyone who wished to help himself to a piece of the *Daffodil* was welcome to take what they wanted. As a consequence, the river site was swarming with scavengers, like flies around a rotten carcass, picking the ship to its bones. "Can yuh *beat* that, my'am? Ah guess *someone* could figger it aht—*ah* shure as hell cahn't!"

Yes, she could figure it out. Whatever might have once been

mounted on her prow, the *Daffodil* remained a symbol of the man Raventhorne hated; that he was now dead made no difference. Lubbock would have been shocked, had he known it, at just how accurate was his analogy of that carcass.

Were it not for the dutiful letters Olivia forced herself to fabricate each week to her family, and for those that arrived in return with gratifying regularity, she would no longer have thought of America. Home, family and future had simply ceased to hold meaning for her. Now there was only the present. He was thinking, her father wrote, of registering Amos's name at Yale, "unless Freddie considers Oxford or Cambridge more fitting." A nursery annex for two was half erected right next to the beach. Sally was busy stitching little swim-suits. A trip was planned to San Francisco this coming summer, perhaps one to England next year to make the acquaintance of Freddie and his family. No doubt by then she too would be there with both her children. The Sacramento farm had been bought up by Greg, who was now married to a Mexican girl and they were about to become proud parents. Dane and Dirk were learning about India from her father; they also wanted to know if it was true that as an English lord's wife she now had to wear a crown, even when she went to bed.

And then, one fine morning, like a messenger from heaven, an angel from the gods, Kinjal arrived!

Olivia was overwhelmed; for a moment or two she could not speak. Before the rains damaged the roads seriously, Kinjal explained, she had decided to spend some time in Calcutta so as to be on hand during Olivia's second confinement. Also, it would be a good time to complete rituals before the mother goddess at the Kali temple in fulfilment of a vow she had taken for the continuing health and prosperity of her family. Olivia knew that Arvind Singh maintained a permanent residence in Kalighat on the canal known as the *adhi Ganga,* the half Ganges, a tributary of the Hooghly and also highly sacred to Calcutta's Hindus. It was now almost a year since Olivia had last seen Kinjal; however active their correspondence, to be once more face to face with her dearest friend, her true confidant, brought for Olivia a resurgence of a joy such as she had not savoured in months. There was so much news to be given and received, so much to be talked about, oh so much!

Kinjal had brought with her generous gifts for her friend and for Amos. Now almost a year old, bursting with boyish energy and undiluted enchantment, Amos was much admired, cosseted and cuddled, and allowed rampant liberties with which to show off all his newly acquired accomplishments. In between, they exchanged volumes of news and talked and laughed until their throats ran dry and their voices cracked. Tarun and Tara, Kinjal told her, were once again with their grandparents in the north. Arvind Singh was totally preoccupied with completing repairs to the mine and with ubiquitous State duties. Relieved of household responsibilities and the onerous burdens of being a conscientious Maharani, if only temporarily, Kinjal seemed marvellously relaxed, her mood reposeful and receptive.

Which was why, that afternoon, Olivia decided to stir a subject she had not meant to until much later. In a way, she dreaded the moment, but what she had planned had to be said sometime and now seemed a better time than later. "You have already done so much for me, Kinjal dearest, that I am ashamed to confess there is still one favour I have to beg of you. Had you not come, in fact, I would have written to plead for your presence." The strangeness that had come over Olivia's face stopped Kinjal from premature intervention. She waited. "As soon as my baby is born, I request you to remove it from my proximity."

"Remove it?" Kinjal was startled. "Remove it where?"

"Wherever it is not within my reach or hearing. I would also be supremely grateful for the provision of a suitable wet-nurse of your recommendation from Kirtinagar. She should be willing to travel to England with the child. I will, of course, also bear all expenses for her subsequent return. Mary will be accompanying them, naturally. The woman will be well taken care of and will suffer no language difficulties."

Olivia's calm matter of factness by no means deluded Kinjal, but nevertheless she was appalled. "You will surrender your child to your husband? With no thought for your own feelings? No, *no,* my poor friend, I will not, I *cannot* be party to such self-inflicted cruelty!"

"Kinjal, I *must* do this!" Olivia said fiercely. "Without it my moral bargain has no meaning." For the moment she felt no pain, only impatience. There would be plenty of time later for mourning. "You see, Kinjal, what I *want* to do is not what I *have* to do anymore. The two have become irreconcilable. Between you and Estelle, who will also arrive shortly, you must not let me weaken. I have no one else upon whom to depend."

"Curses on that moral bargain of yours!" Kinjal cried in rare anger. "It is the mother in me who rebels at the severity of this obscene penance you have devised for yourself!"

"Devised for myself?" Olivia laughed. "Every twist of my

life has been devised *for* me, my friend, or had you not noticed? Circumstances pipe the tune. I merely dance to it."

Silenced, Kinjal searched Olivia's smiling face in immense sorrow. How transformed her lovely, innocent American had become in even less than a year! There was a waspish set to her mouth, thin and hard, that made a mockery of her laugh. The golden eyes, so filled once with honeyed innocence, were like frosted window panes, opaque and glassy. She seemed compulsively restless, finding it impossible to keep her twitching hands still. Where was that mellifluous calm, that gazelle grace that had given her such suppleness? And where was the innocent radiance that had once illuminated that angelic face from within like a Chinese lantern? Even the rich gloss of her glorious chestnut hair had dulled. Gone also was that beguiling openness of manner that had been her most appealing asset. Now there was unattractive smugness, a furtive need to avoid meeting even her friend's eyes squarely, and a sadly distasteful lack of honesty. It was a reversal of personality so cruel that Kinjal liquefied with inner pain and a profound feeling of personal loss.

"*Keep* your child, Olivia!" she begged, tears streaming down her cheeks. "Forget Freddie, forget your satanic bargain—*forget Jai Raventhorne!* Your craving for vengeance corrodes only you; it tarnishes your judgement, distorts all your perspectives—and still harms not a hair of Jai's head. *Take* your two children away to those heavenly islands, Olivia. There you will learn to be content, to laugh again, to love and be loved, to be happy and, perhaps, to live once more in tranquility."

Olivia was vaguely surprised by Kinjal's lack of understanding. Forget Jai Raventhorne? *Now?* When she was so close to levelling the score? When she had waited so long for this, the moment of final reckoning? But then she remembered that, like Estelle, Kinjal too had divided loyalties; she could hardly be expected to abandon one in favour of the other. No, she could not forget Jai Raventhorne. Life revolved around many axes, in many time cycles. There was a time to love, a time to forget. A time to avenge.

But for Kinjal's benefit, she only smiled.

En route on her return journey to Calcutta, Estelle said, she had made an excursion into the Burdwan jungles to visit the grave of her father. With her she had taken a marble tombstone reading:

> Here lies Joshua Adam Templewood, beloved husband of Bridget Lucy née Halliwell, cherished father of Estelle Sarah Sturges. Born June 28, 1793 Anno Domini, died November 15, 1849, here in the wilderness under tragic circumstances. Deeply mourned in abundant love, never forgotten, always missed. "He maketh me to lie down in green pastures."

The day Estelle had installed the headstone at the lonely grave, he would have completed the fifty-sixth year of his life.

Olivia was pained to see Estelle again so desolate, so low in spirits. She talked instead of Arthur Ransome, making inquiries as to how he enjoyed his holiday in Cawnpore. But Ransome too, it appeared, had broken journey to visit the grave on his way up country and that subject was equally hurtful to Estelle. Considering all this, Olivia refrained from making mention of the letter she herself had just received from Lady Bridget.

Since her aunt had left, Olivia had written to her with unfailing regularity once a month but, until now, she had never received any answer. *My darling child,* the unexpected missive had begun,

> With your inborn compassion you will have, I know, forgiven my long silence. I have had nothing of worth for which to put pen to paper, save my love and blessings that are always yours. I rejoice to learn of your happiness, of your son and of the fulfilment I know you have enjoyed in your marriage. That you are again to be a mother I celebrate without words. I have none to express the joy that I feel.

There followed a page from a sermon she had heard and admired at a local church service, but all that Olivia merely skimmed over. It was too depressingly full of the wages of sin, of penances and expiations, of the hellfire and brimstone that awaited all mortals in the hereafter, to make either pleasant or informative reading. What Olivia searched for was personal news of her aunt; it was contained in the final paragraphs of the letter and it twisted Olivia with pity.

I break my one long silence, my beloved niece, to inform you of another that I am about to enter; it will be a state of such blessedness, such rewarding serenity, that I am filled with ecstasy. I have been granted residence in a convent of Our Lady situated on the Yorkshire moors. In her generous and Christian charity, the Mother Superior will administer to me next week an oath of silence whereby I will pledge my life—or whatever remains of it before I am summoned to the Great Meadow beyond—to the humble service of the Lord who is my Shepherd. Do not ever mourn for me, Olivia, or think of me as a refugee from the world. For those of us to whom the gates of the kingdom of man are forever closed, there is another Kingdom, far, far above this miserable one, where there is always rapture.

I pray that you stay forever happy in your life. I cannot forget, even in the midst of my godly devotions, what it is that I owe to you. In my mind, I talk to Sarah every day. At last, at last, I am forgiven! Sadly, what I receive from Sarah I cannot find it in my heart to give to others. In your God-given wisdom you will understand what I mean, and in your understanding, not think too harshly of me. May the Good Lord smile upon your endeavours, dear child, whatever and wherever you might want them to be. I send my warm greetings to dearest Freddie. To you and to Amos, I send all my love. I will pray for the safe delivery of your second child. Think of me sometimes, Olivia, but never, never with grief.

Neither her husband nor her daughter nor Arthur Ransome was mentioned. Olivia wept, mostly for Estelle, unaware that she too had received the news, but from her Aunt Maude. Neither cousin spoke of it to the other.

Mercifully, Estelle's depression did not last beyond the first day or two of her arrival. Because she was naturally cheerful and because her sense of duty towards her cousin was strong, Estelle again forced her own feelings into the background to apply herself to the single-minded aim of making her company useful to her cousin. She informed Olivia, with much amusing detail, that she hated, absolutely *hated,* Cawnpore. It was dreary and dusty, the military wives more so and the civilians even worse. "All they do is complain about the mofussil *all* the time, *ugh!*"

"Like you?" Olivia teased, glad for once at the return of trivia.

"Yes, but they *add* to the drear, I *don't.* And I hate mahjongg. I can never remember which tile goes where, and I'm hopeless at gin and bridge and écarté and all the other silly card-games. John has his nose buried in his wretched garrison; I hardly *see* him." But she said that Arthur Ransome and her parents-in-law got on splendidly, and in his anxiety to make as good a host as possible, John had promised them all a trip to Lucknow to see all those fabulous native palaces. Discreet as always, John's parents asked no questions either about Sir Joshua's death or anything they had witnessed at the reception at Olivia's house.

Olivia was deeply touched by Estelle's return, but she was also nervous. The favour she needed to ask of Estelle was grotesque; Estelle would argue endlessly. She would also talk, inevitably, about Jai Raventhorne and there would be even more arguments then.

With so many friends in town, Estelle spent her first week making social calls, receiving them and partying, if with subdued enthusiasm. Olivia did not begrudge her her gregariousness, knowing how badly she needed a release from her festering grief. Also, it was pleasant to have hordes of young people in and out of the Birkhurst house; the desolate rooms echoed with rare laughter. Knowing now who Amos's father was, Estelle took exceptional care never to expose the child to her friends. With what excuses she fended them off Olivia did not know, but they were evidently effective. Amos, in his nursery suite upstairs, continued to remain undisturbed.

It was on their first quiet evening at home together that Estelle asked, as Olivia knew she would sometime, "So, what's all this about a *hotel?* Are you seriously considering the idea?"

"Yes."

"But how extraordinary! What made you think of such a project?"

"It will be, I hope, a good investment for the future."

"Well, I suppose in a way it's rather sad. I was born in that house, you know." Estelle stifled a yawn, perhaps to avoid any relapse into nostalgia, and said with a quick shiver, "I don't ever want to live there again. It is Uncle Arthur whom I trust to make all my decisions now." She swallowed another yawn. "But I would have thought the house too small for a proper *hotel.* Surely you should have more rooms to offer."

"Yes. We will. We plan a new construction."

"A new construction? Oh my, how grand! Where, in the garden?"

"No. In the servants' compound."

Estelle aborted a third yawn. "You mean, you plan to pull down all those quarters?"

"Naturally. How else do we make enough space for a new building?"

"Well, yes, I suppose that is sensible." She went on to describe, with some relish, a hotel in London where she had eaten with Jai. "It was terribly grand, you know, with *hot* towels and fancy soaps and a menu card as long as a yardstick. And the food was French, all à la this, that or the other. I even tried the *escargots,*" she made a face, "but they were delicious." She spent a moment or two describing more of the gustatory delights, but then something began to scratch at the back of her mind. Frowning, she seemed to be trying to mentally put it into focus; then suddenly she saw it. "Those servants' quarters," she said slowly, "Jai was born in one of them. His mother lived in it with him for eight years."

"Was he? Oh yes. I had forgotten."

Estelle's expression changed. "He . . . he might not want those rooms demolished, you know. I told you how strange he is about everything to do with his mother."

"Well, he's unlikely to be consulted in the matter."

Very gradually understanding dawned. Estelle sat up very straight, no sign of sleep now in her alert eyes. "That isn't what this . . . hotel is all about, is it Olivia? *Is* it to wound Jai that you seek to destroy those quarters?"

Olivia shrugged off her questions. "Sentiments, his or anyone else's, are of no value to me. I see the hotel as a sound business project for Farrowsham, that's all."

"Do you? Well, I don't believe you," she said, acutely distressed. "Uncle Arthur told me about the sale of the *Daffodil* and about that figure-head. Even though I knew how you had hit upon its significance to Jai, I had not intended to bring up the subject. You see, Olivia—despite what you have assumed—I have not and *cannot* forgive Jai entirely, not when Papa's grave is still so fresh. I was *glad* that you could force Jai into making even this minimal reparation. But that was only a matter of money. This, what you do now, is . . . *inhuman.*"

"Humanity and sound business propositions sometimes don't go together, as under other circumstances your brother would be the first to agree."

"Neither do humanity and exploitation!" Estelle cried. "You bought Papa's property *only* to exploit Jai's irrational weakness, Olivia, admit it—a weakness you happened to learn about from *me.* It's so . . . *cruel* to hit him where he is least defended!"

Olivia raised an eyebrow, amused. "My dear, where else would you expect me to hit him—where he is fully defended? Have you not heard what he is attempting to do to Farrowsham?"

Estelle was immediately downcast. "Yes. Uncle Arthur told me."

"And do you consider I should sit back and let him demolish poor, blameless Freddie's company?"

"No, but there must be other ways of retaliation. If you like, I could perhaps—"

"Intercede? Plead for charity? No!" Incensed, Olivia took care not to show it. Tedious debates such as this she had expected; it was to other, more vital matters that she wanted to turn now. "He attacks Farrowsham to punish *me* for having married Freddie—no, don't say anything, Estelle, just listen." She pounced before Estelle could interrupt. "You must see that I cannot allow that, I must fight back. I don't have the resources he has, nor the physical force. To retaliate effectively, I must make use of the *only* weapon available to me—*information.* And it must be used accurately. Mine will be." She raised her heavy, cumbersome body off the settee and stretched the stiffness out of her limbs. "And now, would you join me in a glass of hot milk? Before we retire to bed there is something I wish to tell you."

Estelle knew that Olivia would not now allow her to reopen the subject. Unhappily, swallowing the remainder of her comments, she nodded. The breach between them was still not fully healed. As it was, she had said far more than she had intended. But there was something about Olivia that was now beginning to frighten Estelle. She saw that her cousin's attitude was not entirely unjustified. Jai was behaving shockingly with her, going berserk; yes, she had to retaliate, perhaps even with cruelty—inhuman as it was. What frightened Estelle was not what Olivia plotted to do; it was the openly malicious pleasure she seemed to derive from doing it.

Half an hour later, however, having listened intently to Olivia about quite another project, Estelle was devastated. "To

England?" she gasped. "You will do this for Freddie after the way he has treated you?"

"Don't delude yourself that my motives are noble, Estelle! I do it for my own salvation, for the way I have treated *him.*"

"But how can Freddie dare to expect—"

"Freddie expects nothing. For all I know, he doesn't even expect fatherhood! I do this of my own free will because I must. From you, Estelle, I beg a very special favour: You must ensure with Kinjal that I never lay eyes on my baby. It is upon both of you that I depend to see to its care before it can be safely taken away to England. And whatever happens, you must promise that my baby's birth cry," an ache, a mere shadow of one, streaked across her face and was then gone, "is not within my hearing. That I could not bear. It will make me falter and I mustn't. No, don't cry, Estelle! To succumb to emotion now is to make it even more difficult for me. But if you feel that you cannot help—"

"Of course I can help! And of course I *will!*" Eyes pouring tears, Estelle flung herself at her cousin and hugged her. "Oh, Olivia, how can you even *consider* such a monstrous sacrifice!"

Olivia put her arms around Estelle's heaving shoulders and stroked her hair. "I do not see it as a sacrifice. My loss will be Freddie's gain, and that of my baby. This child, at least, will not have to live deprived of a father. And now, also promise me that you will not talk of this again. Not until the time comes. Argument might convince me otherwise, and I know that would be wrong."

Still sobbing, Estelle nodded tacitly. Her one little seed of brattish discontent—with what malignant fecundity it had germinated this seemingly infinite forest!

The following day was a Friday. Olivia gave the order for the demolitions of the Templewood servants' quarters to commence on the coming Monday morning.

Whatever Estelle's reactions, she now chose to keep them to herself, but young Mordecai Abrahams was delighted. A Jew from Cochin and a building contractor by trade, Abrahams had secured this highly lucrative and prestigious commission through the good offices of his brother, Sol, who was employed at Farrowsham as a messenger. Sol had warned his brother that, unlike plenty of other mems, this one could not be hoodwinked easily with inflated bills and false expenses. Besides, she knew their language well, which meant he had to be careful what he said to his men in her presence. Most important of all, he was to obey her every instruction implicitly. Which is why, when Olivia instructed Abrahams to announce far and wide that the demolitions would start on Monday, he instantly dispatched runners all over Calcutta so that the news became known in every locality. He had no idea why she should issue such an odd instruction. But he did know that all white people were partially *sankhi,* eccentric. If that was the way of their world, considering what she was paying him, who was he to argue?

There was still no word from Jai Raventhorne. Not a hint, not a whisper. But Olivia was not worried. The bait had been cast; she knew it would be taken, but not until the very last, when her already jittery nerves were at the snapping point. The vast quadrangle where hordes of children had once played and crowded families lived crammed into inadequate, unhealthy space still showed signs of life, although not human. Rats, bandicoots, and scavenging cockroaches scuttled about searching for scraps no longer available. The drain that had nauseated her that significant Dassera night two years ago had long dried, but the stubborn stench still lingered. To Olivia's right was that dismal cell in which the old woman had lain coughing her life away, now no doubt dead, cremated to ashes and forgotten. To her left, adjoining the erstwhile cow shed, was the quarter that Arthur Ransome had once pointed out to her as where Jai Raventhorne had been born. In appearance it was no different from the others. Dark, dank and with a small, slatted window, it had a brick floor pitted with rat burrows. Desolation seeped in slimy green fingers through the cracks in its walls, the residue of many monsoons. The smell in Olivia's nostrils was of decay, of death, as in a foetid catacomb. Ironically enough, this decrepit tomb had also been a womb from which new life had emerged.

Had it always been like this? Was it like this on that stormy night of more than three decades ago when that naiad's son's eyes, fashioned by his punitive heredity, had first seen the light of the world? In which corner had lain that child of nature shorn of her innocence, paying the price for a sin that was truly sinless? Clearly in her inner vision, Olivia saw a twisted young form writhing on the pock-marked floor in the throes of that agony that was also the act of life-giving. Nubile fingers clawed the air; a bloated torso, not unlike her own now, thrashed wildly from side to side. Shrill screams of supplication begged someone unseen for mercy; warm, viscous streams of blood snaked across the floor towards Olivia's feet, pouring forth from the battered child-woman not yet seventeen. In her ears Olivia heard the rasping demands of her lungs, the murmured cajolement of midwives, the rain as it lashed on the roof and then sidled in through the ceiling. A hush fell, as from spaces beyond the earth, and hovered awhile. From the depths of that hush emerged a sound, first trifling, then full blooded. It was the cry of a new-born, loud and lusty and angry at being hurled into a hostile world that would never accept it as one of its own.

Blindly, Olivia turned and ran out of the room, limp with sweat. The force of her fantasies was such that she could not breathe. If she had not grabbed the support of a broken column, she would have fainted.

For two days Olivia plunged herself into the soporific diversions of domesticity. She could not afford again to think, to indulge in the luxury of emotionalism, to *deviate.* Thought made her fallible, eroded her will-power. Happenstance had handed her a weapon. It was small but, like a needle, it was sharp. It would pierce unerringly. Nothing—not Kinjal's well-intentioned advice, or Estelle's half love for a half brother, or indeed her own hallucinations—could be permitted to deny her the chance to strike deeply. To keep herself on even keel, Olivia occupied herself with a frenzy of cleaning. She rearranged Amos's nursery, tidied forgotten cupboards, thriftily separated from her linen chest those sheets and pillow covers that could be darned into reuse. Taking a leaf out of her aunt's domestic Bible, she subjected Rashid Ali to several hours of relentless stock-taking in the kitchen store-rooms, leaving him perplexed and considerably disgruntled.

By tea time on Sunday she had exhausted both her energy reserves and her domestic chores, but she was still restless. Estelle had been of great assistance in relieving the load of her self-inflicted duties, but now she was out and not expected until after supper. Olivia rejected another call on Kinjal, regardless of temptation. Kinjal's serene logic would again try to soften her resolve, and Olivia was tired, so tired, of dialectics!

The demolitions were to start early tomorrow morning. *Still*

Raventhorne had not made any move! Olivia's earlier confidence was fast eroding, her brain seething with fresh doubts. Had he seen through her bluff and decided to call it? Was he planning some last-minute trick that she had not foreseen? Or, could it be that despite Estelle's valiant melodramatics, he simply did not care whether or not those miserable quarters were pulled down?

No. Resolutely Olivia checked her irrational doubts. Jai Raventhorne *did* care. He would never allow her to destroy the disreputable husk that had once housed his mother, which to him still embodied her spirit, and was the cradle in which he had been nurtured. It meant that he would make his move tonight. Or not at all!

"I'm going to the Templewood house again, Mary. That sweeper has not yet disinfected the drains and they stink. There is no need to order the carriage, I'll walk. I need the exercise." In her eagerness to expend restless energy, Olivia almost ran out of the house.

The extensive park land across which she had ridden so often fronted the Birkhurst mansion and enjoyed great popularity as an avenue for recreation. Early showers of the monsoons had washed away layers of dust and given the nascent grass the look of a lime green carpet. Children frolicked with armies of ayahs and nannies in exasperated attendance, their parents probably out on the Strand enjoying more adult pleasures. Those who preferred exercise to social chit-chat on the Strand took brisk constitutionals across the park, marching in rhythm as if preparing for a military parade. Smartly outfitted army men from Fort William, contained within the extensive park land, cantered on superbly brushed horses and looked very superior to those unfortunate enough to be on foot. It had been a long time since Olivia had walked across the park. There were many surprised glances as gents doffed their hats and ladies avoided looking at her stomach. Some halted to exchange a few pleasantries, and one or two men from the business district were bold enough to probe cautiously about the hotel.

It was a cool, breezy evening with a fine mist of sporadic rain from scattered clouds that hovered uncertainly overhead. No doubt it would rain more decisively during the night. The leisuredly amble considerably helped to settle Olivia's mind. She felt better for the exercise, her brain clearer. The day-watchman was not yet off duty at the Templewood bungalow. He greeted her unexpected visit with surprise tempered with relief, glad that he had returned when he had from a surreptitious smoke with his cronies around the corner. No, he said, the sweeper was no longer on the premises and yes, he would personally supervise the cleaning of the drains in the morning. Had there been any visitors, any messages? A letter, perhaps? Stoutly he shook his head, swearing that he had been on guard every minute and there had been no one and nothing.

She knew she would have to wait.

Vagrant footsteps and a wandering mind took Olivia aimlessly in the direction of the cook-house. She unlocked the door and went inside, not knowing why or what it was she sought. With no Babulal, no Rehman, no bands of frisky scullery boys, the kitchen looked desolate. There were lathers of black cobwebs everywhere and termites had again mounted assaults on her aunt's sacrosanct larder, the marauding lines of insects at one time considered a calamity of major proportions. The larder itself, scene of so many hot skirmishes between cook and mistress, was as bare as Mother Hubbard's cupboard.

Through the soot- and oil-encrusted wire mesh at the window, Olivia gazed steadily across the deserted wastes of the servants' quadrangle. Long, shadowy fingers crept over it to make a vibrant patchwork of vermilion light and shade. A touch of setting sun turned a heap of rubble into something exotic and unfamiliar. In the mournful silence a pair of geckos chased each other or some choice insect across a kitchen wall with their plaintive cry of *satti, satti, satti,* which the Indians, in their zeal to philosophise everything, interpreted as truth, truth, truth.

Out in the compound against an umbral back-drop, something moved. It might have been a rat or a stray cat or dog or, indeed, merely a trick of the changing light. But it wasn't. Every muscle in Olivia's body tensed; her shallow breathing deepened into rasps, her heart bolted into gallops. Even without being able to see clearly, her every instinct told her that she was not about to be disappointed. At last, Jai Raventhorne had arrived to strike his bargain.

His bargain but on *her* terms!

21

She had not been face to face with him since their encounter in his office. But in a business environment as close knit as in Calcutta, her awareness of his presence was constant. Through the window of her office she had often distinguished the sound of Shaitan's hooves as they thundered past the Farrowsham main entrance, for Raventhorne's day, like hers, started early. Sometimes she had seen him striding along the wharf with that eternal impatience with which he announced his contempt for the world. Once in a while in the early morning she had even heard his voice in all its deep-timbred richness as he read some unfortunate Customs official his fortune, for at that time of day voices carried clearly. In whatever situation she had observed him covertly, it was always he who was in control of it, his authority not for a moment in question.

This was not so now. The picture Jai Raventhorne presented to Olivia in the filtered light of impending dusk was very different. Head slung low between hunched shoulders, he sat on an upturned bucket carelessly left behind by one of the workmen. In one hand he held a twig with which he doodled on the soil around his feet. His elbows were balanced on his knees. Cast downward, his eyes stared at nothing in particular but with unmoving intensity. There was now no sign of the conceit, the hauteur that was such an integral part of his bearing. Save for his right wrist as he doodled, he was still. He had no suspicion of being watched.

The taste in Olivia's mouth was suddenly nectarine sweet.

With careful cat treads she stepped out of the kitchen house to glide silently down the court-yard at his back. Keeping to the darkening verandahs that ran alongside the quarters, she positioned herself as close to him as she could without attracting his notice. A few fat drops of rain plopped down from a visiting cloud; glancing upward, he pulled up the collar of his shirt but otherwise ignored them. In the fractional lift of his head he had revealed his face. It looked harrowed. The taste in Olivia's mouth turned even sweeter.

Softly she called out, "I was expecting you earlier. What took you so long?"

His back straightened. Were it not for the hush of the dusk, she might have altogether missed the hiss with which he pulled in his breath. She sauntered past him unhurriedly and strolled towards the doorway upon which she knew all his energies were concentrated. He remained seated and stared blankly, without recognition, as if tangled in some distant dream not yet shaken off. She had surprised him in a moment of intense privacy: It was on a pilgrimage that he had come. How fortuitous the timing of her own visit!

With a finger-nail Olivia scraped off some splinters from the door jamb. "Ugh! Eaten hollow by termites. It's worse inside, believe me."

He still did not speak. But in the saffron blaze of the dying sun his expression changed. He rose, walked away and turned his back upon her.

"Would you like to see inside for yourself? You will not again have the opportunity. Tomorrow all this comes down, every brick, every roof tile, every last rotten beam." She laughed under her breath. "No? Well, please yourself. My offer of inspection remains until the morning."

His back was like a wall, hard and unbending. She could read fury in its every line and contour. Slicked with sweat, his forearms glistened and in the eerie light that dusk brings they looked metallic. She knew that if he were to turn now, his face would be ravaged. But then he did turn and she was disappointed. He had reconstituted his face into such emptiness that she felt cheated. Raw emotion dispensed with, he loosened as he confronted her.

"Don't be tricked into complacency by a few cheap victories, Olivia." He spoke almost gently. "You will not be able to fight me."

"You think not? And why, might I ask, such an odd delusion?"

"I know not. Unlike you, I am unencumbered by a conscience."

"No longer! In your admirable tutelage I have also unloaded

that unwanted appendage. The rules I too follow now are my own. I devise, I improvise. Like you I too have made a fine art of the rule of thumb." Olivia's voice rang with confidence, but how she hated that minimal quaver she always felt in his presence!

"Indeed!" He smiled and leaned against a pillar. "Street dogs fight very craftily, Olivia. They attack from unexpected directions, which is how they survive as a beleaguered breed."

"Not every street dog wins every fight. Sometimes crafty mongrels too can be outwitted. And as tutor you have already seen how fast I learn!"

"True. But then, a cutting tongue and a bag of wily, childish tricks are not all that are needed in the game, Olivia. You are still vulnerable, although in your brashness you fail to see it, and there are areas of your mind that are still freely accessible to me." His manner was casual. Obviously he did not take her seriously.

"No longer that either!" she countered sharply. "Don't underestimate me now, Jai, as you once did. The mind you think you know exists now in quite another form. Don't misinterpret it."

"Perhaps it always existed in quite another form! I sometimes wonder if I have not always misinterpreted it." He raised a quizzical eyebrow and walked past her into the quarter in which he had once lived. To her astonishment, he reemerged a moment later carrying a pipe and a pouch of tobacco. Olivia felt a small sense of shock; he was used to coming here, perhaps during the hours of night when there would be no risk of exposure. In his audacity, he had stored his belongings in some crevice remembered from his childhood. She felt her skin start to tingle. How foolish of her to have doubted her own instincts or, indeed, his!

"Whatever the misinterpretations, they were mutual," she snapped. "One could say even mutually beneficial."

"And, in your case, also material and tangible! You did well out of your marriage. A pity your husband appears to have benefitted somewhat less, apart from the carnal pleasures of having sired two infants." He took his time lighting his pipe, no longer uneasy in her presence, unconcerned that he had tacitly informed her of his nocturnal visits to the quadrangle in which they stood.

"But then whoredom brings its own benefits to some men," she retorted, hating his nonchalance, his unruffled calm, because she could not fathom it. "And I *have* had the advantage of a highly skilled mentor!"

If Olivia had hoped for the reward of at least a flinch, of some gratifying sign of inner bleeding, she was disappointed again. The brazen reference did not even graze his skin. "You flatter me surely," was all he murmured with a trace of humour but none of embarrassment. "Had the tutorials been better skilled, the Golden Behind might not have earned all those fat bills Donaldson never tired of paying."

It was she who flushed and was furious that she had, but she was glad he had said that. It swept aside the remaining debris from her path, made her task easier. "Whatever Freddie's faults, he is a man of honour, a gentleman, twice the man *you* could ever aspire to be!"

He arched an eyebrow. "Is that why he separates himself from you by half a world? A curious reward for such touching loyalty!" He mocked her with a laugh, but then, all at once, he seemed to tire of the pointless game, of its barbs and lances and futile verbal jousting. With a gesture of exasperation, he spun on a heel and walked away from her. "Why the hell are you still here, Olivia?" he asked wearily. "Why are you also not half a damned world away with this man who is twice what I can ever aspire to be?"

"If my presence disturbs you, that is justification enough! For the rest, it is my business."

"I don't really give a damn where you are." Still no heat, only persisting fatigue. "Your presence is a nuisance, no more, no less." Outside the verandah it had started to rain. A few drops leaked through a crack in the ceiling and made a puddle on the floor. He stood and stared at it fixedly. "I wish you would go, Olivia. England, Hawaii, anywhere. We are unequal adversaries."

Olivia had once prided herself on knowing all his moods in all their subtle shadings. But tonight, she could not recognise any of them. It seemed that nothing she had said had truly touched him. Even his stinging insults had been lazily dispensed, devoid of anger. Not even the fact of her all too obvious pregnancy invoked those familiar expressions of disgust. As he had done so many times before in another age, he had merely removed himself mentally from her reach. And she had allowed herself to be distracted from her purpose.

"We shall see about that," she said shortly. "In the meantime I would like to know why you are on my property without my permission. I presume you trespass with a purpose?"

He puffed thoughtfully at his pipe and dug one hand deep in a pocket. "You still play with toys that are not toys, but your games now are dangerous. You could be badly hurt." He did not answer her question.

"Nothing in my life could hurt me badly again." It was not what she should have said, but having said it she persisted. "Yes, you did have the power to hurt me once, Jai. Once. You don't have it anymore. Nor ever will again."

"And you are certain of that?"

"Entirely! To act outside the rules is not a monopoly, and my skin too is now toughened. No, you will not be able to hurt me again. If you try, you will be disappointed."

It was almost dark. Heavy footsteps sounded in the gathering gloam at the far end of the court-yard. A flickering, lemon light approached, a lantern carried towards them by the nightwatchman. He salaamed, placed the lantern on the ledge between them and withdrew.

"I think you must know that I cannot allow you to demolish these."

Olivia's breath quickened. At last, he nibbled! "And you must know that you cannot stop me!"

"What you mount for my benefit is a charade. Once again you make a fool of yourself, this time with even more pointless bravado."

"Do I?" Her eyes glinted with amber light. "You forget these worthless ruins mean nothing to me. I will raze them to the ground with no compunction whatsoever."

"And you consider they mean something to me?"

Olivia shrugged. "If they do, your interest is incidental."

"Oh, no," he said softly, "my interest to you is vital! You are indeed a fast learner: I compliment you on your efforts at blackmail."

"Blackmail?" Olivia threw him an amused smile. "What a curious notion! *I* didn't invite you here, you arrived of your own accord."

"Which, of course, surprises you?" he inquired casually. Noticing his pipe had gone cold, he tucked it into his belt and crossed his arms. "Mooljee has been sounding the drum hard to tout your hotel hoax. Why not? Your collateral adds power to his lungs. But what if I told you to go ahead and build your hotel, that your little charade does not impress me? That you may pull down these worthless ruins if you wish *with* my blessings, what then?"

"The hotel project is neither a hoax nor a charade, Jai!" The tremble starting in her knees made it difficult to stand. She took a step back to sit on a broken half wall. "That hotel *will* become a reality!"

"Unless?"

She hesitated, then conceded the point. "All right. Unless."

"Ah, so it is blackmail after all!"

"No, merely the use of a tactical advantage I happen to have over you. I call it shrewd business strategy."

He nodded, as if accepting the distinction. "And you seriously believe I will allow myself to be coerced?" He asked the question not with anger or contempt, but merely as if he were truly curious to have an answer.

"You have no option!"

"Options are easily devised."

"They weren't with the *Daffodil* and they won't be now."

But he only laughed.

Covertly, she searched his face jaundiced by the lantern. And once more she felt out of her depth. Was she missing something? Instinct told her that he prevaricated, but today the chameleon colouring tricked the eye with disquieting success. He touched the pipe tucked inside his belt, half lifted it, then shoved it back again—and Olivia's heart skipped a beat. In that small gesture there was infinitesimal but significant and uncharacteristic indecision; it spoke to her only because she *did* know him so well! Behind the smoke-screen of airy nonchalance, she sensed a faint smell of doubt, a frisson of uncertainty. He was suspicious, but he was not sure. And because he knew *her* so well, his intuition warned him that her project was a hoax, the proposed demolitions a bait. But it was her instinct that proved to be right in what he next asked.

"All right. Would you consider selling me this property?"

Olivia knew she had won. Almost. "No. One doesn't sell a tactical advantage that can be exploited with continuing profit," she scoffed.

"Regardless of the consequences?" Her refusal did not disturb him. He had expected it, of course.

"Regardless of anything *you* are capable of conjuring!"

He laughed. "Still as stubborn as that old Kansas mule?"

"No. More so."

He finally lifted his pipe from under his belt and, holding it unlit, sauntered to the edge of the verandah and peered up at the sky. It still drizzled and in the distance was the rumble of thunder. For a while he stood in silence, surrounded by it as if insulated from everything around him. Then he turned and asked very quietly, "What is it that you want from me?"

Only superhuman effort concealed Olivia's exhilaration. It was an unconditional surrender, but she volunteered no reaction. "You already know what I want."

"Yes, but clarify it further for me."

"Leave Farrowsham alone. Restore our credit and carry our cargo in your holds as before."

In her pause he sensed more and lifted a questioning eyebrow. "And is that all?"

"No. I would like a fresh contract drawn up between us giving us more favourable freight rates."

"Anything else?"

Olivia shrugged. "An undertaking, of course, that you will not harass either Farrowsham or Arthur Ransome again."

He sucked in his underlip, nodded and looked quietly amused. "And what do *I* get in exchange for all these generous concessions?"

"If you agree to make them, there will be no demolitions. If you also implement them honourably, I will gift you this property with clear title, to do with as you wish." She waited, breath held back tight in her chest, scarcely daring to expel it for fear of causing ripples, knowing that even a verbal acceptance from him would be his bond. When no response came and he remained silently lost in thought, she asked a trifle impatiently, "Well?"

He started to light his pipe, attention concentrated entirely on the task at hand. "It seems like a fair bargain," he said finally.

She was ecstatic! "I consider so. Then you agree?"

He looked at her and smiled. "No."

"What?" For a moment Olivia thought she had not heard him correctly, but then he repeated himself.

"No, Olivia. I do not agree. I told you I tolerate neither coercion nor blackmail. I meant that. But I do commend your persistence. And your ingenuity. *Those* I find worthy of unqualified admiration."

Olivia forced herself out of her shock of stunned disbelief. "But you yourself admitted that it was a fair bargain!" she cried, shaken out of her complacency.

"True. But then, as you know, I am not a fair man."

She started to tremble. "You reject my offer out of hand despite all this?" She waved a furious hand at the quarter outside which they stood. "You realise that I *do* intend to go ahead with the demolitions, don't you?"

"I realise that you do *intend* to, yes."

"Intend to and *will!* I warn you, Jai—"

"Don't threaten me, Olivia." There was a chill edge to his tone. "That I would tolerate least of all."

"Nevertheless I do *warn* you . . . ," choking with disappointment and a bitter, bitter sense of failure, she sprang to her feet, ". . . first thing tomorrow morning all this starts to come down! Every stone, every termite-riddled, rotten beam, every stinking rat hole—by evening there'll be nothing left of this miserable hovel and those memories that you pretend to cherish. Wiped out will be all that remains tangible of your mother's last wretched, drug-ridden years, her degradations and desperations, of her very *being*—as will be every trace of the birth-place where your own damned life began." She now shook so violently that she had to sit down again, her legs suddenly like jelly. "Take a good look, Jai," she taunted, insane with frustration, "like your broken mother, these mute walls too will merge with the earth tomorrow. Drink in your fill of memories now. There will be no more opportunities."

Seemingly hewn out of stone, he had listened with all intentness but without having given her the reward of even one responsive flicker. "I think you will find that you are mistaken," he remarked composedly. "Every stone that is here now will also be here tomorrow. Not one will be moved."

Olivia laughed in his face. "You can't really believe that, can you? You know you can't stop me!" Behind the corrosive laugh, hot tears threatened but she *willed* them not to fall. She was beside herself with rage.

He sighed. "Ah, but you see, Olivia, I can stop you."

"How? By resorting to old tactics? Vandalism? Sabotage? Terrorism and intimidation?" His continued calm infuriated her, in some way made her feel humiliated even more. She forced her mind into submission, her spasmodic body into stillness. "You will again start to destroy because that is all you know? Because you couldn't bear to be a second-time loser?" She burned with spite, but somehow she manufactured a smile. "I have beaten you once, Jai. I will do so again."

He did not reply. Instead, his stare became long and deep, his maddeningly placid eyes shadowed with strangeness. Olivia stared back, anger throbbing like a pain in every part of her body. She strove to say more but her throat was blocked; she could not raise a voice.

And then, all at once, he was gone.

She was left alone with the shades of night into which he had melted with such suddenness. Her startled eyes followed the invisible path of his departure, her energies too depleted to regroup immediately. She had failed in her ploy; her calculations had been wrong, her instincts fraudulent. Still paralysed with disbelief, her mind simply could not accept defeat. Not at the moment, not yet. For the moment it was that look of strangeness that seemed to fill all her mental horizons, for she had recognised it for what it was and she could not accept that either. That even less than her failure! It was a look of pity. And Olivia was outraged by it. She had tolerated much from Jai Raventhorne, and had now laid herself open to tolerate more.

What she was not prepared to suffer at any price was his *pity!* It was his worst insult to her yet, but that he would soon learn for himself.

Even before the cock crowed the next morning, Olivia sent for Willie Donaldson.

A long night's intense cerebration convinced Olivia that she had not been wrong in her calculations. Her instincts had not lied to her, nor had her knowledge of the man in all his variations let her down. It was merely a new game that he played, one she had not foreseen. If she had miscalculated anything at all, it was the dimensions of Raventhorne's abhorrence of defeat. It would come, of course, but it would come more slowly than she had anticipated.

"Those mercenaries that we have on our pay-roll—how many do they number at the moment?" Like many affluent business houses, Farrowsham too maintained its private security forces.

"Aboot two hundred." Donaldson answered Olivia's question evenly. "Why?"

"And Raventhorne?" She ignored his question.

"I canna say for certain, but I reck'n more."

"How many on duty at our warehouses?"

"Enough. For *current* requirements, that is."

"I see. Well, perhaps we should double the watch round the warehouses and at our office premises. Also, we should start taking some precautions at our properties in Dharamtala, Circular Road, Portuguese Church Street, Chowringhee and Garden Reach. The Bow Bazaar shops and houses all have Indian tenants. They will not be disturbed. But where we—"

"Na disturbed by whom?" Donaldson leaned forward to ask. "And *why?*"

Olivia frowned at his interruption, but she knew that she would have to give him some explanation. And he would demand answers to many questions "By Raventhorne. I learn from an informant of unimpeachable integrity that he might soon be up to more of his tricks. It would be wise to take precautions. What I would like to emphasise is that it is at the Templewood bungalow that we need to concentrate the best of our resources. The area must be patrolled day and night until the demolitions are complete. The guards must have instructions to shoot if sabotage or arson is attempted, or if there is interference with the work. Hire more people if we need them, Mr. Donaldson. If we offer double wages, we can lure away the best men available from other private armies. Anything else?" She deepened her frown in thought and reflected quickly. "No, I think not. The plantation is too far away and the *Seagull* is already at sea on her way to Malaya. All I need are two clear days to complete the demolitions."

But Willie Donaldson did not ask questions. Suddenly, he felt very sick indeed.

She continued, "Should Slocum—or anyone else, for that matter—make inquiries? We should merely take precautions following those hangings yesterday."

Recently, another minor revolt had erupted among a contingent of local native sepoys. Ordered to Burma, they had refused to sail because of official refusal to transport their cooking vessels according to the Hindu code of caste segregation. Rather than lose caste, the men had mutinied, convinced that this was yet another British trick to convert them to Christianity. The rebellion had been brutally quashed and five of the ringleaders hanged publicly. Consequently, unrest simmered in the city, with nationalist sentiments running high. British business houses and residents had been cautioned to guard against retaliatory action by bands of aroused native civilians.

Fort William had issued the warning to the district magistrate as a matter of routine; not even Slocum had taken it very seriously. Certainly no business house had reacted to it quite as strongly as to double watches and hire extra mercenaries. Donaldson did not point all this out to Olivia; she was well aware of it already. But within himself, he started to feel even sicker.

"One more thing." Knowing that Donaldson's pallor was no indication that he was faint hearted, because he was not, Olivia made no more excuses. "Abrahams and his men should be summoned immediately. I want the demolitions to start within the hour."

Estelle, like Donaldson, had turned pale listening to Olivia's confident commands, watching the high red spots on her cheeks and the excitement that had produced them. Unlike him, however, she had no difficulty in locating the germ of the problem.

"You've seen and talked to Jai, haven't you?" As soon as Donaldson had left and they were at the breakfast table, she cornered Olivia.

"Yes." There was no reason to lie to Estelle.

"And he refused your bargain?" She lifted a sarcastic eyebrow.

"For the moment."

"How do you presume that?"

"Once the demolitions start he will change his mind soon enough!"

"He will not change his mind!" Estelle countered emphatically. "He never does. If you truly believed that, why all these elaborate defensive measures?"

Olivia shrugged. "It would be foolhardy to be unprepared. We both know his methods."

Yes. They did—who better than they! It was not, however, Jai Raventhorne's methods that Estelle was concerned about at the moment, it was her cousin's. But she did not say so.

The answer to Olivia's first urgent message was delivered to her by her personal peon soon after breakfast. Mordecai Abrahams was devastated to have to inform her that he was not available to carry out his commission at the Templewood bungalow until the following week. An even more urgent summons had come to him from elsewhere. He had been forced to accept it. *Next* Monday morning, however, without fail at dawn . . . Olivia did not bother with the rest. In a fury, she tore up the note and let loose her temper on the hapless messenger. Then, wasting no more time, she dispatched the peon to three more addresses of contractors from whom she had received estimates for the work. Whichever of them was available was to be brought to the Templewood house without delay, she instructed the man. About charges, he was forbidden to haggle. She would pay twice whatever they demanded.

It was at this point in the still early morning that Olivia had a most unexpected visitor: Ram Chand Mooljee. She was greatly taken aback. Mooljee, she knew, never visited clients; it was they who went to him. In the privacy of the downstairs study where she received him with ill-concealed impatience, Mooljee touched her feet and instantly plunged into vehement self-denigrations. He was a knave, a man to be despised, the son of a moth-eaten camel, a renegade who deserved to be hung—nay, hanging was too good for the likes of him. He should be—

"What exactly is the problem, Mr. Mooljee?" Olivia cut off his tedious self-vilifications with an exasperated gesture. "Is it any special business that brings you here this morning?"

Indeed it was, very special business. "I am ashamed to have to say it, honourable memsahib," Mooljee moaned. "I should have my tongue amputated, my hide flogged." He sighed as if about to cry, took out her satin-covered box from the folds of his voluminous apparel and laid it on the table. "I regret that I can no longer retain your collateral."

"Why ever not?" She was even more surprised.

Remorse forgotten, Mooljee's face went bland. "With no warning, I find myself in a situation of dire financial embarrassment. It is a family matter. I cannot disclose it. But I am in a dilemma, a grave crisis. My wife and children are distraught with worry. I myself—"

"Well, I'm sorry to hear that, Mr. Mooljee," again she diverted the tiresome flow, "but in what way can *I* help you?"

"The help the compassionate memsahib can give me is to return my loan." His jowls drooped in mournful folds. "Were it not for unspeakable family dishonour whereby my community will spit on me—"

"The loan? But of course I will return your loan, Mr. Mooljee! As I have already assured you, the moment my funds from Lloyd's of London—"

"Alas, my need cannot wait, worthy lady!" He wrung his fat hands in abject despair. "I must have the money *today* itself."

"Today?" Olivia was outraged. "That is absolutely impossible! You know very well that I have already paid in full for the property." Not only was she peeved, she was openly sceptical. Ram Chand Mooljee in dire financial straits? He, the richest Hindu merchant in town? "I'm sorry, Mr. Mooljee," she said frigidly, making no secret of her acute displeasure, "but there is no way I can return your loan today. If you *insist* on immediate repayment, I permit you to sell my tiara. As you know very well, it is worth far in excess of what is owed you."

But this too, he said, he could not accept. To go to the market himself would be to reveal his family circumstances, to lose face and reputation. There would be ruinous gossip, his wife would die of shame, his children would drown themselves, his—

"Well, what do you expect *me* to do about the matter?" Olivia demanded angrily. "Sell it myself and give you the money?"

This suggestion he accepted with alacrity. In fact, he suddenly beamed. "That would be very fine, *very* fine, generous lady! Such benevolence to salvage the self-respect of this wretched villain! I am overwhelmed." Delicately he dabbed each eye with a corner of his pleated dhoti.

"Very well then." Livid, she picked up the jewellery box and rose. "I will see what can be done by tomorrow. We will exchange receipts when you send for the money." He accepted her decision with due humility.

Olivia did not, of course, believe a word of Mooljee's story. Moreover, he had wasted her precious time, and far more would be wasted in arranging the quite unnecessary sale of the tiara. Still in a temper, Olivia sent to the office for Bimal Babu and entrusted the job to him. An austere, elderly Bengali who had been with the Agency since its inception, Bimal Babu was someone she knew she could trust implicitly.

As Bimal Babu left with the tiara, Olivia's peon returned. It appeared that none of the contractors she had suggested was free to take on her work in this particular week. Two others he had located were similarly engaged elsewhere and a third said he was too sick to leave his bed.

"Did you offer them double wages?" Olivia asked in increasing frustration. "Or did you haggle?"

"I know the work is urgent, lady memsahib. I did not haggle. I took the liberty of offering even more than double, but they would not budge."

"Did you get the impression that their excuses were genuine?"

The peon lowered his eyes and slowly shook his head.

The suspicion forming in Olivia's mind strengthened. With the return of Bimal Babu and the news that he brought, the suspicion turned into a certainty. He had shown the tiara, he said, to the town's four leading gem merchants, one of whom was his distant relation. Their answers had all been remarkably similar. The tiara was exquisite, and the lady memsahib's credentials were unquestionable. No disrespect was intended, but such a priceless piece would need to be re-evaluated. The formality—which is all that it was—could take up to a fortnight. Could they then offer a loan against the jewellery, Bimal Babu had taken it upon himself to ask? Oh, certainly, but to raise such a large sum of cash would take at least a week. Soon after Bimal Babu's return, a curt note arrived from Willie Donaldson. All at once, it seemed, there was not a mercenary available for hire in the city. Half of those Farrowsham had on its payroll had disappeared overnight. Of the rest, many had reported sick or claimed bereavements. It was astonishing how many grandmothers had died all at once.

The pattern that emerged from all this was clear; It was Raventhorne's hand that was blocking each avenue to make it into a dead end. Of that Olivia was now certain. The harassment was part of his tactics to delay the demolitions, to divert her energies elsewhere, to dissipate her manual resources. Refusing to either be intimidated or to waste her stamina further on useless anger, Olivia instead invoked her logic in a mental climate of calm and examined her options. She could refuse to repay Mooljee with such ludicrous dispatch, but then she would have to return the tiara to him. He would instantly foreclose the mortgage, sell the tiara and cheat her out of a sum much higher than his wretched loan. She could use Farrowsham funds to tide her over in the crisis or apply to Clarence Pennworthy's bank for another loan against the tiara. Both these last two options Olivia rejected. She would not break her vow not to touch Freddie's money for a war strictly her own. And although Pennworthy would certainly sanction her the loan, perhaps even without collateral, he was also Trident's banker. Just as Mooljee disliked "the Eurasian," Pennworthy did too; but, as Arthur Ransome had once pointed out to her, when it came to the crunch, business was business. Both also feared Kala Kanta, and Pennworthy would cunningly invoke as much red tape as possible to delay actually handing her the money.

It was this silent observation that brought to Olivia's mind another of Ransome's long ago remarks. Raventhorne, he had said, had one matchless advantage over the Europeans: He had India on his side. Now, for the first time, Olivia was struck by the stunning validity of that contention. So far, Raventhorne had succeeded admirably in outplaying all her gambits. It was only much later in the day that Olivia suddenly saw one that he had missed, and she pounced on it. "He might have India on his side," she exclaimed, eyes shining again, "but not yet *America!*"

"What?"

Olivia didn't realise she had spoken aloud until Estelle, following all the frenetic comings and goings with gathering alarm, jerked out her monosyllabic query. Olivia laughed. "I was merely wondering why I had not thought of it earlier."

"Thought of what?" How Estelle was beginning to distrust that secretive little smile on her cousin's lips!

"Why, the Seventh Cavalry, of course!"

While Estelle gaped in incomprehension, Olivia signalled Salim to order her carriage and gathered her purse and shawl. Estelle ran up to her and clutched at her arm. "Olivia, *please* don't goad Jai into any more recklessness! You cannot match forces with him, he is far too well prepared."

Olivia stopped in her tracks and gave her a long, thoughtful look. "No. Forces I cannot match. I do see that now. But what I can match—and adequately!—are *wits.* There, my dearest Coz, we are far from unequal."

As Olivia had known he would, Hal Lubbock was delighted to grant all her requests not only without hesitation but with enthusiasm. Yes, he had heard of the vile troubles her Agency was being subjected to by that son of a bitch Raventhorne, and yes, of course he would help—any danged way she suggested. "The gah sure needs his essentials trimmed, beggin' pahdon for mah language, my'am." He added generously that if he, Hiram Arrowsmith Lubbock, could be of any service whatsoever, whah, it would be his danged pleasshah to oblige, bah God it would! A loan? Lubbock laughed. That *sure* would be no problem; as much as she wanted, anytime. But was that *all?* For a moment he looked quite disappointed.

"No, that is not all, Mr. Lubbock," Olivia said. "There is something else."

He brightened. "Jes' name it, my'am—want the gah's teeth knocked back into his throat?"

Olivia smiled. "Thank you for the offer, it really *is* a temptation! But no, that isn't it. What I would be most grateful for is a loan of your workmen. I will need them only for two days, three on the outside."

Lubbock looked astonished. "Yuh want some *furn'ture* built?"

"No. I want some structures demolished. I know that is not their usual line, but they're strong, hard-working and there are plenty of implements in your workshop to suit my purpose. I think they will do the job quite satisfactorily." Still baffled, Lubbock agreed without question. "Thank you kindly, Mr. Lubbock. I will let you know when."

"Sure, but ah could easily start raht away, if yuh want," he suggested hopefully.

Olivia cogitated, then shook her head. "No. There is one more matter that needs to be settled before I commence the demolitions. One last thing, Mr. Lubbock," she paused briefly, "there is likelihood of some . . . trouble at the Templewood site. May I also request your presence there with a shot-gun?"

Lubbock was ecstatic. He hadn't had a single good fight since he had arrived in India and it was about time he did. "Black or white, my'am, bustin' asses is what yours truly does best, and ah owe yuh one, ah surely do!"

If her business with Lubbock had gone smoothly, the second errand that Olivia had devised for herself was fraught with uncertainty. Lubbock she had met openly; her second visit would have to be in stealth and at night. It might be a confrontation and she dreaded it. The letter that her bearer, Salim, had delivered had brought only a noncommittal, lukewarm response. The meeting she sought had not been refused outright. But, Olivia knew, there would be rancour, possibly insults and innuendo. Whether or not she was successful in her quest, she would lose self-respect. But she was prepared for that, for if she achieved her purpose, what she stood to gain was more, far more.

For one, she would have proved that not all of India, perhaps, was on Jai Raventhorne's side after all.

Sujata received her with no outward sign of surprise, for she too was prepared. The midnight eyes, still smooth as satin, seemed startled only at Olivia's odd apparel, a *burqua* such as Muslim women wore to conceal their bodies and faces. Many visitors, especially men, came to call only under cover of night in equal secrecy. Accepting, if not understanding, Olivia's need for stealth, Sujata merely shrugged and, with that sublime grace that was part of her profession, silently invited Olivia into her house. They passed through an archway curtained with glass-beaded strings into a salon, large and dimly illuminated. Impatiently Olivia divested herself of her cumbersome outer garment wet from the spitting rain, since she had chosen to walk part of the way. A servant boy brought in a chair, the only one in evidence. Sujata herself reclined on a somewhat sad-looking mattress. She was as alert as a snake but otherwise inscrutable. Somehow, the minor courtesy of a chair seemed to constitute a snub. It underlined the difference between them, conveyed a delicate contempt.

Positioning herself in the chair, Olivia ignored the slur. "Thank you for consenting to see me. I hope you will forgive the intrusion." She spoke in fluent Hindustani, her face expressionless. "I have come with a proposition that might be of interest to you." She allowed herself the flicker of a smile. "Its benefit will be mutual."

It had not been difficult for Salim to locate Sujata's *kotha,* her courtesan's premises. She was well known in the neighbourhood, and local gossip about her proliferated. But in her profession, it was obvious to Olivia, her success had been modest. It was said that she paid her dues on time and entertained a few regular customers but that her heart was not in her business. The triple-storied house was owned by her but called for repairs; some walls showed exposed brickwork, others badly needed a coat of whitewash. The furnishings, once brocade perhaps, were threadbare; the bolsters and cushions displayed evidence of darning. In a corner, on a well-worn Persian carpet, stood neatly arranged musical instruments, perhaps the very ones Olivia had seen in the Chitpur house.

"Oh?" Sujata's low laugh was insolent. "I would not have thought that the lady memsahib and I could have anything in common."

It was the first time Olivia had heard her speak. She was faintly surprised by the sweetness of her voice, but then she remembered that she was a singer. "On the contrary, Sujata," she said softly, scrutinising closely the woman's smooth, sandalwood face. It was vibrant with colour but beneath the cosmetics and the contrived smoothness, there were lines. The satin eyes showed hard ripples of discontent, no longer liquid with love. The coral mouth with which Olivia had once shared Jai Raventhorne's kisses was puckered into a pout of sourness. She no longer looked young. Perhaps not even twenty-five, she was already tarnished, the shine gone. Strange that this too should be mutual, Olivia thought! "On the contrary, Sujata," she repeated with greater emphasis. "There appears to be a great deal that we do have in common."

Sujata laughed again, a jarring sound. A malicious glance swept over Olivia's stomach. "The lady memsahib likens her situation to mine? I hardly deserve such mockery! Yes, we have both been discarded," a flash of vicious triumph, "but how different our fates are! Could it be that blinded by wealth, fame, a husband, children, all that a woman desires—the lady memsahib has not noticed?" Breathing hard, she turned her angry face away. "Unlike you, I am not married, nor ever can be. Used for three years, I am fit only for *this,* a profession of shame but the only skill that the Sarkar taught me. Unlike you, I will never have children. Those I might will also live ingloriously, despised for want of a father." Kohl-laden eyes spilled over with hate and a deep, inner burning. "You are a white mem. Your kind protects you. You survive the abandonment well, lady memsahib, but don't rub salt into *my* wounds."

"You are wrong, Sujata," Olivia spoke as gently as she could bring herself to. The hate she no longer cared about; it was the anger that interested her. "I too have wounds of my own. What we share is a common cause. Perhaps we both have many private fires to douse."

"I do not have the strength to settle scores with him," Sujata said bitterly. "He is like an elephant, I merely an ant." Reaching for a well-used silver receptacle at her elbow, she spat into it.

"But if you did have the strength, would you be prepared to use it?"

Sujata stared, suspicious and uncomprehending. "Yes. I do not know what the lady memsahib means, but *yes!* If I had the strength, I would use it." Her lips thinned; she looked coarse again. "I would cut out his heart and eat it for reducing me to this!"

"I can give you the strength. It will not be difficult." Taking out a small silken bag from her purse, Olivia started to open it. "Together, we could be invincible."

Speechless at what Olivia now held in her hand, a pair of exquisite emerald earrings, Sujata stared riveted. Against the white of Olivia's palm they glittered like green fire.

"These are yours if you can achieve what I want."

Sujata tore her eyes away from Olivia's hand and swallowed. "What is it that I must achieve?" she whispered dazedly.

"Something quite easy, but patience! First I must be assured that you possess the requisite information."

Having had time—even a few seconds—to think, Sujata was now cautious. "I spoke in haste," she muttered, suddenly nervous. "I would never cut out his heart and eat it."

"You will not be required to! Tell me, do you know the Chitpur house well?"

The question startled Sujata. "The Chitpur house? Of course I know it well! I was sole mistress of it once." Her chin rose with an unconscious pride that was somehow pathetic. "Why?"

"Would you be able to enter it without anyone knowing?"

Her eyes widened. "Yes, but the Sarkar—"

"The Sarkar's ship is being provisioned. Temporarily he resides on board. Bahadur also. The house is negligently guarded, particularly at night. The watchman sleeps, three of the staff are down with the flux and the dogs are also on board the ship. All this has already been ascertained." If Sujata had learned one skill from her Sarkar, she herself had learned another: how to secure and use information as a weapon. The two men she had hired to watch the Chitpur house round the clock and supply her details about the woman she now faced had not come cheaply; but the small fortune she had paid them had provided rich dividends. With luck, the dividends would be even richer. "I presume that you are still familiar with the Sarkar's personal apartment?"

Sujata looked at her with contempt. "Naturally. I shared it with him."

"And his personal belongings?"

"Everything he possessed was in my care." Again that flash of unaware pride, but then the wariness returned. "He has nothing of value because he values nothing material, except for his guns. If stolen, these too he could afford to replace a hundred times. Evidently, the lady memsahib does not know the Sarkar as well as she pretends!"

"There is something that he does value." Olivia dismissed the taunt; it was not to trade insults with this sorry woman that she had spent painstaking days building her dossier of information and risked this visit. "It is this that I wish retrieved. That is, if you can find it."

"If it is there, I will find it. The Sarkar locks nothing." Despite her boast, she looked uneasy and her slitted eyes were questioning, but she could not keep them away from the silken pouch. "A childish prank will only irritate him, no more . . . ," she said uncertainly.

"You might know his body well, Sujata. I am better acquainted with his mind. If anything can be relied upon to mortally wound him, it *is* only this childish prank."

"The lady memsahib talks in riddles," Sujata muttered, turning sullen at the slur suggested by Olivia's remark. Still in the grip of greed, however, she did not think to retaliate. "Before I can give an answer I must know more. I must know everything."

"No! I must have your answer *first.*"

"But the lady mem doesn't understand!" Sujata cried. "I am frightened of the Sarkar. If he ever found out—"

"He will not find out your involvement. The blame will be mine. He will not even think to suspect you." She scanned the frightened face thoughtfully. "I have been informed that you wish to leave town and go to Benares where your mother lives. With these," she picked up the pouch of jewellery, "you could afford all that you wish. You could vanish, leave behind forever this life that you despise. You would no longer be dependent for a living on the lust of men who revolt you. Some day you might even marry, have children." Relentlessly, Olivia continued her cajolings. "You could start that music school that I learn is your life's ambition."

"How have you come to know so much about me?" There was again fear in Sujata's kohl-smeared eyes. "And why?"

"It doesn't matter how. The *why* I have already explained." She opened the silk pouch and dangled the earrings casually.

Hypnotised by the flashes of green fire, Sujata remained riveted, all her yearning concentrated in her eyes. Then, with a wail she buried her face in her palms. "Once I had everything, everything! Then *you* came, and nothing was the same for me again. I lost it all. I was cast out on the streets like an old rag. All because of *you,* white-skinned memsahib! He is of *my* world, not yours." She was distraught. "Why did you not stay with your own kind and let me keep what was *my* due?"

"He did not cast you out onto the streets," Olivia said with cold disdain. "The whole bazaar knows that it was he who set you up in this *kotha,* he who gave you everything you possess."

"But he robbed me of my self-respect, of my future! How can I ever face my community again, my mother, my brothers? As the Sarkar's woman I was somebody; now I am *nothing!*" Desolate, she rocked back and forth on her heels, moaning softly.

Olivia's heat died as quickly as it had arisen. Yet another victim! With an effort she pulled herself together. "Just tell me, Sujata, yes or no?" she asked, feeling soiled and tired.

In control of herself again, Sujata wiped her eyes with a corner of her veil. "I committed the sin of learning to love him. In our profession it is not allowed. For that I must atone. Once I would have cut out my tongue rather than wound him with a harsh word. Today I offer to cut out his heart!" In her painful self-discovery, she gave a small, sour laugh, then said with a sigh of defeat, "My answer is yes. Tell me what I have to do."

The flame of the single lamp in the room spluttered. It seemed that the fuel was exhausted. Amidst the darkening shadows, Olivia replaced the earrings in the pouch. She had not intended to part with them until the bargain was completed, but now she rose and laid the pouch on the mattress beside Sujata. "Yes. I know what you mean, Sujata. We have more in common than you think."

She sat down again and began to dispense her precise instructions.

"Raventhorne will na damage our property," Willie Donaldson said. "But I saw the commandant anyway."

"You went to Fort William?" Olivia asked.

"Aye. This morning. Should trouble arise, they will help."

Donaldson abhorred the situation Farrowsham was in, even more so the fact that there was much that was being kept from him. But, all said and done, he could never let his Agency down, nor the Birkhursts. If Farrowsham was threatened, then that to him was the clarion call. He was honour bound to answer it and do his best.

"What does our man on the *Tapti* report?" In Calcutta's cutthroat corporate world, everyone had informers in everybody else's camp. Donaldson was too shrewd a trader, too seasoned an India hand, not to also have his own spies at Trident. Raventhorne's establishment was tightly knit, hard to penetrate, but then greed being a universal vice (sometimes virtue), with his persistence Donaldson had managed to secrete one wily Indian clerk into Trident's shipping department. The man was now on board the *Tapti* helping the stevedores with the provisioning. Yes, Raventhorne had superior muscle power, but he was not as invulnerable as he thought!

"He says he has na let Raventhorne out of his sight for two days. At night, he keeps watch on the master cabin from one of the longboats on deck. So far, he reports, there are nae moves in the direction we fear. Leastways, na yet."

"Yes," Olivia conceded after some reflection, "I panicked unnecessarily. He will not act openly, nor in any direction we anticipate. It's not that kind of a war."

"Just what kind of a war is it then, Your Ladyship?" Donaldson pounced on that to ask quietly.

Having let slip a comment she should not have, Olivia smiled. "I meant, this is the kind of war in which strategy is the missile, not conventional armaments." She met his quizzical eyes without a blink.

It was Donaldson who first dropped his stare, all his remaining questions unvoiced. She had made a night journey in secret—where? His peon had lost her in the maze of gullies after she had abandoned her carriage. It was that Templewood bungalow that was somehow at the crux—how? And the *Daffodil,* never even claimed by Raventhorne and now stripped bare where she had lain for months—where did *that* fit in? Already disturbed, Donaldson was making an even more disquieting discovery. He was not a coward; in his decades of trade he had fought many battles, some lost, some won. But now he felt fear, not of Raventhorne, who was a known devil, but of this strange, enigmatic woman whose depths he had not been able to plumb at all. He ventured no more questions. He would rather not know the answers.

"Where did you go last night?" If Willie Donaldson considered ignorance bliss, Estelle suffered no such illusions. At luncheon she put the question bluntly to her cousin.

"On an errand."

"Errand where? To whom?"

"A business matter. It doesn't concern you."

Estelle pushed her plate away, her appetite disappearing. "You are determined to have Lubbock's men pull down those rooms?"

"Of course!"

"Don't do it, Olivia. He will turn more rabid." Helplessly, she tried one final appeal. "*Let* me go and see Jai, *please*, Olivia! He will at least let me have my say, I'll force him to. He will not refuse to see me."

"All right. By all means go. In fact, I was about to request you to do precisely that."

Estelle's jaw dropped loose with amazement. "You *were?*" she gasped. "Why?"

"As it happens, I would like you to deliver to him a letter from me." Olivia's tone sharpened. "It will be only a delivery, Estelle, no more. I warn you, *not one iota more!*"

Estelle glared, riven with suspicion. She was no longer sure how far in her malice Olivia could be trusted. "What will you say to him in that letter?"

"I don't know yet. I can only decide that tonight."

Reading nothing in her cousin's expression, Estelle abandoned her efforts to probe. "Anyway, I have not seen Kinjal for a week," she said coldly. "She will be offended. Why don't we both call on her this morning? I would like to get to know her better."

It was a pointed inquiry; neither had Olivia seen Kinjal for a week—but how could she have? She could lie to everyone; she could not lie to Kinjal. Yet, she could not tell her the truth either! "No," she replied lightly enough, "I have other matters to attend to here. Please make my sincere apologies and assure her I will see her soon."

Whatever remorsefulness Olivia felt did not take long to dissipate in the tightness trapped inside her chest. Yes, tonight would decide once and for all the fate of that war Donaldson could not understand. If Sujata failed, then she too would have failed. Sujata was the last wild card in her pack, her final trump—she *must* succeed in that midnight mission! Lying unlocked somewhere in the Chitpur house was Jai Raventhorne's most precious belonging—his *only* precious belonging—that red velvet bundle Estelle had found on the *Ganga*, the bundle in which lay all the splintered memories of a childhood that never was, a mother who might never have been. Raventhorne would never have risked leaving it aboard the *Ganga* after she had docked and then sailed away on another voyage, Olivia calculated, praying passionately that her instincts were accurate.

And once she held that bundle in her hand, Olivia knew, with it she would also hold Jai Raventhorne's soul. Fragments of a missing childhood for fragments of a ruptured life. Yes, it was a fair exchange.

Olivia dispatched a note to Hal Lubbock. If he would be so kind, he should have his men ready for the demolitions on the day after the next.

The moon sinks and then returns
The severed branch grows again
Ponder this, oh fool, and be not troubled
In its own time everything ripens.

The song of the *bauls,* a clan of singing minstrels in Bengal, was plaintive and sweetly melancholy. The words were in a dialect Olivia could not understand, but a helpful passer-by translated them for her into Hindustani. Dropping some coins into the hand of one of the saffron-clad singers, she urged her coachman to drive on. The pearly moistness of a monsoon midday sat heavily in the air. A light rain had come and gone. Left behind was the cool caress of a breeze but also the inescapable pall of humidity. The ambling clip-clop of the horses' hooves pulsed away time in regular beats, somehow making it malinger. Olivia felt calm, a curious calm, nerveless and numb. Only the gripping cramp in her stomach and the restless kicks of the baby disturbed the unrippled surface of her mind. *Please God, don't let the baby come yet, not yet . . .*

For the hundredth time she diverted the thought with reflection.

The velvet bundle had been in her hands soon after midnight. Goaded by her own private demons—as they all were, as they all were!—Sujata had not failed her. She had completed her assignment with faultless skill. As proof of the new ownership of that precious childhood repository, Sujata had left in the same place the silver locket and chain that Olivia had given her for the purpose. Once in possession of the bundle, Olivia had spent the rest of the night in composing her letter to Jai Raventhorne. By seven o'clock in the morning, Estelle had been away with it for delivery aboard the *Tapti.* Even though its composition had taken much time, the letter itself was terse.

> If you will look inside the desk in your bedchamber, the second drawer to the right, you will see why I am not as unequal an adversary as you believe. The game and its rules you devise, but I am still a fast learner. I await your response.

She did not sign the letter. There was no need to.

By eight o'clock Estelle must have made her delivery to Raventhorne; he would have read it at a glance. It was now almost ten. Unable to stay at home while waiting for Estelle to return, Olivia had spent the past three hours driving around aimlessly in her carriage, trying to occupy her errant mind with trivia. But now, frantic with impatience, she ordered the coach back to the house. By the time she arrived home, Estelle had returned from her assignment.

"Did you deliver it?"

"Yes."

"In his hands?"

"Yes."

"And . . . ?" Distorted with anxiety, Olivia's voice sounded shrill.

Estelle did not reply to her question. Instead, she stared at her hard, her face set. "What did you write in that letter, Olivia?"

"It was a private matter. *Tell* me, what—"

"Private or not, I want to know what was in that letter!" Estelle's fists were clenched. Beneath her apparent calm, anger lay waiting.

Olivia shrugged. "I offered him an olive branch. A chance to make peace." She brushed that aside and asked sharply, "What did he say? Tell me what his reaction was, *tell* me, Estelle!"

"He said nothing. Only his face went strange. Strange and dead."

Olivia's breath untangled, exhaled and became normal. She sat down. "And then what did he do?"

Estelle's lips thinned with cutting scorn but she did not release her anger. "Then he put the letter in his pocket and left the ship without a word." She turned her back on Olivia and walked towards the window. "But before he went he stood and looked at me, just looked. I have never seen that look on him before, not even that first night on the *Ganga.* It was not even hate. It went beyond that, and it terrified me." She spun back to face Olivia, her expression stormy. "*Tell* me what was in that damned letter! I know I'm somehow implicated. I have a *right* to know!"

"You are not implicated," Olivia said dismissively, attempting to end the conversation and turning towards the door.

"You've used me again, haven't you, Olivia?" Estelle asked, trembling. "You've again exploited the information I gave you in conf—"

She was cut off by a knock on the door and Mary Ling entered. With an effort, both composed themselves and Estelle took herself off to the other end of the room. Olivia was not entirely annoyed at the interruption. "Yes, Mary? What is it?"

"Begging your pardon, Madam," Mary looked apologetic, "it's past the time for Amos's fruit juice. I only came to fetch him upstairs."

"He's already upstairs, Mary, We've both just returned to the house."

Mary frowned. "He has not returned with you? Amos isn't in the nursery. I've just come from there."

"Returned with us?" Olivia looked blank.

"Yes. Since you sent the coach to fetch him and the ayah, I presumed he must have—"

"*I* sent the coach?" Olivia echoed. "Which coach?"

"Why, the Maharani's, of course! I sent them off myself no more than an hour ago, Madam." She stared at Olivia, puzzled.

"Why on earth should I send the Maharani's carriage for Amos, Mary? Surely you are mistaken! Amos must be upstairs . . . ," she faltered. "He . . . he *must* be . . . !" Dropping the purse she still held in her hand, Olivia turned to run out of the room and up the stairs as fast as her cumbersome weight would allow. Their argument forgotten, Estelle followed, and behind her a pale-faced Mary.

The nursery was empty. There was no sign of Amos.

Gasping with the effort of her climb, Olivia clutched the doorway, her breath coming in huge, gusty wheezes. "I didn't send any coach for Amos, Mary," she whispered again and again in a stupor, "Why should I, why should I . . . ?"

"I . . . w-wouldn't know, M-madam." Mary started to stammer nervously. "They came at about nine. I had just finished the—"

"They? Who?" Olivia went cold, her hands like blocks of ice. "Who, Mary, *who?*"

Now truly frightened, Mary began to tremble. "The . . . the Maharani's coachman and the . . . other man. The note was very c-clear, Madam."

The chill in Olivia's body produced a deathly calm. "Show me the note."

As Mary flung herself at the waste-paper bin and started to scramble inside it, Estelle still stood in the doorway watching in stunned silence, threading and rethreading her hanky between shaking fingers. The note, when found, was just a few words in an untidy scrawl. *I am sending Her Highness's coach to fetch Amos and the ayah.* The initials at the end of the note were a clear *O.B.* And the message had been written on Kinjal's unmistakable cream and gold crested notepaper.

Upright only by force of sheer will-power, Olivia kept persuading herself to discount the reality: *I will not panic, I will not panic.* It is a simple misunderstanding. Amos is indeed at Kinjal's. Amos is in the park with some irresponsible servant. Amos is in the servants' compound watching the cows in the milking shed. No other explanation was possible!

But then Mary gave a gasp and fumbled in the pocket of her

apron, mumbling tearful apologies. "They also brought a letter for M-madam. I'm sorry, I f-forgot to—"

Olivia snatched the envelope out of her hand. It was addressed to her in a handwriting she could not mistake. The note contained within the envelope was briefer than hers but as clear: *You will not see your son again. You have my response.* There was no signature.

Crumpling into Estelle's arms, Olivia started to scream.

22

In giving birth to her second son Olivia almost lost her life. The baby's position in her womb was precarious, its arrival six weeks early and her body's remaining reserves few. With her world blotted out, its light extinguished, she was not aware of Dr. Humphries's valiant battle for her survival. Her own will to fight had died even before the battle had begun. The numbed tract of grey slush that was her brain registered only vague sensation. Half-formed creatures scuttled occasionally from the hide-outs of her semiconsciousness to hunt for footholds, but there *were* none in that limbo. Sometimes, through the black layers of the shroud that cocooned her she could feel pain, terrible pain, but only as if it were somebody else's. And also somebody else's was the voice that, in those terrifying final moments of her ordeal, screamed in a weak whisper, "Take it away before it cries . . ."

Crushed into pulp, beyond awareness and beyond endurance, Olivia slid away into deep, deep unconsciousness. She was not to know yet that her moral debt of honour to her husband and to his family had at last been repaid.

Nor was Olivia to know yet that for those past two days and two nights, while others fought for her to live, Arvind Singh had launched a massive man-hunt for Jai Raventhorne. Throwing the might of his State into the search, he had sent his agents foraging into every corner of the city and the countryside for any snippet of information about Raventhorne and the child. There was none. No one at Trident had any information about their Sarkar's whereabouts, or chose not to have. He was no longer aboard the *Tapti,* still in port, nor was he at either of his homes. The hunt was pervasive, but it was hampered by the need for extreme secrecy. On this Kinjal had insisted. There were already too many rumours about Olivia; to expose her to more would make an even greater mockery of her poor friend's sham of a life.

"He has taken Amos to Assam," Kinjal said. "No one knows the hills like Jai does. Pursuit would be impossible."

"How could he have been so heartless?" Estelle cried, red eyed and stricken. Whatever her other feelings, this act of villainy she could never forgive the half brother she had defended so stoutly. "He could have at least sent word that Amos is safe and not fretting."

"He will not harm the child," Kinjal pointed out in an effort to provide some morsel of comfort. "Wherever he hides them, he will care well for the child."

"But we both know that that is not the point, Kinjal." Estelle's tired, swollen eyes brimmed again. "It is now *both* her children that Olivia is losing. And it is *I* who started it all . . ." Quietly, she again began to cry.

Kinjal said nothing. What was there to say? Both she and Estelle had scarcely left Olivia's bedside over the past forty-eight hours. Assisting Dr. Humphries had been two experienced midwives from Kirtinagar, whose help he had gratefully accepted. Mary Ling, a competent nurse trained by the doctor himself, ran up and down tirelessly performing vital errands. Estelle had sat by her cousin, holding her hand and cooling her perspiration-drenched face with damp napkins. Because she did not show her face to strange men, Kinjal had remained in a far corner, her features draped with a veil, acting as interpreter for the midwives. It had been a frightening ordeal for them all, and Kinjal felt close to tears herself as she and Estelle waited for the doctor to emerge from the birth chamber. Yes, Olivia did stand to lose both her children, but the tragedy was not hers alone; one way or another it was to be equally shared between Amos and his parents. Sadly, what his parents were destined never to share was Amos himself.

"Now, young miss, what was the meaning of all those silly shenanigans in there, eh?" Almost dead on his feet, Dr. Humphries bowed to Kinjal, waited for permission to sit, and subjected Estelle to a look of great severity. Kinjal quickly nodded and, exhausted, he slumped into a chair. "It is a mother's reward after hours of labour to hear the first cry of her new-born. Olivia was delirious. Dammit, what was the need for the infant to be carried away with such unholy haste? I am extremely angry, *extremely!*"

"Olivia was not delirious." Serving him a large snifter of brandy, which he downed almost in a single gulp, Estelle wiped her red rimmed-eyes and blew her nose. She glanced at Kinjal, received a nod, and proceeded to tell him the facts. That Olivia was not to keep her child would be common knowledge soon anyway.

Dr. Humphries was astounded. He lost no time in announcing that he had never heard anything so preposterous in all his years of practice! "That infant is premature! By God's grace he's a healthy little nipper, but you can't subject him to mortal danger by whisking him off to *England* because of someone's idiotic fancy!"

"He will not be 'whisked off,' Dr. Humphries," Estelle assured him earnestly. "Nothing will be done without your express approval and advice. It is only because of you that Olivia has pulled through."

"Oh, fiddlesticks! She's a sturdy filly, she would have pulled through anyway." But he looked pleased. "Well, what is this plan you have then for the child? May I be permitted to know?"

Estelle amplified her explanations without giving him the reason for Olivia's decision. That was irrelevant in the present context. The baby, she told him, was to be moved to a caretaker's lodge on Her Highness's estate in Kalighat. Mary Ling and the wet-nurse, now arrived from Kirtinagar, would care for the child under the Maharani's personal supervision. "We will not arrange passages for England until you give us permission, when you consider that the baby is fit to make the voyage. Mary, the wet-nurse and I will go with him." She started to weep. "I beg of you, please help us, Dr. Humphries. We must do our best, our very best. Or we will have made a travesty of Olivia's noble act of self-denial."

In spite of his shock, he was moved. "Well . . . I can't pretend to understand the situation," he muttered gruffly, "but then, in forty years of anatomy and physiology, I've never been able to make sense of a woman's mind anyway. However," he sighed, "whatever her reasons, your cousin has my sympathy. She is a brave young woman who deserves support. I suppose I too will have to do my mite. But I warn you," he dropped his banter, "neither mother nor child is out of the woods. They will need meticulous care, *meticulous.*"

Suppressing her shyness, Kinjal proceeded to give him her assurances and to answer fully all the probing questions he put to her. Eventually he appeared satisfied. Promising to return in the evening, he left behind many grim warnings and a lengthy list of instructions. He prescribed medications for Olivia's sadly depleted blood, energy and weight; for her mutilated spirit, however, he had nothing. But then, neither did anyone else.

"You will go to England too, Estelle?" Kinjal inquired wonderingly after the doctor had left. "I was not aware of that, but your decision relieves me."

Estelle coloured. "Yes. I wrote and begged John to allow me this final duty to my cousin. He has agreed, of course. I will not be able to rest, Kinjal, until I have delivered Olivia's little one into his father's arms. It will at least help me to hate myself a little less. What small beginnings life's major tragedies have!" she ended sadly.

"Amos . . . ?"

It was Olivia's first and only question in the flickers of returning consciousness. When Kinjal shook her head and turned it away, she heaved a tired little sigh, then slipped back into her private world of silent misery. About her new-born son she made no inquiry.

"Somebody loses a son and somebody gains one," Kinjal said. "Is there no end to the ironies of your cousin's fate?" Olivia's fragile condition and the loss of her will to mend it alarmed both Kinjal and Estelle. Neither had ever seen her at such a nadir, mentally and physically, and neither could think of effective devices to pull her out of the swamp into which she sank deeper daily. "Let us at least be content that in this situation there has been *one* winner."

"Olivia has lost not one but *two* sons," Estelle reminded her, totally unforgiving of the crime that had been committed.

"But Jai does not know that."

"That cannot correct the enormity of the injustice to someone who is already so bereaved," Estelle contested. "I can think of *no* defence for him, not one, however much he was goaded."

Kinjal lowered her head. "To be honest, neither can I, whatever he might have considered his provocations. I merely voice a selfish thought to justify my own reading of him. Surely, I cannot have been totally wrong in that reading."

In the meanwhile, the relentless search for Raventhorne and his hostages continued, but with little success. Almost a week had passed since the abduction; there was still no information that could be considered useful. Had Olivia been aware of the situation, she would have perhaps again recalled Arthur Ransome's remarks of long ago; not only was India again on Raventhorne's side, but ranks had once more been closed against a common enemy, the British. There were plenty of witnesses who swore they had seen him here, there and everywhere, but each testimony conflicted with the other and every one of the leads proved fruitless. Not even Arvind Singh's impeccable reputation and the high regard in which Indian India held him could elicit results. He had offered not thirty but many times those pieces of silver in the hope of inducing treachery, but if a Judas did exist somewhere, he did not step forward.

It was impossible that some rumours should not fly about, but on the whole the abduction remained a fairly well kept secret from at least the European community. But for how long? When the bubble did burst, it would explode with the force of dynamite and the aftermath would be ugly. In the meanwhile, further lies had to be woven and sustained: Because his mother was so ill and the situation would distress him, that Amos had been quietly sent to Kirtinagar was the discreet and plausible explanation given. There could be no further doubt that it was indeed to Assam that Jai Raventhorne had taken the child he must know now to be his son. He had chanced upon a prize the existence of which he had not even suspected. Having secured it with such serendipity, he would not be fool enough to relinquish it. There was no doubt in the minds of either Kinjal or Estelle that Amos would not be returned to his mother. What Olivia thought they did not know; she never spoke about it. But in her sinking health itself was subsumed her conviction.

Only once did she ask about her new son, just as only once she had asked about Amos. "Is he well . . . ?"

"Yes, *very* well," Estelle assured with well-meaning enthusiasm. "He is marvellously cared for and looks bigger every day. His eyes are amber, like yours, not," she giggled, "like Freddie's boiled goose—"

"Don't!" A rare spark of animation returned to Olivia's wasted face. "You must not say any more."

Bursting into tears, Estelle fled, unable to contain her sorrow.

According to his mother's wishes, the infant had been named Alistair.

One further flash of irony had briefly lightened the grim tragedy being unfolded at the Birkhurst mansion. While Olivia lay gripped in the coils of her deathly labour, Hal Lubbock had arrived at the house with a plaintive inquiry. He had waited at the Templewood bungalow for several hours in anticipation of instructions to start the demolitions. Should he proceed now or wait a while longer?

The demolitions! Nobody had had time to give them even an idle thought! In fact, Estelle had known little about her cousin's exact arrangements with Lubbock. "No, Mr. Lubbock, I don't think you should proceed," she said, riven with sorrow. "Those structures no longer need to be demolished."

He looked visibly disgruntled. Done out of a decent fight with an evenly matched opponent rather than some prettified pouf alleged to be a gentleman, he made no secret of his disappointment. "Yuh mean the gah's changed his mind about makin' trouble? Aw, *hell!* Ah was lookin' forward to splashin' his brains all over the doggone brickwork!"

"If you had, Mr. Lubbock, I promise you we would have all stood and cheered," she assured him glumly. "About making trouble, no, Mr. Raventhorne doesn't seem to have changed his mind so don't lose hope yet. The man is truly evil. He will never reform."

But in her categorical condemnation of Jai Raventhorne, Estelle was to be unjustified. One morning in the predawn dark, exactly seven days after the kidnapping, an unfamiliar carriage pulled up outside the gates of the Birkhurst mansion. Having only one function to fulfil, it halted very briefly. Without a word spoken, the coachman summoned the night-watchman. And into his care he silently surrendered Amos, his ayah and a sealed long brown envelope.

It happened to be the morning of Amos's first birthday.

At the Farrowsham offices during this past week there had been grave concern for the rapidly deteriorating health of Lady Birkhurst. But, at the same time, it was impossible not to show some signs of joy at the birth of a second Birkhurst son. The celebration Donaldson arranged was intimate, subdued and discreet and to it were invited the European officials of the Agency and their wives. The Indian employees were given a month's extra wages, baskets of fruits and sweets, and toys for their children. A bottle of champagne was uncorked and then an entire case demolished with remarkable ease. But on the fifth day after the celebration (which also happened to be Amos Birkhurst's first birthday), Willie Donaldson was to rue the fact that his entire stock of choice champagne had been exhausted. Not even one bottle now remained to celebrate what other electrifying news the day was to bring.

It was around noon that Ranjan Moitra arrived and, with customary daintiness, laid before Donaldson a folder containing several formal notifications. A new contract between Farrowsham and Trident had been drafted with concessional freight rates, and awaited Donaldson's approval. The *Tapti,* which was to sail on the morning tide two days hence, had hold capacity for Farrowsham cargo; likewise every subsequent sailing. The Agency's credit facilities were being restored in full and compensation would be made for losses incurred during the freight embargo. The folder also contained a letter of assurance. Since the Farrowsham Agency and Trident had always enjoyed a cordial business relationship, there was no reason to believe that the same cordiality would not continue in the future. It was not an apology, but the closest they could come to one. The notifications and the letter were all signed by Ranjan Moitra. Jai Raventhorne was not mentioned. Through the reading, Moitra sat stone faced and utterly inscrutable. When it was over, he quietly got up and left.

For a long while after he had gone, Willie Donaldson sat frozen, convinced that he was dreaming. His first reaction, when mobility finally returned to his nerveless body, was to fly to the Birkhurst manse and deliver his astounding news without delay. But then, recalling Her Ladyship's sorrowful condition, he restrained himself somehow. Also, he remembered something else. She had predicted it all anyway.

It was the first time in his life that Willie Donaldson came close to fainting. Even in his shaky condition, however, he did not forget every self-respecting Scotsman's essential priorities. Firstly, even though the cost of it might well break his goddam heart, he ordered a fresh case of champagne bought from wherever it might be found for all Farrowsham staff to have their fill. Then he sent a note to Cornelia warning her not to expect him home for at least three days. And finally, he went to the Bengal Club and got gloriously drunk.

All of Donaldson's jubilation was, without his knowledge, being shared at the Birkhurst mansion, but for other reasons. None the worse for the adventure of which he was blissfully unaware, Amos looked fit and well fed and cheerful. The clothes he was wearing were new. Accompanying him was a galaxy of expensive toys, also new, and—a fact the ayah confirmed—with her as companion, the child had not fretted at all.

The fevered inquisition to which the ayah was subjected revealed little that was not already known, except one thing: All along they had been on a boat. She could not tell where, because they had sailed many miles down river before they had anchored. But the region was desolate, with little or no habitation, and there had been tigers and jungle all around. She had been very frightened because she had heard the predators roaring at night.

"The Sunderbans," Kinjal recognised instantly, "the eerie half world where the Hooghly joins the sea. There are thousands of islands and inlets. And it is this wild region that is the home of the royal Bengal tiger."

"In all probability, he used a country craft," Estelle said excitedly, hugging Amos and covering his face with kisses. "How silly of us not to have even thought of that!"

"Even if we had, the area is well nigh impenetrable, certainly on foot. And looking for *a* boat in that morass is like trying to find a particular leaf in a forest."

Yes, the ayah—bewildered by her experience and hugely relieved that it was over—further confirmed, there was a very tall man with eyes "just like baba's." And yes, he had been very kind to them, especially to the child. She herself had been well housed and fed, and permitted to roam freely around the boat with its two small cabins. In any case there had been no one else about save for two oarsmen. The man with the frightening eyes had asked her many questions but had not answered any of hers. What he did mostly was to sit and stare at the baba, playing with him but not saying a word. It was obvious that he knew nothing about children, for when he picked up the boy, which he wanted to do all the time, his hands were clumsy. But there had been in them a great deal of tenderness. And when he had finally released them it had been with reluctance, for he had not been able to hide the tears in his eyes.

Even Dr. Humphries was startled by the sudden spurt in Olivia's hitherto slow process of recovery. Having no knowledge of its true cause, he assigned credit to the veritable pharmacy of medications he had prescribed. Of course, nobody thought to inform him otherwise.

Nevertheless, illness had rendered Olivia's cheeks pale and hollow. It had etched even more deeply the lines of bitterness that had become permanently grooved on either side of her mouth. Without its well-shaped contours, her body looked skeletal; only her breasts, swollen with milk, still retained signs of good health. Each day the milk was extracted by suction with a rubber device and sent for the benefit of the child whose whereabouts were unknown to her and whom she was destined neither to know nor to ever see. Olivia never asked after Alistair, seemingly content in the frequent assurance that he was well, that he too progressed satisfactorily. Outwardly, she had not shown any indications of joy at the return of her precious Amos, still too emotionally depleted to assimilate fully so sudden a shock, so unexpected a miracle. But she had cried softly when she again held him in her arms, still not strong enough to contain his boyish energy. If she rejoiced at all, it was inwardly. Her eyes remained secretive, guarding the concealments of her mind behind steely doors. What she was thinking, no one either guessed or dared to ask. Buried deep within the privacy of her self-constructed citadel, her thoughts continued to be her own.

The sealed brown envelope that had come for her with the return of Amos, Olivia asked to be placed inside her almirah. She showed no desire to learn its contents.

Through the month following Alistair's birth there was no question of visitors for either Olivia or her baby. Doing his "mite" manfully, Dr. Humphries placed an embargo on casual callers, however well meaning. He could not, of course, shield her forever. As her condition improved and it became known that he had permitted her to move out of her bedchamber, it was Kinjal who took over the delicate task of keeping inquisitive visitors away. Everyone in Calcutta knew, of course, that ladies of the royal households of India were surrounded by complex protocol and were in strict purdah. Since the Maharani was now in residence at the Birkhurst mansion, it was naturally not possible to call without a formal invitation. Since no invitations seemed to be forthcoming, except to a select few, stray callers were automatically eliminated. In any case, the community had long accepted, resentfully, that Lady Birkhurst preferred her own company to theirs. "Just as well, my dears," the Spin remarked tartly at the regular Tuesday morning mahjongg meet of the

Gentlewomen's Institute. "After all, she's never really been one of *us,* has she?"

Arvind Singh was one of Olivia's early visitors, soon after the return of Amos. Now aware of all his efforts in her direction, she thanked him warmly with seldom seen emotion. "I am indebted to you for life. I shall never forget your compassion."

Deeply shocked by her dismal appearance, he waved away her words of gratitude as unnecessary and took his courage in his hands. "I have only done my duty as a friend. It is Jai who has been truly compassionate. He returned the child when he need not have. And he has made full reparation to your Agency. Can you not bring yourself to forgive him at least somewhat?"

Olivia's expression closed. She did not answer his question. And he did not ask it again. Painfully aware of the circumstances, neither did he ask after Alistair.

But others did, with the kindest of intentions. Two of those select few who were invited to the house were, of course, Willie and Cornelia Donaldson. Unaware of the cruel realities, they were eloquent and delighted about Alistair's birth. Knowing that their affection for her was genuine and immense, Olivia herself volunteered the news that would soon be common knowledge. "My husband longs to see his son, and so does his mother, who gets older and more frail every day. Since I myself intend to go to Hawaii first, I have arranged for Alistair to be taken straight to England."

The dispirited lie was hardly necessary. Not even the Donaldsons believed it anymore. The Birkhurst marriage, they realised in all sorrow, was over.

Jubilation having settled into placid contentment, Donaldson finally brought himself to speak about the other matter. However raging his curiosity, he knew she would not satisfy it. "We have a new freight contract with Trident," he said, looking at her deeply. "And the credit has been restored."

"Oh? That's good." Olivia had no more interest in Farrowsham. In any case, Estelle had already conveyed the news to her.

"The *Tapti* sailed last week with our cargo, all of it. We have double the space in her bilges, at half the cost." He paused for a reaction. None came. "Trident has three more clippers on order. Smith and Dimon have already laid the keel of the third. They're na being delivered till next year but Moitra's willing to contract one to us exclusively."

"Well, I'm very pleased to hear it, Mr. Donaldson."

Had Donaldson been insensitive and a fool, he would have

been thunderstruck by her lack of response, but he was neither. Sighing, he resigned himself to never learning the truth. But later he confided sorrowfully to Cornelia, "I still dinna ken the kind of war it was, love—but it's na been withoot *some* casualty, na by a *bloody* long-shot."

The month of September, russet and golden and glowingly autumnal in northern hemispheres, was lush and green in the tropics. The rains had swept through, leaving a land verdant and brilliant in its blaze of new growth. Rinsed clean, the skies were endlessly blue and flawless. In apparent gratitude to nature, the soil of India burst forth in an abundance of fruit and flower and fields of fat grain. It was time again to prepare for worship to the goddess Durga and the ten-day feast of Dassera.

It was also time for Estelle, now back from a month-long visit to Cawnpore, to bear Alistair away to his father.

Nourished by the milk of his unknown mother, supplemented with that from the bursting breasts of the wet-nurse, Alistair had thrived. Delighted, the doctor had finally pronounced him absolutely fit for the voyage. One fine morning soon after, Estelle had taken him away, with Mary and the wet-nurse, to the ship that was to carry them all to England. There were no tearful farewells; Olivia had forbidden any demonstrations of emotion. But she did embrace and kiss Estelle with unqualified love and a whispered apology, for now no barriers remained between them. Mentioning finally the letter she had received from her Aunt Maude and the news it contained about her mother, Estelle could only say that she would not seek to disturb her mother's vow of silence; she would beg to merely *see* her once more.

And then, all at once, it was also time for Kinjal to return to Kirtinagar. She had been away almost three months. Her husband had been alone; now her children were back, and they all needed her. Also, there were the Dassera worship rituals and ceremonies to prepare for.

"To leave you alone now is against my better judgement," Kinjal said, anxious. "Will you truly not consider coming with me to Kirtinagar?"

Waving her fan idly in front of her face, Olivia smiled and shook her head. "I must now prepare for my own departure. And

I am not alone. I have Amos. Uncle Arthur returns soon from Cawnpore and I will be busy interviewing new governesses to choose one to take with me to Hawaii."

"But you will surely not leave without at least *one* more visit to us, will you? I would be bereft, my dear, dear, friend if you did."

Olivia's eyes, accustomed to remaining carefully blank these days, suddenly welled. "Of *course* I will come to see you before I leave! How could I ever not? It is you who have been my sanctuary between hope and despair, sanity and madness. If there is anyone with whom I leave part of myself in India, it is you, Kinjal."

The parting, so close, so final, was painful for them both. But, swallowing her heartache Kinjal ventured to ask, "The only one?"

The spark in Olivia's dark, golden eyes died. "Yes. The only one."

"Olivia, you once told me that as recompense for the gratitude your uncle expressed to you, you had asked for a favour in kind. If I have indeed been this sanctuary, then would you consider such a favour for me?" Knowing what might be coming, Olivia turned away. "Before you sail for Hawaii, would you allow Jai to be with his son once more?"

Trembling, Olivia shook her head. "No!"

"I know that you have closed your mind to the subject, but that does not make it go away," Kinjal persisted. "Admit it or not, Jai acted with honour. Having been through it yourself, can you not imagine *his* self-denial, the extent of his sense of loss? He need not have suffered it—certainly, none of us believed that he would. By denying himself so severely, don't you think he has *earned* at least this meagre privilege?"

Panic fluttered across Olivia's face, making it even paler. Weakly, she hid herself behind her fan. "I cannot risk it, Kinjal. You *must* see that I cannot. He relented once, he might not the next time."

"You still cannot trust him?"

"I have steeled myself to live without one son, but if Amos also goes . . . !" Scabs peeled themselves off old wounds, making them bleed anew. How she hated Kinjal for forcing her to face herself again!

"Jai will never hurt you again."

"No, he will never again have the chance to!" Confused,

shaken, pulsating with those pains that would now always be with her, Olivia stumbled to her feet and ran out of the room.

Kinjal abandoned the argument as worthless. As far as Jai Raventhorne was concerned, Olivia was still beyond the bounds of reason.

There comes a time when even pain becomes a habit. Left by herself in the aftermath of everyone's departure—Alistair's departure!—Olivia plunged into a trough of depression. Her love for Amos was consuming, but it could not reduce the enormousness of her loss any more than one limb can compensate for the amputation of another. The abundance of her grief frightened her; it was bottomless. Amos would now never play with the one who had also occupied her womb. She herself would forever stay in ignorance of Alistair's features, never see her own reflection in them, always wondering, wondering. Nor would he know or love the mother who had almost exchanged her life for his and then given him away like an unwanted bundle donated to charity. Would he understand? *Could* he ever? The flesh on his bones was hers; it was her blood that nourished his veins. Yet, their destinies would unfold on opposite sides of the globe, neither touching nor transfusing. Passing by on the same street, they would not recognise each other, forever strangers. Over the years they would perhaps teach themselves to think of each other as dead. But for now, it was as if she had consigned his infant body to earth as a living entity . . .

How could she not still hate Jai Raventhorne?

Arthur Ransome returned from Cawnpore. Abandoning all courtly formality he gathered Olivia in his arms. "Oh my dear child, my poor, dear child . . ." He could say no more.

Against the comfort of his shoulders, cushioned in the warmth of his unquestioning love, she wept. "I have missed you. Oh, how I have missed you!"

"Yes, I know. Estelle told me everything. Had it not been for . . . circumstances, I would have returned earlier. But I could not force myself to do so." Awkwardly, he patted her back, still gruff with sorrow.

She was ashamed of her selfishness. He too had suffered a crippling loss; he was not yet over it. He too needed to be solaced, needed to learn to live with the disability of an amputation. Drying her own tears, Olivia set aside her grief to share in his. They talked of Sir Joshua, of the early days in Canton, the halcyon years when they were young and immortal and invincible. They talked for hours, salving Ransome's wounds with the magic balm of memories. Eventually, they even laughed, for it was inevitable that they should also talk about Hal Lubbock, his unorthodoxies and the business that now flourished.

They did not talk of Jai Raventhorne.

Finally, Ransome sobered again. "Was it wise, my dear, to send your child to Freddie in such infancy?" If he was unhappy about her broken marriage, this act of cruel self-denial he had not been able to understand at all.

"Wise or not, it has been a worthy division," Olivia replied with forced lightness. "You see, now we have one son each." Engrossed in arranging a bowl of exquisite pink roses from her garden, she sounded casual.

Too casual. He now knew her well enough not to be misled by her façades. "Hal told me about those quarters. You stayed the demolitions, I believe."

"Yes. They didn't seem like such a good idea after all."

"And the hotel? Market rumour has it that you've shelved the project indefinitely. I must say I was surprised."

Olivia smiled. The cunning old coot, he was not surprised at all! "I haven't quite made up my mind yet."

He let the lie pass. "And what will you do with the property if you do decide to abandon your project?"

She snipped off another stem and stood back to examine the arrangement through squinted eyes. "I'm not sure. Perhaps sell it. I think you are aware of the marriage portion that Aunt Bridget was kind enough to give me." Ransome nodded. "The money should have gone to my mother, but she rejected it. Over the years the funds have accumulated considerable interest with Lloyd's of London. Half of those funds have now been transferred here so that I could clear all my loans. To be honest, I have no need for more money, but neither do I have any need now for the Templewood property. I am therefore tempted to rid myself of it one way or another. Would you have any objections if I . . . gave it away?"

He looked startled. "My dear, you are its sole owner! You are free to do with it what you wish. But—give it away to whom? Some worthy educational or charitable institution?"

"Something like that."

They shared a silent meal, talk of the Templewood house having now dampened their abortive forays into inconsequentialities. Sweet-sour remembrances again made them morose as spectres walked freely about their minds, reviving long-forgotten incidents. Chains of thoughts forged in the past brought into focus fresh links still too new to ignore. Inevitably, Ransome brought up the subject they had been skirting so carefully all evening.

"There are some rather strange rumours about regarding Jai Raventhorne. Perhaps you have already heard them?"

"No. I no longer involve myself with business matters." Then, because she could not suppress the question, she blurted out, "What kind of rumours?"

"They say he is pulling out from Calcutta."

In the act of pouring the coffee, Olivia's hand stilled. "Pulling out?"

"Yes. That is to say, he is said to be turning over Trident to Ranjan Moitra." He accepted the cup she offered and stared at her hard. "The consensus is that he has not been able to stomach his humiliation at the hands of . . . Farrowsham. He's lost too much face to be able to show what's left of it in the business district."

Olivia rose abruptly from the table and picked up the pair of secateurs with which she had been trimming the rose stems. "And do you subscribe to that too?"

"No." His hard look turned sharper. "Jai might be a bad loser, but he doesn't give a fig for public opinion. He might be foolishly sentimental on occasion, but he is not a weakling. One reverse would not make him renounce everything he has struggled over years to achieve. There is some other explanation for his surprising decision." His eyes bored deeper. "From Estelle I learned about this . . . extraordinary kidnapping of your son. Could it perhaps have something to do with that?"

She managed to look successfully surprised. "No, of course not. Why should it?"

"Yes, why should it?" he echoed. "I was hoping you might be able to answer that. It was a dastardly act, no matter what the provocation. I confess, I was shocked, quite shocked, that Jai could have turned his villainy towards an innocent child."

With a cluck of irritation, Olivia pulled out all the roses from the bowl and angrily started to rearrange them. "He killed his father as surely as if he had pulled that trigger himself, destroyed Aunt Bridget's life, sought to demolish that of an innocent half sister—and you still say that you are shocked?" She laughed.

"His hatred against them was justified," Ransome said with quiet stubbornness. "For what he did to poor deluded Josh I will never perhaps find the generosity to forgive Jai—but, in all conscience, he was not the sole perpetrator."

"Maybe he considers his hatred against me justified too!"

"No doubt. But what justifies *your* excessive hatred against him, Olivia . . . ?" he inquired softly.

He had never approached this, her tallest barrier. But Olivia knew that he was aware that it existed. Still not prepared to lower all barricades, she shrugged and answered with marked coldness, "The justifications are self-evident. He has damaged beyond repair many whom I too loved."

Reminded of his own severe losses, he turned morose again. "He too is damaged beyond repair, Olivia. I somehow sense it. Jai, it seems, has disappeared. At least, no one at Trident is willing to reveal his whereabouts even if they do know them. His houses are padlocked, many of his personal staff have been dispatched back to their villages. The *Ganga* sailed in yesterday but he has not been aboard. The gossip about his vanishing act gets more bizarre by the day. Pennworthy tells me there was little else talked about at the Chamber meeting yesterday." He hesitated as if about to add something more but then changed his mind and fell silent.

The roses finally arranged to her satisfaction, Olivia picked up the delicate Wedgwood bowl and placed it at the centre of the dining table at which Ransome still sat nursing his coffee.

"Well, if he has disappeared," she said with studied indifference, "let us hope this time the disappearance is permanent."

At last I abandon India! Olivia wrote in her long-forgotten diary. *I shed my shackles. The banyan tree can throw down no more roots.*

The black leather-bound diary had once been her constant companion, her nightly confidant. But now, for almost two years, it had lain discarded in a bottom drawer and rediscovered only during the assiduous process of cleaning. In her sudden surge of liberation, Olivia again felt the need to share her sense of release with someone, anyone, even a lifeless notebook.

The *George Washington,* Willie Donaldson assured her with great relief, was a modern vessel, a clipper that plied under an American flag with an American captain and crew. It was well provisioned, had comfortable living space and plenty of portholes for fresh air in the cabins. The vessel was scheduled to dock in Calcutta harbour sometime within the next two weeks. She would then sail shortly for the Pacific and touch Honolulu in record time. With her own affairs already more or less in order, there was little left for Olivia to do except to finalise the appointment of a suitable governess for Amos. Most of the inventories had been completed in the mansion, the strong-rooms sealed and locked, and the neatly labelled bunches of keys handed over to Donaldson for safe keeping. This time she had bowed to his wishes; the mansion would not be let and some of the old retainers would remain to see to its maintenance.

"Surely, one of the bairns will want to return some day and enjoy the rewards of Caleb's endeavours," he had protested in support of his bid to preserve the sanctity of the manse. Olivia had not argued. Yes, perhaps one day Alistair would return to India. She had no right to tamper with his inheritance. Now there remained only the problem of the Birkhurst jewellery to be settled. But that, Olivia decided, she would tackle later.

The girl who appealed most to her as Amos's new governess was a young Anglo-Indian called by the veritable mouthful of Bathsheba Smith Featherstonehaugh, "pronounced," she proudly told Olivia, *"Fanshawe."* The girl came with excellent references from Cornelia Donaldson's sister-in-law in Bombay and was said to be well versed in both child care and household duties. Besides, she was pert, placid and neat, and Olivia liked her infectious smile. Her father, she said, had been an adjutant to a commanding officer in Poona. He had died during the Afghan War. Her mother, whose nationality was obvious from the girl's walnut complexion, had died of the pox soon after. "But I have a grandmother in Newcastle," she said, thrilled at the prospect of a voyage overseas. "She's *English,* you know. Just like my father was."

"And what do you consider yourself to be?" Olivia asked.

She was surprised at the question. "Why, English, of course. Why else should I be wanting to go home?"

That what she thought to be "home" was half a globe away from Honolulu Olivia did not have the heart to tell her yet. But the girl's comment depressed her. Like Amos, she too was of two worlds. Or neither. And for twilight people like them, rejects from both worlds, there were not many options open. For them, however, a third world did exist—and that could only be America, already a mixture of many, and less cruel than most. She decided to hire the girl, shortening her name instantly to Sheba.

It was only after Olivia had finished assigning her new duties to Sheba and writing down for her the child's routine through the day that she suddenly noticed her diary still lying on the table. The breeze had riffled through its pages to reveal one where she had written just two sentences: *Yesterday I met a man. I think I would like to meet him again.* The few words, innocent and unaware, were the same she had once also written in a letter to her father. She had not known then that these innocuous words were destined to be the starting point of an odyssey begun more than two years ago, an odyssey only now being completed. Or, perhaps, being left uncompleted. *My life is finished and yet unfinished.* It was what her aunt had once said to her about herself. The analogy disturbed Olivia.

Unthinkingly, before she was aware of what she was doing, she sat down to flick through the pages of the diary. Her account started excitedly on the day she had disembarked in Calcutta, with her awestruck admiration for the imposing man who was her uncle, with her first meeting with her aunt, with Estelle. As if hypnotised by her handwriting, Olivia re-read her initial impressions, her confusions, her desperate homesickness, her sporadic enthusiasms and irritations and excavations into a land so frightening in its strangeness. Among the cramped notations there was even mention of the intrepid young Englishman Courtenay (or Poultenay!) who had gone native and provoked her visit to the bazaar of the Chitpur Road. In between the writings the diary had many blank pages when she had been too tired or too restless to pen confidences. The last date on which she had written anything—everything!—was the day before Jai Raventhorne had sailed away on his *Ganga* with her cousin Estelle. And with her own future.

The diary was a microcosm of her life in Calcutta, down to today's hasty words of celebration. In re-living that life vicariously through the pages, Olivia realised that she had made a terrifying mistake. Like a jammed drain slowly being unblocked, memories started to trickle through, then expand and gush. With the free flow swept a cascade of debris, forgotten flotsam and jetsam from a life that might never have been. Before she could stop the deluge, her mind flooded. Airless, she felt she was drowning, but then she began to float. In her state of somnambulance, she walked to her almirah to retrieve the sealed brown envelope that had been delivered to her with the return of Amos. Outraged, her mind screamed in protest, but the fingers that cracked open the seal were no longer hers, rebels against the frantic commands of her brain.

Within the brown envelope was contained another, smaller and once white but now soiled and crumpled as if having passed through many hands over many months. Completing the process of her submersion, Olivia tore open the flap and withdrew the single sheet that reposed within. She read the handwriting of which she recognised every stroke, every curl.

> I once told you that I was weak, and you laughed. Reading this you will no longer doubt me. Were I not a coward, you would not have to suffer the pain of having to read these words in a letter. Instead, you would be circled within my arms, encompassed by my tenderness; your ear would be pressed to my heart, listening carefully to its language, to the sounds of love that are above speech, beyond hollow words, eloquent in their silence. I would not be begging forgiveness for the inadequacies of these pathetic sentences behind which I hide because I do not have the courage to face you. And somewhere within your own heart, I know, you would be assured that I love you in defiance of the dictates and limits of all reason.
>
> I take Estelle to England. Why? For these answers, which I do not have the strength to give you, you must go to Arthur Ransome, for he knows everything and more. I do what I do because I must. It is a ritual of exorcism that I perform. To deserve you, I must return to you undiseased. And return I will, my much loved one—that much I beg of you to believe. The pain I inflict on you I give to myself tenfold, but if, in your abundant generosity, you will continue to trust me, to tolerate even this that I have chosen to be, you will have fulfilled the hope that is the life force of this wretched man to whom you have already entrusted everything.
>
> Wherever I go, my beautiful innocent, you go with me, unseen and unheard but always there where I can reach out and touch you. Within six months I shall be back. You must be prepared to receive a man depleted by his loss of you, a man even less whole than he is now. In his supreme arrogance, he will

believe that he is still loved. In his abject humbleness he will know it is not because he deserves but because you disburse with charitable forgiveness.

I wound you, I make gross demands, I explain nothing. I ask of you a sacrifice you cannot understand. Shamelessly, I offer nothing in return except everything that I am and have, and a love far beyond measurable dimensions. I marvel at such pathetic recompense—can it ever be enough for you? Stark reason tells me that what I expect is a madness; selfish instinct comforts me that it is not. In my darkest hour I cling with awe to your reckless assurances, to your promise to trust me, no matter what. I carry you with me, always. I sail away but I also leave myself behind.

Holding in her hand the letter that Jai Raventhorne had written, the letter whose existence she had never believed, Olivia sat through the night at her window, gazing out and beyond into nothingness. She was engulfed in the swirling flood of memories, but by the sheer force of her will-power she fought them and made the tides recede. When the first lavender light of dawn touched the eastern horizon, her mind was again static, her thoughts again in her control. Calmly, she carried the black diary and the letter into her bath-room and, on a corner of the cemented floor, set a light to both. With no perceptible feeling, she sat and watched as they burned down into a tidy pile of ashes. Then she gathered them up and scattered them out of the window into the morning light.

A time to remember, a time to forget. A time to leave behind what one could never return to.

But it was the following night that Olivia's nightmares returned to again desecrate the hours of her sleep.

Astonishingly, the spider was still there. And the cobweb.

At least *a* spider and *a* cobweb. Not having the requisite talent to distinguish one spider from another, Olivia could not say with certitude that this fat, furry little fellow was the same or a remarkably similar descendant. The giant cobweb, however, still barricaded the wooded path near the Maratha Ditch, still looking like a jewelled screen of black lace with the early morning dew. The banyan tree, of course, was the same. Its gnarled roots still made as comfortable a perch as they had more than two years ago. Idly, Olivia sat to observe the single-minded endeavours of the busy little spider who seemed so contemptuous of her presence. His beady head swung from side to side like a pendulum clocking time as he spun out, inch by painstaking inch, silken filaments of exquisite fineness. He occasionally threw her darting, sidelong glances but without pausing in his labours. Olivia was shot through with wistful envy; how idyllic to have but one function in life, one thread of existence in which only the here and now mattered!

Everything in the forest was the same as she had left it on that distant morning. Only Jasmine was missing, now given away to a charitable orphanage, the other Templewood horses and coaches taken over by Hal Lubbock. Also missing, of course, was the barking of the dogs. Instead of Jasmine, Olivia now rode another mare, a blue roan, from Freddie's stables. As for the dogs' barking, if she closed her eyes she could hear even that.

Why was she here this morning? Olivia could think of no reason that logic would accept. To her great joy, Dr. Humphries had at last declared her fit enough to ride again. "But no steeplechasing, my friend," he had warned. "Choose a horse that is a lady, and then ride her like one." She had not been in a saddle for an age and her sense of liberation compounded into rapture. But then, why here, why to this forest? Olivia did not know the answer to the curious question. It seemed that she had been driven here by some intangible and sadistic force lying buried in her unconscious mind.

And by those hideous, recurring nightmares.

During the day, generally, her mind obeyed her entirely. It was during the nights, when she had abdicated conscious control of it that it had got into the habit of playing tricks on her. Suddenly invoked like rabbits out of a conjurer's hat were tiny disjointed fragments that turned into frescos of the past without her permission or participation. There seemed not a word, not the whisper of a thought, not a gesture or a sensation that her secretive mind had not stored and preserved to perfection without her knowledge. In her nightmares, echoes and sounds reverberated with frightening and forgotten fidelity. In her sleep Olivia saw sights, touched surfaces, tasted flavours and inhaled fragrances that no longer should have held any meaning. It was an insanity that had dragged her here this morning, but she could not expel her hallucinations any more than she could break away from the spells that this sorcerer of a forest was casting upon her now.

There was, Olivia recognised with a calmness that amazed her, an inevitability about her recession into the past. It was, perhaps, in its meticulous re-enactment that her salvation lay, her final liberation. She could no longer keep buried those memories that she despised. For her own exorcism, she had to exhume them one by one, examine them from a distance and then inter them to lay them to rest forever. The answer was not concealment; it was bold confrontation.

The pool where the dragon-flies looped and swooped over water-lilies still lay turgid and unmoving and covered with emerald green slime. The *bel* tree was not yet in fruit, but it would be in the spring. *I can tolerate anything you choose to be;* it was here that she had said it. Perched on that boulder, he had said, *I always know where you are. You make it impossible for me to stay away.* Wonderingly, he had asked what was the stubbornness that drove her. *It is a stubbornness called love.* Standing apart from herself, Olivia heard her own voice as she made that commitment as clearly as she heard the yelping of the dogs prancing around her feet. And it was here that he had repeatedly bemoaned his madness. But now, it seemed, that madness was not only his.

In the tedious task of compiling the few remaining inventories at the mansion, Olivia gratefully accepted Arthur Ransome's offer to help. Also, the matter of the Birkhurst jewellery given to her at the time of her marriage could no longer be postponed. With her sailing date approaching rapidly, some decision had to be arrived at and Olivia badly wanted advice. After completing the copious compilations in the kitchen, the provision store-rooms, the stables and the gardeners' sheds, over breakfast Olivia asked Ransome, "Since I do not intend to take the jewellery with me, would it be wise to leave it in the bank vault in Mr. Pennworthy's care? If I do so Donaldson will want to know why I do not take it with me."

Ransome reacted more sharply than Olivia had expected. "Those jewels are yours," he said with categorical conviction. "They *are* yours to take with you legitimately wherever you go. Whatever your differences might be with Freddie, you are still his wife and the baroness. To say nothing of being mother to his two sons."

Perhaps because she was out of kilter, or because of her prevailing emotional imbalances, or maybe because she was suddenly tired of all her deceptions, Olivia decided to now tell Arthur Ransome the entire truth. There had been no end to her lies; she was beginning to be disgusted with them, especially with the tawdry half truths she had been dispensing to this fine man who had given her his sorely needed friendship and love and thus deserved much better. The breakfast completed, Olivia folded her serviette and asked composedly, "Have you ever wondered, Uncle Arthur, why you have never seen Amos closely since the christening even though he is your godchild?"

He frowned, not knowing what to make of the sudden question. "Amos? Well, no. That is to say," he shifted uneasily in his seat and coloured, "yes. As a matter of fact, I have wondered sometimes . . ."

Olivia rose from the table. "You will see him now. Then I will not have to explain the reason." She went out of the room to summon Sheba.

Ransome had not added that the wonderment was, in fact, universal. But then, he was certain that in her perspicacity she was already aware of that. There had been much unkind gossip concerning the reclusivity in which she was bringing up her child. Ransome had never mentioned any of it to Olivia, but he had been hurt by much of what he had heard at *burra khanas* and had, on occasion, defended her stoutly. Not being dense, he had calculated that Amos had enacted in this shadow play—all the nuances of which he could not understand—a quite considerable part far in excess of what was apparent.

A few minutes later, Olivia returned with the child. Now all of fifteen months old, Amos was just starting to find his feet and insisted on making full use of his discovery. He toddled in unsteadily, hanging on to his mother's finger, stumbled once or twice, then sat down heavily with a thud in the middle of the carpet. Leaving him where he was, Olivia walked back to the table and resumed her seat opposite Ransome. Left to his own devices, Amos looked around for a plaything and happily grabbed a cushion to investigate with consuming interest.

Olivia watched Ransome's face carefully, not removing her eyes from it as he sat staring at the child. "Well?"

His stare deepened and his frown intensified. Initially puzzled, his expression slowly changed into something else. Realisation came in stages, then all at once everything clicked into place in his mind and he gasped. "God's blood!" he whispered, aghast. "Am I seeing things, Olivia? Do my eyes deceive me . . . ?"

"No. Your eyes do not deceive you. The person Amos reminds you of so unmistakably is indeed his father. Are any further explanations necessary?"

He shook his head, his face bleached white. For a moment he could not speak.

A corner of the cushion was now in Amos's mouth and imminent destruction was threatened with his teeth. Olivia got up to give the bell rope a tug and then gently removed the object from the child's hands. Incensed at the deprivation, Amos opened his mouth and screamed. But before he could exert his lung power to its full capacity, which was considerable, Sheba had quietly come in, whisked him up in her arms and removed him quickly from the room. The child's lusty bawls continued until the door of the nursery upstairs slammed shut behind them.

"You see?" Olivia commented drily. "The resemblance isn't only skin deep."

The little interlude had allowed Ransome to recollect his scattered wits and contain his reactions, but shock was still writ large across his face. "All these months, all these *years,* how dreadfully you must have suffered!" Disoriented and dazed, he dabbed his forehead with quick, clumsy gestures. "And how severe must have been the strain of sustaining your necessary subterfuges! I . . . I scarcely know what to say . . ."

No moral judgements, no pious censure; Olivia was moved to tears by his unqualified acceptance and simple, spontaneous sympathy. "I married Freddie because I had to marry someone," she said huskily, "and only Freddie was decent—and foolish!—enough to have taken me. Freddie too has suffered, also strained sometimes beyond endurance to sustain *my* subterfuges. Now you see why I had to part with Alistair? And why I consider I have no right to keep the jewellery?"

Enormously saddened, he hung down his head and shook it. "I have had some intuitions about your inner disturbances, my dear. And of course I sensed that you were better . . . acquainted with Jai than you would have had me believe. But *this* was not a prospect I had ever imagined. What agonies you must have been through!" Even baffled and unhappy, he had no difficulty making further deductions. "I presume Jai was not aware of his child's existence when he indulged in that inexcusable act of abduction?"

"No. But he is aware of it now."

Ransome pondered. "Do you think that is why he returned him, having vowed not to in that note?"

"I have no idea," she said coldly. "The workings of his mind are as much a mystery to me as they are to everyone else."

He almost smiled; the workings of Jai Raventhorne's mind she knew as she did her own, but he did not venture to pursue the thought. "But surely he has made contact with you since then? Come forward with offers of, well, help . . . ?"

At that Olivia stiffened. "His help is not required! Amos is my responsibility. And he will remain a Birkhurst."

"Yes, yes, of course. I only meant . . ." Embarrassed, he lapsed into silence and did not complete his sentence. When he spoke again it was with a tangential switch of subject. "Wild rumours still thrive. One is that Moitra is about to make a bid for Templewood and Ransome, whatever little remains of it."

"I see." Her fractional smile was sarcastic. "Since he has not been able to put you on the streets, for his efforts he buys the pleasure of at least removing your name plate—is that it?"

Ransome spread his hands to show his indifference. "Perhaps. I am inclined to let him have that pleasure." Shaking two pills out of the bottle he always carried, he washed them down with a draught of water, suddenly seeming as detached as she. "I feel I too have had enough of India, you know, my dear," he said unexpectedly. "There comes a time when she wants to devour you for all that she has given. She breaks you in body and in spirit. She cannibalises and destroys—as she did Josh and Bridget and, perhaps, even you. All at once I find myself hungering for the placid green pastures of England, where I can graze my last few years away in peace without fear of predators. All at once, Olivia, I too want to go *home* . . ."

Olivia searched his worn face in surprise and sadness. She had never before heard him talk of England as his home. "Where will you go in England? Do you have in mind any special place for retirement?"

"Home!" He laughed sourly. "The tragedy is that it is of a foreign country that I speak of as 'home.' I have a sister in Exeter, but I have not seen her since she was ten. Now she is a grandmother. I doubt if we would even recognise each other anymore. And all my friends are here. My only identity with England is that on the streets I will look no different from anyone else." He heaved a mighty sigh, then clucked, as if in impatience with himself. "Oh . . . *bal*derdash! It is old age that is making me nostalgic. My home, such as it is, is *here.* I have no other. When I die, I would want to be buried in Indian soil next to Josh."

Salim came in bearing a tray of hot tea and Olivia silently set about refreshing their cups. She could think of nothing to say that would not sound false and shallow, but within herself she shared his loneliness. In his own way, he too was a man of two worlds and yet of neither, as were so many other Englishmen estranged from the mother country.

"You must not take my ramblings seriously," Ransome said, shedding his air of dejection and forcing a laugh. "I could never live in England any more than Josh could have done. For one, we both hated those damned umbrellas one is forced to carry everywhere, to say nothing of the diabolical winters and stewed slop they call food. Besides, whatever would I do without my bearer? Good God, I don't even know how to find a pair of socks for myself!" They laughed a little, sipped their cups of steaming tea and lapsed again into trivia to shake off their absurd melancholy. And then, as he rose to go, Ransome suddenly said, "Oh, the wildest rumour of all I have not mentioned to you. Perhaps it will help to cheer you up and dispel the involuntary gloom I have introduced into the morning. Although some say that Jai has gone to earth in Assam in his self-imposed banishment from station, others disagree. It is being bandied about with gathering conviction that Kala Kanta is, perhaps, dead. Now, is that not something to warm the cockles of many hearts, perhaps even yours?"

23

Was he?

The question remained trapped between the layers of Olivia's mind, scavenging its tissue, interfering with all her thoughts. She could not understand its persistence; she was becoming a stranger to herself. To correct the tilt of her world and to retrieve a fine edge of her sanity, she rode fiercely every morning. Her sorties took her far out into the countryside, along the river, to the forests on the other bank of the Hooghly, but despite its exploding seas of humanity, Calcutta to her was a city peopled with ghosts. Everywhere she saw phantoms: in the mango groves, amidst scraggy scrub lands, around the bazaars and the temples and the embankments, most of all along the river embankments. The *Ganga* was again in port, moored at the Trident wharf, which was shrouded in silence. Olivia started to shrink from those re-enactments she had so blithely believed to be the means of her eventual liberation, her salvation from the past. Instead of exorcising her, they were beginning to draw blood again. Ironically, this time her adversary was invincible because it was herself. And yes, her life was unfinished, like a stitched garment with the hems left undone. All other parts of her life had now been neatened; she could not leave those hems unattended.

"Is he dead?"

It was during her final visit to Kirtinagar that Olivia asked Kinjal the question that would not lie dormant. She had brought Amos and Sheba with her for farewells to a family that was now her own. If Kinjal was at all surprised by her question, she took care to conceal it. Instead, she countered with one of her own. "Would it matter to you if he were?"

"No. It is merely a loose end. It needs to be tied."

"And if Jai is dead, will you consider it then tied?"

"Yes. Instantly."

"And if he is not?"

"Then it will take longer."

"Very well then," Kinjal retorted, matching her obstinacy, "since it is of no consequence one way or the other, we will talk about it later."

If there was joy in the reunion, inevitably there were also ripples of consuming sorrow. To soothe the melancholy aches of the long, perhaps permanent, parting ahead, they exchanged wild promises, made enthusiastic plans, shared impossible dreams.

"It has always been my ambition to visit the New World," Arvind Singh said. "Now there is even more incentive to do so. We will bring the children, of course. They would never forgive us if we left them behind."

"Neither would we! But you are used to living in palaces," Olivia teased. "Would you be able to live with us in a grass hut when you come to Hawaii?"

"Certainly. My villagers live in huts made of mud and grass. I have often spent nights with some hospitable family or other."

"Do you still intend to start your little school?" Kinjal asked Olivia.

"Oh yes. I will teach all our children together. And when they are not having lessons we will swim and surf and teach them how to catch fish. Sally will keep our appetites satisfied with taro doughnuts, which are now her specialty, she writes. We will have luaus and sing Hawaiian songs and gather seashells to make necklaces . . ."

They laughed but with forced gaiety, knowing that all this would perhaps never be, but it made the parting more bearable. Relentless in her silence, Kinjal had still not answered Olivia's question until the eve of her return to Calcutta. But then it was Kinjal herself who revived the subject, insisting that her own question be answered with honesty.

"No, it does not matter one way or the other," Olivia reiterated evenly. "I ask only because he has become a habit to my mind. And however pernicious, habits die hard. If these past few chapters of my life are to be closed, as they must be, then I do have a right to know."

"You consider the narrative concluded?"

"Irrevocably! I am the wife of another man, Kinjal. That he chooses not to live with me is irrelevant. I still wear his ring, bear his name, enjoy his material possessions. Besides," she paused, *"He . . .* despises me." She could not bring herself to say Raventhorne's name.

"Jai did not know the truth, Olivia."

"He condemned me without ever trying to find out the truth!"

Kinjal laughed with indulgent amusement. "You wanted him to know the truth yet you dreaded that one day he would! How can you have it both ways, Olivia? And in your strange irrationality you still punish him by denying him his son?"

Olivia swivelled to face her. "I have spent two long years unraveling my miserable complications, Kinjal," she said fiercely. "As far as it can ever be cleared, I have cleared my conscience. And I have honoured my debts, especially to Freddie. I no longer owe anyone anything except," her throat constricted, *"you.* For what is owed to you I can think of no recompense, and to offer any would be an insult. I have valued your judgement and your advice and your help more than I can ever express in words, Kinjal. That you must already know. *But,* I will not consider complicating my life again no matter how persuasive your arguments. I cannot, Kinjal," she concluded quietly, "I cannot."

Kinjal allowed the silence between them to remain undisturbed for a moment, then sighed her resignation. "Very well then. No, Jai is not dead. At least, his body lives. For his spirit I cannot vouch. He too has been to bid us farewell. It seems we are to be abandoned very thoroughly."

Something small, a twitch more than a spasm, nudged Olivia from within. "To bid you farewell?"

"Yes. He too sails away soon. On his beloved *Ganga.* I don't know for where. Perhaps he does not either. Men of the sea return to the sea when they are done with their lives. The ocean is Jai's oyster. He will go wherever the wind blows him, I presume."

They were taking a final stroll in the herb garden, drenched in the evocative scents of mint and marjoram and sharply pungent cloves. In the whitewashed temple with its crowning trident, offerings were being prepared for vespers, the soft bells already tinkling. It would soon be Dassera again. And then would come the immersions.

"Yes. He is good at renunciations," Olivia murmured, her eyes far away on the death throes of the sun and the orange inferno that marked its funeral procession below the horizon. She plucked a sacred *tulsi* leaf and bit into it. It tasted tangy and cleansing. "He will leave without even looking back over his shoulder."

"There is not much for him to look back upon."

"No. Nor for me," Olivia pointed out with an unfeeling smile.

Kinjal did not share in her smile. Instead she halted in her steps and faced Olivia with solemnity. "You have been luckier than Jai, Olivia. You are strong. Your resources have regenerated you. He is crippled by his weaknesses. In the ultimate analysis, it is you who are the survivor, he the victim. And it is you who have won."

Won? Yes. She had won. All that she had set out to achieve. But then why was the taste of victory on her tongue so unsweet? Olivia said nothing.

"Jai sails but he is not yet gone. He has returned from Assam where he has been all this while and is now at his house by the river." Kinjal caught Olivia's arm, the plea in her night-dark eyes very eloquent. "*Let* Jai see his son once more before you leave, Olivia! By returning him when he need not have, Jai deserves *some* gratitude, even if this paltry crumb!"

Olivia took a deep breath and then shook her head. "No, Kinjal."

Then it was time to return to Calcutta.

There were cabin trunks scattered all over the house. Lists of their contents had already been compiled for the insurers but they still had to be sealed, numbered and labelled. Olivia tackled the boring chores without enthusiasm. Part of herself, she felt, had been left behind in Kirtinagar. Her sense of bereavement was so acute that she seemed able to do nothing right. In her disjointedness she labelled all the trunks *Lulubelle,* unaware of the error until it was pointed out by Arthur Ransome, and the rectifications made messes and took hours more to complete. Her list of provisions needed for the voyage Olivia mended and amended so often that Willie Donaldson could not make head nor tail of it. And then, when she discovered that she had accidentally thrown out all the lists of trunk contents over which she had laboured for days and that everything now needed to be unpacked, relisted and repacked for the insurers, Olivia's nerves revolted. She dumbfounded both Ransome and Donaldson by bursting into tears and running out of the room, sobbing hysterically.

There were only three days left before the *George Washington* was to sail.

"Blue Vanda, lady memsahib . . . ?"

Olivia did not remember the flower seller until he suddenly spoke to her. It was her second to last day in India, her last ride in the early morning. Tomorrow the stables were to be cleared, the carriages dismantled and the parts oiled for safe storage, the horses all dispatched to their new homes. Olivia was to be escorted to the docks by Ransome, Donaldson, Lubbock and some of the staff from Farrowsham. Her baggage was finally at the wharves awaiting Customs clearance and loading aboard the American clipper.

Olivia was startled by the approach of the flower seller. She looked around and realised to her surprise that she had somehow arrived at the flower market. The stalls were laden with saffron marigolds, once again in full season. Columns of wild orchids hung by green tendrils and awaited to be implanted in host tree branches. The man held out a gnarled hand around which were twined trailing blue-mauve blossoms. "Another blue Vanda, lady memsahib?" he repeated, smiling persuasively.

Yes, she remembered him. Another ghost, another re-enactment! She was not surprised that he recalled her visit more than two years earlier. Not many Europeans chanced upon this little cranny of a native bazaar. Those who might would certainly be remembered. Besides, that day she had been with someone whom the old man had known well. In answer to his request she shook her head and tried to move on, but somehow she couldn't. Her feet remained where they were, her eyes glued to the flowers trailing from his fingers.

"The other one, it grows well?" he asked. His skin still looked like crushed brown paper, even more so as he smiled.

Olivia tore her eyes away from the blue malignance, her mouth suddenly running dry. "No. It died."

He clucked in sympathy. "Then you must take another to replace it." Before she could refuse, he had thrust the vine into her hand. She gave a small cry, recoiled and dropped it. Hurt, the old man got up to retrieve it from the ground, then parted its flowers to show her the stem. "See, memsahib? No thorns, not one."

Feeling silly and ashamed, Olivia quickly took out a coin from her purse. "I'm sorry. I ruined your flowers. No, of course there aren't any thorns, I was merely startled. Please do let me pay for these, at least. They're lovely but I cannot use them. I leave for my own country soon."

He was unconcerned with her affairs, wholly engrossed in smoothing out the wounded petals. He waved aside the coin she offered. "I cannot take money from you, lady memsahib. You were brought here by Chandramani's boy." Olivia looked blank, so he explained. "The man white people sometimes call Kala Kanta."

"That was his . . . mother's name?" she asked, taken by surprise.

"Yes."

"You knew her?"

"Oh yes. She was my sister's child. Poor, misguided girl! She died very young, very young." He clucked absently and replaced his orchids.

In her sudden confusion at the information, Olivia recalled that he had spoken in Assamese to Jai Raventhorne and there had been affection in the ancient eyes. Raventhorne had not told her that the man was his uncle. But then, he wouldn't have, naturally. "That name . . . Chandramani," she asked, feeling dizzy and steadying herself against his wooden stall, "it means 'jewel of the moon,' doesn't it?"

He nodded in confirmation. "Jewel of the moon," he repeated sorrowfully, pointing towards the sky. "But Chandramani never shone, the unfortunate girl, she never shone."

I must stop this, Olivia thought in her stupor, *I mustn't linger here!* But she still could not move. "Tell me about Chandramani," she heard herself persist.

"There is nothing to tell." He shrugged and settled back on his haunches. "She died many years ago."

"Where, here in Calcutta?"

"Oh yes. She could not be taken back by our people."

"How did she die?"

He shrugged again. "No one knows. Save for the boy. They took away Chandramani's shine, the sahibs did." He spat expertly in the drain. "It was after she died that the boy walked all the way back into the hills, back to his grandfather. But he never spoke of Chandramani, not even to her father. Heart-broken, her mother had already died grieving for her daughter who would never return home." He stopped and squinted at her. "Lady memsahib wants to know all this, why?"

She did not hear his question. Like a marionette speaking in another's voice, she said mechanically, "Yes. He was about ten years old at that time. But your people could not have known him."

"No." He looked at her curiously. "Nor did they recognise him by his appearance. His was a sahib's face, it was not one of ours. But there were other means of identification. He had some of Chandramani's jewellery, although at that time his memory had failed him and he remembered little about his mother or her death. Our elders considered the matter. As always, they were wise and just. It was Chandramani who had sinned, broken tribal law. The child was blameless. He had been rejected by his father's people. He could not be abandoned. The boy's grandfather, a widower now, took him in with joy and loved him, as we all did. But then his grandfather too died and on the very day of the cremation, the boy again vanished. He was always a strange, secretive one, always, and his memory was still not fully repaired. Now, of course, it is all changed. He is a big man. He is Kala Kanta . . ." He stopped to smile and savour a moment of quiet pride, then peered at her short-sightedly, trying to focus her face. "You know him well, lady memsahib, to ask all these long-forgotten questions?"

With a slight jolt, Olivia returned to the present. Picking up the reins of her horse, she finally forced her feet to move. "No. I do not know him well. I was merely indulging my idle curiosity."

He watched her as she hurried away and wondered why the history of a stranger asked for out of idle curiosity should bring grief to the lady memsahib's eyes.

That night Olivia had another nightmare, her most frightening yet. She was walking across the surface of the moon. Beneath her feet, it shone with translucent light. In hand she was carrying a red velvet bundle. Suddenly, the bundle started to move and then to wriggle and squirm frantically. She laid it down, opened it and saw that it was full of scorpions, each one with its tail upraised and ready to sting. Before she could pull away her hand, they had covered it with their crusty bodies and turned it bloody and swollen with their poison. She woke up screaming, fighting them off, and found that she was drenched with sweat.

It was no effort to recognise the significance of the nightmare. It was a reminder of what had to be done and had not been. It was also a reminder of Kinjal's damnably accurate contention;

no, she had not paid all her debts. One remained. Jai Raventhorne had indeed returned her son when he need not have. For that, at least, she would always have to owe him.

Two polished brass carriage lamps burned low on either side of the mahogany front door. The brass knocker, also burnished, was in the shape of a tiger's claw. In its ridged surface Olivia could see her face and it looked distorted, as in a trick fairground mirror. Her hand rose and then dropped again. She shivered and closed her eyes. Silently, she hunted for some helpful prop, some added strength to perform her final mission in Calcutta. She would again be crossing over an uncharted sea, but this, her most feared crossing yet, she knew that she could not, must not, evade. Somehow she had to navigate this last course, somehow. Taking courage from a long, deep breath, she raised her hand again. This time it did not falter.

Before the echoes of her knock had died away, the door slid open on oiled hinges and Bahadur stood before her. Trained never to betray surprise, he only dared to widen his eyes for a barely perceptible fraction of a second. Then, as usual, he bowed low and folded his hands in greeting. Wildly, Olivia prayed that Jai Raventhorne would not be home, that he had left instructions to deny her entry, that he had already sailed away on his *Ganga*. But before she could nerve herself to ask the question, Bahadur had already given her the unwanted answer.

"The Sarkar is by the river with the dogs."

He opened the door wide but Olivia shook her head and stepped back. She indicated that she would prefer to reach the embankment through the garden path and would easily be able to find her own way there. She walked down the path slowly, preparing herself for the ordeal ahead. Above her, as she strolled, tall casuarina and *neem* trees danced in random rhythm. The hand of the moon was on her neck and it felt pleasantly cool on her burning skin. In her nostrils the dankness of the Hooghly was strong and, like all smells, it immediately evoked associated remembrances. Olivia recognised some of the constellations overhead, the clusters of low hanging stars, even the wisps of cloud—all familiar faces in the sudden crowd of memories. Time unwound. It was these very configurations that had ordained her escape from the *burra khana* that long-ago night. Escape! Had she actually ever seen it as that? Around her it was dark, but that flawless inner vision of hers—that traitor!—was like crystal, clear in its image after image of a night that belonged to a previous incarnation.

On the embankment she neither saw nor heard the dogs. Perhaps he had already gone away somewhere by another route? But in that hope too she was disappointed. She saw the white blur of his shirt exactly where prescience had informed her it would be—on those steps by the river. Olivia's breath quickened even as her feet halted. Greedy swallows of air revived her lungs, dispelled her panic and reconstituted her intentions. She had come tonight only to repay a debt, no more, no less. Noiselessly, she slipped behind a bush to give herself time to regularise the erratic gasps of her breath. He lay sprawled across the length of the step, head cushioned on cupped palms, fingers clasped. He stared intently at something, perhaps the opposite bank or the horizon or the silver fringe of a rising moon—it was difficult to tell. Olivia stood and observed him, the moments pulsing by in units of eternity. They were separated by only a few steps, but even those were like symbols of infinity. Sheltered by the bush, Olivia struggled to mentally formulate what it was that she had come to say, but then, all at once, it was he who spoke first.

"You should have told me."

Slowly, he sat up but he did not turn to look behind him because, like a jungle animal, he had perhaps caught her scent on the wind. Or maybe because he had never needed eyes to see her. Or because she was expected. He had known that she would come tonight.

She negotiated the flight of steps to walk into his range of vision, her breath once more even in its cadence. "I could not. I feared that you would want to take him away from me."

He still did not look at her. "Oh yes, you feared rightly!"

Olivia sank down on the step above him, his face well within her sight so that she could examine his expressions. "You could have kept him."

"Yes."

"Why didn't you?"

"*Why* is still your favourite question!"

"Then humour it." She was shocked at how ill and wan he looked.

"My motives are immaterial. You have your son. Be content in that."

No, she could not be content. Not until she had forced him

to verbalise a renunciation as final as that with which he had once sought to disclaim her. "Did you not want to?"

At that he laughed, an empty little sound. "You wish to vindicate your conscience at the expense of mine—is that it? You still want to have your cake and eat it!"

"My conscience needs no vindication," she retorted sharply. "You returned to me what is rightfully mine!"

"True. Nevertheless I will vindicate it." He swung his legs to position himself at the far end of the steps that divided them. "No, I did not want to keep him. Not even I, in all my reprehensibilities, could condone wilfully depriving a child forever of his mother."

He spoke with immense bitterness, and in his lie Olivia felt stirrings of the pain that had recently also been her own. She did not wound him further by challenging his lie. "In that case I misjudged you. I owe you an apology. And some expression of gratitude."

"Is that why you have come? To apologise, to offer thanks?"

Was it? "Yes. It was an undeserved misjudgement. I did not think I would see my son again. It was what you had threatened."

The swift intake of his breath was harsh. "You owe me nothing. Your misjudgement is not undeserved, neither is your mistrust. In my arrogance, I expected far too much." As he turned finally, the moon touched his face; it was gaunt, hollow cheeked. "I never thought to consider why you had married Freddie," he mused wonder-struck. "I never even *thought* to consider that!"

Olivia wanted to get up and walk away, but she could not; there was more to be said. She was trapped by her own intentions. In this final encounter with which she completed her odyssey, she could not leave her pieces unspoken. She gritted her teeth and stayed where she was. The silence was shattered by the barks of the returning dogs. Accepting her as a familiar presence, they came bounding down the steps but with no aggressive overtures. Animals too have memories, after all, which endure well.

"Don't move. They will not harm you." He uttered the warning mechanically, then recalled that once before he had sounded the same caution in the same place, and again he soured. "How different our histories might have been had I walked the dogs in the opposite direction that night!"

"They would have been no different. Fate is spiteful enough to have ensured that we would meet in another time, another place."

He stilled with the force of her cynicism. Already dull, like burnt-out ashes, his eyes dimmed with aches that were involuntarily shared. His tongue too seemed to taste the acrid flavours on hers, his vision also bedevilled by those same phantoms that floated in hers. "Yes, your spiteful fate more than mine!" He was ravaged, the despair also shared. "You were cursed to meet me anyway."

Olivia froze. She was done with the brittle bones of history, done with autopsies on corpses already putrid with decay, done with weighing blame and counter-blame. Fighting for balance, she centred her world with a single touch. But then she immediately sent it awry again with the one subject she had vowed not to invoke. "Why did you have to send me that long-lost letter? It was an act of cruelty."

He shuddered and closed his eyes. "Why do you still have to ask all these questions?" He was too spent for anger. He sounded only beaten. "Because you sail tomorrow and must neatly knot all those unfinished ends your tidy mind has always hated?"

"If you wish."

"Unfinished ends!" He laughed a little, not replying to her question. "Yes, I suppose that is all they can ever be now. You, my own cursed life, my son . . ." Without completing the thought, he rose abruptly to pick up a stone and send it spinning across the water in a fierce spurt of energy.

My son. Olivia went cold. *My* son! For the first time it struck her that if they shared nothing else ever, that pronoun of possession would forever be common property. Angrily she shook off her numbness to steel herself and return to what was relevant. "On your side, the bargain is fulfilled. On mine, it still pends. The Templewood house is yours to take whenever you wish. The quarters remain intact."

He resumed his seat heavily, lilac shadows obscuring his face. "I have now even less need of possessions."

"Nevertheless I return to you what is yours as a . . . birthright." She stopped, swallowed hard and continued. "As is this, which I also return to you." Hands shaking, sick with shame, she placed the red velvet bundle as close to him as she could reach. Initially she had intended to have it sent back to him by messenger after her departure but had then willed herself the courage to do so personally. There, now it was over, this most hideous of all her missions! Now there remained nothing between them, except for that obnoxious pronoun that not even the gods could alter. Somehow she gathered more courage to say what else needed verbalising. "I'm . . . sorry."

He turned on her, all at once enraged. "You are generous in your remorse, but I deserve no such consideration. In war one uses whatever weapon comes to hand—a lesson you no doubt learned from *me.* I beg you, don't humble me anymore!"

"I did not come with the intention of humbling you."

"No. You came only to tie all your loose ends. Are there more?"

"One, perhaps." Her throat felt bruised with the effort of speech. "After tonight we will not meet again. I would not want to part on a note of that hostility, which is now obsolete. I have no more recriminations." One of the slumbering beasts within her stirred, yawned and then scratched—would she want to part at all . . . ? Ruthlessly, she crushed it out of her mind, but in her agitation she stretched a hand towards the black bitch lying near her feet.

"Don't, she is capricious!" Leaning sideways, he had stayed her hand with lightning swiftness. The unplanned contact was like a plunge into icy waters; it jolted both equally. Instantly, he let her hand drop. "No. We will not meet again." In his ready agreement he was callous. "But such nobly granted absolution is hardly the point! Loose end or not, I have a responsibility towards the boy—"

"I want nothing from you!" She sliced him off at once. "I accepted nothing from my husband, save his name. From you not even that is due. My son is my responsibility, mine alone." *My* son. She made no mistake with her own emphasis.

He winced, then threw up his hands in a gesture of abjuration. "I use words badly, you know that. I don't know how to say what I mean with delicacy. I am out of my depth, in a situation that has defeated me. I don't know how not to be offensive."

In his unaccustomed bewilderment he looked vulnerable, like a young bird that has lost its bearings, but Olivia did not weaken. "It is a situation that need not concern you. If it is outside your depth, it is also outside your life. I will manage well on my own."

The reminder of her essential aloneness slammed into him like a sledge-hammer, although that was not what Olivia had intended. He convulsed. With a groan, he covered his face with his hands. "Yes. I know you will manage well, but how will *I?* It is not you I seek to help, Olivia, nor can I, but my own misbegotten self. You see? As always I am selfish and coarse and conceited, with none of those social graces I once paraded before you with such pride. You must bear with me, Olivia, one last time for the sake of . . ." He stopped and looked up. "What is the name of the . . . boy? The ayah knew him only as 'baba.' "

Yes. Kinjal was right. There was a time when he was the rock, she the tide that lapped timidly around it. Now the picture was reversed, as were their functions. It was she who had survived, she who had translated hidden resources into strength. He was unequipped, resourceless, rudderless. And she had been wrong in her conclusions; he had not been spared either. Perhaps he too, like the rest of them, was a victim. Yes, he too, for he was denied even the name of his son. Olivia felt her eyes blur. She started to ache. And somewhere in that ache, somewhere, she felt what could have been grief at what might have been and was not.

"His name is Amos."

"Amos." He held the name in his mouth, balanced on the tip of his tongue, as if tasting an elusive sweetness. "Amos. Yes, he will bear many burdens. It is apt and appropriate. But then, you have always had an impeccable sense of the fitness of things, Olivia. It is one more area in which I stand humbled."

"There are no more scores to be counted, Jai!" She was alarmed by his humility, alarmed by the inner dragons it threatened to unleash. "The past is *dead*—can't you see that?"

"For me there can only be the past. I exist now without a future." His despair erupted with volcanic force, sending him leaping to his feet like one possessed. "In a single glance at my son's face your life unfolded before me like a mural unveiled. A carnal bargain for the privilege of a *name,* a daily lie perpetuated alone in constant fear of exposure, a betrayal never understood, never explained—"

"Stop it!" Blinded by panic, not at his escaping demons but her own, Olivia also sprang to her feet in fury. "I *forbid* you to—"

"And then you sacrificed a second son." In the grip of helpless passion, he remained unhearing, deafened by the roars of his own guilt. "Why? Was that also part of the carnal bargain? Expiation for the crime of a begged and borrowed name?" Raking fingers punished his hair with a rage he could not contain. "And I, blinded by my own arrogance, demanded that you survive on the strength of one miserable *letter* that failed to even reach you. Oh *Christ . . . !* The wrenching turbulence peaked, then started to fade, then died away altogether. "And I called you a whore, a *whore!*" Flattened with horror, his voice could not sustain itself.

"Don't, please *don't!*" Olivia cried, recoiling at the violence of his self-flagellations, stupid with dread at the dimension of her own expanding responses. "*Please* don't say any more, Jai, I *beg* of you!"

But he was beyond recall. "Why did you not run, Olivia—flee, hide, abscond, anything, *anywhere!*" Insane with frustration, he fisted a hand and rammed it against a stone ledge, uncaring of injury. "Why did you not *trust* me, damn you . . . ?"

Anger flared briefly and insulated her from her fear. "Why?" She looked at him with scorn. "Because I did not wish my son to be born a bastard like his father. It was as simple as that."

His head jerked back as if struck. His face became bloodless. Slowly he began to diminish, his rage evaporating. "Yes," he mumbled, devastated, "yes. That was a stupid question. I am raving, Olivia, because I look for a scapegoat and there is none. Because I want to reverse the clock and I cannot. Because I have lost you. My hindsight, you see, is perfect." Embittered again, he surrendered to the uselessness of his guilt. "In my selfish search to redeem at least something of myself, however, I want you to know that I would have returned within six months had I not learned along the way that you had already married Freddie. I had tried once to renounce you; I could not sustain it. It was not within my power to renounce you again. You should also know, if only as an exercise in futility, that to find you I would have ransacked the earth. I would have come to you wherever you were hidden. Wherever."

Olivia knew then that she should not have come. But having come, she also knew that she could not now leave. "Would you have?" she asked dully.

He sighed and bowed his head, weighted down with those burdens he could neither carry nor cast off. "The fact that you are still driven to ask that is my most despicable failure. And my most lethal punishment."

Once again the stubborn fingers of pain crept around Olivia's body, refusing to be repulsed, challenging her resistance. She could not bear his torment any more than she could her own. "Mine or yours, our failures are shared. You could not have known of my circumstances. I had no yardstick with which to measure a man such as you. And time was against us . . ."

Us. How cunningly that word had slipped out, and with what parodic timing in these final moments before they went their separate ways!

Submerged within himself, he did not notice her slip—that

seemingly innocuous little two-letter word that so blithely melded them together again. "As an avenger, I am a travesty. I did not spare even you—the only thing in my life that made it worthy of being lived at all."

For an instant, a mere whisper in time, Olivia was overwhelmed with feeling. So as to force from her sight the nightmare of his face, she squeezed her eyes shut. But it was useless. Every feature of his was etched forever in her brain. Without even opening her eyes she knew that in his, once more, there would be tears.

She sighed and moved away from her feelings. As if in an odd chimera, weightless and airborne she floated out of herself to watch him from above. With dispassion and only vague surprise, she made another discovery. Kinjal had been wrong in her judgement; she had not won after all. She could never have won. And with that discovery came others, a succession of others. She wanted to get up and go to him, to sit by his side, to rest her cheek against that defeated shoulder. She wanted to sprout wings, to soar across those divides that had segregated their destinies so irreversibly, to somehow erase the years of their separate sorrows. She wanted to touch him again, as she once had, to be reassured, warmed, by the closeness of his skin, to gather him in her arms, to solace him. To love him and be loved by him. Released from their fragile, insubstantial moorings, her sensations stampeded. Behind closed lids, she ruffled his disobedient hair, even wilder in the blowing breeze, and in her palm she felt again those long, tapered fingers that had prompted in her such wanton responses. Next to her face she actually felt the rough weave of his ever-present white mull shirt about which she had teased him so often. And through the fabric came the incandescence of the blood that was now also part of her son. With her finger-tips she gently stroked away the pain creased in his forehead. She put an ear to his pocket to listen to his heart; it beat the same rhythm as hers. And once more in her inner hearing was the soundless sound of those words that she had not thought of for so long: *But yes, I do love you . . .*

"There is a loose end that I too must knot."

Startled, Olivia stepped out of her reverie to return to poignant reality. His manic ferments were successfully quelled. He again spoke normally. She decided she wanted no more instigations into insanity, but not wanting them, asked, "Which loose end?"

"I have to tell you how my mother died."

"No!" So much, so late—what was the point?

"Yes. You have unturned each stone of my life. This too must not remain unreversed. You have a right to know."

"I forfeit the right; it is no longer important!"

"It is important." His contradiction was firm but gentle. "You cannot forfeit a right that is not yours alone. Someday my son too will have the right to know; you must then tell him." It was a cruel reminder of their divided destinies and it cut deeply, but he was already lost in that distant world in which had been laid the foundations of their own futures. "She died as she had lived, a woman of no consequence, unloved to the end. The one whiplash she had suffered in order to save me had wounded her badly. For eight years she had not been a day without opium. It ran through her blood; her body craved it like a hunger that nothing else could satisfy. I could not give her any, so the appetite remained unsatiated, and with that hunger it died. Her heart and spirit had died long before. She was not yet twenty-five."

He spoke in an even rhythm, but she saw that each word exacted a toll as buried emotions, never aired, lay quivering just beneath the surface of his control. "Don't!" Olivia entreated. "Let it lie if it is so hurtful."

"Yes, it is hurtful, but it still must be told." Absently, his finger-tips stroked the red bundle beside him, that pathetic little childhood treasury. "She slipped away that very first night after we had left the big house. We had to sleep by the road. The cut on her arm still bled and she was in agony, her brain addled with her need for the little pellets that ensured her silent docility. But that night, before we slept, she told me many things—perhaps because she knew that night would be her last." He got up and turned his back to Olivia. "It was then that I learned for the first time about the opium. And about the identity of my father. The opium was beyond my comprehension, but that the man who had cut her open was my *father* dumbfounded me. I was awe-struck. Before then, you see," restless in his recollections he started to pace, "I had always admired him from a distance—this fine figure of an Englishman who could read and write and command with such consummate ease. I used to watch him for hours, storing away all his actions, his little gestures and mannerisms, and imitating them when I was alone. There were times I wanted to touch him, because to touch an Englishman was to me the ultimate honour. And sometimes he spoke to me, gave me things, tried to be kind. But the sound of his voice petrified me. It was as if an idol from a temple had stepped down and spoken. I could never answer anything he asked and he would turn impatient. Even that impatience I took as an accolade, a reward, for it meant that I was important enough to make him angry . . ." He broke off, as if fearful of emotion, and again contained himself within parameters he had defined for himself.

"I had never seen death," he continued with calmness, regaining his seat, "I was not aware of my mother's. It was a passing water carrier who told me that she was gone, that she must now be consigned to flame. Together we carried her to the river bank and gathered wood. It was damp; it took a long time to light. I did not know what a cremation meant. It was only when the pyre began to burn that I cried. I saw then that she could never return to me."

To his monotone there was only a minimal quiver, nothing more, but Olivia saw how terribly he suffered. "Please don't go on," she begged, suffering with him, "I can't bear to hear any more!"

He turned harsh again. "For the boy you must learn *everything!* You allow me nothing else, let me give him at least this pittance of myself. In giving it I cleanse that infection you once called a canker. So you see," even his laugh was harsh, "in this too I am selfish."

Olivia remained silent. She did not protest again.

"The water carrier went. He had a living to earn." He had sprung up again, his interlocked fingers behind his back twitching. "He left me an empty coconut shell in which to gather the ashes when they had cooled. I did as he had instructed, then cast the shell into the river. The monsoon winds were strong; they carried the shell quickly towards the open sea. I bathed, as I had been told to, and a wandering barber, taking pity, shaved my head and trimmed my nails without charge, as this too, the water carrier had emphasised, was part of the cremation ritual. My wound was still raw and it bled again. I lay down somewhere, I can't remember where, and slept. When I opened my eyes, it was to find myself in the house of a stranger. Many days had passed since my mother died. I could remember none of it. My mind was devoid of all memory."

Ranjan Moitra's house. Olivia knew this but said nothing. Pin-points of heat seared her inner eyelids. The curiously impersonal tone in which he related this most harrowing experience in a child's life—as if he spoke of someone else, someone unknown—was a protective device. Inside, Olivia knew, he bled quietly.

"It was in this strange house that kindness and medication repaired my body. My mind was still blank. They did not know how to repair that. It was only two years later, when I chanced upon some travellers from Assam, heard their language, that a faint glimmer of memory told me that there were people of my own up in the hills. It took me six months to make the journey, but I could not find them, for I did not know who I was looking for. It was someone from the tribe who found me roaming the hills, recognised some of the jewellery I had, which the water carrier had removed from my mother's body before we burned it, and took me to the village. One old man, it appeared, was my grandfather. He cried, took me in, gave me his love and taught me everything he knew. He taught me about the soil, the forests and their fauna, the seasons and their crops; he taught me especially about those majestic tea trees that were, he said, part of my inheritance." In remembering this childhood love, he softened. In his eyes there was a faint smile of tenderness. Then the smile vanished and he was again impassive. "But he was an old man, made older by grief. In time he too died. It was I who closed his eyes, I who lit his pyre. And it was as I stood watching him too turn to ashes that all at once my memory returned to me. I remembered everything—how my mother had died, where and *why.* I remembered the big house, the cell of my birth, the opium pellets, the slash on her arm, all her final words. And I remembered Lady Bridget, Sir Joshua's mother and his whip. But most of all, *most* of all, I remembered Sir Joshua Templewood, my father."

In the nascent moonlight his eyes were like opals, hard and shining dimly. Somewhere, a jackal howled. Others picked up the refrain, obviously celebrating the find of a left-over cadaver. Olivia barely moved as she watched him. There was no question of an intrusion.

"It was then, in that moment of total recall, that I first knew what it meant to hate. It was a frightening emotion, so immense that it seemed to own me, to devour me. And it was then, at my grandfather's pyre, at the age of thirteen, that I made a vow. Not with words, for at that age I had none that were adequate. It was a vow forged in silence, in a hate that far exceeded the limits of speech. From that moment on, my life was preordained. As the lines on these palms," he thrust his hands out at her, "my route was etched and unerasable. There could be no deviations, no obstructions. Nor would I permit any."

His voice trailed but left behind an echo with which the

night seemed to reverberate. Olivia finally let her tears fall unhindered. She knew that what he had divulged to her, this blazing memory carved into the brain of a child, was the very axis around which his life had rotated. Inevitably, hers too. This was the essence of what had made him what he was and, curiously enough, what she had become. This then was the last piece of the jigsaw puzzle, the core of the onion. She now shared with Jai Raventhorne a place in his innermost sanctum—that one vital day in his life that had fashioned his, extinguished that of his father, mutilated the lives of so many others. Ironically, what she would never be able to share with him was his life. The sense of humour of the gods was indeed inexhaustible.

"You were a deviation, Olivia. An obstruction." He now said aloud what he had already spoken in her mind. "I sacrificed you for a crime that was a mere error of geography: You were in the wrong place at the wrong time." The deep grooves on either side of his twisted mouth gleamed even more livid in the moonlight. "And you were foolish enough to love the wrong man."

The only man.

She did not correct him. "We delude ourselves that we have a choice," she said bitterly. "Love, hate—both are competent puppet masters. They pull the strings, we merely strike postures."

Once more he was shaken by the force of her disillusionment. He stood helpless and resourceless, then quickly removed the silver chain he again wore around his neck. Balancing the rectangular box on a palm, he stared at it a moment, then sat down beside her. Deftly, with the edge of a finger-nail, he went around the sides of the pendant and opened it.

"Feel."

With the tip of her forefinger Olivia probed. At first she felt nothing, then a delicate presence, a shadow so fragile as to be almost not there at all. Her gaze on him was questioning.

"If as his only bequest to me my father left me these infernal appendages," he jabbed viciously at his eyes, "then from him my mother had even less. A few strands of hair!" He shut the locket with a sharp snap. "Just these lifeless lengths from that accursed head that had once lain on her shoulder, a souvenir of a love that gave her nothing, took away everything. But she treasured this one pathetic remembrance, cherished it, kept it always around her neck." His voice softened, his eyes once again far-away, probing through the swirling mists of time. "She would sit in that miserable little cell lost in her twilight world of illusory contentment, chiseling away at those toys of hers with gentle strokes, singing to herself in that childish voice I can still sometimes hear. That figure-head of a girl with her arms stretched above her was her most ambitious labour of love, a symbol of that freedom she craved, although in her simplicity she could not have been aware of such a sophisticated concept. That figure-head was of herself, as she had once been, uncaged and unshackled. She lived in a vanished world that existed only in her mind, but with me she shared it often, regressing whenever she could into that lost innocence that was never entirely lost, the one thing he could not take away from her." Unashamed of emotion for once, he brushed his eyes with the back of his hand. "One meagre strand of hair for one meagre life—an inequitable bargain, no? But to her it was acceptable. From him she wanted nothing more."

Olivia searched the face he had restructured into a screen. "And you? What is it that you would have wanted from him?"

To that he reacted sharply. "Everything! And what I wanted I took. I wish I could profess regrets, but I cannot." Patrician in his flash of arrogance, his features cemented.

"He could have killed you twice."

"Empty gestures! They meant nothing." The arrogance started to fade and, tired again, he heaved a sigh. Perhaps he remembered that his hate was wasted now, that the drama was played out and the curtain down. "No," he amended quietly. "Maybe they were not empty gestures. Maybe they did hold some meaning for him, if not for me. I don't know. Now I never will know. Yes, he could have whipped me to death; I expected him to. I was surprised when he stopped. And yes, he missed that first shot deliberately." His small laugh held a touch of macabre humour. "Probably the first time he missed anything he didn't want to. He was an extraordinary marksman."

"You could have shot him too," Olivia reminded him softly.

"Yes." Just that. No more. No explanation. "I could never have felt for him, for *her,* his wife, anything but hate. One way or another, they all conspired to kill my mother. Even Ransome, decent man that he is. And yet . . ." He got up to saunter away from her and stand staring into the dark vacancy of the silent night. "And yet, sometimes when I was very alone, when I was lost and confused and searching for my identity, when I remembered that I had admired him once—I wondered to myself what it might be like to hear a man such as Sir Joshua Templewood call me 'son' . . ."

The hair at the nape of Olivia's neck rose and tingled. In the icy sensation, she numbed. There was a parallel in his words that could not be missed. Someday, sometimes, when Amos too was alone, lost and confused and searching for his identity, would he also wonder what it might be like to be called "son" by an absent father? In the wilderness of her imagination, Olivia saw Amos's dove grey eyes cloud as he too struggled with the same flux of emotions—anger, hate, bitter accusations, heaving resentments, bewilderment. Standing as tall, as stubborn, with the identical bone structure, would Amos too feel the same fleeting sense of loss? Would Jai Raventhorne's denials, his emotional famines, also be his?

Nothing she could give Amos would ever compensate for what had been taken away. Olivia saw the parallel and was chilled, her mind exploding with suspicion, with renewed fears. He had said that deliberately! It was a trick to part her from her son. "Amos is *not* like you!" she flared. "He at least has a *name.* He will never lack an identity!"

He flinched, taken aback by her sudden cruelty. But he did not return it. "Yes," he admitted, again anguished, "you have ensured that."

"He will have *me* to call him son; he needs no one else."

Recognising her fear, he sought to allay it. "I know. It will be enough. Why do you doubt it?"

For her own ravaging fantasies she punished him further. "I want to establish clearly that you will have no claim over Amos, *ever.*"

"I do not make any claim, nor will I." Helplessly he stared at his feet, not knowing where else to in his misery. "I will not try to separate you again, you have my word. I have no place in your life, Olivia. And a child should have a mother. At least a mother."

With a small cry, she buried her face in her hands. She could no longer deny the crux of her agony. She recognised clearly where she was—once again at a cross-road. It was dark and she could not see her way, but she saw that there was more than one. Once more she stood alone. Arctic winds pulled and tore her in conflicting directions. She was blinded by snow; the flurries obscured everything. The elements howled into a storm; with all the will-power at her command, she could not combat it. Where were all her resources? Her resolutions, her infallible sense of logic, that strength on which she prided herself? Frantically she searched; despairingly, she could not locate any of them.

Then slowly, with the grace of a sunset, the storm subsided. The howling winds became tranquil, the flurries of snow cleared.

Above her, the sky shone without a flaw, and ahead as calm and comforting as a country walk, lay the path she knew she must take. She filled with an enormous peace. And in that serenity, with the delicacy of a falling flower, a decision dropped smoothly into her heart. The ease with which it had arrived now astonished Olivia. But then she saw that it had always been there; it was she who had not noticed.

She looked up to find herself encapsulated tight in his unswerving stare. He watched, he waited, already having gleaned the workings of her mind. Abandoning thought, Olivia once more stepped into her dream and floated weightless. "When do you sail?" she asked, or someone asked in her voice.

"Soon."

"Where for?"

"Somewhere. It makes no difference."

"You will run and hide and be able to forget that your son is without a father, as you have always been?"

"I hardly have a choice in the matter!"

The unreality deepened; in her dreamscape, Olivia smiled. "I give you a choice."

The stillness around them was eerie. Even the river appeared not to flow. Within that frozen tableau something moved, then fluttered, then pulsated wildly—a wisp of a hope struggling to survive. He came back to life and voiced it. "You would come with me?"

"Yes."

"Why?" Even in his hope there was despair.

"Why?" Neatly, Olivia rearranged the pleats of her dress over her lap. "I don't know. Perhaps because my life is still not complicated enough. Or because I would want Amos to hear his father call him son. Or . . ." She stopped, unable to unblock her throat.

"Or?"

Her mouth felt rigid, her lips hurt as she spoke words that had remained unused and rusting for so long. "Or because I love you."

He was dazed by disbelief. "After all this, *all this,* you can still say that?"

"Yes, I can still say that."

Gripped by rigor and shuddering, he turned away. "It is still a wasted love, Olivia. I deserve it now even less than I did then." Battling to live, the hope could not and his eyes dulled.

"As it was then, it is still mine to waste."

"No!" He was violent in his rejection. "It would be a senseless, childish display of bravado. I cannot permit it!"

He was slipping away from her! Driven by panic, she flew back into reality. "It would not be bravado! I am not noble like your mother, who wasted her love knowing that it was not returned. I too, like you, am self-seeking. I *know* that you return to me what is given."

Torn between two parts of himself, he stood despairing, arms hanging loosely by his sides. "It can reverse nothing, Olivia, repair nothing. How can I let you risk destruction a second time?"

"For me it will reverse everything—even that clock!—repair everything," she cried, also fighting despair. "You told me, wrote in your letter, that you loved me. It is that love that has been my staff, my talisman, my strength—even if I had lost the faculty to see it." In her pleadings there was déjà vu; they had been here once before. And they had come full circle. "Tell me again, Jai, please tell me again!"

"No! You are the wife of another man."

"But I am also the mother of a child fathered by you, a child fathered in mutual love!"

"Love!" His lip curled in an involuntary sneer. "It was a grudging love tainted by many resentments, Olivia. And I am now even more unholy, stricken by jealousies that live in my entrails like gut rot. For this tarnished love can you bear a lifetime of scandal, of social ostracism?" He was ruthless in his inquisition.

"*You* have borne a lifetime of both!"

"For me, therefore, they are not novelties. I am used to them. I have taught myself how not to let them touch me. Can you?"

"As a discarded wife I already have. They no longer touch me either. And if your love is indeed tarnished, then so be it." In her panic she was again reckless. "Even then I will be a gainer."

He laughed with pitying derision. "You still believe love is the universal panacea? That even tainted it is a world conqueror?"

"No. I know now that it is not. But if one does not expect the perfect, it teaches how to accept the imperfect."

He threw up his arms. "The world outside your charmed circle is not kind, Olivia. It is virulent in its dictates and demands."

"There is no world for me outside you and Amos."

"Oh yes, there is!" He was again brutal. "You still have a husband—and I cannot share you with anyone. With me, Olivia, it is *all.* Or nothing. As in war, so also in love!" His arrogance now was hurtful.

Did he truly reject her? No, no, that could not be—she would not permit it to be! He was only testing her, measuring her courage, experimenting how far she could bend without breaking. He did not see that in doing so he was trying to rationalise the irrational, justify the unjustifiable, resolve by logic that which was insoluble. He forgot that beyond this, beyond words, there was another dimension. Some called it—as *he* had!—an affinity.

Under her breath she laughed. "What a fool you are, Jai Raventhorne! Like me, a Kansas mule." Her tone turned soft as silk. "I've fought my fate, the world, once. I would willingly fight them again, *for* you. What I no longer have the energy to fight again is *you.*" She rose, walked up to him and, tired of not touching him, of loving him from afar, of not loving him at all, surrounded him with her arms. "Have you not learned yet that with me too, always, as in war so also in love—it is all, all, *all . . . ?*"

Shocked, he stood rigid and unmoving in her embrace, not daring to touch her in return, not daring even to breathe. He could not find a voice except to gasp out her name.

For a moment, a spellbound moment, neither could she breathe. Drunk with the heady rush of his well-remembered, never-forgotten muskiness, drowned in the lightest of light whiffs of his faintly tobacco-tinged breath, Olivia almost died of his nearness. Starved for so long, she skimmed feathery lips across the texture of his neck, tasting once more the salt of his skin, holding its sharpness in her mouth, unwilling to let it go. "If you don't want me," she whispered, intoxicated, "then let me hear you say it outright. That, at least, is owed to a woman who has borne you a son."

He was resurrected into life with a spasm. Hesitantly his arms rose and within them, he held her closer to him. "Oh yes, I want you, oh *yes . . . !*" Hopelessly defeated, he was abject in his capitulation. He breathed tumbling incoherencies into the profusion of her hair, on her cheeks, all around her upturned face. "How can you ever know how much you have been wanted?"

"I can if you tell me." She rested an ear against his pocket. Yes, it was still there, safe for her—only for her!—syncopating like a kettle-drum!

"My God, you *still* need it said?" He was again incredulous.

Between open shirt buttons she kissed the hollow of his neck. "Still!"

Bewildered by what he could neither define nor understand, by what he could only feel, he suffocated her with random kisses that made her fight for breath. "There has not been a day, not a fraction of one, when you have not been loved and wanted. Absent or present, you rule my thoughts, command and control me, drive me to despair and in my despair I lose my mind." He forced her away to grip her shoulders and hold her at arm's length. "I am an insufferable, demanding man, Olivia, and still extreme in my reactions. You will not be able to tolerate me for long. And then I will lose you again."

"And you cannot bear to be a loser, is that it?" Unshed tears made her eyes even more bright. "I promised you once to tolerate anything you chose to be. It was a reckless promise, one that was not within my capacity to honour then. It is now. I too need another chance, Jai, I too." The grip of his fingers dug deeply into her flesh. She loosened it to take his hands in hers. "This is the truth, Jai. Why can't you accept it as such?"

He could not match her eloquent persuasions and was stricken with inarticulacy. Frustrated, he gathered her to him roughly, cursing his own incapacities under his breath. "Why, why, why! How many damned whys do you still have left for me?"

"As many as will take to learn you entirely."

"Entirely?" He groaned in his exasperation. "If even I cannot learn myself *partially,* what you assign to yourself is a lifetime of study!"

"Well then, that is perfect," she retorted with abandon, free finally in soul and spirit. "As it happens, I do have a lifetime to spare."

He did not pay heed to her gay insouciance. Still troubled, he was unrelievedly solemn. Raising her chin, he stared into her eyes, enchanted by their dancing lights but nervous at the size of her submission. "Your love awes me, Olivia. I am alarmed by its sheer persistence. At the same time it dazzles me, but I know neither how to love well nor to receive with grace. What I feel for you still angers me, for it is a bondage and I rebel against slavery. You entrust me with so much, *too* much, and I am inadequate as a caretaker." He tried to smile but couldn't. "I would want you to be happy, as . . . as my sister," he stopped and flushed, "as Estelle is happy. But I am unsure what makes the substance of happiness . . ." At a loss again, he shrugged.

Tenderly, she smoothed out the lines of anxiety on his forehead. "For me the substance of happiness is to be with you. Perhaps, if we're lucky, we can both learn to love well again, learn to receive with grace."

Abstracted, he caressed her hair, still frowning. "It will not be easy, Olivia."

She sighed. "No. But then, has it ever been?"

For a long moment he remained unspeaking. Then, disengaging himself, he bent down to retrieve the momentarily forgotten bundle. For a while he held it between his hands. His eyes closed and, soundlessly, his lips moved. He lifted his precious treasury to them and kissed it once. Then, before Olivia could guess his intention, he had thrown it with all his strength into the middle of the river. She gave a startled cry, but he restrained her impulsive move towards it. "Let it go," he commanded, but with profound feeling. "It is time for the dead to bury their dead. I am done with apparitions."

Olivia's eyes filled. "But you loved her!"

"I will always love her," he assured her gently. "One clings to the dead when there is nothing living to turn to. Now, it seems, there are others to love." He brushed her wet lids with his fingertips. "Don't cry. You know I cannot bear your tears and you have cried enough."

Mesmerised by the still-bobbing blur on the surface of the water, she could not wrench her eyes away from it. She was racked with renewed shame. "I must tell you that—"

"Don't say it." He sealed her lips with a finger. "It is part of the past that must now be forgotten."

She removed his hand and stilled it between hers. "But you must know *how* I—"

"I know how. It was Sujata who took it. Isn't that what you want to tell me? You paid her well to."

Olivia gulped, mortified. "How did you—"

"It was surprisingly easy." It might have been her imagination, but something stirred in the depths of those veiled, silverfish eyes, something she had never seen before, a faint twinkle. "I know Sujata's perfume," he explained with halting care. "Wherever she has been it lingers."

Her eyes widened. "You haven't—"

"No." Again he caught her thought before she could complete it. "I have not harmed her, nor will. She has gone to Benares." He sensed Olivia's quick stab of jealousy and caressed it away. "You must forget Sujata now. We have both done things we are not proud of. I more than you, Olivia, I far more than you!"

Forget. Two simple syllables, yet two of the most demanding in the English language. So much to forget! Fleetingly, Olivia's thoughts turned errant again. Theirs would be a hesitant happiness, their hopes stolen from a still-grudging fate, their future touched by fears of the unknown, of the unknowable. Once again she would sail across uncharted seas. There would be doubts and discoveries, resentments and earnest resolutions, inevitably at least some persistent barriers. There would be suspicions and pain, losses and gains—oh yes, gains!—and always with them would be that past never wholly forgotten. It had not yet been fully lived out, perhaps; it would resist healing balms, and some scars would remain, always itching faintly.

And between them, unforgotten and unforgettable, there would be Freddie. And Alistair—as much a part of herself as was Amos.

No. The past could not all be obliterated yet. Its agonies would linger for both, and sometimes also divide them. Within, they would share a world as close to magic as any world could be. But the world they faced outside would be savage in its refusal to forgive. Would she truly be able to bear that? Yes, a hundred times yes! He was justified in his insecurities but wrong in his conclusions. In all this, all this that was yet to come, she had a source of strength that he had not considered: they would never again be on opposite sides.

And without him life had no meaning anyway.

He followed her through the labyrinth of her deep inner silences, tilted his head to a side and raised an eyebrow. With matching intuition, Olivia understood his unasked question. "No." She straightened, squared her shoulders and shook her head. "No second thoughts. Not now, not ever. I was merely trying to tailor the past to fit the future."

"And you are certain that it will fit? A square peg in a round hole?" He was still sceptical.

"No, I am not certain. But if my determination can bring me *you* again, then it can also make a square round. I am, after all, renowned for my resourcefulness."

At that he laughed. Finally. A full-throated laugh, fluid and free flowing, a laugh empty of doubts, filled instead with the wonder of revelation. As he had done once many lifetimes ago, he removed the chain from his neck and fastened it around hers.

"I can still give you nothing that I value more. You wear it now with my mother's blessings." His hands at the back of her neck stroked it, then cupped her face. "With it I bequeath you my past. My future appears to be yours already."

It was a commitment, this time irreversible. And this time, Olivia knew, it would be mutually honoured. She raised the locket to her lips, then, taking his hand, kissed the bruised knuckle with which he had punished himself. "Come. Let us go to the carriage," she said, laying his palm against her cheek. "I have brought your son to return to you."